THE
REDEMPTION
OF ALTHALUS

By David and Leigh Eddings
Published by The Ballantine Publishing Group:

THE BELGARIAD
Book One: Pawn of Prophecy
Book Two: Queen of Sorcery
Book Three: Magician's Gambit
Book Four: Castle of Wizardry
Book Five: Enchanters' End Game

THE MALLOREON
Book One: Guardian of the West
Book Two: King of the Murgos
Book Three: Demon Lord of Karanda
Book Four: Sorceress of Darshiva
Book Five: The Seeress of Kell

BELGARATH THE SORCERER
POLGARA THE SORCERESS

THE ELENIUM
Book One: The Diamond Throne
Book Two: The Ruby Knight
Book Three: The Sapphire Rose

THE TAMULI
Book One: Domes of Fire
Book Two: The Shining Ones
Book Three: The Hidden City

HIGH HUNT
THE LOSERS
THE RIVAN CODEX

THE REDEMPTION OF ALTHALUS

David and Leigh Eddings

THE BALLANTINE PUBLISHING GROUP
NEW YORK

A Del Rey Book
Published by The Ballantine Publishing Group
Copyright © 2000 by David Eddings and Leigh Eddings

www.randomhouse.com/BB/

A Library of Congress Catalog Card Number can be obtained from the publisher upon request.

ISBN 0-345-44398-5

Manufactured in the United States of America

First American Edition: January 2001
First Mass Market International Edition: March 2001

10   9   8   7   6   5   4   3   2

For the sisters, Lori and Lynette,
who have made our lives so much more pleasant.

Thank you, thank you, thank you, thank you, thank you, thank you!!!!!!

PROLOGUE

Now before the Beginning, there was no Time, and all was Chaos and Darkness. But Deiwos, the Sky God, awoke, and with his awakening, Time itself began. And Deiwos looked out upon the Chaos and the Darkness, and a great yearning filled his heart. And he rose up to make all that is made, and his making brought encroaching Light into the emptiness of his kinsman, the Demon Daeva. But in time Deiwos wearied of his labors, and sought him a place to rest. And with a single thought made he a high keep at that edge which divides the Light from the Darkness and the realm of Time from that place where there is no Time. And Deiwos marked that awful edge with fire to warn all men back from Daeva's abyss, and then he rested there in his keep and communed with his Book while Time continued her stately march.

Now the Demon Daeva was made sore wroth by the encroachment upon his dark domain by his kinsman Deiwos, and eternal enmity was born in his soul, for the Light caused him pain, and the orderly progression of Time herself was an agony unto him. And then retreated he to his cold throne in the echoless darkness of the void. And there he contemplated vengeance against the Light, and against his kinsman, and against Time herself.

And their sister watched, but said nothing.

    —*FROM "THE SKY AND THE ABYSS"*
    THE MYTHOLOGY OF
    ANCIENT MEDYO

In defense of Althalus, it should be noted that he was in very tight financial circumstances and more than a little tipsy when he agreed to undertake the theft of the Book. Had he been completely sober and had he not reached the very bottom of his purse, he might have asked more questions about the House at the End of the World, and he most certainly would have asked many more about the owner of the Book.

It would be sheer folly to try to conceal the true nature of Althalus, for his flaws are the stuff of legend. He is, as all men know, a thief, a liar, an occasional murderer, an outrageous braggart, and a man devoid of even the slightest hint of honor. He is, moreover, a frequent drunkard, a glutton, and a patron of ladies who are no better than they should be.

He is an engaging sort of rogue, however, quick-witted and vastly amusing. It has even been suggested in some circles that if Althalus really wanted to do it, he could make trees giggle and mountains laugh right out loud.

His nimble fingers are even quicker than his wit, though, and a prudent man always keeps a firm hand over his purse when he laughs at the sallies of the witty thief.

So far as Althalus can remember, he has always been a thief. He never knew his father, and he cannot exactly remember his mother's name. He grew up among thieves in the rough lands of the frontier, and even as a child, his wit had made him welcome in the society of those men who made their living by transferring the ownership rights of objects of value. He earned his way with jokes and stories, and the thieves fed him and trained him in their art by way of thanks.

His mind was quick enough to make him aware of the limitations of each of his mentors. Some of them were large men who took what they wanted by sheer force. Others were small and wiry men who stole by stealth. As Althalus approached manhood, he realized that he'd never be a giant. Sheer bulk was apparently not a part of his heritage. He also realized that when he achieved his full growth, he'd no longer be able to wriggle his way through small openings into interesting places where interesting things were kept. He would be medium sized, but he vowed to himself that he would not be mediocre. It occurred to him that wit was probably superior to bull-like strength or mouselike stealth anyway, so that was the route he chose.

His fame was modest at first in the mountains and forests along the outer edges of civilization. Other thieves admired his cleverness. As one of them put it one evening in a thieves' tavern in the land of Hule, "I'll swear, that Althalus boy could persuade the bees to bring him honey or the birds to lay their eggs on his plate at breakfast time. Mark my words, brothers, that boy will go far."

In point of fact, Althalus *did* go far. He was not by nature a sedentary man, and he seemed to be blessed—or cursed—with a boundless curiosity about what lay on the other side of any hill or mountain or river he came across. His curiosity was not limited to geography, however, since he was also interested in what more sedentary men had in their houses or what they might be carrying in their purses. Those twin curiosities, coupled with an almost instinctive realization of when he'd been in one place for quite long enough, kept him continually on the move.

And so it was that he had looked at the prairies of Plakand and Wekti, at the rolling hills of Ansu, and at the mountains of Kagwher, Arum, and Kweron. He had even made occasional sorties into Regwos and southern Nekweros, despite the stories men told of the horrors lurking in the mountains beyond the outer edges of the frontier.

The one thing more than any other that distinguished Althalus from other thieves was his amazing luck. He could win every time he touched a pair of dice, and no matter where he went in whatever land, fortune smiled upon him. A chance meeting or a random conversation almost always led him directly to the most prosperous and least suspicious man in any community, and it seemed that any trail he took, even at random, led him directly to opportunities that came to no other thief. In truth, Althalus was even more famous for his luck than for his wit or his skill.

In time, he came to depend on that luck. Fortune, it appeared, absolutely adored him, and he came to trust her implicitly. He even went so far as to privately believe that she talked to him in the hidden silences of his mind. The little twinge that told him it was time to leave any given community—in a hurry—was, he believed, her voice giving him a silent warning that unpleasant things lurked on the horizon.

The combination of wit, skill, and luck had made him successful, but he could also run like a deer if the situation seemed to require it.

A professional thief must, if he wants to keep eating regularly, spend a great deal of his time in taverns listening to other people talk, since information is the primary essential to the art of the thief. There's little profit to be made from robbing poor men. Althalus liked a good cup of mellow mead as much as the next man, but he seldom let it get ahead of him in the way that some frequenters of taverns did. A befuddled man makes mistakes, and the thief who makes mistakes usually doesn't live very long. Althalus was very good at selecting the one man in any tavern who'd be most likely to be in possession of useful information, and with jokes and open-handed generosity, he could usually persuade the fellow to share that information. Buying drinks for talkative men in taverns was something in the nature of a business investment. Althalus always made sure that his own cup ran dry at about the same time the other man's did, but most of the mead in the thief's cup ended up on the floor instead of in his belly, for some reason.

He moved from place to place; he told jokes to tavern loafers and bought mead for them for a few days; and then, when he'd pinpointed the rich men in any town or village, he'd stop by to pay them a call along about midnight, and by morning he'd be miles away on the road to some other frontier settlement.

Although Althalus was primarily interested in local information, there were other stories told in taverns as well—stories about the cities down on the plains of Equero, Treborea, and Perquaine, the civilized lands to the south. He listened to some of those stories with a profound skepticism. Nobody in the world could be stupid enough to pave the streets of his hometown with gold; and a fountain that sprayed diamonds might be rather pretty, but it wouldn't really serve any practical purpose.

The stories, however, always stirred his imagination, and he sort of promised himself that someday, someday, he'd have to go down to the cities of the plains to have a look for himself.

The settlements of the frontier were built for the most part of logs, but the cities of the lands of the south were reputed to be built of stone. That in itself might make the journey to civilization worthwhile, but Althalus wasn't really interested in architecture, so he kept putting off his visit to civilization.

What ultimately changed his mind was a funny story he heard in a tavern in Kagwher about the decline of the Deikan Empire. The central cause of that decline, it appeared, had been a blunder so colossal that Althalus couldn't believe that anybody with good sense could have made it even once, much less three times.

"May all of my teeth fall out if they didn't," the storyteller assured him. "The people down in Deika have a very high opinion of themselves, so when they heard that men had discovered gold here in Kagwher, they decided right off that God had meant for *them* to have it—only he'd made a mistake and put it in Kagwher instead of down there where it'd be convenient for them to just bend over and pick it up. They were a little put out with God for that, but they were wise enough not to scold him about it. Instead, they sent an army up here into the mountains to keep us ignorant hill people from just helping ourselves to all that gold that God had intended for them. Well, now, when that army got here and started hearing stories about how much gold there was up here, the soldiers all decided that army life didn't really suit them anymore, so the whole army just ups and quits so that they could strike out on their own."

Althalus laughed. "That *would* be a quick way to lose an army, I suppose."

"There's none any quicker," the humorous storyteller agreed. "Anyhow, the Senate that operates the government of Deika was terribly disappointed with that army, so they sent a second army up here to chase down the first one and punish them for ignoring their duty."

"You're not serious!" Althalus exclaimed.

"Oh, yes, that's exactly what they did. Well, sir, that second army decided that they weren't any stupider than the first one had been, so they hung up their swords and uniforms to go look for gold, too."

Althalus howled with laughter. "That's the funniest story I've ever heard!" he said.

"It gets better," the grinning man told him. "The Senate of the Empire just couldn't *believe* that two whole armies could ignore their duty that way. After all, the soldiers *were* getting paid a whole copper penny every day, weren't they? The Senators made speeches at each other until all their brains went to sleep, and that's when they took stupidity out to the very end of its leash by sending a *third* army up here to find out what had happened to the first two."

"Is he serious?" Althalus asked another tavern patron.

"That's more or less the way it happened, stranger," the man replied. "I can vouch for it, because I was a Sergeant in that second army. The city-state of Deika used to rule just about the whole of civilization, but after she'd poured three entire armies into the mountains of Kagwher, she didn't have enough troops left to patrol her own streets, much less the other civilized lands. Our Senate still passes laws that the other lands are supposed to obey, but nobody pays any attention to them anymore. Our Senators can't quite seem to grasp that, so they keep passing new laws about taxes and the like, and people keep ignoring them. Our glorious Empire has turned itself into a glorious joke."

"Maybe I've been putting off my visit to civilization for too long," Althalus said. "If they're *that* silly down in Deika, a man in my profession almost *has* to pay them a visit."

"Oh?" the former soldier said. "Which profession do you follow?"

"I'm a thief," Althalus admitted. "And a city filled with stupid rich men might just be the next best thing to paradise for a really good thief."

"I wish you all the best, friend," the expatriate told him. "I was never all that fond of Senators who spent all their time trying to invent new ways to get me killed. Be a little careful when you get there, though. The Senators buy their seats in that august body, and that means that they're rich men. Rich senators make laws to protect the rich, not the ordinary people. If you get caught stealing in Deika, things won't turn out too well for you."

"I never get caught, Sergeant," Althalus assured him. "That's because I'm the best thief in the world, and to make things even better, I'm also the *luckiest* man in the world. If half the story I just heard is true, the luck of the Deikan Empire has turned sour lately, and my luck just keeps getting sweeter. If the chance to make a wager on the outcome of my visit comes along, put your money on me, because in a situation like this one, I can't possibly lose."

And with that, Althalus drained his cup, bowed floridly to the other men in the tavern, and gaily set off to see the wonders of civilization for himself.

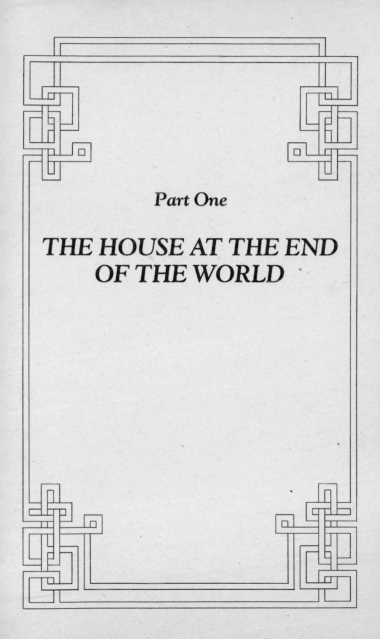

Part One

THE HOUSE AT THE END
OF THE WORLD

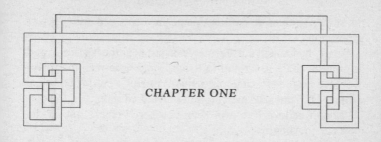

CHAPTER ONE

Althalus the thief spent ten days on the road down out of the mountains of Kagwher to reach the imperial city of Deika. As he was coming out of the foothills, he passed a limestone quarry where miserable slaves spent their lives under the whip laboriously sawing building blocks out of the limestone with heavy bronze saws. Althalus had heard about slavery, of course, but this was the first time he'd ever actually seen slaves. As he strode on toward the plains of Equero, he had a little chat with his good luck about the subject, strongly suggesting to her that if she *really* loved him, she'd do everything she possibly could to keep him from ever becoming a slave.

The city of Deika lay at the southern end of a large lake in northern Equero, and it was even more splendid than the stories had said it was. It was surrounded by a high stone wall made of squared-off limestone blocks, and all the buildings inside the walls were also made of stone.

The broad streets of Deika were paved with flagstones, and the public buildings soared to the sky. Everyone in town who thought he was important wore a splendid linen mantle, and every private house was identified by a statue of its owner—usually so idealized that any actual resemblance to the man so identified was purely coincidental.

Althalus was garbed in clothes suitable for the frontier, and he received many disparaging glances from passersby as he viewed the splendors of the imperial city. After a while, he grew tired of that and sought out a quarter of town where the men in the streets wore more commonplace garments and less superior expressions.

Finally he located a fishermen's tavern near the lakefront, and he stopped there to sit and to listen, since fishermen the world over love to talk. He sat unobtrusively nursing a cup of sour wine while the tar-smeared men around him talked shop.

"I don't believe I've ever seen you here before," one of the men said to Althalus.

"I'm from out of town," Althalus replied.

"Oh? Where from?"

"Up in the mountains. I came down to look at civilization."

"Well, what do you think of our city?"

"Very impressive. I'm almost as impressed with your city as some of the town's rich men seem to be with themselves."

One of the fishermen laughed cynically. "You passed near the forum, I take it."

"If that's the place where all the fancy buildings are, yes I did. And if you want it, you can take as much of my share of it as you desire."

"You didn't care for our wealthy?"

"Apparently not as much as they did, that's for certain. People like us should avoid the rich if we possibly can. Sooner or later, we'll probably be bad for their eyes."

"How's that?" another fisherman asked.

"Well, all those fellows in the forum—the ones who wear fancy nightgowns in the street—kept looking down their noses at me. If a man spends all his time doing that, sooner or later it's going to make him cross-eyed."

The fishermen all laughed, and the atmosphere in the tavern became relaxed and friendly. Althalus had skillfully introduced the topic dearest to his heart, and they all spent the rest of the afternoon talking about the well-to-do of Deika. By evening, Althalus had committed several names to memory. He spent another few days narrowing down his list, and he ultimately settled on a very wealthy salt merchant named Kweso. Then he went to the central marketplace, visited the marble-lined public baths, and then dipped into his purse to buy some clothing that more closely fit into the current fashion of Deika. The key word for a thief who's selecting a costume for business purposes is "nondescript," for fairly obvious reasons. Then Althalus went to the rich men's part of town and spent several more days—and nights—watching merchant Kweso's walled-in house. Kweso himself was a plump, rosy-cheeked bald man who had a sort of friendly smile. On a number of occasions Althalus even managed to get close enough to him to be able to hear him talking. He actually grew to be rather fond of the chubby little fellow, but that's not unusual, really. When you get right down to it, a wolf is probably quite fond of deer.

Althalus managed to pick up the name of one of Kweso's neighbors, and with a suitably businesslike manner, he went in through the salt merchant's gate one morning, walked up to his door, and knocked. After a moment or two, a servant opened the door. "Yes?" the servant asked.

"I'd like to speak with Gentleman Melgor," Althalus said politely. "It's on business."

"I'm afraid you have the wrong house, sir," the servant said. "Gentleman Melgor's house is the one two doors down."

Althalus smacked his forehead with his open hand. "How stupid of me," he apologized. "I'm *very* sorry to have disturbed you." His eyes, however, were very busy. Kweso's door latch wasn't very complicated, and his entryway had several doors leading off it. He lowered his voice. "I hope my pounding didn't wake your master," he said.

The servant smiled briefly. "I rather doubt it," he said. "The master's bedroom is upstairs at the back of the house. He usually gets out of bed about this time in the morning anyway, so he's probably already awake."

"That's a blessing," Althalus said, his eyes still busy. "You said that Melgor's house is two doors down?"

"Yes." The servant leaned out through the doorway and pointed. "It's that way—the house with the blue door. You can't miss it."

"My thanks, friend, and I'm sorry to have disturbed you." Then Althalus turned and went back out to the street. He was grinning broadly. His luck was still holding him cuddled to her breast. The "wrong house" ploy had given him even more information than he'd expected. His luck had encouraged that servant to tell him all sorts of things. It was still quite early in the morning, and if this was Kweso's normal time to rise, that was a fair indication that he went to bed early as well. He'd be sound asleep by midnight. The garden around his house was mature, with large trees and broad flowering bushes that would provide cover. Getting inside the house would be no problem, and now Althalus knew where Kweso's bedroom was. All that was left to do was to slip into the house in the middle of the night, go directly to Kweso's bedroom, wake him, and lay a bronze knife against his throat to persuade him to cooperate. The whole affair could be settled in short order.

Unfortunately, however, it didn't turn out that way at all. The salt merchant's chubby, good-natured face obviously concealed a much sharper mind than Althalus expected. Not long after midnight, the clever thief scaled the merchant's outer wall, crept through the garden, and quietly entered the house. He stopped in the entryway to listen. Except for a few snores coming from the servants' quarters, the house was silent. As quietly as a shadow, Althalus went to the foot of the stairs and started up.

It was at that point that Kweso's house became very noisy. The three dogs were almost as large as ponies, and their deep-throated barking seemed to shake the walls.

Althalus immediately changed his plans. The open air of the nighttime streets suddenly seemed enormously attractive.

The dogs at the foot of the stairs seemed to have other plans, however. They started up, snarling and displaying shockingly large fangs.

There were shouts coming from upstairs, and somebody was lighting candles.

Althalus waited tensely until the dogs had almost reached him. Then, with an acrobatic skill he didn't even know he had, he jumped high over the top of the dogs, tumbled on down to the foot of the stairs, sprang to his feet, and ran back outside.

As he raced across the garden with the dogs snapping at his

heels, he heard a buzzing sound zip past his left ear. Somebody in the house, either the deceptively moon-faced Kweso himself or one of his meek-looking servants, seemed to be a very proficient archer.

Althalus scrambled up the wall as the dogs snapped at his heels and more arrows bounced off the stones, spraying his face with chips and fragments.

He rolled over the top of the wall and dropped into the street, running almost before his feet hit the paving stones. Things had not turned out the way he'd planned. His tumble down the stairs had left scrapes and bruises in all sorts of places, and he'd managed to severely twist one of his ankles in his drop to the street. He limped on, filling the air around him with curses.

Then somebody in Kweso's house opened the front gate, and the dogs came rushing out.

Now *that*, Althalus felt, was going just a little *too* far. He'd admitted his defeat by running away, but Kweso evidently wasn't satisfied with victory and wanted blood as well.

It took some dodging around and clambering over several walls, but the thief eventually shook off the pursuing dogs. Then he went across town to put himself a long way from all the excitement and sat down on a conveniently placed public bench to think things over. Civilized men were obviously not as docile as they appeared on the surface, and Althalus decided then and there that he'd seen as much of the city of Deika as he really wanted to see. What puzzled him the most, though, was how his luck had failed to warn him about those dogs. Could it be that she'd been asleep? He'd have to speak with her about that.

He was in a foul humor as he waited in the shadows near a tavern in the better part of town, so he was rather abrupt when a couple of well-dressed patrons of the tavern came reeling out into the street. He very firmly persuaded the both of them to take a little nap by rapping them smartly across the backs of their heads with the heavy hilt of his short-bladed bronze sword. Then he transferred the ownership of the contents of their purses, as well as a few rings and a fairly nice bracelet, and left them slumbering peacefully in the gutter near the tavern.

Waylaying drunken men in the street wasn't really his style, but Althalus needed some traveling money. The two men had been the first to come along, and the process was fairly routine, so there wasn't much danger involved. Althalus decided that it might be best to avoid taking any chances until after he'd had a long talk with his luck.

As he went toward the main gate of town, he hefted the two purses he'd just stolen. They seemed fairly heavy, and that persuaded him to take a step he normally wouldn't even have considered. He left the city of Deika, limped on until shortly after dawn, and then stopped at a substantial-looking farmhouse, where he bought—and actually paid for—a horse. It went against all his principles, but until he'd had that chat with his luck, he decided not to take any chances.

He mounted his new horse, and without so much as a backward glance, he rode on toward the west. The sooner he left Equero and the Deikan Empire behind, the better. He absently wondered as he rode if geography might play some part in a man's luck. Could it possibly be that his luck just didn't work in some places? That was a very troubling thought, and Althalus brooded sourly about it as he rode west.

He reached the city of Kanthon in Treborea two days later, and he paused before entering the gates to make sure that the fabled—and evidently interminable—war between Kanthon and Osthos had not recently boiled to the surface. Since he saw no siege engines in place, he rode on in.

The forum of Kanthon rather closely resembled the forum he'd seen in Deika, but the wealthy men who came there to listen to speeches seemed not to be burdened with the same notions of their own superiority as the aristocrats of Equero were, so Althalus found that he was not offended by their very existence. He even went into the forum once to listen to speeches. The speeches, however, were mostly denunciations of the city-state

THE REDEMPTION OF ALTHALUS

of Osthos in southern Treborea or complaints about a recent raise in taxes, so they weren't really very interesting.

Then he went looking for a tavern in one of the more modest neighborhoods, and he no sooner entered a somewhat run-down establishment than he became convinced that his luck was once again on the rise. Two of the patrons were involved in a heated argument about just who was the richest man in Kanthon.

"Omeso's got it all over Weikor," one of them asserted loudly. "He's got so much money that he can't even count it."

"Well, of course he has, you fool. Omeso can't count past ten unless he takes his shoes off. He inherited all his money from his uncle, and he's never earned so much as a penny on his own. Weikor worked his way up from the bottom, so he knows how to *earn* money instead of having it handed to him on a platter. Omeso's money flows out as fast as he can spend it, but Weikor's money keeps coming in. Ten years from now, Weikor's going to *own* Omeso—though why anybody would want him is beyond me."

Althalus turned and left without so much as ordering a drink. He'd picked up exactly the information he wanted; clearly his luck was smiling down on him again. Maybe geography *did* play a part in fortune's decisions.

He nosed around Kanthon for the next couple of days, asking questions about Omeso and Weikor, and he ultimately promoted Omeso to the head of his list, largely because of Weikor's reputation as a man well able to protect his hard-earned money. Althalus definitely didn't want to encounter any more large, hungry dogs while he was working.

The "wrong house" ploy gave him the opportunity to examine the latch on Omeso's front door, and a few evenings spent following his quarry revealed that Omeso almost never went home before dawn and that by then he was so far gone in drink that he probably wouldn't have noticed if his house happened to be on fire. His servants, of course, were well aware of his habits, so they also spent their nights out on the town. By the time the sun went down, Omeso's house was almost always empty.

And so, shortly before midnight on a warm summer evening, Althalus quietly entered the house and began his search.

He almost immediately saw something that didn't ring at all true. Omeso's house was splendid enough on the outside, but the interior was furnished with tattered, broken-down chairs and tables that would have shamed a pauper. The draperies were in rags, the carpets were threadbare, and the best candlestick in the entire house was made of tarnished brass. The furnishings cried louder than words that this was *not* the house of a rich man. Omeso had evidently already spent his inheritance.

Althalus doggedly continued his search, and after he'd meticulously covered every room, he gave up. There wasn't anything in the entire house that was worth stealing. He left in disgust.

He still had money in his purse, so he lingered in Kanthon for a few more days, and then, quite by accident, he entered a tavern frequented by artisans. As was usually the case down in the lowlands, the tavern did not offer mead, so Althalus had to settle for sour wine again. He looked around the tavern. Artisans were the sort of people who had many opportunities to look inside the houses of rich people. He addressed the other patrons. "Maybe one of you gentlemen could clear something up for me. I happened to go into the house of a man named Omeso on business the other day. Everybody in town was telling me how rich he is, but once I got past his front door, I couldn't believe what I was seeing. There were chairs in that man's house that only had three legs, and the tables all looked so wobbly that a good sneeze would knock them over."

"That's the latest fashion here in Kanthon, friend," a mud-smeared potter told him. "I can't sell a good pot or jug or bottle anymore, because everybody wants ones that are chipped and battered and have the handles broken off."

"If you think *that's* odd," a wood carver said, "you should see what goes on in *my* shop. I used to have a scrap heap where I threw broken furniture, but since the new tax law went into effect, I can't *give* new furniture away, but our local gentry will pay almost anything for a broken-down old chair."

"I don't understand," Althalus confessed.

"It's not really too complicated, stranger," a baker put in. "Our old Aryo used to run his government on the proceeds of the tax on bread. Anybody who ate helped support the government. But our old Aryo died last year, and his son, the man who sits on the throne now, is a very educated young man. His teachers were all philosophers with strange ideas. They persuaded him that a tax on profit had more justice than one on bread, since the poor people have to buy most of the bread, while the rich people make most of the profit."

"What has that got to do with shabby furniture?" Althalus asked with a puzzled frown.

"The furniture's all for show, friend," a mortar-spattered stonemason told him. "Our rich men are all trying to convince the tax collectors that they haven't got anything at all. The tax collectors don't believe them, of course, so they conduct little surprise searches. If a rich man in Kanthon's stupid enough to have even one piece of fine furniture in his home, the tax collectors immediately send in the wrecking crews to dismantle the floors of the house."

"The floors? Why are they tearing up floors?"

"Because that's a favorite place to hide money. Folks pry up a couple of flagstones, you see, and then they dig a hole and line it with bricks. All the money they pretend they don't have goes into the hole. Then they cement the flagstones back down. Right at first, their work was so shabby that even a fool could see it the moment he entered the room. Now, though, I'm making more money teaching people how to mix good mortar than I ever did laying stone-block walls. Here just recently, I even had to build my own hidey-hole under my own floor, I'm making so much."

"Why didn't your rich men hire professionals to do the work for them?"

"Oh, they did, right at first, but the tax collectors came around and started offering us rewards to point out any new flagstone work here in town." The mason laughed cynically. "It *was* sort of our patriotic duty, after all, and the rewards were nice and substantial. The rich men of Kanthon are all amateur stonemasons now, but oddly enough, not a single one of my pupils has a name that I can recognize. They all seem to have names connected to honest trades, for some strange reason. I guess they're afraid that I might turn them in to the tax collectors if they give me their real names."

Althalus thought long and hard about that bit of information. The tax law of the philosophical new Aryo of Kanthon had more or less put him out of business. If a man was clever enough to hide his money from the tax collectors and their well-equipped demolition crews, what chance did an honest thief have? He could get into their houses easily enough, but the prospect of walking around all that shabby furniture while knowing that his feet might be within inches of hidden wealth made him go cold all over. Moreover, the houses of the wealthy men here were snuggled together so closely that a single startled shout would wake the whole neighborhood. Stealth wouldn't work, and the threat of violence probably wouldn't either. The knowledge that the wealth was so close and yet so far away gnawed at him. He decided that he'd better leave very soon, before temptation persuaded him to stay. Kanthon, as it turned out, was even worse than Deika.

He left Kanthon the very next morning and continued his westward trek, riding across the rich grain fields of Treborea toward Perquaine in a distinctly sour frame of mind. There was wealth beyond counting down here in civilization, but those who had been cunning enough to accumulate it were also, it appeared, cunning enough to devise ways to keep it. Althalus began to grow homesick for the frontier and to devoutly wish that he'd never heard the word "civilization."

He crossed the river into Perquaine, the fabled farmland of the plains country where the earth was so fertile that it didn't even have to be planted, according to the rumors. All a farmer of Perquaine had to do each spring was put on his finest clothes, go out into his fields, and say, "Wheat, please," or, "Barley, if it's not too much trouble," and then return home and go back to bed. Althalus was fairly sure that the rumors were exaggerations, but he knew nothing about farming, so for all he knew there might even be a grain of truth to them.

Unlike the people of the rest of the world, the Perquaines worshiped a female deity. That seemed profoundly unnatural to most people—either in civilization or out on the frontiers—but there was a certain logic to it. The entire culture of Perquaine rested on the vast fields of grain, and the Perquaines were absolutely obsessed with fertility. When Althalus reached the city of Maghu, he discovered that the largest and most magnificent building in the entire city was the temple of Dweia, the Goddess of fertility. He briefly stopped at the temple to look inside, and the colossal statue of the fertility Goddess seemed almost to leap at him. The sculptor who'd carved the statue had quite obviously been either totally insane or caught up in the grip of religious ecstasy when he'd created *that* monstrosity. There *was* a certain warped logic to it, Althalus was forced to concede. Fertility meant motherhood, and motherhood involved the suckling of the young. The statue suggested that the Goddess Dweia was equipped to suckle hundreds of babies all at the same time.

The land of Perquaine had been settled more recently than Treborea or Equero, and the Perquaines still had a few rough edges that made them much more like the people of the frontiers than the stuffier people to the east. The taverns in the seedier parts of Maghu were rowdier than had been the case in Deika or Kanthon, but that didn't particularly bother Althalus. He drifted around town until he finally located a place where the patrons were talking instead of brawling, and he sat down in a corner to listen.

"Druigor's strongbox is absolutely bulging with money," one patron was telling his friends. "I stopped by his countinghouse the other day, and his box was standing wide open, and it was packed so full that he was having trouble latching down the lid."

"That stands to reason," another man said. "Druigor drives very hard bargains. He can always find some way to get the best of anybody he deals with."

"I hear tell that he's thinking about standing for election to the Senate," a wispy-looking fellow added.

"He's out of his mind," the first man snorted. "He doesn't qualify. He doesn't have a title."

The wispy man shrugged. "He'll buy one. There are always nobles running around with nothing in their purses but their titles."

The conversation drifted on to other topics, so Althalus got up and quietly left the tavern. He went some distance down the narrow, cobblestoned street and stopped a fairly well-dressed passerby. "Excuse me," he said politely, "but I'm looking for the countinghouse of a man named Druigor. Do you by any chance happen to know where it is?"

"Everybody in Maghu knows where Druigor's establishment's located," the man replied.

"I'm a stranger here," Althalus replied.

"Ah, that explains it then. Druigor does business over by the west gate. Anybody over in that neighborhood can direct you to his establishment."

"Thank you, sir," Althalus said. Then he walked on.

The area near the west gate was largely given over to barnlike warehouses, and a helpful fellow pointed out the one that belonged to Druigor. It seemed to be fairly busy. People were going in and out through the front door, and there were wagons filled with bulging sacks waiting near a loading dock on one side. Althalus watched for a while. The steady stream of men going in and out through the front door indicated that Druigor was doing a lot of business. That was always promising.

He went on up the street and entered another, quieter warehouse. A sweating man was dragging heavy sacks across the floor and stacking them against a wall. "Excuse me, neighbor," Althalus said. "Who does this place belong to?"

"This is Garwin's warehouse," the sweating man replied. "He's not here right now, though."

"Oh," Althalus said. "Sorry I missed him. I'll come back later." Then he turned, went back out into the street, and walked on down to Druigor's warehouse again. He went inside and joined the others who were waiting to speak with the owner of the place.

When his turn came he went into a cluttered room where a hard-eyed man sat at a table. "Yes?" the hard-eyed man said.

"You're a very busy man, I see," Althalus said, his eyes covering everything in the room.

"Yes, I am, so get to the point."

Althalus had already seen what he'd come to see, however. In the corner of the room stood a bulky bronze box with an elaborate latch holding it shut.

"I've been told that you're a fair man, Master Garwin," Althalus said in his most ingratiating manner, his eyes still busy.

"You've come to the wrong place," the man at the table said. "I'm Druigor. Garwin's establishment's over to the north—four or five doors."

Althalus threw his hands up in the air. "I should have known better than to trust a drunkard," he said. "The man who told me that this was Garwin's place of business could barely stand up. I think I'll go back out into the street and punch that sot right in the mouth. Sorry to have bothered you, Master Druigor. I'll revenge the both of us on that sodden idiot."

"Did you want to see Garwin on business?" Druigor asked curiously. "I can beat his prices on just about anything you can name."

"I'm terribly sorry, Master Druigor," Althalus said, "but my hands are tied this time. My idiot brother made some promises to Garwin, and I can't think of any way to wriggle out of them. When I get back home, I think I'll take my brother out behind the house and brick his mouth shut. Then, the next time I come to Maghu, you and I might want to have a little chat."

"I'll look forward to it, Master . . . ?"

"Kweso," Althalus picked a name at random.

"Are you by any chance a relation of that salt merchant in Deika?"

"He's our father's cousin," Althalus replied glibly. "They aren't talking to each other right now, though. It's one of those family squabbles. Well, you're busy, Master Druigor, so if you'll excuse me, I'll go have some words with that drunkard and then visit Master Garwin and find out how much of the family holdings my half-wit brother's given away."

"I'll see you next time you come to Maghu, then?"

"You can count on it, Master Druigor." Althalus bowed slightly, and then he left.

It was well after midnight when Althalus broke in through the door on Druigor's loading dock. He went on silent feet through the wheat-fragrant warehouse to the room where he'd spoken with Druigor that afternoon. The door to the room was locked, but that, of course, was no problem. Once Althalus was inside the room, he quickly ignited his tinder with his flints and lit a candle sitting on Druigor's table. Then he closely examined the complex latch that held the bulky lid of the bronze strongbox shut. As was usually the case, the complexity had been designed to confuse anyone who might be curious about the contents of the box. Althalus was quite familiar with the design, so he had the latch open in only a few moments.

He lifted the lid and reached inside, his fingers trembling with anticipation.

There were no coins inside the box, however. Instead, it was filled to overflowing with scraps of paper. Althalus lifted out a handful of the scraps and examined them closely. They all seemed to have pictures drawn on them, but Althalus couldn't make any sense of those pictures. He dropped them on the floor and dug out another handful. There were more pictures.

Althalus desperately pawed around inside the box, but his hands did not encounter anything at all that felt anything like money.

This made no sense whatsoever. Why would anybody go to the trouble to lock up stacks of worthless paper?

After about a quarter of an hour, he gave up. He briefly considered piling all that paper in a heap on the floor and setting fire to it, but he discarded that idea almost as soon as it came to him. A fire would almost certainly spread, and a burning warehouse would attract attention. He muttered a few choice swearwords, and then he left.

He gave some thought to returning to the tavern he'd visited on his first day in Maghu and having some words with the tavern loafer who'd spoken so glowingly about the contents of Druigor's strongbox, but he decided against it. The sting of constant disappointments he'd endured this summer was making him very short-tempered, and he wasn't entirely positive that he'd be able to restrain himself once he started chastising somebody. In his present mood, chastisement might very well be looked upon as murder in some circles.

He sourly returned to the inn where his horse was stabled and spent the rest of the night sitting on his bed glaring at the single piece of paper he'd taken from Druigor's strongbox. The pictures drawn on the paper weren't really very good. Why in the world had Druigor bothered to lock them up? When morning finally arrived, Althalus roused the innkeeper and settled accounts with him. Then he reached into his pocket. "Oh," he said, "I just remembered something." He drew out the piece of paper. "I found this in the street. Do you have any idea at all what it means?"

"Of course," the innkeeper replied. "That's money."

"Money? I don't follow you. Money's made out of gold or silver, sometimes copper or brass. This is just paper. It's not worth anything, is it?"

"If you take that to the treasury behind the Senate, they'll give you a silver coin for it."

"Why would they do that? It's just paper."

"It has the seal of the Senate on it. That makes it as good as real silver. Haven't you ever seen paper money before?"

A sense of total defeat came crashing down on Althalus as he went to the stable to pick up his horse. His luck had abandoned him. This had been the worst summer in his entire life. Evidently, his luck didn't want him down here. There was wealth beyond counting in these cities of the plain, but no matter how hard he'd tried, he hadn't managed to get his hands on any of it. As he mounted his horse, he amended that thought. Last night in Druigor's countinghouse, he'd had his hands on more money than he'd likely ever see in the rest of his entire life, but he'd just walked away from it, because he hadn't realized that it *was* money.

He ruefully conceded that he had no business being in the city. He belonged back on the frontier. Things were just too complicated down here.

He mournfully rode his horse to the central marketplace of Maghu to trade his civilized clothes for apparel more suitable to the frontier where he belonged.

The clothier swindled him, but he'd more or less expected that. Nothing down here was ever going to go well for him.

He wasn't even particularly surprised to discover when he came out of the clothier's shop that someone had stolen his horse.

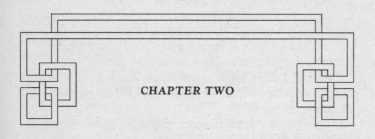

CHAPTER TWO

His sense of defeat made Althalus a little abrupt with the first man who passed his place of concealment late the next night. He stepped out of the shadows, grabbed the unwary fellow by the back of his tunic, and slammed him against a stone wall just as hard as he could. The man sagged limply in his hands, and that irritated Althalus all the more. For some reason he'd been hoping for a bit more in the way of a struggle. He let the unconscious man collapse into the gutter and quickly stole his purse. Then, for no reason he could really justify, he dragged the inert body back into the shadows and stole all the man's clothes.

He realized as he walked down the dark street that what he'd just done was silly, but in some obscure way it seemed appropriate, since it almost perfectly expressed his opinion of civilization. For some reason the absurdity made him feel better.

After he'd gone some distance, however, the bundle of clothes under his arm became a nuisance, so he shrugged and threw it away without even bothering to find out if any of the garments fit him.

As luck had it, the city gates were open, and Althalus left Maghu without even bothering to say good-bye. The moon was almost full, so there was light enough to see by, and he struck out to the north, feeling better with every step. By dawn he was several miles from Maghu, and up ahead he could see the snow-capped peaks of Arum blushing in the pink light of the sunrise.

It was a long walk from Maghu to the foothills of Arum, but Althalus moved right along. The sooner he left civilization behind, the better. The whole idea of going into the low country had been a mistake of the worst kind. Not so much because he hadn't profited: Althalus usually squandered every penny he got his hands on. What concerned him about the whole business was the apparent alienation between him and his luck. Luck was everything; money meant nothing.

He was well up into the foothills by late summer. On a golden afternoon he stopped in a shabby wayside tavern, not because of some vast thirst, but rather out of the need for some conversation with people he could understand.

"You would not *believe* how fat he is," a half-drunk fellow was saying to the tavern keeper. "I'd guess he can afford to eat well; he's got about half the wealth of Arum locked away in his strong room by now."

That got our thief's immediate attention, and he sat down near the tipsy fellow, hoping to hear more.

The tavern keeper looked at him inquiringly. "What's your pleasure, neighbor?" he asked.

"Mead," Althalus replied. He hadn't had a good cup of mead for months, since the lowlanders seemed not to know how to brew it.

"Mead it is," the tavern keeper replied, going back behind the wobbly counter to fetch it.

"I didn't mean to interrupt you," Althalus said politely to the tipsy fellow.

"No offense taken," the fellow said. "I was just telling Arek here about a Clan Chief to the north who's so rich that they haven't invented a number for how many coins he's got locked away in that fort of his."

The fellow had the red face and purple nose of a hard-drinking man, but Althalus wasn't really interested in his complexion. His attention was focused on the man's wolf-skin tunic instead. For some peculiar reason, whoever had sewn the tunic had left the ears on, and they now adorned the garment's hood. Althalus thought that looked very fine indeed. "What did you say the Chief's name was?" he asked.

"He's called Gosti Big Belly—probably because the only exercise he gets is moving his jaw up and down. He eats steadily from morning to night."

"From what you say, I guess he can afford it."

The half-drunk man continued to talk expansively about the wealth of the fat Clan Chief, and Althalus feigned a great interest, buying more mead for them each time the fellow's cup ran dry. By sundown the fellow was slobbering drunk and there was a sizable puddle of discarded mead on the floor near Althalus.

Other men came into the tavern after the sun had set, and the place grew noisier as it grew dark outside.

"I don't know about you, friend," Althalus said smoothly, "but all this mead is starting to talk to me. Why don't we go outside and have a look at the stars?"

The drunken man blinked his bleary eyes. "I think that's a wunnerful idea," he agreed. "My mead's telling me to go see some stars, too."

They rose to go outside, and Althalus caught the swaying man's arm. "Steady, friend," he cautioned. Then they went outside with Althalus half supporting his drunken companion. "Over there, I think," he suggested, pointing at a nearby grove of pine trees.

The man grunted his agreement and lurched toward the pines. He stopped, breathing hard, and leaned back against a tree. "Kinda woozy," he mumbled, his head drooping.

Althalus smoothly pulled his heavy bronze short sword out from under his belt, reversed it, and held it by the blade. "Friend?" he said.

"Hmm?" The man's face came up with a foolish expression and unfocused eyes.

Althalus hit him squarely on the forehead with the heavy hilt of his sword. The man slammed back against the tree and bounced forward.

Althalus hit him on the back of the head as he went by, and the fellow went down.

Althalus knelt beside him and shook him slightly.

The man began to snore.

"That seems to have it," Althalus murmured to himself. He laid his sword down and went to work. After he'd removed his new wolf-skin tunic from the unconscious man, he took the fellow's purse. The purse wasn't very heavy, but his drinking companion's shoes weren't too bad. The trip up from Maghu had left Althalus' own shoes in near tatters, so replacing them was probably a good idea. The snoring man also had a fairly new bronze dagger at his belt, so all in all, Althalus viewed the entire affair as quite profitable. He dragged the man farther back into the shadows, then put on his splendid new tunic and his sturdy shoes. He looked down at his victim almost sadly. "So much for wealth beyond counting," he sighed. "It's back to stealing clothes and shoes, I guess." Then he shrugged. "Oh, well. If that's what my luck wants me to do, I might as well go along with her." He half saluted his snoring victim and left the vicinity. He wasn't exactly deliriously happy, but he was in better spirits than he'd been down in the low country.

He moved right along, since he wanted to be in the lands of the next clan to the north before the previous owner of his fine new tunic awakened. By midmorning of the following day, he was fairly certain that he was beyond the reach of last night's victim, so he stopped in the tavern of a small village to celebrate his apparent change of luck. The wolf-eared tunic wasn't equal to all that unrecognizable wealth in Druigor's countinghouse, but it was a start.

It was in that tavern that he once again heard someone speak of Gosti Big Belly. "I've heard about him," he told the assembled tavern loafers. "I can't imagine why a Clan Chief would let his people call him by a name like that, though."

"You'd almost have to know him to understand," one of the other tavern patrons replied. "You're right about how a name like that would offend most Clan Chiefs, but Gosti's very proud of that belly of his. He even laughs out loud when he brags that he hasn't seen his feet in years."

"I've heard tell that he's rich," Althalus said, nudging the conversation around to the topic that most interested him.

"Oh, he's rich, all right," another confirmed the fact.

"Did his clan happen to come across a pocket of gold?"

"Almost the same thing. After his father was killed in the last clan war, Gosti became Clan Chief, even though most of the men in his clan didn't think none too highly of him on accounta how fat he was. Gosti's got this here cousin, though—Galbak his name is—and Galbak's about seven feet tall, and he's meaner than a snake. Anyway, Gosti decided that a bridge across the river that runs through their valley might make things easier for him when he had to go meet with the other Clan Chiefs, so he ordered his men to build him one. That bridge isn't none too well made, and it's so rickety that it's as much as a man's life is worth to try to cross it. But let me tell you, that's not a river that a man with good sense would want to wade across. The current's so swift that it carries your shadow a good half mile downstream. That rickety bridge is as good as any gold mine, since it's the only way to cross that river for five days' hard travel in either direction, and Gosti's cousin's in charge of it. Nobody who's got his head on straight crosses Galbak. He charges an arm and a leg to cross, and that's how it is that Gosti's got a sizable chunk of the loose money in Arum salted away in that fort of his."

"Well now," Althalus said, "how very interesting."

Different lands required different approaches, and up here in the highlands of Arum our thief's standard plan of attack had always been to ingratiate himself into the halls of men of wealth and power with humorous stories and outrageous jokes. That kind of approach obviously would not have worked in the stuffier cities of the plains where jokes were against the law and laughter was held to be in extremely bad taste.

Althalus knew that tavern stories are almost always exaggerations, but the tales of Gosti Big Belly's wealth went far enough to suggest that there was probably at least sufficient money in the fat man's fort to make a journey there worth the time and effort, so he journeyed to the lands of Big Belly's clan to investigate further.

As he moved north into the mountains of Arum, he occasionally heard a kind of wailing sound far back in the hills. He couldn't immediately identify exactly what kind of animal it was that was making so much noise, but it was far enough away that it posed no immediate threat, so he tried to ignore it. Sometimes at night, though, it seemed very close, and that made Althalus a bit edgy.

He reached the shaky wooden bridge he'd been told about, and he was stopped by a burly, roughly dressed toll taker whose hands and forearms were decorated with the tattoos that identified him as a member of Gosti's clan. Althalus choked a bit over the price the tattooed man demanded for crossing the bridge, but he paid it, since he viewed it in the light of an investment.

"That's a fine-looking garment you've got there, friend," the toll taker noted, looking with a certain envy at the wolf-eared tunic Althalus wore.

"It keeps the weather off," Althalus replied with a casual shrug.

"Where did you come by it?"

"Up in Hule," Althalus replied. "I happened across this wolf, you see, and he was about to jump on me and tear out my throat so that he could have me for supper. Now, I've always sort of liked wolves—they sing so prettily—but I don't like them well enough to provide supper for them. Particularly when I'm going to be the main course. Well, I happened to have this pair of bone

dice with me, and I persuaded the wolf that it might be more interesting if we played dice to decide the matter instead of rolling
around on the ground trying to rip each other apart. So we put up
the stakes on the game and started rolling the dice."

"What stakes?" the bearded clansman asked.

"My carcass and his skin, of course."

The toll taker started to laugh.

"Well—" Althalus began to expand the story. "—I just happen
to be the best dice player in all the world—and we *were* playing
with my dice, and I've spent a lot of time training those dice to
do what I want them to do. Well, to cut this short, the wolf had a
little run of bad luck, so I'm wearing his skin now, and he's up
there in the forest of Hule shivering in the cold because he's running around naked."

The tattooed man laughed even harder.

"Have you ever seen a naked wolf with goose bumps all over
him?" Althalus asked, feigning a sympathetic expression. "Pitiful! I felt terribly sorry for him, of course, but a bet *is* a bet, after
all, and he *did* lose. It wouldn't have been ethical for me to give
his skin back to him after I'd fairly won it, now would it?"

The toll taker doubled over, howling with laughter.

"I felt sort of sorry for the poor beast, and maybe just a little
bit guilty about the whole business. I'll be honest about it right
here and now, friend. I *did* cheat the wolf a few times during our
game, and just to make up for that I let him keep his tail—for de-
cency's sake, of course."

"Oh, that's a rare story, friend!" the chortling toll taker said,
clapping Althalus on the back with one meaty hand. "Gosti's *got*
to hear this one!" And he insisted on accompanying Althalus
across the rickety bridge, through the shabby village of log-
walled and thatch-roofed huts, and on up to the imposing log fort
that overlooked the village and the bridge that crossed the
foaming river.

They entered the fort and proceeded into the smoky main hall.
Althalus had visited many of the clan halls in the highlands of
Arum, so he was familiar with these people's relaxed approach
to neatness, but Gosti's hall elevated untidiness to an art form.

Like most clan halls, this one had a dirt floor with a fire pit in the center. The floor was covered with rushes, but the rushes appeared not to have been changed for a dozen years or so. Old bones and assorted other kinds of garbage rotted in the corners, and hounds—and pigs—dozed here and there. It was the first time Althalus had ever encountered pigs as house pets. There was a rough-hewn table across the front of the hall, and seated at that table stuffing food into his mouth with both hands sat the fattest man Althalus had ever seen. There could be no question about the man's identity, since Gosti Big Belly came by his name honestly. He had piglike little eyes, and his pendulous lower lip hung down farther than his chin. A full haunch of roasted pork lay on the greasy table in front of him, and he was ripping great chunks of meat from that haunch and stuffing them into his mouth. Just behind him stood a huge man with hard, unfriendly eyes.

"Are we disturbing him at lunchtime?" Althalus murmured to his guide.

The tattooed clansman laughed. "Not really," he replied. "With Gosti, it's a little hard to tell exactly which meal he's eating, since they all sort of run together. Gosti eats all the time, Althalus. I've never actually seen him do it, but there are some here who swear that he even eats while he's asleep. Come along. I'll introduce you to him—and to his cousin Galbak, too."

They approached the table. "Ho, Gosti!" the tattooed man said loudly to get the fat man's attention. "This is Althalus. Have him tell you the story of how he came by this fine wolf-eared tunic of his."

"All right," Gosti replied in a deep, rumbling voice, taking a gulp of mead from his drinking horn. He squinted at Althalus with his little piglike eyes. "You don't mind if I keep eating while you tell me the story, do you?"

"Not at all, Gosti," Althalus said. "You *do* appear to have a little gaunt spot under your left thumbnail, and I certainly wouldn't want you to start wasting away right in front of my eyes."

Gosti blinked, and then he roared with laughter, spewing

greasy pork all over the table. Galbak, however, didn't so much as crack a smile.

Althalus expanded the story of his dice game with the wolf into epic proportions, and by nightfall he was firmly ensconced in the chair beside the enormous fat man. After he'd told various versions of the story several times for the entertainment of all the fur-clad clansmen who drifted into the hall, he invented other stories to fill the hall of Gosti Big Belly with nearly continuous mirth. No matter how hard he tried, however, Althalus could never get so much as a smile out of the towering Galbak.

He wintered there, and he was more than welcome to sit at Gosti's table, eating Big Belly's food and drinking his mead, as long as he could come up with new stories and jokes to keep Gosti's belly bouncing up and down with laughter. Gosti's own occasional contributions obviously bored his clansmen, since they were largely limited to boasts about how much gold he had stored away in his strong room. The clansmen had evidently heard those stories often enough to know them all by heart. Althalus found them moderately fascinating, however.

The winter plodded on until it was finally spring, and by then Althalus knew every corner of Big Belly's hall intimately.

The strong room wasn't too hard to locate, since it was usually guarded. It was at the far end of the corridor where the dining hall was located, and three steps led up to the heavy door. A massive bronze lock strongly suggested that things of value were kept inside.

Althalus noticed that the nighttime guards didn't take their jobs very seriously, and by midnight they were customarily fast asleep—a condition not uncommon among men who take large jugs of strong mead to work with them.

All that was left to do now was to wait for the snow to melt—and to stay on the good side of Gosti and his sour-faced giant cousin. If all went well, Althalus would be in a hurry when he left. Galbak had very long legs, so Althalus didn't want deep snow in the passes to slow him down enough for Galbak to catch up with him.

Althalus took to frequently stepping out into the courtyard to check the progress of the spring thaw, and when the last snow-drift disappeared from a nearby pass, he decided that the time had come for him to take his leave.

As it turned out, the strong room of Gosti Big Belly wasn't nearly as strong as Gosti thought it was, and late one night when the fire in the pit in the center of the hall had burned down to embers and Gosti and his clansmen were filling the corners with drunken snores, Althalus went to that strong room, stepped over the snoring guards, undid the simple latch, and slipped inside to transfer some ownership. There was a crude table and a sturdy bench in the center of the room and a pile of heavy-looking skin bags in one corner. Althalus took up one of the bags, carried it to the table, and sat down to count his new wealth.

The bag was about the size of a man's head, and it was loosely tied shut. Althalus eagerly opened the bag, reached his hand inside, and drew out a fistful of coins.

He stared at the coins with a sinking feeling. They were all copper. He dug out another fistful. There were a few yellow coins this time, but they were brass, not gold. Then he emptied the bag out onto the table.

Still no gold.

Althalus raised the torch he'd brought with him to survey the room—maybe Gosti kept his gold in a different pile. There was only the one pile, however. Althalus picked up two more bags and poured their contents onto the table as well. More copper sprinkled with a little brass lay on the now-littered table.

He quickly emptied out all the bags, and there wasn't a single gold coin in any of them. Gosti had hoodwinked him, and he'd evidently hoodwinked just about everybody in Arum as well.

Althalus began to swear. He'd just wasted an entire winter watching a fat man eat. Worse yet, he'd believed all the lies that slobbering fat man had told him. He resisted the strong temptation to return to the hall and to rip Gosti up the middle with his dagger. Instead he sat down to pick the brass coins out of the heaps of copper. He knew that he wouldn't get enough to even begin to pay him for his time, but it'd be better than nothing at all.

After he'd leached all the brass out of the heaps of copper, he stood up and disdainfully tipped the table over to dump all the nearly worthless copper coins onto the floor, and left in disgust.

He went out of the hall, crossed the muddy courtyard, and walked on through the shabby village, cursing his own gullibility and brooding darkly about his failure to take a look into the strong room to verify the fat man's boasting.

Fortune, that most fickle Goddess, had tricked him again. His luck hadn't changed after all.

Despite his bitter disappointment, he stepped right along. He hadn't left Gosti's strong room in a very tidy condition, and it wouldn't be long until the fat man realized that he'd been robbed. The theft hadn't been very large, but it still might not be a bad idea to cross a few clan boundaries—just to be on the safe side. Galbak had the look of a man who wouldn't shrug things off, and Althalus definitely wanted a long head start on Gosti's hard-faced cousin.

After a few days of hard travel, Althalus felt that it was safe enough to stop by a tavern to get a decent meal. Like just about everyone else on the frontiers, Althalus carried a sling, and he was quite skilled with it. He could get by on an occasional rabbit or squirrel, but he was definitely in the mood for a full meal.

He approached a shabby village tavern, but stopped just outside the doorway when he heard someone saying, "—a wolf-skin tunic with the ears still on." He stepped back from the door to listen.

"Gosti Big Belly's fit to be tied," the man who'd just mentioned the tunic went on. "It seems that this Althalus fellow'd just spent the whole winter eating Gosti's food and drinking his mead, and he showed his gratitude by sneaking into Gosti's strong room and stealing two full bags of gold coins."

"Shocking!" somebody else murmured. "What did you say this thief looked like?"

"Well, as I understand it, he's about medium sized and he's got a black beard, but that description fits about half the men in Arum. It's that wolf-eared tunic that gives him away. Gosti's cousin Galbak is offering a huge reward for the fellow's head, but for all of me, he can keep his reward. It's those two bags of gold this Althalus fellow's carrying that interest me. I'm going to track him down, believe me. I'd like to introduce him to the busy end of my spear, and I won't even bother to cut off his head to sell to Galbak." The man gave a cynical laugh. "I'm not a greedy man, friends. Two bags of gold are more than enough to satisfy me."

Althalus stepped around to the side of the tavern to swear. It was the irony of it all that stung so much. Gosti desperately wanted everybody in Arum to believe that he was rich. That absurd reward offer was nothing more than a way for the fat man to verify his boasts. Gosti, still eating with both hands, was probably laughing himself sick right now. Althalus had stolen no more than a handful of brass coins, and now he'd have to run for his life. Gosti would get the fame, and Althalus now had Galbak on his trail and every man in Arum looking for him—with a knife.

Obviously though, he was going to have to get rid of his splendid new tunic, and that *really* bit deep. He went back to the door and peeked inside to identify the man who'd just described him. What had happened had been Gosti's doing, but Gosti wasn't around to punish, so that loud-mouthed tavern loafer was going to have to fill in for him.

Althalus etched the man's features in his mind, and then he went outside the village to wait and watch.

Dusk was settling over the mountains of Arum when the fellow lurched out of the tavern and came wobbling out to the main trail that passed the village. He was carrying a short spear with a broad-bladed bronze tip, and he was whistling tunelessly.

He stopped whistling when Althalus savagely clubbed him to the ground.

Then Althalus dragged him back into the bushes at the side of the trail. He turned the unconscious man over. "I understand you've been looking for me," he said sardonically. "Was there something you wanted to discuss?"

He peeled the man's knitted smock off the limp body, removed his own splendid tunic, and regretfully dropped it on his would-be assassin's face. Then he put on the shabby tunic, stole the man's purse and spear, and left the vicinity.

Althalus didn't have a very high opinion of the man he'd just robbed, so he was fairly certain that the idiot would actually wear that tunic, and that might help to muddy the waters. The description the fellow had been spreading around had mentioned a black beard, so when the sun rose the following morning, Althalus stopped by a forest pool where he could see his reflection in the surface of the water and painfully shaved with his bronze dagger.

Once that had been taken care of, he decided that it might be prudent to continue his northward journey along the ridgelines rather than in the canyons. His shave and his change of clothing had probably disguised him enough to conceal his identity from people who were searching for somebody with a black beard and a wolf-eared tunic, but a fair number of men had stopped by Gosti's hall during the preceding winter, and if some of those guests were among the searchers, they'd probably recognize him. And if *they* didn't, Gosti's cousin Galbak certainly would. Althalus knew the Arums well enough to be certain that they'd stay down in the canyons to conduct their search, since climbing the ridges would be terribly inconvenient and there weren't many taverns up on top where they could rest and refresh themselves. Althalus was positive that no real Arum could ever be found more than a mile away from the nearest tavern.

He climbed the ridge with a sense of bitterness dogging his heels. He'd make good his escape, of course. He was too clever to be caught. What really cankered at his soul was the fact that his escape would just reinforce Gosti's boasts. Gosti's reputation as the richest man in Arum would be confirmed by the fact that the greatest thief in the world had made a special trip to Arum just to rob him. Althalus mournfully concluded that his bad luck was still dogging his heels.

Up on the ridgeline, the sodden remains of last winter's snowdrifts made for slow going, but Althalus slogged his way north. There wasn't much game up here on the ridges, so he frequently went for days without eating.

As he sourly struggled north, he once again heard that peculiar wailing sound he'd first noticed back in the mountains on his way to Gosti's fort the previous autumn. Evidently it was still out there, and he began to wonder if maybe it was following him for some reason. Whatever it was, it was noisy, and its wailing cries echoing back from the mountainsides began to make Althalus distinctly edgy.

It wasn't a wolf; Althalus was sure of that. Wolves travel in packs, and this was a solitary creature. There was an almost despairing quality about its wailing. He eventually concluded that it was most probably the mating season for that particular creature, and that its mournful, hollow cries were nothing more than an announcement to others of its species that it would really like to have some company along about now. Whatever it was, Althalus began to fervently wish that it'd go look for companionship elsewhere, since those unearthly cries of absolute despair were beginning to get on his nerves.

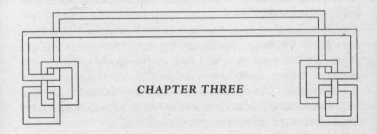

CHAPTER THREE

Althalus was in a somber mood as he slogged north along the ridgelines of Arum. He'd had setbacks before, of course. Nobody wins every time. But always in the past his luck had returned in short order. This time had been somehow different. Everything he'd touched had gone sour. His luck had not just deserted him, she seemed to be going out of her way to ruin everything he attempted. Had he done something that'd turned her love to hate? That gloomy thought hounded him as he came down out of the mountains of Arum into the deep-forested land of Hule.

Hule is the refuge of choice for men who are the unfortunate victims of various misunderstandings in the surrounding lands. Helpful men who "just wanted to give your horse some exercise" or were "just taking your silver coins out into the light to polish them for you," found sanctuary in Hule. There's nothing resembling a government or laws of any kind there, and in a land where there aren't any laws, there's no such thing as a lawbreaker.

Althalus was in a foul humor when he reached Hule, and he felt a great need for the companionship of people of his own kind with whom he could be completely open, so he made his way directly through the forest to the more or less permanent encampment of a Hulish man named Nabjor who brewed good mead and sold it at a fair price. Nabjor also had several plump young ladies available for the convenience of customers who might be feeling lonely for conversation or consolation.

There's a hushed quality about the vast forests of Hule. The trees of that land of the far north are giants, and a traveler can wander under the endless canopy of their outspread limbs for days on end without ever seeing the sun. The trees are evergreens for the most part, and their fallen needles blanket the ground in a deep, damp carpet that muffles the sound of a traveler's footsteps. There are no trails in the land of Hule, since the trees continually shed their dead needles in a gentle sprinkle to cover all signs of the passage of man or beast.

Nabjor's congenial camp lay in a small clearing on the banks of a cheerful little stream that giggled its way over brown rocks, and Althalus approached it with some caution, since a man reputed to be carrying two heavy bags of gold tends to be very careful before he enters any public establishment. After he'd lain behind a fallen tree watching the camp for a while, Althalus concluded that there were no Arums around, so he rose to his feet. "Ho, Nabjor," he called. "It's me, Althalus. Don't get excited; I'm coming in." Nabjor always kept a heavy-bladed bronze axe close at hand to maintain order and to deal with interlopers who might have some questions about his own indiscretions, so it was prudent not to surprise him.

"Ho! Althalus!" Nabjor bellowed. "Welcome! I was beginning to think that maybe the Equeros or the Treboreans had caught you and hung you up on a tree down there."

"No," Althalus replied with a rueful laugh. "I've managed to keep my feet on the ground so far, but only barely. Is your mead ripe yet? That batch you had the last time I passed through was just a trifle green."

"Come and try some," Nabjor invited. "This new batch came out rather well."

Althalus walked into the clearing and looked at his old friend. Nabjor was a burly man with dun-colored hair and beard. He had a large, bulbous nose, shrewd eyes, and he was dressed in a shaggy bearskin tunic. Nabjor was a businessman who sold good mead and rented out ladies. He also bought things with no questions asked from men who stole for a living.

The two of them clasped hands warmly. "Sit you down, my friend," Nabjor said. "I'll bring us some mead, and you can tell me all about the splendors of civilization."

While Nabjor filled two large earthenware cups with foaming mead, Althalus sank down on a log by the fire where a spitted haunch of forest bison sizzled and smoked. "How did things go down there?" he asked, returning to the fire and handing Althalus one of the cups.

"Awful," Althalus said glumly.

"That bad?" Nabjor asked, seating himself on the log on the other side of the fire.

"Even worse, Nabjor. I don't think anybody's come up with a word yet that really describes how bad it was." Althalus took a long drink of his mead. "You got a good run on this batch, my friend."

"I thought you might like it."

"Are you still charging the same price?"

"Don't worry about the price today, Althalus. Today's mead is out of friendship."

Althalus lifted his cup. "Here's to friendship then," he said and took another drink. "They don't even make mead down in civilization. The only thing you can buy in the taverns is sour wine."

"They call *that* civilized?" Nabjor shook his head in disbelief.

"How's business been?" Althalus asked.

"Not bad at all," Nabjor replied expansively. "Word's getting around about my place. Just about everybody in Hule knows by now that if he wants a good cup of mead at a reasonable price, Nabjor's camp is the place to go. If he wants the companionship of a pretty lady, this is the place. If he's stumbled across something valuable that he wants to sell with no embarrassing questions about how he came by it, he knows that if he comes here, I'll be glad to discuss it with him."

"You're going to fool around and die rich, Nabjor."

"If it's all the same to you, I'd rather live rich. All right, since that's out of the way, tell me what happened down in the low country. I haven't seen you for more than a year, so we've got a lot of catching up to do."

"You'd better brace yourself, Nabjor," Althalus warned. "This isn't going to be one of those happy stories." Then he went on to describe his misadventures in Equero, Treborea, and Perquaine at some length.

"That's *awful!*" Nabjor said. "Didn't *anything* turn out well?"

"Not really. Things were so bad that I had to waylay men coming out of taverns to get enough money to pay for my next meal. My luck's gone sour on me, Nabjor. Everything I've touched for the past year and a half's turned to ashes on me. I thought for a while that it was because my luck hadn't followed me when I went down into the low country, but things didn't get any better when I got to Arum." Then he told his friend about his misadventures in the hall of Gosti Big Belly.

"You really *do* have a problem, don't you, Althalus?" Nabjor observed. "It's your luck that's always made you famous. You'd better see what you can do to get back on the good side of her."

"I'd be more than happy to, Nabjor, but I don't know how. She's always been so fond of me that I didn't have to take any special pains to keep her in my pocket. If she had a temple someplace, I'd steal somebody's goat and sacrifice it on her altar. But the way things have been going here lately, the goat would probably kick my brains out before I could cut his throat."

"Oh, cheer up, Althalus. Things have got to get better for you."

"I certainly hope so. I don't see how they could get any worse."

Just then Althalus heard that almost despairing wail again, far back in the trees. "Do you have any idea what sort of animal makes that kind of noise?" he asked.

Nabjor cocked his head to listen. "Can't quite place it," he admitted. "It wouldn't be a bear, would it?"

"I don't think so. Bears don't go around singing in the woods that way. I heard that beast howling for days on end while I was up in Arum."

"Maybe it's heard about Gosti's lies and it's following you to rob you of all your gold."

"Very funny, Nabjor," Althalus said sarcastically.

Nabjor smirked at him. Then he took their cups back to the crock to refill them. "Here," he said, coming back to the fire and holding one of the cups out to Althalus, "smother your laughter with this and quit worrying about animals. They're afraid of fire, so whatever it is out there howling among the trees isn't likely to come in here and sit down with us."

Althalus and Nabjor had a few more cups of mead, and then the thief noticed that his friend had a new wench in his camp. The wench had wicked eyes and a provocative way of walking. He decided that it might be sort of nice if he and the wench got to know each other a little better. He was very much in need of friendship just now.

And so Althalus remained in Nabjor's establishment for quite some time to enjoy the entertainments available there. Nabjor's mead was plentiful, there was usually a haunch of forest bison on a spit near the fire in case anyone grew hungry, and the wench with wicked eyes was talented. Not only that, other thieves, almost all of them old friends and acquaintances, stopped by from time to time, and they could all spend happy hours together, bragging, talking shop, and engaging in friendly dice games. After this past year, Althalus really needed some relaxation to unwind his nerves and restore his good humor. His stock in trade was witty stories and jokes, and a grumpy man can't tell jokes very well.

His meager supply of brass coins was not inexhaustible, however, and after a time his purse grew very slender, so he regretfully concluded that he'd probably better start thinking about going back to work.

And then along toward the end of summer on a blustery day when the racing clouds overhead were blotting out the sun, a man with deep-sunk eyes and lank, greasy black hair rode into Nabjor's camp on a shaggy grey horse. He slid down from the back of his weary mount and came to the fire to warm his hands. "Mead!" he called to Nabjor in a harsh voice.

"I don't know you, friend," Nabjor said suspiciously, fingering his heavy bronze axe. "I'll have to see your money first."

The stranger's eyes hardened, and then he wordlessly shook a heavy leather purse.

Althalus squinted speculatively at the stranger. The fellow was wearing a kind of bronze helmet on his head that reached down the back of his neck to his shoulders, and there were thick bronze plates sewn onto his black leather jerkin. He also wore a long, hooded black cloak that looked rather fine and that Althalus was sure would fit *him*, if the stranger happened to drink too much of Nabjor's mead and drift off to sleep. The man also had a heavy-bladed sword tucked under his belt and a narrow bronze dagger as well.

There was an oddly archaic look about the stranger's features that made his face appear to have been only half finished. Althalus didn't really pay too much attention to the stranger's face, though. What he was really looking for were the characteristic clan tattoos of the Arums. At this particular time Althalus thought it might be prudent to avoid Arums. The stranger, however, had unmarked hands and forearms, so our thief relaxed.

The black-haired stranger seated himself on a log across the fire pit from where Althalus lounged and looked penetratingly at the thief. It might have been some trick of the light, but the dancing flames of the fire were reflected in the stranger's eyes, and that made Althalus just a bit edgy. It's not every day that a man comes across somebody whose eyes are on fire. "I see that I've finally found you," the stranger said in a peculiarly accented voice. It appeared that this man was not one to beat about the bush.

"You've been looking for me?" Althalus said as calmly as possible. The fellow *was* heavily armed, and as far as Althalus knew, there was still a price on his head back in Arum. He carefully shifted his own sword around on his belt so that the hilt was closer to his hand.

"For quite some time now," the stranger replied. "I picked up your trail in Deika. Men down there are still talking about how fast you can run when dogs are chasing you. Then I tracked you to Kanthon in Treborea and on to Maghu in Perquaine. Druigor's still trying to figure out why you just dumped all his money on the floor and didn't steal any of it."

Althalus winced.

"You didn't know that it was money, did you?" the stranger asked shrewdly. "Anyway, I followed you from Maghu up into Arum, and there's a fat man up there who's looking for you even harder than I am."

"I sort of doubt that," Althalus said. "Gosti wants people to think he's rich, and I'm probably the only man around who knows that there's nothing in his strong room but copper pennies."

The stranger laughed. "I thought there was something that didn't quite ring true about the way he kept going on about how you'd robbed him."

"And just why have you spent all this time looking for me?" Althalus asked, getting to the point. "Your clothing says Nekweros, and I haven't been there in years, so I'm sure I haven't stolen anything from you recently."

"Set your mind at rest Althalus, and slide your sword back around your belt so the hilt doesn't keep poking you in the ribs. I haven't come here to take your head back to Gosti. Would you be at all interested in a business proposition?"

"That depends."

"My name's Ghend, and I need a good thief who knows his way around. Are you at all familiar with the land of the Kagwhers?"

"I've been there a few times," Althalus replied cautiously. "I don't care very much for the Kagwhers. They have this habit of assuming that everyone who comes along is there to sneak into their gold mines and just help himself. What is it that you want me to steal for you? You look like the kind of man who can take care of things like that for himself. Why would you want to pay somebody else to do it for you?"

"You're not the only one with a price on his head, Althalus," Ghend replied with a pained expression. "I'm sure I wouldn't care much for the reception I'd get if I happened to venture into Kagwher just now. Anyway, there's someone in Nekweros who's holding some obligations over my head, and he's not the sort I'd want to disappoint. There's something he really wants over in Kagwher, and he's told me to go there and get it for him. That puts me in a very tight spot, you understand. You'd be in the same sort of situation if someone told you to go get something for him and it just happened to be in Arum, wouldn't you?"

"I can see your problem, yes. I should warn you that I don't work cheap, though."

"I didn't expect you to, Althalus. This thing my friend in Nekweros wants is quite large and very heavy, and I'm prepared to pay you its weight in gold if you'll steal it for me."

"You just managed to get my undivided attention, Ghend."

"Are you really as good a thief as everyone says you are?" Ghend's glowing eyes seemed to burn more brightly.

"I'm the best," Althalus said with a deprecating shrug.

"He's right about that, stranger," Nabjor said, bringing Althalus a fresh cup of mead. "Althalus here can steal anything with two ends or with a top and a bottom."

"That might be a slight exaggeration," Althalus said. "A river has two ends, and I've never stolen one of those; and a lake has a top and a bottom, but I've never stolen one of those either. What exactly is it that this man in Nekweros wants badly enough to offer gold for it—some jewel or something like that?"

"No, it's not a jewel," Ghend replied with a hungry look. "What he wants—and will pay gold for—is a book."

"You just said the magic word 'gold' again, Ghend. I could sit here all day and listen to you talk about it, but now we come to the hard part. What in blazes is a book?"

Ghend looked sharply at him, and the flickering firelight touched his eyes again, making them glow a burning red. "So *that's* why you threw all of Druigor's money on the floor. You didn't know that it was money because you can't read."

"Reading's for the priests, Ghend, and I don't have any dealings with priests if I can avoid it. Every priest I've ever come across promises me a seat at the table of his God—*if* I'll just hand over everything I've got in my purse. I'm sure the dining halls of the Gods are very nice, but you have to die to get an invitation to have dinner with God, and I'm not really *that* hungry."

Ghend frowned. "This might complicate things just a bit," he said. "A book is a collection of pages that people read."

"I don't have to be able to read it, Ghend, to be able to steal it. All I have to know is what it looks like and where it is."

Ghend gave him a speculative look, his deep-sunk eyes glowing. "You may be right," he said, almost as if to himself. "I just happen to have a book with me. If I show it to you, you'll know what you're looking for."

"Exactly," Althalus said. "Why don't you trot your book out, and I'll have a look. I don't have to know what it says to be able to steal it, do I?"

"No," Ghend agreed, "I guess you don't at that." He rose to his feet, went over to his horse, reached inside the leather bag tied to his saddle, and took something square and fairly large out of the bag. Then he brought it back to the fire.

"It's bigger than I thought," Althalus noted. "It's just a box, then, isn't it?"

"It's what's inside that's important," Ghend said, opening the lid. He took out a crackling sheet of something that looked like dried leather and handed it to Althalus. "That's what writing looks like," he said. "When you find a box like this one, you'd better open it to make sure it has sheets like that one inside instead of buttons or tools."

Althalus held up the sheet and looked at it. "What kind of animal has a hide this thin?" he asked.

"They take a piece of cowhide and split it with a knife to get thin sheets," Ghend explained. "Then they press them flat with weights and dry them so that they're stiff. Then they write on them so that other people can read what they've put down."

"Trust a priest to complicate things," Althalus said. He looked carefully at the neatly spaced lines of writing on the sheet. "It looks sort of like pictures, doesn't it?" he suggested.

"That's what writing is," Ghend explained. He took a stick and drew a curved line in the dirt beside the fire. "This is the picture that means 'cow,' " he said, "since it's supposed to look like a cow's horns."

"I thought learning to read was supposed to be difficult," Althalus said. "We've only been talking about it for a few minutes, and I already know how to read."

"As long as all you want to read about is cows," Ghend amended, half under his breath.

"I don't see anything about cows on this page," Althalus said.

"You've got it upside down," Ghend told him.

"Oh." Althalus turned the page and studied it for a little while. Some of the symbols carefully drawn on the parchment chilled him for some reason. "I can't make any sense of this," he admitted, "but that's not important. All I really need to know is that I'm looking for a black box with leather sheets inside."

"The box we want is white," Ghend corrected, "and it's quite a bit bigger than this one." He held up his book. The cover of the book had red symbols on it, ones that chilled Althalus.

"How much bigger than yours is the book we want?" he asked.

"It's about as long and as wide as the length of your forearm," Ghend replied, "and about as thick as the length of your foot. It's fairly heavy." He took the sheet of parched leather from Althalus and almost reverently put it back inside the box. "Well?" he said then. "Are you interested in the proposition?"

"I'll need a few more details," Althalus replied. "Just exactly where is this book, and how well is it guarded?"

"It's in the House at the End of the World over in Kagwher."

"I know where Kagwher is," Althalus said, "but I didn't know that the world ended there. Exactly where in Kagwher is this place? What direction?"

"North. It's up in that part of Kagwher that doesn't see the sun in the winter and where there isn't any night in summer."

"That's a peculiar place for somebody to live."

"Truly. The owner of the book hasn't lived there for many, many years, so there won't be anybody there to interfere with you when you go inside the house to steal the book."

"That's convenient. Can you give me any kind of landmarks? I can move faster if I know where I'm going."

"Just follow the edge of the world. When you see a house, you'll know it's the right place. It's the only house up there."

Althalus drank off his mead. "That sounds simple enough," he said. "Now, then, after I've stolen the book, how do I find you to get my pay?"

"I'll find you, Althalus." Ghend's deep-sunk eyes burned even hotter. "Believe me, I'll find you."

"I'll think about it."

"You'll do it then?"

"I said I'll think about it. Now, why don't we have some more of Nabjor's mead—since you're the one who's paying."

Althalus didn't feel very well the next morning, but a few cups of Nabjor's mead quieted the shaking in his hands and put out the fire in his belly. "I'll be gone for a while, Nabjor," he told his friend. "Tell the wench with the naughty eyes that I said good-bye and that I'll see her again someday."

"You're going to do it then? Go steal that book thing for Ghend?"

"You were listening."

"Of course I was, Althalus. Are you really sure you want to do this, though? Ghend kept talking about gold, but I don't remember that he ever showed you any. It's easy to say 'gold,' but actually producing some might be a little more difficult."

Althalus shrugged. "If he doesn't pay, he doesn't get the book." He looked over to where Ghend lay huddled under his excellent black wool cloak. "When he wakes up, tell him that I've left for Kagwher and that I'm going there to steal that book for him."

"Do you really trust him?"

"Almost as far as I could throw him," Althalus replied with a cynical laugh. "The price he promised me sort of hints that there'll be some fellows with long knives nearby when I demand my pay. Besides, if somebody offers to pay me to steal something for him, I'm always certain that the thing's worth at least ten times what he's offering me to steal it. I don't trust Ghend, Nabjor. There were a couple of times last night after the fire had burned down when he looked at me, and his eyes were still on fire. They were glowing bright red, and the glow wasn't a reflection. Then there was that sheet of parched leather he showed me. Most of those pictures were sort of ordinary, but some of them glowed red the same way Ghend's eyes did. Those pictures are supposed to mean words, and I don't think I'd like to have anybody saying those particular words to me."

"If you feel that way about it, why are you going to take on the job, then?"

Althalus sighed. "Normally I wouldn't, Nabjor. I don't trust Ghend, and I don't think I like him. My luck's turned sour on me here lately, though, so I sort of have to take what comes along— at least until fortune falls in love with me again. The job Ghend offered me is fairly simple, you know. All I have to do is go to Kagwher, find a certain empty house, and steal a white leather box. Any fool could do this job, but Ghend offered it to me, so I'm going to jump on it. The job's easy, and the pay's good. It won't be hard to do it right, and if I *do* pull it off, fortune might change her mind and go back to adoring me the way she's supposed to."

"You've got a very strange religion, Althalus."

Althalus grinned at him. "It works for me, Nabjor, and I don't even need a priest to intercede for me and then take half my profits for his services." Althalus looked over at the sleeping Ghend again. "How careless of me," he said. "I almost forgot to pick up my new cloak." He walked over to where Ghend lay, gently removed the black wool cloak, and put it around his own shoulders.. "What do you think?" he asked Nabjor, striking a pose.

"It looks almost as if it's been made for you," Nabjor chuckled.

"Probably it was. Ghend must have stolen it while I was busy." He walked back, digging several brass coins out of his purse. "Do me a favor, Nabjor," he said, handing over the coins. "Ghend drank a lot of your mead last night, and I noticed that he doesn't hold his drink very well. He won't be feeling too good when he wakes up, so he's going to need some medicine to make him feel better. Give him as much as he can drink, and if he's feeling delicate again tomorrow morning, get him well again with the same medicine—and change the subject if he happens to ask what happened to his cloak."

"Are you going to steal his horse, too? Riding's easier than walking."

"When I get so feeble that I can't do my own walking, I'll take up begging at the side of the road. A horse would just get in my way. Keep Ghend drunk for a week, if you can manage it. I'd like to be a long ways up into the mountains of Kagwher before he sobers up."

"He said that he's afraid to go into Kagwher."

"I don't think I believe him on that score either. He knows the way to that house up there, but I think it's the house he's afraid of, not the whole of Kagwher. I don't want him hiding in the bushes when I come out of that house with the book under my arm, so keep him drunk enough not to follow me. Make him feel good when he wakes up."

"That's why I'm here, Althalus," Nabjor said piously. "I'm the friend of all men when they're thirsty or sick. My good strong mead is the best medicine in the world. It can cure a rainy day, and if I could think of a way to make a dead man swallow it, I could probably even cure him of being dead with it."

"Nicely put," Althalus said admiringly.

"Like you always say, I've got this way with words."

"And with your brewing crocks. Be the friend of Ghend then, Nabjor. Cure him of any unwholesome urges to follow me. I don't like to be followed when I'm working, so make him good and drunk right here so that I don't have to make him good and dead somewhere up in the mountains."

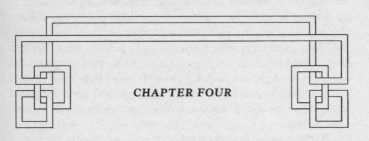

CHAPTER FOUR

It was late summer now in deep-forested Hule, and Althalus could travel more rapidly than he might have in less-pleasant seasons. The vast trees of Hule kept the forest floor in perpetual twilight, and the carpet of needles was very thick, smothering obstructing undergrowth.

Althalus always moved cautiously when traveling through Hule, but this time he went through the forest even more carefully. A man whose luck has gone bad needs to take extra precautions. There were other men moving through the forest, and even though they were kindred outlaws, Althalus avoided them. There weren't any laws in Hule, but there *were* rules about behavior, and it was very unhealthy to ignore those rules. If an armed man doesn't want company, it's best not to intrude upon him.

When Althalus was not too far from the western edge of the land of the Kagwhers, he encountered another of the creatures who lived in the forest of Hule, and things were a little tense for a while. A pack of the hulking forest wolves caught his scent. Althalus didn't really understand wolves. Most animals don't bother to waste time on things that aren't easy to catch and eat. Wolves, however, seem to enjoy challenges, and they'll chase something for days on end just for the fun of the chase. Althalus could laugh at a good joke with the best of them, but he felt that the wolves of Hule tended to run a joke all the way into the ground.

And so it was with some relief that he moved up into the highlands of Kagwher, where the trees thinned out enough to make the forest wolves howl one final salute and turn back.

There was, as all the world knows, gold in Kagwher, and that made the Kagwhers a little hard to get along with. Gold, Althalus had noticed, does peculiar things to people. A man with nothing in his purse but a few copper coins can be the most good-natured and fun-loving fellow in the world, but give him a little bit of gold and he immediately turns suspicious and unfriendly and spends almost every waking moment worrying about thieves and bandits.

The Kagwhers had devised a charmingly direct means of warning passersby away from their mines and those streams where smooth, round lumps of gold lay scattered among the brown pebbles just under the surface of the water. Any time a traveler in Kagwher happened across a stake driven into the ground with a skull adorning its top, he knew that he was approaching forbidden ground. Some of the skulls were those of animals; most of them, however, were the skulls of men. The message was fairly clear.

So far as Althalus was concerned, the mines of Kagwher were perfectly safe. There was a lot of backbreaking labor involved in wrenching gold out of the mountains, and other men were far better suited for that than he was. Althalus *was* a thief, after all, and he devoutly believed that actually working for a living was unethical.

Ghend's directions hadn't really been too precise, but Althalus knew that his first chore was going to be finding the edge of the world. The problem with that was that he wasn't entirely sure what the edge of the world was going to look like. It might be a sort of vague, misty area where an unwary traveler could just walk off and fall forever through the realm of stars that wouldn't even notice him as he hurtled past. The word "edge," however, suggested a brink of some kind—possibly a line with ground on one side and stars on the other. It was even possible that it might just be a solid wall of stars, or even a stairway of stars stretching all the way up to the throne of whatever God held sway here in Kagwher.

Althalus didn't really have a very well-defined system of belief. He knew that he was fortune's child, and even though he and fortune were currently a bit on the outs, he hoped that he'd be able to cuddle up to her again before too long. The ruler of the universe was a little distant, and Althalus had long since decided to let God—whatever his name was—concentrate on managing the sunrises and sunsets, the turning of the seasons, and the phases of the moon without the distraction of suggestions. All in all, Althalus and God got along fairly well, since they didn't bother each other.

Ghend had said that the edge of the world lay to the north, so when Althalus reached Kagwher, he bore off to the left rather than climbing higher into the mountains where most of the gold mines were located and where the Kagwhers were all belligerently protective.

He came across a few roughly clad and bearded men of Kagwher as he traveled north, but they didn't want to discuss the edge of the world for some reason. Evidently this was one of the things they weren't supposed to talk about. He'd encountered this oddity before, and it had always irritated him. Refusing to talk about something wouldn't make it go away. If it was there, it was there, and no amount of verbal acrobatics could make it go away.

He continued his journey northward, and the weather became more chill and the Kagwher villages farther and farther apart until finally they petered out altogether, and Althalus found himself more or less alone in the wilderness of the far north. Then one night as he sat in his rough camp huddled over the last embers of his cooking fire with his new cloak wrapped tightly around his shoulders, he saw something to the north that rather strongly told him that he was getting closer to his goal. Darkness was just beginning to settle over the mountains off to the east, but up toward the north where the night was in full bloom, the sky was on fire.

It was very much like a rainbow that had gotten out of hand. It was varicolored: not the traditional arch of an ordinary rainbow, but rather a shimmering, pulsating curtain of multicolored light, seething and shifting in the northern sky. Althalus wasn't very superstitious, but watching the sky catch on fire isn't the sort of thing a man can just shrug off.

He amended his plans at that point. Ghend had told him about the edge of the world, but he'd neglected to mention anything about the sky catching on fire. There was something up here that frightened Ghend, and Ghend had not seemed to be the sort of man who frightened easily. Althalus decided that he'd continue his search. There was gold involved, and even more importantly, the chance to wash off the streak of bad luck that had dogged his steps for more than a year now. That fire up in the sky, however, set off a very large bell inside his head. It was definitely time to start paying very close attention to what was going on around him. If too many more unusual things happened up here, he'd go find something else to do—maybe over in Ansu, or south on the plains of Plakand.

Just before sunrise the next morning he was awakened by a human voice, and he rolled out from under his cloak, reaching for his spear. He heard only one voice, but whoever was talking seemed to be holding a conversation of some kind, asking questions and seeming to listen to replies.

The conversationalist was a crooked and bent old man, and he was shambling along with the aid of a staff. His hair and beard were a dirty white, he was filthy, and he was garbed in scraps of rotting, fur-covered animal skins held together with cords of sinew or twisted gut. His weathered face was deeply lined, and his rheumy eyes were wild. He gesticulated as he talked, casting frequent, apprehensive glances up at the now-colorless sky.

Althalus relaxed. This man posed no threat, and his condition wasn't all that uncommon. Althalus knew that people were supposed to live for just so long, but if someone accidentally missed his appointed time to die, his mind turned peculiar. The condition was most common in very old people, but the same thing could happen to much younger men if they carelessly happened to miss their appointment. Some claimed that these crazy people had been influenced by demons, but that was really far too complicated. Althalus much preferred his own theory. Crazy people were just ordinary folk who'd lived too long. Roaming around after they were supposed to be lying peacefully in their graves would be enough to make anybody crazy. That's why they started talking to people—or other things—that weren't really there, and why they began to see things that nobody else could see. They were no particular danger to anyone, so Althalus normally left them alone. Those who were incapable of minding their own business always got excited about crazy people, but Althalus had long since decided that most of the world's people were crazy anyway, so he treated everybody more or less the same.

"Ho, there," he called to the crazy old man. "I mean you no harm, so don't get excited."

"Who's that?" the old man demanded, seizing his staff in both hands and brandishing it.

"I'm just a traveler, and I seem to have lost my way."

The old man lowered his staff. "Don't see many travelers around here. They don't seem to like our sky."

"I noticed the sky myself just last night. Why does it do that?"

"It's the edge of things," the old man explained. "That curtain of fire up in the sky is where everything stops. This side's all finished—filled up with mountains and trees and birds and bugs and people and beasts. The curtain is the place where nothing begins."

"Nothing?"

"That's all there is out there, traveler—nothing. God hasn't gotten around to doing anything about it yet. There isn't anything at all out beyond that curtain of fire."

"I haven't lost my way then after all. That's what I'm looking for—the edge of the world."

"What for?"

"I want to see it. I've heard about it, and now I want to see it for myself."

"There's nothing to see."

"Have you ever seen it?"

"Lots of times. This is where I live, and the edge of the world's as far as I can go when I travel north."

"How do I get there?"

The old man stabbed his stick toward the north. "Go that way for about a half a day."

"Is it easy to recognize?"

"You can't hardly miss it—at least you'd better not." The crazy man cackled. "It's a place where you want to be real careful, 'cause if you make one wrong step when you come to that edge, your journey's going to last for a lot longer than just a half a day. If you're really all that eager to see it, go across this meadow and through the pass between those two hills up at the other end of the grass. When you get to the top of the pass you'll see a big dead tree. The tree stands right at the edge of the world, so that's as far as you'll be able to go—unless you know a way to sprout wings."

"Well then, as long as I'm this close, I think I'll go have a look."

"That's up to you, traveler. I've got better things to do than stand around looking at nothing."

"Who were you talking to just now?"

"God. Me and God, we talk to each other all the time."

"Really? Next time you talk to him, why don't you give him my regards? Tell him I said hello."

"I'll do that—if I happen to think of it." And then the shabby old fellow shambled on, continuing his conversation with the empty air around him.

Althalus went back to his camp, gathered up his belongings, and set out across the rocky meadow toward the two low, rounded hills the old man had indicated. The sun rose, climbing

above the snowy peaks of Kagwher, and the night chill began
to fade.

The hills were darkly forested, and there was a narrow pass
between them where the ground had been trampled by the
hooves of deer and bison. Althalus moved carefully, stopping to
examine the game trail for any unusual footprints. This was a
very peculiar place, and it was entirely possible that unusual
creatures lived here. Unusual creatures sometimes had unusual
eating habits, so it was time to start being very careful.

He moved on, stopping frequently to look around and listen,
but the only sounds he heard were the songs of birds and the
sluggish buzzing of a few insects just starting to come awake
after the chill night.

When he reached the top of the pass, he stopped again for
quite a long time to look to the north, not because there was anything to see in that direction, but because there wasn't. The game
trail went on down through a narrow patch of grass toward the
dead snag the crazy old man had mentioned, and then it stopped.
There wasn't anything at all beyond that tree. There were no distant mountain peaks and no clouds. There was nothing but sky.

The dead snag was bone white, and its twisted limbs seemed
to reach in mute supplication to the indifferent morning sky.
There was something unnerving about that, and Althalus grew
even more edgy. He walked very slowly across the intervening
stretch of grass, stopping quite often to bring his eyes—and his
spear—around to look toward his rear. He'd seen nothing threatening so far, but this was a very unusual place, and he didn't
want to take any chances.

When he reached the tree, he put his hand on it to brace himself and leaned out carefully to look down over the edge of what
appeared to be a precipice of some kind.

There wasn't anything down there but clouds.

Althalus had been in the mountains many times before, and
he'd frequently been in places that were above the clouds, so
looking down at the tops of them wasn't really all that unusual.
But these clouds stretched off to the north with absolutely no
break or occasional jutting peak for as far as he could see. The

world ended right here, and there was nothing past here but clouds.

He stepped back from the tree and looked around. There were rocks lying here and there, so he lifted one that was about the size of his head, carried it back to the tree, and heaved it as far as he could out over the edge. Then he cocked his head to listen.

He listened for a long time, but he didn't hear anything. "Well," he murmured, "this must be the place."

He stayed some distance back from the Edge of the World and followed it off toward the northeast.

There were places where tumbling rock slides had rolled down from nearby mountainsides to spill over the edge, and Althalus idly wondered if those sudden avalanches might have startled the stars. That thought struck him as funny for some reason. The notion of stars whirring off in all directions like a frightened covey of quail was somehow vastly amusing. The cold indifference of the stars sometimes irritated him.

In the late afternoon he took his sling and picked up several round stones from a dry creek bed. There were hares and beaver-faced marmots about, and he decided that some fresh meat for supper might be an improvement over the tough strips of dried venison he carried in the pouch at his belt.

It didn't take too long. Marmots are curious animals, and they have the habit of standing up on their hind legs beside their burrows to watch passing travelers. Althalus had a good eye, and he was very skilled with his sling.

He chose a small grove of stunted pines, built a fire, and roasted his marmot on a spit. After he'd eaten, he sat by his fire watching the pulsating, rainbow-colored light of God's fire in the northern sky.

Then, purely on an impulse that came over him just after moonrise, he left his camp and went over to the Edge of the World.

The moon gently caressed the misty cloud tops far below, setting them all aglow. Althalus had seen this before, of course, but it was different here. The moon in her nightly passage drinks all color from the land and sea and sky, but she could not drink the

color from God's fire, and the seething waves of rainbow light in
the northern sky also burnished the tops of the clouds below. It
seemed that they almost played there among the cloud tops, with
the moon's pale light encouraging the amorous advances of the
rainbow fire. All bemused by the flicker and play of colored light
that seemed almost to surround and enclose him, Althalus lay in
the soft grass with his chin in his hands to watch the courtship of
the moon and the fire of God.

And then, far back among the jagged peaks of the land of the
Kagwhers, he once again heard that solitary wailing that he'd
heard before in Arum and again in the forest outside Nabjor's
camp. He swore, rose to his feet, and went back to his camp.
Whatever was out there was obviously following him.

His sleep was troubled that night. The fire of God in the
northern sky and the wailing back in the forest were somehow
all mixed together, and that mixing seemed to have a significance that he couldn't quite grasp, no matter how he struggled
with it. It must have been along toward dawn when his dreams of
fire and wailing were banished by yet another dream.

Her hair was the color of autumn, and her limbs were rounded
with a perfection that made his heart ache. She was garbed in a
short, archaic tunic, and her autumn hair was plaited elaborately.
Her features were somehow alien in their perfect serenity. On his
recent trip to the civilized lands of the south, he had viewed ancient statues, and his dream visitor's face more closely resembled the faces of yore than the faces of the people of the
mundane world. Her brow was broad and straight, and her nose
continued the line of her forehead unbroken. Her lips were sensual, intricately curved, and as ripe as cherries. Her eyes were
large and very green, and it seemed that she looked into his very
soul with those eyes.

A faint smile touched those lips, and she held her hand out to
him. "Come," she said in a soft voice. "Come with me. I will
care for you."

"I wish I could," he found himself saying, and he cursed his
tongue. "I would go gladly, but it's very hard to get away."

"If you come with me, you will never return," she told him in her throbbing voice, "for we shall walk among the stars, and fortune will never betray you more. And your days will be filled with sun and your nights with love. Come. Come with me, my beloved. I will care for you." And she beckoned and turned to lead him.

And, all bemused, he followed her, and they walked out among the clouds, and the moon and the fire of God welcomed them and blessed their love.

And when he awoke, there was a sour emptiness in him, and the taste of all the world was bitter, bitter.

He continued on toward the northeast for the next several days, and he almost hoped that at some point he might see a peak or even a low-lying shadow emerging from the perpetual cloud beyond the Edge of the World to prove that this was *not* the place where everything ended. But nothing ever emerged, and he gradually and with great reluctance was forced to concede that the sharp brink he followed was indeed the very Edge of the World and that there was nothing beyond but cloudy emptiness.

The days grew shorter and the nights more chill as Althalus followed the Edge of the World, and he began to look at the prospect of a very unpleasant winter looming ahead. If he didn't come to the house Ghend had described very soon, he'd have to pull back, seek some kind of shelter, and lay in a supply of food. He decided that the first snowflake that touched his face would send him south in search of someplace to hole up until spring. He began to keep his eyes directed toward the south in search of a break in the mountains, even as he continued along the Edge of the World.

Perhaps it was because his attention was divided that he didn't even see the house until he was quite close to it. The house was made of stone, which was unusual here on the frontier, where most houses were made of logs or thatched limbs. Moreover, such houses as he had seen in civilized lands had been made of limestone. *This* house, however, had been built of granite blocks, and granite would eat up at a ferocious rate the bronze saws that slaves used to cut limestone.

Althalus had never seen a house like this one before. The

granite house at the Edge of the World was enormous, bigger even than the log fort of Gosti Big Belly back in Arum or the temple of Apwos in Deika. It was so huge that it rivaled several nearby natural spires for sheer size. It wasn't until he saw windows that he finally accepted the fact that it really *was* a house. Natural rock formations *do* break off into square shapes from time to time, but a natural formation with windows? Not very likely.

It was about noon on a short, overcast late autumn day when Althalus first saw the house, and he approached it with some caution. Ghend had told him that it was unoccupied, but Ghend had probably never been here, since Althalus was still convinced that Ghend was afraid of the house.

The silent house stood on a promontory that jutted out from the Edge of the World, and the only way to approach it would be to cross the drawbridge that had been built to span the deep chasm that separated the house from the narrow plateau that lined the precipice where the world ended. If the house was indeed deserted, the owner would certainly have devised some way to raise that drawbridge before he'd left. But the drawbridge was down, almost inviting entry. That didn't ring true at all, and Althalus ducked down behind a moss-covered boulder to gnaw at a fingernail and consider options.

The day was wearing on, and he'd have to decide soon whether to just walk on in or wait until night. Night was the native home of all thieves; but under these circumstances, might it not be safer to cross that bridge in the daylight? The house was unfamiliar, and if the place was indeed occupied, the people inside would be alert at night, and they would know exactly how to slip up behind him if he tried to sneak inside. Might it not be better to openly cross the bridge and even shout some kind of greeting to the unseen occupants? That *might* persuade them that he had no evil intent, and he was fairly sure that he could talk fast enough to keep them from immediately hurling him into the void beyond the promontory.

"Well," he muttered, "I guess it's worth a try." If the house was indeed empty, all he'd be wasting was his breath. He still had lots of that, and trying to sneak in at night might be a very good way to cut it short. A show of friendly innocence really seemed to be the best approach right now.

Acting on that, he rose to his feet, took up his spear, and walked on across the bridge, making no effort to conceal himself. If anyone was in the house watching, he'd certainly see Althalus, and a casual saunter across the bridge would shout louder than words that he had no unsavory motives.

The bridge led to a massive arch, and just beyond that arch lay an open place where the ground was covered with closely fitting flat stones with weeds growing up through the cracks. Althalus braced himself and took a tighter grip on his spear. "Ho!" he shouted. "Ho, the house!" He paused, listening intently.

But there was no answer.

"Is anybody here?" he tried again.

The silence was oppressive.

The main door of the house was massive. Althalus poked his spear at it a few times and found it to be quite solid. Once again the warning bell sounded inside his head. If the house had been empty for as long as Ghend had suggested, the door should have completely rotted away by now. All sorts of normal rules didn't appear to be in force here. He took hold of the massive ring and pulled the heavy door open. "Is anybody here?" he called once more.

He waited again, but again there was no answer.

There was a broad corridor leading back into the house beyond the doorway, and there were other corridors branching off from that main one at regular intervals, and there were many doors in each corridor. The search for the book would obviously take longer than he'd thought.

The light inside the house was growing dimmer, and Althalus was fairly certain that evening was rapidly descending. He was obviously running out of daylight. The first order of business now was to find a secure place to spend the night. He could begin his search of the house tomorrow.

He looked down one of the side corridors and saw a rounded wall at the far end, which hinted strongly that there might be a tower there. A tower room, he reasoned, would probably be more secure than a chamber on the ground floor, and the notion of security in this peculiar structure seemed fairly important just now.

He hurried down the hall and found a door somewhat larger than those he'd previously passed. He rapped his sword hilt against the door. "Ho, in there?" he called.

But of course there was no answer.

The door latch was a bronze bar that had been designed to slip into a hole chipped deep into the stone door frame. Althalus tapped its knob with the butt of his sword until it cleared the hole. Then he poked the point of his sword into the edge of the door, flipped the door open, and jumped back, sword and spear at the ready.

There was nobody behind that door, but there were steps leading upward.

The likelihood that these hidden steps just *happened* to be behind a door Althalus had just *happened* to notice in passing was very, very slim. The clever thief had a profound distrust of things that came about by sheer chance. Chance was almost always a trap of some kind, and if there *was* a trap in this house, there almost had to be a trapper.

There wasn't much daylight left, however, and Althalus didn't really want to meet whomever it was at night. He drew in a deep breath. Then he tapped the first step with the butt end of his spear to make certain that the weight of his foot wouldn't bring something heavy down on top of him. It was slow going up the stairs that way, but the careful thief methodically checked every single step before he put his foot on it. Just because ten steps had been perfectly safe, there were no guarantees that the eleventh wouldn't kill him, and the way his luck had been going lately, it was better to take some extra precautions.

He finally reached the door at the top of those hidden steps, and he decided not to rap this time. He tucked his sword under his left arm and slowly pushed the latch back until it came clear of the stone door frame. Then he took hold of his sword again and nudged the door open with his knee.

Beyond the door there was one room, and one only. It was a

large, circular room, and the floor was as glossy as ice. The whole house was strange, but this particular room seemed stranger still. The walls were also polished and smooth, and they curved inward to form a dome overhead. The workmanship that had created this room was far more advanced than anything Althalus had ever seen before.

The next thing he noticed was how warm the room seemed to be. He looked around, but there was no fire pit to explain the warmth. His new cloak wasn't necessary here.

Reason told him that the room should not be warm, since there was no fire and there were four broad windows, one looking out in each direction. There should be cold air blowing in through each of those unglazed windows, but there was not. That wasn't at all natural. Winter was coming, so the air outside was bitterly cold; but it wasn't coming in, for some reason.

Althalus stood in the doorway carefully looking over every bit of the domed, circular room. There was what appeared to be a very large stone bed against the far wall, and the bed was covered with dark, thick-furred bison robes. There was a table made of the same polished stone as the floor and walls, and the table rested on a stone pedestal in the center of the floor, and there was an ornately carved stone bench beside that table.

And there, resting on the precise center of that gleaming tabletop, was the book Ghend had described.

Althalus cautiously approached the table. Then he leaned his spear against it, and with his sword firmly gripped in his right hand, he rather hesitantly reached out with his left. Something about the way Ghend had handled that black-boxed book of his back in Nabjor's camp had suggested that books should be approached with extreme caution. He touched his fingers to the soft white leather of the book's enclosing box, and then he snatched his hand away to grab up his spear as he heard a faint sound.

It was a soft, contented sort of sound that seemed to be coming from the fur-covered bed. The sound was not exactly continuous, but seemed to change pitch slightly, going in and out almost like breathing.

Before he could investigate, though, something else happened that took his attention away from that soft sound. Twilight was deepening outside the windows, but it was not growing dark in this room. He looked up in astonishment. The dome above him had begun to glow, growing slowly brighter and perfectly matching its brightening to the pace of the increasing darkness outside. The only source of light other than the sun, the moon, and the shimmering curtain of God's light at the Edge of the World was fire, and the dome over his head was not on fire.

Then that contented sound coming from the bed grew even louder, and now that the light from the dome over his head was growing brighter, Althalus could see the source of that sound. He blinked, and then he almost laughed. The sound was coming from a cat.

It was a very dark cat, almost black, and it blended so well into the dark fur of the bison robes on the bed that his cursory glance when he'd first entered the room had missed it entirely. The cat lay on its belly with its head up, though its eyes were closed. Its front paws were stretched out on the robe in front of its short-furred chest, and they were making little kneading motions. The sound that had so baffled Althalus was the sound of purring.

Then the cat opened its eyes. Most of the cats Althalus had seen before had looked at him with yellow eyes. This cat's eyes, however, were a brightly glowing green.

The cat rose to its feet and stretched, yawning and arching its sinuous back and hooking its tail up. Then the furry creature sat down, looking into the face of Althalus with its penetrating green eyes as if it had known him all its life.

"You certainly took your own sweet time getting here," the cat observed in a distinctly feminine voice. "Now why don't you go shut that door you left standing wide open? It's letting in the cold, and I just *hate* the cold."

CHAPTER FIVE

Althalus stared at the cat in utter disbelief. Then he sighed mournfully and sank down onto the bench in absolute dejection. His luck hadn't been satisfied with everything else she'd done to him. Now she was twisting the knife. *This* was why Ghend had hired somebody else to steal the book instead of doing it himself. The House at the End of the World didn't need guards or hidden traps to protect it. It protected itself and the book from thieves by driving anyone who entered it mad. He sighed and looked reproachfully at the cat.

"Yes?" she said with that infuriatingly superior air all cats seem to have. "Was there something?"

"You don't have to do that anymore," he told her. "You and this house have already done what you're supposed to do. I've gone completely insane."

"What in the world are you talking about?"

"Cats can't talk. It's impossible. You aren't really talking to me, and now that I think about it, you're probably not really even there. I'm seeing you and hearing you talk because I've gone crazy."

"You're being ridiculous, you know."

"Crazy people *are* ridiculous. I met a crazy man on my way here, and he went around talking to God. Lots of people talk to God, but that old fellow believed that God talked back to him." Althalus sighed mournfully. "It'll probably all be over before long. Since I'm crazy now, it shouldn't be very long until I throw myself out of the window and fall on down through the stars forever and ever. That's the sort of thing a crazy man would do."

"What do you mean by 'fall forever'?"

67

"This house is right at the end of the world, isn't it? If I jump out that window, I'll just fall and fall through all that nothing that's out there."

"Whatever gave you the ridiculous idea that this is the end of the world?"

"Everybody says it is. The people here in Kagwher won't even talk about it, because they're afraid of it. I've looked out over that edge, and all there is down there is clouds. Clouds are part of the sky, so that means that this edge is the place where the world ends and the sky starts, doesn't it?"

"No," she replied, absently licking one of her paws and washing her face. "That's not what it means at all. There *is* something down there. It's a long way down, but it *is* there."

"What is it?"

"It's water, Althalus, and what you saw when you looked over that edge is fog. Fog and clouds are more or less the same thing—except that fog's closer to the ground."

"You know my name?" That surprised him.

"Well, of *course* I know your name, you ninny. I was sent here to meet you."

"Oh? Who sent you?"

"You're having enough trouble holding on to your sanity already. Let's not push you off any edges with things you aren't ready to understand just yet. You might as well get used to me, Althalus. We're going to be together for a long, long time."

He shook off his momentary dejection. "No," he said. "I think I've had just about enough of this. It's been just wonderful talking with you, but if you'll excuse me now, I think I'll just take the book and go. I'd love to stay and chat some more, but winter's going to be snapping at my tail feathers all the way home as it is."

"And just how did you plan to leave?" she asked calmly as she started to wash her ears.

He turned sharply to look around. But the door through which he had entered the room wasn't there anymore. "How did you do that?"

"We won't be needing it anymore—for a while at least—and

it was letting in the cold air, since you were too lazy to close it behind you when you came in."

A brief panic clutched at the thief's throat. He was trapped. The book had lured him into this place, and now the cat had trapped him, and there was no way out. "I think I'll kill myself," he said mournfully.

"No you won't," she said quite calmly, beginning to wash her tummy. "You can try, if you like, but it won't work. You can't leave, you can't jump out of the window, and you can't stab yourself with your sword or your knife or your spear. You might as well get used to it, Althalus. You're going to stay right here with me until we've done what we're supposed to do."

"Then I can leave?" he asked hopefully.

"You'll be required to leave. We have things we need to do here, and then there are other things that have to be done in other places, so you'll have to go do them."

"What are we supposed to do here?"

"I'm supposed to teach, and you're supposed to learn."

"Learn what?"

"The Book."

"How to read it, you mean?"

"That's part of it." She began to wash her tail, hooking it up to her tongue with one curved paw. "After you learn how to read it, you have to learn how to use it."

"Use?"

"We'll get to that in time. You're having enough trouble here already."

"I'll tell you something right here and now," he said hotly. "I am *not* going to take any orders from a cat."

"Yes, actually, you will. It may take you a while to come around, but that's all right, because we've got all the time in the world." She stretched and yawned. Then she looked herself over. "All nice and neat," she said approvingly. Then she yawned again. "Did you have any other silly announcements you'd like to make? I've finished everything that I have to say."

The light in the dome overhead began to grow dim.

"What's happening?" he demanded sharply.

"Now that I've got my fur all nice and neat, I think I'll take a little nap."

"You just woke up."

"What's that got to do with anything? Since you're obviously not ready to do what you're supposed to do, I might as well sleep for a while. When you change your mind, wake me up and we'll get started." And then she settled back down on the thick-furred bison robe and closed her eyes again.

Althalus spluttered to himself for a bit, but the sleeping cat didn't so much as twitch an ear. Finally he gave up and rolled himself up in his cloak near the wall where the door had been, and he too went to sleep.

Althalus held out for several days, but his profession had made him a high-strung sort of man, and the forced inactivity in this sealed room was beginning to fray his nerves. He walked around the room several times and looked out the windows. He discovered that he could put his hand—or his head—through them quite easily, but when he tried to lean out, something that he couldn't see was in his way. Whatever that something was kept out the much colder air outside. There were so many things about this room that couldn't be explained, and the thief's curiosity finally got the best of him. "All right," he said to the cat one morning as daylight began to stain the sky, "I give up. You win."

"Of course I won," she replied, opening her bright green eyes. "I always do." She yawned and stretched sinuously. "Now why don't you come over here so that we can talk?"

"I can talk from right here." He was a little wary about getting too close to her. It was clear that she could do things he couldn't understand, and he didn't want her to start doing them to him.

Her ears flicked slightly, and she lay back down. "Let me know when you change your mind," she told him. And then she closed her eyes again.

He muttered some choice swearwords, and then he gave up, rose from the bench beside the table, and went to the fur-robed bed. He sat down, reached out rather tentatively, and touched her furry back with his hand to make sure that she was really there.

"That was quick," she noted, opening her eyes again and starting to purr.

"There's not much point in being stubborn about it. You're obviously the one who's in control of things here. You wanted to talk?"

She nuzzled at his hand. "I'm glad you understand," she said, still purring. "I wasn't ordering you around just to watch you jump, Althalus. I'm a cat for now, and cats need touching. I need to have you near me when we talk."

"Then you haven't always been a cat?"

"How many cats have you come across who know how to talk?"

"You know," he bantered, "I can't for the life of me remember the last time."

She actually laughed, and that gave him a little glow of satisfaction. If he could make her laugh, she wasn't entirely in control of the situation here.

"I'm not really all that hard to get along with, Althalus," she told him. "Pet me now and then and scratch my ears once in a while, and we'll get along just fine. Is there anything you need?"

"I'll have to go outside to hunt food for us before long," he said, trying to sound casual about it.

"Are you hungry?"

"Well, not right now. I'm sure I will be later, though."

"When you're hungry, I'll see to it that you have something to eat." She gave him a sidelong look. "You didn't *really* think you could get away that easily, did you?"

He grinned. "It was worth a try." He picked her up and held her.

"You aren't going anywhere without me, Althalus. Get used to the idea that I'm going to be with you for the rest of your life— and you're going to live for a very, very long time. You've been chosen to do some things, and I've been chosen to make sure you do them right. Your life's going to be much easier once you accept that."

"How did we get chosen—and who did the choosing?"

She reached up and patted his cheek with one soft paw. "We'll get to that later," she assured him. "You might have a little trouble accepting it right at first. Now then, why don't we get started?" She hopped down from the bed, crossed to the table, and without any seeming effort leaped up and sat on the polished surface. "Time to go to work, pet," she said. "Come over here and sit down while I teach you how to read."

The "reading" involved the translation of stylized pictures, much as it had in Ghend's book. The pictures represented words. That came rather easily with concrete words such as "tree," or "rock," or "pig." The pictures that represented concepts such as "truth," "beauty," or "honesty," were more difficult.

Althalus was adaptable—a thief almost has to be—but the situation here took some getting used to. Food simply appeared on the table whenever he grew hungry. It startled him the first few times it happened, but after a while, he didn't even pay attention to it anymore. Even miracles become commonplace if they happen often enough.

Winter arrived at the Edge of the World, and as it settled in, the sun went away and perpetual night arrived. The cat patiently explained it, but Althalus only dimly understood her explanation. He could accept it intellectually, but it still seemed to him that the sun moved around the Earth instead of the other way around. With the coming of that endless night, he lost all track of days. When you get right down to it, he reasoned, there simply weren't any days anymore. He stopped looking out the windows altogether. It was almost always snowing anyway, and snow depressed him.

He was making some progress with his reading. After he'd come across one of the pictures often enough, he automatically recognized it. Words became the center of his attention.

"You weren't always a cat, were you?" he asked his companion once when the two of them were lying on the fur-covered bed after they'd eaten.

"I thought I'd already told you that," she said.

"What were you before?"

She gave him a long, steady look with her glowing green eyes. "You aren't quite ready for that information yet, Althalus. You're fairly well settled down now. I don't want you to start bouncing off the walls the way you did when you first arrived."

"Did you have a name—before you became a cat, I mean?"

"Yes. You probably wouldn't be able to pronounce it, though. Why do you ask?"

"It just doesn't seem right for me to keep calling you 'cat.' That's like saying 'donkey' or 'chicken.' Would it upset you if I gave you a name?"

"Not if it's a nice name. I've heard some of the words you use when you think I'm asleep. I wouldn't like one of those."

"I sort of like 'Emerald,' because of your eyes."

"I could live with that, yes. I had a very nice emerald once— before I came here. I used to hold it up in the sunlight to watch it glow."

"Then you had arms before you became a cat, and hands as well," he said shrewdly.

"Yes, as a matter of fact, I did. Now would you like to make some guesses about how many and where they were attached to me?" She gave him an arch look. "Stop fishing, Althalus. Someday you'll find out who I really am, and it might surprise you. But you don't need to know that right now."

"Maybe I don't," he said slyly, "but every now and then, you make a slip, and I keep track of those slips. It won't be too long before I know pretty much what you used to be."

"Not until I'm ready for you to know, you won't," she told him. "You need to concentrate right now, Althalus, and if I used my real form here in the House, you wouldn't be able to do that."

"That bad?"

She snuggled up against him and started to purr. "You'll see, pet," she said. "You'll see."

Despite her rather superior attitude—which Althalus strongly suspected had been a part of her original nature—Emerald was an affectionate creature who always wanted to be in close physical contact with him. He slept on the thickly furred bison robes on the stone bed, and she always snuggled up to him, purring contentedly. Right at first he didn't care for that, so he made a practice of covering himself with his wool cloak and holding it tightly around his neck. Emerald would sit quite calmly at the foot of the bed watching him. Then, as he started to drift off to sleep and his grip relaxed, she would silently creep up the bed until she was just behind his head. Then she would skillfully touch her cold, wet nose to the back of his neck, and Althalus would automatically flinch away from that surprising touch. That was all she needed to burrow down under the cloak, and she would settle down against his back and purr. Her purring was really very soothing, so he didn't mind having her there. She seemed to get a great deal of entertainment out of the game, though, so Althalus continued to clench his cloak up around his neck so that she could surprise him in the same way each time they slept. It didn't really cost him anything, and as long as it amused her . . .

She had one habit, though, that he really wished she'd get over. Every so often, Emerald seemed to develop an overpowering urge to bathe his face—usually when he was sound asleep. His eyes would suddenly pop open, and he'd realize that she had her paws firmly wrapped halfway around his head to hold him in place while she licked him from chin to forehead with her rough, wet tongue. He tried to jerk away from her the first few times, but as soon as he started to move, she'd flex her paws slightly, and her claws would come out. He got the point almost immediately. He didn't really care for those impromptu baths, but he learned to endure them. There are always adjustments to be made when two creatures set up housekeeping together, and aside from a few bad habits, Emerald wasn't really all that hard to get along with.

Although the permanent night that blanketed the far north had taken away anything he could really call "day," Althalus was fairly sure that the routine they followed probably coincided rather closely with the rising and setting of the sun farther to the south. He had no real reason for that belief and no way to verify it, but it seemed to him that it made more sense to think of it that way.

His "days" were spent at the table with the Book open before him and with Emerald seated beside the Book, watching. Their conversations were largely limited to his pointing at an unfamiliar symbol and asking, "What's this one mean?" She would tell him, and he'd stumble along until he came to another unintelligible picture. The parchment sheets were loose inside the white leather box, and Emerald became very upset if he got them back in the wrong order. "It doesn't make any sense if you mix them up like that," she'd scold him.

"A lot of it doesn't make sense anyway."

"Put them back the way you found them."

"All right, all right. Don't tie your tail in a knot." That remark always seemed to trigger one of their little mock tussles. Emerald would lay her ears back, crouch low over her front paws with her bottom raised up and swinging back and forth ominously while her tail swished. Then she'd leap on his hand and mouth it. She'd never extend her claws, and though she growled terribly, she never actually bit him.

His best response to that was to take his other hand and thoroughly stir up her fur. She seemed to *hate* that, since it took her quite a while to comb everything back in place with her tongue.

Since Emerald was a cat—at least for right now—she had a keen sense of smell. She insisted that Althalus should wash frequently—every time he turned around, it seemed. A large tiled tub filled with steaming water would quite suddenly appear near their bed, and after the first few times, Althalus would sigh, rise from his seat, and begin removing his clothes. In the long run, he'd found, it was easier to bathe than it was to argue with her. As time went on, he even began to enjoy soaking in hot water before supper every day.

A peculiar notion came to him that winter, brought on perhaps by the continual darkness. He was still not entirely convinced that he wasn't crazy, having possibly gone insane because he'd missed his time to die—just like the mad old man who'd talked to God. But maybe he hadn't missed it after all. What if somewhere back in Hule, or maybe after he'd come up into the mountains of Kagwher, someone had slipped up behind him with an axe and chopped his head open, and he was dead? If it'd happened quickly enough, he wouldn't have even realized it, so his ghost had just kept on walking. His body was probably lying somewhere with its brains dribbling out of its ears, but his ghost had continued on toward this house, totally unaware that he was really dead. It hadn't been Althalus who'd encountered the crazy man who talked to God, and he hadn't really reached the Edge of the World and watched the fire of God. That was just something his ghost had thought up.

Now his ghost had reached its final destination, and it would remain here in this closed room with Emerald and the Book forever. If his theory was correct, he'd crossed over into the afterlife. Everyone knows that the afterlife is filled with all sorts of strange things, so there was no point in getting excited about a room that stayed warm and comfortable and well lit without any trace of fire, and no real need to start bellowing, "impossible" every time he turned around and something unusual happened. The whole business was just his own personal afterlife.

All things considered, though, this particular afterlife wasn't so bad. He was warm and well fed, and he had Emerald to talk to. He might have wished that there was some of Nabjor's mead around someplace, or that some sister of the naughty-eyed girl in Nabjor's camp might pay him a call now and then, but as time went on, those things became less and less important. He'd heard some pretty terrible stories about the afterlife, but if it didn't get any worse than it was right now, Althalus felt that he could learn to be dead with it—he realized that "learn to live with it" didn't exactly fit in with his current situation. The one thing that nagged him was the total lack of any possibility of hunting down the man who'd killed him. Since he was now an insubstantial ghost, he wouldn't be able to hack the rascal to pieces. But then he realized that he might just be able to haunt his unknown assailant, and that might be even more satisfying than butchering him.

He wondered if he might be able to persuade Emerald to agree to that. He could promise her that they could come back here to their private afterlife after he'd haunted his murderer to death, but he was almost positive that she wouldn't put much store in promises made by the ghost of a man so famous for lying every chance he got. After he'd thought his way through the idea, he decided that he wouldn't mention the notion to his furry roommate.

Then the sun came back to the roof of the world, and the notion that he was dead began to fade. Eternal darkness sort of fit in with his concept of an afterlife, but the return of the sun made him almost feel that he'd been reborn.

He could read the Book fairly well by now, and he found it more and more interesting. One thing did sort of bother him, though. Late one spring afternoon, he laid his hand on the Book and glanced at Emerald, who appeared to be sleeping with her chin resting on her paws as she lay on the table beside the Book. "What's his real name?" he asked her.

Her green eyes were sleepy when she opened them. "Whose name?" she asked.

"The one who wrote the Book. He never comes right out and identifies himself."

"He's God, Althalus."

"Yes, I know, but which one? Every land I've ever visited has its own God—or its own set of Gods—and they all have different names. Was it Kherdhos, the God of the Wekti and Plakands? Or maybe Apwos, the God of Equero? What *is* his name?"

"Deiwos, of course."

"Deiwos? The God of the Medyos?"

"Of course."

"The Medyos are the silliest people in the world, Emerald."

"What's that got to do with anything?"

"You'd think that the people who worshiped the real true God would have better sense."

She sighed. "It's all the same God, Althalus. Haven't you realized that by now? The Wekti and Plakands call him Kherdhos because they're interested in their herds of sheep or cows. The Equeros call him Apwos, because they concentrate most of their attention on the lakes. The Medyos are the oldest people in this part of the world, and they brought the name with them when they first came here."

"Where did they come from?"

"Off to the south—after they learned how to herd sheep and plant grains. After they'd lived in Medyo for a while, they expanded out into those other places, and the people in the new places changed God's name." She rose to her feet and stretched and yawned. "Let's have fish for dinner tonight," she suggested.

"We had fish last night—and the night before."

"So? I like fish; don't you?"

"Oh, fish is all right, I suppose, but I get a little tired of it after we've eaten it three times a day for three straight weeks."

"Fix your own supper," she flared.

"You know perfectly well that I don't know how to do that yet."

"Then you'll just have to take whatever I put on the table, won't you?"

He sighed. "Fish?" he asked with a certain resignation.

"What a wonderful idea, Althalus! I'm *so* glad you thought of it."

There were many concepts in the Book that Althalus couldn't understand, and he and Emerald spent many contented evenings talking about them. They also spent quite a bit of time playing. Emerald *was* a cat, after all, and cats like to play. There was a kind of studied seriousness about her when she played that made her absolutely adorable, and she filled up most of the empty places in his life. Every so often she'd do something while she was playing that was so totally silly that it seemed almost human. Althalus thought about that, and he came to realize that only humans could be silly. Animals generally took themselves far too seriously even to suspect that they were being ridiculous.

Once, when he was concentrating very hard on the Book, he caught a slight movement out of the corner of his eye and realized that she was creeping up on him. He hadn't really been paying much attention to her, and she'd only let that go on for just so long before she'd assert herself. She came creeping across the polished floor one furtive step at a time, but he knew that she was coming, so he was ready for her when she pounced, and half turning, he caught her in midair with both hands. There was the usual mock tussle, and then he pulled her to his face and held her tightly against it. "Oh, I *do* love you, Emmy!" he said.

She jerked her face back from his. "Emmy?" she hissed. "EMMY!?!"

"I've noticed that people do that," he tried to explain. "After they've been together for a while, they come up with pet names for each other."

"Put me down!"

"Oh, don't get all huffy."

"Emmy indeed! You put me down, or I'll claw off one of your ears!"

He was fairly sure she wouldn't, but he put her down and gave her a little pat on the head.

She turned sort of sideways, her fur bristling and her ears laid back. Then she hissed at him.

"Why, Emmy," he said in mock surprise, "what a thing to say. I'm shocked at you. Shocked."

Then she swore at him, and that really surprised him. "You're actually angry, aren't you?"

She hissed again, and he laughed at her. "Oh, Emmy, Emmy, Emmy," he said fondly.

"Yes, Althie, Althie, Althie?" she replied in a spiteful tone.

"Althie?"

"In your ear!" she said. Then she went off to the bed to sulk.

He didn't get any supper that night, but he almost felt that it might have been worth it. He now had a way to respond when she started acting superior. One "Emmy" would immediately erase the haughty look on her face and reduce her to near-inarticulate fury. Althalus carefully tucked that one up his sleeve for future use.

They declared peace on each other the next day, and life returned to normal. She fed him a near banquet that evening. He understood that it was a peacemaking gesture, so he complimented her after about every other bite.

Then, after they'd gone to bed, she washed his face for quite some time. "Did you really mean what you said yesterday?" she purred.

"Which particular thing I said were you thinking of?" he asked.

Her ears went back immediately. "You said you loved me. Did you mean it?"

"Oh," he said. "That. Of course I meant it. You shouldn't even have to ask."

"Don't you lie to me."

"Would I do that?"

"Of course you would. You're the greatest liar in the whole world."

"Why, thank you, dear."

"Don't make me cross, Althalus," she warned. "I've got all

four paws wrapped around your head right now, so be very nice to me—unless you'd like to have your face on the back of your head instead of the front."

"I'll be good," he promised.

"Say it again, then."

"Say what, dear?"

"You know what!"

"All right, little kitten, I love you. Does that make you feel better?"

She rubbed her face against his and started to purr.

The seasons turned, as seasons always do, although the summers were short and the winters long up here on the roof of the world, and after they'd gone around several times, the past seemed to recede until it was only a dim memory. In time, the days plodded by unnoticed as Althalus struggled with the Book. He began to spend more and more of his time staring up at the glowing dome overhead as he pondered the strange things the Book had revealed.

"What *is* your problem?" Emerald demanded irritably once when Althalus sat at the table with the Book lying almost unnoticed on the polished surface in front of him. "You're not even pretending to be reading."

Althalus laid his hand on the Book. "It just said something I don't understand," he replied. "I'm trying to work it out."

She sighed. "Tell me what it is," she said in a resigned tone. "I'll explain it to you. You still won't understand, but I'll explain anyway."

"You can be very offensive; did you know that?"

"Of course. I'm doing it on purpose—but you still love me, don't you?"

"Oh, I guess so."

"You *guess* so?"

He laughed. "Woke you up, didn't I?"

She laid back her ears and hissed at him.

"Be nice," he said, putting out his hand and scratching her ears. Then he looked back at the troublesome line. "If I'm reading this right, it says that all the things Deiwos has made are of the same value in his eyes. Does that mean that a man isn't any more important than a bug or a grain of sand?"

"Not exactly," she replied. "What it really means is that Deiwos doesn't think of the separate parts of what he's made. It's the whole thing that's important. A man's only a small part of the whole thing, and he's not really here for very long. A man's born, lives out his life, and dies in so short a time that the mountains and stars don't even notice him as he goes by."

"That's a gloomy thought. We don't really mean anything, do we? Deiwos won't even miss us after the last one of us dies, will he?"

"Oh, he probably will. There were things that used to be alive, but they aren't anymore, and Deiwos still remembers them."

"Why did he let them die out, then?"

"Because they'd done everything they were supposed to do. They'd completed what they'd been put here to attend to, so Deiwos let them go. Then too, if everything that had ever lived were still here, there wouldn't be any room for new things."

"Sooner or later, that'll happen to people as well, won't it?"

"That's not entirely certain, Althalus. Other creatures take the world as they find it, but people change things."

"And Deiwos guides us in those changes?"

"Why would he do that? Deiwos doesn't tinker, pet. He sets things in motion and then moves on. All the mistakes you make are entirely yours. Don't blame Deiwos for them."

Althalus reached out and ruffled her fur.

"I *wish* you wouldn't do that," she said. "It takes forever to get it all straight again."

"It gives you something to do between naps, Emmy," he told her, and then he went back to the Book.

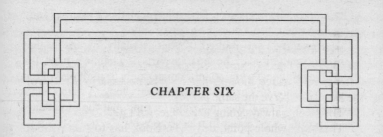

CHAPTER SIX

The past receded even more in his memory as the Book claimed Althalus. By now he could read it through from end to end, and he'd done that so often that he could recite long passages from memory. The more it sank into his memory, the more it altered his perception of the world. Things that had seemed very important before he'd come here to the House at the End of the World were no longer relevant.

"Was I really that small, Em?" he asked his companion one evening in the early autumn of another of those interminable years.

"What exactly are we talking about here, pet?" she asked, absently washing her ears.

"I was convinced that I was the greatest thief in the world, but along toward the end there, I wasn't really much more than a common highwayman hitting people on the head so that I could steal their clothes."

"That comes fairly close, yes. What's your point?"

"I could have done more with my life, couldn't I?"

"That's why we're here, pet," she told him. "Whether you like it or not, you *are* going to do more with it. I'm going to see to that." She looked directly at him, her green eyes a mystery. "I think it's time for you to learn how to use the power of the Book."

"What do you mean, 'use'?"

"You can make things happen with the Book. Where did you think your supper comes from every night?"

"That's your job, Em. It wouldn't be polite for me to stick my nose into that area, would it?"

"Polite or not, you *are* going to learn, Althalus. Certain words from the Book carry the sense of doing things—words like 'chop' or 'dig' or 'cut.' You can do those things with the Book instead of with your back if you know how to use it. Right at first, you'll need to be touching the Book when you do those things. After some practice, though, that won't be necessary. The idea of the Book will serve the same purpose."

"The Book's always going to be here, isn't it?"

"That's the whole point, dear. The Book has to stay here. It wouldn't be safe to take it out into the world, and you have things you have to do out there."

"Oh? What kind of things?"

"Little things—saving the world, keeping the stars up in the sky where they belong, making sure that time keeps moving. Things like that."

"Are you trying to be funny, Em?"

"No, not really. We'll get to those things later, though. Let's try the easy ones first. Take off your shoe and throw it over by the bed. Then tell it to come back."

"I don't think it'll listen to me, Emmy."

"It will if you use the right word. All you have to do is put your hand on the Book, look at the shoe, and say '*gwem.*' It's like calling a puppy."

"That's an awfully old-fashioned word, Emmy."

"Of course it is. It's one of the first words. The language of the Book is the mother of your language. Your language grew out of it. Just try it, pet. We can talk about the changes of language some other time."

He dubiously pulled off his shoe and tossed it over by the bed. Then he laid his hand on the Book and said *"gwem"* rather half-heartedly.

Nothing happened.

"So much for that as an idea," he muttered.

"Command, Althie," Emerald said in a weary tone. "Do you think a puppy would listen if you said it that way?"

"Gwem!" he sharply commanded his shoe.

He didn't really expect it, so he wasn't ready to fend the shoe off, and it hit him squarely in the face.

"It's a good thing we didn't start with your spear," Emmy noted. "It's usually best to hold your hands out when you do that, Althalus. Let the shoe know where you want it to come to."

"It actually works!" he exclaimed in astonishment.

"Of course it does. Didn't you believe me?"

"Well . . . sort of, I guess. I didn't think it'd happen quite that fast, though. I kind of expected the shoe to come slithering across the floor. I didn't know it was going to fly."

"You said it just a little too firmly, pet. The tone of voice is very important when you do things this way. The louder and more sharply you say it, the faster it happens."

"I'll remember that. Getting kicked in the face with my own shoe definitely got my attention. Why didn't you warn me about that?"

"Because you don't listen, Althie. It's just a waste of breath to warn you about things. Now try it again."

Althalus put miles on that shoe over the next several weeks, and he gradually grew more proficient at altering the tone of his voice. He also discovered that different words would make the shoe do other things. *"Dheu"* would make it rise up off the floor and simply stand in front of him on nothing but air. *"Dhreu"* would lower it to the floor again.

He was practicing on that one day in late summer when an impish kind of notion came to him. He looked over at Emerald, who was sitting on the bed carefully washing her ears. He focused his attention on her, set his hand on the Book, and said, *"dheu."*

Emerald immediately rose up in the air until she was sitting on nothing at all at about the same level as his head. She continued to scrub at her ears as if nothing had happened. Then she looked at him, and her green eyes seemed very cold and hard. *"Bhlag!"* she said quite sharply.

The blow took Althalus squarely on the point of the chin, and it sent him rolling across the floor. It seemed to have come out of nowhere at all, and it had rattled him all the way down to his toes.

"We don't do that to each other, do we?" Emerald said in an almost pleasant tone of voice. "Now put me down."

His eyes wouldn't seem to focus. He covered one of them with his hand so that he could see her and said *"dhreu"* in an apologetic sort of way.

Emerald settled slowly back to the bed. "That's much better," she said. "Are you going to get up, or did you plan to lie there on the floor for a while?" Then she went back to washing her ears.

He more or less gathered at that point that there were rules and that it wasn't wise to break them. He also realized that Emerald had just demonstrated the next step. She hadn't been anywhere near the Book when she'd knocked him across the room.

He continued to practice with his shoe. He was more familiar with it than with his other possessions, and it didn't have any sharp edges, as some of the others had. Just to see if he could do it, he put a pair of wings on it, and it went flapping around the room blundering into things. It occurred to him that a flying shoe would have been a sensation in Nabjor's camp or Gosti Big Belly's hall. That had been a long time ago, though. He idly roamed back through his memory, trying to attach some number to the years he'd spent here in the House, but the number kept evading him for some reason.

"How long have I been here, Em?" he asked his companion.

"Quite some time. Why do you ask?"

"Just curious, I suppose. I can barely remember a time when I wasn't here."

"Time doesn't really mean anything here in this house, pet. You're here to learn, and some of the things in the Book are very difficult. It took your mind a very long time to fully grasp them. When we came to one of those, I'd usually let your eyes sleep while your mind worked. It was a lot quieter that way. Your arguments were with the Book, not with me."

"Let me see if I understand this. Are you saying that there've been times when I went to sleep and didn't wake up for a week or more?"

She gave him one of those infuriatingly superior looks.

"A month?" he asked incredulously.

"Keep going," she suggested.

"You've put me to sleep for years on end?" he almost screamed at her.

"Sleep's very good for you, dear. The nice thing about those particular naps is that you don't snore."

"How long, Emmy? How long have I been penned up in here with you?"

"Long enough for us to get to know each other." Then she heaved one of those long-suffering sighs. "You *must* learn to listen when I tell you something, Althalus. You've been here in this house long enough to learn how to read the Book. That didn't really take too long, though. It was learning to understand the Book that took you so much time. You haven't quite finished that yet, but you're coming along."

"That means that I'm very, very old, doesn't it?" He reached up, took hold of a lock of his hair, and pulled it down so that he could see it. "I can't be *that* old," he scoffed. "My hair hasn't even turned white yet."

"Why would it do that?"

"I don't know. It just does. When a man gets old, his hair turns white."

"That's the whole point, Althalus. You haven't grown old. Nothing changes in this house. You're still the same age as you were when you first came here."

"What about you? Are you still the same age you were as well?"

"Didn't I just say that?"

"If I remember right, you told me once that you haven't always been here."

"Not always, no. I was somewhere else a long time ago, but then I came to wait for you." She glanced back over her shoulder at the mountain peaks looming out beyond the south window. "Those weren't there when I first came," she added.

"I thought mountains lasted forever."

"Nothing lasts forever, Althalus—except me, of course."

"The world must have been very different back in the days before those mountains," he mused. "Where did people live back then?"

"They didn't. There weren't any people then. There were other things here instead, but they died out. They'd done what they were supposed to do, so Deiwos let them go. He still misses them, though."

"You always talk about Deiwos as if you knew him personally."

"Yes. As a matter of fact, we're very well acquainted."

"Do you call him 'Deiwos' when you're talking together?"

"Sometimes. When I really want to get his attention I call him 'brother.' "

"You're God's sister?" That startled Althalus.

"Sort of."

"I don't think I want to push that any further. Let's go back to what we were talking about before, Em. Just how long have I been here? Give me a number."

"Two thousand, four hundred, and sixty-seven—as of last week."

"You're just making that up, aren't you?"

"No. Was there anything else?"

He swallowed very hard. "Some of those naps I took were a lot longer than I'd thought they were, weren't they? That makes me just about the oldest man in the world, doesn't it?"

"Not quite. There's a man named Ghend who's quite a bit older than you are."

"Ghend? He didn't really look all that old to me."

Her green eyes went very wide. "You know Ghend?"

"Of course I do. He's the one who hired me to come here and steal the Book."

"Why didn't you *tell* me?" she almost shrieked at him.

"I must have."

"No, as a matter of fact, you didn't. *You idiot!* You've been sitting on that for the last twenty-five hundred years!"

"Calm down, Emmy. We're not going to get anywhere if you turn hysterical." He gave her a long, level look. "I think it's just about time for you to tell me exactly what's going on, Emmy—and don't try to put me off this time by telling me that I won't understand or that I'm not ready to know certain things yet. I want to know what's going on and why it's so important."

"We don't have time for that."

He leaned back on his bench. "Well, we're just going to *take* the time, little kitten. You've been treating me like a house pet for quite a while now. I don't know if you've noticed, but I don't have a tail, and even if I did, I probably wouldn't wag it every time you snapped your fingers. You don't have me completely tamed, Em, and I'm telling you right here and now that we aren't going any further until you tell me just exactly what's going on."

Her look was very cold. "What is it that you want to know?" Her tone was almost unfriendly.

He laid one hand on the Book. "Oh, I don't know," he said. "Why don't we start out with everything? Then we can move on from there."

She glared at him.

"No more deep, dark secrets, Emmy. Start talking. If things are as serious as you seem to think they are, then *be* serious."

"Maybe you *are* ready to know what's going on," she conceded. "How much do you know about Daeva?"

"Just what it says in the Book. I'd never even heard of him before I came here. He's very angry with Deiwos, I gather. Deiwos seems to be sorry that he feels that way, but he's going to keep on doing what he's doing whether Daeva likes it or not—probably because he has to."

"That's a novel interpretation," she said. She mulled it over a bit. "Now that I think about it, though, there seems to be a lot of truth in it. Somehow you've managed to redefine the concept of evil. In your view, evil's no more than a disagreement about the way things are supposed to be. Deiwos thinks they're supposed to be one way, and Daeva thinks they're supposed to be another."

· "I thought I just said that. It's the business of making things that started the fight then, isn't it?"

"That might be an oversimplification, but it comes fairly close. Deiwos makes things because he *has* to make them. The world and the sky weren't complete the way they were. Deiwos saw that, but Daeva didn't agree. When Deiwos does things to make the world and the sky complete, it changes them. Daeva believes that's a violation of the natural order. He doesn't want things to change."

"What a shame. There's not much he can do about it, though, is there? Once something's been changed, it's been changed. Daeva can't very well go back and *un*change it, can he?"

"He seems to think so."

"Time only moves in one direction, Emmy. We *can't* go back and undo something that happened in the past just because we don't like the way it turned out."

"Daeva thinks he can."

"Then both of his wheels just came off the axle. Time isn't going to run backward just because he wants it to. The sea might run dry and the mountains might wear down, but time runs from the past to the future. That's probably the only thing that won't change."

"We can all hope that you're right, Althalus, because if you aren't, Daeva's going to win. He'll unmake everything Deiwos has made and return the earth and sky to what they were at the very beginning. If he can make time go backward, then things he does now will change things that happened in the past, and if he can change enough of the past, we won't be here anymore."

"What's Ghend got to do with all of this?" Althalus asked her suddenly.

"Ghend was one of the early men who came to this part of the world about ten thousand years ago. That was before men had learned how to cook certain rocks to make copper or how to mix tin with copper to make bronze. All their tools and weapons were made of stone, and Ghend's Chief put him to work cutting down trees so that the tribe could plant grain. Ghend hated that, and Daeva approached him and persuaded him to abandon Deiwos and worship *him* instead. Daeva can be very persuasive when he wants to be. Ghend's the high priest of the Demon Daeva, and the absolute master of Nekweros." Emerald looked up suddenly. Then she sinuously flowed down from the bed, crossed the floor, and jumped up to the sill of the north window. "I should have known," she said in an irritated voice. "He's doing it again."

"Doing what?"

"Come here and see for yourself."

He rose and crossed to the window. Then he stopped, staring incredulously. There was something out there, and there wasn't supposed to be. The world didn't seem to end there anymore. "What *is* that?" he asked, staring at what appeared to be a white mountain.

"Ice," she replied. "This isn't the first time it's happened. Every so often Daeva and Ghend try this way to slow things down—usually when they think Deiwos is getting too far ahead of them."

"That's a lot of ice, Em. When I was coming here, the clouds were a long way down. Did that water down there start rising?"

"No. It froze solid a long time ago. It snows on it every winter, and the snow doesn't melt anymore. More snow piles up and presses down on it, and it turns to ice."

"How thick is it?"

"About two miles—maybe three."

"I meant how thick, Em, not how far away."

"So did I. Once it gets thick enough, it'll be above the level of what you call the Edge of the World. Then it'll start to move. It'll grind down mountains and spill down onto the plains. Nothing can stop it, and people won't be able to live in this part of the world anymore."

"Have you seen this happen before?"

"Several times. It's just about the only way Ghend and Daeva have to interrupt what Deiwos is doing. We're going to have to change our plans, Althalus."

"I didn't know we *had* a plan."

"Oh, we've got a plan, all right, pet. I just hadn't gotten around to telling you about it yet. I thought we had more time."

"You've already had twenty-five hundred years, Em. How much more did you think you were going to need?"

"Probably about another twenty-five hundred. If you'd told me about Ghend earlier, I might have been able to adjust things. Now we're going to have to cheat. I just hope it doesn't make Deiwos angry with me."

"Your brother's awfully busy, Em," Althalus said piously. "We shouldn't really pester him with all the picky little details, should we?"

She laughed. "My thought exactly, pet. We were *made* for each other."

"Are you only just now coming to realize that? The simplest way for us to cheat would probably be for me to just slip on over to Nekweros and kill Ghend, wouldn't it?"

"That's an awfully blunt way to put it, Althalus."

"I'm a plainspoken man, Em. All this dancing around is just a waste of time, because that's what it's going to come down to in the end, isn't it? Ghend wanted me to come here and steal the Book so that he could destroy it. If I kill him, we can destroy *his* Book, and then Daeva has to go back and start all over."

"How did you find out about Daeva's Book?" she asked sharply.

"Ghend showed it to me back in Nabjor's camp."

"He's actually carrying it around out in the real world? What's he thinking of?"

"Don't ask me to tell you what somebody else is thinking, Em. My guess is that he knew that I'd never seen a book before, so he brought one along to show me what they look like. The pictures in his Book weren't at all like the ones in ours, though."

"You didn't touch it, did you?"

"Not the Book itself. He handed me one of the pages, though."

"The pages *are* the Book, Althalus. You've touched both Books with your bare hands?" she demanded, shuddering.

"Yes. Is that significant?"

"The Books are absolutes, Althalus. They're the source of ultimate power. Our Book is the power of pure light, and Ghend's Book is the power of absolute darkness. When you touched that page from his Book, it should have totally corrupted you."

"I was moderately corrupt already, Em, but we can sort that out later. What do you think about my idea? I can slip across the border into Nekweros without anybody ever seeing me. Once I've put Ghend to sleep, I'll burn his Book, and that'll be the end of it, won't it?"

"Oh, dear," she sighed.

"It *is* the simplest solution, Em. Why complicate things when you don't have to?"

"Because you probably wouldn't get more than a mile past the border, pet. Ghend's about seventy-five hundred years ahead of you. He knows how to use his Book in ways you couldn't even imagine. Using a Book is a very complicated process. You have to be so totally immersed in the Book that the words come to you automatically." She looked at him speculatively. "Do you really love me, Althalus?" she asked.

"Of course I do. You shouldn't even have to ask. What's that got to do with what we were just talking about?"

"It's crucial, Althalus. You have to love me totally. Otherwise, this won't work."

"What won't work?"

"I think I know a way for us to cheat. Do you trust me, pet?"

"Trust you? After all the times you've tried to creep up and pounce on me from behind? Don't be ridiculous."

"What's that supposed to mean?"

"You're sneaky, little kitten. I love you, dear, but I'm not foolish enough to trust you."

"That's only playing, so it doesn't count."

"What's love and trust got to do with getting rid of Ghend and his Book?"

"I know how to use our Book, and you don't; but you can do things out there in your world, and I can't."

"That sort of defines the problem, I guess. How do we get around it?"

"We break down the barriers between us, but that means that we have to completely trust each other. I have to be able to get inside your mind so that I can tell you what you have to do and which word from the Book you have to use to do it."

"Then I just tuck you in my pocket and we go kill Ghend?"

"It's a little more complicated than that, Althalus. You'll understand better, I think, once we're inside each other's minds. The first thing you have to do is empty your mind. Open it up so that I can get in."

"What *are* you talking about?"

"Think about light, or dark, or empty. Turn your mind off."

Althalus tried to empty his mind of thought, but that almost never works. The mind can be like an unruly child. Tell it to stop, and it works that much faster.

"We'll have to try something different," Emerald said, her ears laid back in irritation. "Maybe . . . ?" she said a bit uncertainly.

"Go to the south window. I want you to look south at the mountains of Kagwher. Pick out the closest one and count the trees on it."

"Count trees? What for?"

"Because I said so. Don't ask silly questions. Just do it."

"All right, Em, don't get so excited." He stood up and went to the south window. The nearest peak was only a mile or so away, and he started counting the snow-covered trees up near the top. The snow blurred the outlines of the trees, and that made counting them very difficult.

"Move over just a little." Her voice seemed to be murmuring in his right ear, and he jerked his head around in surprise. He couldn't feel her on his shoulder, but he could almost feel her warm breath on the side of his face.

Emerald was still sitting on the bed a dozen feet away. "I asked you to move over, pet," her voice sounded inside his head. "I need a little more room."

"What are you *doing*?" he exclaimed.

"Shush. I'm busy."

He felt a kind of surging inside his head as if something were moving around in there. "Quit fidgeting," her voice told him. "I'm not taking up that much room."

Then the sense of intrusion began to fade and he felt the gentle rumble of her purring within his mind. *Now you are mine,* her purring gloated.

"What's going on?" he demanded in alarm.

You don't have to talk out loud anymore, pet, she breathed inside his mind. *Now that I'm in here, I can hear your thoughts; and you can hear mine, if you'll just take the trouble to listen.*

"How did you *do* that?"

Just think the words, Althalus. There's an awful echo in here when you think them and say them at the same time.

Are you really in there? He sent his thought inward.

My awareness is. It's also over on the bed, but it's easy to be in two places at once with your mind. There was a kind of tickling sensation over his left ear. *It's bigger in here than I thought it'd be. You're more clever than I'd imagined, and you're really rather poetic.*

Will you quit rummaging around in there?

Not a chance, pet. Cats are curious. Didn't you know that?

How did you manage to break through so quickly? I thought this was going to take a long time.

So did I, to be honest. I was pushing at the barrier before you started counting. I couldn't get through it, though. As soon as you started counting trees, the barrier went down.

Does that mean that I'll have to say "one-two-three" every time I want to talk with you this way?

Not anymore, pet. I'm in now, and you'll never get rid of me.

It's going to take some getting used to. I've never had somebody inside my head before.

Is it really that unpleasant?

Not really.

Now I'll be with you wherever you go.

I wasn't going to leave without you, Em. I'd been meaning to talk with you about that. I'm not going anywhere without you, kitten—even if that means that the world goes all to smash. The world doesn't matter; you do.

Please don't say things like that, Althalus. Her voice inside his head had a melting sort of tone. *You're making it very hard for me to think.*

Yes, I noticed that. He considered it. *When you get right down to it, though, this is where we've been going since I first came here, isn't it? You started out by talking to me out loud, and a talking cat isn't the most natural thing in the world. All we've done is take that one step further, so now you won't have to waste all those thousands of years teaching me how to use the Book. We could leave right now if winter weren't settling in.* He looked at her with one raised eyebrow. "Now that you've opened the door, all sorts of things are coming through," he said aloud. "I don't want to seem critical, Em, but you shouldn't really be having those kinds of thoughts, you know."

She glared at him for a moment. Then she jumped down from the bed and stalked away.

"Are you blushing, Em?" he asked mildly.

She turned and hissed at him.

Part Two

THE GATHERING

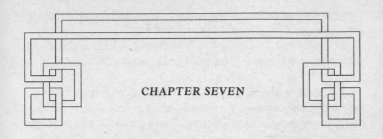

CHAPTER SEVEN

"Stay out of there, Althalus! What's in there is none of your concern!"

"You're the one who opened the door, Em," he replied mildly. "It swings both ways, you know."

"Just mind your own business and quit snooping. You have to start paying closer attention. When I tell you which word to use, I'm sending a picture of what the word's going to do. You *must* have the picture in your mind as well as the word. The word's just a sound, pet. Nothing's going to happen if all you're doing is making noises. Now try it again."

"How much longer is it before we have to leave?"

"About a month—six weeks at the most. As soon as spring arrives, we go, whether you're ready or not."

"We have to pick something up in Arum?"

"The Knife, yes."

"Is that the knife I'll use when I kill Ghend?"

"Will you *stop* that?"

"Isn't that what this is all about? Ghend's interfering with what Deiwos is trying to do, so I'm supposed to get rid of him. It's not really all that uncommon, Em. I've done it before. I'm primarily a thief, but I'll take on a murder if the pay's right. I thought that's what you had in mind."

"It most certainly is *not*!"

"It *is* a simple solution, Em, and you wouldn't even have to get your little paws dirty. We go to Arum and pick up the knife. Then I go to Nekweros and cut Ghend's throat with it."

"That's not what it's for, Althalus. It has writing on the blade.

There are some people we're going to need, and we'll recognize them because they'll be able to read that writing."

"Isn't that just a little exotic? Talk to your brother and find out who these people are. Then we'll chase them down and get on with this."

"It doesn't work that way, Althalus. Situations change. If things have happened one way, we'll need certain people. If they've happened in another way, we'll need different people. Circumstances decide exactly who we're going to need."

"Wouldn't that mean that the writing on the knife blade changes as the circumstances change?"

"No. It's not the writing that changes, pet. It's the reading."

"Wait a minute. Doesn't the writing mean the same thing to everybody?"

"Of course it doesn't. Everybody who reads *any* writing gets a different meaning from it. When *you* look at the writing on the blade, you'll see a certain word. Other people will see a different word. Most people won't see words at all—only decorations. The people we want will see a word, and they'll say that word out loud."

"How will we know that they've read it right?"

"We'll know, pet. Believe me, we'll know."

The tag end of winter dragged on for the next month or so, and then one night a warm wind blew in from the southwest, cutting the snow away almost overnight. Althalus stood at the south window watching the muddy brown streams overflowing their banks as they ripped their way down the mountainsides of Kagwher. "Did you do that, Em?" he asked.

"Do what?"

"Call up that wind that's melting all the snow."

"I don't tamper with the weather, Althalus. Deiwos doesn't like it when we do that."

"If we don't tell him, maybe he won't notice. We're already cheating, Em. What's one more little cheat? Maybe we should work on that a bit. You teach me how to use the Book, and I'll teach you how to lie, cheat, and steal." He grinned at her.

"That isn't funny, Althalus!" she flared.

"I sort of liked it. How about a little wager on which of us can corrupt the other first?"

"Never mind."

"Corruption's a lot of fun, Em. Are you sure you wouldn't like to try it?"

"You stop that!"

"Think it over, Em, and let me know if you change your mind."

They were both edgy for the next week while they waited for the spring runoff to subside. Then, after the mountain streams had returned to their banks, Althalus gathered up his weapons and they made ready to leave.

He pulled his cloak over his shoulders and looked around. "I guess that's everything," he said. "I'm going to miss this place. It's the first time I've ever had a permanent home. Do you think we'll be able to come back some day?"

"I think so, yes. Shall we leave?"

He picked her up, reached back, and spread the hood of his cloak. "Why don't you ride back there, Em?" he suggested. "Once we get outside, I might need to have both hands free in a hurry."

All right, her voice murmured in his head. She crawled up over his shoulder and down into the baglike hood. *This should work out just fine.*

"Will other people be able to see you when we get outside?"

If we want them to. If we don't, they won't.

He looked at the curved wall and saw that she'd put the door back.

No questions or comments? Her silent voice sounded disappointed.

"Oh, I'm sorry, Em. How's this?" He threw himself back in an exaggerated posture of amazement. "Astonishing!" he exclaimed. "There seems to be a hole in that wall! And somebody even covered that hole with a door! Would you fancy that?"

She hissed in his ear.

He laughed, opened the door, and started down the stairs.

He remembered something as they were crossing the drawbridge. "This might not mean anything, Em," he said, "but I'll tell you anyway, since you always seem to tie your tail in a knot when I mention something that doesn't seem very important. There was some kind of animal following me when I first came here. I never saw it, but I could definitely hear the silly thing."

What did it sound like?

"It was a sort of wailing sound, but not quite like the howl of a wolf. I heard it off and on all the way here."

A kind of despairing scream? The kind of cry a man might make if he'd just fallen off a cliff?

"That comes close. It wasn't a man, though."

No, it probably wasn't.

"Should I have hidden so that I could get a look at it?"

You wouldn't have really wanted to see that creature. It's something that Ghend sent to follow you, to make sure you were doing what he wanted you to do.

"Ghend and I are going to have a little talk about that one of these days. Will that thing still be waiting out there on the other side of the bridge?"

It might be. There's not much we can do if it is.

"I could chase it down and kill it."

You can't kill it. It's a spirit. Is killing always your first answer to every problem?

"Not *every* problem, Em, but I *can* kill things—or people— when the situation calls for it, and I don't get all weepy about it. It's part of the business I'm in. If I do my job right, I don't *have* to kill anybody, but if something goes wrong . . . ah, well."

You're a terrible person, Althalus.

"Yes, I know. Isn't that why you hired me?"

Hired?

"You want something done, and you want me to do it for you. One of these days before long we'll have to discuss my wages."

Wages?

"I don't work for nothing, Em. That's unprofessional." He continued on across the bridge, his spear at the ready.

You want gold, I suppose? she asked in an accusatory tone.

"Oh, gold's all right, I suppose, but I'd really rather get paid in love. Love can't be counted, so it's probably even more valuable than gold."

You're confusing me, Althalus.

"I was trying hard enough."

You're teasing me, aren't you?

"Would I do that? Me? Little old lovable me?"

They reached the other side of the bridge, and Althalus stopped, listening intently for the wailing sound of Ghend's sentinel, but the forest and mountains remained silent. "It must have gotten bored," he said.

Maybe, her voice murmured dubiously.

He turned to take one last look at the House, but it wasn't there anymore. "Did you do that?" he demanded.

No, it takes care of that itself. You were able to see it when you came here because you were supposed to. Nobody else needs to see it, so they can't. Let's go to Arum, pet, she said. Then she stirred around inside the baglike hood of his cloak until she was comfortable and went to sleep.

They covered about fifteen miles that day, traveling along the brink of the precipice Althalus still thought of as the Edge of the World, despite the frozen glaciers that now loomed off to the north. As evening approached, they took shelter in a clump of stunted trees, and Althalus built a fire. Then Emmy provided him with the words that produced bread and a roasted chicken.

Not too bad, she observed, nibbling at a piece of chicken, *but isn't it a little overdone?*

"I don't criticize *your* cooking, Em."

Just a suggestion, pet. I wasn't criticizing.

He leaned back against a tree, stretching his feet out to the fire. "I think there's something you need to know, Em," he said after some reflection. "Before Ghend hired me to go steal the Book, I was having a run of bad luck. It might have worn off by now, but nothing was working for me the way it was supposed to."

Yes, I know. I thought the paper money in Druigor's strongbox was a nice touch, didn't you?

He stared at her. "It was *you*? You were behind all that bad luck?"

Of course. If your luck hadn't turned sour, you wouldn't even have considered Ghend's proposition, would you?

"And before that, you were the one responsible for all the *good* luck I was so famous for?"

Well, of course it was me, pet. If you hadn't had such a streak of good luck, you wouldn't even have recognized bad luck when it came along, would you?

"You're the Goddess of Fortune, aren't you, Em?"

It's a sideline, pet. We all play with the luck of certain people. It's a way to get them to cooperate.

"I've been worshiping you for years, Emmy."

I know, and it's been just lovely.

"Wait a minute," he objected. "I thought you said that you didn't know that it was Ghend who hired me to steal the Book. If you were perched right on my shoulder to play games with my luck, how could you have missed it?"

I wasn't quite that *close, Althalus. I knew that* somebody *was going to do it, but I didn't know it'd be Ghend himself. I thought he'd have some underling take care of it—Argan, maybe, or Khnom. I'm sure it wouldn't have been Pekhal.*

"Who are they?"

Ghend's underlings. I'm sure you'll meet them before this is all over.

"You almost got me killed in Equero, you know. Some of those arrows came awfully close when I was running across Kweso's garden."

But they didn't hit you, did they? I wasn't going to let anything happen to you, pet.

"That notion of paper money was your idea, wasn't it? Nobody could actually believe that paper's worth anything."

The idea's been around for a while. People who are in the business of buying and selling things write little notes to each other. They're a sort of promise to pay, and they're not as cumbersome as gold. The people of Maghu have sort of formalized the idea.

"Were you the one who arranged for Gosti Big Belly to lie to me about what was in his strong room?"

No. That might have been Ghend. He had as much reason as I did to want you to be unlucky right then.

"I wondered why everything was turning so sour. I had people pouring trash on my luck from both sides of the fence."

Isn't it nice to have everybody so concerned about you?

"Then my luck has changed back now?"

Of course it has, Althalus. I'm your luck, and I'll love you all to pieces—as long as you do just exactly as I tell you. She patted his cheek then with one soft paw.

A few days later they reached the place where the dead tree stood. "It's still here?" Althalus was a bit startled.

It's a landmark, pet. We sort of like to keep it here as a reference point.

They turned south there and traveled down through Kagwher for a week or so. Then late one afternoon they crested a hill and saw a rude village huddled in the next valley. "What do you think, Em?" Althalus said back over his shoulder. "Should we go on in and talk with a few people? I've been out of touch for quite a while, so it might not be a bad idea to find out what's happening in the world."

Let's not leave memories of our passing lingering behind us, pet. Ghend has eyes and ears everywhere.

"Good point," he agreed. "Let's sleep here, then. We can slip past that village before daybreak tomorrow."

I'm not really sleepy, Althalus.

"Of course not. You've been sleeping all day. I'm the one who had to do the walking, and I'm tired."

All right, we'll rest your poor little legs here, then.

Althalus wasn't really all *that* tired, however. There was something about the rude village below that had immediately caught his eye when he'd crested the hill. There was a corral on the southern edge of the village, and there were horses in that corral and a number of rude saddles laid over the top rail. It was still a long way to Arum, and riding would probably be faster—and easier—than walking.

He decided not to burden Emmy with his plan. He *was* a master thief, after all, so he was perfectly capable of stealing a horse and saddle without any help—or commentary.

He fixed supper, and after they'd eaten, they curled up under his cloak and went to sleep.

What are you doing? Emmy asked with a sleepy thought as he was preparing to leave not long after midnight.

"I thought we should get an early start and slip past that village before the people woke up. Traveling at night's the best way I know of to avoid being seen."

You don't mind if I sleep a bit longer, do you?

"Not at all, Em," he said. "Just curl up in your little pouch and go back to sleep."

She squirmed around in the hood of his cloak as he started out. Then she got settled in and purred herself back to sleep.

She woke up rather abruptly, however, when Althalus nudged his new horse into a loping canter. *I suppose I should have guessed,* she murmured.

"We *are* on a sort of sacred mission, aren't we, Em?" he replied with a tone of high-minded justification. "We're going out to save the world. It's only right and proper that the people along the way should lend a hand, isn't it?"

You'll never change, will you, Althalus?

"Probably not, no. Go back to sleep, Em. I've got everything under control now."

Once they were mounted, they made good time, and they crossed out of Kagwher into the vast forest of Hule a couple of days after Althalus had acquired the horse.

There were villages here and there in the deep wood of Hule now, and that offended Althalus. Hule was *supposed* to be wild, but now grubby little men had come here to contaminate it. The villages were squalid-looking collections of rude huts squatting on muddy ground and surrounded by garbage. They weren't much to look at, but what *really* offended Althalus were the tree stumps. These wretched intruders were cutting down trees. "Civilization," he muttered in tones of deepest contempt.

What? Emmy asked.

"They're cutting down trees, Em."

Men do that, pet.

"Little men, you mean. Men who are afraid of the dark and invent ways to talk about wolves without actually saying the word 'wolf.' Let's get out of here. The sight of that trash heap makes me sick."

They passed a few other villages on their way south, and the opinion he'd formed about the people who lived in those villages didn't improve very much.

His humor began to improve as they rode up into the foothills of Arum. He was fairly certain that no matter how civilized man became, it was highly unlikely that they'd come up with a way to chop down mountains.

They rode some distance up into the foothills, and on the second day, as evening settled over the mountains, Althalus rode back from the narrow track a ways and set up their night's camp in a small clearing.

Could we have fish tonight, pet? Emmy asked once he had their fire going.

"I was sort of thinking about beef."

We had beef last night.

He was about to say something, but suddenly laughed instead.

What's so funny?

"Haven't we had this conversation before? It seems that I can remember long talks about having the same thing six or eight days in a row."

That was different.

"I'm sure it was." He gave in. "All right, dear, if you want fish, we'll have fish."

She began to purr in happy anticipation.

Althalus slept well that night, but just before dawn he awoke quite suddenly as some almost forgotten instinct warned him of approaching danger. "Somebody's coming, Em." He jarred her awake with the urgent thought.

Her green eyes opened immediately, and he felt her send out a searching thought. Then she hissed.

"What's the matter?" he demanded.

Pekhal! Be careful, Althalus. He's very dangerous.

"Didn't you tell me that he's one of Ghend's people?"

Ghend's animal would come closer. There isn't much humanity left in Pekhal. I'm sure he'll try to kill you.

"Lots of people have tried that, Em." He rolled out from under his cloak, reaching for his bronze-tipped spear.

Don't try to fight him, Althalus. He's a total savage and very vicious. He'll try to talk his way in close enough to reach you with his sword. I'd imagine that he's looking for breakfast along about now.

"He eats *people*?" Althalus exclaimed.

That's one of his nicer habits.

"I think I remember a way to make him keep his distance," Althalus said with a bleak sort of grin.

There was a crashing sound back in the undergrowth, and Althalus slipped behind a tree to watch.

The man was huge, and his face was almost subhumanly brutish. He was bulling his way through the bushes, and he was swinging a large sword that obviously wasn't made of bronze. "Where are you?" he roared in a hoarse, animal-like voice.

"I'm more or less here," Althalus replied. "I don't think you need to come any closer."

"Show yourself!"

"Why would I want to do that?"

"I want to see you!"

"I'm not really all that attractive."

"Show yourself!" the beast roared again.

"If you say so, neighbor," Althalus replied mildly. He stepped out from behind the tree, looking intently at the heavily armed savage. Then he said, "*dheu.*"

The brute rose up off the ground with a startled oath.

"Just a precaution, friend," Althalus explained urbanely. "You seem a bit bad-tempered this morning—somebody you ate, no doubt."

"Put me down!"

"No, I don't think we'll do it that way. You're fine just where you are."

The grotesque brute began swinging his sword at the air around him as if trying to slash at whatever was holding him suspended.

"You don't mind if I have a look at that, do you?" Althalus asked. Then he held out his hand and said, *"gwem!"*

The huge sword spun out of the giant's hand and then drifted obediently down to Althalus. "Very impressive," Althalus said, hefting the heavy weapon.

"You give that back!"

"No. Sorry. You don't really need it." Althalus stuck the heavy sword into the ground and then neatly filched the brute's dagger and purse from his belt as well.

Pekhal began roaring, his face contorted with savage fury.

Althalus lifted his hand. *"Dheu,"* he said again.

Pekhal rose about another twenty feet into the air. His face blanched, his eyes went very wide, and he stopped moving entirely.

"How's the view from up there?" Althalus was beginning to enjoy this. "Would you like to take a look at things from a few miles higher up? I can fix that, if you wish."

Pekhal gaped at him, his eyes filled with sudden terror.

"Do we understand each other, friend?" Althalus asked. "Now, then, the next time you see Ghend, give him my regards and tell him to quit playing around like this. I don't work for him anymore, so he has no claim on me." Althalus picked up his new purse and dagger. He tucked the purse in his pocket, pulled his new sword out of the turf, and tapped its heavy-blade with the hilt of the dagger. It made a ringing sound. Then he tested the sword edge with his thumb. It seemed much sharper than his bronze sword. "Very nice," he murmured. Then he looked up at Pekhal. "I certainly want to thank you for the gifts, friend," he said pleasantly. "All I have to give you in return are my old weapons, but since you're so much nobler than I am, I'm sure you won't mind." He stowed away his bronze weapons. "We'll have to do this again one of these days," he called. "You have yourself a very nice day now, hear?"

Are you just going to leave him up there? Emmy asked critically.

"Oh, I'd imagine he'll set along about the same time the sun does, Em. If he doesn't come down today, he probably will tomorrow—or the next day. Why don't we have a bite of breakfast and move on?"

She was trying to stifle her laughter without too much success. *You're awful!*

"Fun, though, don't you think? Is that half-wit the best that Ghend can come up with?"

Pekhal's the one Ghend summons when brute strength and savagery seem to be called for. The others are much more dangerous.

"Good. This might get kind of boring otherwise." He looked closely at his new dagger. "What is this metal?" he asked.

People call it steel, she replied. *They learned how to forge it about a thousand years ago.*

"I was a little busy just then. That's probably why I missed it. Where does this metal come from?"

You've seen all those red rocks in Plakand, haven't you?

"Oh, yes. Plakand's red from one end to the other."

There's a metal called iron in those rocks. Men couldn't smelt it out of those rocks until they learned how to make hotter fires. Iron is harder than bronze, but it's brittle. It has to be mixed with other metals to make weapons or tools.

"It's completely replaced bronze, then?"

For most things, yes.

"It might be better than bronze, but it's not as pretty. This grey's sort of depressing."

What on earth has that got to do with anything?

"It's a question of aesthetics, Em. We should always strive to fill our lives with beauty."

I don't see anything beautiful in something that was designed to kill people.

"There's beauty in everything, Em. You just have to learn to look for it."

If you're going to preach at me, I think I'll just curl up and go back to sleep.

"Whatever you wish, Em. Oh, before you doze off, though, do you happen to know which clan here in Arum has that knife we're looking for? If I'm going to have to search every man in these mountains for it, we could be here for quite a while."

I know where it is, pet, and you've been there before. You're even rather famous in the clan that has the Knife.

"Me? I try to avoid fame whenever I can."

I wonder why. You do *remember the way to the hall of Gosti Big Belly, don't you?*

"Is *that* where the knife is?"

Yes. The current Clan Chief has it. He doesn't know how he came by it or how important it is, so he keeps it in the room where all his spare weapons are.

"Is that a coincidence of some sort? I mean, that the knife's in Gosti's hall?"

Probably not.

"Would you care to explain that?"

I don't think so. The word "coincidence" always seems to start religious arguments for some reason.

For the next several days, they traveled along the ridgeline Althalus had followed to make good his escape from Gosti, and they finally reached the high pass that overlooked the canyon where Gosti's hall had stood. The rough log fort had been replaced by a large stone castle. The rickety toll bridge that had been the source of Gosti's meager wealth was gone, and the bridge that now spanned the rushing stream was a structure of stone arches. Althalus turned his horse off the trail and rode back into the trees.

Aren't we going down? Emmy asked.

"It's almost evening, Em. Let's wait and go down in the morning."

Why?

"My instincts tell me to wait, all right?"

Oh, well, she replied with exaggerated sarcasm. *We* must *obey our instincts, mustn't we?*

"Be nice," he murmured. Then he dismounted and went over to the edge of the trees to look at the settlement outside the castle. Something struck him as peculiar. "Why are the men all wearing dresses?" he asked.

They call them kilts, Althalus.

"A dress is a dress, Em. What's wrong with leggings like mine?"

They prefer kilts. Don't be picking any fights with them about their clothing. Keep your opinions to yourself.

"Yes, ma'am," he replied. "You'll want fish for dinner again, I suppose?"

If it's not too much trouble.

"And if it is?"

That's just too bad, isn't it?

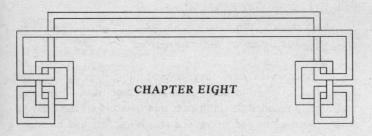

CHAPTER EIGHT

Althalus and Emmy woke early the next morning, but they waited until the villagers started stirring before Althalus mounted his horse and rode through the woods to the trail that led on down to the settlement. He noticed that the houses were more substantial now than they'd been last time he'd been here.

They reached the settlement just as a husky fellow in a dirty kilt came out of one of the houses near the wall of the castle. He was stretching and yawning, but when he saw Althalus riding toward him, his eyes became suddenly alert. "You there—stranger," he called.

"Were you talking to me?" Althalus replied innocently.

"You don't live here, so you're a stranger, aren't you?"

Althalus made some show of looking around. "Why, blast my eyes, I do believe you're right. Isn't it strange that I hadn't noticed that myself?"

The man's suspicious look softened, and he started to chuckle.

"Was it something I said?" Althalus asked, feigning wide-eyed innocence and climbing down from his horse.

"You're a humorous fellow, I see."

"I try. I've found that a little humor smooths over the awkward moments when I first meet somebody. It lets people know that I'm not really a stranger, but only a friend they haven't met yet."

"I'll have to remember that one," the now openly grinning man said. "And what might your name be, friend I haven't met yet?"

"I'm called Althalus."

"Is that supposed to be a joke?"

"That wasn't what I had in mind. Is there something wrong with it?"

"There's a very old story in our clan about a man named Althalus. Oh, my name's Degrur, by the way." He held out his hand.

Althalus shook hands with him. "Pleased to meet you. What's the gist of this story about that other Althalus?"

"Well, as it turned out, he was a thief."

"Really? What did he steal?"

"Money, I'm told. The Clan Chief back in those days was named Gosti Big Belly, and he was the richest man in the world."

"My goodness!"

"Oh, yes. Gosti's strong room was filled to the rafters with gold—until Althalus came along. Anyway, this Althalus could tell jokes so funny that they made the walls laugh. Then, late one night after everybody in the hall had drunk himself to sleep, the thief Althalus broke into Gosti's strong room and stole every single gold coin there. The story says that he had to steal twenty horses just to carry it all away."

"That's a lot of gold."

"It was indeed. I'd imagine that the story's been exaggerated a little over the years, though, so there probably wasn't all *that* much gold in the strong room."

"I'm sure you're right, Degrur. I heard a story once about a man who was supposed to be as big as a mountain."

"I'm going on to the hall," Degrur said. "Why don't you come along, and I'll introduce you to our Chief? I think he'd really like to meet a man called Althalus."

"Probably so that he can keep his eye on me. My name might raise a few suspicions around here."

"Don't worry, my friend. Nobody takes those old stories seriously anymore."

"I certainly hope not."

"Would it alarm you if I told you that you've got a cat peeping out of the hood of your cloak?"

"No, I know she's there. I was camped up in the mountains, and she wandered in—probably to steal some food. We sort of took to each other, so we're traveling together for a while. What's your Chief's name?"

"Albron. He's young, but we think he's going to work out fairly well. His father, Baskon, spent most of his time facedown in the nearest ale barrel, and a drunken Clan Chief tends to make mistakes."

"What happened to him?"

"He got roaring drunk one night and went up to the top of the highest tower to challenge God to a fight. Some say that God took him up on it, but I think he just wobbled and fell off the tower. He splattered himself all over the courtyard."

"Everybody dies from something, I suppose."

They went on to the courtyard of the stone castle. Althalus noticed that it was paved, much as the courtyard of the House at the End of the World had been. Degrur led the way up the steps to the massive door, and they proceeded down a long, torchlit corridor to the dining hall.

There were bearded men sitting at a long table there, eating breakfast off of wooden plates. Althalus glanced around as he and Degrur approached the table. The bleak stone walls were decorated with battle flags and a few antiquated weapons, and the logs burning in the fire pit crackled cheerfully. The stone floor had obviously been swept that morning, and there weren't any dogs gnawing bones in the corners.

Neatness counts, Emmy's voice murmured approvingly.

Maybe, he replied, *but not for very much.*

"My Chief," Degrur said to the kilted man with shrewd eyes and a clean-shaven face at the head of the table, "this traveler was passing through, and I thought you might want to meet him, since he's very famous."

"Oh?" the Clan Chief said.

"Everybody's heard of him, my Chief. His name's Althalus."

"You're not serious!"

Degrur was grinning openly now. "That's what he told me, Albron. Of course, if that's really his name, he might have lied about it to put me off my guard."

"Degrur, that doesn't make any sense at all."

"I just woke up, my Chief. You don't expect me to make sense when I first get up, do you?"

Althalus stepped forward and bowed elegantly. "I'm pleased to make your acquaintance, Chief Albron," he said. Then he looked around the hall. "I see that you've made some improvements since my last visit."

"You've been here before?" Albron asked with one quizzically raised eyebrow.

"Yes—quite some time ago. The Chief in those days used to keep pigs in this hall. Pigs are nice enough animals, I suppose—good to their mothers and all—but they don't make very good house pets. And the dining hall isn't really the place to keep them—unless you like your bacon *very* fresh."

Albron laughed. "Is your name really Althalus?"

Althalus sighed with feigned regret. "I'm afraid so, Chief Albron," he replied theatrically. "I was positive that your clan had forgotten me by now. Fame can be *so* inconvenient sometimes, can't it, my Lord? Anyway, since my dreadful secret's out in the open, and if you're not too busy, maybe we can get right down to cases here. Has your clan managed to amass enough gold since my last visit to make it worth my while to rob you again?"

Chief Albron blinked, and then he burst into laughter.

Althalus pushed on. "Since you already know my dreadful secret, there's no point in beating about the bush, now is there? When would it be most convenient for you to have me rob you? There'll be all that shouting and running around and organizing pursuits, and the like. You know how disruptive a robbery can be sometimes."

"You carry your age very well, Master Althalus," Chief Albron noted with a grin. "According to that story we all heard when we were children, you robbed Gosti Big Belly several thousand years ago."

"Has it been that long? My goodness, where *does* the time go?"

"Why don't you join us for breakfast, Master Althalus?" Albron invited. "Since you plan to rob me of all my gold, you're going to need a few dozen horses to carry off all your loot. We could discuss that over breakfast. I've got a few spare horses, and some of them even have all four of their legs. I'm sure we can strike a bargain on them. Just because you're planning to rob me, it shouldn't get in the way of our doing business together, should it?"

Althalus laughed and joined the group of men at the table. They bantered back and forth over breakfast, and after they'd eaten, the young Chief Albron offered Althalus a tankard of something he called ale.

Never mind, Emmy's voice murmured.

It wouldn't be polite to refuse, Em, he sent back his silent reply. Then he lifted the tankard and drank.

It took all of the self-control he could bring to bear to keep from spitting the awful stuff onto the floor. Good, rich mead was one thing, but Albron's ale was so bitter that Althalus almost choked on it.

Told you. Emmy's voice sounded smug.

Althalus carefully set the tankard down. "This has all been

very entertaining, Chief Albron," he said, "but there's a question I need to ask you."

"The best escape route to take after you've robbed me?"

Althalus laughed. "No, my Lord. If I really *were* that other Althalus, I'd have planned my escape before I even came down here. As you've probably noticed from my clothes, I'm not an Arum."

"That *had* sort of crossed my mind, Master Althalus."

"Actually I come from over to the east in Ansu, and I've been trying to track something down for several years now."

"Something valuable?"

"Well, not to anybody else, probably, but it's something I need to have to lay claim to an inheritance. My father's older brother is the Arkhein of our region."

"Arkhein?"

"It's a title of nobility, my Lord—sort of an equivalent to your own title. Anyway, my uncle's only son—my cousin—had an argument with a bear a few years back, and not many men win those kinds of arguments, since the bears of Ansu are very big and very bad tempered. Anyway, my cousin lost the argument, and since his father, my uncle, only had the one son, his title's going to be vacant after he dies."

"And you'll succeed him? Congratulations, Master Althalus," Albron said.

"It's not quite that cut and dried, my Lord," Althalus said, making a sour face. "I've got another cousin, the son of my father's younger brother, and he and I were both born in the same summer. We Ansus don't have a very precise calendar, so nobody can really be sure which one of us is the eldest."

"Wars tend to break out over things like that."

"My uncle, the Arkhein, realized that too, my Lord. That's when he called my cousin and me to his castle and told us *very* firmly to stop recruiting armies and forming alliances. Then he told us a story. It seems that many years ago one of our ancestors had owned a very pretty dagger. There'd been one of those little wars that break out in Ansu from time to time, and our ancestor had gotten himself killed. Then, after the sun had gone down, the

scoundrels who lurk around the edges of every battlefield like
vultures came out to rob the dead."

"Oh, yes," Albron said, nodding grimly.

"You've seen the same sort of thing yourself, I gather.
Anyway, one of those scoundrels picked up our ancestor's
dagger. It didn't have any jewels in the hilt or anything, but it was
ornamental enough that the rascal thought he could probably
sell it for enough to make it worth his while. Our uncle told my
cousin and me that he was proposing a sort of contest. Whichever one of us could track down that dagger and bring it back to
him would be the one who'd get his title." Althalus sighed dramatically. "I've been running hard ever since that day. You would
not *believe* how interesting life can be when you're looking for
an antique with one eye and watching for assassins with the
other."

"Assassins?"

"My cousin's a bit lazy, my Lord, so the idea of wandering
around the world looking for an ancient knife doesn't light any
warm fires in his heart. He seems to feel that it'd be much easier
to have me murdered than it'd be to try to win a race with me.
Anyway, to get to the point here, I happened across a fellow who
told me that he'd been in your arms room once, and he said that
he was almost certain that he'd seen a knife there that fit the description of the one I'd just told him about." Althalus cast a
covert look at Chief Albron. The story he'd just conjured up out
of whole cloth seemed to have fired the Clan Chief's imagination. Althalus was quite pleased to discover that he hadn't lost
his touch.

Chief Albron rose to his feet. "Why don't we go have a look,
Arkhein Althalus," he suggested.

"I'm not the Arkhein yet, my Lord," Althalus amended.

"You will be if that dagger's in my armory. You're a well-
spoken man with a civilized sense of humor, Althalus. Those are
noble qualities, and your cousin's an absolute knave. I'll do
everything in my power to see to it that you inherit your uncle's
title."

Althalus bowed. "You honor me, my Lord," he said.

Wasn't that all just a little thick? Emmy's voice suggested.

I know these Arums, Em, so I know exactly what kind of story to tell them. Actually, that was a very good one. It had a threat of civil war, a hero, a villain, and a quest fraught with danger. What more does a good story need?

A little bit of truth might have added something.

I don't like to contaminate a good story with truth, Em. That'd be a violation of my artistic integrity, wouldn't it?

Oh, dear. She sighed.

Trust me, little kitten. That knife's as good as in my hands already, and I won't even have to buy it. Albron's going to give it to me outright, along with his blessing.

Albron's armory was a stone-walled chamber at the back of his castle, and it was littered with all kinds of swords, axes, pikes, helmets, daggers, and shirts made of chain.

Albron introduced Althalus to a blocky, kilted fellow with a bristling red beard. "This is my armorer, Reudh. Describe this dagger you're looking for to him."

"It's about a foot and a half long, Master Armorer," Althalus told the red-bearded man, "and it's got an odd-shaped blade—sort of like a laurel leaf. There's a design etched into the blade. From what I understand, the design's actually writing in some ancient language that nobody understands anymore."

Reudh scratched his head. "Oh," he said then. "It's *that* one. It's very pretty, but it's a little ornate for my taste. I prefer more businesslike weapons."

"It's here, then?"

"Well, it *was*. Young Eliar came here to arm himself before he went off to that war down in Treborea. He took a fancy to that knife, so I let him take it."

Althalus gave Chief Albron a puzzled look. "Have you got a quarrel of some kind with somebody in Treborea, my Lord?"

"No, it's a business arrangement. In the old days the low-landers were always trying to persuade the Clan Chiefs of Arum to agree to alliances with them—alliances where we'd do the bleeding and they'd get the profit. There was a conclave of all the Clan Chiefs of Arum about fifty years ago, and the Chiefs all agreed that there weren't going to *be* any more of those alliances with the lowlanders. The way things are now, if the lowlanders need soldiers, they have to rent them."

"Rent?"

"It works out very well for us, Master Althalus. We don't ally ourselves with anybody during those wars, so we don't get swindled out of our share when the war's over. It's all strictly business now. If they want soldiers, they pay for them—in advance—and we won't accept promissory notes or paper money. They pay in gold, and they pay *before* any of our men start marching."

"How did the lowlanders take that?"

"From what I've heard, their screams of outrage were echoing off the moon. The Clan Chiefs of Arum have held firm, though, so now the lowlanders either pay, or they fight their own wars." Albron scratched his chin reflectively. "We're a warlike people here in Arum, and there was a time when almost anything could set off a clan war. It's not that way here anymore. There hasn't been a clan war in Arum for forty years."

Althalus grinned at him. "Why burn down your neighbors for fun when you can set fire to Perquaine and Treborea for profit?" he said. "Which Treborean city bought the services of this young Eliar?"

"Kanthon, wasn't it, Reudh?" Albron asked. "Sometimes I lose track. I've got men involved in a half dozen little wars down there right now."

"Yes, my Lord," Reudh replied. "This was Eliar's first war, so you sent him off to one of the quiet ones so he could get his feet wet in shallow water his first time out. That war between Kanthon and Osthos has been simmering for the last ten centuries, and nobody's taking it very seriously."

"Well," Althalus said, "I guess I get to go to Kanthon then. There's something to be said for that, I suppose."

"Oh?" Albron asked.

"It's open country down there in Treborea. I don't want to offend you, my Lord, but there are too many trees here in Arum for my taste."

"Don't you like trees?"

"Not when one of my cousin's assassins might be hiding behind any one of them. Flat, open country's sort of boring, but some boredom might give my nerves a bit of a rest. Here lately they've been stretched as tight as a bowstring. What does Eliar look like?"

"He's sort of gangly," the red-bearded armorer said. "He's only about fifteen years old, so he's still growing. If he lives, he'll probably turn into a fairly respectable warrior. He isn't any too bright, but he might outgrow that. He's got a lot of enthusiasm, and he's convinced that he's the greatest warrior alive."

"I'd better hurry, then," Althalus said. "Young Eliar sounds like a fellow who's just brimful of incipient mortality."

"Nicely put, Master Althalus," Albron said admiringly. "That description fits just about every adolescent male in the whole of Arum."

"They're good for business, though, aren't they, Chief Albron?"

"Oh, yes." Albron smirked. "I can usually get double price for the young ones."

Althalus and Emerald left Albron's castle the next morning and traveled south. *Do you know the way to Kanthon?* Emmy asked as they rode on down the canyon.

"Of course, Em. I know several ways to just about every city in the world."

And several other ways to get out of them?

"Naturally. Getting out of town in a hurry is sometimes very necessary for people in my profession."

I wonder why?

"Be nice, Emmy. Where do we go after we get the Knife away from Eliar?"

I haven't the faintest idea.

"What?"

Don't worry, Althalus. The writing on the Knife will tell us where to go.

"I thought the words on the blade were there to identify the people we're going to need."

That's part of what they say, but only part of it. The writing on the blade is much more complex than that, pet, and its meaning changes with the circumstances. It tells us where to go, who we need to find, and what we're supposed to do next.

"It sounds to me as if it's almost like the Book."

Sort of, yes. The Knife changes in subtle ways, though, and the Book doesn't. Let's move along, Althalus. We have a long way to go.

They rode down onto the plains of Perquaine, and after about a week they reached the city of Maghu. There had been many changes in Maghu since Althalus had last been there, but the ancient temple was still the most prominent building in town. As they rode past it, Althalus was a bit startled by Emmy's reaction. She was riding, as always, in the hood of his cloak, and she laid back her ears and hissed at the temple. "What was that all about?" he asked her.

I hate that place! she replied vehemently.

"What's wrong with it?"

It's grotesque!

"It's a little fancy, but not much more than other temples I've seen."

I'm not talking about the temple, Althalus. I'm talking about the statue inside.

"You mean the one with all those extra bosoms? It's just the local Goddess, Em. You don't have to take it so personally."

It is personal, Althalus!

He could feel her fuming outrage, and he looked sharply back over his shoulder at her. A sudden notion struck him, and he sent a probing thought into that part of her mind she'd always insisted was personal and private. He was stunned by what he found. "Is *that* who you really are?" He gasped.

I've told you to stay out of there!

"You're Dweia, aren't you?"

Amazing. You even pronounced it right. Her tone was snippy. She was definitely not in a good humor.

Althalus was awed. "Why didn't you tell me?" he demanded.

It wasn't any of your business who I am.

"Do you really look anything like that statue?"

Like a brood sow, you mean? Like a whole herd of brood sows?

"I was talking about the face, not all those extra . . ." He groped for an inoffensive word.

The face isn't accurate either.

"A fertility Goddess? What's fertility got to do with anything?" he asked.

Would you like to rephrase that question, while you still have your health?

"Maybe I should just drop it."

Wise decision.

They rode out of Maghu, and Althalus struggled with what he'd just discovered. In a peculiar sort of way, it began to make sense. "No biting," he said to Emmy. "Just tell me if I've got this straight. Deiwos makes things, right?"

So?

"After he's made them, though, he goes on to make other things, and he turns the things he's already made over to you. You're the one who keeps them alive by making sure that they all have offspring—or whatever." Then another thought came to him. "That's why you hate Daeva so much, isn't it, Em? He wants to destroy everything Deiwos made, but you want to preserve it—to keep it alive. Is there a reason why your names all begin with the same sound? Deiwos, Dweia, and Daeva? Might that mean you're Daeva's sister as well as the sister of Deiwos?"

It's a little more complex than that, Althalus, but you're nibbling around the edges of it. There are some men coming up the road toward us.

Althalus looked on ahead. "Maybe you'd better pull your head in until I find out who they are."

As the men came closer, Althalus saw that they were wearing kilts. Most of them were also wearing bloody bandages, and several were hobbling along with the aid of wooden staffs. "Arums," he muttered to Emmy. "The markings on their kilts suggest that they're members of Albron's clan."

What are they doing here in Perquaine?

"I don't know, Em. I'll ask them." Althalus reined in his horse and waited as the wounded men hobbled closer.

The man at the front of the column was tall, lean, and dark haired. He had a bloody bandage wrapped about his head and a sour look on his face.

"You gentlemen are a long way from home," Althalus said by way of greeting.

"We're trying to do something about that right now," the sour-faced man said.

"You're of Albron's clan, aren't you?"

"How did you know that?"

"The markings on your kilts, neighbor."

"You don't look like an Arum to me."

"I'm not, but I'm acquainted with your customs. It looks as if you've run into some trouble."

"That sort of covers it, yes. Chief Albron hired us out to work in a war over in Treborea. It was supposed to be a quiet little war, but it got out of hand."

"It wasn't by any chance that little squabble between Kanthon and Osthos, was it?" A cold lump began to settle somewhere in the vicinity of Althalus' stomach.

"You've heard about that one?"

"We've just come from Chief Albron's hall."

"We?"

"My cat and me," Althalus explained.

"A cat's an odd traveling companion for a grown man," the lean man observed. He glanced back at his battered troops. "Rest a bit." He barked out the command. Then he sank down onto the grass at the side of the road. "If you've got a little time, I'd sort of like to know what's up ahead of us," he said to Althalus.

"Of course." Althalus swung down from his saddle. "My name's Althalus, by the way."

The wounded warrior gave him a startled look.

"It's just a coincidence," Althalus explained. "I'm not really *that* Althalus."

"I didn't really think so. I'm called Khalor, and I'm the Ancient of what's left of this group of Albron's clansmen."

"You don't look all that ancient to me."

"It's a Treborean title, friend Althalus. We're supposed to try to fit in when we come down into the low countries to fight their wars for them. Back at home they call me Sergeant. Did you happen across any groups of armed men on your way out of the mountains?"

"Nothing out of the ordinary, Sergeant Khalor—a few hunters is about all. I think you'll be able to get home without any trouble. From what your Chief told me, the clans of southern Arum are more or less at peace with each other. What happened to you and your men?"

"Albron hired us out to the Kanthons about six months or so ago. Like I told you before, it was supposed to be a quiet little war. About all we were supposed to do was march around in places where the Osthos could see us—the usual sorts of things, you understand—flex our muscles, wave our swords and axes, shout war cries, and all the other foolishness that impresses the lowlanders. Then the feeble-minded fool that sits on the throne of Kanthon got carried away and ordered us to invade the territory of the Aryo of Osthos." The Sergeant shook his head in disgust.

"You couldn't talk him out of it?"

"I tried, Althalus. God knows I tried. I *told* him that I didn't have enough men for that and that he'd have to hire ten times as many as he already had before I could mount an invasion, but the silly ass wouldn't listen. Don't ever try to explain military reality to a lowlander."

"You got yourself trounced, I take it?"

"Trounced only *begins* to cover it. I got a mud puddle stomped into my backside, if you want to know the truth. Unfortunately, we took the Osthos by surprise when we marched across their frontier."

"Unfortunately?"

"They didn't expect us to do that, so they weren't ready for us. That gave the idiot in Kanthon all sorts of wild delusions, and he ordered me to lay siege to the city of Osthos itself. I didn't have enough men to set up a picket line around the place, much less lay siege to it, but the jackass in Kanthon wouldn't listen to me."

Althalus started to swear.

"When your vocabulary begins to run dry, I can give you

whole platoons of interesting things to say about my former employer. I've been inventing new swearwords for the last two and a half weeks. You seem to be taking this sort of personally."

"Yes, I am. I've been looking for a young fellow who's under your command. His name's Eliar. He doesn't happen by any chance to be among your wounded, does he?"

"I'm afraid not, Althalus. I'd imagine that Eliar's long dead by now—unless that savage girl down in Osthos is still slicing very tiny pieces off of him."

"What happened?"

"Eliar was very enthusiastic about this business; you know how young fellows are in their first war. Anyway, the Aryo of Osthos had ordered his troops to fall back every time they saw us. Eliar and some of my other green troops thought that meant that they were cowards instead of men who had a very clever leader. When we reached the walls of the city, the Osthos just closed their gates and invited us to try to get in if we thought we could. I had this cluster of young enthusiasts on my hands, and they were all jumping up and down and frothing at the mouth and begging me to mount an assault on the walls. Eliar was the one who was screaming the loudest, so I put him in charge and ordered him to take a run at the gate and see how many of his men he could get killed."

"That's a blunt way to put it, Sergeant."

"It's the only real way to find out if a young leader's got sand in his craw. Eliar was a nice boy, and the other young fellows all sort of followed his lead. That's part of my job. I'm supposed to keep an eye on these natural leaders and put them into situations where they can prove whether or not they've got what it takes to lead troops. Getting some of your people killed is part of the business of command. Well, to cut this short, Eliar and his puppies all went rushing across the meadow toward the city gate screaming and waving their weapons as if they thought they could frighten the walls into falling down. When they were about fifty paces from the gate, it swung open, and the Aryo of Osthos personally led out his troops to give my howling little barbarians a quick lesson in good manners."

"By hand, I assume," Althalus added in a gloomy voice.

"Also by foot. They tramped all over my little boys. Eliar was right in the thick of things, naturally, and he was really doing quite well until he came up against the Aryo himself, who just happened to be armed with a battle-ax. Eliar took a wild swing at the Aryo's head with his sword, and the Aryo blocked it with his ax. Eliar's sword broke off just above the hilt, and I thought, 'Well, good-bye, Eliar.' But the boy surprised me—and he probably surprised the Aryo even more. He threw what was left of his sword right at the Aryo's face and went for his dagger. Before the Aryo could regain his balance, Eliar was all over him, and he was working that dagger double time. He must have stabbed that poor nobleman two dozen times, and he left a gash as wide as his hand with every stab. I didn't really think that ornamental dagger of his was worth all that much, but it certainly leaves big holes in people if a man uses it right. The Aryo's men swarmed Eliar under, of course, and they took him and some of his men prisoner and went back into the city with them."

"Who was this woman you mentioned before?"

"The Aryo's daughter. There's a girl who can probably cut glass with her voice from a mile away. We could hear her very clearly when her father's soldiers carried his body to her. We even heard her when she ordered the soldiers to come out of the city and chop us into little pieces. I didn't think real soldiers would take orders from a woman, but Andine's got the kind of voice you can't really ignore." Khalor winced. "It seems that I can still hear her. But for all I know, I really can. You've never *heard* a voice like that one. It's only been two and a half weeks, and she might very well be still screaming about how many yards of our entrails she wants draped over every tree in the vicinity."

"Andine?" Althalus asked.

"That's her name. It's a pretty name for a pretty girl, but she's got a very ugly mind."

"You've seen her?"

"Oh, yes. She stood up on top of the city wall to gloat while her soldiers butchered us. She kept screaming for more blood and waving Eliar's dagger around. She's a total savage, and she's the ruler of Osthos now."

"A *woman*?" That startled Althalus.

"She's no ordinary woman, Althalus. That one's made out of steel. She was the Aryo's only child, so they're probably all bowing to her and calling her 'Arya Andine.' If Eliar's lucky, she just had him killed outright. I sort of doubt that, though. More probably, she's been carving pieces off him with his own knife and making him watch while she eats them. I wouldn't be at all surprised to hear that she's trying to come up with a way to cut out his heart so fast that he'd still be alive long enough to watch her eat it right in front of his face. Stay away from that one, Althalus. I'd advise you to give her forty or fifty years to cool down before you go anywhere near her."

CHAPTER NINE

"**W**hy should we care if she kills him, Em?" Althalus asked aloud. "It's the Knife we want, not some half-grown little boy from Arum."

When are *you going to learn to look beyond the end of your nose, Althalus?* Her tone was a bit snippy, and there was enough condescension in it to be offensive.

"That's about enough of that, Em," he told her crisply.

Sorry, pet, she apologized. *That* was *a little nasty, wasn't it? What I'm getting at is that everything is connected. Nothing happens in isolation. Eliar's probably some crude, unschooled barbarian from the backcountry of Arum, but he* did *pick up the*

Knife back in Albron's arms room. It might have been a whim, but we can't be sure of that until we test him. If he can't read what's written on the blade, we'll pat him on the head and tell him to run along home. If he can *read it, though, he'll have to come with us.*

"What if he's like I was before I came to the House? I couldn't even read my own name back then."

I noticed. It won't matter whether he can read or not. If he happens to be one of the selected ones, he'll know what the writing means.

"How will we know if he's got it right?"

We'll know, pet. Believe me, we'll know.

"Why don't you enlighten me? Tell me what the word on the blade is."

It varies. It'll mean something different to each person who reads it.

"Emmy, that doesn't make any sense at all. A word's a word, isn't it? It's supposed to have one specific meaning."

Does the word "home" have a specific meaning?

"Of course it does. It means the place where a man lives—or maybe the place he originally came from."

Then it has a different meaning for each person, doesn't it?

He frowned.

Don't beat yourself over the head with it, pet. The word that's carved into the Knife's blade is a command, and it tells each one of the people we have to locate to do something different.

"It can't just be one word, then."

I didn't say that it was. Each reader will see it differently.

"It changes, then?"

No. It's permanent. The writing stays the same. It's the reading that changes.

"You're starting to give me a headache, Em."

Don't brood about it, Althie. It'll make more sense to you once we get the Knife. Our problem right now is getting the Knife— and Eliar—away from Andine.

"I think I've already got the answer to that one, Em. I'll just buy them from her."

Buy?

"Pay her to give them to me."

Althalus, Eliar's a person. You can't buy people.

"You're wrong about that, Em. Eliar's a captured soldier, and that means that he's a slave now."

That's disgusting!

"Of course it is, but that's the way things are. I'll have to rob a few rich people to get enough gold to buy Eliar and the Knife. If Arya Andine's as dead set on butchering Eliar as Sergeant Khalor seems to think she is, I'll need *lots* of gold to persuade her to sell him to me."

Maybe, she murmured, her green eyes going distant. *But then again, maybe not. If we use the Book right, she'll be more than happy to sell him to us.*

"I've come across vindictive ladies before, Em. Believe me, it'll take a *lot* of gold. If Sergeant Khalor was anywhere at all close to being right, she's developed a strong appetite for Eliar's blood by now. Let's see if we can find some rich man's house. I'll rob him and then we can go make Andine an offer."

There are other ways to get gold, Althalus.

"I know—mining it out of the ground. I don't care for doing it that way. I've seen a lot of deep holes in the mountainsides of Kagwher, and from what I hear, only about one in a hundred has turned up even a speck of gold."

I believe I can improve on those numbers, pet.

"I still don't like chopping at the ground, Em. It makes my back hurt."

That's because you don't get enough exercise. Let's move right along. We have several days' travel ahead of us before you get to start digging.

"There isn't any gold down here in the low country, Em."

There is if you know where to look. Ride on, my brave boy, ride on.

"Was that supposed to be funny?"

They rode south across the parched grain fields of Perquaine for the next several days, moving at a steady canter. It was about midafternoon on the third day after their meeting with Sergeant Khalor when Althalus reined in and dismounted.

Why are we stopping? Emmy asked.

"We've been pushing the horse a bit. I'll walk alongside to give him a rest." He looked around at the sun-baked fields. "Skimpy," he observed.

What is?

"This year's crop. It looks to me as if it's hardly going to be worth the trouble to harvest it."

It's the drought, pet. It doesn't rain much anymore.

"We should be getting close to the coastline, Em. It always rains along the coast."

We're a long way from where the coast is now, pet. We talked about that back in the House, remember? The ice locks up more of the world's water every year. That causes the drought and lowers the sea level.

"Are we going to be able to repair that?"

What do you mean?

"Melt the ice so that things go back to the way they're supposed to be."

Why do men always want to tamper with the natural order of things?

"When something breaks, we fix it, that's all."

What gave you the absurd idea that it's broken?

"It's not the way it was before, Em. To our way of looking at things, that means that it's broken."

Now *which one of us is thinking the way Daeva thinks?*

"Drying up the oceans and turning the world into a desert doesn't make things better, Em."

Change doesn't necessarily mean improvement, Althalus. Change is just change. "Better" and "worse" are human definitions. The world changes all the time, and no amount of complaining's going to stop it from changing.

"The seacoast shouldn't move around," he declared stubbornly.

You can tell it to stop, if you'd like. It might *listen to you, but I wouldn't make any large wagers on it, if I were you.* She looked around. *We should reach the place we're looking for sometime tomorrow.*

"Have we been looking for someplace special?"

Sort of special. It's the place where you're going to start working for your living.

"What an unnatural thing to suggest."

It'll be good for you, love—fresh air, exercise, wholesome food . . .

"I think I'd sooner take poison."

They set up a rudimentary camp in a scraggly thicket some distance back from the road that evening and started out again shortly after dawn.

There it is, Emmy said after they'd ridden for a couple of hours.

"There what is?"

The place where you do some honest work, pet.

"I wish you'd stop rubbing my nose in that." He looked across what appeared to be a long-abandoned field at a kind of knoll, sparsely covered with stunted, tired-looking grass. "Is that it?" he asked.

That's the place.

"How can you tell? It's just a hill. We've passed dozens of others just like it."

Yes, we have. This one isn't an ordinary hill, though. It's the ruins of an old house that's been covered with dirt.

"Who buried it like that?"

The wind. The ground's very dry now, so the wind picks up dirt and carries it along until it comes to something that blocks it. That's where it drops the dirt.

"Is that the way all hills get built?"

Not all of them, no.

Althalus squinted at the rounded hillock. "I think I'm going to need some tools. I'll dig if you insist, Em, but I'm not going to do it with my bare hands."

We'll take care of it. I'll tell you the word to use.

"I still think it'd be easier just to rob somebody."

There's more gold in that hill than you're likely to find in a dozen of the houses we've passed. You say that you'll need gold to buy Eliar and the Knife from Andine. All right, there's the gold. Go dig it up.

"How do you know there's gold there?"

I just do. There's more gold in those ruins than you've ever seen before. Fetch, boy, fetch.

"That's starting to make me a little tired, Em."

If you'd do as you're told the first time, I wouldn't have to keep telling you over and over again. You're going to do what I tell you to do eventually anyway, so why not just do it immediately instead of arguing with me?

He gave up. "Yes, dear."

Good boy, she said approvingly. *Good boy.*

She gave him instructions on how to manufacture a shovel with a single word and then directed him to a spot about fifty paces up the south side of the slope. As he led his horse up the hill, he saw some very ancient limestone building blocks half buried in the soil. They'd obviously been sawed square when the house had been erected, but wind and weather had rounded them to the point that they were almost indistinguishable from native stone. "How long ago was the house abandoned?" he asked.

About three thousand years ago. The man who built it started out in life as a plowman. Then he went up into Arum before anybody else went up there. He wasn't really looking for gold, but he found some.

"Probably because he got there first. Why did he go to Arum if he didn't know there was gold there, though?"

There'd been a slight misunderstanding about the ownership of a certain pig. His neighbors were a little excited about it, so he decided to go up into the mountains for a while to give them time to calm down. I'm sure you understand. This is the place, pet. Get down off the horse and start digging.

He dismounted, lifted Emmy out of the hood of his cloak, and set her on his saddle. Then he took off his cloak and rolled up his sleeves. "How deep do I have to dig?" he asked.

About four feet. Then you'll hit some flagstones, and you'll have to pry them up. There's a little cellar under the stones, and that's where the gold is.

"Are you sure?"

Quit wasting time and start digging, Althalus.

"Yes, dear." He sighed and very reluctantly thrust his shovel into the dirt.

The drought had made the soil dry and sandy, so digging wasn't really as hard as he'd thought it would be.

I wouldn't throw the dirt so far down the hill, pet, Emmy suggested after a while. *You'll have to shovel it all back in the hole when you've finished.*

"What for?"

To keep somebody from finding the gold you'll have to leave behind.

"I'm not going to leave any, Em."

How do you plan to carry it?

"You're sitting on him, love. He's a strong horse."

Not that strong, he isn't.

"How much *is* there here?"

More than our horse can carry.

"Really?" Althalus began to dig faster.

After about a half hour, he struck the flagstones Emmy had told him about. Then he widened out the hole he'd dug to give himself some more room. He leaned his shovel against the side of the hole, knelt on the stones, and began to probe between them with his bright steel dagger. "Exactly what am I looking for here, Em?" he asked. "These flagstones fit together so tight that I can't get my knife into the cracks."

Keep looking, she instructed. *The one you want to find fits a little more loosely.*

He kept poking until he found it. The dirt the patient centuries had blown in had sifted down into the cracks between the stones, and it took him a while to dig it out with his dagger point. Then he resheathed his dagger, took the shovel, and began to pry.

The stone lifted out rather easily, followed by a rush of stale-smelling air. There was an open space of some kind below the flagstones, but it was too dark down there to see anything. He pried up another stone to let in more light.

There were tightly piled stacks of dust-covered bricks in the cellar, and a hot surge of disappointment came over him. But why would anyone take so much trouble just to hide bricks? He reached down through the hole and brushed the dust away from one of the bricks.

He stared at it in absolute disbelief. The brick that had been concealed by centuries of dust was bright yellow.

"Dear God!" Althalus exclaimed, brushing away more dust.

He's busy right now, Althalus. Could I take a message?

"There must be tons of it down here!"

Told you, she reminded him smugly.

The gold had been cast into oblong blocks, each about the size of a man's hand and slightly thicker. They weighed about five pounds apiece. Althalus found that he was trembling violently as he lifted the blocks out of the hole and laid them on the flagstones.

Don't get carried away, Althalus, Emmy suggested.

"Twenty?" He said it with a great reluctance.

I don't think the horse would want to carry any more.

Althalus forced himself to stop at twenty of the gold blocks. Then he replaced the flagstone, shoveled all the dirt back into the hole, and uprooted a number of nearby bushes. He replanted the bushes in the freshly dug-up dirt to conceal his private gold mine.

Then he fashioned a couple of bags, put ten blocks of gold in each, tied them together, and hung them across his horse's back just behind his saddle. Then he remounted, whistling gaily.

You're all bubbly this afternoon, Emmy noted.

"I'm stinking rich, Em," he said exuberantly.

I've been noticing that for several days now. You're long overdue for a bath.

"That's not what I meant, little kitten."

It should have been. You're strong enough to curdle milk.

"I told you that hard work didn't agree with me, Em," he reminded her.

They crossed the River Osthos late that afternoon and made camp on the Treborean side. To keep the peace, Althalus bathed, washed his clothes, and even shaved off the past month's growth of beard. Emmy definitely approved of that. They rose early the following morning, and three days later they caught sight of the walls of the city of Osthos. "Impressive," Althalus observed.

I'm sure they'll be glad you approve. Emmy's whisper sounded inside his head. *How did you plan to gain entry into the palace?*

"I'll come up with something. What's the word for 'stay away'?"

"Bheudh." *Actually* "bheudh" *means "to make someone aware of something," but your thought when you say the word should get your meaning across. Why do you ask?*

"I'll have to go about on foot to locate certain officials, and I'd rather not have some rascal steal my horse. He's very dear to me right now."

I wonder why.

Althalus rode some distance away from the road, and with Emmy's instruction, he converted five of his gold blocks into coins marked with the idealized picture of a stalk of wheat, which identified them as having come from Perquaine. Then he rode into the city, where he stopped by a clothier's shop and bought himself some moderately elegant garments to disguise his rustic origins. Emmy chose not to comment when he emerged from the shop.

He remounted and made his way to the public buildings near the palace to listen and to ask questions.

"I wouldn't go anywhere near her, stranger," a silver-haired old statesman advised when Althalus asked him about the procedure for gaining an audience with Arya Andine.

"Oh?" Althalus said. "Why's that?"

"She was difficult before her father's death, but now she's graduated from difficult to impossible."

"Unfortunately, I have some business I have to discuss with her. I'd planned to talk with her father, the Aryo. I hadn't heard that he'd died. What happened to him?"

"I thought everybody knew. The Kanthons invaded us a month or so back, and they sent their mercenaries down here to lay siege to our city. Our noble Aryo led our army outside the walls to chase those howling barbarians off, and one of the scoundrels murdered him."

"My goodness!"

"The murderer was captured, naturally."

"Good. Did Arya Andine have him put to death?"

"No, he's still alive. Arya Andine's still considering various ways to send him off. I'm sure she'll come up with something suitably unpleasant—eventually. What line of business are you in, my friend?"

"I'm a labor contractor," Althalus replied.

The statesman gave him a quizzical look.

Althalus winked slyly at him. " 'Labor contractor' sounds so much nicer than 'slave trader,' wouldn't you say? I'd heard about the assault on your city, and I understand that your soldiers captured several of the attackers. I thought I might stop by and take them off your hands. The owners of the salt mines in Ansu are paying a lot of money for strong, healthy slaves right now. Captured soldiers bring a premium price in the salt mines, and I pay in good gold. Do you think Arya Andine might be interested?"

"The word 'gold' is very likely to get her attention," the courtier agreed. "She'll want to keep Eliar, the young fellow who killed her father, but she'd probably be willing to sell the others to you. What might your name be, my friend?"

"I'm called Althalus."

"A very ancient name."

"My family was sort of old-fashioned."

"Why don't we step over to the palace, Master Althalus?" the courtier suggested. "I'll introduce you to our impossible Arya."

The old gentleman led the way to the palace gate, and he and Althalus were immediately admitted. "The soldiers will look after your horse, Master Althalus," the silver-haired man said. "Oh, my name's Dhakan, by the way. I tend to forget that strangers don't know me."

"I'm pleased to make your acquaintance, Lord Dhakan," Althalus said, bowing politely.

Emmy, who'd been sitting rather primly on the saddle of their horse, dropped sinuously to the stones of the courtyard.

"Your pet, Master Althalus?" Dhakan asked.

"She tends to look at it the other way around, my Lord," Althalus replied. "Cats are sort of like that."

"I have a pet turtle myself," Dhakan said. "He doesn't move very fast, but then, neither do I."

Osthos was an ancient city, and the throne room was truly magnificent. It had a marble floor and stately columns. At the far end was a raised dais backed by crimson drapes, and there was an ornate throne on that dais. Imperious Andine, Arya of Osthos, sat upon that throne. She was quite obviously not paying the slightest bit of attention to the droning speech being presented by a stout man wearing a white mantle. The speech was a diplomatically gentle suggestion that the young Arya wasn't paying enough heed to affairs of state.

Andine was young—very young, in fact. Althalus judged her to be no more than fifteen years old. Everyone else in her throne room had white hair, the only exception being a similarly youthful kilted Arum, who was chained to a marble column at one side of the dais. *That* young fellow was receiving imperious Andine's undivided attention. She was looking directly at him with her huge, almost black eyes, and she was absently toying with a large laurel-leaf dagger.

That's the Knife, pet, Emmy silently exulted.

"Is that the murderer chained to that post?" Althalus whispered to Dhakan a bit incredulously.

"Sick, isn't it?" Dhakan replied. "Our glorious, but slightly warped, leader hasn't let him out of her sight since the day he was captured."

"Surely she has a dungeon."

"Oh, yes, indeed she does. The other prisoners are all there. For some strange reason, our little girl longs for the sight of the young ruffian. She never talks to him, but she never takes her eyes off him. She sits there playing with that knife and watching him."

"He looks just a bit nervous."

"Wouldn't you be?"

Then Emmy, her tail sinuously flowing back and forth, daintily crossed the marble floor and went up onto the dais.

What are you doing? Althalus sent a startled thought at her.

Stay out of this, pet, her voice came back. Then she raised herself up, putting her front paws on the marble throne, and meowed inquiringly at the young Arya.

Andine jerked her eyes off her captive and looked at the green-eyed cat at her knee. "What an adorable kitten!" she exclaimed. "Where did you come from, Puss?"

"My apologies, your Highness," Althalus said, stepping forward. "Emmy, you come back here."

Arya Andine gave him a puzzled look. "I don't believe I know you," she said. Her voice was rich and vibrant, the kind of voice that stirs a man's spirit.

"Permit me, your Highness," Dhakan said, stepping forward and bowing slightly. "This is Master Althalus, and he's come here to discuss a business matter."

Emmy gave another inquiring meow.

"Did you want to come up here into my lap, Puss?" Andine asked. She leaned forward and picked Emmy up. She held the cat out and looked into her face. "My," she said in her rich voice, "aren't you adorable?" Then she put the cat in her lap. "There," she said, "was that what you wanted?"

Emmy started to purr.

"Master Althalus here is a businessman, Arya Andine," Dhakan said. "He deals in captives, and since he heard about the recent attack on our city, he's stopped by to inquire about the possibility of buying those barbaric Arum prisoners from you. I recommend that you give him a hearing, your Highness."

"What on earth would you do with them, Master Althalus?" Andine asked curiously.

"I have a number of contacts in Ansu, your Highness," Althalus replied. "The owners of the salt mines there are always in the market for strong young men. A salt mine uses up workers at a ferocious rate."

"You're a slave trader, then?"

Althalus shrugged deprecatingly. "It's a living, your Highness. Slaves are a valuable commodity. I buy them in places where they're an inconvenience and take them to places where they can be put to work to pay for their keep. Everybody benefits, really. The one who sells them to me gets gold, and the one who buys them gets laborers."

"What do the slaves get?"

"They get fed, your Highness. A slave doesn't have to worry about where his next meal's coming from. He gets fed even when the crops fail or the fish aren't biting."

"Our philosophers tell us that slavery's an evil."

"I don't concern myself with philosophy, your Highness. I take the world as I find it. I'm prepared to offer ten Perquaine gold wheats for every able-bodied young captive you'd care to sell."

She stared at him in astonishment. "That's a noble price, Master Althalus," she said in that throbbing voice.

"I buy the best, your Highness, so I pay the best. I don't deal in children or old men or young women. I buy only young, strong, healthy men who can put in a good day's work." He glanced over at the youthful Arum chained to the marble pillar. "With your permission, your Highness," he said, bowing slightly. He walked over to the pillar where Eliar sat disconsolately on the marble floor in chains. "On your feet!" Althalus barked.

"Who says so?" Eliar replied sullenly.

Althalus reached out, took Eliar by his hair, and jerked him into a standing position. "When I tell you to do something, do it," he said. "Now open your mouth. I want to see your teeth."

Eliar tightly clamped his mouth shut.

"He's a bit stubborn, Master Althalus," Andine said. "I've been trying *ever* so hard to cure him of that."

"It takes a certain amount of firmness to break a slave's spirit, your Highness," Althalus advised her. Then he took his dagger from his belt and pried Eliar's teeth apart with it. "Good healthy teeth," he noted. "That's a promising sign. Bad teeth usually mean that the slave's got something wrong with him."

Eliar made a lunge at Althalus, but his chains brought him up short.

"He's a little stupid," Althalus observed, "but that can be cured. Boy," he said to the captive, "didn't your Sergeant ever explain to you that it's foolish to attack an armed man with your bare hands? Particularly when you're chained up."

Eliar was straining at his chains, trying to pull himself free.

"Good muscle tone there, too," Althalus said approvingly. "I'd pay a premium for this one, your Highness."

"That one isn't for sale," Andine replied rather intensely. Her voice had taken on a steely note, and her huge black eyes burned.

"Everything's for sale, your Highness," Althalus replied with a cynical laugh.

Don't push it just yet, Althalus, Emmy's purring voice murmured in his mind. *I'm still working on her.*

Do you think you can bring her around?

Probably. She's young enough to be impulsive. Ask to see the other captives. You'll probably have to buy them all to get Eliar.

"We can discuss this one later, your Highness," Althalus said to the Arya. "Do you suppose I might be able to take a look at the others?"

"Of course, Master Althalus," Andine replied. "Show him the way to the dungeon, Lord Dhakan."

"At once, your Highness," the silver-haired old gentleman replied. "This way, Master Althalus."

The two of them left the throne room.

"Your Arya's a beautiful young woman, Lord Dhakan," Althalus observed.

"That's the only reason we tolerate her, Althalus. She's pretty enough that we can overlook her flaws."

"She'll settle down, Dhakan. Marry her off, that's my advice. After she's had a few babies, she'll start to grow up."

There were nine kilted young Arums in the dungeon, and some of them were still nursing wounds they'd received during the battle outside the walls of Osthos. Althalus made some show of inspecting them. "Not bad, on the whole," he said as he and Dhakan were returning to the throne room. "That one she's got chained to the post is the key to the whole arrangement, though. He's the best of the lot. If we can persuade her to include him, I'll make her an offer. If she won't agree, I think I'll have to go elsewhere."

"I'll speak with her, Althalus," Dhakan promised. "You might want to describe the conditions the slaves have to live in once they get to the mines of Ansu. Exaggeration wouldn't hurt. Our little girl hungers and thirsts for revenge. Let's persuade her that the life of a slave in a salt mine is far, far worse than anything she can think of to do to him here. That might just tip the scales. Be eloquent, Althalus. Linger on unspeakable horrors if you possibly can. Our dear Andine is topful of passions, and passionate people make hasty decisions based on whims. I'll help as much as I can. I want that young Eliar out of Osthos and out of Andine's sight. If she refuses to sell him to you, I'll have to come up with a way to kill him. I *have* to get rid of him."

"Trust me, Dhakan," Althalus said confidently. "When it comes to buying and selling, I'm the very best." Then he sent his thought out to Emmy. *Have you got her yet, Em?* he asked.

I'm getting closer.

See if you can stir some interest in the salt mines.

What for?

So I can tell her some horror stories.

You're going to lie to her, I take it?

No, I'm going to tell her the truth. Unless things have changed, the salt mines of Ansu are worse than the deepest pits in Nekweros. Dhakan thinks that might turn the trick here. Nudge her hard, Em. If she doesn't sell Eliar to us, Dhakan's going to have him killed.

When Althalus and Dhakan entered the throne room, they saw that Andine had laid the laurel-leaf dagger aside and that she was concentrating all her attention on Emmy. She was smiling, and her smile was almost like the sun coming up. Even when she'd been scowling at Eliar, she'd been beautiful, but when she smiled, her beauty made Althalus go weak in the knees.

Dhakan went up to the dais and spoke quietly with his young ruler at some length.

Andine shook her head vehemently several times. Then Dhakan beckoned to Althalus.

Althalus approached the throne. "Yes, my Lord?" he asked Dhakan.

"I think we should get down to cases here, Master Althalus," Dhakan declared. "What's your offer?"

"Nine Perquaine wheats apiece for the ones you've got down in the dungeon," Althalus replied.

"You said ten!" Andine's voice suddenly soared. Sergeant Khalor's description of that voice appeared to have been a slight understatement.

Althalus held up one finger. "The price is subject to amendment, your Highness," he said. "If you're willing to include the one you have chained here, I'll slide it up. I'll pay you eighty-one gold wheats for the nine in the dungeon. If you're willing to add this one, I'll pay you a hundred for the lot."

"That's a difference of nineteen pieces of gold. He isn't worth that much!" Her voice rose again.

"He's prime stock, your Highness. When I reach Ansu, I'll put him out front for the mine owners to look at. They'll buy the lot just to get him. I know good merchandise when I see it. I could sell cripples if I could wave Eliar in the buyer's face."

"What's it like down there in those salt mines?" she asked. "How would you describe them?"

Althalus feigned a shudder. "I'd really rather not, your Highness," he replied. "Over to the east, in Wekti, Plakand, and Equero, criminals beg to be executed when they're sentenced to be sold into the salt mines as a punishment for murder and the like. Being sent into those mines is far worse than a death sentence. If a slave's unlucky, he'll last for ten years down there. The lucky ones die in just a few months."

"Why don't we talk about that?" Andine almost purred.

Althalus described conditions in the salt mines at some length, exaggerating only slightly. He mentioned the prevalence of blindness, the frequent cave-ins during which lucky slaves were crushed to death. He covered the darkness, the perpetual chill, the continuous choking dust, and dwelt at some length on the burly men with whips. "All in all," he concluded, "murderers and the like are very wise to prefer hanging to the mines."

"Then you'd say that being sent to the salt mines is a fate worse than death?" Andine said, her lovely eyes all aglow.

"Oh, yes," Althalus assured her. "Much, much worse."

"I *do* believe we can strike a bargain here, Master Althalus," she decided. "A hundred gold wheats for the lot, you say?"

"That was my offer, your Highness."

"Done, then—if you'll throw in your cat."

"I beg your pardon?"

"I want this lovely little cat. If you let me have her, we've struck a bargain."

CHAPTER TEN

*D*o as she says, Althalus. Emmy's thought cut through his startled dismay.

I most certainly will not! he shot back.

You don't really think she can keep me here, do you? Make her throw in the Knife, though.

How am I going to manage that?

I don't care. Think something up. That's what I'm paying you for, remember? Oh, one other thing. When you get the Knife from her, just tuck it under your belt and don't look at it.

Why?

Can't you ever *do as you're told without asking all these questions? I don't want you to look at the Knife until after we're out of here. Just do it and don't argue.*

He gave up. *Yes, dear,* he said silently.

"What's the problem, Master Althalus?" Andine asked, gently stroking the purring cat in her lap.

"You took me by surprise, your Highness," he replied. "I'm really very fond of my cat." He scratched his chin. "This puts the whole transaction on a different footing. The slaves are just merchandise; including Emmy changes things. I think I'll need something in addition to the slaves before I'd be willing to part with her."

"Such as?"

"Oh, I don't know." He pretended to think about it. "It really ought to be some personal possession of yours. I'm much too fond of my cat to include her in some crass commercial transaction. I'd have trouble living with myself if I just sold her outright."

"You're a strange man, Master Althalus." Arya Andine looked at him with her luminous eyes. "What sort of possession of mine would satisfy your delicate sensibilities?"

"It doesn't have to be anything of great value, your Highness. I didn't pay anything for Emmy. I just picked her up along the side of the road a few years ago. She's very good at worming her way into someone's affections."

"Yes, I noticed that." Andine impulsively lifted Emmy up to hold her against her own face. "I just *love* this cat," she said in that throbbing voice of hers. "Choose, Master Althalus. Name your price."

Althalus laughed. "You really shouldn't say things like that, your Highness," he advised her. "If I weren't an honest businessman, I could take advantage of your sudden attachment to my cat."

"Name your price. I *must* have her."

"Oh, I don't know—anything, I suppose. How about that knife you've been toying with? You seem to have a certain attachment to it. That's all that matters, really."

"Choose something else." Andine's eyes grew troubled.

"Ah . . . no, your Highness, I don't think so. My cat for your knife. You won't value her if you haven't given up something that you cherish for her."

"You bargain very hard, Master Althalus," she accused.

Emmy reached out one soft paw and gently stroked the Arya's alabaster cheek.

"Oh, dear," Andine said, pressing Emmy against her face. "Take the knife, Master Althalus. Take it. I don't care. Take anything you want. I *must* have her." She seized up the laurel-leaf dagger and tossed it to the marble floor in front of the dais.

"If it please your Highness, I'll see to the details," the silver-haired Dhakan said smoothly. Quite obviously, Dhakan was the one who really ran things here in Osthos.

"Thank you, Lord Dhakan," Andine said, rising to her feet with Emmy cradled possessively in her arms.

"You be a good cat now, Em," Althalus said, bending to pick up the Knife. "Remember—no biting."

"Does she bite?" Andine asked.

"Sometimes," Althalus replied, tucking the Knife under his belt. "Not very hard, though. Usually it's when she gets carried away while we're playing. Snap her on the nose with your fingernail and she'll quit. Oh, I should probably warn your Highness: don't be too surprised if she decides to give your face a bath. Her tongue's a bit rough, but you get used to it after a while."

"What's her favorite food?"

"Fish, of course." Althalus bowed. "It's been a pleasure doing business with your Highness," he said.

The clinking of the long chain started to irritate Althalus before he and the ten young Arums even reached the main gate of Osthos. It was a continual reminder that he wasn't alone anymore, and he didn't really like that.

Once they were outside the city, Althalus sent a searching thought back toward the palace. This was the farthest he'd been from Emmy in the last twenty-five centuries, and he didn't like that either.

I'm busy right now, Althalus, her thought came back to him.

Don't bother me. Go to that place where we made the coins and wait for me there.

Do you have any idea of how long you'll be?

Sometime tonight. Keep Eliar, and turn the others loose.

I just paid a lot of money for them, Em.

Easy come, easy go. Point them toward Arum and send them home. Get them out from underfoot.

The walls of Osthos were still in sight when Althalus turned his horse aside and rode across an open field to the small grove of oak trees where he and Emmy had converted the five bars of gold. As his horse plodded across the field, Althalus prudently manipulated his hearing and directed it back toward his slaves to hear what they were up to.

"—only one man," he heard Eliar whisper. "As soon as we get away from the city, we'll all jump on him at once and kill him. Pass it on to the others. Tell them to wait for my signal. Up until then, we'd all better act sort of meek. Once we've got him alone, we'll get unmeek."

Althalus smiled to himself. "I wonder why it took him so long," he murmured to himself. "That notion should have come to him hours ago." Obviously, he was going to have to take some steps here to discourage certain loyalties.

They reached the grove of trees, and Althalus dismounted. "All right, gentlemen," he said to his captives, "I want you to sit down and listen. You're right on the verge of making some hasty decisions, and I think there's something you should know first." He took the key to their chains and freed the young man at the end of the line. "Come out here in front of the others," he told him. "You and I are going to demonstrate something for your friends."

"You're going to kill me, aren't you?" the boy asked in a trembling voice.

"After what I just paid for you? Don't be silly." Althalus led the boy out to the center of the clearing. "Watch very closely," he instructed the others. Then he held his hand out, palm up, toward the shaking boy. *"Dheu,"* he said, raising his hand slowly upward.

The slave gave a startled cry as he rose up off the ground. He continued to rise, going higher and higher into the air as Althalus rather overdramatically continued to lift his hand. After a few moments the boy appeared to be only a tiny speck high above them.

"Now then," Althalus said to his gaping slaves, "what lesson have we just learned? What do you suppose would happen to our friend up there if I let go of him?"

"He'd fall?" Eliar asked in a choked voice.

"Very good, Eliar. You've got a quick mind. And what'd happen to him when he came back down to earth?"

"It'd probably kill him, wouldn't it?"

"It goes a long way past 'probably,' Eliar. He'd splatter like a dropped melon. That's our lesson for today, gentlemen. You don't want to cross me. You want to go a long way to *avoid* crossing me. Does anybody need any further clarification?"

They all shook their heads violently.

"Good. Since you all understand just exactly how things stand, I suppose we can bring your friend down again." Althalus said *"dhreu,"* slowly lowering his hand as he said it.

The boy descended to the ground and collapsed, blubbering incoherently.

"Oh, *stop* that," Althalus told him. "I didn't hurt you." Then he went down the chain, unlocking each slave's iron collar, leaving only Eliar still chained up. Then he pointed north. "Arum's off in that direction, gentlemen. Pick up your distracted friend there and go home. Oh, when you get back, tell Chief Albron that I've found the knife I was looking for and that Eliar's going to be coming with me. Albron and I can settle accounts on that somewhere on down the line."

"What's that all about?" Eliar demanded.

"Your Chief and I have a sort of agreement. You'll be working for me for a while." Althalus glanced at the others. "I told you to go home," he said. "Why haven't you left yet?"

They were running the last time he saw them.

"Aren't you going to unchain me?" Eliar asked.

"Let's hold off on that for a little while."

"If you've got an agreement with my Chief, you don't have to keep me chained up like this. I'll honor his word."

"The chain makes it easier for you, Eliar. As long as you're chained up, you won't have to struggle with any difficult moral decisions. Do you want something to eat?"

"No," the boy answered sullenly. Eliar appeared to be very good at sullen. Aside from his pouty expression, he was a fairly handsome young man, tall and blond haired. Despite his youth, he had fairly bulky shoulders, and his kilt revealed powerful legs. It was easy to see why the other young Arums in Sergeant Khalor's detachment had accepted this young fellow as their leader.

Althalus looped the boy's chain around an oak tree, locked it securely, and then stretched out on the leafy ground. "You might as well catch a few winks," he advised. "I expect we'll have a long way to go and not much time, so we'll be a little short on sleep in the not-too-distant future."

"Where are we going?" Eliar asked as curiosity evidently won out over sullenness.

"I haven't got the foggiest idea," Althalus admitted. "I'm sure Emmy will tell us when she gets here, though."

"Your cat?"

"Things aren't always what they appear to be, Eliar. Go to sleep."

"Can I have some bread or something?"

"I thought you said you weren't hungry."

"I changed my mind. I really could eat something."

Althalus called up a loaf of bread and tossed it to his captive.

"How did you do that?" Eliar exclaimed.

"It's just a little trick I picked up a few years back. It's no great thing."

"That's the first time *I've* ever seen anybody do it. You're not exactly like other people, are you?"

"Not very much, no. Eat your supper and go to sleep, Eliar." Then Althalus settled back and drifted off to sleep.

Emmy ghosted silently into the oak grove not long after midnight and found Althalus just waking up. *Aren't we being a bit irresponsible, pet?* she chided him.

"About what?"

I sort of thought you'd be keeping an eye on Eliar.

"He's not going anyplace, Em—not unless he plans to take that tree with him."

Did you have any trouble persuading his friends to leave?

"No, not really. They were scheming a bit on our way here, but then I showed them that it wasn't a good idea."

Oh? How?

"I picked one at random and did the same thing to him that we did to Pekhal a few weeks ago. They got my point almost immediately. Then I unchained them and told them all to go home. They left in quite a hurry."

Show-off.

"I know the way Arums think, Em. They're intensely loyal, so I had to do something spectacular enough to dispel that loyalty. I didn't think we'd want them lurking back in the bushes watching for a chance to ambush us. I managed to get my point across to them."

Have you got the Knife?

He patted the hilt protruding from his belt. "Right here," he replied.

Come out into the moonlight, she told him, leading the way out of the grove.

"What are we doing?"

You're going to read the Knife.

"I take my orders from you, Em, not from this antique."

Just a precaution, Althalus. The Knife'll make sure you don't lose interest along the way.

"What's the matter? Don't you trust me?"

Trust you? Her laugh was sardonic.

"That wasn't very nice, Em."

Just take the Knife out and read it, Althalus. Let's get on with this.

He drew the Knife out from under his belt and held it out in the moonlight. The inscription engraved on the blade was complex and very formal, with interlocking lines that twined around each other. The writing was not the distinctly separated pictographs Althalus had seen in the Book, but seemed somehow to flow together. He had no difficulty picking out one single word, however, since it glowed with a pale light.

What does it say? Emmy asked intently.

"Seek," he answered promptly.

There was a soft, musical sound that seemed to soar higher and higher, enclosing, enveloping, almost caressing him. It was so beautiful that it brought sudden tears to his eyes.

And now you are mine, Emmy gloated.

"I already was, Em. Is the Knife really singing?"

Oh, yes.

"What for?"

To let me know that you've been chosen. And, *of course, that you'll do exactly as I tell you to do.* She gave him a sly look. *Sit, Althalus,* she said.

He immediately sat down.

Stand up.

He scrambled to his feet. "Stop this, Emmy!" he said sharply.

Dance.

He began hopping around. "I'm going to get you for this, Em!" he threatened.

No, you won't. You can stop dancing now. I just wanted to show you what the Knife can do. You'll be able to do the same sort of thing with it—just in case Eliar or any of the others we'll pick up later start getting out of hand.

"That could come in handy." He looked even more closely at the Knife's blade. "That one word is all I can make out. It jumps right out of the middle of those other squiggles."

The other "squiggles" are intended for others.

"Why can't *I* read them?"

Nobody can read it all, Althalus. Some of those words were intended for people who lived thousands of years ago, and others are there to be read by people who won't even be born for several thousand more. Our current crisis isn't the only one in the history of the world, you know.

"It's enough to get *my* attention. Did it tell you where we go next?"

That'll come after Eliar reads his instructions. Everything in its proper time and place.

"Anything you say, dear." He frowned slightly. "Let's see if I've got this straight. Nobody except certain people can read the Knife, right?"

Exactly.

"Everybody else just sees those squiggles that look like some meaningless decoration?"

Didn't I already say that?

"What would happen if I showed it to Ghend—or Pekhal, or Khnom?"

The screams would probably be very loud. The sight of the Knife causes unbearable pain to the agents of Daeva.

"Well, now," he said, grinning. "Maybe I'd better not use the Knife to cut bacon with, then."

You wouldn't!

"Only teasing, Em. That Knife's going to be *very* useful, I think. I believe I'll keep it very close."

Sorry, pet. You aren't the one who's supposed to carry it.

"Who is?"

Probably Eliar.

"Are you absolutely sure I can control him? He *is* a professional killer, Em, so the first thing he's likely to do if I hand him the Knife is stab me in the belly with it."

There aren't really any absolutes in life, Althalus.

"Oh, thanks, Em," he said sarcastically.

It's a safe wager. The chance that he'll kill you is about the same as the one for the sun coming up in the west this morning.

"I suppose I'd risk a little money on that one. Why don't we wake him up and have him read to us?"

Let him sleep. After he reads the Knife, we'll find out where we're supposed to go next, and we'll have to leave immediately. Let's not start wandering around in the dark.

He shrugged. "You're the one in charge, Em." Then he looked at her curiously. "What did you do to Andine to bring her around? She didn't really want to sell Eliar to me."

I persuaded her to love me more than she hated him.

"I thought you couldn't do that sort of thing out here."

I didn't create her love, pet. All I did was encourage it. Andine's very young and very passionate. She loves—and hates—with her blood and bones, and she loves even more intensely than she hates. All I had to do to unleash her love was to be adorable. I'm an expert at that, if you'll recall.

"I still think you're cheating, Em."

No, not really. Andine's very pretty, and she smells nice. She's soft and warm, and that voice of hers throbs like a bell. She's very easy to love, and she responds to love with love of her own. I didn't cheat her, Althalus. I did love her—and I still do.

"I thought you were supposed to love only me."

What a ridiculous idea. Just because I love her, it doesn't mean that I love you less. My love is boundless, you know.

"But now you've managed to sneak away from her, and that means that I've swindled her out of Eliar, the Knife, and you—all in the same day. I really think we should get out of here, Em—almost immediately."

She won't wake up until morning; I've seen to that. When she does wake up, the first thing she'll do is search her whole palace for me. The idea of sending out her soldiers won't come to her until later.

"Are you sure?"

Trust me.

Eliar woke up just before dawn, and he'd evidently forgotten that he was securely attached to the tree, because he started struggling with his chain before he was fully awake.

"Stop that!" Althalus barked sharply. "You'll hurt yourself."

Eliar quit fighting. He held up one of his wrists and jingled the chain. "You don't need to keep me locked up anymore," he said. "I've already told you that if you really *do* have an agreement with my Chief, I'll do what you tell me to do. If you're lying about it, you'll have to answer to him."

"Now you're starting to make some sense," Althalus said approvingly. "I thought I might have to rattle your teeth a little bit before you started to get the point."

"I'm a good soldier, and I follow my Chief's orders. I don't have to get any points or understand anything. I just have to do what I'm told to do."

"I think we'll get along just fine," Althalus said. "Hold out your hands. Let's get rid of those silly chains."

Eliar held out his wrists, and Althalus freed him.

Eliar stood up, stretching and yawning. "I didn't sleep too well," he said. "Those stupid chains jingled and rattled every time I moved. What am I supposed to call you? Sergeant, maybe? I *won't* call you Master, no matter what you do to me."

"If you ever call me Master, I'll braid all your fingers and toes together. My name's Althalus. Why don't you call me that?"

"Is that really your name? There's an old story in our clan about a man named Althalus."

"I know. Chief Albron thought it was just a coincidence, but he was wrong." Althalus made a wry face. "My name's about the only part of the story your people got right. The rest of it's the biggest lie I've heard in my whole life—and I've heard some very big lies in my time. Let's get it right out into the open, Eliar. I *am* the one who robbed Gosti Big Belly about twenty-five hundred years ago, but Gosti didn't have any gold in his strong room, just copper and a little brass. He wanted people to believe that he was the richest man in the world, so he spread some wild lies about how much gold I'd stolen from him. You wouldn't *believe* how much trouble that caused me."

The boy scoffed. "Nobody can live *that* long."

"I didn't think so myself, but Emmy cured me of that. Let's stick to the point here. Can you read?"

"Warriors don't waste their time on that nonsense."

"There's something you *have* to read."

"I just told you that I don't know how, Althalus. You'll have to read it to me."

"It won't work if we do it that way." Althalus took the Knife out from under his belt and held it out to Eliar. He pointed at the complex engraving on the blade. "What does this say?" he asked.

"I can't read. I told you that."

"Look at it, Eliar. You can't read it if you don't look."

Eliar looked at the leaf-shaped blade, and he jerked his head back, startled. "It says, 'Lead'!" he exclaimed. "I can actually read it!" Then he shrank back as the song of the Knife touched him.

"Pretty, isn't it?" Althalus said.

Emmy had been sitting nearby, watching. She rose and came over to where they were seated. She looked very closely at Eliar, who was still staring at the Knife with a befuddled expression. *Tell him to do something, Althalus,* she suggested. *Let's make sure that you can control him before you give him the Knife.*

Althalus nodded. "Stand up, Eliar," he said.

The boy immediately scrambled to his feet. He swayed a bit and put one hand to the side of his head. "It made me a little dizzy," he confessed.

"Dance," Althalus told him.

Eliar started to jig, his feet pattering on the ground.

"Stop."

Eliar quit dancing.

"Put both hands up over your head."

"Why are we doing this?" the boy asked, raising his hands.

"Just making sure that it works. You can put your hands down. Did you notice anything peculiar just now?"

"You kept telling me to do things that were sort of silly," Eliar replied.

"If they seemed silly, why did you do them?"

"I'm a soldier, Althalus. I always do what the man in charge tells me to do. If he tells me to do silly things, he's the one who's silly, not me."

"That sort of takes a lot of the fun out of this, doesn't it, Em?" Althalus said aloud. "Did the Knife force Eliar to jump around, or was it just his training?"

Eliar gave Emmy a surprised look. "How did your cat get away from Andine?" he asked curiously.

"She's sort of sneaky."

"Andine's going to be *very* angry about that. Maybe we should leave in sort of a hurry—right after breakfast."

"Are you hungry?"

"I'm always hungry, Althalus."

"Why don't we eat, then?" Althalus held the Knife out to the boy. "Here. You're the one who's supposed to carry this. Tuck it under your belt and don't lose it."

Eliar put his hands behind his back. "You should probably know that I was planning to kill you last night before we got to know each other. You might want to think it over a little before you just hand me back my knife like that."

"You aren't going to try to kill me now, though, are you?"

"No. Not now."

"Why not?"

"You're the man in charge, Althalus. Your arrangement with Chief Albron sort of makes you my Sergeant. A good soldier *never* tries to kill his Sergeant."

"Then I haven't got a thing to worry about. Take the Knife, Eliar, and let's eat."

"What a great idea," Eliar said enthusiastically, tucking the Knife under his belt.

"Bacon? Or maybe ham?"

"Whichever one you can make the quickest."

Althalus made some ham and a loaf of black bread. Then he produced a very large cup of milk.

Eliar started to eat as if he hadn't had anything for a week.

Althalus made more. *How long can he keep this up?* he silently asked Emmy.

I'm not really certain, her reply came back. She watched Eliar eat with a slightly bemused look in her large green eyes. *See if you can distract him enough to get him to show me the Knife. I need to find out where we're supposed to go next.*

"Eliar," Althalus said, "you can keep chewing, but Emmy needs to take a quick look at your Knife."

Eliar mumbled something.

"Don't talk with your mouth full," Althalus told him. "Just take the Knife out from under your belt and show it to her."

Eliar shifted the chunk of ham he'd been eating to his left hand, wiped the grease off his right hand on the grass, and drew out his Knife. Still chewing, he held the Knife out to Emmy.

She glanced at it briefly. *Awes,* she said.

Isn't it in ruins? Althalus asked.

So?

Just thought I'd mention it, that's all. I'll go saddle my horse.

Emmy had gone back to watching Eliar eat. *There's no real hurry, Althalus.* Her silent response sounded slightly amused. *From the look of things, our boy here's just getting started.*

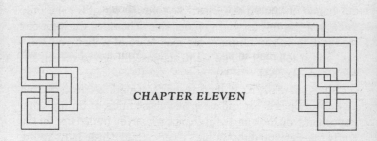

CHAPTER ELEVEN

"Just exactly where's this war?" Eliar asked as he trotted along beside Althalus' horse, "and what kind of people are we going to be fighting?"

"War?" Althalus asked.

"People don't rent soldiers just for show, Althalus. I'm fairly sure you didn't go to all the trouble of getting me away from Andine just because you were lonesome. Sergeant Khalor always told us that we should find out as much about the people we're going to be fighting as we possibly can."

"Your Sergeant's a very wise man, Eliar."

"We all looked up to him—even though he could be awfully picky about details sometimes. I'll swear that he can talk about one speck of rust on a sword for half a day."

"Some soldiers are like that, I suppose," Althalus said. "I don't get all that excited about it myself. A rusty sword kills somebody as well as a polished one does."

"We're going to get along just fine," Eliar said, grinning broadly. "Now, then, who am I supposed to fight?"

"The war we're involved with isn't exactly like an ordinary

war—at least not yet. We haven't quite reached the point of armies and battlefields."

"We're still choosing up sides?"

Althalus blinked, and then he laughed. "That might just come closer to what we're doing than anything I've heard so far."

Watch your mouth. Emmy's thought had a slight edge to it.

Althalus laughed again. "That's why we absolutely *had* to get our hands on the Knife, Eliar," he told the boy. "It's the only thing that can tell us who's on our side. The ones we want can read it. Others can't. Emmy can read more of it than you and I can, and it tells her where we're supposed to go to recruit the people we'll need."

"She's not really a cat, then, is she? My mother's got a cat, but all her cat does is eat and sleep and chase mice. If Emmy's that important, you took an awful chance when you traded her for the Knife the way you did. Andine's a very strange little lady. You're lucky she didn't chain Emmy to her bedpost."

"The way she had you chained to that pillar in her throne room?"

Eliar shuddered. "That was a real bad time for me, Althalus. The way she used to look at me gave me the wibblies. She'd sit there for hours playing with my knife and staring right straight at me. Women are very strange, aren't they?"

"Oh, yes, Eliar. Indeed they are."

Shortly before noon, Althalus noticed a farmstead some distance back from the road they were following, and he turned into the lane that led toward the house. "Let's get you mounted, Eliar," he said.

"I can keep up with you on foot, Althalus."

"Possibly, but we've got a long way to go. I'll talk with the farmer here and see what he's got to offer."

While Althalus spoke with the seedy-looking farmer, Eliar carefully examined the farm horses in the large corral behind the farmhouse. "This one," he said, rubbing the ears of a large sorrel horse.

The farmer started to object, but he changed his mind when Althalus jingled his purse.

"You paid him too much," Eliar said as they rode away from the farm.

"The money doesn't really mean anything."

"Money always means something, unless you just made it up in the same way you make up the food we eat." Then he looked sharply at Althalus. "You *did*, didn't you?" he demanded. "You just reared back, waved your hand, and there was a great big pile of gold, wasn't there?"

"No, as a matter of fact, I—" Althalus stopped, his eyes suddenly going very wide. *Can I do that?* he sent his startled question at Emmy, who was dozing in the hood of his cloak.

Probably, yes.

Then why did you make me dig it up?

Honest work's good for you, pet. Besides, it doesn't exactly work that way. Food's one thing, but minerals are quite a bit different.

Why?

They just are, Althalus. There's a certain balance involved that we shouldn't tamper with.

Would you like to explain that?

No, I don't think so.

They rode hard for the next couple of days until they were some distance away from Osthos, and then they slowed to give their horses a bit of rest. The plains of Treborea, drought-stricken and barren under the hot summer sun, were depressing, so Althalus passed the time telling Eliar slightly elaborated stories about his adventures back in the days before he'd gone to the House at the End of the World. Like all Arums, Eliar enjoyed good stories, and he was exactly the kind of audience that warmed Althalus' heart.

Althalus *did* cheat just a little, though, as they rode along. Every time Eliar's attention started to wander, a chicken leg or a chunk of still-warm bread would immediately recapture it. The arrangement worked out rather well, actually.

Emmy, however, found long naps much more interesting than the stories, for some reason.

Eliar more or less took over the care of their horses when they set up camp each night. Althalus produced the hay and oats their mounts needed, and not infrequently he was obliged to provide water for them as well. Eliar did the actual work, though, and the horses seemed quite fond of him. All in all, Althalus rather liked the arrangement.

They passed the walled city of Leupon a few days later, crossed the River Kanthon, and entered the lands of the Equeros. The lake country was not as parched as the plains of Perquaine and Treborea had been, and the population there had not been forced to huddle around slowly diminishing water holes or along river-banks.

It took them about ten days to cross Equero, and then they entered mankind's ancestral homeland of Medyo. Five days later they reached the place where the River Medyo forked and where the ruins of the city of Awes were located.

"What happened here?" Eliar asked as they stood on the west bank of the river waiting for the barge that—for a price—ferried travelers across to the ruins.

"There was a war, I'm told," Althalus replied. "The way I understand it, back in those days the priesthood ruled all of Medyo and the surrounding lands. They got a little too greedy finally, and the army decided that the world might be a nicer place without so many priests, so they marched in to see if they could arrange that. The priests had an army of their own, and those two armies had some extended discussions in the streets of Awes."

"It must have been a long, long time ago. They've got full-grown trees standing in the streets over there."

Althalus, Emmy's voice murmured, *I need to talk with Eliar directly, so I'm going to borrow your voice. I think it might be easier if he's holding me while we do this.*

Why's that?

Just do it, Althalus, she replied. *Don't keep asking silly questions.*

Althalus took her up and held her out to their youthful companion. "Here," he said. "Emmy wants to talk to you. Hold her."

Eliar put his hands behind his back. "I think I'd rather not," he said.

"You'd better get over that. Take her, Eliar."

"I don't understand cat talk, Althalus," Eliar protested, taking Emmy with obvious reluctance.

"I'm sure she'll make you understand."

Get out of the way, Althalus, Emmy's voice commanded. *Count trees or something. I'm going to be using your voice, so don't interfere.* Then Althalus heard his own voice saying, "Can you hear me, Eliar?" His voice seemed lighter, and it had a higher pitch.

"Of course I can hear you, Althalus," Eliar replied. "You're only a few feet away. Your voice sounds a little odd, though."

"I'm not Althalus, Eliar," the voice coming from Althalus' lips said. "I'm just using his voice. Look at me, not at him."

Eliar looked down at Emmy with astonishment.

Emmy wrinkled her nose. "You need a bath," she said.

"I've been a little busy, ma'am," the boy replied.

"You can pet me, if you'd like," she suggested.

"Yes, ma'am." Eliar began to stroke her.

"Not quite so hard."

"Sorry, ma'am,"

"He's such a nice boy," Emmy murmured in her borrowed voice. "All right, Eliar, listen to me very carefully. There's a distinct chance that we'll encounter enemies over there on the other side of the river. What do you do when you meet an enemy?"

"Kill him, ma'am."

"Exactly."

"Emmy!" Althalus overrode her usurpation of his voice.

"Stay out of this, Althalus. This is between the boy and me. Now, then, Eliar, we'll be meeting priests over there. I want you to show the Knife to every one of them we meet. Can you pretend to be stupid?"

Eliar made a rueful kind of face. "Ma'am," he said, "I'm a country boy from the highlands of Arum. We *invented* stupid."

"I'd really prefer it if you called me 'Emmy,' Eliar; we don't have to be so formal. This is the way I want you to do this: When we talk to a priest, put on your best Arum expression and hold the Knife out for him to see. Then you say, 'Excuse me, yer priestship, but kin you tell me what's wrote on this here knife?' "

"Probably not with a straight face, Emmy," Eliar said, laughing. "Is there really anybody in the whole world who's *that* simpleminded?"

"You'd be surprised, Eliar. Practice saying it until you can do it without coming down with the giggles. Now, most of the priests won't be able to make any sense out of what's written on the Knife. They'll either admit that they can't read it, or they'll pretend to be too busy to take the time. The one we're looking for will read it in exactly the same way you did when *you* read it, and the Knife will sing to you as soon as he reads it aloud."

"I sort of thought that was what was going to happen, Emmy. What's this got to do with enemies, though?"

"If you *do* happen to show the Knife to an enemy, he'll scream and try to cover his eyes."

"Why?"

"Because the sight of the Knife will hurt him—probably more than anything has hurt him in his entire life. As soon as somebody does that, drive the Knife right into his heart."

"All right, Emmy."

"No problems? No questions?"

"No, Emmy, none at all. You're in charge of things. If you tell me to do something, I'll do it. Sergeant Khalor always told us that we're supposed to obey orders immediately without asking any stupid questions, and your orders are really very simple. If somebody screams when I show him the Knife, he'll be dead before the echo fades away."

Emmy reached up one soft paw and stroked his cheek. "You're such a good boy, Eliar," she purred.

"Thank you, Emmy. I try my best."

"I hope you've been listening very carefully, Althalus. Maybe you should have taken some notes for future reference. It saves *so* much time when people know how to follow orders without all the endless discussion I get from *some* people I know."

"Can I have my voice back now?"

"Yes, pet, you may. I'm done with it—at least for right now. I'll let you know when I need it again."

The barge took them across the west fork of the River Medyo, and they rode into the ruins of the city. The priests who lived there wore cowled robes, for the most part, and they had built crude hovels among the ruins. There were some noticeable differences between the various groups of priests. Those who lived in the northern part of the ruins wore black robes, the ones in central Awes were robed in white, and the ones closest to the river fork wore brown. Althalus noted that they tended not to talk to each other very much—except to argue.

"No, you've got it all wrong," a black-robed priest from the northern end of town was saying to a fat priest in a white robe. "The Wolf was in the ninth house when that happened, not the tenth."

"My charts don't lie," the chubby priest replied hotly. "The sun had moved to the fourth house by then, and that definitely moved the Wolf to the tenth."

What are they talking about? Althalus silently demanded of Emmy.

Astrology. It's one of the cornerstones of religion.

Which religion?

Most of them, actually. Religion's based on a desire to know what's going to happen in the future. Astrologers believe that the stars control that.

Are they right?

Why would the stars care what happens here? Besides, most of the stars the priests argue about don't actually exist anymore.

I think that one missed me, Em.

The stars are fire, and fires eventually burn out.

If they're burned out, why are the priests still arguing about them?

Because they don't know that they've burned out.

All they have to do is look, Em.

*It doesn't quite work that way, Althalus. The stars are a lot far-
ther away than people realize, and it takes a long time for their
light to reach us. Probably about half of what you see when you
look up at night isn't really there anymore. To put it another way,
the priests are trying to predict the future by looking at the
ghosts of dead stars.*

Althalus shrugged. *It gives them something to do, I suppose.*
He looked around at the ruined buildings and rubble-strewn
streets. The robed and cowled priests were moving about singly
or in small groups, but there were more conventionally dressed
men in Awes as well. He saw one man who'd set up what appeared to be a shop next to a partially collapsed wall. The man
had a rough table with pots, pans, and kettles on it.

"Welcome, friends," the fellow said hopefully, rubbing his
hands together. "Look and buy. Look and buy. I have the best
pots and kettles in all of Awes, and my prices are the lowest
you'll find in any shop here."

Be careful, Althalus, Emmy murmured in his mind. *That's
Khnom. He works for Ghend.*

Then Ghend knew that we were coming here?

*Maybe not. He might have just spread his agents out to watch
for us. Fix Khnom's face in your mind. We'll probably run across
him again.*

"Was there anything in particular you were looking for, friend?"
the ostensible merchant asked. He was a small-sized man, and
he seemed to be very careful not to look Althalus in the eye.

"Actually, I need some information, neighbor," Althalus replied. "I'm not familiar with the proprieties here in Awes. Can I
just set up shop in any ruined building that's empty?"

"That wouldn't be a good idea," the merchant advised. "Most
of the business that goes on here in Awes takes place in this
middle part of town, and the White Robes who control it sort of
expect a 'donation' from you before you open for business."

"A bribe, you mean?"

"I wouldn't use that word to their faces. Pretend to be some religious simpleton. All priests love feeble-minded parishioners."

Khnom cast a sly, sidelong glance at Althalus to see how his somewhat sacrilegious remark had gone over.

Althalus kept his face bland. "What are their feelings about us pitching our tents at the back of the shop?" he asked.

"They'd rather that we didn't—and you probably wouldn't want to. They pray a lot, and they're noisy about it. The rest of us businessmen have a sort of community over by what's left of the east wall of the city."

"How do these priests get the money to buy anything?"

"They sell horoscopes to gullible people who believe in that nonsense, and they charge a fairly steep price."

"Good. They swindle their parishioners, and then we swindle them. I love doing business with a man who devoutly believes he's more clever than I am. Thanks for the information."

"Glad I could help. Do you need any pots or pans?"

"Not right at the moment, no. Thanks all the same."

He knows who you are, Althalus, Emmy's voice warned.

Yes, I know. He's clever, I'll give him that, but he's not really a merchant.

How did you know that?

He didn't once ask me what line I was in. That's the first question any *merchant asks. No merchant wants a competitor right across the street. Should we get rid of him? Eliar and I could kill him right now.*

No. You two aren't the ones who are supposed to deal with Khnom. Just be careful around him, that's all.

"Where do we go now?" Eliar asked.

"There's a merchant community over by the east wall," Althalus replied. "We'll set up camp there and start looking for the one we want first thing in the morning."

"Could you make me some soap?" Eliar asked as they led their horses off down the rubble-strewn street.

"Probably. Why?"

"Emmy wants me to take a bath. Is that the first thing that pops into every woman's mind? Every time I'd visit my mother back home, those were usually the first words that came out of her mouth."

"You don't like bathing, I take it?"

"Oh, I'll bathe if it really gets necessary, but once a week's usually enough, isn't it? Unless you've been cleaning the stables, of course."

"Emmy's got a very sharp nose, Eliar. Let's neither of us go out of our way to offend her."

You, too, Althalus, Emmy's voice murmured.

I don't need a bath, Em, he silently protested.

You're wrong. You definitely need a bath. You've been riding for several weeks now, and you've got a very horsey fragrance about you. Bathe. Soon. Please.

They started out early the following morning, and after a few awkward starts Eliar became more proficient. His open, boyish face helped quite a bit as he hopefully approached each hooded priest with his question. Most of the priests, Althalus noticed, refused to come right out and admit that they couldn't read the alien script carved into the Knife's blade. Their usual response was a brusque, "I'm too busy for that kind of nonsense." Several they encountered, however, offered to translate—for a price. One hollow-eyed fanatic launched a blistering denunciation, declaring that any script he couldn't read was obviously the handwriting of the devil himself.

Althalus and Eliar left him in the middle of the street still preaching to nobody in particular.

"Here comes another one," Eliar said quietly. "Maybe we can start making wagers about what they'll say when I show them the Knife. This one looks like an 'I'm too busy' sort of fellow to me."

"I'd put him in the 'I'll have to charge you for a reading' crowd," Althalus replied, grinning.

"What gives him away?"

"He's cockeyed. He's got one eye on the sky watching for Deiwos and the other on the ground looking for a penny that somebody might have dropped."

"I just hope he's not like the last one. The next one who calls my knife an instrument of the devil is going to get my fist in his face."

The priest approaching them up the empty street had a gaunt, hungry look about him, and his disconnected eyes and wild hair gave him the appearance of a lunatic. His shabby brown robe was filthy, and there was a powerful odor about him.

"Excuse me, your Worship," Eliar said politely, going up to the cockeyed holy man. "I just bought this knife, and it seems to have some kind of writing on the blade. I never got around to learning how to read, so I can't tell what it says. Could you help me out?"

"Let me see it," the priest growled in a harsh, rasping voice.

Eliar held out his laurel-leaf dagger.

The sudden scream was shockingly loud, echoing from the ruined walls of nearby buildings. The ragged priest stumbled back, covering his eyes with his hands and screaming as if he'd just been dipped in boiling pitch.

"I hope you won't take this personally, your Worship," Eliar said, driving the Knife directly into the shrieking priest's chest.

The scream cut off abruptly, and the dead man collapsed with not so much as a twitch.

Althalus spun, his eyes searching every vacant window and doorway. As luck had it, they were alone. "Get him out of sight!" he barked at Eliar. "Hurry!"

Eliar quickly put the Knife away, seized the fellow's wrists, and dragged him behind a partially collapsed wall. "Did anybody see us?" he asked just a bit breathlessly.

"I don't think so," Althalus replied. "Come here and keep watch. I want to search the body."

"What for?" Eliar stood up. His hands were trembling slightly.

"Calm down," Althalus told him. "Get a grip on yourself."

"I'm all right, Althalus," Eliar said. "It's just that he startled me when he started screaming like that."

"Why did you apologize before you killed him?"

"Just trying to be polite, I guess. Mother taught me to mind my manners. You know how mothers are."

"Watch the street. Let me know if somebody happens along."

Althalus roughly searched the body, not really knowing what he might be looking for, but the dead man's pockets had absolutely nothing in them. He kicked a bit of rubble over the body, and then he came back out into the street.

"Did you find anything?" Eliar asked. His voice still sounded a little excited.

"Calm down," Althalus told him. "If you're going to do this, do it right. People who are all worked up make mistakes."

Then a black-robed priest came striding up the rubble-littered street toward them. He was a fairly young man, and his hair was a rich auburn color. His dark eyes were flashing indignantly. "I saw what you just did!" he said. "You men are murderers!"

"Shouldn't you get a few details before you start making accusations like that?" Althalus said calmly.

"You killed him in cold blood!"

"My blood wasn't particularly cold," Althalus said. "Was yours, Eliar?"

"Not really," Eliar replied.

"The man was *not* a priest, Reverend Sir," Althalus told their accuser. "Quite the opposite—unless Daeva's set up a priesthood of his own here lately."

"Daeva!" The youthful priest gasped. "How did you know that name?"

"Is it supposed to be a secret?" Althalus asked mildly.

"That information is *not* supposed to be in the hands of the general population. Ordinary people aren't equipped to deal with it."

"Ordinary people are probably much wiser than you think they are, Reverend," Althalus told him. "Every family has a few black sheep. There's nothing really unusual about it. Deiwos and Dweia aren't really happy that their brother went astray, but it wasn't really *their* fault."

"You're a priest, aren't you?"

"You make it sound almost like an accusation," Althalus said, smiling slightly. "Eliar and I sort of work for Deiwos, but I wouldn't go quite so far as to call us priests. The man Eliar just put to sleep was one of the people who work for Daeva. As soon as we discovered that, we killed him. There's a war in the works right now, Reverend. Eliar and I are soldiers, and we're going to fight that war."

"I'm a soldier of Deiwos, too," the priest asserted.

"That hasn't been established yet, my young friend. There's a little test you'd have to take first. That's what you just saw happen here. The fellow lying over behind that wall didn't pass the test, so Eliar killed him."

"The stars haven't said anything about a war."

"Maybe the news hasn't reached them yet."

"The stars know everything."

"Maybe. But maybe they've been told to keep the information to themselves. If I happened to be the one who's running this war, I don't think I'd be scrawling my battle plans across the sky every night, would you?"

The priest's eyes grew troubled. "You're attacking the very core of religion," he accused.

"No. I'm attacking a misconception. You look at the sky and imagine that you're seeing pictures up there, but they aren't really pictures, are they? They're just disconnected points of light. There isn't a raven up there, or a wolf, or a serpent, or any other imaginary picture. The war's right here, not up there. But this is all beside the point. Let's find out if you really *are* one of the soldiers of the Sky God."

"I have taken a vow to serve him," the priest asserted devoutly.

"Did he ever get around to telling you whether or not he accepted your vow?" Althalus asked slyly. "Maybe you don't qualify."

The auburn-haired young man's eyes grew troubled.

"You're filled with doubts, aren't you, friend?" Althalus said sympathetically. "I know that feeling very, very well. Sometimes your faith falters and everything you want to believe seems to be nothing but a mockery and a deception—some cruel joke."

"I *want* to believe! I try so hard to *make* myself believe."

"Eliar and I are here to make it easier for you," Althalus assured him. "Show him the Knife, Eliar."

"If you say so," Eliar said obediently. He looked at the troubled priest. "Don't get excited about this, your Worship," he said. "I'm going to show my Knife to you. I'm not threatening you with it or anything. There's some writing on the blade that you're supposed to read to us. If you can't read it, we'll shake hands and part friends. If you *do* happen to see a word on the blade, you'll be joining us. This is that test Althalus was talking about."

"Just show him the Knife, Eliar," Althalus said. "You don't have to make a speech to him."

"He gets grouchy sometimes," Eliar told the now-baffled priest. "He's the oldest man in the world, and you know how grouchy old men get sometimes. We'd better get down to business before he starts jumping up and down and frothing at the mouth."

"Eliar!" Althalus almost shouted. "Show him the Knife!"

"You see what I mean about him?" Eliar said. He took the Knife out from under his belt and pointed at the complex engraving on the blade. "This is what you're supposed to try to read," he explained. "The word sort of jumps right out at you, so you don't really have to work at it too hard."

"Eliar!" Althalus almost pleaded.

"I'm just trying to help him, Althalus." Eliar held the hilt of the dagger firmly in his fist and turned his hand to hold the blade directly in front of the trembling priest's pale face. "What does it say, your Worship?" he asked politely.

The youthful priest went paler still, as if every drop of blood had drained from his face. "Illuminate," he replied so reverently that it seemed almost a prayer.

The dagger in Eliar's fist broke into joyful song.

"I *knew* he was the one, Althalus," Eliar said in an offhand sort of way. "That's why I was trying to sort of ease him into it. You're a fairly good Sergeant, but sometimes you're just a little rough. You ought to work on that, if you don't mind my saying so."

"Thanks," Althalus replied in a flat, almost unfriendly way.

"It's part of my job, Althalus," Eliar replied, tucking the Knife back under his belt. "I'm sort of your second in command, so if I see a way to do things better, I'm supposed to suggest it to you.

You don't have to listen if you don't want to, of course, but I'd be letting you down if I didn't say it, wouldn't I?"

Don't say anything, Althalus, Emmy silently commanded.

Althalus sighed. *Yes, dear,* he replied in a resigned tone.

CHAPTER TWELVE

The auburn-haired young priest had sunk limply down onto a mossy stone, and he sat staring at the ground in a kind of distracted wonder.

"Are you all right?" Eliar asked their new companion.

"I have seen the word of God," the priest replied in a trembling voice. "Deiwos has spoken to me."

"Yes," Eliar replied. "We heard him, too." Then he amended that. "Well, actually we heard the Knife, but since it's God's Knife in the first place, it sort of amounts to the same thing, I guess."

"Why did the Knife make that sound?" The priest's voice was still shaking and filled with awe.

"I think that's God's way of letting us know that you're the one we've been looking for. My name's Eliar."

"I'm known as Bheid," the priest replied, looking into the young Arum's face with a puzzled expression.

"I'm pleased to make your acquaintance, Bheid," Eliar said, grasping the priest's hand.

"Aren't you a bit young to be a holy man?" Bheid asked. "Most holy men I've known are much older."

Eliar laughed. "Nobody's ever called me a holy man before, and I'm not, really. I'm just a soldier who happens to be working for God right now. I don't really understand what's going on, but that's all right. A soldier doesn't have to understand. He just has to do as he's told."

Bheid started to rise, but Eliar put one hand on his shoulder. "It might be better if you sat still for a while," he suggested. "If you're feeling at all the way I did when I first read the Knife, you're probably a little wobbly right now. God's got a very loud voice. I'm sure you noticed that."

"Oh, yes," Bheid replied fervently. "What are we supposed to do now?"

"You'll have to ask Althalus here. He's the only one who can talk to Emmy, and Emmy's the one who makes the decisions."

"Who's Emmy?"

"As I understand it, she's the sister of God, but right now she sort of looks like a cat, and she spends all her time sleeping in that hood Althalus has on the back of his cloak. It's sort of complicated. Emmy's older than the sun, and she's very sweet, but if you make a mistake and cross her, she'll swat the end of your nose right off."

Bheid looked at Althalus. "Is this boy all right?" he asked.

"Eliar?" Althalus replied. "I think so. Of course he hasn't had anything to eat for an hour or two, so he might be a little light-headed."

"I don't understand any of this at all," Bheid confessed.

"Good. That's the first step toward wisdom."

"This might all make more sense if I knew your sign, Althalus—and Eliar's as well. If I can cast your horoscopes, I'll probably know just who you are."

"Do you actually believe that, Bheid?" Althalus asked.

"Astrology's the core of all religion," Bheid told him. "Deiwos has written our destinies in the stars. The duty of the priesthood is to study the stars so that we can give man the word of God. What's your sign? When were you born?"

"A very long time ago, Bheid," Althalus said with a faint

smile. "I don't think you'd have much luck trying to cast my horoscope, because the stars have changed a lot since then. They had different names, and the people who looked at the skies didn't see them in the same combinations that you do. Half of the Wolf was the bottom of something the old sky watchers called the Turtle, and what astrologers call the Boar now was the top half."

"That's blasphemy!" Bheid exclaimed.

"I wouldn't worry about it too much, Bheid. Those astrologers all died, so they won't be able to accuse you."

"That's not what I meant."

"I know, but *they'd* see it that way, wouldn't they?" Althalus put his hand on Bheid's arm. "There aren't *really* any pictures in the sky, you know. As I said before, the stars aren't connected to each other to make pictures for us to look at, but you've already guessed that, haven't you? That's why you're having your crisis of faith. You *want* to believe that there's a wolf and a boar and a dragon up there, but when you look, you just can't really see them, can you?"

"I *try*." Bheid almost wept. "I try so very hard, but they just aren't there."

"Things have just been rearranged, Bheid. You won't have to look at the sky anymore, because Eliar's got the Knife of Deiwos. The Knife will tell us where to go next."

"Are we going to leave Awes?"

"I'm sure we are. We have a long way to go, I think."

You're wasting time, Althalus. Emmy's voice crackled inside his head. *You and Bheid can speculate about the stars on the way back to Osthos.*

"Osthos!" Althalus protested out loud. "Emmy, we just came from there!"

Yes, I know. Now we have to go back.

"Were you talking with Emmy just now?" Eliar demanded. "Did she say that we have to go to Osthos again? I can't go back there, Althalus! Andine would have me killed if I went back!"

"Is there something wrong?" Bheid asked, sounding very confused.

"We just got our marching orders," Althalus told him. "Eliar's a little bit unhappy about them."

"Did something happen just now that I missed?"

"Emmy just told me that we have to go to Osthos."

"I'm not sure I understand all this talk about somebody named Emmy."

"Emmy's the messenger of Deiwos—sort of. It's a bit more complex than that, but let's keep it simple for right now. Deiwos tells Emmy what he wants done. Then she tells me, and I pass it on."

"We're taking orders from a cat?" Bheid asked incredulously.

"No, we're taking orders from God. We can talk about that on our way to Osthos, though. Emmy wants us to start getting ready to leave." Althalus glanced about. "Let's pile some more rocks on top of that dead man so that he's not quite so visible. Then we'll go pick up your belongings, and I'll buy you a horse. We'll leave first thing in the morning."

They concealed the body more thoroughly and started off through the ruins toward the northern end of Awes. "Who's this Andine person you were talking about?" Bheid asked Eliar.

"She's the ruler of Osthos," Eliar replied. "She wants to kill me."

"Whatever for?"

"Well," Eliar replied with a slightly pained expression, "I *did* sort of kill her father, I guess, but it was during a war, and that kind of thing happens during wars. I was just doing my job, but Andine took it personally. I didn't really mean anything by it. I was just following orders, but she can't quite understand that, I guess."

"Did any of that make any sense to you?" Bheid asked Althalus with a perplexed look.

"You almost had to have been there," Althalus told him. "It was all very complicated. We can talk about it on our way to Osthos."

They went to the northern end of Awes where the black-robed priests stayed, picked up Bheid's blankets and his few other belongings, and then returned to the rudimentary camp where Althalus and Eliar had spent the previous night. Then Eliar and Bheid went to the corral of a horse trader and returned with a mount for their newest member.

"I'm awfully hungry, Althalus," Eliar said hopefully. "Could we have beef tonight instead of fish?"

"I'll make a fire," Bheid offered.

"That won't be necessary," Althalus told him. Then he called up a fairly large beef roast and several loaves of bread.

Bheid jerked back with a startled oath.

"Makes your hair stand on end, doesn't it?" Eliar chuckled. "I was almost afraid to eat the first supper he made that way, but the food he makes with words is really very good." Eliar started to eat with a great deal of enthusiasm.

"How do you do that?" Bheid asked Althalus in an awed voice.

"Emmy calls it 'using the Book,' " Althalus replied. "She taught me how to do it back in the House at the End of the World where the Book is."

"Which Book?"

"The Book of Deiwos, of course."

"You've actually *seen* the Book of Deiwos?"

"Seen it?" Althalus laughed. "I *lived* with it for twenty-five hundred years. I can recite it from end to end, forward or backward, and from side to side, if you'd really care to hear it that way. I think I could even recite it upside down if I put my mind to it."

"Exactly how is it that the Book of Deiwos makes it possible for you to perform miracles?"

"The Book's the word of God, Bheid. It's written in a very antique language that's sort of like the language we speak now, but not exactly. The words from the old language make things happen. If I say 'beef,' nothing happens, but if I say '*gwou,*' we get supper. There's a little more involved in the procedure, but that's the core of it. I spent a lot of years committing the Book to memory." He tapped his forehead. "I've got it in here now, so I don't have to carry it with me—which isn't permitted, of course. The Book has to stay in the House. It wouldn't be safe to carry it out into the real world. You'd better eat your supper before it gets cold."

Eliar had several more helpings, then they talked a bit more before rolling up in their blankets to sleep.

It was Awes. Althalus was sure that it was Awes, but it had no buildings. He could clearly see the fork of the River Medyo, but a grove of ancient trees had somehow replaced the ruins. He wandered for a time under those mighty oaks, and then he looked toward the west and saw people far off in the distance. As he watched them coming across the grassy plain toward the place where he stood, he seemed to hear a faint wailing sound coming from very far away. There was a lost, despairing quality to that wailing that seemed to wrench at his very soul.

And then the people he'd seen reached the far bank of the river, and he could see them more clearly. They were dressed in the skins of animals, and they carried spears with stone points.

He rolled over, muttering and groping under his blanket for the rock that had been gouging his hip. He finally located it, threw it away, and slid easily back into sleep.

There were crude huts under the oak trees now, and the fur-clad people moved among those huts, talking, talking, talking in hushed and fearful tones. "He comes, he comes, he comes," the people said. "Make ready for his coming, for he is God." And the faces of some of the people were exalted, and the faces of others were filled with terror. And still they said, "He comes, he comes, he comes."

And Ghend moved among them, whispering, whispering. And the people pulled back from Ghend with fear upon their faces. But Ghend paid no heed to their fear, and his eyes burned, burned.

And Ghend lifted his face and looked upon Althalus with his

burning eyes. And the eyes of Ghend seared at the soul of Althalus. And Ghend spoke then, saying, "It is of little moment, my thief. Run, Althalus, run, and I shall pursue you down the nights and down the years, and the Book shall avail you not, for I shall deliver you up to the throne of Daeva, and you—even as I—shall serve him down all the endless eons. And when the eons end, we shall turn and follow them back to their beginning. And then shall we turn again, and behold, they shall not be as they were before."

The wailing sound rose to an awful shriek.

Althalus started up, sweating profusely. "God!" he exclaimed, trembling violently.

"Who was he?" Bheid's terrified voice came out of the darkness. "Who was that man with eyes of fire?"

"You saw him, too?" Eliar asked, his voice also trembling.

Step aside, Althalus. Emmy's voice inside his head had a crisp, no-nonsense quality about it. *I need to talk to them.*

Althalus felt himself being rather rudely thrust aside. "Eliar," Emmy said, "tell Bheid who I am."

"Yes, ma'am," Eliar responded. "Bheid," he said, "that's Emmy talking. She does that now and then. Althalus might still be there, but she's using his voice."

"The cat?" Bheid said incredulously.

"I wouldn't think of her as a cat, exactly," Eliar advised. "That's just the way she hides what she really is. Her real form would probably blind us if we looked at her."

"Hush, Eliar," Emmy said gently.

"Yes, ma'am."

"What you've all just experienced, gentlemen, wasn't exactly a dream," Emmy told them. "Althalus has met Ghend before, so he'll be able to tell you about him—after I've finished using his voice. What you saw just now wasn't a dream, but it wasn't real, either. It's what Ghend—and Daeva—want to *make* real."

"Who were those people we saw?" Bheid asked in a trembling voice.

"The Medyos—the first ones who came to this part of the world ten thousand years ago. They brought the worship of Deiwos with them when they came here, but Daeva's trying to change that. He's trying to alter things so that the first Medyos worship *him* instead of his kinsman Deiwos."

"But that's impossible," Bheid protested. "Once something's happened, it *can't* be changed."

"Keep a very firm grip on that thought, Bheid," she advised. "It might help. Daeva doesn't seem to agree with you, though. He believes that he *can* change the past—by changing the present. That's why we're being gathered together. We're supposed to prevent what Daeva's trying to do. This *will* happen again. You'll see things that didn't really happen, and you won't always be asleep when you see them."

"This just stopped being fun, Emmy," Eliar complained. "If these wide-awake dreams come popping out of nowhere the way *that* one did, how can we tell what's real and what's not?"

"Because of the wailing," she replied. "When you hear that wailing off in the distance, it's a sure sign that Ghend's trying to alter the past. You'll *also* know when the wailing starts that you're not in the present. You may be in the past or in the future, but you aren't in the place called now."

Althalus looked off to the east where the first faint hint of the new day was touching the horizon. "It's almost daybreak," he told his companions. "Let's gather up our things and get ready to start."

"We *are* going to have breakfast, aren't we?" Eliar asked in a worried tone.

Althalus sighed. "Yes, Eliar, we'll have breakfast."

The sun was just coming up when the barge ferried them across the west fork of the river, and they rode toward the west. After they'd gone a few miles, Bheid trotted his horse up beside Althalus. "Can we talk?" he asked.

"I guess that's permitted," Althalus replied.

"How did you find out where the Book of Deiwos was located?" Bheid asked. "I've been hearing stories about it for years now. Arguments about that Book have been going on for centuries. Most of my teachers said that the Book was actually the night sky, but some said that it really did exist. Evidently those were the ones who were right."

"Yes," Althalus replied, "there really *is* a Book."

"How did you find it? Did God come to you in a vision?"

Althalus laughed. "No it wasn't God who came to me. It was Ghend."

"Ghend?"

"He looked me up and hired me to steal the Book for him. It was Ghend who told me where the House was."

"Why would any honest man agree to something like that?"

"An honest man probably wouldn't have, but I don't have that problem. I'm a thief, Bheid."

"A thief?"

"That's a man who steals things. I'm probably the best thief in the world, so I've got a good reputation. Ghend tracked me down and told me that he'd pay me if I stole the Book for him. Then he told me where it was."

"The House at the End of the World?"

"Well, that's what it's called. It's built on the edge of a cliff up in northern Kagwher, and it's the biggest house I've ever seen. It's almost completely empty though. As far as I could tell, there's only one room that has any furniture in it. That's where the Book was. Of course, Emmy was there, too. She scolded me for being late, and I thought for certain that I'd gone mad. She told me to stop being silly, and then she taught me how to read."

"From the Book of Deiwos?" Bheid asked reverently.

"It was the only Book there."

"What does it look like?"

"It's a box covered with white leather. The pages are stacked inside the box. Emmy used to come all unraveled if I mixed up the pages. Anyway, I learned how to read the Book, and then Emmy and I found a way to speak to each other without using our voices. Then we left the House to go find the Knife. We discovered that Eliar had it. He's a mercenary soldier, and he was fighting in that war between Kanthon and Osthos that's been going on for forty or fifty generations now. Eliar was leading an attack on the walls of Osthos, and he killed the Aryo during the fighting. The Aryo's daughter, Andine, didn't like that at all, and since Eliar'd been taken prisoner, she started thinking about all sorts of interesting things to do to him. I posed as a slave trader and bought him from her. Then we came here to find you. Now we're going back to Osthos to find somebody else."

"How long ago was it? When Ghend hired you, I mean?"

"Emmy says it was twenty-five hundred years ago. From what she tells me, people don't age in the House. It's just as well, really. If I'd aged normally, I'd have a white beard about twelve miles long by now."

"Is Emmy *really* the sister of God?"

"That's what she tells me. Her name's Dweia, but she says she doesn't actually look much like that statue in her temple in Maghu."

"You worship a female God?" Bheid's eyes bulged in outrage.

"I don't worship her, Bheid. I love her, but I don't worship her. Worship means absolute obedience, and it involves a lot of groveling. I do what Emmy tells me to do most of the time, but I don't spend much time on my knees. We argue all the time, actually. Emmy likes to argue—almost as much as she likes to sneak up and pounce on me."

"May I touch her?" Bheid asked in an almost reverent tone.

"Emmy," Althalus said back over his shoulder. "Wake up. Bheid wants to rub your ears."

Emmy poked her sleepy-eyed face up out of his hood. "That would be nice," she murmured.

Althalus reached back, lifted her out of his hood, and held her out to Bheid. "Go ahead and hold her, Bheid," he said. "She'll steal your soul, of course, but why should you be any different from Eliar and me?"

Bheid jerked his hand back.

"I'm only joking, Bheid," Althalus said.

Are you really all that certain, pet? Emmy asked, her green eyes turning sly.

Bheid's hands were trembling as he took her from Althalus, but he relaxed when Emmy started purring.

"When are we going to stop for lunch?" Eliar called from behind them.

They rode on across western Medyo, keeping off the main roads whenever possible. The sudden appearance of the cockeyed man back in Awes indicated a likelihood that Ghend had agents everywhere. Althalus knew that they could deal with those agents, but unnecessary killings went against his grain. A really good thief shouldn't have to kill people.

It was midsummer by the time they approached the bridge across the west fork of the River Osthos, and Althalus prudently turned aside from the road and led Eliar and Bheid into a grove of trees some distance upstream.

Em, he said silently after they'd dismounted, *just exactly who are we supposed to find there in Osthos?*

Guess, she replied rather smugly.

Don't do that, he scolded.

You've already met her, pet.

He blinked. *You're not serious!* He almost said it out loud. *Oh, yes.*

How are we supposed to get inside her palace?

You're the thief, Althalus, she replied. *If you can steal things, I'm sure you'll be able to steal one little girl.*

Emmy, her palace is guarded by an army. One little squeak out of her and I'll have thirty armed men climbing all over me.

Then we'll just have to make sure she doesn't squeak, won't we? She considered it. *I think we'd better leave Eliar and Bheid here—and your horse. We'll want to move very quietly. I'm a cat, and you're a thief. We know how to be quiet; they don't.*

How long have you known that Andine would be joining us?

Since the moment Eliar read the Knife.

Why didn't we pick her up before we went to Awes?

That would have been out of sequence, pet. Everything must be in its proper place and time.

Althalus glanced at Eliar, and he remembered the way Arya Andine had looked at the boy. *I think your brother's got a very warped sense of humor, Em,* he said.

Why, Althalus, she said, *I'm shocked at you. Shocked.*

It was well past midnight when Althalus and Emmy slipped into Andine's palace in the center of Osthos. This time, Emmy chose to walk rather than ride, and she moved on silent feet ahead of the thief, passing warnings back to him. Once they were inside the massive palace, she led him to the Arya's private quarters. *She's asleep,* Emmy advised. *There are two guards outside her door. Encourage them to take a little nap.*

How?

Try "leb."

Will that work?

It always has before. After we leave, you'd better wake them up again, though. People might think it's a little peculiar if they sleep for fifty or sixty years the way you used to do back in the House.

Is that the way you did it?

Of course. Step right along, Althalus. The night won't last forever, you know.

The pair of guards at Andine's door were still standing, but their chins had sagged down onto their chests and they were snoring softly. Althalus reached past them and took hold of the door handle.

Then Emmy hissed.

"What's the problem?" he whispered.

Argan!

"What's an Argan?"

It's a who, not a what. This guard on the left is Argan.

"Is that name supposed to mean anything to me?"

I mentioned him before. Argan's another one of Ghend's underlings.

"That's convenient." Althalus reached for his dagger.

Put that away, Emmy said in a disgusted tone.

"It's a nice, simple solution, Em."

Perhaps, but how do you plan to solve the problem that'll come up later?

"Which problem is that?"

Returning him to life when he absolutely must *be alive and well.*

"I didn't follow that."

I didn't really think you would. Put the knife away, Althalus. You aren't the one who's supposed to deal with Argan—any more than you were the one who's supposed to deal with Pekhal or Khnom. Just leave him alone.

"Hold it, Em. Doesn't this mean that Ghend knew we were coming here?"

Probably, yes.

"How did he find out?"

Probably because Daeva told him.

"How did Daeva find out?"

The same way I did, of course. We hear things that you can't, Althalus. I know *about people like Khnom and Pekhal and Argan, and* Daeva *knows about people like Eliar and Bheid and Andine. They're significant people, and significant people give off a certain sound that we can hear. Just leave Argan alone. Let's get Andine and get out of here before Argan wakes.*

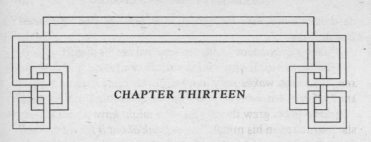

CHAPTER THIRTEEN

The moon was full, and its pale light streamed in through the open window of the Arya's bedroom to fall upon the sleeping girl's face. Her mass of dark hair spilled out over her pillow, and sleep had softened her imperious expression, making her seem very vulnerable and very, very young.

As silent as a shadow, Emmy flowed up onto the bed and sat beside the sleeping girl's pillow. Her green eyes were a mystery as she regarded the face of her sometime mistress. Then she started to purr.

How do we get her out of here? Althalus asked silently. *I suppose I could carry her, but—*

She'll walk, Emmy replied. *Look around and find her some clothes and a dark cape.*

Doesn't she have to be awake to walk? And won't she start screaming even before her eyes are open?

I know what I'm doing, Althalus. Trust me. Get her some clothes.

Althalus poked around until he found boots, a well-made cloak, and clothing suitable for travel. When he turned, he saw Andine sitting on the edge of the bed. Her huge eyes were open, but they obviously saw nothing.

Just bundle up her clothes, Emmy said. *I'll have her dress herself once we're outside the city. The cloak should be enough for now.*

Andine stood up, her eyes still blank, and she was holding Emmy in her arms. Althalus draped the cloak about her shoulders. *How long can you keep her asleep like this?* he asked Emmy.

As long as I need to.

Six or eight weeks might not be a bad idea. If the first face she sees when she wakes just happens to be Eliar's, things might start to get noisy.

Emmy's eyes grew thoughtful. *You might have a point there,* she murmured in his mind. *Let me think about it for a bit. Shall we go?*

They led their sleeping captive out into the corridor, and Althalus stopped briefly to examine the face of the sleeping Argan. Ghend's henchman had yellow hair and regular features.

What are you doing? Emmy asked.

I want to be sure I'll recognize him when I see him again, Althalus replied grimly.

They went back down the corridor, and after they'd rounded a corner, Althalus reached back and woke Argan and his companion. Then he silently led the Arya of Osthos out of her palace.

They moved quietly through the darkened streets of Osthos. Althalus used *"leb"* to put the gate guards to sleep, and they left the city.

"I think you were right, Althalus," Emmy said as Andine woodenly dressed herself. "It might be better to keep her mind asleep until we cross over into Perquaine. By noon tomorrow, her soldiers are going to be looking under every bush in Treborea for her."

They soon rejoined Eliar and Bheid, and Eliar looked rather closely at the young woman who probably still wanted desperately to kill him. "Is she all right?" he asked with a note of concern in his voice. "I mean, you didn't have to hurt her, did you?"

"Emmy put her to sleep," Althalus replied. "It'll probably be better to keep her that way until we get her out of Treborea."

"She won't be able to sit a horse in her present condition," Bheid suggested.

"I'll take care of her," Eliar said. "I'll sit her on my horse in front of me. I can keep her from falling off."

"All right," Althalus agreed. "She's your responsibility. Take care of her. Let's move out. I want to put some distance between us and Osthos by morning."

They crossed the River Maghu just to the north of the Perquaine city of Gagan two days later and moved into the drought-stricken countryside to the west. Arya Andine had remained semiconscious, and Eliar had been strangely solicitous of her throughout the journey. He held her in place in front of him as they rode and lifted her on and off his horse with a peculiar gentleness. He fed her at mealtimes, and his own appetite seemed to have fallen off considerably.

"Is it my imagination, or is he behaving just a bit oddly?" Bheid asked Althalus after they'd crossed the river.

"Eliar takes his responsibilities very seriously," Althalus replied, "and he's always volunteering because he wants to be helpful. He'll probably outgrow that in time."

Bheid chuckled. "From what you've told me, I don't think he should be quite so close to Andine when she wakes up. If she hates him as much as you say she does, she'll probably try to reach down his throat and jerk out his heart as soon as she lays her eyes on him."

"We'll find out before long, I expect. Emmy's going to wake our little girl this evening, and you and I should probably be on our toes when Eliar holds the Knife out for her to read. She might take that as an invitation."

They took shelter in the ruins of a long-abandoned house late that afternoon, and Althalus called up beef for supper before Emmy could suggest fish. Eliar, as he had since they'd left Osthos, cut up Andine's supper and fed her carefully. She sat placidly with her hands folded in her lap, opening her mouth as he held each bite to her lips, much as a sparrow chick might.

After they'd eaten, Emmy commandeered Althalus' voice again to give them their instructions. "I want you to be standing directly in front of her with the Knife right in front of her eyes when I wake her, Eliar. That way she'll see the Knife before she sees you. Once she reads the Knife, she'll be more or less compelled to do as she's told. She might rant and rave a bit, but she won't try to kill you."

Eliar seated their captive on a square stone block by their fire, took out the Knife, and stood in front of her with the blade before her eyes. Emmy leaped up into the girl's lap, nestled against her, and purred.

The life flowed back into the Arya's huge dark eyes.

"Can you tell me what that peculiar writing says, your Highness?" Althalus asked her, pointing at the Knife.

"Obey," Andine said almost automatically.

The Knife sang joyously, and Emmy purred all the louder.

Andine's expression was at once baffled and stunned. Then she seemed to realize suddenly that Emmy was in her lap. She seized the cat up in her arms and held her tightly. "Naughty cat!" she scolded. "Don't you *ever* run away like that again. Where have you been?"

Then she looked at the ruins around them in utter astonishment as the Knife continued its song. "Where am I?" she demanded.

"You'd better stay seated, your Highness," Althalus suggested. "You'll probably be a bit dizzy right at first."

The Arya, however, didn't appear to be listening. She was staring at Eliar instead. *"You!"* she said sharply. She dropped Emmy and sprang directly at the young Arum, both of her hands extended clawlike at his face. "Assassin!" she shrieked.

Then she reeled and would have fallen had Eliar not caught her. "Be careful, your Highness!" the boy exclaimed. "You'll hurt yourself!"

"Let me take care of her, Eliar," Bheid suggested. "Let's get her calmed down a bit."

"I can do it, Bheid," Eliar protested. "She can't really hurt me, you know."

"Maybe not, but the sight of you might be hurting *her*. I'm sure she'll come around, but it might be best if you stayed clear of her for a while."

"He's probably right, Eliar," Althalus agreed. "The girl's a little emotional."

"A *little*?" Eliar said. Then he sighed a bit regretfully. "Maybe you're right, though. I'll stay away from her for a few days."

Althalus and Bheid reseated Andine by the fire, and Emmy leaped up into the girl's lap again.

"Where are we?" Andine asked in her vibrant voice.

"Perquaine, your Highness," Althalus replied.

"Perquaine? That's impossible!"

"I wouldn't be too quick to start throwing that word around, your Highness," Bheid advised her. "Althalus here can do almost anything, and Emmy can do even more."

"I don't believe I know you," she said.

"My name is Bheid," he introduced himself. "I'm a priest. Well . . . I was until Althalus called me."

"Just what's going on here, Master Althalus?" the girl demanded. "I thought you were taking the slaves you bought from me to the salt mines of Ansu."

"I sort of lied about that, your Highness," he admitted blandly. "Eliar was the only one I really needed. I told the rest of them to go home."

"You *thief*!" Her voice rose, soaring dramatically.

"That's a fairly accurate description, yes," he agreed. "Let's clear the air here just a bit. You've just entered the service of Deiwos, the Sky God."

"That's absurd!"

"Andine," he said firmly. "What was the word you read on the Knife?"

"It said, 'obey,' " she replied.

"Exactly. Now hush. Don't interrupt me when I'm explaining things to you. I'm the teacher; you're the student. I'm supposed to teach. You're supposed to sit there and look stupid."

"How *dare* you!"

"Shush, Andine!"

Her eyes went very wide. She struggled, fighting the compulsion he'd just laid upon her, but no sound came from her mouth.

"I have a feeling that might prove to be useful from time to time," Bheid murmured as if to himself.

"That'll do, Bheid," Althalus told him.

"Sorry."

Althalus patiently explained the situation to his reluctant pupil. "It gets easier to accept after a while," he assured her after he'd finished. "I thought I'd gone insane when Emmy first got her paws on me, but that passed—eventually. She has her little ways, as you probably already know."

"What do you mean?" the girl asked.

"Wake up, Andine. Would you have *really* sold Eliar to me unless something very powerful had gotten its little paws on your heart? Killing him was the only thing on your mind that day when I walked into your palace. Then Emmy jumped up into your lap and started purring at you. After about a half hour of that, you'd have given me the entire city of Osthos for her, now wouldn't you?"

"Well . . ." Andine looked helplessly at the cat in her lap. "She's so adorable," the girl said, catching Emmy up in her arms and snuggling her face up to the furry captor of her heart.

"You noticed," Althalus said drily. "Don't try to fight her, because she always wins. Just give her all your love and do as she tells you to do. You might as well, because she'll cheat to get what she wants if she has to."

I think that's about enough, Althalus. Emmy's voice crackled crisply in his mind.

Yes, dear, he replied. *Did you happen to read the Knife when Eliar showed it to Andine?*

Of course.

Where do we go next?

Hule.

Hule's a big place, Em. You didn't by any chance happen to pick up the name of the one we want, did you?

We don't need the name of this one, pet. He'll find you.

"You two are talking to each other again, aren't you?" Eliar asked a bit wistfully.

"She was just giving me our instructions. We have to go to Hule."

Eliar's eyes brightened. "We'll be passing through Arum then, won't we? Do you think I might have time to stop and say hello to my mother? She worries about me a lot."

"I think we can arrange that," Althalus agreed. "I don't think you should tell her what we're doing, though."

Eliar grinned. "I'm pretty good at that. There were a lot of things I did when I was just a boy that I didn't tell her about. I didn't come right out and lie to her, of course. A boy should never lie to his mother, but now and then things sort of slipped my mind. You know how that can happen."

"Oh, yes." Althalus laughed. "Things have been slipping my mind for as long as I can remember."

"I'm sort of hungry, Althalus," Eliar said. "I've been so busy taking care of her Highness here that I seem to have missed a few meals. I'm absolutely starving."

"You'd better feed him, Althalus," Bheid suggested. "We don't want him wasting away on us."

"You might ask her Highness if she'd like something, too," Eliar added. "I couldn't get her to eat very much at all at lunchtime."

Andine was staring at them.

"You missed all that, didn't you, Andine?" Bheid said a bit slyly. "After Emmy put you to sleep, Eliar looked after you like a mother hen with only one chick. He spent more time feeding you than he spent feeding himself, and food's very important to young Eliar just now. If you watch him closely, you can almost see him grow."

"What are you talking about? He's a grown man."

"No, he's only a boy," Bheid corrected her. "He's probably not much older than you are."

"He's bigger than any man in Osthos."

"Arums are bigger than Treboreans," Althalus told her. "The farther north you go, the taller people get—maybe so that they're tall enough to see over all the snow that piles up in the north."

"If he's only a boy, what was he doing in a war?"

"He comes from a warrior culture. They start earlier than civilized people do. It was his first war, and it was supposed to be a quiet one. The half-wit who sits on the throne in Kanthon got carried away, though, so he ordered the soldiers he'd hired from Eliar's Clan Chief to invade your father's territory. It was a stupid thing to do, and it wasn't supposed to happen. It was *his* fault that your father got killed, not Eliar's. Eliar was only following orders. The whole business was the result of a series of stupid mistakes, but that's what most wars are all about, I guess. Nobody ever really wins a war, when you get right down to it. Do you think you could eat something? You don't really have to, but Eliar's worried about how little he was able to get you to eat on our way here from Osthos."

"Why should he care?"

"He feels responsible for you, and Eliar takes his responsibilities very seriously."

"You put me in the care of that monster?" Her voice soared. "I'm lucky he didn't kill me!"

"He wouldn't do that, Andine—quite the opposite, actually. If somebody had threatened you along the way, Eliar would have killed *him*, not you, or he'd have died trying."

"You're lying!"

"Go ask him."

"I wouldn't talk to him if my life depended on it."

"Someday it might, Andine, so don't lock yourself in stone on this issue."

Let it lie, Althalus, Emmy's voice told him. *She isn't ready for this yet. Keep those two apart for now. Turn her over to Bheid for a while. I'll stay with her and try to get her past this.*

Should I buy her a horse?

Let's get her settled down a little first.

You think she might try to run away?

The Knife won't let her do that, pet, but she doesn't want to face the truth about what Eliar really is, so she might try to override the compulsion, and that could cause her a great deal of pain. Let Bheid know what's going on and have him help her along. You stay with Eliar and keep him away from Andine. Let's sort of tiptoe around the children until they settle down.

* * *

They rode north through the drought-ravaged fields of Perquaine, and Althalus and Bheid rather carefully kept some distance between Eliar and Andine. Althalus soon realized that the auburn-haired young priest was very intelligent, and once he'd been cured of the notion that astrology really had any significance, he was able to apply his intellect more usefully. "Is it my imagination, Althalus," he asked one evening when they were alone, "or is there something brewing between the children? They never look each other in the face, but their eyes are always sort of straying back to each other, for some reason."

"They're at that age, Bheid," Althalus replied.

"I don't quite follow."

"*That* age. They're both adolescents—with all that's implied in the word 'adolescent.' This is a very trying time for them—and even more trying for you and me, I'm afraid."

"Yes," Bheid agreed. "I sort of noticed that myself."

"They're both having urges right now. The simplest way to deal with that would be for you to perform a wedding ceremony. We could give them a week or so to explore the differences between boys and girls, and then we could get back to business."

Bheid laughed. "We might have a little difficulty persuading Andine to go along with that notion. She's like a little teapot, isn't she? Always right on the verge of blowing off her lid."

"Nicely put, Bheid," Althalus noted. "Eliar's an uncomplicated little boy and Andine's just the opposite. I rather imagine that Emmy has plans for them, though."

"Has she said anything to you about that?"

"She doesn't really have to. Emmy and I have been together for long enough for me to get occasional hints about her intentions. It's part of her nature to bring boys and girls together. You might want to keep that in mind, Bheid. She's probably already shopping around to see if she can find a wife for you."

"I'm a priest, Althalus. The men in my order don't marry. It's one of the vows we take."

"You might want to give some thought to joining another order, then. If Emmy decides to marry you off, she *will* marry you off, whether you like the idea or not."

* * *

It was when they were approaching Maghu that Emmy spoke quite sharply to Althalus, her silent voice echoing in his mind. *Up ahead!* she said urgently.

What is it?

That man standing off to the left side of the road. It's Koman, Althalus. Put your guard up. He'll try to get inside your mind.

Another of Ghend's underlings?

Yes—and probably the most dangerous one of all. Get between him and Eliar. The boy's not equipped to deal with him.

And I am? What do I do?

Put yourself between him and the others. Look him in the face and count trees.

Again with the counting trees, Em?

Not quite. Skip numbers.

You missed me there, Em.

Jump from six to eight. Then go back to three. Scramble the numbers the way you'd scramble eggs.

What's that supposed to do?

It'll distract his mind from what he's attempting. He'll try to creep inside your mind. If you're throwing out-of-sequence numbers at him, he won't be able to concentrate—on you or on any of the others. He'll be looking for information, and we don't want him to get any. Block him out, Althalus.

I hope you know what you're doing, Em. And please don't tell me to trust you again.

The man at the side of the road had a harsh-looking face and a short white beard. His eyes, Althalus noticed, burned in almost the same way Ghend's eyes had that night in Nabjor's camp. Althalus reined his horse in slightly and looked directly at the harsh-faced man.

Althalus began to count silently. *One, two, three, four, nine hundred and forty-two, eight, nine, twelve.*

The man at the side of the road blinked. Then he shook his head as if trying to clear it.

Nineteen, eighty-four, two, four, six, fifty-two.

The man Emmy had identified as Koman glared at Althalus with smoldering hatred.

"Are we having fun yet?" Althalus asked drily, then continued. *Eleven million and a quarter, thirteen, ninety-seven and six-eighths, forty-three—*

The man called Koman stalked away muttering to himself.

"Always nice talking with you, friend," Althalus called after him. "We'll have to do this again sometime—real soon."

The fractions were a stroke of absolute genius, pet. Emmy's thought actually purred.

I thought you might like them, Althalus said.

Where in the world did you come up with the notion?

He shrugged. *I just made it up,* he said. *I thought that if whole numbers bother him, bits and pieces of numbers should drive him wild.*

They stopped by a farm on the outskirts of Maghu, and Althalus bought a rather sedate mare for Andine. The Arya wasn't particularly impressed by her mount, but despite Emmy's assurances that the volcanic girl with her dramatic voice was resigned to her situation, Althalus had prudently decided to mount her on a horse that wasn't likely to run very fast.

Then they left the lands of the Perquaines and rode up into the foothills of Arum. Bheid and Andine rode side by side along the way, and the auburn-haired priest spent days trying to explain just exactly why the snow on the mountaintops of Arum didn't melt in the summer sun. Andine's teachers had evidently been great believers in logic, so despite the evidence of those white-tipped mountains, she continued to argue that since the peaks were closer to the sun, it *had* to be warmer up there.

After three days of that, Bheid gave up.

They reached the valley where Chief Albron's fort stood shortly after noon on a glorious summer day, and Althalus had a brief word with Eliar. "Keep your visit with your mother sort of brief, Eliar," he advised. "You know that place a few miles on ahead where there's a waterfall in the river?"

"Quite well. We used to go swimming in the pool at the foot of the falls," Eliar replied.

"We'll make camp there. Try to catch up with us before dark."

"I'll be there," Eliar promised. Then he turned aside and rode down into the valley.

"Well," Andine said sardonically, "I'm sure that's the last we'll see of *him*."

"Why do you say that?" Althalus asked her.

"Because he'll run off and hide."

"I rather doubt that."

"The only reason he's stayed with us is because you have some kind of hold on him. He's a murderer, and murderers can't be trusted. *And* you let him keep that precious knife you need so much. You can kiss that good-bye, too, Master Althalus."

"You're wrong on all counts, Andine. Eliar's a soldier, and he always follows orders. He'll rejoin us before nightfall, and *he's* the one who's supposed to carry the Knife. He just wants to visit his mother, that's all."

"I'm getting very tired of hearing about his mother," she flared.

"They're very close, Andine," Bheid told her. "I've talked often with Eliar since we met. His father was killed in a war several years ago, and Eliar became his mother's only support. He was a little young to go off to war, even for an Arum, but his mother needed his soldier's pay to keep eating. In a peculiar sort of way, Eliar went off to war as a way to show his love for his father—and his mother. Your father was unlucky enough to get in his way while he was showing his veneration for his parents. Isn't that sort of what you were doing when you were planning to kill him before Althalus came along?"

"It's not the same thing at all, Bheid," she flared. "My father was the Aryo of Osthos. Eliar's father was just a common soldier."

"And do you believe that Eliar loved his father less than you loved yours? We all love and revere our parents, Andine, and the peasant or common soldier loves—and grieves—as deeply as the aristocrat. You might want to think about that just a bit before you launch yourself into your next tirade."

*   *   *

They set up camp in a grove of fir trees near the waterfall, and Andine spent the afternoon by herself sitting on a log and watching the tumbling water.

"I think you might have touched a nerve there, Bheid," Althalus said. "Our little Arya seems to be reconsidering some of her preconceptions."

"Class distinctions are an impediment to understanding, Althalus," Bheid told him, "and anything that interferes with understanding should be discarded."

"You might want to give some thought to keeping that particular opinion tucked up under your arm, Bheid," Althalus advised. "It won't make you very popular in certain quarters."

As Althalus had predicted, Eliar rejoined them just as the sun was going down. The boy was in high spirits. Arya Andine seemed on the verge of several spiteful remarks, but evidently Bheid's little sermon had taken some of the wind out of her sails, and she finally announced that she had a splitting headache and was going to bed.

Summer was winding down to its dusty conclusion when they came down out of the northern foothills of Arum and rode into the vast forest of Hule. In spite of all that had happened, Althalus felt good to be back. He'd once told Emmy that the House at the End of the World had been the closest thing he'd ever had to a permanent home, but he now realized that his declaration hadn't been entirely true. No matter how far he traveled, he always felt very good when he returned to Hule, and he finally came to realize that more than anyplace else, Hule was his home.

They rode some distance back into the forest of gigantic trees, and Althalus was pleased and almost surprised that he still knew his way around in the woods. For some reason, he *wasn't* surprised when he discovered that a place he remembered very well was still there and that the more recent settlers in Hule had yet to contaminate it with rude huts, muddy streets, and the stumps of trees. "We'll stop here," he announced to his companions.

"We still have a fair amount of daylight, Althalus," Bheid pointed out.

"We'll have time to get settled in, then. This is the place."

"I didn't quite follow that," Bheid confessed.

"The Knife told us to go to Hule, Bheid. This *is* Hule."

"Wasn't it Hule ten miles back? And won't it still be Hule ten miles up ahead?"

"No, I don't think so. I'll see what Emmy has to say about it, but I'm sure this is the place. This is where it all started, my friend. This is the place where Ghend hired me to go to the House at the End of the World to steal the Book of Deiwos for him. This is where Nabjor's camp used to be. Emmy and I used to have long talks about coincidence back in the House. We never did settle the matter, but I've got a very strong feeling that *some* things that seem to be pure chance or coincidence aren't that at all. They're things that were intended to happen. When Emmy read the Knife and told me that it said 'Hule,' this was the first place I thought of, and I rather imagine that I was supposed to. It's one of those significant places, Bheid, so let's stay here for a bit and find out if significant events need significant places to happen in."

I think you're starting to get the hang of this, pet, Emmy silently congratulated him.

After they'd set up their camp, Althalus poked around a bit to see if the centuries had left any traces of Nabjor's establishment. He eventually came to the narrow crevice between two large standing boulders where Nabjor had brewed his mead. There was a mound of stones near the back of the crevice, and lying on top of the mound were the much-pitted remnants of a large bronze battle-ax. Even in its present condition, Althalus recognized it. He sighed. "At least somebody cared enough about you to give you a decent burial, old friend," he said to the grave. Then he smiled. "I'd tell you quite a story if you were still here, Nabjor. You always liked a good story, didn't you? I *do* wish you were still here. A few cups of your mead would go rather well right now. Maybe when this is all over, we'll be able to sit on a cloud somewhere drinking your mead, and I'll tell you all about the House at the End of the World."

He sighed again. "Sleep well, old friend," he said.

It was just past midnight, and their fire had burned low. Althalus wasn't even particularly surprised when his seemingly dormant instincts warned him that someone was creeping up on their camp. He silently rolled out from under his blankets and slipped into the darker shadows away from the fire.

"You heard it, too?" Eliar's whisper came out of the shadow of a gigantic tree.

Even *that* didn't surprise Althalus. "I think it's the one we've been waiting for," he whispered back. "He might try to run. Stop him, but don't hurt him."

"All right."

They waited, scarcely breathing. Then Althalus heard a very faint scuffing sound back in the forest. "He's not very good," he whispered to Eliar.

"What's he doing?"

"He's trying to sneak up on our camp—probably to steal whatever he can lay his hands on. He's fairly inept about it if he can't move any more quietly than that. He'll go to where the horses are."

"Is he going to try to steal our horses?"

"Probably. Work your way around to the far side and come up on him from behind. I'll slip over to the horses. He won't see me, so I'll surprise him. If he gets away from me, you grab him."

"Right." Eliar faded into the shadows.

It wasn't particularly difficult to apprehend the would-be thief. When he reached the place where the horses were tied, Althalus was waiting for him in the shadows, and Eliar was no more than a few feet behind him. They grabbed him from the front and back almost simultaneously. "He's just a little boy, Althalus!" Eliar said, easily holding their struggling captive.

"Yes, I noticed." Althalus took the child by the scruff of the neck and hauled him to the fire.

"I didn't do anything!" the child protested in a shrill voice, struggling to get free.

"That's probably because you're too clumsy for this line of work," Althalus told him. "What's your name?"

"I'm called Althalus," the boy answered a bit too quickly.

Eliar doubled over with sudden laughter. "Pick another name, boy," he chortled. "The man who's holding you by the back of the neck is the *real* Althalus."

"Really?" the boy answered in astonishment. "I thought he was just an old legend."

"What's your real name, boy?" Althalus demanded. "No more lies. Tell me your name."

"I'm called Gher, Master Althalus." The boy stopped struggling.

"Show him the Knife, Eliar," Althalus said. "I think Gher here is the one we've been waiting for."

Eliar drew out the Knife. "What does the writing on this knife blade say, Gher?" he demanded.

"I can't read, sir."

"Try."

Gher squinted at the Knife. "It looks to me as if it says 'deceive,' " he said dubiously. "Is that anywhere close at all?"

The Knife, however, had burst into joyous song.

"It sounds close enough to me," Eliar congratulated their newest member. "Welcome, Gher."

CHAPTER FOURTEEN

"Things haven't been too easy since my father finally drank himself to death last year," Gher said. "I ran errands for Dweni—he keeps a tavern not far from here. He let me eat the scraps from his table and sleep in the shed at the back of his tavern. A lot of thieves drink in Dweni's tavern, and I'd listen to them talking, but I knew enough not to ask questions. Was I doing something wrong when I tried to sneak up on your camp, Master Althalus?"

"Didn't the notion of moving quietly ever occur to you?"

Gher sort of hung his head. "I thought you were all asleep."

"You're still not supposed to make so much noise. You were crashing around like a drunken bear."

"Do you suppose you might have the time to give me a few pointers?" Gher asked hopefully.

"We'll see."

Gher had muddy blond, tangled hair, and he was dressed in castoffs that he'd evidently tried, without much success, to patch. His clothing was filthy, and his face and hands and hair weren't much better.

"You have no family at all, then?" Eliar asked.

"Not that I know of, no. Of course, my father couldn't remember very much along toward the end there. He might have had some brothers or sisters, but he never told me about them. He was too drunk most of the time to make sense."

"What about your mother?"

"I don't know for sure if I ever had one."

Eliar choked on that just a bit. "Aren't you feeling just a little dizzy?" he asked.

"No. Should I?"

"I did the first time *I* read the Knife."

"I'm fine. Do you work for Master Althalus here?"

"You could put it that way, yes," Eliar replied.

Bheid came into the firelight. "I heard the Knife singing," he said. Then he stared at Gher. "Is *this* our newest acolyte?"

"That's what the Knife tells us," Althalus replied.

"He's only a child!" Bheid objected.

"You can talk to the Knife about that, if you'd like. I don't choose them, Bheid. I just hunt them down. His name's Gher."

"What word did he read?"

"It was 'deceive,' wasn't it, Althalus?" Eliar asked.

"That's the way I heard it."

Bheid frowned. "Seek, lead, illuminate, obey, and deceive," he went down the list. "That last one doesn't seem to fit. I don't quite follow the logic there."

"Emmy can explain it," Eliar told him. "Emmy can explain anything."

"What *are* you people doing?" Andine demanded crossly, coming into the light. "How am I supposed to sleep with all this noise going on out here?"

"We were just getting to know our latest recruit, Andine," Althalus replied.

"This?" she said, looking disdainfully at Gher. "Is *this* the best we can do?"

"All shall be revealed in time," Bheid said with mock piety.

"Go preach your sermons someplace else, Bheid," she flared. She looked Gher up and down. "Did he crawl out from under a rock, perhaps? Or did he just come slithering out of the nearest cesspool?"

"Do I have to take that from her, Master Althalus?" Gher demanded with a certain heat.

Turn him loose, Althalus, Emmy's voice whispered.

Won't that make the rest of the night a little noisy? he objected.

Just do it, pet.

Whatever you say, Em. Althalus looked at the boy. "Feel free to respond, Gher. Brace yourself, though. Our beloved Andine has an expressive—and penetrating—voice."

"What's that supposed to mean?" Andine demanded, her voice going up several octaves.

"We love your voice, your Highness," he replied with a straight face. "You need to work on your crescendos just a bit, though. You might think about some deep-breathing exercises. Get some bottom under your voice so that you don't have to move from a whisper to a shriek quite so fast. It'll be much more impressive once you learn to control it." He glanced at Gher. "Was there something you wanted to add, boy?" he asked.

"I just wanted to tell her that I don't much care for that nose-up-in-the-air way she talks," Gher replied. He looked Andine in the face. "All right, lady, I'm woodsy. So what? If you don't like the way I look, don't look at me. I don't have any parents, and I wear rags because that's all I can find to wear. I don't see where that's any of your business, though. I'm too busy staying alive to worry about how I look, and if you don't like it that way, well, that's just too bad."

Move over Althalus. Emmy's tone was brisk. *I'm going to take care of something right now.* He felt her roughly shouldering his consciousness out of her way.

Andine was gaping at Gher. "People don't talk to me that way!" she gasped.

"Not to your face, maybe," Gher shot back, "but I think if you'd close your mouth and listen to other people once in a while, you might find out what they *really* think of you. But you don't want to know, do you? I wasn't raised in a palace the way you were, lady. I grew up in a garbage heap, so I don't have fancy manners."

"I don't have to listen to this!"

"Maybe you don't have to, but you really should. I breathe in and out the same as you do, lady, and you don't own the air, so it belongs to me as much as it does to you. Just back away, lady. You make me even sicker than I make you."

Andine fled.

Did you *do that?* Althalus silently demanded.

Of course, Emmy replied. *I told you that I'd have to go through you to do these things. Gher's going to work out just fine, Althalus.* Emmy paused. *I think you* should *clean him up just a bit, though,* she added.

They stayed in Nabjor's old camp for several days introducing Gher to his new situation. The boy was quick, there was no question about that. In a different time and place, Althalus might have taken him under his wing as an apprentice, since he recognized an enormous potential. It took a while, however, to persuade Gher that regular bathing would keep the noise down. With Emmy's help, Althalus conjured up some clothing for their recruit, and that made him look much less like the runoff from a passing rag cart.

Andine avoided Gher almost religiously until the morning of the boy's fourth day in the camp. Then she came to the fire with a determined look on her face and a comb and a pair of scissors in her hands. "You!" she said to him. She pointed at a stump. "Sit. There. Now."

"What are you going to do to me?"

"I'm going to fix your hair. You look like a haystack."

"I can smooth it down if it bothers you."

"Hush. Sit."

Gher looked quickly at Althalus. "Do I have to take orders from her?" he asked.

"I would, if I were you. Let's keep peace in the family, if we can."

"How can you even see through all of this?" Andine demanded, taking hold of the shock of hair that hung down over Gher's forehead. Then she started combing and cutting, frowning in concentration. For some reason she seemed to be taking her task very seriously.

Gher apparently wasn't used to haircuts, so he squirmed a bit as Andine barbered at him for all she was worth. "Sit still!" she commanded. She combed and snipped for almost an hour,

frequently stepping back to look critically at her handiwork.
"Close," she said finally, reaching out to snip off a stray hair.
Then she looked at Althalus. "What do you think?" she asked.

"Very nice."

"You didn't even look!" Her voice went up an octave or so.

"All right, all right. I'll look. Don't get excited."

Gher's shaggy hair was neatly trimmed and well combed now.
Andine had cut his forelock into straight bangs, and the rest of
his hair ended at his collar line in the fashion Althalus had seen
in Osthos. "Really not bad at all, your Highness," he said.
"Where did you learn barbering?"

"I used to trim my father's hair for him," she replied. "Shaggy
hair makes my fingers start to itch."

"At least he doesn't look quite so much like a sheepdog anymore," Bheid noted.

Andine took Gher firmly by the chin and looked him straight
in the face. "You're presentable now, Gher," she told him.
"You're clean and you've got new clothes and a decent haircut.
Don't go out and play in the mud."

"I won't, ma'am," Gher promised. He looked at her almost
bashfully. "You're awfully pretty, ma'am," he blurted, "and I
didn't really mean everything I said to you the other night."

"I knew that," she said with a little toss of her head. Then she
stroked his freshly trimmed hair and kissed his cheek. "Run
along now, Gher," she told him. "Go out and play, but don't muss
your hair or muddy up your clothes."

"Yes, ma'am," he promised.

Andine looked around, absently clicking her scissors. "Anybody else?" she asked.

Emmy read the Knife that afternoon. "Kweron," she advised Althalus. "We still have one more to pick up, and we'd better
hurry."

They broke camp the next morning and rode northwesterly
through the ancient forest of Hule. Andine, peculiarly, had insisted that Gher ride with her on her placid mare.

"I didn't really think they were getting off to a very good start right there at first," Eliar said to Bheid and Althalus. "Did something happen that I didn't know about?"

"Gher said something to her that night that apparently cut a little close to the bone," Bheid explained. "I'm sure that he's the first commoner she's ever actually encountered. She probably didn't have any idea at all about how miserable the lives of most common people really are. Gher's a bit quick with his tongue, and our little Princess was probably surprised that he even knows how to talk at all. The haircut and the ride on her horse are her way of apologizing to him for any past injustices."

"You've got some fairly radical opinions for a member of the priesthood, Bheid," Althalus suggested.

"The goal of mankind should be justice, Althalus. In their hearts, men really want to be just and kindly, but other things get in the way. It's the duty of the priesthood to keep man on the right course."

"Isn't it just a little early in the day for these dense philosophical discussions?" Althalus asked.

"It's never too early—or too late—to learn, my son," Bheid proclaimed sententiously.

"Now, that's *really* offensive."

Bheid gave him a mischievous little smirk. "I'm glad you liked it," he said.

It was early autumn in Kweron, and the leaves of birch and aspen were beginning to turn. Althalus hadn't been into these particular mountains very often, largely because there'd been very few people in Kweron when he'd met Ghend and gone to the House at the End of the World. The villages here were small and crudely built, and the people who lived in them seemed fearful and withdrawn.

"They aren't very friendly here, are they?" Eliar asked as they rode along the muddy single street of another hamlet. "Back home, everybody comes out to gawk at strangers who come through, but these people all go hide."

"The Kwerons are reported to be a superstitious lot," Bheid

told him. "I've heard that they grow violent if somebody's shadow happens to touch them. I think it might have something to do with how close Kweron is to Nekweros. Legends tell us that some fairly awful things come creeping out of Nekweros now and then."

"Has Emmy told you where we're going yet?" Eliar asked Althalus.

"I'm sure she'll get around to it eventually," Althalus replied.

They rode steadily westward for the next week and came down out of the mountains to the jagged shoreline of the long, narrow inlet that marked the western edge of Kweron. The inlet, like the sea at the Edge of the World in Kagwher, was filled with ice.

We're getting closer, Althalus, Emmy's voice murmured late one afternoon. *Let's pull back into the woods a ways. Set up a camp of sorts, and then you, Bheid, and I had better drift into a couple of those villages down by the edge of the inlet.*

What are we looking for, Em?

A witch.

You're not serious!

The local people call her a witch, but she isn't really. We'll want to talk with the priests in these little towns, and Bheid knows how to talk to other priests. Don't throw the word "witch" around in front of the others. It's one of those words that turns people's heads off.

They rode back into the forest, and Althalus spoke briefly with Bheid. Then he told Eliar, Andine, and Gher to wait. "Bheid and I are going to snoop around a bit," he told them. "These Kwerons are sort of peculiar. I'd like to get the lay of the land before we all go trooping into these villages."

Then Althalus and the auburn-haired young priest rode back to the main trail. *I need to talk to him, pet,* Emmy said. *Why don't you take a little nap or something?*

Very funny, Em.

Just step aside, Althalus. You can listen, if you want, but stay out of it. Then she sort of shouldered him out of the way again. "Bheid?" she said.

Bheid looked sharply at Althalus. "Is that you, Emmy?" he asked in a startled tone.

"Yes. Put on your priestly expression and brush up on your astrology just a bit. When we go into these villages, I want you to look up the local priest in each one. Introduce yourself and tell them that you've come here to verify something that you've read in the stars."

"I might need something a little more specific, Emmy," he said.

"Tell them that if you're reading the stars right, there's going to be a fairly big avalanche around here in the near future."

"Will there really be one?"

"I can almost guarantee it, Bheid. I'll have Althalus bring down a whole mountain if we really need one that big. I want you to act very concerned. You've traveled halfway across the world to warn the people. Make a big fuss. Get excited. Throw in the word 'disaster' every time you get the chance. Then, after Althalus has spilled a few acres of boulders down a mountainside, everybody around here's going to believe that you're a holy savior, and they'll all trust you."

Bheid looked a bit puzzled. "Exactly what are we building up to here, Emmy?"

"One of the villages around here has somebody chained up that they believe is a witch, and they're planning a big celebration when they burn her at the stake. You're going to persuade them to turn her over to you instead. Tell them that you're going to take her back to Awes for interrogation."

"That might be a bit tricky, Emmy," he said dubiously.

"Not really. Just tell them that the priesthood in Awes needs to know what Daeva's plans are so that they can take steps to counter those plans. Make dramatic noises about the fate of the world, eternal darkness, hordes of demons rushing up out of Hell, and assorted other foolishness. I'll have Althalus punctuate your speeches with thunderclaps and earthquakes and maybe a few heavenly trumpets."

"Emmy!" he protested.

"Yes? Was there some problem with that?"

"What you're talking about is pure fakery!"

"So what?"

"I'm a priest, Emmy, not a charlatan! We can't just make things up this way."

"Why not?"

"I'm supposed to tell the truth."

"It *is* the truth, Bheid. All you're going to do is simplify things so that simple people can understand."

"Is this woman we're going to rescue really a witch?"

"Of course not. She's one of *us*—or she will be as soon as she reads the Knife. We *have* to have her, Bheid. We'll fail if she's not with us."

"You're forcing me to violate one of my most sacred vows."

"Oh, I'm sorry. We won't do it that way then. We'll just kill everybody in this part of Kweron instead. You'll be standing waist-deep in blood, but your soul will be all nice and clean. Won't that make you proud?"

"Monstrous!"

"It's entirely up to you, Bheid. You can either be a swindler or a butcher. Take your pick." She paused. "Quickly, quickly, Bheid. Choose which it's to be so that we can get on with this. If we're going to kill all these people, we'd better get to killing."

Aren't you coming down on him a little hard, Em? Althalus murmured to her from the back corner of his mind.

He is *going to learn to do as he's told, pet. The words each of you pick up from the Knife apply to* all *of us. You aren't the only one who's seeking, and Andine's not the only one who must obey. We all seek, and we all obey.* Then she spoke aloud to their very troubled young priest. "Well, Bheid, what's it to be? Lies or blood?"

"What choice do I have?" he said helplessly. "I'll lie to them."

"That's nice," she approved.

They rode down into a crude village that had probably been the home of fishermen before the coming of the ice. Althalus climbed down off his horse and approached one of the residents, a thickly bearded man leading a placid ox. "Excuse me," Althalus said to the man, "do you happen to know where I might find the local priest?"

"There's the church right over there. He might not be awake yet, though."

"I'll wake him," Althalus said. "My Reverend Master here needs to talk to him."

"He doesn't like to be roused out of his bed."

"He'll like getting buried alive a lot less."

"Buried alive?" the bearded man exclaimed.

"By the avalanche."

"What avalanche?"

"The one that's going to come rolling down the side of that mountain before long. Thanks for the information, friend. Have yourself a real fine day."

"You weren't supposed to say that, Althalus," Bheid hissed when the worried man with the ox was out of earshot.

"Preparation, Bheid," Althalus explained. "A few awful rumors are always useful in these situations."

The local priest was a tall, untidy man with melancholy eyes, and his name was Terkor. "I haven't studied astrology as deeply as I probably should have, Brother," he confessed to Bheid. "This is a remote place at the outer edge of civilization. I care for the sick, comfort the bereaved, and mediate local squabbles. That doesn't leave me much time for study. What have you seen in the stars?"

"The Dragon has moved into the seventh house," Bheid replied glibly, "and with the moon in the ascendancy, there's a great potential for a natural disaster. I'm sure you recognize the signs."

"I'll have to take your word for it, Brother," Terkor admitted. "That's at a level of complexity far beyond my poor understanding."

"The Dragon is one of the three Earth signs," Bheid explained, "and the moon carries strong hints of instability— earthquakes, avalanches, and the like. Anyway, as soon as I plotted the course of the Bear, I realized that the disaster was going to strike here in Kweron. I had an obligation to come here to warn you, so my servant and I immediately went to horse. Thank the Gods that we reached you in time."

"You're a noble man, Brother. Most men I know wouldn't have taken the trouble."

"It's my duty, Brother. That's why I read the stars—to warn my fellow men when these things are destined to occur. Most of my fellow priests in Awes concentrate on casting horoscopes for other men for pay. I watch the stars for hints of these disasters instead."

"Were you able to pick up any signs about what kind of disaster this is going to be?"

"The position of the moon sort of hints that a mountainside's going to give way."

"An avalanche? Dear Gods!"

"That's what I'm reading, yes. Some of my brothers in Awes believe that a comet's going to strike the Earth, but I don't agree with them. The Rooster's in the wrong house for a comet."

"Comet or avalanche, it doesn't matter much which one's going to fall on us, Brother," Terkor said. "Either one would kill a lot of my neighbors."

Bheid looked around as if to make sure that they were alone. "Has anything particularly unusual happened here lately, Brother Terkor?" he asked. "I'm reading the presence of some great evil in this vicinity. The stars seem to be combining to respond to that evil."

"Nekweros is over on the other side of the inlet, Brother Bheid," Terkor said rather drily. "That's about as evil as anything's likely to get."

"No, Brother Terkor. This is something here on the Kweron side. It may be concealed, though."

"It *might* be that witch Brother Ambho recently exposed in the village of Peteleya a mile or so on down the coast to the south. Brother Ambho's a very enthusiastic witch-hunter."

"A *witch*?" Bheid exclaimed in mock horror.

"Brother Ambho seems to think she's a witch. His evidence isn't really very convincing, just between you and me. Her name's Leitha, and Ambho plans to burn her at the stake at sunrise tomorrow."

"Praise Deiwos!" Bheid exclaimed. "I arrived in time to talk him out of *that* notion."

"I doubt it, Brother Bheid. Ambho's got his heart set on burning her. He's an enthusiast about witch burning."

"I'll change his mind," Bheid said bleakly.

"I question that. Ambho's an absolute fanatic when it comes to witches."

"Are you telling me that word of last year's decision hasn't reached here yet?" Bheid demanded. "There was a solemn conclave of the high clergies of all faiths, and the decision was unanimous. All witches *must* be sent to Awes for interrogation. What's your Exarch *thinking* of? Word of that decision was supposed to be disseminated immediately."

"Kweron's a long way from Awes, Brother Bheid," Terkor replied. "I doubt if our Exarch even knows where it is. Why are we supposed to send our witches to Awes instead of burning them?"

"We *must* have the opportunity to question them, Brother Terkor. Witches are in league with Daeva. If we can persuade them to talk, we'll be able to determine what the demon's plans are. The fate of humanity may hinge on our getting those answers."

"I've never known a witch yet who was willing even to admit that she *was* a witch."

"That's because you don't know how to question them. There are holy objects in Awes. No servant of the evil one can bear to look upon them. The pain the sight of those sacred objects causes witches and others in league with Daeva is so intense that they'll tell us everything they know if we'll just remove the object from their sight. If we can put our hands on just two or three witches, we'll know Daeva's innermost thoughts."

"Evidently our beloved Exarch didn't think we needed to know about that," Terkor said.

"We *must* go to Peteleya and persuade Brother Ambho to turn this accursed woman over to us so that I can take her to Awes for questioning. The fate of mankind may hinge on it."

"I'll get my horse," Terkor said, and he quickly went out.

"You're very smooth, Bheid," Althalus said admiringly.

"I *hated* that," Bheid said. "Terkor's a good man."

"Yes, he is," Althalus agreed. "You didn't really deceive him that much, though, Bheid. The fate of man might very *well* depend on what we're doing. He's doing the right thing for the wrong reasons, but it's still the right thing."

"You're going to have to be *very* eloquent to persuade Ambho to turn Leitha the witch over to you, Brother Bheid," Terkor said as they rode south. "He has a reputation for building bonfires under people without too much in the way of proof that they're really witches. All he really needs are a couple of accusations, and he'll start building fires. If I were you, I'd make some issue of what you've read in the stars. If I'm following what you told me, there's some connection between this disaster and the witch of Peteleya."

"You might be right about that, Terkor," Bheid agreed. "The stars have been known to do that on occasion. Their messages are warnings, and very often they conceal solutions in their warnings." He reached inside his tunic and drew out his rolled-up map of the stars. "Let me look at this again," he said.

"If it doesn't quite fit, *make* it fit," Althalus muttered softly.

"Right," Bheid whispered his agreement. "Warn Emmy that I might need a few rocks rolling down one of these mountains to get my point across."

The priest of Peteleya was a lean, cadaverous-looking man with a perpetually outraged expression on his face. His reputation had become widespread in western Kweron as the result of his witch-burning activities, and the idea of turning his captive over to Bheid didn't exactly fit into his notion of the way things ought to be done. "The conclave of Awes has no authority over me, Bheid," he declared almost belligerently.

"Perhaps not, Ambho," Bheid replied coldly, "but the stars *do*. Ignore their warning at your own peril. Under what sign were you born?"

"The sign of the Boar," Ambho replied a bit nervously.

"I thought as much. The stars have warned us about the men of the Boar."

"You have the nerve to insult my sign?" Ambho's eyes bulged.

"You Boars are stubborn," Bheid said flatly. "Sometimes the stars have to fall down around your ears to get your attention." Then he threw up his hands. "I have done as the stars commanded," he declared. "I've warned you. If you choose not to listen, what happens to you isn't on *my* head."

The word you want is "twei," *pet,* Emmy murmured to Althalus. *Think of a deep, booming sound when you say it. Be a little careful with that one, though.*

Althalus turned to look at the mountain that loomed over the village of Peteleya. *"Twei,"* he commanded softly.

The thunder came echoing up from miles beneath the surface of the earth. The sound was so deeply pitched that it seemed almost that it was felt, rather than heard. It subsided slowly, fading off toward the northwest.

"What was that?" Ambho exclaimed.

"I rather think it was your final warning, man of the Boar," Bheid replied. "I'd suggest that you make your peace with God. I don't imagine that any of us will see the sun go down this evening if you refuse to turn your witch over to me."

"That was just a coincidence," Ambho scoffed.

"There's no such thing as coincidence, my Brother. Everything that happens, happens by design. Choose, Ambho, choose, and know that the life or death of every living soul in Peteleya hangs on your choice."

Althalus nudged the earth again, a bit more firmly this time.

The cracking that came from beneath their feet was much like the sound that frozen trees in the far north make when the sundering frost explodes them, and the very earth shuddered.

Some fairly large rocks came bouncing down the steep mountainside.

"The next one should probably do it," Althalus said calmly, squinting up at the mountain. "Farewell, Master Bheid. It's been a pleasure serving you. If we're lucky, the rock slide will kill us all instantly. I *hate* the notion of being buried alive, don't you?"

"Take her!" Ambho almost screamed. "Take the witch to Awes, but make it stop!"

"Somehow I almost *knew* he was going to say that," Althalus said to nobody in particular.

CHAPTER FIFTEEN

Leitha the witch had flaxen hair that seemed filled with an inner light, and her skin was very pale, almost like the fine marble so prized by sculptors. She was tall and slender, and her eyes were of the deepest blue, large and luminous and very wise. She was chained to a stone pillar in the center of Peteleya, a pillar much blackened by previous fires.

Her expression as they came to release her seemed unconcerned, but her eyes held a great injury.

"This is but a reprieve, witch," Ambho said in his harsh voice as he roughly unchained her. "The priests of the holy city of Awes will question you most severely, and they will force you to answer their questions about your foul master. Then you will burn."

"I have no master, Ambho," she replied in an untroubled voice. "I am not as you are. I have seen your soul, priest, and it is vile. What burns there is your doing, and not mine—nor the doing of all the others you have consigned to the flames. Your lust is the only evil here, and you cannot drive it away by burning the objects of your lust as you have sought to do. Your vow is violated by your every thought, and the flames in which you shall burn are far hotter than the flames you have built for us. Go from this place and cleanse your soul."

Ambho stared at her, his haggard face filled with sudden guilt and self-loathing. And then he turned and fled.

Althalus paid an outrageous price for a horse for Leitha, and then he and Bheid bade the priest Terkor farewell and rode back up into the wooded hills. When they were out of sight of the village, Althalus reined in. "Let's get rid of those chains right now," he said, dismounting and helping Leitha down from her horse. He examined the crude lock on the chain that bound her hands together. Then he unsnapped it, removed the girl's chains, and in a fit of sudden rage hurled them back into the bushes as hard as he could.

"Thank you, Althalus," she said quietly.

"You know my name?" He was a bit surprised.

"I do now."

Oh, dear, Emmy murmured.

"What?" he asked, baffled.

"Dweia knows that I can hear your thoughts, Althalus," Leitha said with a faint smile. "I think it bothers her."

"You can do *that*?" Bheid exclaimed.

"Yes. It's always puzzled me that others can't."

"So *that* was why Ambho wanted to burn you at the stake."

"Not really. Ambho had taken a vow of chastity, and he kept having thoughts that violated that vow. He chooses to blame those who unwittingly stir those thoughts rather than accept the blame for them himself. Many people do that, I've noticed."

"You have a great gift, Leitha."

"I suppose so, if you want to look at it that way. I'd be very happy to give it to you, if I could. The silence must be lovely." She looked directly at Emmy then. "There's no real point in trying to hide it, Dweia," she said. "They'll all know sooner or later. That was the mistake I made in Peteleya. I tried to hide this so-called gift, and look what it almost got me."

Get out of the way, Althalus, Emmy ordered.

"I can hear you without his voice, Dweia," Leitha said. "I don't think I really want to join you."

I don't think you have much choice, Leitha, Althalus heard Emmy reply.

Leitha sighed then. "Perhaps not," she said in a melancholy tone.

"What's happening?" Bheid asked Althalus in a baffled voice.

"The ladies are talking," Althalus explained. He tapped his forehead with one finger. "In here," he added. "It's a little crowded in there right now." He looked around. "Let's move along," he said. "I'd like to get back to the others before dark."

Twilight was settling down over the foothills of western Kweron when they rejoined Eliar, Andine, and Gher at the camp back in the trees.

"Is she the one?" Gher asked Althalus.

"Emmy seems to think so," Althalus replied.

"She's awfully pretty, isn't she?"

"Yes, she is. That almost got her burned alive. The priest in her village had a habit of burning pretty girls at the stake. Pretty girls gave him naughty thoughts, and he seemed to believe that using them for firewood was the best way to get rid of those thoughts."

"Did you kill him?" Gher demanded fiercely.

"I gave it some thought, but Emmy talked me out of it. I love Emmy dearly, but she can get so unreasonable sometimes. She doesn't approve of killing anything you don't plan to eat."

"If you want me to, I'll talk with Eliar. Then you could sort of distract Emmy, and Eliar and I could sneak back to that village and kill the priest."

"She'd find out," Althalus said rather sadly. "Then she'd yell at us for at least a week."

I heard that, Althalus. Emmy's voice was accusatory.

I'm not at all surprised, Em. If you'd keep your nose out of things that don't concern you, you wouldn't hear so much that offends you.

Do you think you could shorten Gher's leash just a bit? He's an absolute savage.

I rather like him. Do we want to have Leitha read the Knife this evening?

Let's wait until morning. I think I'd better work on her just a bit. She really doesn't want any part of what we're doing.

Did any of us?

Behave yourself, pet.

Yes, dear.

The forest was dark and tangled, and the sky was steely grey. Althalus had lost his way, though he could not remember exactly where he'd been going before he'd entered this gloomy wood. His mind seemed to wander, and each time he tried to bring it back into focus, the hollow sound of wailing blotted out his thoughts, leaving him to grope mindlessly through the tangled vines and brush. It seemed that there was no end to this forbidding forest, but with a kind of helpless resignation he grimly pushed on.

His mind became suddenly alert, and he struggled up through thought and memory as tangled as the dark wood itself even as the hollow wail pulled him back into the depths of the world Ghend had woven about him like the web of some dark spider.

"She comes," the trees sang. "She comes," the vines replied. "She comes!" the hollow sky shrieked. "Fall down before her in abject surrender!"

And Ghend walked once more through the wood and across the plain as the day wore on back to sunrise. "And how shall *you* greet her, my thief?" Ghend demanded of Althalus as his eyes took fire.

"I shall defy her," the thief replied, "even as I defy you, and even as I defy your master."

"Your puny defiance is of no moment, Althalus," Ghend of the burning eyes declared in tones of deepest contempt. "For Gelta, Queen of the Night, shall overcome you, and I, servant of Darkness, shall bear you down into the pit, and Daeva, master of all, shall claim your soul."

And Althalus laughed. "Your illusion has no truth, Ghend, but cling to it if you must. Hold your illusion tightly to your breast, and be as wary as a man can be. But in spite of all your care, I shall filch your illusion from out of your arms and turn the sun once more into its proper course. Time will not return to the place it has left behind. Your illusions are folly, and your curses hollow. I cast my defiance into the teeth of the Queen of the Night, and I cast my defiance into your teeth, servant of Darkness, and even more I cast my defiance into the teeth of him who is *your* master, but never mine."

And Ghend screamed.

And Althalus woke up.

Are you mad? Emmy almost shrieked at him, her voice reverberating inside his head.

That's a little hard for me to know, Em, he replied calmly. *Crazy people don't know that they're crazy, do they? I think we talked about that back in the House a few times. I just thought it might be sort of interesting to turn the tables on Ghend. He's trying to play with reality, but I'm a master at that. I know all sorts of ways to change the rules of any game he can devise.*

You shouldn't be so surprised, Dweia, Leitha's soft voice murmured. *Isn't this why you hired him in the first place?*

You're not supposed to be in here, Leitha! Emmy said sharply.

Just curious, Dweia, Leitha replied. *You can't really keep me out, you know.*

"Do you ladies suppose you could go someplace else to discuss this?" Althalus asked. "I'd like to get some sleep, and you're making a great deal of noise in there."

The sun was coming up when they awoke again, and Althalus took Eliar and Bheid out into the woods to make a quick search of the surrounding area. "This isn't exactly friendly territory, gentlemen," he cautioned them. "The Kwerons themselves don't pose much of a threat, but we're a little too close to Nekweros for my comfort." He'd decided to keep Ghend's visit during the night to himself.

When they returned to camp, they found Andine and Leitha deep in some kind of discussion and Gher sitting nearby with a bored look on his face. The boy's face brightened when he saw them. "Did you find anything?" he asked hopefully.

"We saw a deer," Eliar replied. "No people, though."

"Let's feed the horses, gentlemen," Althalus suggested. "Then I'll see about some breakfast."

"I was starting to think you'd forgotten," Eliar said. "I was just about to remind you."

"What are the ladies talking about, Gher?" Bheid asked as they walked over to where the horses were picketed.

"Clothes, mostly," Gher replied. "Before that, they were talking about hair. They seem to be getting along fairly well. Of course, Emmy's lying in Andine's lap, so she might be keeping them from getting into any arguments."

"Emmy *is* a girl cat, Gher," Eliar reminded him. "She might be interested in clothes and hair, too."

After they'd tended to the horses, they rejoined the ladies, and Althalus made breakfast for them.

"Isn't that the strangest thing you ever saw?" Eliar said to Leitha.

"Very peculiar," she agreed, watching with a certain surprise as Eliar fell on his breakfast enthusiastically.

"He's a growing boy," Bheid explained to her.

After Eliar's third helping of breakfast, Emmy spoke briefly to Althalus. *Let's show Leitha the Knife, pet,* she suggested. *I'm almost certain I know where we're supposed to go next, but let's play by the rules.*

All right, dear, he replied. He looked at Leitha. "We've got a little formality we should get out of the way, Leitha," he told her. "You're supposed to read the Knife along about now."

"It won't really hurt, Leitha," Andine told her new friend. "It's a little surprising, that's all. It made me a little dizzy, but it didn't seem to bother Gher at all. Do you know how to read?"

"Yes," Leitha replied. "The script I read isn't quite the same as yours, but I don't think that's going to make any difference."

Eliar wiped his mouth on his sleeve and took out the Knife.

"I'm not threatening you or anything, Leitha," he assured her. "There's something written on the blade that you're supposed to read."

"Yes," she said. "Show it to me."

Eliar held the Knife out to her in his left hand.

"You've got it upside down," she told him.

"Oh," he replied, switching hands. "Sorry. What does it say to you?"

" 'Listen,' " she replied quite simply.

The song of the Knife seemed somehow richer this time, and even more profound. Eliar looked just a bit startled.

Then Leitha reached out and laid her hand on his wrist. "Don't take it away just yet," she said, still looking intently at the shining blade.

Then she began to tremble, and she swayed as if about to fall.

Bheid quickly caught her.

"Don't do that, Leitha," Emmy scolded, usurping Althalus' voice.

"I'm sorry, Dweia," Leitha replied in a shaken voice. "I had to *know*. There's so *much* there."

"Too much to take in all at once, dear," Emmy replied. "I was right, Althalus. It's time for us to go back home."

"That's a long way, Em," he said dubiously, "and winter's not very far off."

"I have it on the very best authority that we'll make it, pet."

"I made it almost too easy for Ambho back in Peteleya," Leitha was telling Andine as they rode up into the mountains. "I amused the other village girls by telling their fortunes. I knew what they were thinking and what they really wanted, so I could go a little further than promising them all rich husbands, fine houses, and whole platoons of children. Ambho twisted that around to convince the village elders that I was a witch."

"What's it like?" Andine asked curiously. "Hearing the thoughts of others, I mean?"

"Disturbing," Leitha replied. "What people say and what they're thinking don't always exactly match. We're much closer to being animals than most of us would care to admit." She looked around to make sure that Eliar was ahead and well out of earshot. "Your feelings about *him* are very confused, aren't they, Andine? One side of your thought wants to slaughter him because he killed your father, but another side finds him physically very attractive."

"I do *not*!" Andine protested, blushing furiously.

"Yes you do, Andine." Leitha smiled. "It's not your fault, you know. This is what I was talking about when I told you that we're all part animal. Maybe someday we should talk it over with Dweia. She's the one who arranges those things—or so I understand." Leitha looked over at Emmy, who was watching and listening with a great deal of interest from her usual place in Althalus' hood. "Did you want to join in, Dweia?" she asked with artful innocence.

Never mind, Emmy replied shortly.

"Why do you use that other name when you talk to Emmy?" Andine asked curiously.

"It's who she really is, Andine," Leitha said, shrugging, "and she's not really a cat. In her own reality, she looks much as we do—except that she's much more beautiful."

"She cheats."

"Of course she does," Leitha replied. "Don't we all? Don't we put soot on our eyelashes to make them look longer? Don't we pinch our cheeks to make them look rosier? Dweia's a girl, the same as you and I are. She's a much better cheat than we are, though."

That will do, Leitha, Emmy said quite firmly.

"Well, aren't you?" Leitha's blue eyes went innocently wide.

I said that will do!

"Yes, ma'am." Then Leitha laughed.

I don't want any clever remarks from you either, Althalus.

"I didn't say anything, Em."

Well, don't.

They crossed the mountains of Kweron and rode down into Hule without incident. Despite Emmy's reassurances, Althalus pushed their horses as much as he dared. The idea of being caught by an early snowstorm in northern Kagwher didn't appeal to him very much. Better, he felt, to arrive a week or so early than half a year late.

They avoided the few settlements in Hule and made good time. Despite his objections to "civilization," Althalus was forced to admit that roads *did* make travel somewhat easier and much faster.

It was late autumn by the time they reached the foothills of Kagwher, and they'd been together as a group for more than a month now. They'd all grown accustomed to Andine's vocal extremes and to Eliar's overwhelming interest in food. Althalus and Bheid had smoothed over some of Gher's rough edges, and on several occasions they'd found Leitha's special ability quite useful, particularly when they wanted to avoid contact with local inhabitants. Leitha's melancholy was no longer quite so pronounced, and she and the sometimes explosive Andine had grown very attached to each other.

They turned toward the northeast at the indistinct frontier between Hule and Kagwher, and they more or less followed the same route Althalus had taken some twenty-five centuries earlier on his journey to the House at the End of the World.

"Things were a lot different then," he reminisced to Bheid one afternoon when they were nearing the precipice he still thought of as "the Edge of the World."

"It *was* quite a while back, Althalus," Bheid noted.

"Why, I *do* believe you're right," Althalus replied in mock astonishment.

"All right," Bheid said, laughing. "I was being obvious, wasn't I? Sometimes I get this overpowering urge to preach little homilies."

"When we get to the House, the Book may cure you of that." Then Althalus remembered something. "Are you still examining the stars every night, Bheid?" he asked, trying to make the question sound casual.

"It's a habit, I guess. I still can't quite shake off the notion that the stars control our destinies."

Althalus shrugged. "It's a clean, inexpensive hobby, I suppose, so watch the sky all you want. You might start paying particular attention to the north. I think the northern sky may have a surprise for you before too much longer."

"Oh, I'm very familiar with that part of the sky, Althalus. I'm sure there's not much up there that'll surprise me."

"We'll see." Althalus squinted off to the southwest. "We'd better start looking for a place to camp," he said. "Sunset's not too far off.

They reached the Edge of the World about two days later.

"How could you have possibly believed that the world came to an end here?" Andine asked Althalus. "There are all those white mountains out there."

"They weren't there then, your Highness," Althalus explained.

"I've asked you not to call me that," she told him.

"Just practicing my good manners, Andine," he told her.

"Well, don't practice on me. You don't have to keep reminding me what a silly girl I used to be."

They made their camp by the dead tree at the Edge of the World, and Althalus called up fish for supper.

"Fish?" Gher objected. "Again?"

"We sort of have to keep Emmy happy, Gher," Eliar explained. "Fish is supposed to be good for you, anyway."

Why haven't you told them, pet? Emmy asked Althalus.

I don't want to spoil the surprise, kitten, he replied innocently.

You're being childish.

He shrugged. *Advancing age, no doubt. Please don't interfere. I want to see their faces when it happens.*

When are you ever going to grow up, Althalus?

Never, I hope.

"Eliar," Althalus said after supper, "why don't you and Gher gather up a little more firewood? We'll need some in the morning."

"Right," the young Arum agreed, rising to his feet. "Come along, Gher."

The two of them went back across the narrow strip of grass to a grove of stunted trees to pick up limbs. After a little while Gher cried out sharply. "Althalus!" The boy's voice was shrill. "The sky's on fire!"

"My, my," Althalus replied blandly. "Imagine that."

"That was cruel, Althalus," Leitha scolded him. "Why didn't you tell them about the northern lights?"

"I thought they might enjoy the fire more if they discovered it for themselves," he replied.

They all went to look, of course. The fire of God was particularly bright that night, shimmering and pulsating in great undulating waves in the northern sky.

"What *is* that?" Andine demanded, her voice frightened.

"It's called by many names," Leitha replied, "and people have many explanations for it. Some of the explanations are very far-fetched, and religion always seems to play some part in them."

Bheid was gaping at the seething light to the north.

"Which astrological house would you say that's in, Bheid?" Althalus asked slyly.

"I . . . I couldn't say." Bheid faltered. "It keeps moving."

"Do you suppose it might be a portent of some kind?"

"He's teasing you, Bheid," Leitha told the young priest. "Nobody in northern Kweron even pays any attention to those lights anymore."

"They stretch all the way across the north?" Bheid's voice was trembling.

"Evidently so. I didn't know you could see them here as well as in Kweron."

"Does that light burn every night?"

"You can't see it so much when its cloudy, and it's much more visible at certain seasons."

"You knew this was going to happen, didn't you, Althalus?" Bheid accused.

"I was fairly sure we'd notice it eventually," Althalus replied. "I found it moderately interesting the first time I saw it." Then he remembered something he hadn't thought of for a very long time. "I was on my way to the House at the End of the World to steal the Book the first time I saw it. I was fairly superstitious at the time, and I was positive that the fire in the sky was God's way of warning me away. Then one night I went over to the Edge of the World and looked out. The moon was up, and there were clouds down below the edge. I lay down in the grass and watched the moonlight and God's fire playing along the top of those clouds. It was probably the most beautiful thing I'd ever seen. Then that night I had a dream about a very beautiful lady who told me that if I went with her she'd care for me forever. I have my suspicions about the source of that dream." He sent a quick, sly glance back over his shoulder at Emmy.

Would I do that, pet? she asked with exaggerated innocence. *Little old me?*

Leitha laughed.

"How much farther is it, Althalus?" Eliar asked on a chill, cloudy afternoon a few days later. "I'm starting to smell snow in the air."

"We're fairly close now," Althalus replied, squinting off to the south. "These mountains are starting to look very familiar."

"What's that?" Andine exclaimed as a familiar, haunted, wailing sound began to faintly echo from the nearby peaks.

"Let's close up here," Althalus commanded. "That's Ghend out there. We don't want to be spread out just now."

"Ghend? Himself?" Bheid asked, his voice alarmed.

"Maybe, maybe not. Any time you hear that screaming, though, you'll know that Ghend or one of his underlings isn't very far away."

"No," Leitha said, "not far at all. She's very impressive, but her horse seems to have wandered."

Althalus looked sharply at the pale girl from Kweron.

"She's out there," Leitha said calmly, pointing toward the north.

The clouds had built up beyond the Edge of the World—dirty grey clouds that seethed and boiled in the vagrant air currents rising off the ice below, and a dark figure sat astride a black horse on a roiling pinnacle of cloud.

The figure was quite obviously a woman. Her gleaming, tight-fitting breastplate made that abundantly clear. Her black hair streamed in the wind and she held an archaic-looking spear. There was a large sword with a wide, curved blade at her belt. Her features were angular and very cold. "I am Gelta, Queen of the Night," she declaimed in a hollow voice.

"You are the *image* of Gelta," Leitha corrected, "and quite insubstantial. Go back to Ghend and tell him that he should carry his own messages."

"Have a care, mind leech," the dark figure spat. "Speak not so to me, or I shall give you cause to regret your words."

"We go to the House at the End of the World," Leitha replied quite calmly. "If you wish to discuss this further, visit us there— if you dare."

Try "dhreu," rather sharply, pet, Emmy suggested. *It might not bother Gelta, but her horse may not care for it all that much.*

Althalus chuckled. Then he looked at the heavily armed Queen of the Night. "Better hold on," he called to her. Then he snapped, *"Dhreu!"*

Her horse screamed as they fell down through the clouds and vanished.

Well, that's the last of them, Emmy said complacently. *I was sort of wondering when she was going to show up.*

"You knew we'd see her?" Leitha asked.

Of course. Symmetry, Leitha. We've encountered all the others along the way. Ghend would never have left Gelta out.

"Is it just coincidence that there are as many of them as there are of us?" Althalus asked.

Of course not. Emmy started to settle back in.

"We'll be meeting them all again, won't we, Dweia?" Leitha asked.

Naturally, Emmy said. *That's what this has all been about, dear Leitha.*

"Will you be able to talk out loud again when we get back to the House, Em?" Althalus asked.

Yes. Why?

"Just curious. It'll be sort of nice not to have you ladies using my head for a meeting hall."

Eliar was looking at Leitha with an awed sort of expression. "I'm very glad you're on our side, ma'am," he said. "You don't back away from anybody at all, do you?"

"Not often, no."

"Let's move along," Althalus said. "There won't be any more of Ghend's surprises once we go inside the House."

They reached the House at the tag end of a blustery morning when tattered clouds had been spitting stinging pellets of snow at them since daybreak.

"It's enormous!" Bheid exclaimed, staring at the vast granite structure.

"Just a little place Emmy and I like to think of as home," Althalus replied. "Let's get in out of this wind."

They crossed the drawbridge, the hooves of their horses clattering on the thick, heavy planks.

"Why did you leave the drawbridge down when you came out?" Eliar asked Althalus. "That's an open invitation to anybody who happens by."

"Not really," Althalus disagreed. "The only people who can see the House are the people who are *supposed* to see it."

"It's right out in the open, Althalus."

"Not to the people who aren't supposed to see it, it isn't." Althalus led them into the courtyard and swung down from his horse.

"You know where the stables are, don't you, Althalus?" Emmy asked, speaking aloud in her own voice.

"She *talks*!" Andine exclaimed.

"Oh, yes," Althalus chuckled. "I'm sure that before too long you'll wish she didn't."

"Take care of the horses, Althalus," Emmy said very firmly. "I'll take the ladies inside out of the weather." She climbed out of the hood of his cloak and dropped silently to the flagstones. "There's fresh hay in the stable. Unsaddle the horses and feed them. Then come inside. We'll be in the tower."

"Yes, dear," he replied.

Emmy, her tail moving sinuously, led Andine and Leitha inside while Althalus and the others took the horses across the courtyard.

"That's going to take a bit of getting used to," Bheid observed.

"Oh, yes," Althalus agreed, unsaddling his horse. "When I first came here, I was positive that the House had driven me insane. Sometimes I'm still not completely certain that all my wheels are running in the same direction."

The House had a familiar smell to it when Althalus led Bheid, Eliar, and Gher inside and down the corridor to the stairs that went up to the room at the top of the tower.

"It's really quite warm, isn't it?" Bheid said, unfastening the front of his cloak. "These halls aren't the least bit drafty."

"Whoever built it did a very good job," Eliar agreed.

"I'm sure he'll be glad you approve," Althalus noted.

"Who *did* build it, Althalus?"

"The one who lived here, most likely. He likes to do things himself—or so his Book says."

They reached the door at the top of the stairs, and Althalus rapped. "May we come in?" he called.

The door opened—by itself, evidently.

"What was that all about?" Emmy asked.

"Eliar's been giving me lessons in manners."

Emmy, Andine, and Leitha were seated on the bison-robe-covered bed, and the dome overhead was glowing faintly.

"It's good to be back home," Althalus said, removing his cloak.

"Don't get all settled in, pet," Emmy told him. "I've made some other arrangements."

"What's wrong with staying right here, the way we used to?"

"Have you happened to notice that there are two different kinds of people in our little group, pet? We have these girl people here with me, and you have those boy people over there with you."

"All right," he said.

"Were you aware of the differences between boy people and girl people?"

"I said, 'all right,' Em!"

"In most places it isn't considered nice for girl people and boy people to sleep together until after certain formalities have been attended to. Did you know that, pet?"

"Does she do that a lot?" Gher asked.

"All the time," Althalus said sourly.

"Go back downstairs, Althalus," Emmy said in a pleasant tone. "There's a large room on the right-hand side. That's where the boy people are going to sleep. Do *not* try to open the door on the left-hand side of the stairs where the girl people and I are going to sleep, because if you do, I'll claw off the front of your head."

The room to the right of the stairs was large and well furnished. Althalus had peeked into that room once when he'd first come to the House centuries before, and it'd been totally empty. Now that Emmy could use the Book herself rather than going through him, she'd evidently given her creativity full rein. The floor of the room was carpeted, there were drapes at the windows, and there was a fair amount of heavy, ornate furniture. The beds were large, with blankets and pillows, and there was a massive table in the center of the room with four large chairs. There was a cheery fire in the large fireplace, and as Althalus had more or less expected, a large bathtub in one corner.

"I hadn't realized that Emmy could be quite so . . ." Bheid groped for a word.

"Snippy, you mean?" Althalus supplied. "Oh, yes, Emmy comes from the capital city of snip. What would you gentlemen like for supper?"

"Anything but fish," Gher said quickly.

"I'd sort of like beef, myself," Eliar suggested, "lots and lots of beef."

* * *

Althalus could not seem to get to sleep. He'd returned to the House, but without Emmy curled up beside him purring softly, he couldn't drift off.

He finally gave up, threw off his blanket, and went out into the corridor. The House seemed the same, but without Emmy it was empty for him. He sourly went up the stairs to the familiar room at the top.

He stood at the north window looking out at the ice with a sour discontent rankling at him.

Then he heard a soft sound coming from behind him, and everything was all right again. The sound of Emmy's purring welcomed him home.

"Come," he heard her say. "Come with me, pet, and I will care for you."

And he turned, filled with more than astonishment.

The girl from his ancient dream sat on the bison-robed bed beyond the table where the Book of Deiwos lay, and her face and form were more beautiful than he remembered.

"Come to me, my beloved Althalus," she purred. "I will care for you."

Part Three

DWEIA

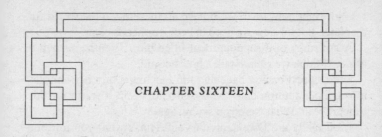

CHAPTER SIXTEEN

Her face was still the face that had sung in his dreams for two thousand and more years: a face of ancient, serene perfection. She rose, and her green eyes penetrated his soul even as her rounded arms reached out to possessively clasp him in a fierce embrace.

His senses reeled in that embrace, and he was lost in her kiss.

How long they remained in each other's arms he would never know, and then as he held her closely to him he heard a very familiar sound, and it filled him with a kind of wonder. The Goddess who had permeated his dreams had always been with him here in the House, and their lives were inseparably interwoven. So much that had been strange before was now clear to him. "You're doing that to let me know that we've always been together here, aren't you?" he said to her.

"What on earth are you talking about, Althalus?"

"You're purring, Emmy."

"I most certainly am *not*!" she exclaimed, and the purring stopped.

Althalus smiled inwardly and stored that away. Their game obviously wasn't over yet. "Maybe it was only my imagination," he said. Then he once more kissed her soft, perfect mouth, and she began to purr again.

"Talk to me, Althalus," she told him, pulling back.

"What?"

"Things are getting just a little intense."

"I thought that was what you had in mind."

231

"Not right now, love. We'll have all the time in the world for that later, but for now we need to keep our heads clear."

A hot surge of disappointment filled him. Then he pushed it aside. "I think we *should* talk a bit," he said.

She stepped back a pace and ran her fingers up her temples through her autumn hair. "My," she said, "isn't it warm for this time of year? What were you saying again?"

"You really are Dweia, aren't you? That's what you told me when we were passing through Maghu, anyway."

"And you even remembered. Amazing."

"Be nice," he said almost from force of habit. "What I'm getting at here is whether or not the others are going to see you in the same way that I do. Or will you be Dweia for me and Emmy for them?"

"That might be just a little difficult, Althalus. I could probably *do* it, but what'd be the point?"

"Your reality's just a bit overwhelming, you know. The others all have things they need to do here, and they'll probably have to concentrate. Won't a divine distraction sort of get in their way?"

She laughed a silvery little laugh and impulsively threw her arms about him. "How sweet!" she said, kissing him again. "You want to keep me all to yourself, don't you?"

"Well," he said sheepishly, "that might have been part of it, I guess, but I still think we ought to talk it over. It's very hard to concentrate when you're around, Dweia."

"Why, thank you, kind sir," she said with a little mock curtsey.

"Will you please be serious? I think there might be a problem here that we'd better look at. Andine and Leitha are both probably going to turn bright green when they see you, and trying to talk to Eliar or Bheid while you're around is going to be almost like shouting down a well. Just the sight of you is very likely to blot out everybody's mind."

"I'm not doing it on purpose, love. My brothers and I exist on a different level of reality, and that always seems to come blazing through, even when we try to hide it. If you'll think back a bit, you'll probably remember that flashes of it came through even when I was Emmy the cat. I'm affectionate by nature, and it always seems to show."

"I still think it might be better if you put your fur back on, Em. The children have to be able to think while we're here, and they won't be able to do that in the presence of a perpetual sunrise."

"That's part of what we have to do here, Althalus. The others have to get used to having me around. It's far better to turn their heads off *here* than it'd be to turn them off in the middle of a crisis out there in the real world."

"Maybe." Althalus was still very dubious about the whole notion. "There's another thing, too," he said. "Aren't you going to be rather conspicuous when we go back outside the House? I think you're going to attract a lot of attention out there."

She shrugged. "Back to Emmy the cat, then."

"Is that your own idea, or has your brother forbidden you to go outside in your real form?"

"Forbidden?" Her tone was flat, even unfriendly.

"Well, he *is* God, after all."

"So am I, Althalus, and *nobody* tells me what I can or can't do. Emmy's *my* idea, not my brother's. I use her when I want to sneak. You should know all about sneaking. It's part of your trade, and it's also part of mine. Neither one of my brothers needs to know what I'm doing, and sneaking *keeps* them from knowing." She laughed a sly little laugh. "Every now and then, I sneak up on Deiwos, and he doesn't even know that I've been there."

"You and Deiwos are very close, aren't you?"

"Not really. We have different interests, so we don't have very much to talk about. We say hello to each other when we pass, and that's about as far as it goes."

"Being a God sounds very lonely."

"It isn't. We have our thoughts for company." She gave him a smoldering sort of look. "And now I have you as well as my thoughts, don't I?"

"Oh, yes. And you'll never get rid of me." Then a thought came to him. "If you and your brothers are so totally complete, why's Daeva trying to change everything? What does he expect to get out of it?"

"It goes back a long, long way, Althalus," she replied pensively. "Daeva destroys—but only the things Deiwos and I permit him to destroy. That immediately reduces him. He's the rag man of the universe, gathering up our castoffs. In a certain sense, he's the God of Nothingness, and that leaves him empty and alone in the dark. Deiwos joys in creation, and I joy in mothering everything he makes. There's not much joy in emptiness, though, so when Daeva's loneliness became more than he could bear, he sought out Ghend to find companions to fill the emptiness. I think Ghend was the wrong choice for my brother."

"You pity him, don't you, Dweia?"

"A little, yes. I'm notorious for being soft-hearted."

Althalus glanced at the east window and saw that the morning star had risen. "It's almost time to wake the children," he said. Then he scratched his chin. "You're probably right about the sleeping arrangements," he agreed, "but wouldn't a sort of neutral dining room give them a place to gather together? When you start putting high walls between boy people and girl people, they spend most of their time trying to think of ways to climb those walls. If we let them mingle at mealtimes and up here in this room, they might even pay attention to you when you're trying to teach them. A little closely supervised mingling might help to keep certain urges under control. Is this making any sense at all?"

"Very good sense, Althalus; sometimes you surprise me. Why don't you go ahead and set up a dining room near the places where we sleep. I'll wait up here for you. That way, you'll be able to prepare them a little for the new Emmy."

"That's probably a good idea, too."

"Oh, as long as the subject of mealtime's come up, there's one other thing."

"What's that?"

"When I sit down at your table, I don't want to see fish."

"I thought you loved fish."

"Emmy's the one who loves fish, Althalus. I can't stand the sight of it, myself."

Althalus "made" some fairly luxurious furniture for their dining room. It cost him no more effort than a trestle-based table and rude benches, and he rather thought that pleasant surroundings might encourage "the children" to linger and socialize. He felt that if they were close-knit when they went back across the drawbridge, things might go more smoothly. Then, to increase their fondness for the place, he made a breakfast fit for a King.

He woke them by knocking on their doors and then waited in the hall outside the dining room like an expectant innkeeper. "Hurry right along," he told them as they emerged from their sleeping quarters. "Emmy's waiting for us upstairs, and you all know how cranky she gets when we're late."

"Isn't she going to eat with us anymore?" Eliar asked.

"Not this time," Althalus replied. "She wanted to give me a chance to warn all of you that she's not Emmy the cat anymore."

"She's not?" Eliar sounded injured. "I *like* Emmy!"

"Wait until you see her now."

"She hasn't taken her *true* form, has she?" Leitha gasped.

"Oh, yes," Althalus replied fervently. "She's Dweia now, and I think she's going to take some getting used to." Then he felt a faint touch brush his mind.

"Oh, dear," Leitha said, biting her lip.

"What's wrong?" Andine asked.

"Is that what she *really* looks like?" Leitha demanded of Althalus.

"It's probably fairly close. I have a very good eye for details."

"Oh, dear," Leitha said again.

"What is it, Leitha?" Andine looked puzzled.

"We're crows now, Andine."

"She can't be *that* beautiful, can she?"

"She's even worse," Leitha mourned.

"Couldn't we talk about this while we're eating?" Eliar demanded, hungrily eying the groaning table.

"Eliar's right," Althalus told them. "Let's eat breakfast before it gets cold. Then we'll all go upstairs and I'll introduce you to Dweia."

"I don't think I'm really very hungry." Leitha sighed.

After breakfast, they all nervously followed Althalus up the stairs to the circular room at the top of the tower.

Dweia was standing at the marble table with her hand lying almost absently on the Book. She wore a white gown of an ancient style that left her arms bare to the shoulders, and her sunset hair streamed down her back. Her perfect face was a mystery. "Good morning, children," she greeted them.

There was a sort of stunned, awkward silence as they all gaped at her.

"Are you *really* our Emmy?" Gher asked finally.

"Yes, Gher," she replied gently. "I hid behind Emmy for a while, but that isn't necessary anymore, so I've stopped hiding." She gave Althalus a sly, sidelong glance. "Our glorious leader here was a bit concerned about the changeover. He was positive that my unspeakable perfection would reduce you all to gibbering lunacy." She paused, cocking her head as if listening intently. "How odd," she said. "I don't seem to hear a single gibber. Could it be that Althalus was wrong? Is it possible that he underestimated your comprehension?"

"All right," Althalus conceded sourly. "I was wrong. You don't have to beat it into the ground."

"Of course not. Beating things into the ground is your department, isn't it?"

"Are you actually God's sister?" Bheid asked in a voice trembling in awe.

"That depends on your point of view, Bheid," she replied with a faint smile. "From where I sit, Deiwos is God's brother. I'm sure he doesn't see it in those terms, but that's *his* problem, isn't it? The three of us—Deiwos, Daeva, and I—all look at things from a slightly different perspective. In my own personal view, Deiwos makes things for me to love, and Daeva hauls out the trash."

"That's a novel set of definitions, Divinity," Leitha noted. "Have you presented them to your brothers lately?"

"It'd just be a waste of time, Leitha. My brothers are both too impressed with themselves to look at things the way they really are. They can be so tiresome sometimes." She looked at them, her eyes slightly narrowed. "I see that you've all sort of adjusted to the situation, so maybe it's time for us to get to work. Make some furniture, Althalus. We might as well be comfortable."

"Anything you say, Dweia."

"Would it be at all possible for you to grow a few freckles or something, Divinity?" Leitha asked. "You're making life terribly difficult for poor Andine and me, you know."

"We're not really in competition, Leitha," Dweia suggested gently.

"What an unworldly attitude," Andine murmured.

"How are we to address you?" Bheid asked when they were all seated in the comfortable chairs Althalus had made.

"Can't you pronounce 'Dweia,' Bheid?" Leitha asked him with feigned curiosity.

"Some orders of the priesthood tell us that it's forbidden to speak the name of God," Bheid explained.

"They're wrong," Dweia told him. "The small mind tries to conceal its inadequacy in senseless formality and endless disputes about meaningless trivia. You're above that, Brother Bheid, or you wouldn't be here. I have a name. Please use it. It's very confusing when somebody looks at the sky and says, 'Oh, God.' My brothers and I can never be sure which of us he's talking to." She laughed then. "That started a whole new religion in Plakand once," she recalled. "When all three of us answered a priest at the same time, he took it to be a revelation, and three-headed idols began popping up all over Plakand."

"Some orders of the priesthood denounce statues of God," Bheid said with a troubled look. "They tell us that no one can really see God."

"You can see me, can't you?" Dweia asked. "Actually, the statues don't concern us too much—except for that monstrosity in Maghu." She paused, her hand resting on the Book. "We're getting a little far afield," she noted. "I think it might be best to put things in their simplest terms right at the beginning here so that we're all starting from the same point. The three of us— Deiwos, Daeva, and I—have always existed, and we seldom agree with each other about anything."

"A war of the Gods, you mean?" Eliar asked.

"There are only three of us, Eliar," she said. "I'd hardly call that a war. As long as only the three of us were involved, our disagreements generated some interesting arguments and not much else. We were civil to each other when we met—which wasn't very often—and we more or less let it go at that. Then humans came along and everything changed. Other creatures take the world as they find it, and so does most of mankind. There are a few humans, however, who have urges to tamper—to change things. Some of the changes are good; some aren't. But it's human nature to try them just to find out if they'll work."

"When has this happened?" Bheid asked.

"The arguments have been going on forever, but humans came to this part of the world about ten thousand years ago, searching for open land where they could grow wheat. Probably nothing has changed the world as much as wheat. It guaranteed the survival of humans, and it kept them in one place long enough to build villages and towns, and that's how civilization began. Anyway, primitive humans came up out of the south— below Meusa and Plakand. There was a vast tropical forest in their original homeland, and chopping down all those trees with stone axes to make room for farmland didn't appeal to them very much, so they came north in search of open country."

"That was ten thousand years ago?" Bheid asked.

"Ten thousand or so," she replied. "Calendars back then weren't very good, and my brothers and I don't pay very much attention to time. As it happened, Ghend was one of those early settlers in Medyo. He's always had a very high opinion of himself, and that used to irritate his chief. The chief always seemed to think of Ghend when some particularly dirty job came along, and no matter how hard Ghend tried to obey his chief's commands, his efforts were never quite good enough to satisfy his ruler. His resentment bloomed like a well-watered weed, and he soon hated his chief. It's a gloomy sort of story that's been repeated over and over again down through the centuries. Ghend's puffed-up sense of his own worth made it impossible for him to see just how absurd he was sometimes. I think that if he'd been able to laugh at himself, things might have turned out differently; but he couldn't laugh, and that opened the door for Daeva. It didn't take very long. Daeva offered glory and power and immortality, and Ghend accepted it all quite eagerly. Then, just to reinforce his grasp on Ghend's soul, Daeva took him to Nahgharash to corrupt him even more."

Leitha gasped. "Not *there*!" she exclaimed.

"Where else?" Dweia said. "Nahgharash *is* the seat of Daeva's power, after all."

"I don't think I've ever heard of it," Eliar said.

"It's a place in Nekweros," Leitha told him. "It lies deep under the earth, and it's a place of unspeakable horror."

"Only if Daeva wants it to be that way, Leitha," Dweia corrected. "Daeva was trying to enslave Ghend, so he provided him with anything he wanted. As far as Ghend was concerned, Nahgharash was a place of infinite delight. At first, Daeva was almost like a servant to Ghend, but as his grasp of Ghend's soul became more firm, that changed. Time means nothing in Nahgharash, and Daeva's infinitely patient; so by the time Ghend left, Daeva was the master, and Ghend was the servant."

"Do his eyes really burn the way they did in that dream we all had back in Awes?" Eliar asked.

"Oh, yes," Althalus told him. "Ghend could light his path through the darkest wood with only his eyes."

"It's the mark of Daeva," Bheid explained confidently.

"Not entirely," Dweia disagreed. "The fire in Ghend's eyes is his, not Daeva's. Anyway, once he had Ghend totally under his control, Daeva sent him back to Medyo with the same command the Knife gave Althalus."

"Seek?" Althalus asked. "What was he supposed to look for?"

"The same things you were, dear," Dweia replied. "There

were certain people Daeva needed, and he ordered Ghend to go find them. We've encountered those people, so you know who they are."

"Pekhal and those others?"

"Exactly. Pekhal was the first, and winning him over wasn't much of a problem. It was about nine thousand years ago when Ghend came out of Nahgharash and went back to Medyo. Pekhal was a murderer who lurked around the outskirts of several villages in central Medyo killing anybody who happened by carrying anything that took his fancy: clothes, food, weapons—anything of the slightest value. He even killed people who had nothing—if he happened to be hungry."

"You're not *serious*!" Andine exclaimed.

"It was more common in those days than most people realize, Andine, and Pekhal was an absolute savage. Ghend used *his* book to subdue the brute, and then he won him over with assorted diversions and entertainments we don't really need to talk about."

"Have you ever seen this Pekhal fellow, Master Althalus?" Gher asked.

"Emmy and I came across him in Arum when we were looking for the Knife," Althalus replied. "The years haven't improved him very much."

"You should have killed him when you had the chance."

"I was told not to. I guess it didn't exactly fit in with Emmy's plans."

"You know perfectly well that wasn't the reason, Althalus," Dweia said.

"Whatever you say, dear," he replied blandly. "Who did Ghend recruit after he'd gotten Pekhal under control?"

"Khnom came next," she replied, "but that was after the Medyos had expanded into Wekti, Plakand, and Equero. That expansion took fifteen hundred years, but Ghend's very patient, so he waited. Khnom lived in Ledan in Equero, and he was a notorious cheat. He dealt mostly in flax, but the bales of flax he bartered had a lot of common weeds mixed in. The citizens of Ledan finally drove him out of their town and let it be known in the other cities that he wasn't to be trusted. All gates were closed to him, and an outcast's chances of survival were very remote back in those days. Ghend and Pekhal found him hiding in a willow thicket near the lakeshore, on the verge of starvation. Ghend didn't have much trouble recruiting him, since he really didn't have any other place to go."

"He was selling pots and pans when Althalus and I met him in Awes," Eliar recalled.

"He was *pretending* to be selling pots and pans," Althalus corrected. "Actually, he was there to keep an eye on us."

"Khnom's a born cheat who can change his face and manner at the drop of a hat," Dweia told them. "He can be charming and very ingratiating, but only a fool would trust him."

"This is turning into a very good story," Gher said enthusiastically. "Which one of Ghend's bad people came next?"

"Gelta."

"The lady in the iron shirt whose horse stands on clouds?"

"That's the one. She was the queen of a warrior clan in Ansu about six thousand years ago."

Bheid frowned. "Wouldn't that have been a bit unusual in Ansu?" he asked. "As I understand it, the men of Ansu don't really believe that women are human."

"You saw her, Bheid," Dweia reminded him. "She's as big as any man, and far more savage. She's a homely woman with a pockmarked face and a big nose. She grew up in the company of her father's warriors, so she thinks more like a man than a woman. She waded through blood to reach her throne, and any man who made an issue of her gender didn't live long enough to see the sun go down."

"How in the world did Ghend ever manage to convert a woman like that?" Bheid asked.

"He offered her power, Bheid. Gelta has lots of appetites, but her hunger for power goes far beyond the others. Ghend offered empire and dominion in exchange for her soul, and Gelta was sure that she was getting a bargain."

"Which one came next?" Eliar asked.

"It was a thousand years before he found the next one," Dweia replied. "The Deikan Empire came into prominence after the religious wars of the fifth millennium had sent Medyo into decline. There was a priest of the Equero god Apwos living in the city of Deika early in the sixth millennium. His name was Argan, and he violently disagreed with his high priest on some obscure aspects of astrology. The high priest finally ordered him to recant, and Argan refused. Then the high priest asserted his authority and expelled Argan from the priesthood."

"Dear God!" Bheid gasped. "That's dreadful!"

"Argan thought so, too. The center of his life had been removed, and he was sunk in absolute despair. Ghend picked him the way you'd pick a ripe apple from a tree."

"Is there really a God named Apwos?" Gher asked.

"It's a variation of 'Deiwos,' " Dweia explained. "The name 'Apwos' means 'Water God,' and 'Kherdhos' means 'Herd God.' The Medyos looked at the sky, the Equeros looked at their lakes, and the Wekti and Plakands looked at their herds of sheep or cows. They use different names, but they're talking about the same God."

"Do they know that?"

"Not really," Dweia replied with a shrug. "I've had about a dozen different names since this all started. Anyway, Ghend's last recruit was living in Regwos about three thousand years ago, and he has the same gift Leitha has."

"I'd hardly call it a gift," Leitha objected.

"Koman feels differently about it. Regwos is a troubled land. It was originally colonized by Osthos, but the land's not good, and there's very little gold there."

"We still have a few settlements along the coast," Andine supplied, "but they cost us far more than we ever get out of them. They're nothing but a burden."

"Koman used his gift to probe for secrets," Dweia continued, "and then he sold them. He happened to meet Ghend, and he liked what he found in Ghend's mind. He didn't have to be enlisted; he volunteered." She smiled then. "Althalus did something horrible to poor Koman when we met him," she recalled. "Leitha might appreciate it more than the rest of you."

"Emmy warned me that Koman was going to try to sneak into my mind," Althalus explained. "She told me to start counting, but to put the numbers out of their proper sequence—one, two, three, seventeen, nine, forty-three, and so on. Then, just to make it more interesting, I added a few fractions—seven and five-eighths, ninety-two and twelve thirty-seconds, and some other combinations. Koman didn't seem to find that very entertaining, for some reason."

Leitha's eyes went suddenly very wide, and she shuddered. "Please, Althalus," she begged. "Promise that you'll *never* do that to me!"

"Would it really be so painful?" Andine asked her friend.

"It'd be *awful*!" Leitha shuddered again. "How did Koman react when you did that to him, Althalus?"

"As I recall, it sent him off down the road talking to himself, and he was using some very colorful language."

"Isn't it almost lunchtime?" Eliar asked suddenly.

"It's only been a few hours since breakfast," Andine reminded him. Her voice seemed oddly gentle, and there was no hint of her usual derision or open hostility toward the young Arum.

"I know that the way I talk about food all the time must get tiresome for the rest of you," Eliar half apologized with an embarrassed expression, "but I just can't help it. An hour or so after I've eaten, I'm starving again."

"Why not stuff your pockets full of food, Eliar?" Gher suggested. "That way, you'd always have something to nibble on when you got hungry."

Eliar's face was shocked. "Oh, I couldn't do *that*, Gher!" he protested. "Eating in front of the rest of you would be *terribly* bad mannered!"

Then Andine burst forth with peal upon peal of rich laughter that filled the tower with music.

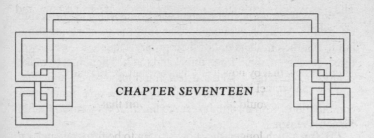

CHAPTER SEVENTEEN

The House was strange for the others, but this was home for Althalus, and it was good to be back. Dweia continued her leisurely lectures on the history of the world, but Althalus didn't really pay much attention. He felt that he knew enough about the world already. If she wanted to waste time giving history lessons, that was up to her, and they wouldn't be going anywhere until spring anyway.

Then, after a few weeks had passed, a peculiar idea came to him, and he waited until he and Dweia were alone in the tower to bring it up.

"Deiwos built the House, didn't he?" he asked her.

"The word you want is 'made,' not 'built.' There's a difference, you know."

"Did he give it to you?"

"No, I snitched it."

"Dweia!"

She laughed. "That got your attention, didn't it? Deiwos came here to think things over after he'd spun the stars out of his thought. Then he went back out and left the House behind. Since he wasn't using it anymore, I just moved in—as Emmy the cat."

"What if he decides that he wants it back?"

"That'll be just too bad. The House is mine now, Althalus. If Deiwos wants a House, he can go make another one someplace else—on the moon, maybe."

"Does he know that you feel that way about him?"

"He should. I've told him often enough. He made this world

and peopled it. That's all he's supposed to do. It's mine now, and he's just underfoot."

"We won't be leaving until spring, will we?"

"The seasons aren't really all that relevant here, pet. You should know that by now. We'll leave when we're ready."

"We can't travel in the dead of winter, Em."

"How much would you care to wager on that, Althalus?" she asked slyly.

"Before much longer, the snow's going to be fifteen feet deep, and the sun won't come up anymore. I'd say that more or less pens us up in here."

"Not really. Watch, Althalus. Watch and learn."

"That's really irritating, Em."

"I'm glad you liked it," she replied smugly.

"Is this going to go on much longer, Master Althalus?" Gher asked quietly while they were eating lunch a few days later.

"This what, Gher?"

"All this business about who was doing what thousands of years ago in places I never heard of before. You don't have to tell Emmy I said this, but it's getting awfully boring. Who cares about what happened in the Deikan Empire five thousand years ago?"

"I went there once," Althalus told the boy. "That was before I came here and Emmy got her paws on me. The merchants of Deika were all very rich, but they didn't have very good sense. I sort of thought that might provide all kinds of opportunities for somebody in our profession. The idea of stupid rich men gives me a warm little glow."

"What happened?" Gher asked eagerly.

Althalus told him a much-embroidered version of the adventure in Kweso's house. Gher proved to be a perfect audience, and Althalus was enjoying himself enormously when Dweia suggested that it was time to go back to work.

As they started up the stairs, Althalus noticed that Andine had a sly little smirk on her face, and he remembered that the girl had drawn Dweia off to one side before they'd all sat down to lunch. A faint smile was also playing about the corners of Dweia's lips. Something was obviously afoot here.

"There's something I don't quite understand," Bheid said while Dweia was recounting the history of Treborea. "You've hinted several times that the coastline of the southern sea has been changing."

"Yes, it has."

"What can possibly change a coastline? I'd always thought that things like mountains and coastlines were fixed and immutable."

"Oh, good grief no, Bheid," Dweia replied, laughing. "They change all the time. The whole world's in a constant state of flux. Mountains rise and fall like the tides, and the slightest change of climate can move a coastline hundreds of miles. An individual man's not alive long enough to see those changes, but they *are* taking place. The southern coast's been expanding for over two thousand years now." Then she turned and pointed toward the north window. "It's because of that ice up there."

"How can ice this far north have any effect on the southern coast?"

"Ice is frozen water, isn't it?"

"Of course."

"There's only so much water. The amount's constant. Some of it's in the seas, some's in the air as rain clouds, and some's locked up in the glaciers. Every so often there's a change in the weather. It gets colder, and the glaciers start to grow. More and more of the world's water is locked up in the glaciers, and there's less and less water in the seas or in the clouds. It doesn't rain as much anymore, and the sea level starts to drop. That's what changes the coastline. The seas off the south coast have always been shallow, so as the water recedes, more and more land is exposed."

"The works of God are wondrous," Bheid recited sententiously.

"I'm sure my brother would be pleased to hear that," Dweia said drily.

"Deiwos rules."

"I was talking about my other brother."

Bheid stared at her in horror.

"This particular change in the weather is Daeva's doing," she told him. "These are interesting times. Daeva's gathered up his people, and I've gathered mine. We're standing right on the brink of a very nice war, Bheid, and Daeva's doing everything he possibly can to give Ghend the advantage. The seas are running away, and when those glaciers start to move, the mountains are going to be ground down into mole hills. The drought will bring famine, and empires will collapse. Isn't that exciting?"

"It's the end of the world!" Bheid exclaimed.

"Not if we win, it won't be."

"Gives you a nice, warm sense of your own importance, doesn't it, Bheid?" Leitha suggested slyly. "Save the world, boy! Save! Save!"

"That'll do, Leitha," Dweia scolded the pale girl.

"It was too good an opportunity to pass up, Dweia," Leitha apologized.

"Isn't it just about time for—?" Eliar started.

Andine was sitting in the chair beside his, and Althalus had noticed that she'd been watching the young Arum quite closely all afternoon. She touched his wrist with one hand and offered him a fairly large piece of cheese with the other. Eliar took the cheese almost absently and began to eat.

Andine's little smile was rather like the sun coming up.

Dweia flicked a quick glance at Althalus, and her purring thought came into his mind. *You saw that, didn't you?* she asked.

Of course, he silently replied. *Did you tell her to do that?*

It was actually her own idea. She has a little bag of tidbits under her chair. Every time Eliar's stomach starts to growl, she's going to feed him. If you look closely, you'll probably notice that he doesn't even realize that he's eating. Andine said that she came up with the notion as a way to keep him from interrupting, but I think there might be a little more to it than that. In a peculiar sort of way, it's something along the lines of Gher's haircut.

She's a very complicated little girl, isn't she?
Indeed she is, Dweia agreed. *Fun, though.*

"How long have we been here, Althalus?" Eliar asked several days later as they were all going up the stairs to the room in the tower.

"A month at least," Althalus replied.

"That's what I thought, too. Is something peculiar happening outside?"

"Peculiar?"

"The days should be getting shorter, but as nearly as I can tell, they aren't."

"Dweia's playing with things, that's all."

"I don't understand."

"I don't either—not entirely, anyway. She's tampering with time. Most probably what's happening is that we're living the same day over and over again—except that different things happen each time we go through that day."

"Would it do me any good to say that's impossible?"

"Not much, probably. Ghend's moving around out there, and we've got to be ready to spoke his wheel every time he tries something. The trouble is that we aren't ready yet. That's why Dweia brought us back here to the House. Time here moves the way she wants it to. If it takes us years to get ready, she'll give us those years, but when we go back outside, it'll only be a day or so later than it was when we came here."

"Except that we'll all be about fifteen years older."

"I don't think it works that way, Eliar."

"I don't understand."

"Don't feel alone."

"Will you *please* stop browsing, Leitha?" Dweia said later that morning.

"I can't control it," Leitha confessed, sighing. "I wish I could. As soon as I look at someone or hear someone talking, this whatever it is seems to home in. Then somebody else says something, and it goes after him. I don't *want* to do it, but it acts on its own."

Dweia opened the Book. "Let's do something about that right now," she said. "Your gift—if we want to call it that—is so completely random that it's totally out of control." She leafed through several of the early pages in the Book. Then she apparently found the page she wanted. "Here we are," she said, lifting out the page. "This is how Deiwos dealt with the same problem. His answer's a little simpler than mine is, so it might be better if you start here. Later on, I'll show you how *I* do it."

"I'll try anything, Dweia," Leitha said fervently. "I don't *want* this thing in my mind." She took the crackling parchment sheet from Dweia and looked at it. "I thought I'd be able to read this," she said, frowning. "But the letters aren't the same. I can't make it out at all."

"It's a very archaic form, Leitha," Dweia told her. "There's a faster way. Just lay the sheet down on the Book and then put the palm of your hand down on it."

"You want me to read with my hand?" Leitha asked incredulously.

"Unless you'd rather use your foot. Just try it, Leitha."

The pale blond girl dubiously set the page down on the white-covered Book and placed the palm of her hand on it. Her blue eyes widened as total comprehension filled them. "It can't be *that* simple," she objected.

"Why not try it and find out?" Dweia suggested.

Leitha sat back and closed her eyes. Her expression became almost inhumanly serene. Then her eyes opened very wide as she drew in a sharp breath.

Then she suddenly screamed.

"You went too far, Leitha," Dweia told her, "and just a little too fast."

"Everything's so empty!" Leitha said in a shuddering voice. "There's nothing there anymore!"

"You just went too high, dear. You want to go above it, but not quite *that* far above. You'll get better at it with practice. All you're really doing is aiming your gift. You want to point it slightly over the heads of everybody around you. You'll still hear that slight murmur that you've been listening to all your life, but you won't hear the actual thoughts. When you *want* to hear them, just point your gift straight at the one you want to hear."

Leitha shuddered. "What was that awful emptiness?" she demanded.

"The sound of nothing, Leitha. You *were* pointing it at the ceiling, you know."

"Did that make any sense to anybody else?" Eliar asked, his expression baffled.

"Leitha's got an extra set of ears, that's all," Gher replied. "She can hear what we're thinking—even when she doesn't want to. Emmy just taught her how to point her ears someplace else. Anybody can see that."

Leitha gave the boy a startled look. "How could you possibly have known that?" she asked.

"I don't know," Gher confessed. "It just seemed to make sense, that's all. Of course, I've been dodging you ever since we first met."

"Dodging?"

"I could feel what you were doing, ma'am, so I'd just step out of your way and let you zing right past me."

Dweia was staring at the boy in absolute astonishment.

"Well, well, well," Althalus murmured.

"What's that supposed to mean?" Dweia demanded.

"Nothing, dear," Althalus replied innocently. "Nothing at all."

"Isn't it just about time for us to—" Eliar started.

Andine gave him a piece of fruit, and he stopped talking.

"Just keep the rest of them entertained, dear heart," Dweia told Althalus. "I'll be taking them aside one by one to explain certain things to them."

He gave her a puzzled look.

"It's faster that way, Althalus. They'll open their hearts to me if we're alone. Doing that in front of others is a little embarrassing. Everyone has flaws they'd prefer not to expose to the whole community."

"I take it that you don't agree with the notion of open confession."

"It's one of man's sillier ideas. Announcing one's sins in public is a form of exhibitionism. It serves no purpose, and it wastes time."

"I thought we had all the time in the world."

"Not *that* much, we don't."

"What are they talking about, Master Althalus?" Gher asked, looking at Dweia and Bheid, who were sitting together at the table with the Book open before them.

"I'd sort of imagine that Dweia's clearing Bheid's mind of a number of misconceptions. Bheid was trained for the priesthood and for astrology. There's a lot of nonsense in his mind that Dweia's getting rid of."

"Does anybody really believe in that astrology business?" Gher asked.

Althalus shrugged. "People want to know what's going to happen next. They think astrology tells them. It's wrong most of the time, but people keep on believing anyway."

"Isn't that sort of stupid?"

"Moderately stupid, yes, but most people need to believe in *something*. There are a few who don't, but they're a bit unusual."

"I've never believed very much, myself. The sun's probably going to come up tomorrow, and spring usually comes after winter, but just about everything else happens by accident."

"That comes fairly close, I'd say. I used to believe in luck, but Dweia's sort of cured me of that."

Gher suddenly chuckled. "Andine just did it again," he said. "Eliar doesn't even realize she's feeding him, does he?"

"Probably not," Althalus agreed. "Eliar's a nice, uncomplicated boy. As long as she keeps the food coming, he doesn't ask any questions—or even pay much attention to what she's doing."

"What I don't understand is why she does it. Back when I first joined you folks, she didn't like him at all. Now she hovers over him all the time."

"She's mothering him, Gher. Women do that a lot, I've noticed. She hated him at first, but that's changing."

"I'm glad she's picking on him now, instead of me," Gher said. "I was starting to get real tired of all those haircuts."

After several days, Dweia left Bheid alone with the Book and turned her attention to Andine. Many of those discussions were quite audible. The Arya of Osthos was a beautiful young lady with dark hair and huge dark eyes, but her emotions leaned in the direction of explosive. The Knife had instructed her to "obey," and that didn't suit her at all.

Althalus had unobtrusively moved his chair to a place near the door, and he spent most of his time watching the others, being careful not to be too obvious about it.

"What are you doing, Althalus?" Dweia asked him late one afternoon when they were alone in the tower.

"Watching, Em. Watching and learning. Isn't that what you told me to do?"

"What have you learned so far?"

"We've picked up a very strange collection of people, little kitten, and they aren't altogether what they seem to be at first glance. Except for Gher, most of them aren't very happy about what they're supposed to be doing. Andine absolutely hates the word 'obey,' and Eliar's very uncomfortable with 'lead,' since he knows he's not ready to command an army yet."

"That isn't what 'lead' means in this situation, pet, but we'll be getting to that in a bit. What have you learned about the others?"

"I think you might have been a little abrupt with Bheid. Once you threw out astrology, you set him adrift. He doesn't know what to believe anymore—and he's right on the verge of believing in nothing. He's positive that 'illuminate' means that he's supposed to preach, and a sermon about nothing might be a little hard to compose."

"He doesn't quite understand yet, Althalus," she replied. "When the time comes, he will. What about Leitha?"

"*That's* the one who worries me. She puts on a bright face, and she makes clever remarks, but she read something on the Knife that she probably wasn't supposed to. The others aren't entirely certain about what the Knife told them to do; Leitha *knows*. She knows *exactly* what she has to do, and who she has to do it to. She's not happy about it, Em. Life hasn't been good to her so far, and she's almost certain that it's going to get worse."

"She's much stronger than she appears, Althalus. She'll need some help at some point, so stay close to her. Be ready to give her that help."

"That's awfully cryptic, Em," he accused.

"You were told to 'seek,' Althalus. I'm sure you'll find a way to help her—if you seek hard enough."

Dweia and Gher were sitting near the east window, deep in conversation. Eliar was telling Andine war stories by the south window, and she was obviously feigning a look of vapid admiration and handing him occasional tidbits of food. Leitha had joined Bheid at the marble table, and they were both deeply engrossed in the Book. This left Althalus more or less to his own devices. He stood at the north window looking out at the mountains of ice out beyond the End of the World. Despite everything Emmy had told him, Althalus still thought of that chasm to the north as the end of everything. He was more comfortable with that, since it seemed to give the world a definite boundary. He didn't much care for the implications of the word "infinity."

"You still think of me as a witch, don't you, Bheid?" Althalus heard Leitha ask their young priest.

"Of course not," Bheid replied. "Whatever gave you that idea?"

"I know that you don't like me."

"That's ridiculous, Leitha. I like you very much. You're one of my true companions."

"You make me sound like a piece of furniture," she accused.

"I don't exactly see where this is going," he confessed.

"You're the only man I've ever met who doesn't seem to be aware of the fact that I'm a woman."

"I'm aware of it, Leitha. It's not all that important to what we're supposed to do, but I *am* aware of it."

"You don't think about it, though." She sighed. "Ever since the end of my childhood, the men in our village all looked at me in a certain way, and they all had certain kinds of thoughts."

"The kind that the priest, Ambho, had, you mean?"

"Exactly. Every man in town had certain thoughts about me."

"You *are* very beautiful, Leitha."

"Why, thank you, kind sir," she mocked.

"Whatever gave you the idea that I don't like you?"

"You don't have the same kind of thoughts about me that other men have."

"Those thoughts are vile, Leitha. It's the duty of a priest to suppress vile thoughts."

"Ah, perhaps that's it. It's making me very uncomfortable, though, Bheid. You despise those vile thoughts, and when you suppress them, what comes in my direction is hatred. Your hatred is directed at the thoughts, but it seems in my mind to be directed at *me*."

"That's certainly not what I'd intended."

"I think I may have a solution."

"I'd be happy to hear it, Leitha."

"Relax that iron-hard suppression a bit and let a few of those vile thoughts out."

"What?"

"Not *too* vile, of course. That would disturb the both of us. A few itty-bitty vile thoughts wouldn't hurt anything." She smiled winsomely and held up her thumb and forefinger as if measuring something very small. "If you were to keep them only about so big, they wouldn't violate your vow, but they'd be naughty enough to let me know that you're aware of the fact that I'm a woman. I think 'modestly vile' is what you should aim at. It wouldn't contaminate you, and it'd make me *ever* so much more comfortable."

Bheid stared at her for a moment, and then he smiled gently. "Of course, Leitha," he promised. "I think I can manage 'modestly vile,' if it'll make you feel better. That's what friends are for, isn't it?"

Her answering smile was radiant.

Keep your nose out of it, Althalus, Dweia's purring voice told him.

Whatever you say, dear.

"The onset of the glaciers has produced a drought that's causing great turmoil in the lands to the south," Dweia was telling them a few days later. "Wealth and power and mighty cities are meaningless if there's nothing to eat. That's the key to Ghend's plan, of course. Chaos is his ally, and the glaciers create chaos."

"I think you told me once that this has happened before," Althalus said.

"Yes. This is about the fourth glacial age in the past several million years. Occasionally they've been the result of changes in weather patterns or the movement of ocean currents. Daeva caused this one, though. It's a crucial part of Ghend's plan to so completely disrupt the various empires to the south that the people will turn to anybody who can offer stability. Civilization's right on the brink of collapse, and a general revolution's looming on the horizon."

"*My* people would never rebel against *me*!" Andine exclaimed.

"I wouldn't be all that certain, dear," Dweia disagreed. "Ghend has people stirring up the citizens of Osthos right now, and your war with the Kanthons just made it easier for them."

"*We* didn't start that war!"

"I know. Althalus and I met Eliar's sergeant—Khalor—on our way from Arum to Osthos, and he kept referring to the Aryo of Kanthon as a half-wit. I think that if we wanted to delve into the matter, we'd find that one of Ghend's henchmen was behind a number of the Aryo's military decisions."

"Sergeant Khalor *was* a little unhappy about that war," Eliar remembered. "He had all sorts of interesting names for the Chief of the Kanthons."

Andine's huge eyes narrowed speculatively. "That sort of means that it was *Ghend* who murdered my father, doesn't it?"

"He was the one who was ultimately responsible, yes," Dweia replied.

"Eliar?" Andine said then in her most appealing and winsome manner.

"Yes, Andine?"

"Would you like to come to work for me?"

"I didn't quite follow that."

"I need a good professional soldier right now. I pay very well—both in money and other benefits." She laid a lingering hand on his bare knee.

"I'd have to talk with my Chief, Andine, but I'm sure we could work something out. What exactly is it that you'd like to have me do?"

"I'd be *ever* so grateful if you'd track this Ghend person down and butcher him for me—and I want to be there to watch while you do it. I want blood, Eliar—lots and lots of blood. And I'd really like to hear some very loud screams. How much do you think that might cost me?"

"I wouldn't *think* of charging you for *that*, Andine," he assured her. "We're friends now, and it wouldn't be at all polite for me to take money from you for a simple little favor like that, would it?"

Andine gave a little squeal of delight, threw her arms about Eliar's neck, and kissed him fervently. "Isn't he just the *nicest* boy you've ever seen?" she demanded of the rest of them.

Dweia looked pensive the following morning. She sat at the marble table in the tower room with her hand lying on the Book and her green eyes lost in thought.

Althalus and the others filed in as usual and quietly took their seats.

"I want you all to pay very close attention," Dweia told them. "You all know about 'using' the Book, and about how Eliar 'uses' the Knife. Now it's time for you to learn how to 'use' the

House." She rose and looked at them. "This may be difficult for you, and some of the things I'm going to tell you will be very hard for you to accept, but you'll have to trust me. I've suggested a number of times that the House isn't really here, but that's not entirely accurate. The House *is* here, but it's everywhere else as well."

"Do you mean that it moves around?" Gher asked incredulously.

"Not exactly," she replied. "It doesn't have to move, Gher. It's everywhere—all at the same time. You've all noticed how big the House is, I'm sure."

"Oh, yes," Althalus said. "When I first came here to steal the Book, I was sure it'd take weeks to search every room."

"Actually, it would have taken you centuries, Althalus, and even then you'd have only scratched the surface. For right now, let's just say that the House is the world, but that's an oversimplification. It's quite a bit bigger than that. When I say that the House is everywhere, I really mean *everywhere*. When Deiwos first made it, this room was all there was, and he went out from here to make everywhere else, and he made a door to each of those places. That's why the House kept growing, and that's why the doors—not the rooms—are important. Let me give you an example. If Andine wanted to stop by her throne room to speak with her High Chamberlain, Lord Dhakan, she could saddle her horse, ride on down through Kagwher, slip past Kanthon, and eventually reach Osthos. There's another way, though. She could go down the hallway that leads to the south, open a certain door right here in this House, and step through that door into her throne room."

"It can't be *that* simple!" Bheid exclaimed.

"No, actually it isn't. Not only does she have to go through the right door, but she also must *believe* that it's the right door. The key to the door is belief."

"And if she *doesn't* believe?" Gher asked.

"She walks into an empty room," Dweia said, shrugging. "When I said that belief is the key, I meant exactly that."

"It's an act of faith, then?" Bheid suggested.

"Exactly. We make things so by *believing* that they are so."

"There are people out there who believe all kinds of very strange things, Dweia," Eliar objected. "Those things aren't true just because they *believe* they're true, are they?"

"They're true for *them*."

"That's why it's a lot better not to believe in anything, Eliar," Gher told him. "That way things don't get all mixed up."

"It makes the world a little lonely, though, doesn't it?" Eliar asked.

"You learn to live with it."

"Mankind *must* believe in something, Gher," Bheid told the boy.

"Why?"

"Because . . ." Bheid faltered.

"We have a long way to go with Gher, don't we?" Leitha asked.

"I'd say so, yes," Althalus agreed. "But he's a good little boy, so he'll be patient and show us the way."

"That's not what I meant, Althalus."

"I know, but you're just getting started."

"That will *do*, Althalus," Dweia said quite firmly.

"Yes, dear."

Gher was frowning. "Ghend can do this, too, can't he?" he asked. "I mean, he's got that place in Nekweros, and it's got doors the same as this house does too, doesn't it?"

"Yes. It's called Nahgharash."

"That's how he—or those others—can keep popping out of nowhere, isn't it? That's going to make this all very interesting."

"Define 'interesting,' " Dweia told him.

"Fun," Gher said. "Ghend pops up here; we pop up there; and nobody knows just exactly where anybody else is—or who he'll have with him—when he shows up. This'll be the funnest game anybody's ever come up with."

" 'Funnest'?" Eliar asked. "I don't think there is such a word."

"You understood what I meant, didn't you?" Gher asked.

"I suppose I did, but—"

"Then that makes it a word, doesn't it?"

"This one's going to give me headaches, I think," Dweia said.

"It's Osthos!" Andine exclaimed when Eliar opened the door at the far end of one of the long, dimly lighted corridors in the south wing of the House.

"Just look, Andine," Dweia commanded. "Don't go through right now. We don't have enough time to go looking for you."

Althalus noticed that the threshold of the doorway was rather hazy, but everything beyond the doorway was sharp and clear. A cobblestoned street led past a number of the shops he'd seen the last time he'd been in Osthos, and then the street went slightly up a hill to Andine's palace.

"You'd better close the door, Eliar," Dweia suggested. "It's letting in the time."

"Ma'am?" Eliar asked in a puzzled tone of voice.

"We don't want time to move just yet. We aren't prepared. We still have quite a bit of ground to cover, and we need to have time stand still until we're ready."

"I really don't understand this, Emmy," Eliar said, closing the door.

"You don't have to just yet."

"You speak of time as if it were some kind of weather, Divinity," Leitha observed.

"They're sort of similar, Leitha." Dweia paused, looking curiously at the pale girl from Kweron. "Tell me, dear," she said. "Why do you persist in calling me 'Divinity' the way you always do?"

"It's a term of respect, Divinity," Leitha replied, her blue eyes open very wide.

"No, Leitha, it isn't. You don't really respect anybody. You're doing it to tease me, aren't you?"

"I wouldn't think of teasing a Goddess, Dweia," Leitha protested.

"Oh, yes you would. I don't really mind, of course, but I thought we should clear it up."

"That takes a lot of the fun out of it," Leitha protested.

"I don't mind a little teasing, Leitha. It's a way of playing. I spent a very long time as Emmy the cat, so I know all about playing. One of these days I'll show you."

"I'll be good," Leitha promised.

"I sort of doubt that. Take us to Kanthon, Eliar."

They spent about a week exploring the possibilities of the doors in the House—at least it *seemed* like a week. Althalus had decided not to pursue the difference between "seems" and "is."

Eliar served as their guide during these excursions. Dweia's explanation of the process wasn't very detailed. The Knife was involved in some way, Althalus gathered. Whatever his inspiration may have been, Eliar unerringly led them to the correct door when Dweia suggested that they look at some other place. "I haven't got the faintest idea of *how* I know which door we want," Eliar confessed. "I just do. Emmy says *'Agwesi,'* and I immediately know which door I'm supposed to open. Half the time, I don't even know which country the place is in."

"You don't really have to know, dear boy," Andine said fondly. "The Knife told you to 'lead,' didn't it? That's exactly what you're doing. Don't change a thing. We all love you just the way you are." She gently stroked his cheek. Andine couldn't seem to keep her hands off Eliar for some reason.

Finally, Dweia suggested that they return to their classroom. "We've more or less taken care of everything we needed to attend to here," she told them. "We know how to use the House—at least partially—and a few other things are in place now, so it's time for us to go back out."

"Partially?" Gher asked shrewdly. "Doesn't that sort of mean that the House can do some other things as well as take us from place to place?"

"Let's hold off on that for now," Dweia said.

"I'm really curious, Emmy," the boy said. "I think I've got an idea—well, sort of, anyway. Would it bother you if I just threw it into the air and we all took a look at it?"

"It takes quite a bit to bother me, Gher. Go ahead and throw it out."

"You said that the House plays with time—I mean, time moves or doesn't move the way you want it to."

"Yes."

"Well, the House plays with distance by using the doors, doesn't it?"

"It's a little more complex, but that more or less sums it up, yes."

"If it's playing with distance that way, can't it play with time the same way?" He paused for a moment. "I'm not saying this too well, am I? You told us that the House is everywhere—all at the same time."

"Yes. Go on."

"It's Every*when* then, too, isn't it? What I'm getting at is that there's probably a door to last week somewhere in the House— or one that leads to next year. Am I making any sense at all with this?"

Dweia's eyes grew troubled. "You aren't really supposed to be asking that kind of question yet, Gher."

"You just said 'yet,' Emmy," the boy said with a certain note of triumph. "That sort of means that we'll get to that part on down the line, doesn't it?"

Dweia's green eyes narrowed. "It's my turn to ask a question, Gher," she said.

"I probably wouldn't be able to answer it, Emmy. I'm just a country boy, remember."

"Let's find out, shall we? Distance is space, isn't it?"

"Well . . . Sort of, I guess."

"What's the difference between space and time?"

Gher frowned slightly. "As far as I can tell, there *isn't* any difference. They're the same thing, aren't they?"

Dweia drew in a sharp breath. "Who have you been talking with, Gher?" she demanded. "Where did you get that idea?"

"It just came to me, I guess. When you said 'space' instead of 'distance,' several things sort of clicked together. Did I say something I wasn't supposed to say, Emmy? I'm sorry if it upset you."

"It didn't upset me, Gher. It just surprised me, that's all. The unity of space and time is something very few people have realized yet."

"I've been thinking about it ever since Eliar told me about that dream you all had back in Awes," Gher explained. "Then when we started using the doors to hop around in space, I sort of came up with the notion that maybe Ghend was using *his* doors to hop around in time, and if hopping is hopping, it wouldn't make any difference whether you were hopping in space or hopping in time. That sort of told me that there isn't any difference—that space and time are the same thing. It didn't make much sense at first, but it sort of fits together now. When you get right down to it, it explains a whole lot of things, doesn't it?"

"Dear God!" Bheid exclaimed in an awed voice.

"Yes?" Dweia replied.

"I wasn't . . . I mean, I was just . . ." Bheid floundered.

"You really shouldn't throw the word 'God' around like that, Bheid," she scolded. "It's very distracting. Does what Gher just said bother you for some reason?"

"Is this boy human?" Bheid asked, looking at Gher with an awed expression. "His thought goes so far beyond mine that I can only understand about half of what he's talking about."

"He *is* a bit unusual," Dweia conceded.

"Unusual or not, he's still our Gher," Andine said. She reached out and playfully mussed Gher's hair. "He's just a tousle-headed little boy who definitely needs to take a bath."

"I just took one last week, ma'am," Gher protested.

"It's time for another one."

"Already?"

"It doesn't really hurt, Gher," Andine said. Then she laughed, threw her arms about the boy, and hugged him to her.

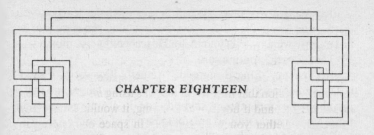

CHAPTER EIGHTEEN

"They won't believe you, Brother Bheid," Eliar told their priest. "We Arums are trained *not* to believe anything the lowlanders tell us. We don't believe in your wars, we don't believe in your customs, and we don't believe in your Gods."

"Your lives are empty, then."

"The money sort of fills that up—at least that's what Sergeant Khalor told us."

"He must be a very evil man."

"You're wrong, Bheid," Althalus disagreed. "Sergeant Khalor's a very good soldier who knows enough not to believe people when they talk about heavenly rewards instead of the money in advance. The Arums work only for pay, and that makes it nice and simple."

"Where can we possibly get enough money to hire all the Arums?"

"I've got a secret little gold mine, Bheid," Althalus replied. "I can buy the whole of Arum—several times over, probably. The Arums are the best soldiers in the world, and they know how to train other people to be fairly good as well. That's what we *really* need. The ragtag armies of the rest of the world fight for their beliefs, which can change with the seasons. The Arums fight for gold, which never changes. A platoon of Arums can train an entire army to be fairly good soldiers in about two months. Then they'll be able to give that army advice about strategy and tactics. Eliar here is only about fifteen years old, and he already knows more about tactics than most of the generals in the low country."

Eliar made a wry face. "When Sergeant Khalor teaches, you learn—one way or the other—and the first thing you learn is to do just exactly what he tells you to do. He teaches by fist, mostly."

"That's cruel," Andine said.

"No, ma'am," Eliar disagreed. "Actually it's a form of kindness. My Sergeant was teaching us how to stay alive, and that's just about the kindest thing anybody can do. People get killed in wars. My Sergeant trained me not to be one of them."

"Then it's a kind of love?"

"I don't think I'd go *that* far. He wanted us to stay alive so that he'd have enough men when the next battle came along. The most important part of strategy is keeping your men alive. If you take care of your men, they'll take care of you."

"Have we more or less finished here in the House, Dweia?" Althalus asked.

"For now, yes."

"Then we might as well go talk with Chief Albron. His clan isn't the biggest one in Arum, but he knows us, so we'll be able to talk with him without all the tiresome introductions."

"My Chief *is* highly respected by the other Clan Chiefs, Althalus," Eliar asserted.

"I'm sure he is, and he and I got along quite well. Of course, I *did* sort of lie to him about the Knife, but I should be able to clear that up without too much trouble. The really important thing here is that only a Clan Chief can call for a general conclave of the Chiefs of Arum, and we won't have time to visit every clan in the entire country. We need to talk to them all at the same time, and Albron's the key to that."

"The arms room might be best, Eliar," Althalus said to the young Arum that evening at supper. "I don't think we should just suddenly appear in the street outside your Chief's castle. Ghend probably has eyes everywhere. Do you think you could manage that?"

"I *think* so," Eliar replied. "I haven't tried it yet, of course, but I get the feeling that I could even pick which part of a room I want to come out in."

"Would a suggestion upset anybody?" Leitha asked.

"It wouldn't bother me," Eliar replied, filling his plate again.

"I'm supposed to do that for you, Eliar," Andine objected. "Now put that back and give me your plate."

"Yes, ma'am," he said apologetically.

"Aren't people going to be a little startled if we all just suddenly appear out of nowhere?" Leitha asked.

"Is there some way around that?" Bheid asked her.

"Why not just go in through the door? We'll be going through a door anyway, so it'll seem more natural to us—and to anybody on the other side."

"Make it so that this side of the door is here and that side of the door is there?" Gher asked.

"Nicely put, Gher," Leitha complimented the boy.

"Thank you, ma'am." Gher dipped his head slightly. "Maybe sometime, though, we *could* just pop out of nowhere."

"Why would we want to do that?"

"Because it'd be funner that way," Gher said, grinning. "I'd love to see somebody's eyes pop out." Then he looked at Althalus. "That'd be a slick way to rob somebody, wouldn't it, Master Althalus? You know—pop out, grab his purse, and then pop back in again. We could steal most of the money in the world that way—and never really leave home."

"Well, now," Althalus said in an almost dreamy voice. "Well now indeed."

"Never mind," Dweia told him flatly.

Andine set Eliar's plate down on the table in front of him. "Eat it before it gets cold, Eliar," she instructed.

"Yes, Andine," he replied, picking up his spoon.

There was something slightly unnerving about the intensity of Andine's expression as she watched Eliar eat. Althalus shuddered slightly and looked away.

"When did you get back home, Eliar?" Rheud, the kilted, red-bearded armorer asked when they all trooped in through the door to his arms room.

"Just now, Rheud," Eliar replied.

Althalus felt just a bit light-headed as he stepped through the doorway. There seemed to be a peculiar sort of dislocation involved in stepping across all those miles.

Just relax, Althalus, Emmy the cat purred softly to him from her customary place in the hood of his cloak. Althalus realized that it was ridiculous, but he *had* missed Emmy during the past several weeks.

I wasn't sure it was really going to work, Em. Looking through a doorway at a place hundreds of miles away is one thing, but crossing all those miles with a single step is something altogether different.

You didn't trust me?

Of course I did, Em—at least out in front.

But not in back, I see.

Talking about it is one thing, Em. Actually doing it is something else.

It gets easier as you go along. Pay attention, Althalus. Don't let Eliar blurt out any trade secrets.

"I see that you found our boy, Master Althalus," Rheud said. "Did he have that knife you were looking for?"

"Oh, yes," Althalus told him. "It was a little complicated, but everything's pretty much the way it's supposed to be now."

"You don't seem to be traveling alone anymore," Rheud observed, stroking his bristling red beard and eying Andine and Leitha.

"Just a few old friends I hadn't met before," Althalus replied. "Is Chief Albron in the main hall right now?"

"He should be," Rheud replied. "He usually lingers over breakfast. He's all business first thing in the morning, and he says that he can get about half of his day's work done before he leaves the table. Did your cousin's assassins give you any trouble down there in the low country?"

"No, not really," Althalus replied. "I managed to give them the slip."

"You might want to thank our Chief for that," Rheud told him. "He sent out the word that anybody asking questions about you—or about that fancy knife—was to be detained. You definitely came down on the good side of Chief Albron, Master Althalus."

"We got along well. Did he intercept very many of my cousin's henchmen?"

"There *were* a few," Rheud replied. "There was one bulky sort of fellow with no forehead to speak of who was a bit of a problem, I understand. From what I hear, it took a dozen men to swarm him under."

"Oh?"

"He said that his name was Pegoyl, or something like that."

"Pekhal, maybe?"

"That might have been it, yes. The clansmen who took him in charge finally just slapped an iron collar around his neck and hitched him to a team of six oxen to drag him here—after they discovered that a two-ox team couldn't budge him."

"Is he still here, Rheud?" Eliar asked intently.

"No, he managed to escape—ate his way through the door of the dungeon, some men say. You're lucky you didn't come across *that* one, Master Althalus. He was more animal than man."

"I know," Althalus replied. "I've met him. It's been good talking with you again, Rheud. I'd better go see if I can catch your Chief before he finishes his breakfast. I've got a little business proposition for him."

"Albron's always ready to talk business."

Althalus led them back out into the corridor.

"Interesting," Bheid said. "You must be making Ghend very nervous, Althalus, if he's got his primary henchmen out looking for you."

"That's a little hard to say for certain, Bheid. Pekhal may be acting on his own. I didn't treat him too well the last time we met. He might have taken it personally."

"May I carry Emmy?" Andine asked, her huge, dark eyes filled with a kind of longing.

Althalus felt a sudden, hot, irrational surge of jealousy. "I think we'd better leave her where she is," he replied. "She might want to give me some instructions when we talk with Eliar's Chief."

"That's a cheap excuse," Andine flared.

"Just let it go, Andine," he replied wearily.

Chief Albron was still seated at the breakfast table in the main hall when Althalus and the others entered. "Why, blast my eyes if it isn't Master Althalus!" the kilted young Chief exclaimed, rising to his feet.

"It's a pleasure to see you again, Chief Albron," Althalus replied with a florid bow.

"Now maybe we can get to the bottom of what happened down there in Osthos," Albron said. "I see that you still have Eliar with you."

"Yes, he's been quite useful. Oh, speaking of that, I think I still owe you for his services."

"We can settle that later. What in the *world* were you doing down there? Those boys you sent home all kept babbling sheer nonsense when they got here."

"We might want to discuss that privately, Chief Albron," Althalus replied cautiously. "There's quite a bit going on that you should know about, and some of it's on the peculiar side."

"Eliar!" a stern voice barked from the far end of the table. "Have you forgotten your manners?"

Eliar winced. "Sorry, Sergeant Khalor," he said quickly. "I didn't want to interrupt."

"That's no excuse! Report!"

"Yes, sir!" Eliar drew himself up into a rigid posture and snapped a smart salute to Chief Albron. "Soldier Eliar reporting, sir!" he announced.

Albron returned the salute. "You're still growing, I see, Eliar," he noted, "and you seem to be filling out quite a bit."

"Yes, sir!"

"Relax, boy," Albron said, smiling. "Your mother told me that you'd paid her a visit late last summer. Why didn't you report in then?"

"I ordered him not to, Albron," Althalus stepped in. "We were on a sort of secret mission, and I didn't want any unfriendly eyes catching sight of our boy. That's one of the things we'll want to talk about when we're alone."

"You're definitely stirring up a lot of curiosity, Althalus. Why don't we adjourn to my study where we can talk more freely? I feel a long, interesting story in the works here—and I'd really appreciate an introduction to these two lovely young ladies."

"If I might suggest it, maybe Sergeant Khalor should sit in," Althalus said. "I think he's going to be involved before long, so he might as well hear this from the beginning."

One of Albron's eyebrows went up.

"I'm hiring, Chief Albron," Althalus said bluntly. "Are you interested?"

"I'm always ready to talk business, Althalus," Albron replied, rubbing his hands together.

"What *really* happened in Osthos, Eliar?" Sergeant Khalor demanded as they all followed Chief Albron down a long, torchlit corridor toward the back of the stone castle. "Your friends were very confused when they finally got home."

"I'm not really all that sure myself, Sergeant Khalor," Eliar confessed. "There were a lot of things going on that I didn't understand back then, and they still don't make too much sense. Althalus bought me and the others from Andine. He told her that he was going to sell us to the Ansus to work as slaves in the salt mines."

"As I remember it, Andine wanted to drink all your blood along about then. What made her change her mind?"

"Emmy took care of that."

"Who's Emmy?"

"She works with Althalus. I think I'd better let him explain that: if I tried, I'd get it all scrambled. There's a whole lot going on that I don't understand."

The room Chief Albron had called his study was a comfortable sort of chamber with a large fireplace and a rush-strewn floor. It had a number of books, as well as quite a few scrolls, on a long shelf. "Do you read very much, Althalus?" the kilted young Chief asked.

"I've studied quite a bit, Albron—mostly one fairly large book. You've got quite a few volumes here."

"A hobby of mine. I've taken a fancy to Treborean poetry here lately."

"And who's your favorite?" Andine asked.

"I rather like the sweep of the epics of Sendhri, madam," Albron replied, "one of the major poets of Kanthon."

"You're wasting your time, Chief Albron," she told him vehemently. "Kanthonese poetry isn't worth the parchment it's written on."

"Our dear Arya has opinions, Chief Albron," Leitha said with a faint smile.

"Arya?"

"How forgetful of me," Althalus said. "Chief Albron, the dark-haired young lady with the musical voice is Arya Andine, the ruler of Osthos. The blond lady with the clever tongue is Leitha, the witch of Kweron."

"Witch?" Albron's eyes looked startled.

"I'll get you for that, Althalus," Leitha threatened. "Actually, Chief Albron, it was a misunderstanding. Our local priest had some unpriestly appetites, and since he was so unspeakably holy, he assumed that any young lady who stirred those appetites absolutely *had* to be a witch. He had some plans to use me for firewood, but Althalus and Bheid persuaded him not to do that."

Chief Albron bowed. "My house is honored, ladies," he said formally.

"Young Bheid here is a priest of Deiwos from Awes in Medyo," Althalus continued, "and the boy's name is Gher. He's from Hule, and I'm training him to be a thief."

"You have an oddly assorted group of companions, Althalus. Oh, by the way, did you ever find that knife you were looking for?"

"Oh, yes. Eliar's got it tucked under his belt right now."

"I thought you were going to take it to your uncle back in Ansu."

"Ah . . . Actually, the story I told you when I was here last time wasn't entirely true." Althalus made a slight face. "When you get right down to it, Albron, I just made it up out of whole cloth. If I'd tried to tell you why I *really* needed the Knife, you'd have had me chained up as a dangerous lunatic. I hate to admit it, but I'm sort of working for God."

"You struck me as a man with better sense than that, Althalus. Is *that* what this is all about?"

"I'm afraid so. It wasn't really my idea, but God has ways to make people do what she tells them to do."

"She?"

"It's fairly complicated."

Albron shook his head with an expression of profound disbelief. "I thought better of you. You aren't going to have much luck here in Arum, I'm afraid. We *don't* get involved in religious wars. They're too messy, for one thing, and we'd rather not have our young men coming home after a war with assorted lunacies sticking out of their ears. Arums fight for money, not for religion."

"I'm *paying* money, Albron, and nobody has to believe in anything to work for me." Althalus reached into his tunic and took out two of the oval bars of his gold. "Do *these* sort of get your attention, Chief Albron?" He handed the bars to the startled Chief.

Albron hefted the two bars. "Well, now," he said, breaking into a broad grin. "I'd say that these *definitely* give us something to talk about."

"I rather thought you might see it that way. I'm offering gold, Albron, not eternal life or a seat at God's supper table. There's a war in the works, and I need soldiers, not converts."

"If you can keep it on that footing, Althalus, I'd guess that every clan in Arum's going to fall in behind you."

Althalus took back his two bars of gold. "Now, then," he said, "as a demonstration of my sense of financial responsibility, why don't we settle up the Eliar account? How much do I owe you for his services this past summer?"

"What's the going rate, Sergeant Khalor?" Albron asked his officer.

"Oh, two gold pieces ought to cover it, my Chief," the kilted Khalor replied.

"Two?" Althalus protested. "He's only a boy!"

"He's got leadership potential, Althalus."

"I'm not buying potential, Khalor. I'm buying what he is right now. One silver penny ought to cover that. He may become a general later, but that's off in the future."

"You took him without Chief Albron's permission," Khalor pointed out. "There's a penalty involved in that."

"He was a captive—and Andine was on the verge of cutting him up into little pieces."

"That's true," Khalor conceded, "and you *did* sort of save his life, I guess. I might be able to go as low as one gold piece."

"A half gold piece. Nothing higher."

"Fifteen silver pennies," Khalor countered.

"Twelve."

"Just to keep this on a friendly footing, why don't we say thirteen?"

"Remind me never to trade horses with you, Sergeant Khalor," Althalus said sourly. "All right—thirteen, then."

"I think Sergeant Khalor might be just about due for a promotion," Chief Albron mused.

"I don't know that we need to go into any extended details here, Chief Albron," Althalus said somewhat later. "When you get right down to it, we're not so much fighting for *our* religion as we're fighting *against* somebody *else's*. There's a man named Ghend who wants to convert the whole world to the worship of *his* God. We're going to prevent that. Ghend's formed little secret groups of his converts in most of the lowland countries, and those cults are stirring up rebellions. The official armies down there are mostly ceremonial. They're very good at polishing their armor, but not much good in a fight. That's why I'm here. Arums are *real* soldiers, and I want to hire them to train and advise the lowlanders to fight their own wars—at least *this* one."

"You're asking me to put myself out of business, Althalus," Albron objected.

"Not really. After we've smashed Ghend's armies, things should go back to normal. The princes of the low countries will still break out in rashes of ambition, and they'll come here to Arum to hire professionals to do their fighting. It's a matter of economics, Albron. It's very expensive to train and maintain any army. Even when there's no war, you have to keep feeding them. It's cheaper in the long run to hire Arums."

"How big is your treasury, Althalus?" Albron asked.

"Big enough—I hope. How long do you think it's going to take to gather the Clan Chiefs together for a general conclave? I'd like to talk to them all at one time."

"Next spring's probably as early as they can all make it," Albron replied. "Once the passes are snowed in, nobody travels in Arum."

Althalus feigned a thoughtful expression. *Will that be soon enough, Em?* He sent his silent question back over his shoulder.

That's more or less what I'd planned, Althalus, she replied. *I know Arums well enough to realize that it takes them a while to get started. Ghend isn't quite ready yet either, so I'd say that the war won't start until about the middle of next summer.*

I'll check my schedule and see if I can work it in, he told her.

The rivers rushed cold and clear through the canyons, and eagles soared on high, and wolves stalked the forests.

The mountains and forests were silent, silent. And then from afar came the wailing of utter despair. And with that wailing, the people came out of the west. Crude they were, clad in half-rotten hides of beasts, and red were their tools and weapons—axes and mattocks of ruddy copper.

And Ghend walked among the people, whispering, whispering, and his eyes burned the ruddy flame of copper.

And the people were afraid.

But Ghend urged them on, and to the rivers they went, and behold, gold was in the rivers, and Ghend commanded them, saying, "Seek the gold, O ye people, and offer it up to Daeva, who is your God, for gold is fair in the eyes of Daeva, and he will bless ye in that ye offer it unto him."

And the people fell to hard toil, searching the rivers for yellow gold, and all the while, the wailing echoed from the mountainsides, and the people were afraid, afraid as they toiled.

"Noisy night, wasn't it?" Althalus said to the shaken Chief Albron the following morning.

"Were you having nightmares, too?" Albron asked.

"Oh, yes—and so was everybody else, most likely. That's not all that unusual, you know. An overripe piece of meat in the stew can do strange things to everybody at the supper table. This particular nightmare didn't grow out of rotten meat, though. It was a present from Ghend. You saw a group of frightened people dressed in fur and carrying copper tools, right?"

"How could you possibly know that?"

"I had the same dream, Albron. Most likely everybody in the castle had that dream. Ghend's done this before. He's trying to change reality. That's what this upcoming war's all about. Ghend wants to change some things that we don't want changed, so we're going to stop him."

"How in the world can you stop somebody with *that* kind of power?" Albron's face had gone ashen, and his hands were trembling.

"I sort of thought I might kill him just a little bit," Althalus replied. "People usually cooperate with you after you've killed them."

"Would you like to borrow my sword?" Albron offered. "Did you hear that dreadful howling sound during *your* dream?" he asked, shuddering.

"Oh, yes," Althalus replied fervently. "Any time you hear that, you'll know that Ghend's playing tricks with your mind and that what you're seeing is something that *he* thought up."

"How did you find *that* out?"

"You don't really want me to answer that, Albron. You're a confirmed skeptic, and if I told you where I got this information, you'd think that I was trying to convert you. I'm not a missionary. I don't tamper with the beliefs of other men. That isn't why Dweia hired me. She hired me because I'm the finest thief who ever lived."

"You're getting paid to do this?"

"Of course. It's very unprofessional to work for nothing. Oh, speaking of that, I'll be gone for the next few days. I think I'd better pay a little visit to my gold mine—unless you and the other Chiefs of Arum would care to accept my promissory note. I'd be happy to sign, of course, but—" He broke off, grinning broadly.

"If it's all the same to you, my friend, why don't we keep all accounts current?" Albron replied.

"I rather thought you might look at it that way. My name might be responsible for that. Isn't it one of the commandments of the Arum religion not to trust anybody named Althalus?"

"It's right up at the top of the list, my friend."

"Perquaine?" Eliar objected the next morning after he, Althalus, and Bheid had returned to the House. "There isn't any gold in Perquaine, Althalus."

"That depends on where you look," Althalus replied. "It's not a natural gold deposit, Eliar. It's a treasure room in the ruins of an old house."

"How did you find it?" Bheid asked him.

"Emmy took me there when we were on our way to Osthos. How much detail do you need to find the right door, Eliar?"

"Not too much, really," Eliar answered. "Emmy and I practiced a bit before we all went to my Chief's castle. *You* have to know exactly where you want to go, but I don't."

"That doesn't make any sense, Eliar," Bheid objected.

"I know. I told Emmy the same thing, but she showed me that I was wrong. The Knife's involved in it somehow. If Althalus has a sort of picture of the place in his mind, the Knife picks up that picture and tells me which door I'm looking for. I guess the Knife can do the same sort of thing Leitha does. It reaches out and picks the information it needs out of people's minds. Then it tells me where to go. Emmy wasn't really too clear when she was telling me how it worked. You know how she is sometimes. She said that it wasn't important for me to know *how* it worked, just that it *would*."

"That's our Emmy, all right," Bheid said. "And there's a lot more to that Knife than she's told us, I think."

"Someday we might want to talk with her about that," Althalus said. "For right now, though, let's grab our shovels and go dig up some gold."

Eliar led them to a corridor in the south wing of the House, and about halfway along that corridor, he stopped in front of a door that looked exactly like all the others. "This is it," he said, opening the door.

Just beyond the door was a road, and Althalus saw the familiar hill off to the right. "This is the place, all right," he told his friends. "We want to go around to the south side." He stepped through the doorway out onto the road and made a large mark in the dirt at the side of the road with his shovel.

"What's that for?" Eliar asked him.

"To let us know exactly where the doorway is."

"I know where it is, Althalus."

"Let's not take any chances. It'll be a long walk back to the House if we lose that door."

They went around to the south side of the hill, and Althalus led the way up to the spot he'd concealed the previous spring. He stuck his shovel into the ground. "This is it, gentlemen. Start digging. We need to go about four feet down. Don't throw the dirt too far away. We'll probably need to fill the hole back in before we leave."

"Why?" Bheid asked curiously.

"To hide the gold we'll leave behind."

"Aren't we going to take all of it?"

"I hope not. It shouldn't take *that* much to hire the Arums."

"How much *is* there?"

"I'm not entirely sure. All I took last time was a hundred or so pounds. We know how to get here now, so if we need more, we can always come back. Let's start digging, gentlemen."

It took them about a quarter of an hour to get down to the flagstone floor, and then Althalus probed around with his dagger until he found the loose-fitting flagstone. He pried it up, reached down into the hidden cellar, and lifted out one of the oval-shaped blocks. Then he blew the dust off the block to reveal the rich yellow metal.

"Dear God!" Bheid breathed reverently, staring at the block of gold in Althalus' hands.

"Pretty, isn't it?" Althalus said. "Here, hold it while I make a lantern. I really don't know how big this cellar is. It's fairly dark down there." He handed the bar to Bheid and made a lantern with the word "*lap*." He lit it and held it down into the cellar. "Give me your hand, Eliar. I don't want to break my leg jumping down."

The cellar was about eight feet deep, and the stacks of gold bars stretched back into the shadows in all directions. "My goodness," Althalus murmured softly.

"Is there quite a bit of it down there?" Eliar called from up above.

"I don't think we're very likely to run out," Althalus replied. "Climb out of the hole, Eliar. I'll hand the bars up to Bheid and then he can give them to you. Stack them in a pile a ways back from the edge of the hole. Bheid, keep count. I think two hundred and fifty should cover current expenses."

"Are there *that* many down there?" Bheid asked in an awed voice.

"It won't even scratch the surface, Brother Bheid. We're moving way out past rich this morning, gentlemen. Let's step right along here. I want the gold back in the House and this hole covered up again before the sun goes down, so let's get cracking."

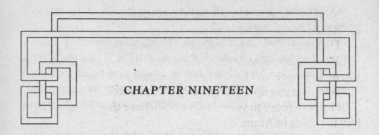

CHAPTER NINETEEN

"Why not just leave it in bars?" Eliar asked as the three of them sat in the tower staring at the carefully stacked wealth they'd brought to the House.

"Most people have never seen a bar of gold," Bheid explained. "They recognize coins, because they probably handle them every day."

"You could be right about that, I suppose," Eliar conceded, "but why Perquaine coins?"

Bheid shrugged. "Perquaine coins are a standard all over the known world. I've been told that their weights are very precise, and the Perquaines don't adulterate the precious metals that go into their coins, the way others do."

Eliar eyed the stack of bars. "This is going to take quite a while, isn't it?" he asked.

"Not really," Althalus told him. "Emmy showed me some shortcuts the last time we did this."

"When was that?"

"Just before I bought you from Andine." Althalus scratched at his ear. "Maybe I'd better make some stout kegs first, though. Twenty thousand coins might just be a few too many to carry in my purse."

"Are you busy right now, Albron?" Althalus asked the young Clan Chief the next morning after breakfast.

"Not really. Why?"

"There's something I'd like to show you."

"All right. Where is it?"

"Not too far," Althalus replied evasively.

"It's snowing outside, you know."

"That shouldn't be any problem. Shall we go?"

Eliar and Bheid were waiting for them in the corridor outside Rheud's armory, and Eliar straightened and saluted his Chief.

"What are you up to, Althalus?" Albron asked suspiciously.

"I want to prove to you that I really *do* have the wherewithal to hire the clans of Arum."

"You're keeping your gold in my armory?"

"Not exactly. We have to go through the armory to get to the place where I keep it, though. Take us through the door, Eliar."

"We go through here, my Chief," Eliar said, opening the armory door. Then he led them across the threshold into the tower room of the House.

"This isn't my armory!" Albron exclaimed, looking around in astonishment.

"No, it's not," Althalus replied.

"Where are we?" Albron's eyes were wild.

"It's a different sort of place, Albron. Don't get all excited. You're perfectly safe."

"We just took a sort of shortcut to get here, my Chief," Eliar said. "There's no danger here. This is probably the safest place in the whole world."

"This is what I brought you here to see, Albron," Althalus said, gesturing at the stout wooden kegs lined up along the curving north wall. "After you've seen what's in those kegs, we can go back to your castle."

Albron was still wild-eyed, and his hand was on the hilt of his sword. "What sort of—" He broke off quite suddenly when Bheid opened one of the kegs, reached in, and lifted out a handful of gold coins. The priest raised his hand and slowly let the tinkling coins cascade back into the keg.

"Pretty, aren't they?" Althalus murmured.

"Are all those kegs filled with—" Albron broke off as Bheid scooped more coins out and once again let them fall in that musical cascade.

"Why don't you look for yourself, Albron?" Althalus invited.

"Open every keg. Pour them out on the floor, if you want. That's why we came here. It doesn't really matter how we got here. That's a little detail you don't need to concern yourself with. The point of this morning's excursion is to prove that I'm not trying to hoodwink you and the other Clan Chiefs. I *do* have gold, and I *am* prepared to spend it. Feel free to examine the coins. Bite them or tap them on the wall to make sure that they really *are* gold. I've been told to present my credentials to you, and I thought this might be the quickest way to do that."

Albron was thoughtfully bouncing one of the coins on his palm. "The weight's right," he mused. Then he examined the coin. "Newly minted, too. Are they all the same?"

"Look for yourself. It might take you a while, but we've got lots of time."

Albron let the coins in his hand spill back into the open keg. Then he opened several of the others and slipped both hands into each one. "Your credentials are very convincing, Althalus," he said. Then he laughed. "I feel like a little boy in a candy shop," he admitted. "Money's just a word, really. The actuality of this much gold is sort of staggering." He kept lovingly sliding his hands into the kegs. "I *love* the feel of it!"

"You're convinced that I've been telling you the truth?" Althalus asked.

"How could I *not* be convinced?" Then Albron almost reluctantly drew his hands out of the kegs and looked out the north window at the mountains of ice beyond the End of the World. "We aren't in Arum, are we?" he asked shrewdly.

"No, we aren't. We're a long ways from Arum." Althalus laughed. "Don't get any ideas, Albron. You can't lay siege to this House, because you'll never be able to find it."

"I wasn't thinking about that—well, not too seriously, anyway. It isn't wise to show an Arum that much gold all in one place at one time, Althalus."

"Would you like to see some of the rest of the House?"

"I think I would, yes. You've managed to stir my curiosity."

"Good. I'll give you the grand tour then, and we can talk about this and that as we go along."

"We'll wait here," Bheid said.

"I was just about to suggest that," Althalus replied, leading Albron to the door.

The two of them went down the stairs, and Althalus showed the kilted Arum Chief the dining hall and the bedrooms. "Quite luxurious," Albron observed.

Althalus shrugged. "Places to eat and sleep," he said indifferently.

"You seem to be in a peculiar mood today, my friend," Albron noticed.

"It's the House," Althalus replied, leading Albron down a long corridor. "I always feel different when I'm here."

"Do you come here often?"

"This is only about the third time, but the first two visits were quite extended."

"That's a cryptic sort of answer."

"I know. It almost has to be that way, though. The House is something on the order of a temple, and I've been firmly told *not* to make an issue of that."

"You're taking orders from that young priest?"

"No. He takes orders from *me*. I get mine a bit more directly. You're a skeptic, Albron, and I've been ordered not to tamper with that. I didn't bring you here to try to convert you."

They continued down the corridor, opening doors and looking into empty rooms. "This is a very peculiar place, Althalus," Albron said. "It seems to go on forever, but almost all the rooms are empty."

"Only when I don't need them. If we happen to get company, I can furnish them."

"Don't you have any servants?"

"No. I don't need any."

"Trying to get information out of you is like trying to squeeze water out of a stone," Albron accused.

"I'm sorry. I've got quite a few restrictions hanging over me right now—trade secrets and all that sort of thing, you understand."

Albron looked pensive. "I think I should be alarmed about all of this, my friend, but for some reason, I'm not. I have no idea of where I am or how I got here, but oddly enough, that doesn't bother me in the slightest. I'm also getting some very peculiar notions."

"Oh?"

"It just occurred to me that you *might* just be the *real* Althalus."

"Is there an imitation one running around?"

"Very funny," Albron said drily. "All that joking about your name when we first met wasn't really a joke, was it?"

"Some of it was—but not all."

"You really *are* the same Althalus who robbed Gosti Big Belly some three thousand years ago, aren't you?"

"Actually it was only about twenty-five hundred. Don't make it any worse than it already is."

"How on earth did you manage to live so long?"

"I was sort of encouraged to keep on breathing," Althalus replied drily. "Are you really sure you want to hear about what happened?"

"Go ahead and tell me the story, Althalus. I'll decide how much to believe later."

"All right, then. I was a thief, Albron. That was back before men had learned how to make steel. Anyway, my luck had turned sour on me, and I was having a terrible time of it. I was passing through Arum, and I heard about how rich Gosti was, so I went to his log fort and entertained him with stories and jokes all through one winter. When spring came and all the snow melted, I robbed him—but believe me, that's *not* how I got those twenty kegs of gold. Gosti was a fat braggart who wanted the world to believe that he was rich. Most of his fabled treasure was nothing but copper pennies."

"I've always wondered about that," Albron admitted.

"You don't have to wonder anymore. Anyway, after I'd made good my escape, I met a man named Ghend, and he hired me to steal a book for him. The book was here in the House, so I came here. The Goddess Dweia was waiting for me when I got here. I didn't *know* she was a Goddess, because she appeared to be a cat."

"That same cat who rides in the hood of your cloak?"

"That's her. I called her Emerald because of her green eyes, and when she started talking to me, I was positive that I'd gone crazy. I got over that, though, and she taught me how to read. Then I spent all those years studying that book Ghend had wanted me to steal for him. I can do a lot of things that other men can't do because of all the time I spent studying that particular book. To keep this short, Emerald—or 'Emmy'—and I came out of the House last spring and started tracking down the people we needed: Eliar and the others. After we'd found them all, we came back here to the House for some fairly intense education, and that's when Dweia let us see who she *really* is."

"I can't believe I'm listening to all of this," Albron said, shaking his head. "Worse yet, I almost believe it."

Althalus gave him a sly, sidelong look. "I'm a master story-teller, Albron. It's one of the tricks I use to get close to rich people. I kept poor, fat old Gosti giggling for one whole winter just so that I could rob him." Then he looked around. The corridor *seemed* empty. He was almost sure, however, that it wasn't. "This is probably going to get me in trouble," he said then, "but out of courtesy, I think I should tell you that this conversation is almost certainly being manipulated."

"Manipulated? How?"

"I really wouldn't know exactly how, but you're asking all the right questions, and I'm giving you all the right answers. When Dweia told me to bring you here this morning, I thought she just wanted me to show you all those kegs of gold. Now I'm not so sure. Maybe the gold was just bait to get you here so that we could have this particular conversation. I'm almost positive that she's somewhere nearby, and that she's feeding you questions and feeding me answers. For some reason she wants you to know what happened here. She doesn't want to convert you, but she *does* want you to have certain information."

"Aren't you being just a bit overly suspicious, Althalus?"

"Use your head, Albron. Would anybody in his right mind believe the wild story I just told you?"

Albron laughed a bit sheepishly. "Now that you mention it . . ." He left it hanging in the air.

Althalus! You stop that! Emmy's voice crackled inside his head, and he laughed with sudden delight.

"What's so funny?" Albron asked.

"I just received some fairly snippy confirmation of what I was just saying," Althalus replied. "I was told in no uncertain terms not to pursue this any further."

"I didn't hear anything."

"You wouldn't have. Emmy talks to me in here." Althalus tapped his forehead. "She came up with that idea before we left the House last spring. I spent about half a year with this cat riding around in the hood of my cloak telling me exactly what to do. I didn't really *need* all those instructions; I can make up my own lies. But Dweia seems to have this overpowering urge to tinker." Althalus shrugged. "Of course she's female, and all women seem to be that way. Delegating authority seems unnatural to women. First they tell you to do something, and then they keep sticking their noses into it while you're trying to do it, and all they're really doing is getting in the way."

"Isn't talking about her that way going to get you into trouble?"

"What's she going to do to me? She needs me too much to set me on fire or turn me into a toad. She knows that I love her, and love's more important to Dweia than blind obedience or slavish fawning. She and I argue all the time, but argument's a form of playing, and Dweia spent so much time as Emmy the cat that playing's second nature to her."

"I think I'd like to meet her."

"Not if you want to keep your soul, you don't. I think the reason for this particular conversation has been to enlist your aid when the conclave meets. I'm not even going to mention religion. I'm going to talk about politics instead so that this whole thing sounds like an ordinary war. I guess I'm supposed to lie to them, and you're supposed to confirm those lies. You don't have to *believe* anything I've just told you—actually it'll probably be better if you don't—but for some peculiar reason, you have to *know* about it. Look at it this way, Albron. We're going to pull off a hoax. I'm doing it for religious reasons and you're doing it for money, but we're still in partnership; so it's important that we understand each other."

"Now you're starting to make sense, Althalus," Albron said, grinning broadly. "If we keep it on that basis, we'll get along just fine." He held out his hand. "Partners?" he suggested.

"Partners it is," Althalus agreed as they shook hands.

It snowed steadily for the two weeks following Chief Albron's visit to the House, and all of Arum turned white. The passes were all clogged with snow, and Albron's messengers to the other clans were obliged to literally claw their way through the drifts to return to the castle in central Arum.

"It's more or less as I'd expected, Althalus," Albron said one snowy afternoon when the two of them were alone in the Chief's study. "Most of the Clan Chiefs are coming to the conclave."

"*Most* of them?"

"There are ten clans altogether, but the clans of Deloso and Agus have sent excuses. I didn't really expect them to attend. Their lands are located over on the eastern fringe of Arum, and the rest of us think of them as more Kagwher than Arum. There's a lot of intermarriage back and forth across that frontier, so those two clans have never really been pure Arum. They're small clans, anyway, and they aren't very good warriors. I don't think we'll miss them all that much." He rolled his eyes upward. "I know *I* won't. I don't like Deloso, and I *despise* Agus."

"Oh?"

"They both spend all their time toadying up to the mine owners in Kagwher, because that's where all their money originates. Their clans are wholly committed to guarding the mines in Kagwher. They don't march, and they don't fight. They just stand guard. They're fat and lazy, and they're willing to work for short pay, since just standing around isn't very strenuous."

"I think we can get along without them. Are there any peculiarities about the other clans I should know about?"

"We're Arums, Althalus. We're *all* peculiar. We have no culture and very few manners. No Arum has ever written a line of poetry or composed a song. We're pure barbarians."

"I think you're being a little hard on yourself, Albron."

"Wait until you meet the others. I'm sure you'll immediately notice that we all defer to Delur. If it weren't for the fact that his clan's the largest in Arum, we wouldn't pay a scrap of attention to him. He's about eighty years old, and it pleases him to look upon himself as the Chief of the Clan Chiefs. The old fool even wears a crown. His clansmen are very good soldiers, so the rest of us put up with him. He's a tiresome, senile old windbag, but I'll fawn all over him and flatter him outrageously because he's the key to what we're trying to accomplish. Once I win Delur over, the rest will probably fall in line. We don't really need him personally, but we *do* need the number of good men he can put in the field."

"You know him, Albron, so I'll leave him to you."

"Good. That way I'll earn my commission."

"Commission?"

"You *were* planning to pay me a bounty for each Chief I recruit, weren't you, Althalus?"

"We can bounce that around later. Tell me about the other Chiefs."

"Gweti's clan is almost as large as Delur's, but Gweti's not very well liked. He's greedy and very stingy. He pays his clansmen the lowest wages in all of Arum, and he makes them buy their own weapons. His clansmen hate him, but they put up with him because he's their Chief. He's a scrawny fellow with greying hair and a pinched-in face. He spends most of his time counting his money, and he's got a musty sort of odor to him."

"And you don't like him, I gather."

"Whatever gave you *that* idea, Althalus?" Albron replied with mock surprise. "I'm almost certain that Gweti has his good points. Just because I've never *seen* any of them doesn't mean that he hasn't got any.

"Oh, I think I'd better warn you about Twengor," Albron continued. "He's big, burly, and belligerent. He'll pick a fight at the drop of a hat, so be careful what you say around him. He drinks too much, and his normal speaking voice is a loud bellow. He's got a bristly black beard that sticks way out in front of him, and I don't think he's taken a bath in the past dozen years. His clansmen would follow him into Hell, though. He's unbelievably lucky in a fight, and when he hires his clan out, it's the whole clan. He won't hire out a platoon or a battalion. With Twengor, it's all or nothing, and he personally leads his men."

"An enthusiast, I take it?"

"At least an enthusiast, and his nephew, Laiwon, is almost as bad, so we have two clans of enthusiasts."

"They belong to different clans? Isn't that a bit unusual? I thought a clan was an extended family."

"It *was* that way a few hundred years ago. Back then, it was all one clan with an east branch and a west branch—connected by a narrow trail that passed through a deep gorge. Then about two hundred years ago, an avalanche blocked that trail, so there wasn't any way for them to stay in touch. After a while, there were two clans instead of one. Now that the clan wars are over and done with, it's safe for them to travel through the lands of other clans to visit each other. There's a certain amount of intermarriage between those two clans now, and I sort of suspect that after Twengor drinks himself to death or gets unlucky in a fight, Laiwon's going to try to reunite the clans—probably by cutting a new road through that gorge."

"The politics of Arum are more complicated than I'd thought."

"Wars are a summer pastime, Althalus. Politics is a year-round entertainment. The southern clans—Smeugor's and Tauri's—are fairly large, but they're not the best soldiers in the world. They're too close to civilization, I think. The lowlanders won't hire them for serious wars, anyway. Smeugor and Tauri put their men to work building fine palaces and good roads, so their people are better qualified as builders than they are as soldiers. Smeugor and Tauri can't quite seem to be able to decide just exactly what they are. They try to impress the lowlanders by pretending to be

Arums, and they try to impress *us* by pretending to be civilized lowlanders."

"Neither fish, nor fowl, nor good red herring?" Althalus suggested.

"Exactly. Their word's not to be trusted, I'm afraid. They'll take your money in a flash, but it might be quite a while before any of their men show up on a battlefield."

"I'll keep that in mind." Althalus made a quick count. "That's nine clans counting yours, Albron. Who's the Chief of the last one?"

Albron made a sour face. "Neigwal," he replied with some distaste. "I probably couldn't prove it, but I suspect that he might be some bastard descendant of our own beloved Gosti Big Belly. The Gods know that he's at least as fat as Gosti was—and almost as bright. His health isn't very good though, so he probably won't be around for much longer."

"What's the matter with him?"

"He's eating himself to death," Albron replied bluntly. "He's too fat to get through an ordinary door, and he wheezes like a broken bellows after the slightest exertion. I'm sure he won't come to the conclave, but his son Koleika usually fills in for him. Koleika's as lean as his father's fat. He's got a huge lower jaw, and he almost never says anything. He's the *real* Chief of the clan, but he pretends that he has to get his father's approval on all his decisions. That gives him the chance to see which way the wind's blowing before he commits himself."

"You Arums aren't nearly as simple and uncomplicated as everyone seems to believe, are you?"

"Not by half, Althalus. Your advantage lies in those twenty kegs of gold you've got stacked up back in the House. Ride that horse just as hard as you can. Let them see gold at every opportunity. Juggle it and jingle it while you're talking, and they'll go along with almost anything you suggest. You're an entertaining fellow, partner, but it's your gold that they'll find more interesting. The dullest man in the world is charming beyond belief when he's pouring gold coins from one hand to the other."

* * *

The winter dragged on interminably with snowstorm following snowstorm with dreary regularity. Althalus passed the time instructing Gher in the fine art of picking pockets. The boy was quick, there was no question about that, but his mind sometimes wandered off in strange directions. "Pay attention, Gher," Althalus scolded the boy on one occasion. "That little grab you just made was unbelievably clumsy."

"I'm sorry, Master Althalus. An idea just came to me, and I got sort of distracted."

"What sort of idea?"

"Ghend's trying to make everything in the world different by going back through Everywhen and playing games with what really happened, isn't he?"

"That's what Dweia says, yes."

"If Ghend can do that, couldn't we do it, too?"

"Probably—if Dweia decides to let us."

"There isn't any problem with that. You can make Dweia do almost anything you want her to do. She starts purring every time you touch her. Andine sort of behaves the same way around Eliar. Maybe someday you could explain that to me. I don't exactly understand what's going on when people get grown-up. Anyway, if Ghend changes things back in Everywhen, you're going to just follow along behind him and change them right back again, aren't you?"

"More than likely, yes."

"Wouldn't it be easier to just take a trip back into Everywhen and kill Ghend's father? Then Ghend wouldn't even be here anymore, would he?"

Althalus blinked.

"Wouldn't that be the easiest way to murder somebody? You don't have to kill *him*. You just go back and kill his father." Gher frowned. "Of course, you wouldn't have any reason to want to murder him in the first place then, would you? I mean, what'd be the point of murdering somebody who never lived at all? But that isn't what distracted me when I bumped you while I was picking your pocket. What I was thinking about was some way to get around Ghend. He's going backward in Everywhen, but couldn't we go forward instead?" The boy frowned. "This isn't coming out very well, is it? What I'm getting at is that if *this* happens now, it makes *that* happen next week."

"It's called 'cause and effect,' Gher."

"I suppose," Gher said absently. "Let's say that you pick up a rock from one place and put it down over there in another place, all right?"

"If you say so."

"But let's say that you go forward in Everywhen and put it right back where it was. Wouldn't that sort of make it so that you hadn't moved it in the first place? That's where I start to hit a problem. If you did it like that, you'd be doing something and *not* doing it both at the same time."

"You're starting to give me a headache again, Gher."

"Let me work on it some more, Master Althalus. I'm almost sure I can come up with *some* way to do it."

"What'd be the point?"

Gher looked at him with astonishment. "Can't you *see* it, Master Althalus? If we did that to Ghend—made him do something and not do something at the same time like that—wouldn't it sort of freeze him right there as if he'd suddenly been turned to stone? You could use him for a hat rack after that. What I'm really getting at, though, is that I'm almost sure that time's not a straight line. I think it's a circle instead, and if we change anything that happens anywhere around that great big circle of Everywhen, it'll change everything else, won't it? Isn't that just about the funnest idea you've ever heard? We can change everything that's ever happened anytime we want to."

"Why me?" Althalus moaned, burying his face in his hands.

It was early the following spring when a mud-smeared Arum arrived at Albron's castle to advise him that Chief Delur would arrive the following day.

"He's early, isn't he?" Althalus noted. "Some of the passes are still clogged with snow."

"That wouldn't particularly bother Delur, my friend," Albron replied. "His clan's the biggest one in all of Arum, and he likes to rub our noses in that. He probably just sent out a few hundred men to tramp out a trail through the snow in the passes. He's too old to ride a horse, so he does his traveling in a litter or a sled. He doesn't pay much attention to the elements. He more or less believes that he's something on the order of the King of Arum, so I'm sure he wants to get here and take charge before the other Clan Chiefs arrive."

"Will the other Chiefs pay much attention to him?"

"They'll pay a lot more attention to your gold, but we *will* want to win him over because of the number of men he can put in the field. I'll flatter him and put on an air of obsequious respect. That'll put him in the mood to go along with us, and your kegs of gold should clinch the arrangement."

"That's what they're for, Albron. You can win a lot of arguments with twenty kegs of gold."

Chief Delur was a tall old man with snow-white hair and a long white beard. When he was thinking about it, he stood stiffly erect as if he had a straight pole strapped to his back. When his attention wandered, however, his posture began to droop as if the weight of his years were crushing him. His outer garments were made of luxurious fur, Althalus noted as the old Chief painfully rose from the sled that four of his burly clansmen had pulled into Chief Albron's courtyard, and the steel helmet he wore was encircled by a wide band of gold that was only a step short of being a crown.

"Well met, my son Albron!" The old man greeted his host in a voice that was no longer booming or hearty.

"My house is honored, Great Chief," Albron replied with a floridly courtly bow. "We had not expected your arrival this early."

"Your message stirred a great curiosity in me, my son," the old man replied. Then he threw a sly look at his retainers. "Moreover, it seemed to me that the men of my household suffered for want of exercise, and that perchance a little jaunt through the mountains might clear their minds and strengthen their bodies that they might better serve me—forasmuch as they all assure me that serving me is their only reason for living."

That brief flicker of irony suggested to Althalus that Albron's assessment of Chief Delur hadn't been entirely accurate. Delur was not *quite* as senile as the other Chiefs appeared to believe he was. Althalus quietly decided to watch the old man rather carefully and to form his *own* opinion.

"Let us go inside, Great Chief," Albron was saying. "The season is raw and inclement, and the fires in my hall burn bright and warm to welcome you."

CHAPTER TWENTY

It was just before midnight on a blustery day a week or so later when Emmy roused Althalus from a sound sleep by touching her nose to the back of his neck. Her nose was as cold and wet as it had always been, and he jerked away from it in the traditional way. "I *wish* you wouldn't do that," he grumbled.

"As long as it works, why change it? Go wake the others, Althalus. There are some things we need to talk about—back at the House."

He threw off his blankets, dressed, and went down the corridor to rouse his friends.

"Is something wrong?" Bheid asked quietly when they gathered out in the hall.

"I'm not sure. She didn't tell me, but she wants to talk to us—in private. Take us to the House, Eliar."

"All right." Eliar led the way to the armory, opened the door, and led them into the familiar tower room.

"Do we have a problem of some kind, Emmy?" Gher asked Dweia after she'd resumed her real form.

"Not really. I just thought we should talk about how we're going to present our offer to the Clan Chiefs, that's all. Things might go more smoothly if we all tell the same story. Quite obviously we won't be able to tell them what's *really* happening. If Albron's right, the Arums don't like to get involved in religious wars, so we'll have to invent something political for their entertainment."

"If you're looking for a war, Dweia, I'd be more than happy to lend you mine," Andine offered. "The notion of all the clans of Arum marching on the city of Kanthon gives me a warm little glow."

"It's a simple solution," Bheid agreed. "The Arums already know about that perpetual war between Osthos and Kanthon, so we won't have to invent some tedious history to explain our need for a vast army."

"And I'll be available to present a stirring plea for their assistance in crushing the degenerates of Kanthon," Andine added.

"It's got a lot to be said for it, Dweia," Althalus said. "Andine *is* the Arya of Osthos, so it stands to reason that she'd have the key to the treasury in her pocket. That'd explain where we got the gold—just in case one of the Clan Chiefs really cares."

"Are you any good at all when it comes to speaking in public, Andine?" Leitha asked her tiny friend.

"Have you been asleep for the past several months, Leitha?" Andine asked archly. "I'm *always* speaking in public. Did you *really* think my dramatic way of speaking was an accident? My voice is the most finely tuned instrument in all of Treborea. I can sing the birds down out of the trees with it, and make stones weep, if I really want to. I probably don't need those kegs of gold. Give me half an hour and a little room and I'll mobilize the Arums with my voice alone."

"She could be right about that," Eliar said. "Back when she had me chained to that post in her throne room, she made a lot of speeches about me, and she even convinced *me* that something awful should happen to that monster Eliar."

"It all more or less fits together, Dweia," Althalus conceded. "We'll have Albron introduce her, and then she makes a stirring plea for aid. Then she can turn it over to me, and I'll give them the details and make the offer. Albron knows what's *really* going on, so he'll be able to make introductions and smooth over any rough spots." He leaned back in his chair. "There *is* a slight inconsistency, though. It wouldn't really be normal for a ruler to make a plea like this in person, would it? Isn't that what diplomats are for?"

"Whatever gave you the idea that I'd behave the way other rulers would?" Andine demanded. "I almost *never* do expected things. It goes sort of like this, Althalus. Despite the violent objections of all my advisors, I've thrown caution to the winds, and with only a few retainers, I've traveled to Arum to make my plea for help in my ongoing war with the villainous Kanthons. At great personal risk, I've braved the dangers of a troubled world to go to Albron's castle to present my case to the noble Clan Chiefs. I'm so unbelievably courageous that you and everybody else who'll be there can hardly stand to be in the same room with me."

"Isn't that just a shade melodramatic?" Bheid objected.

"I'm going to be speaking to Arums, Brother Bheid," Andine pointed out. "I'd take a different approach with Perquaines or Equeros. Arums are a melodramatic people, and I'll give them a performance they'll never forget. Just ask Albron to introduce me and then get out of my way. I'll *own* those Chiefs within a half an hour."

"Aren't we being just a bit overconfident?" Leitha asked.

"Not a bit, Leitha," Andine replied. "I'm the very best."

"Excuse me," Gher said.

"Go ahead, Gher," Althalus told him. "Is there something you'd like to add?"

"Well, wouldn't that be just a little *too* simple? What I'm getting at is would the Arums believe that it'd take *that* many soldiers to run all over just *one* city?"

"He's got a point there, Althalus," Eliar agreed. "Sergeant Khalor told us that the lowlanders always try to get by with hiring just as few soldiers as they possibly can. I think we're going to need a bigger war to make the Clan Chiefs believe us."

"It's the only war I've got right now," Althalus replied.

"Well, not really," Gher disagreed. "There's the one between you and Ghend, isn't there?"

"That's a religious war, Gher. Didn't you hear Albron when he said that Arums don't get mixed up in wars that're based on religion?" He shook his head. "We've got to stick to politics and leave religion out of it."

"Why not just say that the Kanthons are working for the Nekweros? Or that they're on the same side, or something? From what Leitha says, nobody really knows very much about the Nekweros—except that they're real scary. Couldn't we sort of say that there's a King or something in Nahgharash who wants to take over the whole world and that he's managed to talk the silly fellow in Kanthon into joining up with him? Wouldn't that be sort of close to what's *really* going on? And shouldn't a good lie have a certain amount of truth mixed up in it? If the only war we talk about is the one between Lady Andine and the nitwit in Kanthon, the story's just a little too short. Shouldn't there be sort of an open end in it, something we can't quite explain?"

"I think you'd better look to your tail feathers, Althalus," Leitha suggested. "I'd say that the boy's gaining on you."

A warm wind swept across the mountains of Arum the night after Althalus and his friends returned to Chief Albron's castle, and it cut the snow out of the passes the way a hot knife cuts butter. The melting snow sent all the streams out of their banks, and after the floods had subsided, the rest of the Clan Chiefs began to arrive.

Koleika, the heir apparent to the gross Chief Neigwal, was the first to reach Chief Albron's castle. Koleika was lean, with jet black hair and a jutting lower jaw. He was a somber man dressed in leather, and he wore snug leather trousers rather than the traditional kilt of most Arums. He spoke very seldom, and when he did, he had the peculiar habit of never permitting his upper lip to move. Upon his arrival, he spoke briefly with Albron and then largely kept to himself.

A few days later, Smeugor and Tauri, the Chiefs of the two southern clans, rode in. Smeugor was stout, with a fiery red face that was a sea of angry red pimples interspersed with deep scars. He affected an air of forced gaiety, but his narrow eyes were cold and as hard as agates. Tauri had sparse yellow hair and no trace of a beard. He evidently thought of himself as a ladies' man. He wore elegant lowlander garb that wasn't too clean, and he eyed every female in Albron's hall with open lasciviousness. Even as Koleika had, Smeugor and Tauri largely kept to themselves after their arrival.

"I'm catching some hints of ancient hostilities in the air, Albron," Althalus told their host somewhat later. "Is there something going on that I should know about?"

"It's a leftover from the old clan wars, Althalus," Albron conceded. "No Clan Chief really trusts any of the others. This conclave you've asked me to arrange is a break with tradition, and the others are quite suspicious about the whole thing. The history of Arum is a melancholy repetition of deceptions, betrayals, and open murders. We're always on our guard when we enter the territory of another clan. If I hadn't made an issue of your gold, most of the others would probably have begged off. Things should liven up when Twengor arrives."

Chief Twengor—big, burly, and vastly bearded—was roaring drunk when he reached Albron's castle, and his nephew, Chief Laiwon, rode closely beside him to steady his swaying uncle and keep him from falling off his horse. Twengor bawled ancient drinking songs as he rode, sending off-key echoes bouncing down the gorge. Laiwon was an abrupt young man who definitely stood in his more famous uncle's shadow.

Chief Gweti was the last to arrive, and Althalus noticed immediately that the other Chiefs went out of their way to avoid him. Gweti had an overly large head but a very tiny face that barely covered a quarter of it. This gave him a sort of pinched-in look. His bulging eyes shifted continually, and he had a nervous tic in one cheek. When he spoke, his voice sounded very much like the bleating of a sheep.

"I thought they'd all be more like Albron," Andine said to her friends with a slightly worried frown, "but these others are howling barbarians, aren't they?"

"Are we having some doubts about our oratorical ability, dear?" Leitha asked her friend.

"No, not really," Andine replied. "I think I'll have to change my approach, that's all. Albron's relatively civilized, but I think any degree of subtlety might be a bit beyond these others. I may have to beat them over the head with a club to get their attention."

"I just can't wait to hear your speech, Andine."

"To be perfectly honest about it, Leitha, neither can I," Andine replied, still looking worried.

The kilted Clan Chiefs of Arum and their sizable retinues gathered in Albron's hall for breakfast on the morning after Gweti's arrival, and the noise level was quite a bit higher than usual. Albron liked a certain amount of decorum at mealtimes, but some of the other Clan Chiefs were a bit on the rowdy side. After breakfast, Albron suggested that the chiefs and their immediate advisors should gather in some quieter place to discuss the reason he had issued the call for a conclave.

The conference room to which he led them was near the back of his castle, far away from the noisy near riot in the dining hall. The room was secure, well guarded, and *not* in one of the towers. An old Arum folktale had concerned a mass assassination that had once taken place in a tower, so by tradition, all meetings of the various Chiefs took place on the ground floor. There was a table in the center of the room with large chairs for the Chiefs and smaller chairs behind them for assorted advisors. The twenty kegs Althalus and Eliar had brought from the House were stacked unobtrusively in one corner, and there were chairs for Althalus and his friends at the lower end of the table where they could face the assembled Chiefs.

"What's this all about, Albron?" Twengor demanded in his

bellowing voice. "Nobody's called a general conclave for over a century."

"I've been approached by the ruler of one of the city-states of Treborea," Albron replied. "It seems, gentlemen, that there's an employment opportunity in the wind."

"And you're sharing it with the rest of us?" Gweti bleated. "Are you out of your mind?"

"The ruler in question wants to hire more soldiers than I can provide, Gweti," Albron replied. "When you get right down to it, all of us put together don't have enough men. There's work enough—and gold enough—for every able-bodied man in the whole of Arum."

"I just *love* to hear somebody talk about gold," Gweti said, with a dreamy look coming over his pinched face.

"I take it that these outlanders are the emissaries of the ruler you spoke of?" Koleika said, looking at Althalus.

"I was just getting to that," Albron replied. "Lowlanders have some strange customs. Improper as it might seem to us, it's not uncommon down there for a woman to occupy a throne."

"That's *sick*!" Twengor boomed. "I'll listen to this, but you just went down a notch or two in my estimation, Albron." He turned his bloodshot eyes to the stack of kegs in the corner. "Why don't we broach one of those?" he suggested. "This all might go more smoothly if we've got some ale to wash it down with."

"They aren't ale kegs, Twengor," Albron replied with a faint smile, "but what's inside might make it easier to swallow the fact that the person who wants to hire us is a woman."

"I'll be leaving now," the taciturn Koleika announced, rising to his feet.

"A very *rich* woman, Koleika," Albron added. "Shouldn't you hear her offer before you rush off?"

"Turning down a lot of gold won't make you very popular among your clansmen, Koleika," Chief Laiwon pointed out. "Open rebellions sometimes break out when a chief makes that sort of blunder."

Koleika scratched at his outthrusting jaw. "All right," he said, sitting back down. "I'll listen, but I'm not making any promises."

"I wouldn't have any trouble working for a woman," Chief Gweti bleated, "as long as she's rich enough. I'd work for a rich goat, if he offered me enough gold."

"Goat?" Andine's voice was indignant.

Leitha touched the small girl's arm. "Later," she murmured.

"I think this brings us directly to the core of the matter," Albron continued smoothly. "The young lady who appears to be right on the verge of clawing out Chief Gweti's eyes is Arya Andine of Osthos, and she'd like to talk to us about gold."

"I'm going to steal some of your thunder here, Althalus," Andine murmured. "You may have to revise your speech just a bit." Then she rose to her feet, her huge dark eyes smoldering.

"Pretty little thing, isn't she?" Tauri observed to Smeugor, "and she's got a lot more to offer than just gold."

"I was noticing that myself," the pimple-faced Smeugor leered.

"Do I look goatish enough to suit you, Chief Gweti?" Andine asked.

"Poor choice of words, perhaps," Gweti bleated. "Can you find it in your heart to forgive me?"

"Not immediately, Chief Gweti," Andine replied. "I think I'll send you to bed without any supper tonight, and we can talk about it again tomorrow." She paused then, fixing each Chief with her luminous eyes. "Let's not waste any time here, gentlemen. I want to show you something, and then we'll talk about it." She turned slightly. "Eliar," she said, "would you be so good as to open one of those kegs over there for me?"

"Of course, Andine," Eliar replied. He rose, went to the stack of kegs, and removed the lid from one of them.

"Pour it out on the floor," she commanded.

"On the floor?"

"That's the part of the room on the bottom, Eliar. The sides are called walls, and we call the top the ceiling. Pour, Eliar, pour."

"If you say so." Eliar took the keg and tipped it slowly, spilling out a cascade of bright yellow coins that tinkled musically on the floor.

"Pretty, aren't they?" Andine said to the startled Chiefs.

They didn't answer. Althalus noticed that most of them weren't even breathing.

Eliar shook out the last of the coins. "It's empty, Andine," he reported.

"Pour out another one, then."

"Yes, ma'am." He took up another keg.

Two kegs later, Andine held up one hand. "That should be enough for right now," she told him, eying the heap of coins on the floor. Then she smiled winsomely at the assembled Clan Chiefs of Arum. "Have I managed to get your attention yet, gentlemen?" she asked archly.

"I don't know about the others, but you've got *mine*, Princess," Gweti choked.

"Maybe I'll let you have your supper after all, Chief Gweti," she said in her throbbing voice. "See, gentlemen, I'm not really all that hard to get along with." Then her tone changed to become almost a challenge. "The whole point of this little display, gentlemen, is that I'm hiring. Are you interested?"

Old Chief Delur was trembling uncontrollably. "My clan is yours to command, Imperial Arya!" he declared.

"Isn't he just the dearest old gentleman in the world?" Andine said fondly.

"Who did you want us to kill, little girl?" Twengor demanded. "Give me his name, and I'll bring you his head."

"Astonishing!" Andine said in mock amazement. "Everybody says that making speeches is difficult. I didn't seem to have any trouble at all."

"Any speech goes over better with musical accompaniment, Andine," Leitha suggested. "And Eliar plays the gold keg like a world-renowned virtuoso."

"It's the most beautiful music *I've* ever heard," Koleika said fervently. "I'm glad I stayed for the concert."

"I'm just a silly little girl," Andine told them, "So I'll let my Lord High Chamberlain give you all the tiresome details. Now that I've earned your love, I'm certain that you just can't *wait* to do as I ask."

"And what might that be, your Highness?" Gweti asked.

"Oh, I don't know. Would 'Burn! Fight! Kill!' be too much to ask?"

"I don't have any problems with that," Chief Laiwon said. "Just say the word, Arya Andine, and burn, fight, kill it is."

Althalus was a bit nonplused as he rose to his feet. "My beloved Arya appears to have pulled the rug out from under me," he told the Clan Chiefs with a rueful expression. "*I* was the one who was supposed to show you that lovely gold."

"Always trust a woman to seize any opportunity to show off her attributes," Tauri said with a knowing laugh.

"Maybe that's it," Althalus conceded. "Anyway, I was supposed to describe the situation to you first and *then* pour out gold to let you know that she was ready to pay. She's managed to steal my main talking point."

"She *did* get our undivided attention, though, Chamberlain Althalus," Albron said easily. "I think it's safe to say that we've already been enlisted. All that's left for you to do is identify the unlucky people who've crossed her."

"Well," Althalus said, "her finger's currently pointed at Kanthon, but it goes perhaps a little further. The Aryo of Kanthon *thinks* he's right on the verge of becoming the ruler of the whole of Treborea, but thinking isn't his strong point. 'Half-wit' is probably the kindest thing anybody's ever said about him."

The Chiefs laughed.

"Actually, the Kanthons have been duped by the Nekweros. My beloved ruler knows this. Don't let her wide-eyed innocence deceive you, gentlemen. Her mind is sharper than any knife, and she knows exactly who the *real* enemy is. Agents from Nahgharash have been enlisting troublemakers in every land in the low country, and my Arya would be *ever* so grateful if you'd slaughter those troublemakers just a little bit."

"Isn't 'slaughter' an absolute, Chamberlain Althalus?" Albron asked. "I don't see exactly how you could half slaughter somebody. Anyway, after we're wading knee-deep in blood, she wants us to invade Nekweros, right?"

"Later, perhaps," Althalus replied. "Arya Andine thinks it

might be best to dispose of any hostile forces to our rear before we mount an assault on Nahgharash. She seems to believe that neatness counts for something."

"Neat might be nice," Twengor half bellowed, "but I like her 'Burn! Fight! Kill!' idea much more. Wouldn't that be a great motto to put on a battle flag?" He roared with half-drunk laughter.

"This is going to be more complicated than that, Chamberlain Althalus," the pimple-faced Smeugor said pointedly. "We can bluster as much as we like, but the simple fact is that you're not talking about a siege or a single battle. You're talking about a general war stretching from Ansu to Regwos. We Arums are the finest warriors in the world, but are we really ready for *that* kind of war?"

"Smeugor's right," Tauri joined in quickly. "Gold's very nice, but a man has to be alive to spend it. A war like this would spread us so thin that we wouldn't have a chance in the world of winning."

"If you feel that way about it, Tauri, stay home," Twengor boomed. "I've never lost a fight in my life, and I'd attack the sun if the pay was right."

That particular argument lasted for most of the rest of the day. Smeugor and Tauri kept raising more and more objections, hammering on the fact that there weren't enough Arums to fight a general war. Twengor and the others scoffed at that notion, but the two southern Clan Chiefs kept coming back to it.

"It's getting late, gentlemen." Chief Albron stepped in smoothly as the sun was setting. "Why don't we adjourn for supper? We can discuss this further tomorrow."

"Our host is correct, my sons," old Chief Delur intoned. "Let us to table and then to bed, that we may think more clearly on the morrow."

"Well put," Koleika murmured, with no hint of a smile.

"You must be mistaken, Leitha!" Albron exclaimed later that evening when they'd left the Clan Chiefs carousing in the dining hall.

"No, Chief Albron," the pale girl replied firmly. "Smeugor and Tauri are both working for Ghend."

"Should we kill them?" Gher said.

"I think you'd better put a leash on this boy, Althalus," Albron suggested. "I can't think of a quicker way to start a clan war than killing those two."

"It'd also slam the door on something that might be very useful," Althalus mused. "Since I know that they're working for Ghend, they provide a perfect way to pass false information to him. I can use them to lead Ghend around by the nose."

"Only for so long, Althalus," Bheid pointed out. "After they've sent him down the garden path a few times, he's bound to have them both killed."

"What a shame," Althalus sighed with mock regret. "Of course that'd mean that the clans of Smeugor and Tauri would be morally obliged to go to war with Ghend's clan, wouldn't they? And isn't that more or less what we really want anyway? We'll all be terribly sorry, of course, but you know what people say about clouds and silver linings. I'm almost certain we'll be able to bear our grief. After all, we're terribly brave, aren't we?"

The Clan Chiefs gathered again in the room at the back of Albron's castle immediately after breakfast the next morning. "Where's the gold?" Chief Gweti demanded in an alarmed bleat.

"We put it in a safe place," Althalus replied. "We certainly wouldn't want some thief to steal it, would we?"

"May the Gods forbid!" Gweti replied fervently.

"I have it on the best authority that they will," Althalus replied. "I take it then that you gentlemen have decided that you'd like to go to work for my beloved Arya?"

"Right after the haggling," Twengor said. He looked at Andine. "How much are you willing to pay, little lady—and for how long?"

"I've enlisted the aid of a certain Sergeant Khalor," Andine replied. "He's one of Chief Albron's most experienced officers, and he knows far more about these details than I could ever hope to know. He'll make certain that *I* don't get cheated. *You* gentlemen are going to have to look out for yourselves."

"I've heard of him," Gweti said with obvious disappointment. "I was sort of hoping—"

"That you could swindle me personally, Chief Gweti?" she asked archly. "You wouldn't really take advantage of a poor, innocent little girl, would you?" She fluttered her eyelashes at him.

He sighed with a certain resignation. "No, I suppose not."

"Isn't he a dear?" Andine said fondly. "Leitha and I'll leave you gentlemen to your entertainments then. As I understand it, haggling about prices can grow quite emotional, and it involves some highly colorful language that innocent ladies shouldn't hear. Enjoy yourselves, gentlemen—but no hitting." Then she swept from the room with Leitha close behind her.

Sergeant Khalor adamantly held his ground on "standard fee" as the basis for negotiation, despite some shrill objections. Gweti in particular wanted to hold out for a fairly exotic "fee-for-service" arrangement. Chief Gweti had obviously done some computations, and he realized the "standard fee" would put a fair amount of those twenty kegs beyond his reach. That seemed to cause him something very much akin to physical pain.

"Actually, Chief Gweti, I'm being generous," Khalor pointed out. "We're hiring every man you can muster. If he can stand up, see lightning, and hear thunder, we'll pay for him. I won't push for a discount on cripples as I probably should. We're honorable Arums, noble Chiefs. How would it look to the rest of the world if we cheated an innocent young girl?"

"Who cares what the rest of the world thinks?" Gweti demanded.

"*You* should, Chief Gweti," Khalor told him. "If the word gets around that you're a cheat, nobody's ever going to want to do business with you again. Your soldiers will stay at home, and you'll still have to feed them. You'll be old and grey and up to your eyebrows in debt before anybody out there will ever hire men from you again."

"The good Sergeant speaks truly, son Gweti," Chief Delur intoned pompously. "The prosperity of all Arum might well hinge upon what we do here in this day. As all men know, Arum soldiers are the best to be found across the wide, wide world, but if Arum Chiefs are dishonorable men, who will ever come to these sacred mountains again with gold to deal with us? Take less, my sons, that ye may gain more."

Althalus was closely watching Smeugor and Tauri, who were sitting somewhat apart from the Chiefs and holding a whispered conversation. They seemed to be a bit worried about something. Andine's blatant display on the previous day appeared to have taken them off guard.

Althalus let his gaze drift across the faces of the clansmen seated directly behind the pair of wayward chiefs, and he saw some hints of a certain dissatisfaction there. Smeugor and Tauri, it appeared, weren't overly popular with the members of their clans, and their obvious dismay with Andine's "show everybody the gold" strategy was arousing a certain disaffection. Althalus tucked that notion away for future use. For right now, Smeugor and Tauri might be very useful, but when they started to be *un*useful, a well-coordinated mutiny might be a quick solution to the problem.

The haggling continued for most of the rest of the day as each Clan Chief struggled to find reasons to increase his share of the gold, but Sergeant Khalor held fast to his original offer based on numbers alone. Stubbornly, he kept repeating, "So much a head," almost as if he were buying a herd of sheep. The Chiefs of the smaller clans protested vigorously, but Khalor ignored claims of "better training," "more enthusiasm," and "superior weaponry" and concentrated on numbers. Finally, he put it to them bluntly. "That's my offer, gentlemen. You can take it or you can leave it. If Arum doesn't have enough men for us, we can probably find recruits in Kweron or Kagwher. I'm sure that if I mention all the profitable looting that's likely to be going on during this war, I won't have much trouble finding enough soldiers to fill up the ranks of this army. I'd rather have Arums, but I'll take what I can get."

Their resistance more or less collapsed at that point.

"Oh, one other thing," Khalor added. "Payment will be on delivery. I won't pay for promises. I'll see the bodies right in front of me before I'll open the purse."

"That's not the way it's done!" Gweti objected. "Our word's *always* been accepted in the past!"

"Not this time, Chief Gweti," Khalor told him. "I'm buying men, not promises."

Albron leaned closer to Althalus. "I told you that Khalor was very good, Althalus," he said slyly. "Don't you think his services might be worth a premium of some kind?"

"Certainly, Albron," Althalus agreed placidly. "I'll tell you what I'll give you by way of a premium. I'm the one who owns that gold mine, so I can buy almost anything, but I'll give you my absolute promise that I won't make any attempt whatsoever to hire Khalor right out from under you. How's *that* for a premium?"

It was well past midnight when Emmy woke Althalus in the usual way, and her nose hadn't grown any warmer or drier, he noticed. "We have to go to the House, Althalus," she said quite urgently.

"Trouble?" he asked.

"Ghend's making his move. We aren't quite ready yet, but we're going to have to respond."

Althalus dressed and went down the torchlit hallway to rouse his friends. They went through the armory door again and up the stairs to the tower.

"Wekti's right on the verge of collapse," Dweia told them. "We're going to have to deal with that."

"Wekti?" Bheid said. "Who cares about Wekti? It's nothing but one vast sheep pasture."

"If Wekti falls, Plakand will as well, Brother Bheid," Dweia said crisply. "Then they'll march on Medyo. Awes is on the eastern frontier of Medyo, and *this* time there won't be *anything* left after the battle's over. The destruction of Awes has always been a part of Ghend's plan."

"How are we going to get enough men there to make any difference, Emmy?" Eliar asked. "It's a month or more from Arum to Wekti."

"Use the doors," Gher suggested.

"I *can't* bring Arum soldiers to the *House*, Gher," Eliar objected.

"You probably won't have to bring them *to* the House, Eliar," Gher said. "Just take the House to them instead—well, not the *whole* House. A couple of doors ought to turn the trick."

"Would you like to explain that?" Eliar said with a certain exasperation.

"I've been sort of working on this," Gher admitted, "so maybe I jumped over a few things. We don't really want all the Arums to know about the House and the doors, but I think I know of a way to pass them through so that they won't even know they've been here. We'll need a lot of bushes, though."

"Bushes?"

"To kind of hide what we're doing. It sort of goes like this. You're leading this army of Arums, you see, and you march them along a path that goes through a big thicket of bushes. You've got a door hidden in that thicket, and they march on through the door, and they're in the House—only they don't know it, because we've piled more bushes up in the hallway outside the door they've just come through. Then you keep on—" He stopped, frowning slightly. "Oops," he said.

"What's wrong?" Eliar asked.

"I think I missed something. The doors aren't really wide enough. I mean, if you've got a whole lot of people, and they can only go through one at a time—" He shook his head. "Maybe I'd better work on this some more."

"Don't worry about the doors, Gher," Dweia told him. "That's my department. They'll be as wide—or as narrow—as I want them to be."

"That'd be *great*, Emmy!" he exclaimed. "You could fix it so that a door's so narrow that *I'm* the only one who could wiggle through."

"You're wandering, Gher," Leitha told him. "Finish one thought before you jump off to another one. You've got an army out in the hallway. What are you going to do with them?"

"Oh, that's right. I was sort of thinking that Eliar leads them through a door they can't even see into the House here, but they don't know that they're *in* the House because the bushes hide it. Then they go to another door and walk out into this Wekti place. They start over here, and they end up over there, but they don't even know it."

"Except that they start out in the mountains and end up in the flat country," Eliar objected.

"The House can take care of that. Since it's Everywhen, it can make the trip through those bushes last for as long as Emmy wants it to last. The soldiers are going to *think* they've been walking through those bushes for weeks and weeks, but when they come out, it'll only be a minute or so later. *We'll* know that, but *they* won't." He looked at Dweia. "Could we do it that way, Emmy?" he asked her.

"I think we can, yes," she replied. "What started you to thinking about this, Gher?"

"The other day I was sort of listening when that Chief with the squoze-in face was talking with the one with the big jaw. He thought it was going to be real neat that he'd get paid for whole weeks when his soldiers wouldn't be doing anything but walking. Then I got to thinking about how the House can make distance and time turn into the same thing. The House is kind of like a shortcut, but I don't think we want those people to know about it. Some of them would probably get all excited, and maybe try to use it in ways we wouldn't want them to. Then I came up with the notion of the bushes. They won't know anything at all about the House, because they won't even know that they've been here. Wouldn't it sort of work out that way, Emmy?"

Dweia was smiling fondly at him. "You're an absolute treasure, Gher," she said. "I believe I owe you quite a few hugs and kisses for this particular idea."

Gher blushed furiously. "Just a thank-you would be enough, Emmy," he protested. "I don't really like all that hugging and kissing business. It's all gooey and sticky, and it makes me *real* uncomfortable."

"Gooey and sticky get more interesting after you grow a little older, Gher," Andine told him. Then her huge eyes moved slowly to Eliar's face, and a wicked little smile touched her lips. She didn't say anything, but for some reason, Eliar's face turned bright red.

Part Four

ELIAR

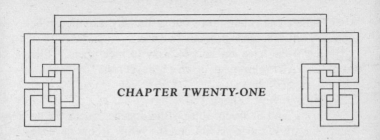

CHAPTER TWENTY-ONE

A summer storm had been raging across the mountains of Kagwher with roiling clouds, staggering lightning bolts, and sharp cracks of thunder that seemed almost to shake the very stones of the eternal House at the End of the World. Wind-driven rain had swept the battlements, but not long after midnight the storm passed, and the sliverlike moon emerged from behind the clouds to look down upon a world washed all clean by the savage storm.

Dweia stood at the north window in all her perfection, and her green eyes were a mystery.

"Just exactly what's Ghend doing in Wekti, Dweia?" Althalus asked her.

"The trouble's coming from the north, Althalus," she replied, turning back to look around the room where they all had gathered. "Ghend sent Gelta to southern Ansu to stir up the tribes along the frontier. She dominated those tribes back in the fourth millennium, and she's the central figure in their mythology. Her return appears to be miraculous, and the southern Ansus are convinced that she's an immortal War Goddess. They'll follow her blindly, and if we don't stop her, she'll crush Wekti within a month."

"How did she persuade the Ansus that she's really the same Gelta who led them six thousand years ago?" Althalus asked. "The Ansus aren't very bright, but that should have been a little hard to swallow, even for them."

"Ghend arranged a few demonstrations, pet," Dweia replied.

"After Gelta came riding down out of the sky, skepticism became very unfashionable in southern Ansu."

"Do the Wekti have any sort of army to meet them?" Eliar asked. "Enough to slow them down a little, at least?"

Bheid laughed.

"What's so funny?" Eliar asked.

"Wekti's a land of sheep, Eliar," Bheid said. "That's the domain of the white-robed priests, and the White Robes have elevated 'meek' to an art form. The Wekti won't defend themselves. The apostate White Robes have seen to that."

"Do you suppose we could discuss theology some other time, Bheid?" Althalus suggested. "I need facts, not denunciations. Where's the capital of Wekti, and who rules?"

"Maybe I *was* getting a little sidetracked," Bheid apologized. "The government of Wekti's located in the old provincial capital of Keiwon. The city dates back to the days of the Deikan Empire, and the titular ruler's a direct descendant of the last imperial governor."

"Titular?"

"He's a joke, Althalus. His official title is 'Natus,' which is supposed to mean 'father.' Shepherds have some very odd notions. His name's Dhakrel, and he's a figurehead with no real authority. He wears a golden crown, dresses himself in an antique Deikan toga, and carries a scepter. He's a pudgy, balding man of middle years with a mind uncontaminated by thought. He never leaves the palace, and neither do any of his 'Royal Proclamations.' The sycophants in his court all tell him how important he is. His face appears on Wekti coins, and that's just about the entire extent of his significance."

"Who's really in charge, then?" Andine asked.

"Exarch Yeudon."

"Exarch? Is that some title of nobility?"

"It's a theological title, Princess. Each of the three orders is ruled by an Exarch. The term roughly translates as 'the priest of the priests.' Yeudon's the real power in Wekti, so he's the one we'll have to deal with. He's a brilliant man, but he's shrewd, devious, and not to be trusted."

"Then they don't have any kind of army at all?" Eliar pressed.

"Two ceremonial legions in Dhakrel's palace," Bheid answered. "They're fat, lazy, and probably completely useless. They carry swords but don't know how to use them, and if you marched them for more than a mile, they'd probably all collapse and die of sheer exhaustion."

Eliar was frowning. "What about the ordinary people? Could we make decent soldiers out of *them*?"

"I doubt it," Bheid said. "They're shepherds, and they're more sheep themselves than they are human. A loud noise would send them running off in all directions, bleating in terror. The average Wekti spends his days cuddling lambs to his breast and composing bad poetry—and worse songs—about his love for the shepherdess in the next valley."

"Do we really have to get involved with these people, Emmy?" Eliar asked, turning to Dweia. "It doesn't seem to me that they're worth the trouble."

"We don't have much choice, Eliar," the Goddess replied. "Ghend already controls Nekweros in the west. You might want to talk with Sergeant Khalor about your strategic position when your enemy controls lands on both sides of you. We won't be defending Wekti so much as we'll be defending our eastern flank."

"I guess I hadn't thought of that," Eliar conceded.

"We'd better go to Keiwon and talk with this Yeudon," Althalus decided.

Bheid laughed. "The war's probably going to be over before we get the chance to do that," he said.

"I didn't quite follow that."

"The White Robes are obsessively traditional, Althalus. It takes about six months to gain access to Yeudon. We'd have to wade our way upstream through whole platoons of self-important church functionaries before we'd even get close to the Exarch."

"I could use a door," Eliar suggested.

"I don't think we want to wave the doors around in unfamiliar places," Althalus replied. "Ghend might have spies in Keiwon."

He looked speculatively at Bheid. "Who's the headman of your order?" he asked.

"Exarch Emdahl."

"If he happened to send a messenger to Keiwon to speak with Yeudon, that messenger wouldn't have much trouble bypassing the usual procedures, would he?"

"Probably not, but it'd take a week at least to get in to see my Exarch to explain the situation to him."

"Your Exarch's a busy man, Bheid. We don't need to bother him. Who'd normally carry his message to Yeudon?"

"Probably a Scopas—one of the nobles of our church."

"Do they wear any special garb?"

"Their robes aren't made of burlap, if that's what you mean." Bheid plucked at the front of his roughly woven black robe. "And they wear scarlet sashes about their waists."

"Congratulations on your promotion, Scopas Bheid," Althalus said.

"We can't do that!"

"Why not? If all it takes is a change of clothes to open doors, I'll spin you several yards of gold cloth."

"It's forbidden!"

"In Awes, probably, but we aren't going to Awes, Bheid. We're going to Keiwon. Your order has no authority in Keiwon, so the rules don't apply there, do they?"

"That's pure sophistry, Althalus."

"Of course it is. Sophistry's the basis of any good religion. Didn't you know that? Would you need any credentials aside from the costume?"

Bheid started to object further, but then his eyes narrowed. "It might just work," he admitted. "It goes against everything I've been taught, but—"

"Our purpose is noble, Scopas Bheid. Our means to achieve that purpose aren't particularly important." Then Althalus looked at Dweia. "Are you coming with us?" he asked her.

"I think you can manage things this time without my help, Althalus. The girls, Gher, and I will wait here."

"Suit yourself," he said, rising to his feet. "Let's go find the door to Keiwon, Eliar."

Dawn was just peeping over the rolling hills of Wekti when Eliar led Althalus and Bheid through a door that opened out into a small clump of willows off to the side of the road that came up from the south. Althalus went to the edge of the trees to look at the city.

Keiwon lay a hundred miles or so upstream from the ancient ruins of Awes, and it was on the east bank of the River Medyo. It had that second-rate quality about it that was characteristic of all provincial capitals. In many ways it was no more than an imitation Deika, complete with a forum, a palace, and a temple— except on a reduced scale. The architecture was uninspired, and there was a wooden quality to the statues. The provincial governors who had ruled Wekti for centuries had been bureaucrats from the imperial city of Deika, and no secondary bureaucrat is ever burdened with artistic integrity—or any other kind, for that matter. They had wanted Keiwon to resemble Deika as closely as possible, and as a result, Keiwon did not soar as Deika had. It huddled instead.

The temple of Kherdhos adjoined the gubernatorial palace, and that too was a reflection of Deika, Althalus recalled, though he hadn't spent much time in the official part of Deika twenty-five centuries ago when he'd gone there to rob the salt merchant Kweso. The similarities gave him that peculiar sense of having done all of this before, and he idly wondered if Exarch Yeudon might possibly keep a few dogs somewhere in his temple.

Bheid looked decidedly uncomfortable in his new finery. "How do you want me to proceed here, Althalus?" he asked.

"I'd try for arrogance, Bheid. Do you think you could manage that?"

"I suppose I could try."

"Don't suppose, Bheid, *be*. You have to act the part if you're going to pull this off. You're carrying a vital message from Exarch Emdahl to Exarch Yeudon, so let it be known that you'll kill anybody who stands in your way."

"Kill?"

"You don't have to do it, Bheid. Just threaten. You're wearing the garb of one of the nobles of your order. Bull your way through."

"Just exactly what *is* the message I'm carrying? Maybe I should write it down."

"Absolutely not. You don't want it to fall into the wrong hands. It's a verbal message, and it's for Yeudon's ears only. It should probably go something like this. Your Exarch has recently discovered that the Demon Daeva has begun his campaign to conquer the world, and since your Exarch's so unspeakably holy, he's set aside his traditional animosity for the apostate White Robes to rush to their aid in the upcoming war with the powers of darkness."

Bheid blinked.

"We need *some* kind of reasonable explanation for the horde of barbaric Arums who'll be arriving in Keiwon tomorrow or the next day, don't we? I'm sort of scraping this off the wall right now, so it's got a few rough edges. We can smooth those out as we go along. Yeudon probably already knows that there are Ansus massing on his northern frontier, but you'll behave as if you're bringing him alarming news. Try to look horrified and mention a few things that'll get his undivided attention—end of the world, invasion from Hell by demon hordes, the sun going out like a snuffed candle, that sort of thing. Then you'll introduce Eliar as the spokesman for the clans of Arum, and you'll tell Yeudon that I'm a sort of business manager who's holding the purse strings of our sacred mission to save the world from the powers of darkness."

"Isn't that just a little thick, Althalus?"

"Of course it is. I'm just giving you a broad outline. Feel free to amend and improvise as you see fit, Brother Bheid. Unleash your creative imagination. After the way you handled Ambho back in Kweron, I have absolute confidence in your ability to lie convincingly."

Bheid winced. "I'm not really supposed to lie to people," he protested.

"When you get right down to it, this lie comes dangerously close to the real truth of the matter. We actually *are* offering aid, and this upcoming war *is* a struggle between good and evil. All I'm suggesting is that you forget to mention a few things that Yeudon's probably incapable of understanding. If you were to come right out and tell him the bald truth, he'd probably have you locked up as a dangerous lunatic. Just give him as much truth as you think he can handle and gloss over the rest. Tell him that the Arums are coming to fight his war for him, and he'll welcome you with open arms. We need to get our foot in the door, Bheid, and this is the quickest way I know of to do that." He glanced at the newly risen sun. "Let's go on into town," he said. "The White Robes in the temple should be stirring by now."

Bheid assumed a harsh, imperious expression when they entered the temple, and he spoke abruptly to the minor church functionaries as he demanded to be taken immediately to Exarch Yeudon. Althalus watched, but said nothing. Given a bit of training, he mused, Brother Bheid appeared to have some potential for an entirely different profession.

Not *all* of the White Robes leaped to do Bheid's bidding, however. There was an officious-looking priest seated at a small table in the anteroom outside the Exarch's study who had that well-remembered down-the-nose expression that had so irritated Althalus back in Deika. "You'll have to wait your turn," he told Bheid in a lofty tone of voice.

"If this fool doesn't get to his feet immediately, I want you to kill him, Eliar," Bheid said flatly.

"You're in charge, my Scopas," Eliar replied, drawing the Knife.

"You *wouldn't!*" The officious doorkeeper scrambled to his feet and stopped looking down his nose.

"That's a little better. Now go tell your Exarch that Scopas Bheid is here with an urgent message from the Exarch of the Black Robes. The fate of the world may not *totally* depend on how quickly you obey, but *your* fate does. Now move."

The terrified priest in the white robe scrambled to the Exarch's door.

"Got his attention, didn't I?" Bheid murmured with a grin.

"You're doing just fine, Bheid," Althalus told him. "Don't change a thing."

"The Exarch will see you, Reverend Sir," the chastened official said with an obsequious bow.

"It's about time," Bheid said. Then he led Althalus and Eliar into Yeudon's ornate study.

The room was lined with many shelves where books and scrolls were stored, and there were lambskin rugs here and there on the polished stone floor. Exarch Yeudon was a thin, almost emaciated man in a cowled white robe. He had silvery hair and a deeply lined face that wore a slightly amused expression. "What took you so long, Scopas Bheid?" he asked with a faint smile.

"Have we met before, your Eminence?" Bheid asked.

"Not personally, Scopas, but I've been receiving progress reports—somewhat hysterical ones, actually—ever since you came into the temple. I was about half expecting you to kick down my door."

"I'll admit that my manner may have been just a trifle uncivil," Bheid confessed. "The importance of my Exarch's message seems to have unhinged my sense of courtesy. I apologize for that."

"No apologies necessary, Scopas Bheid. Would you have *really* had Brother Akhas killed?"

"Probably not," Bheid said. "But over the years, I've found that the word 'kill' opens doors almost immediately."

"It certainly woke up Brother Akhas. Tell me, Scopas Bheid, what could possibly be so important that you felt obliged to offer general murder to bring it to my attention?"

"There's trouble brewing on your northern frontier, your Eminence," Bheid said gravely.

"We're aware of that, Scopas Bheid. Was there anything else?"

"The trouble may be more serious than it appears on the surface, your Eminence. It's serious enough at any rate that it's moved my Exarch to offer assistance."

"Did the sun go out while I wasn't watching?" Yeudon said

with a surprised look. "What could possibly have shaken Emdahl so much that he's going *this* far?"

"Have you perhaps heard of a man named Ghend, your Eminence?" Bheid asked carefully.

Yeudon's face went dead white. "You're not *serious*!" he exclaimed.

"I'm afraid so, your Eminence. We Black Robes have sources of information that aren't always available to White Robes or Brown Robes. Exarch Emdahl discovered just this past week that the tribes of southern Ansu are being stirred up by several of Ghend's underlings. Evidently Gelta, the Queen of Night, is planning to invade Wekti."

"Daeva's finally making his move then," Yeudon said in a trembling voice. "He's coming out of Nahgharash."

"So it would seem, your Eminence. *That* was the information that moved Exarch Emdahl to discard his customary hostility to your order to offer his aid. The various orders don't agree about very much, but we *do* agree that Daeva's our ultimate enemy."

"We're lost, Scopas Bheid," Yeudon despaired. "We're priests, not soldiers. There's no way we can meet those savages from Ansu."

"Exarch Emdahl's well aware of that, your Eminence, and he's already taken steps to bring in a people who *are* qualified to make war. He opened the treasury of our order to hire mercenary soldiers from Arum. They'll reach Wekti very soon, and even Gelta and Pekhal may have trouble dealing with *those* howling barbarians."

"Howling barbarians?" Eliar objected.

"A relative term, Eliar," Bheid apologized. He turned back to the pale-faced Yeudon. "This kilted young man is Eliar, and he's the representative of the Clan Chiefs of Arum. I prevailed upon him to come with me to confirm my words and to go to your northern frontier to make a preliminary survey of the terrain for the Generals of the approaching army."

"You move very fast, Scopas Bheid," Yeudon noted.

"I have all the demons of Hell snapping at my tail, your Eminence," Bheid said wryly. "That encourages me to step right along. This other gentleman is Master Althalus, the one who dispenses money. He's widely traveled in many lands, and he's an expert in getting things done in the most efficient manner. To put it in the bluntest terms, he knows which officials can be bribed to cooperate."

"You Black Robes are more devious than I'd thought," Yeudon said.

"We're the oldest of the orders, your Eminence," Bheid said rather sadly, "and we've had more experience in the *real* world than the White Robes or the Brown Robes. Your orders are innocent of the innate corruptibility of most of mankind. We Black Robes lost all our illusions eons ago, and a world without illusions is a very bleak place. We see the world as it really is, not as we'd like it to be. Our motives are ultimately as pure as yours, but our methods are sometimes a bit cynical. We'll use whatever it takes to achieve our goals in an imperfect world."

"Maybe I should take lessons," Yeudon said.

"Watch, your Eminence," Althalus told him. "Watch and learn." Then he grinned roguishly. "And since we're allies, we'll even give you a special rate for your education."

"Back to the House?" Eliar asked when they'd returned to the thicket outside the walls of Keiwon.

Althalus frowned slightly. "Let's go see Albron first," he decided. "I think we'd better get things started. I want an advance party in Keiwon by tomorrow morning. Gelta's not the sort to dawdle around. She could come crashing across that frontier any day now, so let's be ready for her."

Eliar had prudently marked the location of the door, and they passed through the House to reach Chief Albron's study.

"I was hoping you'd stop by, Althalus," Albron said. "There's something we need to talk about."

"Oh?"

"I've been cudgeling myself over the head about something ever since the conclave, and I can't for the life of me come up with any way to get around a notion that might possibly send Dweia right straight up the wall."

"I try to avoid that if I possibly can. What's the problem, Albron?"

"I think we're going to have to let Sergeant Khalor know about the doors."

"*What?*"

Albron raised one hand. "Hear me out, my friend," he said. "When we brush aside all the nonsense about rank and station, Khalor's the one who'll *really* be commanding our forces, and if he doesn't know about those doors, he won't be able to take full advantage of the strategic edge they'll give us. When you get right down to it, Althalus, it's far more important for *him* to know about them than it was for *me* to know."

"My Chief has a point, Althalus," Eliar said. "Sergeant Khalor's the best in all of Arum, and if we tell him the secret of the doors, he'll be able to use that in ways none of the rest of us could even begin to imagine."

"I'll have to talk it over with Dweia," Althalus said dubiously.

"You *do* understand my point, though, don't you?"

"Oh, *I* understand right enough. Floating the notion past Dweia might take bit of doing, though."

"There's nothing in Wekti to work with, Dweia," Althalus told her that evening when they were alone in the tower. "If Bheid's evaluation comes even close, there isn't anybody with a back-bone in the entire county."

"They might surprise you, love," she disagreed.

"I don't think I'll get my hopes up very much." Then he braced himself. "One other thing. Albron said something that we might want to consider."

"Oh? What was that?"

"The key man in what we're going to try in Wekti—and any other place where Ghend has things afoot—is likely to be Sergeant Khalor. We might be the ones with the grand ideas, but Khalor's the one who's going to have to carry them out."

"He seems competent enough to me."

"He's a good soldier, right enough." Althalus hesitated.

"There isn't any easy way to say this, Dweia, so I'll put it to you straight out. Albron thinks that we should show Khalor how the doors work."

"It makes sense," she replied almost indifferently.

"Emmy!" he protested.

"I said all right, Althalus. Go ahead and show Khalor how we use the doors."

"Aren't you going to object at all?"

"Did you want me to object?"

"Well, no, but I was positive you would."

"Why should I?"

"I thought that the House and what we can do with the doors was some kind of deep, dark secret."

"Where on earth did you get *that* absurd idea? Ghend knows all about the doors. He has doors of his own in Nahgharash, and he can do the same things we can by using *his* doors. Why should we hide the doors from our friends when our enemies already know about them? That wouldn't make any sense at all, would it?"

"What's going on here, my Chief?" Sergeant Khalor demanded, looking around at the long corridor. "This isn't the arms room."

"No, Sergeant, it's not," Albron replied.

"Where are we? And how did we get here?"

"It's a part of the world that very few people know about, Sergeant," Althalus told him. "There *is* an explanation for what we just did, but it's very complicated—and more than a little tedious. Why don't we just say that certain normal rules don't apply here and let it go at that? Now, if you decided that you wanted to go back to the city of Kanthon down in Treborea, how would you get there?"

"I'd steal a horse and ride southeast for several weeks. Why would I want to go back to Kanthon, though?"

"I just picked it at random, Sergeant. I know you've been there and that you'd recognize the place if you saw it. I happen to know another way to get there. Lead us to Kanthon, Eliar."

"Right. It's on down this hall a ways."

Sergeant Khalor looked suspiciously at his young protégé, but made no comment.

"Here it is," Eliar said finally, opening the door.

Sergeant Khalor looked briefly at the city beyond the threshold. "That *looks* like Kanthon, all right," he said almost indifferently. Then he looked at Albron. "Don't we have anything better to do, my Chief? This is all very entertaining, but I've got some troops I've got to get ready for a long march."

"You don't believe that really *is* Kanthon down there, do you, Sergeant?" Althalus suggested.

"Oh, of *course* it's Kanthon, Althalus," Khalor said with heavy sarcasm. "Everybody *knows* that natural laws don't apply to people like you. Why don't we take a quick hop to the back side of the moon so that you can show me the sights?"

"Would you like to go into the town for a while, Sergeant?" Albron asked him.

"If I walk through that painting, I'll rip it, my Chief."

"It isn't a painting, Khalor. That really *is* the city of Kanthon."

"Have you been drinking?" Khalor asked bluntly.

"There's a thought," Althalus said. "Why don't we go on into town and see if we can find a tavern?"

Eliar led them across the threshold onto the road leading toward the gates of the city, pausing briefly to mark the location of the door.

The look of skepticism began to fade from Khalor's hard-bitten face as they approached the gates of Kanthon. "It's that blond girl from Kweron—Leitha—isn't it?" he guessed. "She really *is* a witch after all, isn't she?"

"If it makes you comfortable to think so, Sergeant," Althalus replied. "Now then, the point of this overdone theatrical display has been to suggest something that you might find quite useful. Do you really want a cup of ale right now? We can go into town and have a few, if you want, but if you can hold off for a while, there are a couple of other things I'd like to show you."

"The ale can wait," Khalor said shortly. He squinted at Althalus. "If this is some sort of game, Master Althalus, I'm going to be very, very disappointed in you. Why don't we look at some other town? But this time *I'll* decide which town."

"All right. Which town would you like to see?"

Khalor looked suspiciously at Albron and Eliar. "Bhagho," he said shortly.

"Where in the world is Bhagho?" Albron asked. "And when were you ever there?"

Khalor grinned at Althalus. "*That* sort of spokes your wheel, doesn't it? You haven't had time to create your illusion, have you?"

"No, I haven't. You're a shrewd man, Khalor. Let's go to Bhagho, Eliar."

Sergeant Khalor spent the next hour naming towns scattered across most of the lowland countries, and Eliar obediently led them to each one.

"There *has* to be some sort of trick involved in this," Khalor said finally, "but I'll be hanged if I can see how you're doing it."

"And if it's not a trick?"

"Then I've gone crazy."

"Just for the sake of argument, let's say that it's not a trick and that you haven't gone crazy. Then let's say that you're leading a platoon of soldiers—or an army, for that matter—and you want to take that army from Chief Albron's castle to some city halfway across the world. Wouldn't it be sort of useful to have *this* way to travel?"

"If this works the way it *seems* to work, I could put my Chief on the throne of the whole world!" Khalor exclaimed.

"Now *that's* an interesting thought," Albron mused.

"Never mind," Althalus said firmly.

There was an excited young shepherd in Exarch Yeudon's study when Eliar led Althalus, Bheid, and Khalor into the room. The shepherd had fiery red—almost orange—hair, and he wore a sheepskin tunic. "They were mounted on horses, your Eminence," the young man was shouting, "and they were killing my sheep!"

"Calm yourself, Salkan," the silver-haired Exarch told him, motioning Bheid and the others to remain silent.

"I showed them, though," the shepherd said fiercely. "I killed three of them. That'll teach them to leave my sheep alone."

"I'm fairly sure that the three you killed won't bother you again," Yeudon murmured. "There are some people at the door, Salkan. Would you mind waiting outside for a moment?"

"Perhaps he should stay, your Eminence," Althalus suggested. "He has some information I think we're going to need."

"You certainly move around, Scopas Bheid," Yeudon observed.

"My Exarch encourages diligence, your Eminence," Bheid replied. "He insists, actually. This is General Khalor, the commander of the Arums who approach your western frontier even now. We've brought him on ahead to introduce him."

"Your Eminence," Khalor said with a curt nod of his head. "Would it be all right if I spoke with your young visitor? He's actually seen our enemies, and I'd like to get some details."

"Of course, General Khalor," Yeudon replied.

"Your name is Salkan?" Khalor asked the redhead.

"Yes, sir."

"How many horsemen were there in the party that attacked you?"

"At least a dozen," Salkan replied. "I was a little excited, so I didn't really count them."

"Where exactly were you grazing your sheep?"

"Up near the frontier—not that you can really tell exactly where the frontier is up there. It's just open pastureland, so there's no boundary of any kind."

"I think I'll have to fix that," Khalor said, "but we can get to it later. Now, these men who attacked you—what kind of weapons did they have?"

"Spears," Salkan replied.

"Short ones? Or were they long?"

"Pretty long."

"Were they throwing them? Or were they riding along stabbing your sheep with them?"

"That's the way they were using them. I don't remember any of them throwing their spears."

"Were they carrying any other kinds of weapons?"

"I think they had curved swords."

"Were any of them carrying axes?"

"Not that I saw."

"If they were on horseback and you were on foot, how did you manage to kill those three?"

"I used my sling, sir. All Wekti shepherds carry slings. We have to drive off packs of wolves every so often, so we practice with our slings all the time."

"Where do you aim?"

"Usually for the head."

"You don't carry spears or bows?"

"They'd just get in the way, sir. A sling doesn't weigh hardly anything, and you can find good rocks anywhere."

"I thought the sling was just a child's toy."

"Oh, no, Sergeant Khalor," Althalus told him. "I carried a sling for years myself when I was younger. It kept me eating on a regular basis."

"Could a man kill a horse with one?"

"Easily. The bone between a horse's eyes isn't very thick. I haven't used a sling for a long time, but I'm fairly certain I could drop a horse in midstride from a hundred paces."

"That's a little hard to swallow, Althalus."

"I've taken rabbits at fifty paces—and a horse *is* quite a bit bigger than a rabbit."

Sergeant Khalor suddenly grinned broadly. "I think my job just got a lot easier. You were dead wrong, Althalus. The Wekti *do* have an army, and it's exactly the force I'm going to need."

"I'm not sure I follow your reasoning, General Khalor," Yeudon said with a puzzled look.

"Infantry's at a distinct disadvantage in a fight with cavalry, your Reverence," Khalor explained. "Mounted men can move faster than my foot soldiers can, and they use the bulk of their horses to push us back. I'll build the standard earthworks along the top of the hills and line the hillsides with pointed stakes and trip lines, but that'll be mostly for show. Our enemies are cavalry units, and they'll charge up the hillsides to attack my trenches. As soon as they come in range of your shepherds' slings, though, they'll stop."

"Our religion frowns on the killing of our fellow men, General."

"Young Salkan here killed three, didn't he?"

"That was in the defense of his sheep, General. In those circumstances, killing men *is* permitted."

"Don't worry, your Reverence. I don't *want* your shepherds to kill men. I want them to kill horses. Our enemies are cavalry, and they've probably spent their whole lives on horseback. They're so bowlegged by now that they can scarcely walk. After your shepherds kill their horses, though, they'll *have* to walk to reach my trenches. Their spirits will already be broken, and they'll be fighting—uphill—in a manner they aren't accustomed to. I'll have them for lunch."

"How do you know that their spirits are going to be broken?"

"A cavalryman gets very attached to his horse, your Eminence. He loves his horse even more than he loves his wife. We'll be facing an army of blubbering cripples trying to charge uphill through obstacles and in a hailstorm of arrows and javelins. Very few of them are going to reach my trenches. I'd better go have a look at the ground and find a suitable location for the earthworks."

"Won't it take quite a long time to dig trenches all the way across northern Wekti?" Yeudon asked.

Khalor shrugged. "Not too long, really. I have a lot of men, your Eminence, and they'll dig diligently, since the trenches are the only defense they'll have to keep them alive."

"We've still got some daylight," Althalus said when they returned to the House, "so we've got time enough to go have a look at the ground. Bheid, why don't you go tell Dweia what we've accomplished so far today? Don't make *too* big an issue of killing horses, though; she's sort of sentimental sometimes. Tell her that we'll be back in a little while. All right, Eliar," he continued, "let's go look at northern Wekti."

It was a murky afternoon when Eliar led Althalus and Khalor through a door that opened out onto a grassy hillock. Sergeant Khalor looked around. "No trees," he said.

"That's why people call it grassland, Sergeant," Althalus told him. "We call the places with trees *forests*."

"You really ought to try to get over that, Althalus. My point was that we'll need stakes, so we'll have to bring them with us when we come here."

"Althalus!" Eliar hissed. "Pekhal's out there someplace!"

"Where?"

"I'm not sure. He's close, though. The Knife's singing to me."

"Why don't you see if you can get it to be more precise."

Eliar closed his hand around the Knife hilt, and a look of intense concentration crossed his face. "They're right on the other side of this hill," he whispered.

"They?"

"I think it's Ghend who's with him."

"Take us back to the House! Now!"

"But—"

"Do as he says, Eliar!" Khalor snapped in a half whisper.

"Yes, sir."

Eliar led them back to the place where the door was located, and they went through it to emerge back in the corridor of the House. "Where do we want to go now, Althalus?" Eliar asked.

"I'm not sure if this is going to work, but I want you to find a door that's about ten feet from where Ghend and Pekhal are standing. Then open the door as quietly as you can. I don't want to go *through* the door, though. What I want to do is stand here in the corridor and listen to what they're saying."

"Now *that's* something I hadn't even thought of," Khalor said admiringly. "Do you think you can manage that, Eliar?"

"I'm not sure, Sergeant. We can try, I suppose." Eliar put his hand on the door next to the one they'd just used. "This one feels about right," he whispered. He slowly turned the handle and inched the door open.

Just beyond that door Althalus saw Ghend and Pekhal standing in knee-high grass. The sky to the west was an angry red, and seething black clouds raced across that fiery sunset. Beyond the two men, Althalus could see a vast encampment that spread out over the next valley.

Ghend still wore that peculiarly archaic helmet he'd worn in Nabjor's camp, and his burning eyes flashed angrily at the brutish Pekhal. "I want you and Gelta to stop all this playing around. Quit running across the border to murder everybody you come across."

"We're just taking out scouting parties, Master," Pekhal replied.

"Of *course* you are. Sometimes she's even worse than you are. Put a leash on her, Pekhal. Tell her to stay on her own side of the border. How long will it be until the rest of her army's in place?"

"Two weeks at least. She's got three tribes that haven't arrived yet."

"Tell her that she's got *one* week. We've got to move before Althalus can fortify that frontier. Tell her to pull back and stop these raids across the border. We move in one week, whether you and Gelta are ready or not. I've *got* to stay ahead of Althalus."

"You worry too much about him," Pekhal scoffed harshly.

"You'd better *start* worrying, Pekhal. He's moving faster than I thought he possibly could. He's learning more about that House every day. Now pull back and quit raiding down into Wekti. All you're doing is alerting him."

"Yes, Master," Pekhal replied sullenly.

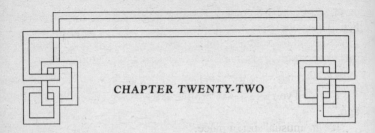

CHAPTER TWENTY-TWO

"Shut the door, Eliar," Althalus whispered.

Eliar nodded and quietly closed the door.

"Well, Khalor?" Althalus asked the hard-bitten Sergeant. "Have we got time enough to be ready for them?"

Khalor squinted thoughtfully. "It'll be close," he said, "but with a little luck . . ." He shrugged.

"I've always been sort of lucky," Althalus said, "but just to be on the safe side, I think we'd better have a talk with Dweia."

"Who's he?" Khalor asked.

"He's a she, Sergeant," Eliar said, "and I think you're going to like her."

"Where does she live?"

"Right here," Althalus told him. "This is her House."

"She's a noblewoman, then?"

"She goes quite a ways past noble, Sergeant," Eliar said.

Althalus led them along the corridor to the granite stairs at the base of the tower. "She stays here—most of the time," he said as they started up.

When they reached the top of the stairs, they found the others there. Dweia, Andine, and Leitha were deep in a discussion about hairstyles, Bheid was reading the Book, and Gher was staring out the north window at the mountains of ice with a bored look of discontent.

"How nice of you to stop by, Althalus," Dweia observed drily.

"Busy, busy, busy," he replied.

"Stop that!"

"Sorry. We've been jumping around quite a bit. This is Sergeant Khalor. He'll be commanding our forces in Wekti."

"Sergeant." Dweia greeted their guest with a slight inclination of her head.

"Ma'am," he replied. "You have quite a house here."

"I'm glad you like it. My brother left it to me quite some time ago."

"It's an unusual sort of place."

"Indeed it is, Sergeant," she said, with a peculiar smile touching those perfect lips.

"We've made quite a bit of progress in Wekti," Althalus reported. "I'm sure Brother Bheid's told you about our conference with Exarch Yeudon. The Exarch's a little suspicious about our motives, but he's in no position to argue with us. Sergeant Khalor here looked over the ground where we're going to meet the Ansus, and he thinks it'll be defensible after he puts up some earthworks. Oh, I almost forgot. We saw Ghend."

"You *what*?" Her tone was decidedly unfriendly.

"He looked well. We didn't get the chance to talk, but I'm sure he'd have sent his regards to you if we had."

"You're starting to make me cross, Althalus."

"Althalus came up with a way to use the doors that hadn't even occurred to me," Eliar broke in eagerly. "Did you know that if you open one of those doors near where some people are talking, you can stand out in the hall and hear what they're saying?"

"I suppose you could," she replied. "I have alternatives available to me, so I've never really needed to do it that way."

"What makes it so good is that the people you're listening to don't even know you're there. As long as you stay on your side of the door, they can't see you."

"How did you come up with *that* particular notion?" Dweia asked Althalus curiously.

"My shady background, probably," he replied. "The point, though, is that we were eavesdropping while Ghend was giving Pekhal a fairly thorough dressing-down. It seems that Pekhal and Gelta have been amusing themselves by raiding down into

Wekti, and Ghend spoke quite firmly to Pekhal about that. Then he ordered the brute to start the invasion one week from today."

"Can you be ready for them, Sergeant?" Dweia asked.

"I think so, ma'am. Once we get some troops up along that frontier, I'll send out scouts. I'd like to know whether I'll be facing cavalry or infantry."

"It'll probably be both," she said. "Pekhal's a foot soldier, and Gelta's spent most of her life on horseback."

"That's useful to know, ma'am. Althalus here tends to gloss over details sometimes."

She smiled. "I know," she said. "He can be *very* offensive sometimes, can't he?"

Khalor shrugged. "He's useful right now, ma'am, so I can put up with his little quirks. I think his whole problem springs from his notion that he's amusing. When you get right down to it, he's not really that funny, but I suppose I can learn to live with him."

Althalus gave Khalor a hard look.

"Is everybody teasing you, Althie?" Leitha asked with feigned sympathy. "Poor baby."

"I gather that you're the one in charge, ma'am," Khalor said to Dweia.

"More or less. Althalus usually does what I tell him to do— eventually. Will taking orders from a woman disturb you, Sergeant?"

"Not particularly. I'd rather take orders from a clever woman than a stupid man, but we're facing a policy decision right now. I'll handle strategy and tactics, but I'll need to know what policy you want me to follow."

"Could you clarify that, Sergeant?"

"Our enemies, Pekhal and Gelta, are going to make their move next week, and I'm going to meet them. Just how far do you want me to go? I can give them bloody noses and let it go at that, if you want."

"But you'd rather not do it that way, I gather."

"No, ma'am, I wouldn't, but I'm not involved in the political side of this war. A good soldier avoids politics and religion, but if all you want me to do is spank them and send them home, we'll do it that way."

"But you wouldn't like it."

"No, ma'am. If all I do is rough them up a little, they'll be back again next month, and I'll have to tie up troops I might need someplace else just to guard that frontier."

"What's the alternative?"

"Annihilation, ma'am. If I kill everything that moves along that border, I won't have to go back and do it again. It's brutal and messy, but this is a war, not a tea party. You're a lady, and ladies are tender-hearted. My best advice, though, is for you not to put any restrictions on me."

"Burn, fight, kill?"

"Exactly."

"All right, Sergeant, your leash is off."

"You and I are going to get along just fine, ma'am," Khalor said with a steely smile.

Despite Khalor's impatience, Dweia insisted that they all stay for supper. "The ladies are feeling sort of left out, love," she explained privately to Althalus. "Let's keep peace in the family, if possible."

"I'm a little pressed for time, Dweia."

"You're forgetting where you are, pet. These golden moments won't interfere with your schedule at all, since time here moves—or doesn't—as I tell it to."

The ladies took a while—quite a while—to dress for dinner, and then they all sat down to what could only be called a banquet.

Andine reverted to hovering, and she filled Eliar's plate three times before he advised her that he was "full clear up to here" with a gesture in the vicinity of his throat.

"How long's that been going on?" Khalor asked Althalus.

"Quite a while now."

"I was sort of wondering why Eliar's been having trouble concentrating here lately. The same sort of thing's happening between the priest and the witch, isn't it? Do you think you could persuade Dweia to hold off on the weddings until *after* the war? Married men don't make good soldiers."

"She's sort of keeping things under control," Althalus said. "I think she agrees with you on the issue of mixing wars and weddings, Sergeant." Then he looked across the table at Dweia. "Would you be offended if we talked shop while we eat?" he asked her.

"As long as you don't get *too* graphic," she replied.

"I think we'd better have Eliar take Brother Bheid back to Keiwon," Althalus said. "There's a redheaded shepherd there that Sergeant Khalor's going to need when the fighting starts. We'll want him to gather up as many other shepherds as he can lay his hands on and start them toward the frontier."

"You're going to actually make them walk?" Bheid asked.

"We aren't going to need them for several days, so let's keep them out from underfoot until the earthworks are complete. If they make it to the trenches on time, fine. If they're still too far away on the day before the invasion, Eliar can use the doors to get them where they need to be."

"Should I stay in Keiwon with Bheid?" Eliar asked.

"No. Just take him to Keiwon and come right back. You have to take Khalor and me to see Albron. We need to decide which clan we want to use to build those fortifications, and I might need some kind of authorization to start that clan marching."

"A keg or two of those gold coins is probably all the authorization you're going to need, Althalus," Khalor snorted. "I think I'm going to use Gweti's clan to build the fortifications, and the word 'gold' gets Gweti's complete attention."

"Let's pay attention to the courtesies, Khalor. I don't want to offend Chief Albron."

"Excuse me," Gher said. "I just had an idea."

"Brace yourself, Sergeant," Althalus warned Khalor. "Gher can be *very* creative when it comes to using those doors. Some of his ideas are so complicated that half the time I don't even understand what he's talking about. Go ahead, Gher."

"This war's not the only one we'll have to fight, is it?"

"I'm sure it's only the first one. There'll be others."

"Then wouldn't it be a good idea to start *all* the Arums marching right now?"

"Where to?" Khalor asked curiously.

"That doesn't really matter."

"I don't exactly follow you, young man."

"Well, it takes a little while for them to get started, doesn't it? I mean, they've got to gather up their equipment, say good-bye to their lady friends, get drunk a time or two, and things like that. Isn't that sort of the way it goes?"

"It's pretty close to that, yes."

"The time might come sometime later when one of Ghend's people surprises us, so we might need a lot of soldiers in a hurry. If they're already marching up and down the hallways here in the House, Eliar can pop them through a door, and they'll be right where we need them in about a minute."

"You mean just walk them around in circles?" Eliar asked in a puzzled tone.

"Why not? Wouldn't that fix it so that Emmy won't have to trick them into thinking that they've been walking for months and months? Some of them really *will* be walking for a long time. They'll be right here any time you need them. You'll have seven or eight armies right in your pocket, and you can take them out any time you need them."

"Can we *do* that?" Khalor asked Althalus incredulously.

"I don't see why not. We might have to work out a few details, but the basic idea's perfectly sound."

"Did I leave something out, Althalus?" Gher asked.

"We'll have to tell them where they're going, Gher. We almost have to let them know where the war is before they start."

Gher shrugged. "Tell them they're going to Fiddle-Faddle or Hippety-Hop to fight a war against the Whiz-Bangs or the Furpleinians. Make up some names. The way I understand it, the Arums don't really care *where* the war is or *who* they're going to fight. All they're interested in is getting paid."

"I *knew* there was something wrong with this idea," Althalus said triumphantly.

"Did I miss something?" Gher looked a little crestfallen.

"The unpleasant word 'pay' just cropped up, Gher. As soon as they start walking, I have to start paying."

"But you'll be paying for the time out there, and it's shorter out there than it is here—or longer, maybe. If you start counting it all up, I think you'll find out that you're paying less. Besides, you said that when you went into that storeroom where you keep your gold, the light from your lantern wouldn't even reach the walls. If the place is *that* big, you've got so much gold that it doesn't even mean anything anymore."

Althalus stared at the boy. The urgency that'd been in Ghend's voice when he'd given Pekhal his orders had strongly suggested that he was afraid. Althalus had assumed that *he* was the one Ghend feared. Evidently that wasn't quite true. This tousle-haired little boy who hadn't even seen his tenth birthday yet was the one who *really* frightened Ghend.

That's all right, Althie, Emmy's voice murmured inside his mind. *I still love you—even if you have just been outclassed.*

"There are better warriors in Arum than Gweti's clan, my Chief," Khalor was saying to Albron a few hours later in the smooth-shaven Chief's study, "but they're the best when it comes to field fortifications."

Albron nodded. "Gweti likes it that way," he noted. "He adores stalemates, since he gets paid by the day instead of the job. His men are far more expert with shovels than they are with swords."

Khalor nodded. "I don't really like them very much, but in this situation, they're exactly what I'm going to need. I *don't* want somebody like Twengor. He's too unpredictable for this kind of battle."

"What's your overall strategy, Sergeant?" Albron asked.

"I'm still working on some of the details, my Chief, but I've got a few surprises for Pekhal and Gelta up my sleeve."

"Oh?"

"As it turns out, the Wekti aren't *quite* as meek as we all thought they were. They're quite militant when it comes to pro-tecting their sheep. They use slings—and I'm not talking about some child's toy. We came across one young fire eater who killed three of Pekhal's mounted men when they attacked his herd."

"With a *sling*?" Albron seemed startled.

"A rock right between the eyes kills a man—or a horse—even faster than a sword in the belly, my Chief. Gelta's Ansus are cavalrymen, and that had me a little worried. My cares are all gone now, though. The Ansus may *start* their attack on horseback, but they'll be on foot by the time they reach the trenches. Then the Ansus—who don't know a thing about infantry tactics—are going to have to attack uphill on foot."

"Very shrewd, Sergeant."

"That's only the start, my Chief. I'm going to put old Chief Delur's clan somewhere close to the battlefield on the west side, and I know quite a few people down in Plakand. The Plakanders are even better horsemen than the Ansus, and I'll hire a cavalry army down there. They'll sweep up around the east side of Wekti. They've got a week, so they'll be in place when the battle starts. I'll let Pekhal's Ansus wear themselves out trying to attack Gweti's fortifications, and *then* I'll signal Delur's men and the Plakanders, and they'll rush the Ansus from behind. I don't think there'll be very many survivors, my Chief."

"Brilliant, Khalor! Brilliant!"

"I rather liked it myself, my Chief. I'd like to borrow your sister's husband, Melgor, though. I'm going to be scampering around like a dog with his tail on fire setting everything in motion, and Chief Gweti encourages his men to take their time while they're digging trenches. I think I'll need somebody on that line to crack the whip over them every so often. Those earthworks absolutely *must* be in place before the week's out—even if it means that poor pinch-faced Gweti has to get by with short pay."

"I'll take care of that, Sergeant," Albron said, obviously trying to make it sound casual.

"You said what?"

"I think it's time for me to get my feet wet, Khalor. I spend all my time here making business arrangements. You know, I've never actually taken part in a single one of the wars I've hired you out to fight since my father died. I'm tired of being nothing but a businessman. I want to be a real Arum."

"You aren't good enough, Albron," Khalor told his Chief bluntly.

"I'm a quick learner, Khalor. Whether you like it or not, I *am* the Chief, and I *am* going to Wekti to crack the whip over Gweti's ditchdiggers."

Khalor winced. "Would you agree to taking Melgor along to advise you, my Chief—and to flex his muscles when some Gweti man starts to argue with you about how long it takes to throw a shovelful of dirt out of a trench?"

"I don't really get along all that well with my sister's husband, Khalor. I *am* a Chief, and I *do* know how to give orders. I'll take care of the trenches, Sergeant." Then he grinned almost boyishly. "I'm being just a little childish about this, aren't I?"

"A little, yes. What brought this on, my Chief?"

"The excitement, Khalor. Despite all the hours I have to spend adding up columns of figures and counting stacks of pennies, I'm still an Arum, and when the horns blow, my blood starts to race. This might just be the most important war in the history of the world, and I'm *not* going to be left out."

Khalor sighed. "No, my Chief," he said in a resigned tone of voice, "I guess you won't be at that."

Eliar returned from Keiwon early the following morning. "Exarch Yeudon didn't like it very much," he reported. "I guess he thought that none of his shepherds were going to have to do any of the fighting. He really likes the idea of having other people do his work for him. Bheid changed his mind for him, though."

"Oh?" Althalus asked.

"It was sort of along the lines of, 'If you aren't interested enough to do some of the fighting, the rest of us won't bother either.' Yeudon got the point almost immediately. Where do we go now?"

"Gweti's hall. Let's get his ditchdiggers to the Wekti border as soon as possible." Althalus looked inquiringly at Dweia, who sat at the table idly leafing through the pages of the Book. "Was

Gher at all close to being right when he was talking about the doors to Everywhen?" he asked her.

"More or less," she replied. "Why do you ask?"

"I think I'm going to need more time than I've really got. I like the notion of having all the clans of Arum roaming around in the halls of the House here, but it's going to take quite a while to set it all up. If Eliar can take me through the door to last week to give me time enough to get the clans moving, everything'll be in place before Pekhal and Gelta mount their attacks. I don't like it when the hours start nipping at my tail feathers, though. When that happens, people start making mistakes."

"We'll take care of it, dear. Get Gweti's men started, and then come back here. I'll need to explain some things to Eliar. The doors to Everywhen are a bit different from the doors to Everywhere, and there's a different procedure involved."

"All right. Pick up one of those kegs of gold, Eliar, and let's go to Gweti's house."

Eliar put his hand on the hilt of the Knife for a moment and frowned slightly. Then he nodded, almost as if someone—or something—had just spoken to him. "It's just a ways down the hall from Chief Albron's door," he said. Then he took up one of the kegs and led Althalus and Khalor down the stairs.

"How long have you two been married, Althalus?" Khalor asked as they started down the hall.

"What?" Althalus asked.

"You and the lady who's in charge of everything. You're married, aren't you?"

"Where did you get *that* idea?"

"You aren't?" Khalor said incredulously. "You both *behave* as if you're married."

Althalus laughed. "I guess we do at that," he conceded. "I'm sure we'll get around to that eventually, but there are a few technicalities we'll have to take care of first. Getting her family's permission might be a little tricky."

"This is the door," Eliar said.

"What's on the other side?" Althalus asked him.

"The big door that opens into the hall where Gweti calls his men in to get their orders."

"You'd better let me do the talking, Althalus," Khalor suggested. "I broke Gweti to harness at the conclave, so I know how hard I have to jerk his reins to point him in the right direction."

"And you enjoy it, too, don't you, Khalor?" Althalus suggested with a wicked grin.

"Tweaking Gweti's nose *is* one of my favorite pastimes, Althalus," Khalor chuckled.

Eliar led them through the door into a musty-smelling and very large hall where Chief Gweti was sitting hunched over a rough table, counting pennies.

"I've come for your men, Chief Gweti," Sergeant Khalor announced brusquely.

Gweti quickly tried to hide the pennies on the table in front of him. "You surprised me, Sergeant," he said. Then a look of sly cunning came over his pinched-in face. "I'm glad you stopped by," he said then. "There's something we overlooked during the negotiations at the conclave."

"Oh? I thought we'd pretty much covered everything. It's so much per day per man, right?"

"Oh, that part's all right," Gweti said quickly, "but we overlooked the rent on their weapons. Good swords and axes are expensive, Sergeant."

"We'll provide the weapons, Chief Gweti." Althalus stepped in.

"But—" Gweti started to protest.

"We're renting bodies, Gweti, not the cheap swords in your storehouse."

"What about their boots?" Gweti asked almost desperately. "It's a long way down to the low country, and my men are certain to wear out their boots along the way."

"I'll take care of that, too. Quit trying to swindle me, Gweti. You're out of your class. Did you want to talk about how much you plan to pay us for the rations your men are going to eat along the way?"

"That's absurd!" Gweti's eyes bulged.

"They're *your* men, Gweti. Feeding them is *your* responsibility, not mine. If half of them starve to death, that's your problem. Those are the terms, Gweti. I'll pay so much per man per day, and I'll trade you the rations for the weapons and boots and we'll call it even."

"That isn't fair!" Gweti protested.

"Life's that way sometimes. Make up your mind, Gweti. If an even trade doesn't suit you, I'll go see Chief Delur, and you can go back to fondling those pennies. Quickly, Gweti. I'm a little pressed for time just now."

Eliar set the keg down on Gweti's table, opened it, and took out a handful of gold coins.

"You're not being very—" Gweti began to protest. He broke off suddenly as Eliar let the tinkling gold coins dribble out of his hand back into the keg.

"Done?" Althalus demanded bluntly.

"All right, you thief," Gweti snarled. "We have an agreement."

"How long will it take to gather your clansmen?"

"They're already here, Chamberlain Althalus. I'll order them to march just as soon as you pay me. I want one month in advance."

"Don't be silly. One week."

"Totally unacceptable!"

"Pick up the keg, Eliar," Althalus said. "Let's go see Chief Delur."

"All right, all right," Gweti said. "Don't get excited. One week it is."

"Always a pleasure doing business with you, Chief Gweti," Althalus smirked. "Pay him, Eliar, and let's get started. Arya Andine doesn't like to be kept waiting."

"You're running me ragged, Althalus," Eliar complained when they were all back in the House a few hours later. "This jumping back and forth between Everywhere and Everywhen has got me stretched so thin that light's starting to shine right through me."

"Just do what he tells you to do, Eliar," Sergeant Khalor ordered, "and stop feeling sorry for yourself." He looked at Chief

Gweti's wooden-faced, kilted clansmen plodding along the corridor. "They look about half asleep," he observed.

"At least half," Althalus agreed. "Their minds are busy, though. Right now they think they're marching through the mountains of Kagwher. They're out of touch with real time. In the last half hour or so they believe they've set up camp about a dozen times. They'll be in Wekti before the day's out, but they'll be positive they've been marching for a month or more. Stay with them for now. Bark a few orders now and then so they know you're here. Stay away from the north wing of the House, though. Chief Delur's men are going to be roaming up and down the corridors there within the next hour."

"How are you managing to keep this all straight?"

"It *is* a little complicated, Khalor, but I'm a professional swindler, so I'm used to complications." Althalus chuckled.

"What's so funny?" Khalor asked.

"Gher was right. I'm paying Gweti and the other Chiefs for the time that passes where *they* are, and the House deletes all the time they'd normally spend marching through the mountains. I think Gweti's going to be terribly disappointed when I return his men to him after only a couple of weeks have passed."

"You've got the soul of a thief, Althalus," Khalor accused.

"Why, thank you, Sergeant."

"It wasn't intended to be a compliment."

"That sort of depends on your point of view. All right, Eliar, let's go back to last week again. I've got some special plans for Smeugor and Tauri."

"Oh?"

"I want them to be totally out of any possible contact with Ghend, so I think I'll insist that they lead their men personally instead of just turning the job over to some Captain. I want those two right under my thumb."

Althalus was close to exhaustion by the time he and Eliar had managed to get all the clans of Arum to the House, and he collapsed into his chair at the dinner table. "I could sleep for a week," he declared.

"Probably not," Dweia disagreed. "I'd guess a day and a half at most. Don't try to deceive us, Althie. You're having the time of your life."

"It *is* sort of fun," he admitted. "I haven't really done anything all that strenuous today, but I've been to so many places that it's all a blur. I've hit eight clans of Arum since sunrise, and I've lost count of how many times I've passed through the House."

"There's one thing left that we need to settle, Althalus," Andine said. "If you think that Leitha and I are going to just sit here twiddling our thumbs while you menfolk are out there playing, you'd better think again. *Next* time you go out, we *are* going with you."

"Oh no, you're not," he told her. "I'm *not* going to put you two in that kind of danger from *both* sides."

"What's that supposed to mean?"

"It has to do with that 'boy-people and girl-people' business. I've been hiring soldiers, not choir boys, and soldiers tend to be *very* direct when they want something. You and Leitha'd probably be in more danger from the Arums than you'd be from the Ansus."

"Why don't you let me take care of this, Althalus?" Dweia suggested. "Eat your supper and then get some sleep. You've got another busy day ahead of you tomorrow."

The voice of the spirit of darkness wailed, wailed, and the echo of its wailing lay dark and heavy on the rolling lands of the Ansus.

In the valley below, men did war upon each other with stones. Sharp were the stones, and bright was the blood, and it filled the heart of Pekhal with delight to see the blood.

And behold, stern-faced Gelta, Queen of the Night, did mount the hill astride her midnight horse. And her ax of stone did weep, weep the blood of her fallen foes.

"They flee!" the Queen of the Night exulted. "All do flee before me, my beastlike comrade. And so it shall be always, always. No man of humankind dares face my wrath."

"Thou art my true sister, Queen of the Night!" bestial Pekhal spake. "For it seemeth me that the taste of blood is as sweet upon *thy* tongue as it is upon mine. We will feast this night upon the flesh of our foes, and the night shall be filled with our rejoicing."

"And whither shall we go upon the morrow, brother mine?" the scar-faced Queen of the Night demanded in her harsh voice. "All of Ansu is mine, mine, and which land or city shall next fall beneath mine invincible will?"

"Direct thy wrath most keenly at that city men call holy," spake bestial Pekhal, "and fill thy belly with exultation, for behold, I shall stretch forth mine hand into time yet to come, and I shall arm thee and all thine hosts with weapons of wonder. Cast aside thy weapons of stone, Queen of the Night, for I shall arm thee and thine with steel, and Awes shall cast aside Deiwos at thy command, and they shall instead bow down to thee and to me and to our Master, Ghend; and behold, the temples of Deiwos shall ring with praise of Daeva, and the altars thereof shall run red with sweet, sweet blood!"

"Awes *will* be mine, dear brother," the Queen of the Night gloated in savage ecstasy. "Deiwos shall be cast out, and Daeva shall reign supreme over all the world!"

And the despairing wail rose above the plain in an exultant shriek, and the heart of the Queen of the Night was full, full.

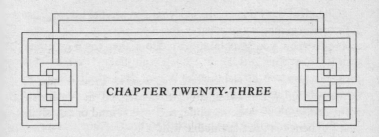

CHAPTER TWENTY-THREE

They were subdued the following morning at breakfast. "Did we all have the same dream again?" Gher asked Dweia in a shuddering voice.

She nodded.

"I thought so," the boy said. "There was that howling noise off in the distance. It didn't really happen that way, did it? What I mean is, when those two were talking to each other way back then, that wasn't the way things *really* went. They were changing things, weren't they?"

"They didn't like the way things turned out, so they went back and altered them," Dweia replied. "Gelta was never able to conquer all of Ansu, and she didn't even know Pekhal until much later."

Pale blond Leitha's face was filled with horror.

"What is it, dear?" Andine asked her in a concerned voice. "That little meeting wasn't very nice, but . . ." She hesitated.

"Their conversation only touched the surface, Andine. What was going on in their minds was far, far worse."

"You can *do* that?" Bheid exclaimed. "They were just an illusion. Could you actually *hear* the thoughts of illusions?"

"It was impossible *not* to hear them, Bheid," she told him in a sick voice. "Pekhal and Gelta are worse than animals. That dreadful slaughter filled them both with unspeakable lust."

"I wouldn't pursue that, Leitha," Dweia said quite firmly. "Push what you heard away. It was only a dream, after all, and it was probably directed at *you* even more than at the rest of us."

"Me?"

"Ghend knows who you are and what you can do, Leitha. That little performance was probably for *your* benefit. Ghend was trying to show you something so hideous that you'd be afraid ever to use your gift again. Steel your heart, Leitha. This probably won't be the last time he'll try it. He's afraid of you, so he'll do everything he possibly can to keep you from doing what you're supposed to do."

"There *is* something we should think about," Althalus said.

"Oh? What was that?" Dweia asked.

"Ghend's probably been working on his invasion for quite some time, wouldn't you say?"

"Obviously."

"Then he's almost certainly got people in the court of the Natus of Wekti and in the Temple of Kherdhos who work for him, hasn't he?"

"I'm sure he has."

"Then Andine was right. She and Leitha almost have to go with us to Wekti."

"Absolutely out of the question," Bheid declared. "It's too dangerous."

"We can protect them, Bheid," Althalus told him. "My point was that we need to have Leitha in Keiwon. I *have* to know who Ghend's people are there."

"If we're so worried about taking girl people with us, why not just dress them in boy-people clothes?" Gher suggested.

"Gher," Andine said gently. "Girl people don't *look* exactly like boy people. We have slightly different shapes." She drew in a deep breath to make her point. "You see what I mean?" she suggested, making a vague gesture at the front of her dress.

Gher blushed bright red. "Oh," he said. "Well, wouldn't looser clothes sort of . . ." He floundered, blushing even more brightly.

Andine giggled wickedly.

"That's not nice, dear," Leitha scolded. Then she looked at Eliar. "Chief Albron has servants, hasn't he?" she asked.

"I wouldn't exactly call them servants," Eliar replied. "He's got stable boys who take care of his horses, and there are people in his kitchen who carry food to him and like that. He takes care of most of the things he wants done by himself."

"The people in Wekti wouldn't know about that, though, would they?"

"Probably not, no."

"Then they wouldn't know that Albron doesn't have servants in the usual sense, would they?"

"I doubt it."

Leitha looked Andine up and down. "Would you please stand up for a moment, dear?" she asked.

Andine rose. "What are we doing here, Leitha?"

"You're very small, aren't you?" Leitha pursed her lips.

"That isn't *my* fault."

"Would you go stand beside her, Gher?" Leitha requested.

"Yes ma'am, if you want me to." Gher rose and went around the table to Andine.

"I sort of thought they might be about the same size," Leitha said. "If we dressed them in identical clothes and hid Andine's hair under some kind of cap—"

"You mean dress up like page boys?" Andine asked. "Could we get away with that, Althalus?"

"It *might* work," he replied, "particularly if Albron took a few other liveried retainers with him to Wekti. I'll speak with Yeudon about suitable quarters. Those retainers wouldn't be soldiers, so they wouldn't be going up to the trenches with their Chief. We'll be able to conceal Leitha in that group, and she should be able to locate any turncoats."

"Are you going to be a page boy, too, Leitha?" Andine asked her friend.

"I'm taller than you and Gher, dear," Leitha replied. "I'd have a little trouble passing as a ten-year-old." She stroked her face speculatively. "How do you think I'd look if I wore a false beard?" she asked them.

Bheid howled with laughter, and Leitha turned on him, her eyes flashing angrily. "Stop that!" she snapped at him.

"There's something else we'll need to attend to before you all leave for Keiwon," Dweia said thoughtfully.

"Aren't you going with us, Em?" Althalus asked.

"I think it might be better if I stayed here. I can keep an eye on our enemies from the window and let you know if they're planning any surprises."

"That window's a long way from Wekti, Em."

"It was a long way from Deika that night Kweso's dogs were chasing you, pet, and I didn't have any trouble seeing what was happening. The window's where I *want* it to be, Althalus. Come and see for yourself." She rose and led him to the window.

The mountains of Kagwher weren't there anymore, and Althalus found himself looking down at rolling grassland. "Is that Wekti?" he asked.

"Northern Wekti, yes—up near the Ansu frontier. This is probably in the general vicinity of where we'll be fighting the battle. Now then, Sergeant Khalor will be commanding our forces during the battle, and I think we'll want him here instead of down there on the ground. He'll be able to see better, for one thing, but there's a far more important reason."

"Oh?"

"Ghend's henchman, Koman, shares Leitha's gift, and if Khalor's anywhere on the battlefield, Koman will pick up any order he gives before it even leaves his mouth. Koman *can't* hear anything that happens here, though."

"Won't it be a little hard for Khalor to give orders from here in the House, though? He can shout fairly loudly, but that's a long way down, Em."

"That's why we're going to need another door." She reached out and patted the stone wall beside the window. "Right here, I think. It won't be quite like the other doors in the House, so you'd better make it look a bit different so that Eliar knows that it's sort of special."

"Where's it supposed to go, Em?"

"Where we want it to go—usually to the spot Khalor can see from the window. Eliar's going to carry his Sergeant's orders to our forces down there on the ground."

"I don't see much advantage to that, Em. Koman can hear Eliar as well as he can hear Khalor, can't he?"

"Only if he knows where Eliar is, and if Eliar's using our door, he'll be popping in and out so fast that Koman won't be able to home in on him. We'll experiment a bit, but let's get the door in place. Make it an arch, Althalus, and give it brass hinges and an ornate handle so that Eliar knows that it's no ordinary door. Use '*peri*.' It's a bit more formal, and we'll use the word 'portal' when we speak of it, instead of the word 'door.' It's important for Eliar to think of it differently. Make the door, Althalus."

"Whatever you say, Em." He thought back and remembered an arched doorway he'd seen in Dweia's temple in Maghu. He concentrated on that image and said, "*Peri.*"

"Very nice, Althalus," she complimented him when the door appeared. "I think that's exactly what we want." Then she turned and looked across the room to where Eliar and Gher were sitting. Gher was talking excitedly, and Eliar looked a bit confused.

"Eliar," Dweia said, "come over here to the window. I want to show you something."

"Right away, Emmy," Eliar replied, coming to his feet.

"The rest of you should probably look as well," she told the others in the room.

They all trooped on over to the window.

"A new door?" Andine observed. "Where does this one go?"

"Down there," Leitha replied, gesturing toward the window.

"That's not Kagwher, is it?" Bheid asked, peering out the window.

"No," Dweia told him. "It's northern Wekti, and it's probably where we'll be fighting the Ansus. This new portal's not like the other doors in the House. They're attached to a specific place, but this one opens any place we'll want it to. When the battles begin, we're going to station Sergeant Khalor at this window, and Eliar's going to carry his orders down to the battlefield." She looked at Leitha. "How long does it usually take you to home in on one specific person's thought, dear?"

"That depends on where he is and how many other people are around him, Dweia—and how noisy things are in the vicinity," Leitha replied. "I think it'd be very difficult in the middle of a battle."

"I thought so myself. If Eliar uses this door to carry Sergeant Khalor's orders to the men on the ground, he'll be there and back before Koman can even begin to locate him."

"Excuse me," Gher said. "Did I understand what you were saying, Emmy?" he asked. "I mean is that door beside the window *really* the door to any place at all?"

"Pretty much, yes."

"And to Everywhen, too? I mean, could Eliar go to that big church in Keiwon thirty years ago through *that* one door?"

"Yes. Why do you ask?"

"What a neat door!" Gher exclaimed. "Why don't you try that thing we were just talking about with this special door, Eliar?"

"We could try it, I suppose," Eliar said dubiously. He frowned. "I'm not sure what that place would look like."

"I don't think it'd look like anything at all, Eliar. That's sort of what it means. Try it, and let's see what happens."

"All right, Gher." Eliar's eyes went distant, and he reached for the ornate brass handle.

The door suddenly changed. The brass hinges and solid planks disappeared, and the archway became a formless hole filled with absolute darkness.

"NO!" Dweia's voice was almost a scream.

"I was only trying—" Eliar started to explain.

"Stop. Push that thought away! And don't *ever* do that again!" The very walls seemed to shake with the intensity of her voice.

Eliar flinched back, and the portal returned to its former state.

"What did you do, Eliar?" Andine demanded.

"It wasn't my idea," Eliar defended himself. "Gher wanted to see what the door to Nowhere and Nowhen looked like."

"Stay completely away from that idea, Eliar!" Dweia commanded. "Don't ever even *think* about it again."

"It can't be all *that* dangerous, can it?" Gher sounded a bit frightened.

"*Think,* Gher. Think about what you just asked Eliar to do. What would lie beyond that door he almost opened?"

"Nothing all that dangerous. Wouldn't it just be empty? I wanted to see what nothing looked like. I'd been thinking about

Everywhere and Everywhen, and I turned the idea over to look at the other side of it. That's when I got the notion of Nowhere and Nowhen. Wouldn't that just be the door to Empty?"

"Exactly. Emptiness is hungry, Gher, so it swallows whatever comes near it—people, houses, moons, suns, and stars. Stop experimenting, Gher. From now on, don't even mention these wild ideas to Eliar until you've talked them over with me first. The door you just told him about is the one door we *never* open."

"I wish I had a donkey," Eliar said, grunting under the weight of the keg he was carrying along the streets of the cow town of Kherdon in northwestern Plakand.

"We've got one," Khalor told him with a grin. "His name's Eliar."

"How did you meet this man we've come to see?" Althalus asked the Sergeant.

"We were on the same side in a war a few years back," Khalor replied. "We worked out some coordinated tactics to use against the army of Kapro up in Equero. My infantry would hold the Kapros in one place, and Kreuter's cavalry would hit them from behind."

"That's his name?"

"Kreuter, yes. He's a Tribal Chief over in eastern Plakand. He's primarily a cattleman, but he picks up money on the side by hiring his horsemen out to fight wars in the civilized lands. After the Plakands heard about how the clans of Arum were getting rich as mercenaries, they decided to give it a try themselves. Kreuter and I get along well together. I know I can trust him, so he's the one I thought of when I came up with the idea of hitting the Ansus from the rear with cavalry. If Kreuter tells me he's going to be someplace at a certain time, I know he'll be there when I need him."

"You've made a lot of contacts over the years, haven't you, Sergeant?"

"I've been in a lot of wars in a lot of places, Althalus, so I've got friends in most of the low countries."

"Are you sure this Kreuter's going to be here?"

"He comes here every summer to sell cows to the cattle buyers from the civilized lands. If he isn't here yet, he's on his way—or he's just left. I'll check around town and find out. If he hasn't arrived—or he's on his way home—we'll be able to chase him down. Those doors were *made* for this sort of thing." Khalor stopped in front of a log building with a crudely painted sign representing a bunch of grapes hanging over the front door. "This is Kreuter's favorite tavern," he said. "Let's try here first."

Inside, the tavern was a dingy place with a strong smell about it. Although it was still early morning, there were a fair number of noisy patrons.

"We're in luck," Khalor said. "That's Kreuter over there in the corner." He squinted at the big man seated on a rough bench. "Better yet, he seems to be fairly sober. Let's go talk with him."

They pushed their way through the crowd to where the burly Chief sat. Kreuter had muddy blond hair and a beard that appeared to have been squared off at the bottom with a sharp knife. He had oxlike shoulders and huge hands.

"Well, bless me if it isn't my old friend Khalor!" the burly man said. "What are you doing here in Plakand, Khalor?"

"Looking for you, as a matter of fact. How've you been lately?"

"Can't complain. What's afoot?"

"Have you sold your cows yet?"

"Just yesterday. I thought I'd take a few days off to celebrate before I rounded up my men for the trip home."

"I caught you before you got too far along, then. Have you got any serious plans for the next month or so?"

"Not really. Is something in the wind?"

"I've got a little war in the works. I think I'm going to need some cavalry, and I thought of you right off. Are you interested?"

"We can talk about it. Where *is* this war of yours, Khalor? My men and I just finished a long cattle drive, so if your war's over in Perquaine, the money'd have to be very good."

"The money's good, Kreuter, and the war's almost on your doorstep."

"Oh? I haven't heard any noises of that kind lately. Where is it?"

"North Wekti."

"There's nothing in Wekti worth fighting about."

"Except for its location. The southern Ansus seem to have gotten bored with life, so they decided to sweep down through Wekti to make a strike into Medyo and Equero for fun and profit. The people I'm working for would rather the Ansus didn't, and they certainly don't want the war crashing around inside their cities. I've set up a defense line across northern Wekti to hold back the invasion. If we leave it that way, I'm looking at a long, tedious summer."

"So you want me to come at them from the rear, I take it?" Kreuter surmised.

"It worked when we fought the Kapros," Khalor said with a shrug. "The Ansus are going to be piled up against my fortifications, so they won't be able to get away from you when you hit them from behind. I'm getting paid for the job, not by the day, so there's no point in dragging it out."

Kreuter squinted at the ceiling. "The Ansus aren't really as good as they seem to think they are, and their horses are pretty scrubby," he mused. "Is the pay good?"

"I'm not complaining about it."

"A short war for good pay, and home by autumn, eh, Khalor?"

"If we can work it that way."

"I think you can count me in, my friend."

"I'll need to have you in position in five days," Khalor told him, "and I'd like to have you swing out wide to the east, so the Ansus won't know you're coming."

"You're being obvious, Khalor. I know how to do this. Now, then, let's talk about the pay. How long's it going to be until I see some money?"

"About as long as it's going to take this young fellow here to get his wooden purse open," Khalor replied with a broad grin.

"I don't think I've ever heard of a wooden purse before," Kreuter said.

"It's all the rage lately, Chief Kreuter," Althalus told him. "Open the purse, Eliar, and let's get down to business here."

"It's sort of expected, Exarch Yeudon," Chief Albron said apologetically as they trooped into the fairly spacious apartment the priests of Kherdhos had prepared for the Arum Chief. "Ever since the clans of Arum started fighting wars in the civilized lands, we've been contaminated by their way of thinking. To be perfectly honest with you, I'd have preferred to leave these servants at home. I don't *need* page boys or a resident soothsayer when I'm fighting a war, but for some reason, appearances have gotten to be more important than reality."

"It's the curse of civilization, Chief Albron," Yeudon said. He smiled faintly. "If you think an Arum Chief is burdened with servants, try the life of a high-ranking churchman." Then he looked curiously at the robed and hooded figure of Leitha. "Do you Arums *really* put much store in soothsayers?" he asked.

"We used to. Some of the more backward Chiefs won't even change their shirts without consulting their soothsayer first. I've more or less outgrown that. If it's all right, I'll leave my page boys, soothsayer, and valet here when I go up to the trenches. Speaking of that, I'd better change into my work clothes and get started. The Exarch of the Black Robes didn't hire me for my social graces."

"I'll leave you to your preparations then, Chief Albron," Yeudon said. He bowed slightly and then left the apartment.

"You're very smooth, Chief Albron," Andine said approvingly, looking around the rather splendidly furnished apartment. The Arya of Osthos wore scarlet livery identical to Gher's, and her long hair was tucked up under her baglike cap.

"I've occasionally visited the civilized world, Princess," Albron said, shrugging, "so I know how the game's supposed to be played."

"Are you picking up any hints of Ghend's spies, Leitha?" Bheid asked the hooded blond girl.

"Quite a few," she replied, pushing back her hood. "Ghend has a few people over in the palace of the Natus, but they're mostly concentrated here in the temple. Ghend seems to know that Natus Dhakrel doesn't loom very large here in Wekti."

"Is there anything significant afoot here in the temple?" Althalus asked her.

"Not really. The ones Ghend's planted here are spies, not plotters. I wouldn't advise sharing too much with Yeudon, though. A couple of Ghend's people are quite close to him, and he might let a few things slip."

"We'd more or less planned to keep him at a distance anyway," Albron said. "You'd better pull your hood up again, Leitha," he advised.

"It's a little warm," she complained.

"I'm sorry, but an Arum soothsayer always keeps his face concealed. I guess it's supposed to add to the mystery." He laughed slightly. "That's what gave me the idea of disguising you as a soothsayer in the first place. Chief Twengor's father had a soothsayer who guided him for thirty years, and it wasn't until after that soothsayer died that they discovered that she wasn't a man."

"It's better than pasting on a false beard, Leitha," Andine said.

"I was sort of looking forward to swashing and buckling and twirling my mustache," Leitha said, sounding slightly disappointed.

"I'm sure you'd have been very convincing," Andine said, "right up until you started to walk."

"What's that supposed to mean?"

"You swish, dear."

"I what?"

"Swish. All sorts of things move when you walk. Have you ever noticed that, Brother Bheid?" she asked.

Bheid's face turned slightly red.

"I thought I noticed you noticing," Andine said. "You *definitely* get his attention when you walk past him, Leitha."

"Really?" Leitha said with feigned astonishment. "You should have mentioned that, Bheid. If you enjoy swishing so much, I'd be more than happy to—"

"Do you suppose we could talk about something else?" Bheid interrupted her.

"Let's leave the children to their entertainments, Althalus," Chief Albron suggested. "Khalor's waiting for us in the trenches."

"Right," Althalus agreed.

Eliar put his hand on the door latch and concentrated a moment. Then he opened the door and led the way into the raw-earth-smelling ditch Chief Gweti's men were digging across the open pastures of northern Wekti.

"Ah," Sergeant Khalor said when he saw them. "Any problems down in Keiwon, my Chief?"

"Things went smoothly, Sergeant," Albron replied. He looked around. "They're making better progress than I'd thought they would," he observed.

"Gebhel knows his business, my Chief," Khalor replied.

"Gebhel?"

"He's the Sergeant of Gweti's people. As soon as he gets out from under his Chief's thumb, he does things right. Gweti always tells his men to drag things out as long as they can. They smile and nod to keep him happy and then they ignore him. I talked with Gebhel as soon as they got here, and he had his surveyors out staking the trench line almost before I finished. He's a very methodical sort of fellow, and he's done this before." Khalor turned and pointed toward the east. "This ridgeline sort of wanders along that dry streambed, and it's just about perfect for our purposes. We'll have a steep slope leading uphill to our earthworks, and that's always an advantage. Things almost always roll downhill, and Gebhel's got some very interesting ideas about various things we'll be able to roll down into the teeth of the Ansus when they try to charge our earthworks. I'll introduce you to him, and he'll explain things. I'd listen very carefully, my Chief. Gebhel's an absolute genius when it comes to trench warfare."

"Not as good as *you* are, certainly."

"Better, my Chief. He isn't much good when it comes to attacking, but he's a master of defense. He forces his enemy to come to *him*. It's not the best way to *win* a war, but it's a very good way to keep from *losing*. It drags things out quite a bit, but that makes Chief Gweti happy. Most of the time, Gebhel's enemies give up and go away after a few months of mounting futile—and costly—attacks against his earthworks."

"That's as good as winning, Sergeant."

"Sometimes, maybe, but probably not this time. I've already taken care of that, though. I want Gebhel to hold this line, and nothing else. I've got other forces that'll take care of the attacks that are going to exterminate the Ansus. Come along, Chief Albron. I'll introduce you to Gebhel; then Eliar, Althalus, and I have to go back to the House. I want to move old Chief Delur's men to Elkan in north Equero so that they'll be in position on our western flank when the time comes."

Sergeant Gebhel was a blocky man with a bushy beard and a bald head. His kilt revealed legs as thick as tree trunks. He spoke in a dry, deep voice without very much emotion. "I'm pleased to meet you, Chief Albron," he said rather unconvincingly. "Has Khalor explained the situation to you?"

"We're here to dig trenches," Albron said.

"That wasn't what I was talking about. You *do* know that *I* give the orders here, don't you?"

"Of course, Sergeant. I'm here to learn, not to lead. I'm studying war, Sergeant Gebhel. Khalor tells me that you're the best there is when it comes to defense, so I've come here to learn from you."

"This isn't exactly a schoolhouse, Chief Albron," Gebhel growled. "I won't have time to give lectures."

"I'll stay out from underfoot, Sergeant," Albron promised. "I can learn most of what I need to know by just watching."

"I've got some other fish to fry," Khalor told them, "so I'll leave you gentlemen to your ditchdigging. I'll be back in a little while."

Althalus, Eliar, and Khalor stood in a doorway leading off one of the halls in the north wing of the House. "Are you sure this is the right door, Eliar?" Khalor asked. "I don't see anybody coming yet."

"This is the door we want, Sergeant," Eliar insisted. "Chief Delur's men should be coming along soon."

Khalor grunted. Then he looked curiously at Althalus. "Just exactly what is it that Delur's men think they're looking at when they're wandering around through these halls?" he asked.

"The mountains of Kagwher," Althalus replied.

"They can't see the walls or the ceiling or the hallway?" Khalor pressed.

"No. They're seeing trees and mountains and sky. It's a form of suggestion, Sergeant. If I started talking about how hot it's been lately, you'd start to sweat before long."

"Are you the one who's doing this to them?"

Althalus laughed. "I'm good, Khalor, but I'm not *that* good. Dweia's taking care of it. It's her House, so it more or less does what she tells it to do. Just exactly who are we waiting for?"

"A certain Captain Dreigon. He's the one who's leading Chief Delur's clansmen. He and I've worked a couple of wars together before. He isn't quite as good at trenches as Gebhel is, but he's a master when it comes to surprise attacks."

"Here they come," Eliar said quietly, pointing down the hall.

A large group of kilted men were plodding rather aimlessly toward them, led by a bleak-faced man with silver-grey hair.

"What kept you, Dreigon?" Khalor called out to him.

"I was picking berries, Khalor," the bleak-faced man replied sardonically. "What are you doing up here?"

"Just making sure you wouldn't be late for the party. If you've got a few minutes, maybe we should talk."

"All right," Dreigon agreed. He turned. "You men keep going. I'll catch up later." Then he pulled off his helmet and looked around. "I *hate* the mountains," he said. "They're pretty to look at, but they're not too pleasant to walk through."

"Truly," Khalor agreed.

"How's Gebhel doing with the trenches?"

"He's a bit ahead of schedule. You know how Gebhel is." Khalor made a wry face.

"Oh, yes," Dreigon agreed. "I think he's part mole, sometimes. We were on opposite sides in a war down in Perquaine a few years back, and I had to attack his earthworks. *That* turned out to be moderately unpleasant. What are we coming up against this time, Khalor?"

"Cavalry—at least for right now. I've got a hunch there'll be infantry involved as well, but my scouts haven't located them yet."

"Any guesses yet about when?"

Khalor nodded. "We got lucky. One of my scouts wriggled through the brush and eavesdropped on a planning session. We've got four days until the fun starts."

"How about where? *When*'s nice, but *where*'s just as important."

"I'm still working on that part."

"Work faster. Gebhel's trenches can probably hold out for a couple of weeks, no matter *what* gets thrown at him, but I need a location—soon. If I have to run my men fifty miles to get to the battlefield, they'll be a little winded by the time they get there."

"You're fairly close to the city of Elkan in northern Equero right now, Dreigon," Khalor said. "You'll probably have a day or so to pause and regroup when you get there. I'll let you know as soon as I find out anything meaningful about where the main attack's going to hit Gebhel's trenches."

"Do that, Khalor. I really *hate* being late for a war."

"It wouldn't be the same without you, my friend."

There was a great deal of activity on the slopes below Gebhel's partially completed trenches when Eliar took Khalor and Althalus back through the door to northern Wekti, and Chief Albron was wearing a rather self-satisfied expression. "Ah, there you are," he greeted them. "Did you get Captain Dreigon and his men to Elkan?"

"They'll be there by tonight, my Chief," Khalor replied. "Have any of those shepherds got here yet?"

"Gebhel's scouts have seen a couple of advance parties of them. Take a look down that slope, Sergeant. I persuaded Gebhel to add something to that forest of sharp stakes his men were planting."

Khalor climbed up out of the trench and looked down the slope. "Bushes?" he asked. "What's the point of weaving bushes in amongst the stakes?"

"That's no ordinary bush, Sergeant," Albron told him. "The local Wektis call it 'the shrub from Hell.' It's a bramble with three-inch thorns—almost like steel needles. They grow wild along the river. I accidentally brushed up against one of the blasted things a few hours ago, and as soon as I got the bleeding under control, I thought they might be an interesting addition to our barricade out front."

"You didn't try to *order* Gebhel to use them, did you?"

"I know better than that, Sergeant," Albron said. "I just handed him a limb from one of the cursed things and said, 'Isn't this interesting?' He got the point—six or eight points, actually—almost immediately."

"It was only a suggestion, then?"

"Precisely. I know a lot more about politics than I do about war, Sergeant. I didn't put Gebhel's nose out of joint, if that's what you're worried about. He's still giving orders, but now he listens when I make suggestions."

"You're better at this than I thought you'd be, my Chief." Then Khalor looked down the slope again. "Why did you and Gebhel thin out the stakes in the places where there aren't any bushes, though? You've given the Ansus natural highways right up to your front door."

"They aren't highways, Sergeant. They're funnels. After the Ansu cavalry hits those bushes, they're going to be riding *very* unhappy horses. No amount of spurring or whipping will persuade their mounts to dash into *those* barricades. The Ansus are going to be forced to find easier routes upslope. Gebhel and I *gave* them those easy routes. As soon as the shepherds get here, we'll concentrate them at the upper end of those funnels. We'll have them wait until the front ranks of the Ansus are about halfway up the hill. Then they'll jump up all at once and pick them off by the dozen. The ones coming along behind are going to have dead horses rolling down all over the top of them. Gebhel's almost positive that the combination of the bushes, the funnels, and the slings will totally demoralize the Ansus and keep them out of our trenches. Can you think of anything we've left out?"

Khalor was scowling. "Don't rush me," he grunted. "I'm working on it."

"Work all you want, Sergeant," Albron boasted. "We've covered everything. We'll still be here when your friends arrive."

"That's all that matters, my Chief. If you and Gebhel can hold them here, I'll get Kreuter and Dreigon into position. We'll wait until the Ansus are fully engaged, and then I'll instruct Dreigon's infantry and Kreuter's cavalry to charge the Ansu rear. We'll grind them into dog meat right there on that hillside."

"Our Chief is really very good, isn't he, Sergeant?" Eliar said enthusiastically.

"Oh, shut up, Eliar!" Khalor snapped.

"Yes, my Sergeant," Eliar said obediently, concealing a sly grin behind his hand.

Althalus was growing more and more edgy as time moved on. Gebhel's trenches were little more than shallow ditches at this point, and Althalus could see no way that they could possibly be completed in the time remaining. "We've only got three more days, Eliar," he told his young friend after supper in Chief Albron's apartments in the temple at Keiwon. "If Gebhel's trenches aren't ready, Gelta's going to ride right over the top of him."

"Sergeant Khalor says that Gebhel's a lot farther along than he seems to be, Althalus," Eliar replied. "I guess the really hard part when you're digging a trench is cutting down through the sod. Once the sod's out of the way, the rest of the job's easy, and it goes a lot faster. As I understand it, now that Gebhel's men have cleared the sod, half of them will keep digging, and the other half will be driving in the stakes and setting up other obstacles to the front of the trench. Sergeant Khalor's sure that they'll be ready when the time comes."

Then Andine burst through the door. "Eliar!" she exclaimed. "I have to go back to Osthos immediately."

"Calm down, Andine," Althalus told her. "What's this all about?"

"Leitha's been gathering information here, and she's managed to uncover Ghend's plans. His next move is going to be a renewal of that war in Treborea. The half-wit in Kanthon is already massing his forces. I *have* to go to Osthos and warn my Chamberlain. This running around and popping in and out of doors is very entertaining, but I *do* have responsibilities in Osthos. Please, Althalus, take me home!"

You'd better do as she says, Althalus, Dweia's voice murmured in his mind. *Things probably aren't quite as bad as she seems to believe, but you'd better pacify her.*

What's Ghend really up to?

I think he's trying to spread us out. He's still ahead of you, Althie, but not by very much. He's trying to confuse you, I'd imagine. This attack on Osthos might be a ploy to pull us out of position. He knows about Leitha's gift, so he might have his people here in Keiwon feeding false information to her.

He may know about Leitha, Althalus replied, *but I don't think he knows about Gher. That little boy's idea of putting all the clans of Arum in the House has arranged things so that I can field an army anywhere in the world at a moment's notice.*

Don't get overconfident, Althie. This new war in Treborea might be bogus. But we can't be positive. Take Andine home so that she can warn Lord Dhakan, but then bring her right back to Keiwon. I don't *want that girl running around loose out there.*

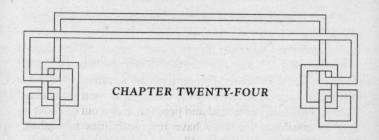

CHAPTER TWENTY-FOUR

It was early the following morning when Eliar led Althalus and Andine through the door into Lord Dhakan's study high in the palace at Osthos.

The silver-haired Chamberlain looked up from his desk angrily. "Who gave you permission to—" He broke off. *"Eliar?"* he asked incredulously. "What on earth are *you* doing here?"

"Just following orders, my Lord," Eliar replied.

"And Althalus?" Dhakan said. "Is that really you?"

"It was the last time I checked, Lord Dhakan. You're looking well."

"I'm still breathing, if that's what you mean. I thought you were going to sell Eliar into the salt mines in Ansu."

"I decided to keep him instead, my Lord. He's a very useful young fellow now and then."

"You don't even recognize me anymore, do you Dhakan?" Andine, still dressed as a page boy, said archly.

"My Arya!" he exclaimed, coming to his feet. "Where have you been? I've been tearing the world apart looking for you for over a year now!"

Andine rushed to him and threw her arms about his neck impulsively. "Dear, dear Dhakan!" she exclaimed. "I've missed you so very much!"

"I don't understand this at all, Althalus," Dhakan said. "What have you done to my Arya?"

"Well, I sort of borrowed her, Dhakan."

"I think the word is 'abducted,' Althalus," Dhakan corrected.

"It wasn't his fault, dear Dhakan," Andine told him. "He was acting on orders from the one we both serve now."

"You've changed, Arya Andine."

"Grown up a bit, you mean?" She laughed then. "How in the world were you able to stand me before? I was absolutely impossible."

"Well, a little, maybe," he conceded.

"A *little*? I was a monster. Would you be willing to accept a blanket apology for all the trouble I caused you after I ascended the throne? Your patience was almost inhuman. You should have turned me over your knee and given me a good, sound spanking."

"Andine!"

"Hadn't we better sort of move along?" Eliar suggested. "We've got a lot of things we have to do."

"He's right, Andine," Althalus said.

"Yes. He's so irritating when he's right."

"I gather that your feelings about the young man have changed, my Arya?" Dhakan suggested.

"Well, sort of, yes. Most of the time I don't even want to kill him anymore. Now I feed him instead. It wasn't really his fault that he killed my father, you know. I know whose fault it *really* was now, and Eliar's going to kill *that* one for me. Isn't that nice of him?"

"I don't understand any of this, Althalus," Dhakan admitted.

"The world's going all to smash, Lord Dhakan," Althalus told him, "but my associates and I are going to fix that. You'd better tell him what's about to happen, Andine. We don't really have very much time here."

"I'll be brief," she promised. "The turmoil Althalus spoke of isn't accidental, Dhakan. There's a man in Nekweros who's behind it all, and he has allies all over, stirring up trouble so that he can rule the world. The idiot is in Kanthon's part of that alliance, and it won't be very long before he comes knocking at the gates of Osthos again."

"Has the fool hired more Arum mercenaries?"

"No, the Arums aren't available to him. I've already hired every able-bodied man in all of Arum."

Dhakan paled visibly. "Arya Andine!" he exclaimed. "You'll strip the treasury bare! How much did you promise to pay these heathen barbarians?"

"Althalus provided the money, Dhakan. It didn't cost me a penny. You'd better tell him what to do, Eliar. Let him know what to expect."

"Yes, Andine," Eliar said. "It sort of goes like this, Lord Dhakan. We're not sure exactly when the Kanthons are going to invade your territory, but it probably won't be very long. We've got an army, and we'll come to your aid, but we're in the middle of another war right now. We'll have to finish that one before we can come here. I know how good your soldiers are, since I've fought them before."

"I seem to remember that, yes," Dhakan said drily.

"We can't be sure just how big an army the Kanthons are going to throw at you, my Lord, but they'll probably outnumber you by quite a little. You won't be able to hold them back out in open country, so you'd probably better not try. Your best course would be to fight a delaying action. Kill as many of their men as you can without losing too many of your own—little skirmishes, ambushes, that sort of thing. Keep pulling back the way Andine's father did last time. The walls of your city here are the one advantage you've got. Pull your men back inside and close the gates. I promise that I'll come and raise the siege before you run out of food."

"I can't stay, Dhakan," Andine said in her vibrant voice, "so you'll have to hold my city. Please don't let our enemies destroy my Osthos."

"All I can do is try, my Arya," Dhakan said dubiously. "I think time's going to be as much our enemy as the Kanthons, though. The best intentions in the world can't move an army overnight."

"Eliar *will* be here when you need him, Dhakan," Andine told him. "You have my absolute promise on that." Then she impulsively threw her arms about the old gentleman's neck and kissed him soundly. "Until later, my dear, dear friend," she said in her throbbing voice.

* * *

It was about noon on that day when Eliar and Althalus located Sergeant Khalor and Chief Albron in the trenches near the east bank of the River Medyo. "It's not done that way, my Chief," Sergeant Khalor was explaining. "Only an idiot mounts a mass attack along a broad, general front. The normal strategy is to mass your troops at one specific point and then strike like a spear thrust."

"But where?"

"That's the problem, my Chief. We don't *know* where the Ansus are going to hit us. We know that they'll come at us the day after tomorrow, but we can't be certain where their main attack is going to be."

"Can't we make any guesses?"

"I can think of a dozen places where *I'd* attack if I happened to be on the other side. When you're going to mount a main thrust, you always want to choose someplace with terrain features that'll help you—woods to hide your movements, a gentler slope to the hillside, weaker defenses, things like that. Then you pick several places a long way away from there and throw away a few battalions with diversionary attacks. The diversions are intended to draw the bulk of the defenders out of position—*and* to force them to commit their reserves. Then, when you mount your main attack, the defenders don't have any troops left to meet you."

"I see," Chief Albron said thoughtfully. "If I understand you, then, the best strategy would be to just ignore those first attacks and hold fast until the *real* one starts."

"Exactly, but how do you know which one *is* the real one? I was working a war down in Perquaine a few years back, and my opponent was one of those 'let's wait and see' fellows. I outsmarted him by starting my main thrust at first light. I made my diversionary thrusts *after* I was already on top of him. He was so certain that my first attack was only a diversion that he pulled men out of the main fight to meet my false thrusts."

"It's almost like a game, isn't it?"

"It's the best game there is, my Chief," Khalor said with a sudden grin. "The word 'strategy' means outsmarting your enemy, *and* recognizing all the tricks he'll use to deceive you."

Khalor tapped his forehead. "Wars are won *here*, my Chief, not out there in the trenches. Right now I'd give a month's pay to know where Pekhal's going to make his main thrust."

"Really?" Althalus said. "I don't suppose you'd care to put that down in writing, would you, Sergeant?"

"Not when I'm talking to *you*, I wouldn't."

"Spoilsport," Althalus accused him.

"I think I see where you're going with this, Althalus," Eliar said. "You *do* know that Bheid's going to go right through the ceiling if you even suggest it, don't you?"

"Oh, he'll come back down—eventually. I won't really put Leitha into any danger. We'll bring her up here to the trenches tomorrow evening and let her snoop around in Pekhal's mind a bit. We'll have her back in Keiwon before the fighting starts."

"Shouldn't we bring her here this afternoon?" Chief Albron asked. "Wouldn't that give us more time to make preparations?"

"We don't *need* time, my Chief," Eliar reminded him. "That's what the doors are all about."

"Pekhal's got access to doors of his own, most likely," Althalus added. "That's why we don't want Leitha here until about ten or twelve hours before the battle. Ghend knows about Leitha's abilities, so he might try to dupe her with false information. If he's told Pekhal and Gelta to hit our lines *here*, and that's the information Leitha picks up, we'll be massing our forces *here*. If Ghend issues new orders about midnight and the attack comes *there*, we'll be out of position. Even with the doors to help us, it might be touch and go."

"Doesn't that mean that Leitha *has* to find Pekhal?" Khalor asked. "Ordinary soldiers usually don't have any idea of where they really are. Could Pekhal trick her? I mean, if he keeps thinking 'over there' instead of 'right here,' would that deceive her?"

"Pekhal's not bright enough for that," Althalus replied. "*Speaking* a lie is one thing, but *thinking* one is quite beyond his capabilities. Gelta *might* be a bit more convincing, but not by very much. They're primitives, Sergeant, so don't expect anything exotic from them. They're still at the 'burn, fight, kill' level when it comes to strategy, so they won't do anything very complex. We'll find out tomorrow night when Leitha gets here."

"We've got some people coming up from the south," Eliar said. "I think it's Salkan and his shepherds."

"They made good time," Chief Albron said.

"They aren't really carrying very much equipment, my Chief," Khalor pointed out. He shaded his eyes with one hand and stared at the approaching shepherds. "Pitiful," he snorted.

"What?" Chief Albron looked puzzled.

"They can't even march properly. They look like a bunch of schoolboys on holiday. They're wandering all over out there."

"They're picking up rocks, Sergeant," Althalus explained. "The selection of good rocks is fairly important when you're using a sling."

"A rock's a rock, Althalus."

"Not really. I found a perfect rock once, and I carried it for about five years until I found a target worthy of it. It was perfectly round, about the size of a hen's egg, and the weight was exactly right."

"What did you kill with it?" Eliar asked, "A deer, maybe?"

"No, Eliar. I wouldn't waste a rock that good on a deer." Althalus chuckled grimly. "I was in Kagwher when I finally used it. There was a fellow who was chasing me over some picky little thing that wasn't really worth all that much. After a week, I got tired of dodging him, so I gave him my pet rock—right between his eyes—and he stopped chasing me." Althalus sighed. "I still miss that rock," he mourned.

"I won't permit it!" Bheid exploded late the following day in the temple at Keiwon when Althalus explained his plan. "I wouldn't even *consider* letting you put my Leitha into that kind of danger!"

"*My* Leitha?" the blond girl murmured.

"You know what I mean."

"Yes, I think I do. Things seem to be moving right along, don't they? Maybe we should talk about that—*after* I come back from the trenches."

"You're *not* going there! I forbid it!"

"Forbid?" Leitha's usually gentle voice turned steely. "You don't own me, Bheid. 'My Leitha' is one thing. 'Forbid' is quite another."

"I wasn't saying . . ." Bheid floundered for a moment. Then he tried another tack. "I'd really rather you didn't, Leitha," he said in a pleading tone. "I'd go crazy if anything happened to you up there."

"You're already crazy if you think you can order me around."

"Stuck your foot in your mouth, didn't you, Brother Bheid?" Andine suggested. "You should really think your way through things before you just blurt out the first notion that pops into your head."

"I'm not going to put her in any danger, Bheid," Althalus assured the young priest. "There's a whole army in those trenches to protect her, and she'll spend most of the time in the House. All we're going to do is drift up and down the corridors and peek through the doors until she locates Pekhal and Gelta. Sergeant Khalor *has* to know where they're planning their main attack so that he can make preparations to meet them, and Leitha's the one who's supposed to listen. As soon as she finds out what we need to know, I'll have Eliar bring her right back here so that you can spend the next few weeks apologizing and trying to pry your foot out of your mouth." He glanced at the west window. "It's almost time for the sun to go down," he observed. "Let's take Leitha to the trenches, Eliar."

"It's perfectly safe, then?" Andine asked.

"Absolutely," Althalus replied.

"If it's really *that* safe, why don't we *all* go? Brother Bheid can hover over Leitha, and Gher and I can look over your preparations and perhaps make a suggestion or two. *My* suggestions might not be worth very much, but Gher's another story, wouldn't you say?"

"It wouldn't hurt, Althalus," Eliar agreed. "Gher doesn't see the world in the same way the rest of us do, so he might come up with some things that wouldn't occur to anybody else."

He's got a point, pet, Dweia's voice murmured to Althalus.

"I don't care," Althalus said, throwing his hands in the air. "Take us all up to the trenches, Eliar."

"Anything you say, Althalus," Eliar replied.

Eliar looked around rather cautiously when they joined Albron and Khalor in the trench near the banks of the River Medyo. "Where's Gebhel, Sergeant Khalor?" he asked.

"I suggested that he might want to have a look at a stretch of trenches a few miles off to the east," Khalor replied. "I told him that the barricades looked a little weak along there. I know where he is, so we can step around him. Gebhel's a good man, but he's too stodgy to understand any of this." He looked with a certain disapproval at the others trailing along behind Eliar. "This isn't exactly the time or place for a sightseeing tour, Althalus," he said.

"It wasn't really my idea, Sergeant."

"Try to keep them out from underfoot." Then Khalor looked at Leitha, who was still garbed as a soothsayer. "You might want to keep your hood up," he suggested. "Princess Andine looks like a page boy, so she won't attract too much attention, but Gebhel's troops might get excited if they catch a glimpse of you."

"Whatever you think best, Sergeant," she replied. "Just what is it that you want me to discover?"

"All I really need to know is exactly where Pekhal and Gelta have massed their troops. That's *probably* where their main attack's going to be."

"If they've got doors the same as ours, they *could* hit us from someplace else, my Sergeant," Eliar cautioned.

"I know. You'll have to stay on your toes tomorrow, Eliar. Keep the hinges on the door to 'someplace else' well oiled, because you might have to move Gebhel's men in a hurry. We'll start out by putting the bulk of them in the trenches opposite from where the enemy forces are massed. If Pekhal and Gelta jump to someplace else, we'll have to respond."

"What I'm supposed to look for is a large number of soldiers, then?" Leitha asked.

"Twenty or thirty thousand anyway," Khalor replied.

"That shouldn't be too hard. That many people are certain to make a lot of noise." Leitha frowned slightly. "Just to be safe, let's start out in one-mile jumps, Eliar. I haven't practiced much at long-range listening. If I can reach out farther, we can start taking longer jumps."

"I just thought of something," Gher said.

"Have we left something out?" Khalor asked him.

"Well, maybe." Gher looked at Eliar. "You can put one of your doors anyplace you want it, can't you?"

"To within a half inch, Gher. Why?"

Gher reached out and laid his hand on the ground just above the front of the trench. "How about right here?" he asked.

"Good God!" Chief Albron exclaimed. "We never thought of that, did we, Sergeant? They could just step over all our barricades and trip lines and be in our trenches before we even knew they were coming!"

"Maybe not, my Chief," Eliar said. He put his hand on the hilt of the Knife, and his eyes narrowed. "I *think* I know of a way to keep that from happening, but I'll need to talk with Emmy about it."

"Don't mumble, Eliar," Khalor barked. "Spit it out."

"It's all going to depend on just how close *our* doors are to the ones in Nahgharash, Sergeant," Eliar said. "If they come together exactly, all I'd have to do is open *our* door when they open *theirs*."

"Oh, that's just fine, Eliar," Andine said sarcastically. "Then, instead of invading Wekti, they invade the House."

"I can take care of *that*, Andine," he said. "They won't know where they really are, any more than Captain Dreigon knows where *he* is. They'll ride through *their* door over in Nahgharash, pass through *my* door into the House, and then ride through *another* one of my doors that opens back down at the bottom of the hill. If I can get those three doors close enough together, I can probably keep them charging up that hill for the rest of the summer." Then he chuckled.

"What's so funny, Eliar?" Khalor demanded.

"I don't think they'll even see that door, Sergeant, and if I juggle it just right, any arrows they shoot at *our* people will come out down there at the bottom of the hill, so they'll be shooting their own reserves in the back every time one of them bends his bow."

"What a neat idea!" Gher said enthusiastically. "Then our people wouldn't have to do anything at all except stand here and watch while the bad people kill each other off."

"I think we're straying," Khalor said. "Let's stick to the business at hand here, shall we? Are you hearing anything over on the other side yet, Leitha?"

"You *did* know that there are several hundred Ansus about a quarter of a mile upriver, didn't you, Sergeant?" she replied.

Khalor nodded. "I've had people watching them," he said. "They're building rafts. Just before dawn tomorrow they'll probably come floating downriver. They won't get past us, though. Gebhel's made some preparations for a greeting."

"There are also some mounted men ranging along through those hills over on the Ansu side."

"Mounted patrols." Khalor dismissed them. "They aren't important."

"Let's go a mile to the east, Eliar," Leitha said then.

The transition was so brief that Althalus received only a fleeting impression of the House, and they were in the trench again.

Leitha frowned, concentrating. "I'm touching the same people," she said. "Let's try five miles, Eliar."

"Right," he said, and then led them through a door that evidently only he could see.

"I'm still getting the same ones," Leitha fretted. "They're fainter, but they're still the same men. Let's go to ten miles, Eliar. I seem to be able to reach much farther than I'd thought."

"Are you sure you aren't missing anybody?" Khalor asked her.

"I'd hear them if they were anywhere near us, Sergeant," she assured him.

They covered perhaps seventy miles in fairly short order, and

Leitha encountered nothing more significant than a few more mounted patrols.

It was about midnight when she stopped and said, "Here!" in a triumphant voice. Then she frowned again. "No," she said. "I don't think that's the main body you were talking about, Sergeant. There are three or four hundred of them, and they seem to be having some kind of party."

"An old Ansu custom," Khalor told her. "I don't believe any Ansu army in the history of the world has ever mounted a charge stone-cold sober. They're usually roaring drunk when they attack."

"If it's only four hundred or so, this obviously is going to be one of the diversions you mentioned, Khalor," Chief Albron suggested.

"Probably so," Khalor agreed. "Let's move on."

"Wait!" Leitha said sharply.

"What?" Althalus asked her.

"I just touched Pekhal!" she hissed. "And Gelta as well!"

"Where?" Khalor demanded.

"I can't be sure. Just a moment." She raised her face and looked up at the stars.

"I don't think they'd be there, Leitha," Andine said.

"Hush," she said absently. "I'm trying to step over all that drunken babble just to the front. But I'm afraid I've lost them." She frowned, concentrating intensely. Then she smiled. "Oh, *that's* clever," she said almost admiringly.

"What?" Althalus asked her.

"There's a huge cave—acres and acres—about a half mile back in those hills," she replied, "and there are thousands of men and horses in that cave. I'm catching the sense that their main attack *will* come from right here—but not until well after sunrise. The ones who are drinking themselves into a stupor closer to these trenches don't even know about the force in that cave. They think that they're only going to be one of the diversionary attacks you mentioned, Sergeant Khalor. I'd guess that Koman's behind this."

"Who's Koman?" Chief Albron asked her.

"He's one of Ghend's associates, and he shares this 'gift' of mine. It has to be somebody who knows how the gift works. He's put a lot of noise and drunken singing between me and that main force, and the rocks enclosing the cave are muffling the sounds of all those men and horses inside. I might have missed that force entirely if Koman and that defrocked priest, Argan, hadn't come out of the cave for a bit of private conversation. They've got some opinions about Pekhal and Gelta that aren't very flattering, and I get the impression that they rather frequently go off to someplace private to give vent to their feelings. But that's beside the point. This is definitely the place, Sergeant. There'll be a diversionary attack by those rowdies across the way at first light. They'll mill around just out of bowshot, making noise and waving torches and eventually ride off. Then there'll be other diversions in other places after that. Then an hour or so after sunrise, the ones hiding in the cave will—" She broke off suddenly. "Wait!" she hissed. "Something isn't right!" She suddenly gave a startled gasp. "Look out!" she shouted. "They're using their doors!"

Althalus looked around wildly and saw a momentary flicker at the back of the trench. Then Khnom was there, swinging a door open wide. Behind Ghend's little henchman, Althalus caught a brief glimpse of a city made of fire, but then Gelta shouldered Khnom out of her way and rushed into the trench, brandishing her archaic stone ax.

"Eliar!" Althalus shouted. "Behind you!"

But Gelta's crude weapon was already descending toward the back of the young Arum's head.

Eliar half turned in response to Althalus' shouted warning, and Gelta's ax struck the back of his head with a glancing blow. He pitched forward to fall facedown into the dirt at the bottom of the trench.

Gelta shrieked triumphantly even as Khnom rushed forward to drag her back to that hideous portal.

Even as the two of them passed through the open doorway, the voice of Ghend echoed into the trench from the fiery vaults of Nahgharash. "And *that* puts you out of business, doesn't it, Althalus?" Ghend chortled.

And then the portal at the back of the trench vanished, leaving behind only the mocking echo of Ghend's laughter.

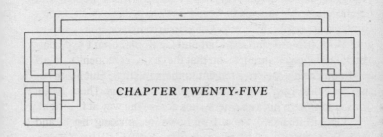

CHAPTER TWENTY-FIVE

"*No!*" Andine shrieked. She rushed to Eliar, fell to her knees beside his limp body, and clasped him to her, weeping uncontrollably.

Get her away from him, Althalus! Dweia's voice crackled inside his mind. *She'll only make it worse!*

He's still alive? Althalus demanded silently.

Of course he is! Move, Althalus!

Althalus firmly pulled the hysterical young woman away from Eliar. "Stop it, Andine," he told her, forcing himself to speak calmly. "He's not dead, but he's badly hurt, so don't shake him around like that."

Move aside, Althalus, Dweia told him. *I have to talk with Leitha.* He felt her push him out of the way. "Leitha," she said, "it's me. I want you to do exactly as I tell you."

"It was all a trick!" Leitha wailed. "I should have known it was too easy!"

"We don't have time for that now. I need to know how badly Eliar's been hurt."

"I've failed, Dweia!" Leitha sobbed. "Everything connected with that cave was nothing more than a trap, and I fell right into it."

"Stop that!" Dweia said sharply. "You'll have to go inside Eliar's physical brain. I have to know exactly what's happening in there."

Leitha's eyes grew distant. "There's nothing, Dweia," she reported in a helpless voice. "His mind's totally blank."

"I said 'brain,' Leitha, not 'mind.' Go in deeper. Get past thoughts and go all the way in. Here, like this." A number of incomprehensible images flickered in Althalus' mind.

"Is that possible?" Leitha asked in astonishment.

"Do it. Don't stand there arguing with me. I *must* know how badly he's been injured."

Leitha's pale face twisted with the intensity of her effort.

"Not that way," Althalus heard his voice say. More images flashed through his awareness.

"Oh," Leitha said, "now I see. I've never done that before." Her face relaxed, and her eyes grew distant. "Blood," she reported. "It's very dark, but he's bleeding at the back of his brain."

"How much? Is it spurting?"

"Not exactly, but it's not just oozing."

"I was afraid of that. We'll need to move him, Sergeant Khalor. Let's get him out of this ditch and into someplace that's warm and well lighted."

"You're not Althalus anymore, are you?" Khalor said, staring at his friend's face.

"It's me, Khalor. I have to go through Althalus. I don't have time to come there myself. Get some men to carry Eliar. Order them not to jostle him around."

"Can you cure him, ma'am? That ugly hag really slammed his head a good one."

"It wasn't quite good enough. He turned his head just as she hit him. We have to move fast, though. Let's get him to someplace where we can work on him."

"Gebhel's got a tent on that hill behind the trench, Sergeant," Albron suggested. "He used it as a command post while his men were digging this stretch of trenches."

"It'll have to do, I guess," Khalor said. "There's no place else nearby. I'll round up some men."

"There are quite a few things going on here that I don't quite understand," Chief Albron said, looking quizzically at Althalus.

"Dweia's speaking to us through Althalus, Chief Albron,"

Bheid explained. "She's in the House, and we're here. There are probably other ways she could do this, but it's quicker—and much less disturbing for the men around us—if she does it this way. A thundering voice coming from nowhere might attract a lot of attention. She's been talking to us through Althalus ever since we first came to know them."

"She *can* cure Eliar, can't she?" Albron asked with a worried frown. "Without those doors of his, we don't have much of a chance here." Then he looked sharply at Althalus. "That's what this was all about from the beginning, wasn't it? All that business with the drunken Ansus across the valley and the cave filled with men and horses was just a trick to lure us to this part of the trenches so that they could kill Eliar. Without Eliar and the doors, we can't possibly defend ourselves."

"That'll change just as soon as we get Eliar back on his feet," Althalus assured him.

"What if we can't?"

"Please don't start with the what-ifs, Chief Albron," Althalus said wearily. "We've got enough to worry about without all those what-ifs muddying the waters."

Gebhel's command post was a large tent with several cots, a crude stove, and a table littered with maps and diagrams. The half-dozen Arums whom Sergeant Khalor had commandeered carried Eliar inside on a hastily improvised litter and gently laid him facedown on one of the cots.

Come in here, Leitha, Althalus heard Dweia silently murmur to the pale blond girl. *You and Althalus are going to have to work together when we do this. Eliar's brain's bleeding, and there isn't any way for it to drain. It might have been better if Gelta'd hit him squarely with that ax. If she'd opened his skull, the blood could run out, but the way it is right now, the blood has no place to go, so it's building up pressure. If that goes on for too long, the pressure will crush his brain, and he'll die.*

Are you saying that we have to pull off the back of his head, Em? Althalus asked incredulously.

Don't be ridiculous, Althalus. All we'll really need to relieve that pressure is one or two small holes in the back of his skull. As soon as Leitha pinpoints the exact location of the bleeding, you'll use a word from the Book to open those holes.

That's all there is to it? Althalus asked. *It sounds awfully mechanical to me—sort of like installing a drainpipe.*

That comes fairly close, yes.

And that'll cure him? That's all it'll take?

Not entirely, but it's the first thing we have to do. We'll get to the rest of it after we've relieved the pressure. Let's move right along: every minute counts right now. The first thing we need is more light. Use "leuk," Althalus. We want the tent roof to glow in the same way the dome in the tower does.

All right. Do we need anything else?

Have somebody fetch one of those Wekti shepherds. We need certain plants to make a poultice and some others to brew up a medicine. The shepherds are more familiar with the local vegetation than the Arums are.

"Gher," Althalus said aloud, "go find that redheaded shepherd Salkan, and bring him here. Hurry."

"Right away," Gher said, bolting from the tent.

We'll have to shave the back of Eliar's head before we can start, Dweia said then.

"Is your razor good and sharp, Bheid?" Althalus asked.

"Of course it is, Althalus."

"Good. Dweia wants you to shave the back of Eliar's head."

"Althalus!" Andine protested.

Put her to sleep, Althalus, Dweia said abruptly. *Use "leb." She's just going to be in the way, and she doesn't need to watch anyway.*

Right, Althalus agreed silently. Then he spoke aloud. "Andine?"

"Yes?"

"*Leb,* Andine. *Leb.*"

Her eyes went vacant, and she slumped senselessly into his arms. He carried her to the other side of the tent and gently laid her on one of the vacant cots.

"How are we going to go about this, Dweia?" Leitha asked.

"As soon as Bheid finishes shaving the back of Eliar's head, you'll locate the exact places where the brain's bleeding. Then you'll put your finger on his head to show Althalus precisely where they are. Then Althalus will very gently grind small holes through Eliar's skull bone with the word '*bher*.' That'll let the blood out and relieve the pressure."

"Has anybody ever done anything like this before, Dweia?" Leitha asked dubiously.

"Not very often, no," Dweia admitted. "Most people who claim to be healers are frauds—or worse—and they have a very limited understanding of how the body really works. Now and then, though, a few very gifted healers have recognized this problem. Unfortunately, they didn't have the right kind of tools. And because they didn't understand the danger of infection, they didn't bother to clean the tools before they started drilling holes in people's heads. Althalus isn't going to use a hammer and chisel or a flint knife. He's going to drill with a word from the Book, and the poultice we'll make should ward off any infection."

I caught a few "shoulds" and "maybes" in there, Em, Althalus noted. *If I wanted to put a wager on this, how good would the chances be?*

About half and half—maybe just a little better. We don't really have a choice, though, do we?

No, I guess we don't at that.

Gher led the fiery-haired Salkan into the tent. "I finally found him," the boy said. "How's Eliar?"

"He's been better," Bheid said, wiping his razor on a crumpled rag.

"Why are you cutting off his hair?"

"Althalus needs to get to skin, and the hair's in the way."

"When Eliar wakes up, he's going to come after you with a club," Gher said. "He's going to look really silly without his hair."

"We have to make a poultice, Salkan," Dweia told the young Wekti, speaking through Althalus, "so we'll need certain leaves and roots. Eliar's been badly injured, and we don't want any infections setting in."

"I've got a fair idea of the things you'll need, Master Althalus," Salkan replied. "I've cured quite a few injured sheep. Your voice sounds a little strange, though. Are you all right?"

"Something just happened that wasn't supposed to happen," Dweia replied. "It made me a little tense. Which plants do you normally use to make a poultice?"

Salkan rattled off some names that Althalus didn't recognize.

"That should come fairly close," Dweia approved. "See if you can find a greenberry tree, though, and bring me some of those berries as well."

"Those berries are poisonous, Master Althalus," the boy warned.

"We'll cook the poison out," Dweia assured him, "and the other ingredients will counter what's left. A greenberry poultice prevents infection, and it stops bleeding. Now, then, there are a few other things I'll need for a medicine we'll be spooning into Eliar's mouth." She identified several other plants for the young shepherd.

"Are you sure you know what you're doing?" Salkan asked dubiously.

"Trust me. Go with him, Gher, and take a basket. Bring back the berries as quickly as you can. They have to cook longer than some of the other ingredients do."

"Anything you say, Emmy," Gher agreed. And then he and Salkan left the tent.

Get a fire going in that stove, Althalus, Dweia instructed, *and put some pots of water on to boil. As soon as the water starts to bubble, use "gel" to cleanse it.*

I thought "gel" meant to freeze something.

Well, sort of.

You're asking me to freeze boiling water? That doesn't make any sense, Em.

It will work, love. Trust me. It's a form of purification. We'll do that several times while we're making the poultice and the medicine Eliar's going to be taking after you drill the holes in his head, and you're going to have to wash your hands in some of that medicine as well. Everything that touches Eliar has to be absolutely clean.

I don't entirely understand, Em.

Clean is good; dirty is bad. Was there any part of that you didn't understand?

Be nice, he murmured silently.

This isn't permanent, is it, Em? Althalus asked, looking at his hands after he'd washed them in the peculiar syrup they'd concocted from several different ingredients. *I might have a little trouble explaining how I came to have green hands.*

It'll wear off in time. Now swab the back of Eliar's head with it, and let's get started. Listen very carefully, Althalus. We're not going to bash our way into Eliar's head, so speak the word "bher" very softly each time. All you want to do the first time is just go through the skin. Then you'll come to a very thin layer of flesh. Say "bher" again, and you'll remove the flesh. Dab away the blood with that linen cloth and swab the wound with more of the green syrup before you start drilling into the bone. Keep flushing out the hole you're drilling to clear away the bone fragments.

We've been through this several times already, Em.

Once more won't hurt. Let's make sure you know what you're doing before you start. I want you to stop immediately when you break through the skull bone. There's a tough membrane between the skull bone and the brain itself. Flush the wound out thoroughly and then swab it again. Only then do you go through the membrane. Do you have any questions at all?

I think we've covered just about everything, Em.

All right. Start drilling.

The bright red spurt of Eliar's blood struck Althalus squarely in the face.

His heart's strong, Dweia observed clinically as Althalus wiped the blood off his face.

How can you tell? Leitha asked, her silent voice echoing in the mind of Althalus.

Every time his heart beats, his head squirts like a fountain.

You ladies are being awfully cold-blooded about this, Althalus accused. *That is Eliar there, you know. We're not just talking about some leaky bucket here.*

Don't be so sentimental, Althalus, Dweia told him. *Pack that wound with the poultice, and then drill another hole on the left side.*

How many do you think we'll need?

That depends on what Leitha finds after we've finished with these two. The poultice should stop the bleeding in these, and then she should be able to discover any other trouble spots.

How exactly does the poultice stop the bleeding, Dweia? Leitha asked curiously.

It's an astringent, dear. It constricts the blood vessels. It's something on the order of the way sour fruit makes your mouth pucker up. That's why we needed the greenberries. They aren't really all that poisonous, but they're so sour that people believe that they almost have *to be deadly. Get back to work, Althalus. You aren't being paid to just stand around.*

Paid? I'm not getting paid, Em.

We'll talk about that some other time. Drill, Althalus. Drill.

"What have you *done*?" Andine demanded, staring at the bandages wrapped around Eliar's head.

"You don't really want to know, dear," Leitha told her. "It was moderately revolting."

"I mean what did you do to me?"

"Althalus put you to sleep, Andine," Bheid told her. "You were very upset, and Dweia wanted to calm you down."

"How much do you love Eliar, Andine?" Dweia demanded, using Althalus' voice again.

"I'd die for him."

"That wouldn't be very useful just now, dear. I want you to administer a medicine to him. It's a bit on the order of the way you've been feeding him lately. You and Bheid are going to have to take care of that, because Althalus and Leitha have to help

Khalor and Albron hold off the Ansus until Eliar's back on his feet."

"Just tell me what to do, Dweia," Andine replied.

"You see that bowl on the table, and that glass tube?"

"Is that some sort of brown syrup in the bowl?"

"It's not exactly syrup, dear. It's a medicine. Eliar has to receive regular doses of it."

"Three times a day, or something like that?"

"No, it's a little more precise than that. Eliar needs very small doses at regular intervals. That's what the glass tube's for. There's a line around the tube to show you just how much to give him. You take the tube, dip it into the medicine as far as that line, and then you put your finger over the upper end of the tube. Then put the tube in Eliar's mouth and lift your finger. That lets the medicine drain into his mouth. Try it once, so that you'll know how to do it."

Andine went to the table, took up the tube, and dipped it into the syrupy liquid. Then she stoppered the end of the tube with her finger. "Like that?" she asked.

"Exactly."

Andine put the tube into Eliar's mouth and lifted her finger. "Oh, that's easy," she said confidently. "How often do I do that?"

"Once every hundred heartbeats."

"Mine?"

"No, Andine. You aren't the one who's sick. That's where Brother Bheid comes in. He'll sit by the other side of the bed with his hand over Eliar's heart so that he can count the beats. Every time he reaches one hundred, he'll tell you to dose Eliar again."

"Why not just give him bigger doses three or four times a day?" Bheid asked.

"The medicine's particularly strong, so an overdose wouldn't be good for him. That's why we need to dose him gradually."

"What exactly does this medicine do?"

"It counteracts the effects of the greenberry poultice that Althalus used to stop the bleeding. The brain needs blood, Brother Bheid, so we don't dare shut off the flow completely. We're walking a very fine line between too much blood and not enough. It's very much like tuning a lute."

"How long do we continue this?" Andine asked.

"Probably ten hours—twenty at most. Pay very close attention—both of you. Those regular doses are absolutely critical. Without them, Eliar might sink deeper into total unconsciousness, and he could stay that way permanently."

"If what you say is true, this might *not* be the place where the main attack's going to hit the trenches," Sergeant Khalor said to Althalus with a worried look on his face. "If all that noise and the cave was some exotic trick to get Eliar to this particular spot so that they could kill him, they might mount their main assault someplace else."

"That could be just a little subtle for Pekhal and Gelta, Sergeant," Althalus disagreed. "Are they still in the cave, Leitha?" he asked the pale girl.

"Yes," she replied. "I'm not getting anything coherent, but there seems to be about the same number of people in the cave."

"It's only a couple of hours until dawn," Khalor mused. "They'd be moving by now if they were planning to hit us from anywhere else. Is there any chance at all that Eliar might be back on his feet by then?"

"I wouldn't count on it, Sergeant," Althalus told him.

"Well, we've fought wars without him before," Khalor said with a slight shrug. "Gebhel's barricades and those Wekti shepherds can hold off assaults anywhere along the trench line until we can bring in reinforcements. If it's the best we can manage, it'll have to do."

Emmy. Althalus sent out a searching thought as he and Leitha moved along the back of the trench line.

Please don't shout, Althalus, she scolded.

Sorry. Can you see what's happening in the tent?

Of course I can.

How's Eliar doing?

The surface bleeding's stopped. He's still oozing a little in a few places, but it's pretty much under control.

Is the rest of his brain getting enough blood?

As far as I can tell, yes.

Good. It'll still be quite a while before he completely recovers though, won't it?

Obviously. Why do you ask?

The notion of having Khalor run this battle from your window fell apart on us when Gelta bashed Eliar on the head, so we're going to have to improvise a bit. Khalor's been telling Gebhel that he's got scouts out front keeping an eye on the Ansus. That wasn't really true, since Khalor was going to do his own scouting from your window. That isn't possible now, so we'll have to rearrange things a bit. Khalor can't get to your window, but you can. I think that means that you're going to have to do the scouting for us. Then you pass what you've seen to me, I'll hand it off to Khalor, and he can use runners to keep Gebhel advised. Won't that more or less give us the same results as what we'd originally planned?

Probably so, yes. Use a few of those Wekti shepherds for runners. A shepherd needs to be fast on his feet. I think Salkan might be a good choice.

That won't make him very happy, Em. That young hothead really wants to unlimber his sling at the Ansus, and in spite of all the pious instructions Yeudon gave him, I'm fairly certain that Salkan has no plans to start wasting perfectly good rocks on horses. I'm sure that he planned to miss fairly often and kill the Ansus instead of their mounts.

That's another reason to get him out of the trenches, pet. Let's not upset Exarch Yeudon any more than we have to. Let's get the runner business all set up and ready to go. Don't dawdle, Althie. Dawn's just over the eastern horizon, so things are likely to start getting noisy before much longer.

"Seventy-seven hundred and seventy-seven, seventy-seven hundred and seventy-eighths," Leitha murmured. "Divided by sixteen and a quarter," she added almost absently.

"What's that fellow in the hood doing, Khalor?" Sergeant Gebhel demanded.

"He's one of my engineers," Khalor lied with a slight shrug. "He's working on a trajectory for the catapults."

"I've *never* been able to understand those people," Gebhel admitted. "They do all their talking in numbers. Sometimes I think they even tell jokes in numbers."

"I don't have much time, Gebhel," Khalor told him. "My scouts have given us the locations of all the places where the Ansus are massing. This place is fairly central, so you might want to set up your command post here."

Gebhel glanced off to the east, where the sky was beginning to grow lighter, and then at the flaring torches across the valley. "Well, this obviously won't be the place where their main attack's going to hit my lines," he said. "Nobody waves torches around like that in a place he wants to keep secret."

"Don't lock your head in stone on that, Gebhel," Khalor cautioned. "That might be what they *want* you to believe."

"That's true," Gebhel conceded. "I've done that myself a time or two."

"Just stay flexible," Khalor cautioned. He turned and pointed toward a hill behind their trenches. "I'm going to set up back there. I've still got scouts out to the front, and we've worked out a set of signals so they can let me know what's going on. I'll have one of those Wekti shepherds bring you any information we pick up."

"How's young Eliar doing?"

"He's still dead to the world. That ugly sow really bashed him a good one. We've got a couple of field surgeons working on him, but it's a little early to tell if he'll fully recover."

"All we can do is hope, I guess," Gebhel said, looking off to the east. "It's coming on toward daylight, Khalor, so we'd all better get to our posts—even though this won't be much of a war. I've fought some stupid people in my time, but these Ansus are pretty much the pick of the litter when it comes to stupidity."

"They're cavalry, Gebhel," Khalor snorted. "Their horses do most of their thinking for them." He glanced at the eastern sky. "It's getting lighter, so I'd better get back up the hill. The young fellow I'll be using as a runner has bright red hair, so you'll know him when you see him."

Gebhel nodded. "Get out from underfoot, Khalor," he said gruffly. "I've got work to do."

"Eliar seems to be stirring a bit," Chief Albron advised Khalor, Althalus, and Leitha when they reached the tent, "and his breathing's stronger."

"We've *got* to get that boy back on his feet," Khalor said. "I've got a huge army piled up in the corridors of the House, but I can't use a single man until Eliar recovers enough to open the doors for them."

"I think Gebhel's good enough to hold off the Ansus for quite a long time, Khalor," Albron replied.

Althalus, Dweia's voice murmured, *take Leitha back into the tent. I need to have a quick look inside Eliar's head.*

All right, Em, he replied silently. Then he spoke aloud. "Let's look in on our boy, Leitha," he suggested.

"All right," she agreed.

Dweia needs to talk with you, he murmured as they entered the tent.

Yes, I heard her.

Move aside, Althalus, Dweia's voice told him.

He sighed. *Yes, dear.*

"Now," Bheid was saying wearily to Andine.

The tiny Arya carefully inserted the glass tube into the young Arum's mouth.

Reach into his head again, Leitha, Dweia instructed. *Tell me what you can see.*

Leitha nodded, and Althalus felt a peculiar sense of reaching out and heard a kind of murmuring. *What's that odd sound?* he asked.

Don't interrupt, Althalus, Dweia's voice told him. *She's busy right now.*

The bleeding seems to have stopped, Leitha reported. *No, wait.* She frowned slightly, and Althalus could feel her reaching out. *There's still one place that's seeping just a bit. It's not very big, and it's deep inside.*

Is his mind awake at all? Dweia asked.

Well—sort of, Leitha replied. *It's a bit disconnected. I think he's dreaming.*

He's starting to come around then, Dweia said thoughtfully. "Brother Bheid," she said then, "it's time to change the procedure. Go to two hundred heartbeats between doses."

"Is he getting better?" Andine said hopefully.

"The bleeding's almost completely stopped, dear," Leitha reported.

"Will he wake up soon?"

"Not for quite some time, Andine," Dweia replied. "He's dreaming now, and that's only the first step. Keep on giving him those regular doses until he starts to stir. Then space them out even more—once every four hundred heartbeats. When he wakes up and starts talking, stop dosing him and call Leitha. Then I'll come back here and have another look at him."

"Wouldn't it be better if you stayed here, Dweia?" Bheid asked.

"Possibly so, but we've got this little war on our hands, too, Brother Bheid. I need to attend to that as well as to Eliar."

Khalor and Albron were looking out across the valley where the drunken Ansus were saddling their horses in the steely first light of dawn.

"How's Eliar?" Albron asked.

"I think he's out of the woods," Althalus replied, "but he could be better."

"I don't want to criticize, Althalus," Khalor said, "but why did you insist that I use Salkan for my runner? He's a nice boy, I suppose, but he can barely tell the difference between a sword and a spear."

"We don't *want* a trained soldier carrying our messages to Gebhel," Althalus explained. "Koman's out there listening, and Salkan's going to be carrying *two* messages every time he runs down to Gebhel's trench. He'll have one message for Gebhel and a different one for Koman. Practice putting on a long face, gentlemen. Dweia's almost certain that Eliar's going to recover, but I'm going to tell Salkan that there's no hope for him. We don't want Ghend to find out that Eliar's not dying. If he's aware of that, he'll throw everything he's got at the trenches to try to finish up before Eliar's back on his feet again. If he's positive that Eliar's dying, he'll take his time and try to hold down his losses. Eliar needs that time to regain his senses, and Salkan's false messages are going to buy us that time."

"Didn't that medicine work?" Salkan asked.

"I'm afraid not, Salkan," Althalus replied somberly. "Eliar's taken a turn for the worse, and I don't think he's going to make it. Sergeant Khalor here needs somebody to take Eliar's place as a runner."

"That's one more reason to kill all those Ansus, isn't it?" the young redhead said fiercely. "I *liked* Eliar. He was my friend, and those people killed him."

"People get killed in wars, Salkan," Sergeant Khalor said gruffly. "It happens."

"What do you want me to do, General Khalor?" Salkan asked, his boyish face hardening.

Althalus drew Leitha off to one side. "Well?" he asked her.

"He's an enthusiast," she replied. "He doesn't really understand what's going on, but he'll do anything we tell him to do. He's terribly excited about this war—and very angry about what happened to Eliar."

"Good. Is he clever enough to notice that certain things don't quite match?"

"I don't think so. He's very excitable—and he's in absolute awe of Sergeant Khalor. He'll do anything Khalor tells him to do, and he's so worked up right now that his thoughts aren't really coherent. I don't think Koman's going to get very much from him—except for the story you just made up about Eliar's condition."

"He's earning his pay, then."

"Are you actually paying him?"

"I might—if it starts to look as if we'll need him in the next war."

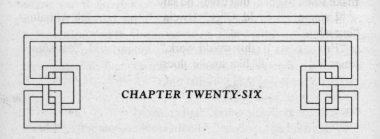

CHAPTER TWENTY-SIX

It was slowly growing lighter in Sergeant Gebhel's trenches and along the opposite ridgeline, but the valley between was in deep shadows. The drunken Ansus on the far slope were building up their bonfires and waving their torches. Their war cries began to echo from the nearby hills.

"Subtlety doesn't seem to be part of the Ansu nature," Chief Albron observed. "Only an idiot would believe that those howling fools over there are the main force."

"Actually, it's not bad, my Chief," Khalor disagreed. "They're overdoing it a bit, but they're fairly drunk. This *is* the place where the main assault's going to hit Gebhel's trenches, and the playacting's supposed to make us believe that nothing serious will happen here. Our main problem is that Gebhel's probably being taken in by the fakery, and I can't tell him about those people in the cave with Koman out there listening to every message I send down to the trenches. At the first hint that we know about the hidden army over there, the enemy Generals will change their plans and hit us from someplace else."

"Gebhel's been around for quite a while, Sergeant Khalor," Althalus told the kilted Arum. "I'm sure he's shrewd enough not to be taken in by the nonsense across the valley."

"I'd still be a lot happier if he had more men in this stretch of his trenches," Khalor said bleakly, "but I don't dare send him any messages that can't be explained."

Gher tugged at Althalus' sleeve. "Ask Emmy if she could make some fog near that cave," he said.

"I suppose I could, Gher," Dweia replied through Althalus, "but why?"

"I'm not sure if this would work," the boy said, "but sometimes fog looks a lot like smoke, doesn't it?"

"Not too much, no. Where are you going with this, Gher?"

"Well, I was sort of thinking that we don't really have any snoopers over there near that cave, and Koman can't hear *us* talking, because Leitha's busy counting bits and pieces of numbers, and that makes him wild. That sort of means that the only thing he can hear is what Salkan's telling Mister Gebhel. If we wanted to, we could tenlike we had one of our snoopers over there and—"

" 'Tenlike'?" Althalus asked in a puzzled tone.

I think he means "pretend like," Althalus, Dweia murmured. *Gher tends to mash things together when he gets excited.*

"Oh. Go ahead, Gher, but don't jump over too many things."

"All right. It goes sort of like this. Emmy puts fog around the front of the cave, see, and Mister Khalor hears from his tenlike snooper that smoke's coming out of the cave, and he right away sends Salkan zipping down to the ditch to tell Mister Gebhel that there's somebody in the cave, but he can't really say how many. Ghend would take a quick look and see the fog, and he'd think that our tenlike snooper wasn't smart enough to be able to tell the difference between fog and smoke, so he'd just think that Mister Khalor'd made a mistake. Mister Gebhel's not the kind who takes chances, though, so he'd bring in extra men because there *might* just be an army in the cave. Ghend might swear a lot because we'd made a mistake, but he wouldn't know that *we* know for certain sure, so he won't have any reason to change his plans, will he?"

Sergeant Khalor squinted off at the eastern sky, scratching thoughtfully at his cheek. "This boy's a treasure, Althalus," he said finally. "Stupid blunders like the one he just described happen all the time in wars, so there's nothing remarkable about it. It'll keep Gebhel right where he is, and Koman won't be able to find anything the least bit unusual about *why* Gebhel's staying put. Ghend loses the element of surprise, and things settle down to a protracted siege of Gebhel's trenches. That should give Eliar all the time he'll need to recover, and once he's back on his feet, we can go back to the old plan."

"Then I done good?" Gher asked eagerly.

"You did just fine, boy," Khalor said, grinning. "Go find Salkan, and we'll get started."

The steel-grey light of dawn began to seep into the valley below Sergeant Gebhel's trenches, and the drunken Ansus on the opposite slope lurched toward their horses in preparation for their mock assault. There was a great deal of laughing involved, for some reason.

"They're behaving as if this is some kind of joke," Chief Albron observed critically.

"In a peculiar sort of way it is, my Chief," Khalor told him. "We aren't supposed to take this mock assault very seriously— at least that's the way it started out. I don't think Ghend's laughing right now, though. I'd imagine that Gher's foggy smoke took a great deal of the fun out of his morning."

The Ansus clambered into their saddles and came galloping down the slope toward Sergeant Gebhel's outer fortifications, mixing laughter with their war cries.

"Is Gebhel just going to ignore this mock attack?" Chief Albron asked.

"I doubt it," Khalor replied. "The Ansus seem to think this is funny, but Gebhel doesn't have too much in the way of a sense of humor. I'm sure he's got a greeting for them."

As the Ansus reached the foot of the slope, Gebhel's catapults lofted baskets full of ten-pound rocks high into the air over the laughing attackers.

"I'll bet that hurts like crazy," Gher observed as the rocks began to rain down on the Ansus.

"I'm sure it does," Althalus agreed.

* * *

"They're getting ready," Leitha announced as the sun began to peep over the eastern horizon. "They'll be coming out of that cave in just a few minutes."

"That's stupid!" Khalor exclaimed. "They know they've lost any chance of surprising us. What's Ghend thinking of?"

"Ghend isn't in the cave, Sergeant," Leitha advised him. "Gelta's the one who's giving the orders."

"That *would* begin to explain it, Sergeant," Althalus noted. "Gelta's *almost* as thick-headed as Pekhal. Does she have any sort of plan at all, Leitha?"

"Nothing very coherent. She's going to lead her forces to the top of that hill over on the other side. Then she'll wait until they're all lined up out in plain sight. She'll order her trumpeters to give us a little concert at that point, and then they'll charge down the hill."

"Typical cavalry behavior," Khalor said, shaking his head. "They always seem to want to make grand entrances on a battlefield. They seem to think it intimidates their enemies."

"Does it?" Althalus asked him.

"Not really, no," Khalor replied, shrugging. "Gher, go tell Salkan to run down to the trench and alert Gebhel. Pass the word that the Ansus are getting ready to charge."

"Right away, Mister Khalor," Gher replied.

"There they come," Althalus said, pointing across the shallow valley.

The Ansu horsemen were cresting the ridgeline on the far side. They paused there, brandishing swords or lances and howling shrill battle cries.

"Typical," Khalor said drily.

"What is, Sergeant?" Albron asked.

"All that posing over there. I'm not sure what it is about sitting on a horse that makes people want to show off. A good soldier keeps his head down until the fighting starts. Those juveniles over there simply can't *bear* the idea of not being noticed. A cavalryman inevitably spends more time and effort saying, 'See me! See me!' than he does fighting."

"It makes them easier targets for the archers, though," Althalus added.

"It does that, right enough," Khalor agreed. "That might explain why only a few cavalrymen live to see their twentieth birthdays." Then he laughed. "Oh, well," he said, "if my enemy wants to be stupid, more power to him."

The trumpets sounded across the valley, and the Ansu horsemen began their charge. They thundered down the slope howling war cries and waving their weapons. Gelta sat astride her black horse on the ridgeline, shouting encouragement and brandishing her ax.

The charge down the far slope was quite impressive as the newly risen sun flashed and glinted from the Ansus' saber blades. Things began to go wrong for the attackers when they reached the bottom of the hill, however. Horses began to tumble and roll across the ground—and not infrequently over the top of their riders.

"What's happening down there?" Albron asked. "I thought the shepherds weren't going to start throwing rocks until the horses got closer."

"Trip lines," Khalor explained. "After that false attack at first light, Gebhel sent some men down there to drive stakes into the ground and stretch ropes between them. The high grass hides those ropes, so the horses can't see them. If those Ansus had any brains, they'd have burned that grass before they mounted their charge. Now they'll have to start being a little more careful. That'll slow them down and make them easier targets for the shepherds."

The Ansu charge had slowed to a walk now, and the war cries were noticeably weaker as Salkan, his red hair aglow in the sunrise, came running back up the hill. "General Gebhel's going to let my boys take the first crack at the Ansus, General Khalor," he said proudly. "I passed the word to them to aim at the horses instead of the people. Some of them weren't very happy about that. They don't seem to be thinking like shepherds anymore."

"Wars tend to do that to people," Kahlor replied.

"They didn't all come out of that cave," Leitha told them. "About a third of them are still in there."

"Reserves," Khalor explained. "Fresh troops—and horses—

for later on in the battle. Are you picking up any foot soldiers anywhere nearby?"

Leitha raised her face slightly, and her eyes grew distant. "Nothing yet," she replied after a few moments. "Is something wrong, Sergeant?"

"They aren't doing this right," Khalor fretted. "Pekhal's not the brightest fellow in the world, but he *should* know that trying to take a fortified position with nothing but cavalry is a serious blunder. Keep an ear out for foot troops, Leitha. Things are going my way now, and I don't want any surprises."

The Ansu charge began to pick up momentum again once the trip lines had been cleared away, and the mounted men veered almost without thinking into Chief Albron's more lightly obstacled avenues.

There was no response from the trenches until the onslaught reached the unobtrusive markers Chief Albron had placed along the side of the slope. Then Salkan's shepherds scrambled up out of the trenches with their slings whirling. At a sharp command from Gebhel, the shepherds sent a hail of stones into the very teeth of the charge.

The chaos along the front of the charge was immediate, and it spread on down the slope as thrashing horses by the score rolled back down the hillside into the ranks of the following cavalry. The squeals of injured horses and the startled shouts of the cavalrymen replaced the war cries, and the attack faltered.

Then the assault collapsed, and the Ansus turned and fled.

Gelta, Queen of the Night, was in full voice, and she was clearly audible. She commented at some length on cowardice. She dwelt on ineptitude. She raised questions about the parentage and probable descendants of her Ansus. Her choice of words was very colorful.

"I don't even know what some of those words *mean*," Chief Albron confessed.

"You're a gentleman, my Chief," Khalor reminded him. "You're not supposed to know what they mean."

"Will they try again?"

"Oh, yes," Khalor replied. "That's the whole point of her oration. I'd guess that there'll be two more attacks before the sun goes down."

"Aren't they going to try to clear away those barricades before they mount another charge?"

"That's what the charges are supposed to do, my Chief," Khalor told him bluntly. "It costs Gelta the life of a man—or a horse—to break off every stake or drag away one of your bushes, but I don't think that bothers her very much."

"Why don't they use catapults—or grappling hooks—to clear the obstructions?"

Khalor shrugged. "It probably hasn't occurred to them yet. You rarely see a cavalry army towing catapults behind them. They seem to feel that it's a sign of weakness."

"He's right, Chief Albron," Leitha said sadly. "The lives of Gelta's men mean absolutely nothing to her. She even enjoys watching them die."

"That's insane!"

"It's even worse than that," Leitha told him. "I'm trying my very best to stay away from some of Gelta's thoughts. The sight of blood—anybody's blood—arouses her in ways I'd rather not talk about."

Driven by the shrieks and curses of the Queen of the Night, the Ansus mounted charge after charge up the stake-studded hillside at a dreadful cost. The bodies of men and horses littered the lower half of the slope. Althalus noted grimly, however, that the senseless-seeming charges were inexorably gnawing away at the defenses. "If she keeps this up, she'll be in the trenches by nightfall, Khalor," he predicted.

"Not hardly," Khalor disagreed. "We didn't hire Gebhel to just stand and watch, you know."

By late afternoon, the frenzied charges of the Ansus had eaten away all but the last few rows of the stakes and their intertwined thorn bushes, and then Gelta's trumpets summoned her forces back to the far hillside.

"Have they given up, General Khalor?" Salkan demanded.

"No, lad," Khalor replied. "They're giving their horses some time to catch their breath, that's all. The barricades are mostly gone now, and it's almost sunset. Gelta's going to mount one more charge, I expect. She's probably convinced that her forces will break through this time."

"We have to do something, General!"

"Gebhel's already done it, Salkan. He's got a fairly nasty surprise waiting for the Ansus when they charge up that hill."

"What kind of surprise?" Chief Albron demanded.

"Watch, my Chief," Khalor told him. "Watch and learn."

The sun was nearing the western horizon when Gelta's trumpets sounded and the Ansus charged. Most of the obstacles had been broken down, and the Ansus galloped up the unobstructed slope, howling victoriously.

Then dozens of stake-studded logs rolled down the hill to greet them.

"That's the main reason for digging your trenches along the ridgelines, Chief Albron," Sergeant Khalor pointed out. "Things don't roll uphill very often. Most of the time, they roll *down*. A twenty-foot log weighs a ton or more. If you bore holes in the log, pound in stakes, and then sharpen the stakes, it's almost certain to make life very unpleasant for anybody in its path once it starts rolling."

"I thought those spiked logs were just a part of the defenses of the earthworks," Albron said.

"It appears that the Ansus thought so, too, my Chief. I'd guess that this is the first time they've ever come up against trained infantry. We have all *sorts* of surprises for them."

The stake-studded logs rolled and bounded down the hill, crushing and maiming horses and men as they went. The Ansu charge faltered, and then the now-terrified horsemen turned their mounts and fled.

On the far hill, the Queen of the Night began to scream curses again.

"I don't think she likes you very much, Mister Khalor," Gher said.

"Isn't that a shame?" Khalor replied with an evil smirk.

"Are you catching any hints at all of Pekhal?" Sergeant Khalor asked Leitha.

"Nothing at all since early this morning, Sergeant," she replied. "I'm catching a few hints that he's gone off."

"I was afraid of that," Khalor said sourly.

"Is something wrong, Khalor?" Chief Albron asked.

"It's my guess that he's gone to fetch some infantry. You saw what happened today. Cavalry's worse than useless in trench warfare. If Pekhal's bringing in an army of infantry, tomorrow's likely to be very unpleasant."

Eliar's starting to wake up, Althalus, Dweia's voice murmured. *Let's go see how he's coming along. Bring Leitha. I might need her.*

All right, Em, Althalus replied. He motioned to Leitha, and the two of them went inside the glowing tent.

"He's stirring a little bit," Andine reported hopefully. "That means that he's going to be all right, doesn't it?"

"We'll see," Dweia replied. "Cut the dosage back to once every four hundred heartbeats now. Some of those herbs are a little dangerous, so we don't want to give him any more of them than we absolutely have to."

"You didn't tell us those herbs were poisonous," Andine accused.

"Almost every medicine is poisonous, Andine—if you take too much of it, anyway. We've been dosing him steadily since last night, so I'm sure we're getting very close to the limit. We won't accomplish very much if we heal his brain and stop his heart, now will we?"

"He seems to be right on the verge of waking up, Dweia," Leitha reported. "He can hear us talking, but he doesn't fully grasp what we're saying."

How long do you think it'll be until he's up and about, Em? Althalus asked silently.

Several days at least—probably as long as a week.

Emmy! he protested. *We've got to have access to the doors! If Pekhal's gathering infantry to assault the trenches, we don't have a week!*

Oh, calm down, Althalus. As soon as Eliar's awake he can open the door to the House. Once he's here, he'll have all the time he'll need to recover fully. I can tamper with time here in the House, you know.

I guess I'd forgotten about that, he admitted. *He won't even have to be able to walk, will he? Bheid and I can pick him up and carry him. All he'll really have to be able to do is reach out and take hold of the door handle. Once he's in the House, you can give him whole months to recover completely, and time here won't move so much as a minute while he's getting well.*

He has a mind like a steel trap, doesn't he, Dweia? Leitha murmured.

All right, Althalus said irritably. *I was a little excited, that's all. Time's been climbing all over me ever since Gelta bashed Eliar in the head. I guess everything's all right now. I'll feel a lot better once Emmy gets time off my back.*

"My head hurts," Eliar said weakly, opening his eyes.

"He's awake!" Andine squealed, throwing her arms around the injured young man.

"Stop that, Andine!" Dweia commanded. "Don't jostle him!"

"I'm sorry," Andine said. "It's just that . . ." She made a face. "You know what I mean."

"What happened?" Eliar asked. "And where are we?"

"Khnom opened a door at the back of the trench, Eliar," Leitha told him, "and Gelta ran out, hit you on the head with her ax, and then ran back again before we could catch her."

"That explains why I've got this headache," the young Arum said.

Gher looked in through the tent door. "I heard Eliar talking," he said. "He's awake, isn't he?"

"Keep your voice down, Gher!" Althalus hissed. "We don't want Salkan to find out that Eliar's on the mend."

"Oh, yes," Gher said, looking around quickly. "I almost forgot about that." He came on into the tent.

"How long have I been dead to the world?" Eliar asked.

"Almost a full day," Bheid told him. "Gelta hit you about midnight yesterday, and you missed the whole day. It's well after sundown now."

"Oh, that's why it's so dark. Is there some reason why we aren't lighting any lamps? Have we got enemies sneaking around looking for us?"

"What are you talking about, Eliar?" Andine demanded. "It's not dark in this tent. The whole roof's glowing."

"You couldn't prove that by me, Andine," Eliar said. "I can't see a thing." He held his hand in front of his face and wiggled his fingers. "Nothing," he said. "I can't even see my own hand. I think I'm blind."

I was afraid of that, Dweia told Althalus silently.

I don't understand, Em, he objected. *Gelta hit the back of his head, not his face. How could a blow on the back of his head do anything to his eyes?*

His eyes are probably perfectly all right, Althalus, but the part of his brain that makes them work is located in exactly the place where Gelta hit him. Evidently, that part of his brain isn't working right now.

Will it heal—eventually? Or is there some way we can repair the damage?

I don't know, Althalus. Eliar's there, and I'm here. If I could just get him back to the House, I might be able to deal with it, but he's the only one who can open the door to the House, and he has to be able to see it to open it.

We're in a lot of trouble, Em. I suppose we could make a litter of some kind and carry Eliar to the House, but it'd take us a month or more to get him there, and by then Ghend's going to have Wekti in his pocket—and most of Medyo as well. After that, he'll march west, and there won't be any way to stop him— particularly since we've got every able-bodied man in Arum locked away in the House.

I'm working on it, Althalus.

Work faster, dear. This isn't too much fun anymore.

"Isn't there *some* way that Dweia could—?" Chief Albron began plaintively.

Althalus shook his head. "Not without the doors. The Knife's the key to the doors, and Eliar's got the Knife, but he can't see to use it. I think she had to arrange it that way to keep her brother Daeva out of the House."

"We aren't dead yet, Althalus," Sergeant Khalor said. "I've sent a courier to Kreuter to tell him to get here as soon as he can. I'm sure Gebhel can hold out until Kreuter gets here."

Then Leitha came out of the tent.

"How's Eliar?" Chief Albron asked.

"Still the same," she replied. "He can't see a thing. I just picked up something you gentlemen should know about. Pekhal's back. He's been to Regwos, and he brought an army of foot soldiers here with him."

"How close are they?" Khalor asked her.

"They're in that cave right now. Pekhal and Gelta are busy making plans for tomorrow."

"I'll need to know as much about those plans as you can pick up, Leitha," Khalor said bleakly, "but I don't think tomorrow's going to be a very pleasant day for us."

Althalus stood in the tent absently watching Andine feed Eliar. *Em.* He sent his silent thought inward.

Yes? her voice returned immediately.

Isn't there some way I could use the Book to fix Eliar's eyes? Maybe if I just told him to see and used the right word, it'd step around the injury and make his eyes work, even if they really don't.

No, Althalus. There might be a remote possibility that you could make him able to see what you're *looking at, but that wouldn't solve our problem, because you can't see those doors. There's a link between Eliar and the Knife that permits him to see—and use—the doors. The only way it could possibly solve*

our immediate problem would be if you could reach into . . ."
She broke off, and there was a long silence.

Have you come up with something, Em? he asked hopefully.

Maybe, she replied. *I don't really like the idea, because I'm almost positive that it'll disrupt something that's very important, but we might not have any choice.*

You're being cryptic, Em.

Don't bother me right now, Althalus. I'm working on something that might get us out of trouble.

Sergeant Khalor and Chief Albron were standing just behind Leitha when Althalus came out of the tent, and they were both watching the pale girl intently.

"Has she managed to pick anything up yet?" Althalus asked the two Arums quietly.

"Nothing specific," Khalor replied. "They're still arguing, I think."

"Do you mind?" Leitha said tartly. "If you're going to talk, go do it someplace else."

"Sorry," Khalor apologized.

They waited, almost holding their breath.

"Ah," Leitha said. "They finally thrashed it out. Ghend had to step on them a little."

"Is Ghend there?" Althalus asked her.

She shook her head. "His voice was for a few moments, but Ghend himself is quite a long ways away."

"What were they arguing about?" Chief Albron asked.

"They're planning a little surprise for Sergeant Gebhel tomorrow morning, and both Pekhal and Gelta wanted to do the surprising. Ghend handed it to Pekhal, and Gelta's not very happy about it."

"What kind of surprise?" Khalor demanded.

"They're going to hit Gebhel's trenches from both sides at first light tomorrow."

"Right and left?" Albron asked.

"No. Front and back."

"That's impossible!" Khalor said.

"Not when Khnom's around, it isn't," Leitha disagreed. "He's going to open a door *behind* Gebhel's trenches, and Pekhal's going to lead his infantry out to attack from there—but only *after* Gelta's cavalry has repeated a few of those futile charges up the slope."

"They cleared most of the slope yesterday," Chief Albron said. "Gelta's charges might not be all that futile."

"No, my Chief," Khalor disagreed. "Gebhel's men have been resetting the stakes, restringing the trip lines, and rebuilding those brush barricades since the sun went down. When the sun comes up tomorrow morning, Gelta's going to be looking at exactly the same problems she had yesterday. She's just been reduced to a diversion, I think. She's supposed to get Gebhel's undivided attention so that Pekhal's infantry attack from the rear will be a complete surprise. Now that we know about it, we can warn Gebhel, and he can take steps." He frowned. "It'll stretch him a bit thin, though. He'll have to pull forces out of the rest of the trenches to deal with Pekhal. Tomorrow might be very interesting." He looked around. "Salkan," he called.

"Yes, General Khalor?" the redhead replied in a sleepy voice.

"Roll out of your blankets, boy. I've got a message I want you to carry down to the trenches."

"Yes, General," Salkan said, yawning.

We need Leitha, pet, Dweia murmured. *I think she may be the key to our current problem—but only if she's willing to cooperate. I can't be sure just how far her "gift" really goes, but it seems to go quite a bit farther than simple eavesdropping. She took the first step when I forced her to separate the concept of thought from Eliar's physical brain to locate his injuries. The next step's likely to be very difficult for her, and she might refuse—or Eliar might. I think you'll have to talk to them, and you might have to talk very fast.*

Just exactly what am I supposed to persuade her to do, Em?

Leitha's passive, Althalus. All she does is listen to other people's thoughts. We'll have to push her a bit to make her reach deeper into Eliar's mind—quite a bit deeper than she goes when she's just skimming over the top of someone's thoughts to pick up secrets—and when she does that, Eliar's going to enter her mind

*as well. That's the point at which she might refuse. Leitha's com-
fortable with the notion of listening to the thoughts of others.
She's been doing that all her life. The idea of having somebody
hear her thoughts could frighten her.*

Why? She should be used to the idea by now.

*The idea of it, yes; the reality, no. Their minds will merge, and
it'll establish a permanent link between them.*

Something on the order of the link between you and me?

*Exactly, and that link might alter certain boy-girl arrange-
ments that she wants to stay exactly as they are. We can hope it
doesn't come to that, but getting Eliar's sight back outweighs
everything else right now.*

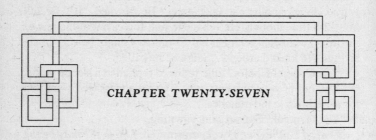

CHAPTER TWENTY-SEVEN

"We've got work to do," Althalus told the others in a
no-nonsense tone as he entered the tent. "Emmy's got
some instructions for you, so pay attention."

Then Dweia shouldered him aside. "Are you getting any glimmers of light at all, Eliar?" she asked.

"Nothing, Emmy," he replied in a hopeless voice. "It's still as
black as the bottom of a well. I don't know how a bang on the
back of the head shut down my eyes, but I can't see a thing."

"The most primitive part of the brain's back there, Eliar. The
senses are there—sight, hearing, smell, and so on. A bug can't
think, but he *can* see. The front of your brain thinks; the back of
it does the simpler things."

"What can we do?" Andine demanded tearfully. "I don't think I've ever heard of a blind man recovering his sight."

"When there's been an injury to the eyes, there isn't much chance, dear," Dweia explained. "Eliar's eyes are perfectly all right, though. His brain was bruised when Gelta hit him with that ax, and it was bleeding. We took care of the dangerous bleeding by drilling holes in the back of his head. It's possible that the bruising that almost killed him is what's interfering with his sight. If it's only bruising, it'll heal itself in time. Once it's healed, he'll be able to see again, and once he can see, he'll be able to use the doors again. Right now, though, he can't, and I have to get him *here* so that I can have a closer look to determine how serious the injury is."

You aren't telling them everything, are you, Em? Althalus asked silently.

Not quite, her voice admitted. *If the damage to that part of his brain's too extensive, he'll probably be permanently blind. Keep that to yourself, Althalus.* Then she pushed him aside and took his voice again. "We *must* get Eliar here to the House," she told the others, "but he's the only one who can use the doors. That's where Leitha comes in."

"How am I supposed to help him see the door to the House?" Leitha asked in a puzzled tone.

"You'll lend him your eyes, Leitha."

"They don't come out, Divinity."

"I know—and he wouldn't be able to use them anyway—any more than he can use his own."

"I don't quite understand, Emmy," Eliar said, raising his head slightly from the pillow.

"Don't jiggle," Andine commanded, gently pushing his head back down onto the pillow. "You'll start the bleeding again."

"What exactly is Eliar thinking right now, Leitha?" Dweia asked.

"Didn't you tell me not to do that?" Leitha asked.

"It's an emergency, dear, so it's all right this time."

"Well," Leitha said, her eyes going distant, "he's very unhappy.

He's sure that he'll be blind for the rest of his life, and he wishes that the blow had killed him."

"Well," Eliar objected, "I suppose I am, I guess. I'm not going to be much good to anybody if I'm blind, am I?"

"You stop that right now!" Andine flared, throwing her arms about him and breaking into tears.

"Calm down, Andine," Dweia told the tiny Arya. "You're just confusing matters. Did you feel anything at all when Leitha went wandering through your mind, Eliar?"

"Well, sort of, maybe. It seemed kind of warm is about all. Does that mean anything?"

"This may not take as long as I'd thought, then. Tell me, Leitha, how exactly do you feel about Eliar?"

Leitha shrugged. "I love him," she replied simply.

"Leitha!" Andine exclaimed.

"Not *that* way, Andine," Leitha said fondly. "I love him in the same way that I love you—or Gher. I feel a bit differently about Bheid, but we can discuss that some other time. We're very much like a family, you know, and it's normal for people to love members of their own families. I encounter that all the time when I go browsing."

"Go just a little deeper, Leitha," Dweia suggested, "and make some noise so that Eliar knows you're there."

A sudden look of revulsion crossed Leitha's face. "You don't know what you're asking, Dweia!" she exclaimed. "I can't do *that*!"

"What's the problem, Leitha?" Bheid asked.

"You don't know what's involved, Bheid," she told him in a horrified tone.

"You're afraid of something, aren't you, Leitha?" Andine asked. "It can't be *that* awful, can it?"

"There *must* be some other way to do this, Dweia," the pale girl said.

"No," Dweia replied, "I'm afraid there isn't. It won't really be all *that* dreadful, Leitha. Eliar's a simple, uncomplicated young fellow, so you won't encounter anything you can't handle."

"But he's a *man*, Dweia."

"I noticed that, yes."

"Will somebody tell me what's going on here?" Eliar asked. "What is it that you want her to do, Emmy? And why's she so upset about it?"

"It's nothing really serious, Eliar," Dweia replied.

"*I'll* explain it to him, Dweia," Leitha declared. "Sometimes you're just a little evasive about certain things." Her voice was flat—even unfriendly.

"Are we keeping secrets here, Em?" Althalus asked.

"She's making a big fuss about nothing," Dweia said irritably.

"*Nothing?*" Leitha said. "You've got a very strange definition of the word 'nothing,' Dweia."

"I think we'd better get this out in the open, Em," Althalus said. "You're trying to do something sneaky, aren't you, little kitten?"

"That's a hateful thing to say, Althalus!" she hissed.

"You just gave yourself away, Em. Exactly what's the problem here, Leitha?"

"If I go as far below the surface of Eliar's mind as she wants me to, I'll never be able to get out again," Leitha replied with a shudder. "Our minds will cling to each other like frightened children, and Eliar and I'll never be truly separate again."

"So? We're all very close to each other anyway, aren't we?"

"Not *that* close, we aren't. Eliar's a man, and I'm a woman. You *did* know that there are differences between men and women, didn't you, Althalus?"

"Be nice," he murmured. "Are you certain that there's no way you'll be able to untangle your mind from Eliar's?"

"Do you think you could untangle yours from Dweia's?"

"It goes *that* far?" Althalus was startled by that.

"Of course it does, Althalus. It's the same thing."

Isn't there some other way we could do this, Em? he asked silently.

No, Althalus. The link between Leitha and Eliar has to be there, or this won't work. The senses are at the deepest level of awareness, so Leitha and Eliar have to be completely merged— in the same way that you and I are.

I see where the problem is now, Althalus said. *Then again, maybe it isn't such a problem, after all. It might even be very useful.*

What are you up to now, Althalus?

Watch, Em. Watch and learn.

I'm getting just a little tired of that, Althalus.

I'm sure you'll get over it. Althalus squinted at the others. "All right, children," he said to them, "mother's come up with an interesting sort of idea that we should consider before we go too much further."

"Mother?" Bheid asked, his face puzzled.

"Isn't she?" Althalus suggested. "You've all seen the way she behaves. She's like a swallow with a nest full of chicks."

"There's a certain truth to that, I suppose," Leitha conceded.

"I rather thought you might see it that way, Leitha," he said. "I'm sort of following up on something you said earlier. We *are* a family of sorts, and that means that Eliar's your brother, and you're his sister, doesn't it?"

"Well . . ." Leitha frowned slightly.

"As you go deeper into Eliar's mind, it *will* establish that link you mentioned, but isn't that link there already? Neither one of you talks about it, but it's there all the same, isn't it? And isn't Andine also your sister? And there's a link there as well, isn't there?"

"I suppose there is," she admitted.

"Then why are you making such a fuss about something that's already in place? You're already locked to Eliar, and you have been ever since we all left Kweron. All you'll be doing now is bringing it out into the open. We *might* even want to expand that later and bring *everybody* into this family get-together. It might just be very useful. Love's a nice sort of thing, Leitha, so don't be afraid of it."

"I get the feeling that I'm being manipulated," Leitha said with a helpless little laugh. "What do *you* think about this, Eliar?"

"I always wondered what it'd be like to have brothers and sisters," he said, smiling a bit shyly. "I have a feeling we have to do this anyway, Leitha. You know how Emmy is, and I'd *really* like to be able to see again."

She gently touched his cheek with one lingering hand. "Why don't we see what we can do about that, brother?" she said fondly.

* * *

Leitha moved quite slowly, almost timidly, and several times both she and Eliar blushed furiously. "It's not really that significant, children," Dweia told them. "Those are just physical differences. They have very little to do with who you really are. All of us are aware of our physical bodies all the time, and that awareness shouldn't bother you." She paused, and Althalus could feel her rummaging around. "Let's start with taste and smell," she suggested. "They're a bit simpler. Go find a flower of some sort, Gher."

"Any old flower?" the boy asked.

"One with a fairly strong smell, if you can find one."

"I'll be right back," Gher promised, dashing from the tent.

Get one of those greenberries, Althalus, Dweia murmured. *Don't say anything about it. Just get it and put it into Leitha's mouth.*

I thought they were poisonous.

Not unless you eat a plateful of them.

Althalus flickered one hand at Leitha to get her attention, and then he touched one finger to his lips.

She nodded.

Althalus went to the rough table and picked up one of the small greenberries. Then he went back to the bed, handed it to Leitha, and pointed at her mouth.

She nodded again and put the berry in her mouth. As her teeth crushed the berry, she winced and puckered her lips.

"That's *awful!*" Eliar exclaimed, contorting his face and trying to spit something out.

"Actually, it's the loveliest thing you've ever tasted, Eliar," Dweia told him. "This is coming along *very* well."

The small yellow flower Gher brought for Leitha to sniff made Eliar break into laughter. "Are you bleeding very much, Gher?" he asked the boy.

"Bleeding?" Gher asked, puzzled.

"That's the flower of the 'shrub from Hell,' isn't it? It's got a smell that's almost as sharp as the thorns."

It's working, isn't it, Em? Althalus said in silent exultation.

It has so far. Now take Leitha aside and whisper something to her. Their noses and mouths seem to be linked. Let's try their ears now.

After Eliar had repeated what Althalus had whispered to Leitha word for word, Dweia told Althalus to tickle Leitha's foot, and that made Eliar jerk *his* foot.

"Four out of four," Dweia said aloud. "Now we come to the really important one. I want you to lay your cheek against Eliar's cheek, Leitha. I want your eyes to be as close to his as possible. Don't think about anything in particular, and just look up at the roof of the tent instead of anyone's face. Let's find out if he can see light before we go on to more details."

Leitha nodded, went to the side of Eliar's bed, and knelt beside it. Then she gently put her face against his.

"I can see!" Eliar exclaimed. "It's not dark anymore!"

"Move your eyes slowly, Leitha," Dweia instructed. "He'll have to adjust to a few things here. Bring your eyes slowly down and look at Andine."

"All right," Leitha said.

"She looks different, for some reason," Eliar complained.

"Leitha doesn't see her exactly the way you do, Eliar," Dweia explained. "Women look at other women in a slightly different way than men do. I don't think we need to talk about that right now, though. Can you see her clearly?"

"She seems to be sort of off-center," Eliar said.

"What do you mean by that?" Andine demanded indignantly.

"He wasn't trying to be insulting, dear," Dweia said. "He's seeing you through Leitha's eyes, and her eyes aren't exactly where his are. It'll take a little while for him to get used to that, but we're past the difficult part now."

Dweia was speaking aloud through Althalus in a calm, matter-of-fact tone, but Althalus winced as her exultation began bouncing off the inside of his head.

"There's nothing there, Eliar," Leitha objected, turning back to the young man sitting on the edge of the cot.

"Please don't look at me, Leitha," he said, shuddering. "It makes my head swim to see myself from where you are."

"I'm sorry," she apologized, quickly looking away. "I still can't see anything that looks like a door, though."

Eliar reached out and patted the empty air between them. "But it's right here. Listen." He patted a little harder, and they could all hear the sound of his hand slapping against wood. Leitha reached out, feeling around the emptiness with her hand.

"You just stuck your arm right through the door!" Eliar exclaimed. "What's happening here, Emmy? That door's as solid as a brick wall, but Leitha just put her hand completely through it."

"The doors only exist for you, Eliar," she explained with Althalus' usurped voice. "They aren't there for anybody else—unless you lead them through. People are walking back and forth through those doors all the time, and they don't even realize it. The Knife's involved, and the Knife complicates things. Can you stand up?"

"I feel fine now, Emmy—except for this headache."

"Stand up slowly. Leitha and Andine can support you and make sure you don't fall. You're going to be using Leitha's eyes, so the door handle's not going to be exactly where your hand thinks it's going to be, so you'll have to feel around to find it. Once you get hold of the handle, open the door, and the three of you can come home."

"Leitha and Andine *will* be coming right back, won't they?" Bheid asked.

"No. They'll be staying here with Eliar and me."

"Wait a minute, Em," Althalus objected. "We need Leitha here. We've already lost the doors. If something should happen and we lose our ears as well, we're going to be in deep trouble."

"I'm going to need Leitha *here* much more than you need her *there*, pet. You can get along without her for a little while, and I can't. I'm not going to argue with you about it, Althalus; *this* is the way we're going to do it."

Leitha and Andine helped Eliar to his feet and supported him as he groped for the door handle that only he could see. Then his hand closed around something. "There it is," he said, and then the three of them stepped out of sight.

"How long will it be until Leitha comes back?" Sergeant Khalor asked in a worried voice.

"There's no way to tell for certain, Sergeant," Althalus replied. "It all depends on how badly Eliar's been injured. If it's just some bruising that needs to heal, it won't be very long. If it's really serious, it could be quite a bit longer. He has to use Leitha's eyes until his own are working again." Althalus kept his tone flat and matter-of-fact.

"I thought Dweia could stop time there in the House," Chief Albron objected.

"That involves the doors, too," Althalus told him. "I'm not sure just exactly what Emmy's going to have to do to him to make his eyes work again, so I imagine time might have to keep moving. It all gets a little complicated."

"Now I've lost my ears, too," Khalor said. "Without Leitha to do my eavesdropping for me, I have no way of knowing what the enemy's going to try next."

"We might have to pull Gebhel entirely out of the trenches, Sergeant," Chief Albron suggested. "He could fall back a few miles and dig in again."

"All that'd do is delay the inevitable, my Chief," Khalor pointed out. "Gelta would keep on charging his front, and Pekhal's infantry would come out behind him through Khnom's doors."

"Can you think of any alternatives, Sergeant?" Althalus asked.

"There *is* a fairly gloomy one," Khalor replied bleakly.

"Oh? How gloomy?"

"It's called 'the last stand,' Althalus, and things don't *get* much gloomier than that." He looked around. "Where's Salkan? He knows the country around here better than I do."

"What are we looking for, Sergeant?" Albron asked.

"A steep hill, my Chief. Gebhel can fortify the top of the hill and hold the enemy off for quite some time—at least until Kreuter gets here. Khnom's doors won't be of any use, because

Gebhel's men are going to be looking out in all directions, so there won't *be* a backside to attack them from."

"Couldn't they just go around Gebhel and march on Keiwon?"

"That wouldn't be a good idea, my Chief. Pekhal and Gelta aren't very bright, but I don't think even *they're* stupid enough to leave an Arum army behind them."

"How long do you think Gebhel could hold out in that kind of situation?" Althalus asked.

Khalor shrugged. "A week, at least—possibly even as long as two—if he's got enough food and water."

"That might be long enough," Althalus mused. "It all depends on whether Emmy can fix Eliar's eyes—and how long it'll take her. Do you think Gebhel can hold out today?"

Khalor nodded. "Since he'll be expecting Pekhal, he'll be able to take steps. He'll still be in his trench when the sun goes down. Then, once it's dark, we'll pull him out and take him to some nice steep hill. The war's not over yet, Althalus. Actually, it's just barely started."

"Gebhel knows what he's doing," Sergeant Khalor told Althalus, Bheid, and Chief Albron as the first faint hints of dawn stained the eastern sky. "We'll be at a bit of a disadvantage without Leitha, but we know enough about the enemy's plans to get by— at least for today."

"And tomorrow?" Albron asked pointedly.

"That'll depend on just how steep a hill Althalus and I can find—and how far to the rear it is."

Gher and Salkan came up the slope from the trenches in the predawn darkness.

"Gher says you wanted to see me, General Khalor," the shepherd said.

"Right," Khalor replied. "You know the country around here fairly well, don't you?"

"I herd sheep in this part of Wekti, General, so I know every bush and rock by its first name."

"Good. I need a large, very steep hill, Salkan—something

right on the verge of being a mountain peak. Is there anything at all like that in the immediate vicinity?"

Salkan frowned. "Daiwer's Tower's a few miles south of here, and it sort of fits that description."

"Who's Daiwer?" Bheid asked.

"He was a crazy hermit who lived around here a few hundred years ago, your Reverence. I'm told that he believed that he was the only man in the world who truly loved God, and that everybody else was an agent of evil. When he first saw that tower, he was certain that God had made it especially for him. It sticks up out of the surrounding pasture land for about a thousand feet, and the walls of it are straight up and down."

"How did he get up there, then?" Khalor asked.

"There's a steep rock slide on the south side of the tower, General. It's hard going, but I've been to the top myself. Anyway, Daiwer climbed up there and lived in a cave up at the top. I understand that he used to roll boulders down the slide anytime anybody tried to get up there. I guess he *really* didn't want company."

"There almost has to be water up there, then," Khalor mused thoughtfully.

"Oh, yes, General Khalor. There's a spring in the back of the cave. I don't know how the water finds its way up there, but it's clear and sweet and cold."

"Just a trickle?" Khalor pressed.

"No, sir. It's more like a fountain."

"What do you think, Khalor?" Althalus asked.

"It sounds very close to what I'm looking for," Khalor replied. "Why don't we go have a look at it?"

"I think we should. Gebhel's men have rounded up a few stray Ansu horses. Why don't you borrow three of them, and then Salkan can take us there so we can look it over."

The three of them reined in their horses as they crested a hill not long after dawn and saw a sheer-sided tower jutting up out of the prairie.

"How did something like that crop up in the middle of all this grassland?" Sergeant Khalor demanded in absolute bafflement as he stared at the peak. "It looks almost like a mountain that went astray."

"I don't think 'how' makes that much difference, Sergeant," Althalus said. "Will it suit our purposes?"

"If we can get to the top, it'll be perfect," Khalor declared. "If Gebhel's got enough food and water, he can hold that place for *years*."

"Not while *I'm* the one who's paying Chief Gweti so much a day for his army, he won't. Let's go take a look at this rock slide. Salkan's part goat, I think, and just because *he* can scramble up the slide, there's no real guarantee that anybody else can."

The three of them returned to the trenches about midday. "If God has teeth, that's probably what one of them looks like, Gebhel," Khalor told the bald and bearded Gweti man. "It juts up out of that grassland for a good thousand feet."

"Steep slope?" Gebhel asked.

"I'd hardly call it a slope, Sergeant Gebhel," Althalus said. "The main tower's straight up and down. There's rubble down at the bottom that sort of slants down to the prairie, and *that* slope's about as steep as anything you'd care to climb. Once you get to the tower itself, nothing but a fly could go up."

"If I can't get my men to the top, what good's it going to be?" Gebhel demanded irritably.

"Oh, there's a way to get up there," Salkan told him. "It looks like part of the peak broke away, so there's a rock slide where that part used to be. It's a lot steeper than the slopes at the bottom, and it isn't very wide, but we managed to scramble up to the top. You can see for *miles* from up there."

"There has to be *something* wrong with it," Gebhel said. "I've never yet found anything that was perfect."

"It hasn't got a roof, Sergeant," Althalus said, "so I suppose you might get rained on every so often. I can make sure you've got food and water, but I won't be able to provide camp followers."

"See?" Gebhel said to Khalor. "I *knew* there was something wrong with the whole idea."

"What's been happening here while we were gone?" Khalor asked in a more serious tone.

"That sow's been wasting her cavalry all morning," Gebhel replied, shrugging.

"No noise or anything from behind your trenches yet?"

"Nothing. I think your spies were blowing smoke in your ears, Khalor. We haven't seen a sign of anything at all moving around behind our trenches—unless you're expecting a surprise attack by rabbits."

"Just keep your reserve forces handy and out of sight, Gebhel," Khalor told him. "You *will* be attacked from the rear by infantry before the sun goes down."

Gebhel shrugged. "If you say so," he said.

"Have you started making plans for your withdrawal from the trenches yet?"

"Who needs a plan to cut and run? As soon as it gets dark this evening, I'll pull my men out of the trenches and go south. Do you want to do me a favor?"

"All you have to do is ask, Gebhel."

"Lend me that young redhead of yours. I want to put a couple of companies of my men on top of God's tooth out there. My people are going to be moving in the dark, and a few bonfires on top of that peak should show them where they're supposed to go."

"That makes sense, I guess."

"Sergeant Gebhel!" one of the men in the trench called. "Here they come again!"

"If you'll excuse me, Khalor, I've got this little war on my hands right now," Gebhel said sourly.

"Of course," Khalor agreed. "Have a nice day, hear?"

"In your ear, Khalor."

"It's Dweia's idea," Althalus lied to Khalor and Albron as the three of them lay concealed in the tall grass not far from the tent. Actually, he hadn't heard so much as a peep from Dweia for the past few hours.

"Sheep?" Albron said incredulously. "I don't quite get the point, Althalus."

"They'll keep Koman from finding out about the men Gebhel's got hidden on the backside of this hill, Chief Albron," Althalus explained. "There's nothing in this world quite as brainless as a sheep, and they bleat all the time. When you get right down to it, a herd of sheep's even better than adding up fractions when you're trying to keep a mind leech like Koman away."

"I'm not going to argue with her about it," Khalor said. "If Dweia says sheep, then sheep it is. Do you think we'll get much warning when Pekhal comes running out through Khnom's doors behind the trenches?"

"Probably not very much."

"Gebhel's made some preparations, Sergeant," Chief Albron assured Khalor. "The backside of his trench line's not *quite* as unprotected as it might appear."

"Gebhel's an expert at that," Khalor agreed. "It's not going to take too much in the way of obstacles to ruin Pekhal's day. Gebhel's reserves are going to be all over him before his men can go fifty feet." Khalor raised his head to look across the valley beyond Gebhel's trenches. "Here comes the hag again," he said.

The Queen of the Night appeared in the center of the army of Ansus lining the far ridge, and the weapon she was brandishing appeared to be that same stone ax that had quite nearly killed Eliar. She paused briefly, looking around to be sure her mounted men were in place, and then she swept her crude, antique weapon forward to point it at Gebhel's trenches. "Charge!" she shrieked. "Kill! Kill! Kill!"

Her army roared its response and spilled down the slope like an unleashed wave, howling and slashing at the air about them with their swords.

Then Althalus caught a faint flicker of darkness on the hillside behind Gebhel's trenches, almost as if a cloud had briefly passed before the sun.

And then, howling triumphantly, Pekhal burst out of nowhere with a savage army of foot soldiers rushing out of the emptiness behind him. "Kill them all!" Pekhal roared.

Khalor calmly identified the attacking army. "Regwos." Then

he rose to his feet and made a long, sweeping motion with his arm to command Gebhel's hidden reserves to attack.

Pekhal and his foot soldiers charged toward the apparently undefended backside of the trench, but at the last possible moment, a forest of slanted, sharp-pointed stakes snapped up out of a thin layer of concealing dirt to face them.

"That *thief*!" Khalor exclaimed.

"Who's a thief?" Albron demanded.

"Gebhel. That's the exact same trick I used on *him* during a war in Perquaine a few years ago."

The sheer weight of Pekhal's army crushed his front ranks forward to impale them on the stakes, and then as the charge faltered, Gebhel's bowmen rose up in the trench to deliver a sheet of arrows directly into the faces of the attacking army.

The Regwos infantry recoiled, and then Gebhel's reserves came charging over the hilltop behind them.

The panic-stricken sheep that had effectively concealed that reserve army from Koman complicated the battle behind the trenches quite a bit. Driven ahead of Gebhel's reserves, they broke over the top of the hill like some huge, white wave and ran blindly down the slope to engulf Pekhal's forces.

"Now *that's* something you don't see very often," Sergeant Khalor observed. "I can't even *remember* the last time I saw a herd of sheep attack somebody's army."

"It's all the rage now, Sergeant," Althalus said. "Fighting sheep are very fashionable this season." He felt a certain disappointment even as he said it. The herd of sheep had been entirely his own idea, but he'd credited it to Dweia to persuade his Arum friends to go along with him. The whole idea had turned out to be even better than he'd thought it might be, but there was no way he could take any credit for it.

It just wasn't fair.

Gebhel's reserves swept down the slope behind the stampeding sheep that had hidden them from Koman, and fell upon Pekhal's disorganized force.

The brutelike Pekhal stood gaping in absolute astonishment as terrified sheep scrambled over his men and Gebhel's force

came along behind their wooly allies, slaughtering every Regwos in sight.

The outcome was never really in doubt, and after a long
animal-like howl of frustration, Pekhal turned, spouting curses
like an erupting volcano, and ran back through Khnom's door to
make good his escape, leaving his army to its inevitable fate.

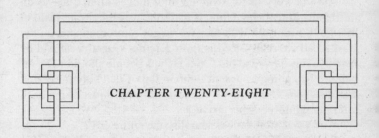

CHAPTER TWENTY-EIGHT

"Now *that's* what I'd call a *real* hill!" Sergeant Gebhel said
in an awed tone when they crested a knoll and saw
Daiwer's Tower jutting up out of the grassland in the pale moonlight. "Where's that rock slide you mentioned, Khalor?"

"It's around on the other side," Khalor told him. "We might
have to set up a defensive perimeter around the base of it,
though. You've got a lot of men, and the slide's not very wide."

"That's the way we want it, Khalor. I don't want a broad
highway leading up to my position. It won't take *too* long for my
men to reach the top, though. My advance party was supposed to
string ropes up the slide, and the rear guard I left in the trenches
should be able to conceal the fact that we've packed up and left.
After what we did to the Ansus yesterday, I'm sure they won't be
expecting our withdrawal. We chewed up most of their infantry
behind my trenches, and bit big pieces out of their cavalry. A re-
treat right after a victory's *very* unusual. They might not even
realize that we've pulled out until tomorrow, and it's going to
take them a while to bring in reinforcements. I hate to admit it,
Khalor, but this notion of yours is strategically sound."

"I'm glad you approve."

"I didn't say I approved. All I said was that it's an interesting strategic innovation."

"Do you think there's any chance that they'll just circle around us and march on Keiwon?" Bheid asked as they started down the knoll toward the tower.

"Anything's possible in a war, I suppose," Gebhel said, "but it wouldn't be very likely. Only an idiot moves on and leaves an unfriendly army behind him. If that's the way they want to do it, though, it's all right with me. We've got reinforcements on the way, so all we really need is time. Kreuter's cavalry should be here in a few days, and old Chief Delur's people shouldn't be far behind. I'm going to just sit tight on top of that silly tower and wait for them. If the enemy takes Keiwon, we'll just take it back after our reinforcements arrive."

"Won't that more or less demolish the entire city?"

"Cities are overrated anyway. It's not *my* city, so I won't lose too much sleep if it gets burned to the ground. I've been burning cities for fun and profit since I was a boy." He looked at Khalor then. "What about food and water?"

"That's one of the things that attracted us to the place, Sergeant Gebhel," Althalus lied smoothly. "Brother Bheid here had heard about a monastic order of the Wekti religion that was just a trifle fanatic about absolute isolation, and there's a fairly large cave up on top with a spring at the back of it. As I understand it, they spent about a decade carrying food—wheat, dried fruit, bacon and dried beef, beans, all the usual things—up that rock slide and storing it in the cave. We looked into that cave when we climbed the tower yesterday, and there are a *lot* of storage bins in there."

"Whatever happened to those monks, anyway?"

Althalus shrugged. "There was an argument about which one of them was going to be the Lord High Whatever of their holy order. It was one of those arguments that started with a lot of shouting and ended up with knives and axes. From what I understand, the dispute was very noisy right at first, but it turned dead quiet after a while."

"God defend us from religion," Gebhel said.

"Amen," Althalus agreed, ignoring the shocked look on Bheid's face.

"Have you heard anything at all from Dweia?" Bheid quietly asked Althalus as they started the climb up the steep rock slide.

"Not so much as a peep," Althalus admitted, "and I don't think it's very likely that I will. Koman's out there eavesdropping, and Emmy's too clever to tell me anything she wants to keep out of his reach."

"Can't you hold him off with halves and quarters and thirds the way Leitha can?"

"Not indefinitely. I'm fairly sure Koman's going to be concentrating on me, because Ghend knows that I'm more or less in charge of things. If I know too much, sooner or later I'll let something slip."

"Did she tell you that she was going to keep you in the dark?"

"She didn't have to. I know Emmy well enough to know the way she thinks. If all it's going to take to restore Eliar's sight is enough time for the bruising to heal, he'll probably be joining us before the day's out. If she has to make some repairs, it might be longer." Althalus kept the possibility that Eliar's blindness might be permanent strictly to himself.

"You're being very calm about this, Althalus," Bheid accused.

"Getting excited won't accomplish very much. Have faith, Brother Bheid. If you believe hard enough, things might even turn out for the best."

"Would it upset you if I worried just a little?" Bheid asked.

"Not if you can keep it to yourself, it won't."

Sergeant Gebhel called a halt after about a half hour on the steep rock slide. "Give me a minute or two to catch my breath, Khalor," he panted.

"Too much soft living in the trenches, Gebhel?" Kahlor suggested slyly.

"I don't see *you* running uphill all that fast."

"It wouldn't be very polite if I just ran off and left you behind, would it?"

"Did you really want to race to the top, Khalor?"

"Not particularly, no. These ropes your advance party strung up the rock slide *are* making this climb a lot more pleasant—particularly in the dark. Salkan brought Althalus and me up this slide yesterday in broad daylight, and I was blowing hard by the time we reached the top."

"What's it like up there?"

"Uninviting, to tell you the truth."

"I didn't plan to invite anybody. Where's this cave with all the food and water inside?"

"On the far side. From the look of things up there, I'd guess that an earthquake or something broke loose a large slab of rock on this side of the tower and it toppled over. That removed the support on this side, and a good part of what used to be on top slid off and followed the slab. That's what formed this rock slide. Evidently the north side's more stable. There's a slope from the top of this slide that runs up to a kind of rocky crag that's a hundred or so feet higher than the rest of the tower. The cave's in the face of that crag, right at the top of the slope."

"If worse came to worst, that cave might turn out to be very useful."

"Let's hope it doesn't come to that."

"That isn't very likely, Khalor," Gebhel said. "The enemy's going to have to come up this rock slide to reach us, and I think I feel a few brand-new rock slides in the offing. It's very hard to concentrate when you've got boulders rolling down over the top of you."

"You're assuming that you're going to get all your men up there before Gelta's cavalry come boiling down from the north," Khalor reminded him.

"There *is* that, I suppose," Gebhel conceded.

"Excuse me," Gher said from a few yards off to the left.

"Brace yourself, Gebhel," Khalor warned. "That boy's a positive wellspring of clever ideas."

"He's hardly more than a baby, Khalor," Gebhel snorted.

"That might be what makes his ideas so interesting. His mind isn't cluttered with preconceptions. Go ahead, Gher."

"Well, the bad lady's soldiers all ride horses, don't they?"

"That's why they're called 'cavalry,' Gher," Khalor replied.

"I suppose," Gher said. "Well, *some* animals that belong to people are used to having fire around—dogs, cats, mostly. But other animals, like horses and cows and sheep, are afraid of fire, and there's miles and miles of grass growing around this rock pile, isn't there? The rock pile won't burn, but the grass probably will, won't it?"

"It might," Gebhel conceded, "but only if there's a strong wind to whip it up. It's an interesting idea, boy, but I don't think it'll work if the weather doesn't cooperate."

Gher looked quickly at Althalus, but Althalus shook his head slightly and laid his forefinger to his lips. Then he spoke aloud. "We can discuss this later, gentlemen," he said. "Shouldn't we concentrate on climbing right now?"

Sergeant Gebhel sighed, and then he continued going uphill, pulling himself hand over hand up one of the ropes snaking down the jumbled rock slide.

"Where does the water go after it bubbles up in the middle of that pool?" Gebhel asked curiously when Althalus took him to the cave to show him the supplies he'd conjured up the previous day.

"I haven't the faintest idea, Sergeant. We were a little pressed for time, so I didn't have the leisure to investigate."

Gebhel scooped up some of the water in his cupped palm and tasted it. "Sweet," he noted.

"Isn't springwater always sweet, Sergeant?" Bheid asked.

"Not really," Gebhel replied, wiping his hand on his kilt. "There's a spring near Chief Gweti's hall that's got a lot of sulphur mixed with the water, and the silly thing's so hot that you can't put your hand in it. This hilltop of yours is looking better and better, Khalor. As soon as my tents get up here, I'll put my men to work building us an encampment around the mouth of this cave."

"We're not exactly planning to set up a permanent residence here, Gebhel," Khalor protested.

"How much would you care to wager on that? I'm sure Chief Gweti's going to absolutely *love* your tower, Khalor. It's got 'stalemate' written all over it, and Gweti wiggles like a puppy every time he hears that word."

By first light, fully a third of Gebhel's men had reached the top of the rock slide, and they had fanned out to line the edges of the slope leading up to the crag on the north side of the summit. As the light gradually increased, the men who were still strung out on the steep path began to move more rapidly, but it was obvious that it'd be well past noon before they all reached the top.

Bheid returned from a ledge that partially encircled the crag on the north end of the tower where he had gone to keep watch. "We've got company coming, Althalus," he reported quietly. "It's still not light enough to see how many, but there are definitely horsemen moving around off to the north."

"So much for the notion that it'd take Gelta a day and a half to miss us," Althalus said sourly. "She's probably standing over Koman with a club, and he's been browsing through Gebhel's rear guard since midnight." Then he wet one of his fingers and raised it, hopefully turning it this way and that. "Nothing," he said. "There's not so much as a trace of a breeze. A nice, cheery grass fire along about now might give us enough time to get the rest of Gebhel's men up the slide before Gelta gets here, but the fire won't spread without a wind to fan it." He ground his teeth together and sent a silent cry out to Dweia. *Emmy!* he called. *I need you!*

There was no answer.

This is important, Em! he tried again. *I'm in trouble!*

The silence in his mind was oppressive. "She won't answer," he said aloud.

"Dweia, you mean?" Bheid asked.

Althalus nodded. "She's cut me off completely—probably to hide Eliar's progress from me."

"Can't you deal with this without her help?"

"I don't know the word I need, Bheid. I don't think the Book ever mentioned the word 'wind.' "

Gher had been standing off to one side. "The Book's on our side, isn't it?" he asked.

"We certainly hope so," Althalus replied.

"Then why would it get all picky about some silly little rule? Isn't there some word that means 'grow' or 'make it bigger,' or something like that?"

"I've used *'peta'* sometimes when I was making food or water," Althalus said dubiously. "I used it fairly often while I was filling that cave with enough food to feed Gebhel's men. What did you have in mind, Gher?"

"Why not just go over to the edge and huff and puff a few times and then say that word? Won't the Book sort of understand what it is that you want?"

"I'm not sure that'd work," Althalus said, frowning.

"You'll never know until you give it a try, Althalus."

"It can't be *that* simple."

"Try it."

"Emmy would have told me if *that's* all it'd take."

"Try it."

"I don't think it'll work, Gher."

"*Try* it."

Althalus dubiously walked over to the sheer brink and drew in a deep breath. Then he blew, much as he would to extinguish a candle, and rather half-heartedly said, "*Peta.*"

Nothing significant happened. "I told you that it wouldn't work, Gher," he said.

"It might have, if you'd said it like you meant it, Althalus," Gher told him. "Do it again, and say the word the right way. The Book needs to know you're serious about this."

Althalus looked sharply at Gher as a faint suspicion began to dawn on him. Then he looked out over the grassland below and blew as hard as he could, mingling the word *"peta"* with the sharp exhalation.

Far below, in the pale light of dawn, he saw the grass suddenly flattened as if mashed down by some enormous hand, and a vast surge spread out almost as a wave upon a stormy sea might.

"Told you," Gher said smugly.

* * *

"There's not even a hint of a breeze, Master Althalus," the red-haired shepherd objected.

"Trust me, Salkan," Althalus told him. "You and your boys light the fires. I'll see to it that there'll be enough wind to make them spread."

Salkan's eyes narrowed suspiciously. "You people aren't like other people, are you?" he asked. "What I mean is that you can do things that nobody else can do, can't you?"

"I'll explain it all to you later, my son," Bheid assured him. "This isn't exactly an ordinary war, and there are things happening that can't be explained in ordinary terms. When Althalus tells you that something's going to happen, it *will* happen, whether it's natural or not."

"Are you some kind of magician?" Salkan asked Althalus.

"Something like that, yes," Althalus admitted.

"Our priests tell us that magicians are in league with Daeva."

"Not all of them," Bheid told him. "Althalus has his faults, but when you get past them, he *is* a servant of God. We aren't endangering our souls by associating with him."

"Are you sure, your Reverence?"

Bheid nodded. "Absolutely, Salkan. Our enemies are the ones in league with Daeva. We're on the good side."

Salkan shrugged. "If you say so. I'm not really very religious, but I didn't want to take any chances."

"Don't dawdle when you and your boys get down there, Salkan," Althalus instructed. "Light up your torches, set the grass on fire, and then join the last of Sergeant Gebhel's men down at the bottom of the slide. I want you and your boys to bring up the rear. A few Ansus might be able to avoid the fires, so keep your slings limber, just in case. Then follow the last of Gebhel's men up the slope, and cut the ropes behind you as you come up."

"Anything you say, Master Althalus," Salkan replied as he turned to rejoin his friends.

"When this is all over, I think I'll steal that boy from Yeudon," Bheid said speculatively. "He might just be very useful on down the line."

"You can worry about that later," Althalus said. "For right now, let's concentrate on living long enough to see the sun go down. Let's go back to your ledge. I need to see what's going on out there, but I don't want Gebhel standing there watching when I kick up some wind."

It only took Salkan and his boys about a quarter of an hour to ring the tower with fire, and then they ran back to join the last few battalions of Gebhel's men at the foot of the rock slide.

"Here she comes," Gher said, pointing toward the north.

Althalus looked out past the sluggish grass fires. Gelta's Ansus, looking much like ants in the distance, were racing across the grassland toward the tower. "I hope this works the way it's supposed to," he muttered, drawing in a deep breath. Then he exhaled the word *"peta"* sharply toward Gelta's charging cavalry.

A soft breeze stirred the grass fires on the leeward side of the tower.

"The fires are starting to spread, Althalus," Gher called, peering over the edge. "We need a stronger wind, though."

"I'm working on it." Althalus drew in another breath and repeated the procedure.

The fires off to each side of the tower flared up, and dark smoke began to stream off to the north. The fires at the foot of the north side of the tower still seemed sluggish, though.

"The tower itself is blocking your wind, Althalus," Bheid reported. "I don't think this is working the way it's supposed to."

"Why don't you point your wind right down the cliff here at those fires that aren't burning as good as the ones at the sides?" Gher suggested.

"I don't think I've ever seen a wind blow straight down."

"Try it."

Althalus gave up and sent *"peta"* howling down the sheer side of the tower.

The sluggish grass fires on the sheltered north side of the tower exploded, boiling out across the plain like some vast tidal wave of flame.

Gelta's Ansus reined in, gaping at the swirling wall of fire bearing down on them. Then, almost as one man, they turned and fled at a dead run.

"I think you can turn your wind off now, Althalus," Bheid shouted over the howling of the gale as he clung to the rocks behind him to avoid being swept off the ledge.

"I'll do that, Brother Bheid," Althalus shouted back, "just as soon as I can think of a way to manage it."

"I don't know, Althalus," Gher admitted. "It just seemed right, for some reason. We work for Emmy, and so does the Book. It wouldn't make any sense for it to start getting nitpicky, would it?" Then the boy frowned slightly. "That really doesn't quite fit, though, does it? I can't read very much, so I don't know too much about books. Maybe it was something else that gave me the idea."

"Such as what?" Althalus demanded over the diminishing gale.

"Emmy doesn't want to talk to you, because you might find out some things she doesn't want Koman to pickpocket out of your head. Maybe it was Emmy who stuck the idea into my noggin—sort of the way Mister Khalor was using Salkan to pass lies to Koman when we were back at the ditch."

"That *would* explain it, Althalus," Bheid agreed. "Dweia can't really hide anything from you, because your minds are too closely linked. Gher would be a perfect vehicle. He's *always* coming up with strange ideas, so you wouldn't even think there was anything very peculiar about his suggestion."

"I probably should have guessed," Althalus admitted. "There was something very Emmyish about the way Gher kept repeating 'Try it' over and over again. I don't really care *where* the idea came from, though, just as long as it worked."

The sun, made bleary by the smoke from the grass fires, rose almost timidly over the eastern horizon as the howling gale subsided to a gentle morning breeze.

"There's not a sign of them anywhere out there," Chief Albron said. "Those grass fires might well have chased them all the way back to Ansu."

"That's probably too much to hope for, my Chief," Khalor said. "It's more probable that they all ran back to that cave." He pulled thoughtfully at one earlobe. "I'd give a pretty penny to know what they're planning, but there isn't much chance of finding out now that Leitha's gone. I can make a few guesses, but I hate to work that way."

"It's something to start with," Althalus said. "What are they most likely to try next?"

"Probably something conventional. I'm fairly certain that they didn't expect us to pull back this way. We'd just bloodied their noses to a fare-thee-well back there in Gebhel's trenches, and under normal circumstances, we'd have held our position. It's highly unusual for an army to turn and run after it's won the kind of victory we pulled off back there, and unusual things on a battlefield tend to make commanders very nervous. It's my guess that they'll send out a few probing attacks to feel us out. They don't want any more surprises, so they're likely to move very carefully for a while."

"You don't expect anything exotic right at first, then?"

Khalor shook his head. "Not for the first few days. We've been springing surprises on them at every turn, Althalus. They didn't expect Gebhel's trip lines, they didn't expect the shrub from Hell, they didn't expect shepherds with slings, and they didn't expect that attack from the rear by Gebhel's reserves. So far, every time they've come up with something, we've come up with something better. They'll approach our new position with a great deal of caution, I think. I know *I* would."

It was midday by the time the last of Gebhel's men reached the top of Daiwer's Tower, and Salkan's shepherds came up behind them. "Should we cut the ropes, General Khalor?" the young redhead called when he reached a spot several yards from the top of the rock slide.

"Why don't you see if you can just pull them up, Salkan," Khalor called back. "Good rope's expensive, so let's not waste it unless we have to."

"We'll try it, General."

"Sergeant Khalor's an Arum through and through, isn't he?" Bheid said to Althalus. "He absolutely hates to waste anything that costs money."

"That doesn't bother me in the slightest, Brother Bheid, since I'm the one who's paying for all of this."

Gher came across the rocky plateau from the place where he'd been throwing rocks off the edge. "I just thought of something," he said.

"Spit it out, boy," Khalor said. "Have you come up with a way to set fire to burned-off grass, by any chance?"

"I don't think you could do that, Mister Khalor—not until next year, anyway. No, this is about the doors."

"We don't *have* any doors right now, Gher," Althalus said.

"No, but the bad people do, and they'll try to use them to hop out right up close to the top of that rock slide, and then, after all of Mister Gebhel's men get real busy trying to hold them back, they'll come popping out someplace behind our people, the way they did back there at the ditches, won't they?"

"That's more or less the way *I'd* do it—if I still had doors," Khalor conceded. "What do you think we should do about it?"

"Well, I got to looking at that bunch of rocks where the cave is. Isn't that a whole lot like a tower stuck on top of another tower? If some of Mister Gebhel's men stayed at the top of the rock slide rolling big rocks down on the bad people and stuff like that, couldn't the rest of them build some sort of fort around the front of the cave and some others could climb up to the top of that bunch of rocks so that they could throw spears and shoot arrows at any bad people running up the slope toward the cave? Wouldn't that tower on top of this big tower be an even better place to fight the bad people than the top of the rock slide?"

"Name your price, Althalus," Khalor said. "I'll pay anything you ask for this boy."

"You're going to get me in trouble talking like that, Sergeant Khalor," Althalus replied.

"It *is* feasible, Khalor," Gebhel conceded reluctantly, "and it's likely to take a lot of the heart out of the attackers. They'll lose thousands fighting their way to the top of the rock slide, and when they *do* get there, they'll see *another* fort they'll have to attack. I think most of them are going to start getting homesick along about then. I know *I* would." He squinted at Khalor. "What are you going to come up with next?"

"Oh, I don't know," Khalor said. "I suppose we *could* build a tower of some kind on top of that crag, if you want."

"And then a tower on top of *that* one? And another, and another? And we just keep on going up and up until we finally have to build a tower with hinges on the bottom?"

"What would we need with hinges, Gebhel?"

"We'd have to be able to tip it over to let the moon go by, wouldn't we?"

"Very funny, Gebhel," Khalor said drily.

"I'm glad you liked it." Gebhel chuckled.

By late afternoon, Gelta's Ansus had returned across the fire-ravaged grassland and totally encircled the tower. Gebhel's men soon discovered that a boulder rolled off the edge of the tower onto the rocks a thousand feet below bounced a long way out from the base of their fortress. They found that to be enormously entertaining.

The Ansus, however, weren't particularly amused, so they withdrew about a half mile.

Sergeant Gebhel came back from the barricade at the top of the rock slide. "Why are those shepherds flinging pebbles down the rock slide?" he demanded.

"For the fun of it, probably," Khalor replied, shrugging. "Why worry about it? The pebbles are free, so it's not costing us anything."

Gebhel grumbled something and went back to rejoin his men.

"Why *are* they doing that, Althalus?" Chief Albron asked.

"It was my idea—sort of," Gher told him. "I got to thinking about doorways. Stuff goes both ways through an open door, doesn't it? And the fellow who opens a door almost has to be standing right behind it, doesn't he? If there's a rock zipping down that slide when Khnom opens his door, it *might* just hit him right smack in the face. If Khnom gets his brains knocked out, the bad people won't have doors anymore, and things go back to being even. I told Salkan that bouncing rocks around among all the boulders on the slide would sooner or later whack into somebody and make him yelp. That way, Mister Gebhel's men might get a little warning that bad people are trying to sneak up on them. Salkan thought it was a real good idea, so he did it."

"How closely were you watching when Pekhal came through Khnom's door back there behind Gebhel's trenches, Bheid?" Althalus asked that evening.

"I *was* paying fairly close attention," Bheid said. "Why do you ask?"

"Did you notice anything at all peculiar just before he came charging out?"

Bheid frowned. "Are you talking about that little flicker?"

"Exactly. I wanted to be sure it wasn't just my imagination. How would you describe it?"

"Oh, I don't know." Bheid groped for a word. "It seemed almost as if some very brief shadow passed over the sun, didn't it?"

"That comes close," Althalus agreed. "I can't confirm this, because Emmy won't talk to me right now, but I wouldn't be surprised if it happens every time anybody uses the doors."

"It *could* happen because the light's not quite the same on both sides of the door, Althalus. It's darker—or lighter—on one side than it is on the other."

"That might explain it. Anyway, I've got a strong suspicion that it happens every time. We've never noticed it before because we were always right in the middle of it, but that flicker might just be all the warning we're going to get before an enemy attack."

Sergeant Gebhel's men spent most of the night building a substantial wall in front of the cave mouth and extending it out to the east and west sides to the tower.

"They work awful fast, don't they?" Gher noted.

"They've had a lot of practice," Althalus replied.

"That's sort of what wars are all about, isn't it?" Gher suggested. "One side builds walls or barricades, and the other side tries to get over the top of them."

"It's part of the long, sad history of man," Bheid told him mournfully. "Sooner or later, everybody tries to come up with some way to keep others out."

"Emmy took care of that a long time ago, didn't she?" Gher said. "*Nobody* gets into *her* House unless she wants them to."

Bheid nodded his agreement. "That chasm at her front door *does* sort of discourage visitors, doesn't it? Actually, it's a variation of the moat that surrounds many fortresses."

"What's a moat?"

"It's sort of like a trench that's filled with water."

"That *would* sort of make it awful hard to get in, wouldn't it? We could do that, too, couldn't we? I mean, Althalus *does* have that spring at the back of the cave, doesn't he?"

Bheid shook his head. "You'd need a river to fill a moat, Gher," he explained.

"Hold it for a moment, Brother Bheid," Althalus said as an idea struck him.

"It's a very nice little spring, Althalus," Bheid said, "but it's hardly a river."

"It might be—when it grows up. I think I'll go have a little talk with Khalor."

"Sometimes you're almost as bad as Gher is, Althalus."

"Why, thank you, Brother Bheid."

"It wasn't intended as a compliment, Althalus."

"Maybe not, Bheid, but that's the way it came out."

"It's an interesting notion, Althalus," Khalor admitted, "but how are we going to explain it to Gebhel? He's got all his men working on that wall. I don't think he'll pull half of them off *that* job to dig a moat."

"I don't think I'll need very much help, Sergeant," Althalus told him. "I know what a ditch looks like."

"You're going to dig it all by yourself?" Chief Albron asked incredulously.

"I *do* have certain advantages, Albron," Althalus reminded

him. "If I say 'ditch' in just the right way, there *will* be a ditch in front of Gebhel's wall."

"And just how do you plan to explain it to him?"

"I hadn't really planned to explain it. We've all been wasting far too much time explaining things. I think I'll try something new this time. I'll just go ahead and do it, and if it makes Gebhel start coming unraveled, that's just too bad. Ghend and his people are starting to irritate me, so I think it's about time to show them just how bad an idea that really is."

Gher came along the ledge at the side of the crag. "I thought the bad people were going to use their doors to get here," he said.

"I'm sure they are," Sergeant Khalor replied.

"Then why are they camped way out there on the flat country? I just saw some little fires a long way from here. They're miles and miles from here."

"Are you sure?" Albron asked.

"It's nighttime, Mister Albron, and you can see a fire—even a little one—from a long ways away when it's dark. Particularly when you're on top of something as high as this."

"Show me," Khalor said shortly. "I don't really need any more surprises. Come along, my Chief. Let's take a look."

"Do you think Dweia might pass the right word to you the way she did last time?" Bheid asked Althalus.

"She won't have to," Althalus replied. "I *know* which word I'll need this time. I've got a fair grip on the simpler words. It's the complex ones that give me trouble. All I need is the word for 'dig,' and I've used that dozens of times. If I'd used my head, I could have made things much easier for us when you and I and Eliar were opening my private gold mine down in Perquaine."

"What about expanding your spring? Do you know the right word to increase the amount of water coming from it?"

Althalus shrugged. "I'll use the same word I used to make the wind blow harder," he said.

"There's quite a difference between wind and water, Althalus."

"Not really. Gher sort of opened my eyes when he suggested

that the Book *wants* to help us. Emmy's the one who's a stickler for fine details. The Book seems to be quite a bit more tolerant. There *will* be a ditch in front of Gebhel's wall, Brother Bheid, and it *will* be full of water when Pekhal's infantry charges. Trust me."

"I *still* think that's a couple of armies out there, Mister Khalor," Gher was saying as the three of them returned. "Those fires are spaced out too even to just be leftovers from the grass fires we set yesterday. Besides, *our* fire went north, and those fires are way out to the east and the west."

"A big fire generates its own wind, boy," Khalor explained patiently. "I've seen whirlwinds spouting out of the top of a fire, and a whirlwind can carry embers in just about any direction."

"I'm sorry, but I think you're wrong."

"You can think anything you want to, Gher," Khalor told him. "Just don't try to grind my face in it."

The sky to the east was growing lighter as dawn approached, and Althalus grew edgier by the moment. He almost jumped out of his skin when Gher said *"ghre"* from just behind him.

"Don't sneak up on me like that, Gher," Althalus scolded.

Gher's expression was absolutely blank, and his eyes were vacant. He pointed at a scrubby bush. *"Ghre,"* he said again. "Say it, Althalus!" he snapped.

Althalus stared at him in total bafflement. *"Ghre?"*

"Don't ask, Althalus—say it!"

The tone was so familiar that Althalus suddenly laughed.

"You're starting to make me cross, Althalus. Look at the bush and say '*ghre*.' "

"Whatever you say, Em," he said, grinning broadly. He waved his hand almost negligently at the bush. *"Ghre."*

The bush instantly sprouted new shoots and leaves as it very visibly became larger and larger, growing on command.

"Now that was *very* sneaky," Althalus said admiringly.

"What was?" Gher asked, his face puzzled.

"You don't know what just happened, do you, Gher?"

"Nothing happened, Althalus," Gher replied. "I just came over here to tell you that I think Mister Khalor's wrong. What are we talking about here?"

"Nothing all that important, Gher," Althalus lied. "Just stay sort of close to me this morning. I think I'll feel a lot better if you're around."

The sun had not yet quite risen when the steady barrage of stones from the shepherds' slings brought a different sound. The clatter of rocks striking rock was replaced by the metallic ring of rocks striking steel. Then a horde of armored men holding shields in front of them came spilling out from behind large boulders scattered across the last fifty yards or so of the slide.

"They're right on top of us!" Bheid shouted.

Gebhel's men, however, didn't appear to be unduly alarmed. Almost casually, they levered loose what had appeared to be their defensive wall of boulders, sending them bounding down the slide directly into the teeth of the charging enemy.

"Fall back!" Gebhel roared, and his army turned and ran up the slope to their defensive wall in front of the cave mouth.

"Oh, *that* was clever," Khalor said admiringly to his bald friend.

"You didn't *really* think I'd try to hold that slide, did you, Khalor?" Gebhel said.

"I thought you might *pretend* for a while."

"I don't waste men just for show, Khalor. The cave's where our food and water are. I'll concentrate on protecting the cave. If our enemies want the top of your silly hill, they're welcome to it. The only part I want is that crag where the cave is."

"Why aren't they doing anything?" Bheid asked about an hour later, when the sun had fully risen and Gebhel's men were all emplaced behind their defensive wall at the foot of the crag.

"They're baffled, Bheid," Khalor explained, "and probably more than a little afraid. Gebhel's outsmarted them at every turn. He hasn't once done what they expected him to do. He holds positions when he shouldn't, and he retreats when there's no reason for it. They have absolutely no idea of what he'll do next."

"Except that whatever it is will probably cost them a lot of their soldiers," Chief Albron added.

"Use '*twei*,' Althalus," Gher, wooden faced and vacant eyed, said in a firm voice.

"I was going to use '*dhigw*,' Em," he disagreed. "I don't think an earthquake's a very good idea up here on top of this tower."

"There's a crack running from east to west about fifty paces to the south of that crag, Althalus," Gher explained woodenly. "If you widen that crack with an earthquake, it'll give you the ditch you want."

"It won't work, Em. I want the ditch just in front of Gebhel's fortification. If I put the ditch that far away, Pekhal's troops will just swim across and continue the attack."

"You're going to do this *my* way, Althalus—eventually. Save your breath and do as I tell you."

He threw his hands in the air. "All right, Em," he gave up.

"Then use '*ekwer*' to pour water into the ditch."

"Yes, dear. I was going to do that anyway, but it's nice to get some confirmation."

"Oh, hush!"

The air seemed to shimmer about halfway down the slope from Gebhel's fortified position, and a huge army of Regwos infantry came charging through Khnom's door.

"Not yet," Gher told Althalus.

"Let me do this, Em. I still think the ditch won't be in the right place, though."

"Trust me."

The enemy foot soldiers, howling triumphantly, charged up the slope toward Gebhel's crude fort, even as archers and shepherds lining the top of the crag showered them with arrows and stones.

"Now, Althalus!" Gher barked.

"*Twei!*" Althalus said sharply, pointing at the ground directly in front of the charging army.

A deep, booming rumble came up from the ground, and the

entire tower seemed to shiver, almost like a wet dog. There was a hideous cracking sound that ripped from east to west across the tower, and the loose earth fell into a wide gap that suddenly opened directly in front of the enemy. The resulting trench was perhaps twenty feet wide and quite nearly as deep.

The enemy charge halted immediately.

Then Pekhal came raging out onto the slope directly below that new obstacle. "Attack!" the brute screamed. "Charge! Charge! Kill them all!"

The soldiers who were carrying scaling ladders rushed forward to push the ladders down into the ditch, and Pekhal's force streamed down into the trench Althalus had just opened.

More and more ladders were pushed down to the men already in the trench, and they were quickly placed against the forward wall so that Pekhal's army could continue its attack.

"What are you waiting for, Althalus?" Bheid demanded. "They're still charging!"

"Let's get as many of them as we can in that trench," Althalus replied calmly.

"You blundered, Althalus!" Chief Albron exclaimed. "Your ditch runs all the way to the edge of the tower on both sides! Your water's going to drain out as fast as it comes in! Those men in the ditch won't even get their feet wet!"

"That sort of depends on how much water I pour into the ditch, doesn't it?" Althalus replied bleakly. He squinted down the slope. "That looks like most of them," he observed, watching the rear ranks of Pekhal's army scrambling down into the ditch. Then he swept his hand down. *"Ekwer!"* he shouted.

The front side of his improvised trench suddenly exploded as a new river burst through into its carefully prepared channel. Unlike most rivers, however, the one Althalus had just created ran both ways, streaming off to the east and to the west, and when those rivers reached the edges of the tower, there were two spectacular waterfalls thundering a thousand feet down to the rocky slopes at the base of the tower.

Pekhal's army, of course, was caught in the savage current,

and they were swept to the brinks of those two thundering water-falls to plunge shrieking in despair to the rocks far below.

"Dear God!" Bheid exclaimed in horror as he saw Pekhal's army literally melt away.

"Look!" Chief Albron shouted. "It's Dreigon! He's coming out of that cave!"

Althalus spun quickly to look in astonishment at Chief Delur's silver-haired captain leading the men of his clan out of the cave to join Gebhel's troops behind the fortifications.

"You didn't expect that, did you, Althie?" Gher said smugly, his voice almost perfectly matching Dweia's.

Pekhal was shrieking insanely on the other side of the raging river that had just swept his army away. He lashed out with his sword, blindly killing any of his men unlucky enough to be near him.

And then, to everyone's stunned disbelief, Eliar emerged out of empty air. The young Arum was fully armed, and he brandished his sword menacingly. "Pekhal!" he roared. "Run now, while you still can! Run, or I'll kill you right where you stand!"

"But you're dead!" Pekhal gasped.

"Not quite," Eliar grated at him. "Choose, Pekhal! Run or die!" And then he started toward the startled savage, his sword held low.

Screaming curses, Pekhal scrambled over the bodies of the men he had just killed, swinging his huge sword.

Althalus shook off his astonishment at this unexpected turn of events to watch very closely as Eliar neatly parried the brute's first massive blow and then lightly flicked his sword across Pekhal's cheek.

Pekhal flinched, his face spurting blood.

Eliar swung again, and Pekhal was only barely able to ward off the blow with his shield.

Without so much as a pause, Eliar swung again. The clanging of the swords quickened, and Althalus found it difficult to separate one swing from the next. Eliar was obviously the better swordsman. Pekhal relied almost entirely on brute strength and rage, but he grew more frenzied and desperate as Eliar blocked or parried his every stroke. Eliar continued to lightly flick his blade across Pekhal's face, drawing blood each time.

Enraged, Pekhal seized his sword hilt in both hands, casting away his shield. He swung a massive overhand blow at Eliar's head, but it slid harmlessly to one side as Eliar neatly diverted it with his blade.

Then Eliar quite suddenly took the offensive, swinging heavier and heavier blows at Pekhal's head and shoulders. In a desperate attempt to protect his head, Pekhal raised his sword and held it in a horizontal position to fend off Eliar's blows.

Then Eliar swung wide, and his sword edge cut smoothly through Pekhal's wrist, sending his sword and hand spinning away.

"Kill him, Eliar!" Sergeant Khalor shouted.

But to everyone's startled disbelief, Eliar dropped his sword and drew the Knife from his belt. He raised it to hold the flat of the blade directly in front of Pekhal's eyes.

Pekhal shrieked, trying to cover his eyes with his remaining hand and the blood-spurting stump of the missing one.

"Go!" Eliar thundered. "Go now, and never return!"

Just then, the terrified Khnom was suddenly thrust violently through his flickering doorway. He dashed forward, seized the maimed and shrieking Pekhal, and dragged him backward.

And then the both of them vanished, and the shimmering flicker of Khnom's door was no longer there.

Part Five

ANDINE

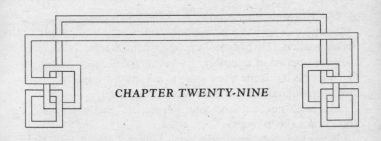

CHAPTER TWENTY-NINE

"How did you get up here, Dreigon?" the kilted Sergeant Gebhel demanded of Chief Delur's silver-haired Captain as they met at the edge of the river that ran both ways to plunge off either side of Daiwer's Tower.

Dreigon shrugged. "Through the caves, of course," he replied. "You *did* know about all those caves under your mountain, didn't you?"

"I know about the one you just came out of," Gebhel said. "Are you trying to tell me that there are more?"

"You must be getting old, Gebhel," Dreigon observed. "This whole mountain's honeycombed with caves. You're lucky *I'm* the one who found them instead of your enemies. If *they'd* known about them, they'd have come out right in your back pocket. You didn't even bother to take a look, did you?"

"Don't grind my face in it, Dreigon," Gebhel said sourly. "I've had a lot on my mind in the last few days."

"That earthquake *definitely* made things exciting down in the caves, let me tell you," Dreigon said, rolling his eyes upward.

"I can imagine," Gebhel agreed.

"Sergeant Khalor," Eliar said as he and the fiery-haired Salkan came over from the eastern waterfall to join them, "your friend Kreuter's down below running all over the top of the Ansus."

"Well, *finally*," Khalor said as they all trooped over to the edge to have a look. "I wonder what took him so long? He should have been here the day before yesterday."

"I didn't know we had horse soldiers," Salkan said to Eliar.

"My Sergeant fights good wars," Eliar told him.

"Sometimes he has a little trouble telling the truth, though," Salkan replied. "He had me convinced that you were dying."

Bheid stepped in smoothly. "It was sort of necessary, Salkan. Our enemies had quite a few spies in our trenches, and we didn't want them to find out that Eliar was getting better."

"You *could* have told me, your Reverence," Salkan replied. "I know how to keep secrets."

"It worked out better this way, Salkan," Bheid told him. "Eliar's your friend, and we wanted you to be very angry about what had happened to him. You might not have been quite as angry if you'd known that he *wasn't* dying. We weren't really lying to you as much as we were using you to send false information to our enemies."

"You Black Robes are a lot sneakier than *our* priests are," Salkan observed.

"Sometimes we have to be, Salkan," Bheid told him. "Church politics can get very complicated sometimes."

"I think I'll stick to taking care of my sheep," Salkan replied. "Every so often, some priest comes by and tries to persuade me to join the priesthood. I've never been very attracted to that sort of thing. I know how to take care of sheep, but taking care of people . . ." He spread his hands. "You know what I mean."

Bheid nodded. "Indeed I do, Salkan," he agreed.

"Your young Eliar's *very* good with his sword, isn't he, Khalor?" Dreigon noted.

Khalor shrugged. "He shows some promise, yes," he replied.

"What was all that business with his dagger, though? He could have split that frothing maniac right down the middle with his sword. Why'd he throw his sword away and go for his dagger?"

"The dagger's an ancient Ansu relic, Captain Dreigon," Althalus lied smoothly. "The Ansus are a superstitious lot, and they all believe that coming within fifty miles of that dagger's just about the worst thing that can happen to anybody. Young Eliar waved it around in front of Pekhal and then let him get away so that he could go back and tell everybody in Ansu that we've got the silly thing. I can almost guarantee that nobody in Ansu's going to come anywhere *near* the Wekti border for at least ten generations—no matter *who* tells them to."

"Using the other fellow's superstitions is a slick way to do business, I guess, but how did *you* get involved in this particular war? Chief Delur tells me that you're an official in the government of Osthos."

"It's all part of the same war, Captain," Althalus explained. "There's a fellow in Nekweros with imperial ambitions, and he's been making alliances with assorted half-wits for quite some time now."

"Have you ever met this so-called Emperor of the World?"

"Once or twice, yes. He and I don't get along very well."

"You should have killed him when you had the chance."

"And put all my Arum friends out of work? That wouldn't be very neighborly, would it, Captain?"

"What I don't understand is how there's suddenly a river in that ditch," Sergeant Gebhel declared, "or how that ditch just suddenly appeared all by itself."

"Oh, that," Althalus replied deprecatingly. "It was nothing, Sergeant. I just reared back and passed a miracle, that's all."

"Oh, *really*?"

"Haven't you ever seen miracles before?"

"I'm serious, Althalus. What *really* happened?"

"You're not going to let me take credit for it, I gather?"

"Not hardly."

"You're taking a lot of the fun out of this, Sergeant. Actually, though, it appears that it was sheer coincidence. This tower's sitting on some very unstable ground, I guess. We should have realized that as soon as we saw it; *something* had to push it up out of the surrounding meadows. Then, too, we didn't bother to explore that cave where the spring is. If we'd gone in a little deeper, we'd have found those caves Captain Dreigon came through. When you've got unstable ground—and caves—you've got a landscape that can change right in front of your eyes. When the roof of a cave collapses during an earthquake, you suddenly have a ditch—without even touching a shovel."

"I guess that makes sense," Gebhel admitted, "but where did the water come from?"

"The same place that spring comes from, probably." Althalus shrugged. "Who cares *where* it came from, Sergeant? It saved our bacon for us."

"Water doesn't run uphill," Gebhel said stubbornly.

"Not usually, no. This is just a guess, but I'd imagine that there's some huge underground river hereabouts that comes down out of the mountains of Kagwher, or someplace. Since the ground around here's unstable, that river was most likely dammed up by an earthquake a few hundred years ago, and the pressure's been building up ever since. This new earthquake turned it loose—just in time to carry off the troops who were attacking your position."

"Pure coincidence?" Gebhel said skeptically.

"We can go back to miracles if coincidence bothers you so much," Althalus suggested.

"Up your nose, Althalus!" Gebhel snorted.

"Why, Sergeant!" Althalus said in mock chagrin. "What a thing to say! I'm shocked at you. Shocked."

As soon as the sun goes down, I think you and the rest of the family should come home, Althalus, Dweia suggested.

Truly, another voice agreed.

Althalus blinked. The second voice in his mind was Andine's. *What's going on here?* he demanded.

The family's getting larger, that's all, Dweia told him. *It gave us something to do while Eliar was recovering. I hadn't really planned for this to happen, but I think it might work out rather well.*

It made Leitha more comfortable, Althalus, Eliar's voice added. *She wasn't very happy about being alone with me, so Emmy invited Andine to come along. It was very crowded inside my head for a while.*

Let's not go into too many details right now, Dweia scolded. *We're leaving Bheid and Gher out, and I don't think we want Koman eavesdropping. Let's wait until evening. Then we'll be able to talk freely.*

* * *

"It's good to be home again," Althalus said, looking around the tower room after they'd returned to the House.

"How long did it *really* take for your eyes to get better?" Gher asked Eliar.

"I started catching some glimmers of light—on my own—after a few days," Eliar replied. "It took a while before I could see very many details, though."

"Emmy must have stopped time, then."

"I wasn't paying too much attention," Eliar conceded. "Other things were happening that were a lot more interesting."

"Maybe you'd better let me explain that, Eliar," Dweia said.

"What made you decide to speak to Althalus through Gher?" Bheid asked her.

"He was available," she replied, "and it seemed sort of appropriate. The whole idea was to conceal what we were doing from Koman. Althalus understood that in fairly short order. If Ghend had known that Eliar was recovering, he'd have done things differently."

"Are there really caves under that tower?" Bheid asked.

"Not nearly as many as Captain Dreigon thinks there are," Eliar replied with a faint smile. "Most of the caves he thought he was marching through are here in the House. After he'd set up his camp out in that big pasture, I led him about a half mile toward your mountain and then slipped him through a door back here in the House. That was about as close as we wanted to get him to Koman. By then, Leitha was camped on Koman's doorstep, and every time he started getting at all close to what we were *really* doing, she'd warn me so that I could do something to throw him off track. At the same time, Andine was watching Kreuter and his Plakands in *their* camp and passing things on to me about *their* plans." He tapped his forehead with one finger. "We had what amounted to a council of war going on in here for most of the night."

Bheid's expression grew a bit wistful.

"You can join us, if you want," Leitha suggested, "and probably even if you don't."

"Not me," Gher announced quite firmly.

"It doesn't hurt, Gher," Andine told him.

"Just leave me out of it."

"He's right," Dweia told Andine. "He's a bit young for certain ideas. Bheid, on the other hand—"

"My thought exactly," Leitha said, giving the priest a sly, wicked look. "Come, Brother Bheid. Come with me. I'll take care of you."

That has a familiar ring to it, Althalus said silently to Dweia.

The old ones are the best, she replied with a slight shrug.

It was about midafternoon, and Althalus was standing at the window watching Kreuter's cavalry running roughshod over the Ansu horsemen around the foot of Daiwer's Tower.

They're even better than Sergeant Khalor said they were, aren't they? Eliar observed silently, joining Althalus at the window.

"You don't have to do that here, Eliar," Althalus told him, speaking aloud.

"It got to be sort of a habit, I guess," Eliar replied. "It's quite a bit faster, isn't it? You can just hand over a whole idea without fumbling around looking for the right words to make it clear."

"How are you feeling?" Althalus asked. "You were in fairly bad shape when you and the ladies left to come back here to the House."

"I'm fine now, Althalus. I get headaches now and then, but Emmy says that's only natural. My hair's even starting to grow back. Have you seen any sign at all of Gelta?"

Althalus shook his head. "I think she's given up on this particular war, so she ran off and left her Ansus to fend for themselves."

"If word of that gets out, she'll have a lot of trouble recruiting new troops."

"What a shame. Isn't that Kreuter coming up the rock slide?"

Eliar peered out the window. "It sort of looks like Kreuter, yes." Then the young Arum frowned. "Is that a woman he's got with him?"

"I think you're right, Eliar. It's a long ways down, but it *does* look a lot like a woman. I think maybe you and I'd better go on down there and see what's afoot." He turned slightly. "Emmy," he called, "Eliar and I are going back to Wekti for a while. Kreuter's coming up that rock slide—probably to collect the rest of his pay. I want to talk with him a bit. We might need him later."

"Don't be late for supper, Althalus," she replied.

"No, ma'am. Let's go, Eliar."

Eliar nodded and reached for the handle of his special door.

"I think you're the luckiest man in the world, Khalor," the burly Kreuter declared as he came puffing up the last few yards of the rock slide. "This silly mountain you stumbled across is probably what they had in mind when they invented the word 'unassailable.' I know *I* wouldn't want to attack it."

"Are you bringing your womenfolk to war with you now, Kreuter?" Sergeant Khalor asked curiously.

"This is my niece, Astarell," Kreuter replied, introducing the tall, dark-haired young lady coming up the slide with him. "Her father—my brother—died recently, and I pretty much have to take her under my wing until I can kick some sense into her older brother."

"One of those family disputes?"

"My nephew's a thoroughgoing scoundrel. He arranged a marriage for Astarell—for money—that was so inappropriate that I was tempted to kill him. I didn't find out about it until after you and I had our little discussion in Kherdon, so I didn't have any choice but to bring her along."

"*That's* why it took you so long to get here."

"Don't be silly, Khalor. Astarell here can ride a horse better than just about any of my men. I'd have been here several days ago if you hadn't kept changing your mind."

"You said what?"

Kreuter clambered up the last few feet of the rock slide with his niece close on his heels. "First you sent a messenger who said 'Hurry.' Then one came running up and said 'Wait.' I was just about ready to turn around and go back to Plakand."

"I only sent *one* messenger, Kreuter."

"Well, two of them reached me."

"I'd say that somebody on the other side was playing games," Althalus said. "We might want to come up with some way to prevent that in the next war. Our enemy seems to have some very efficient spies."

"Passwords might help a bit," Kreuter's niece suggested.

"Not when the enemy spies are as good as they seem to be, my Lady," Chief Albron disagreed. "Oh, my name's Albron, by the way."

"My manners seem to be slipping," Khalor apologized. "This handsome young devil's my Clan Chief, and he invited himself along to study war."

"He hasn't been in the way all that much," Gebhel noted. "His 'shrub from Hell' was quite useful back in the trenches."

"Why are they all wearing dresses, uncle?" Astarell asked curiously.

"I never got around to asking, child," Kreuter replied blandly. "I'm sure they've got a reason for it. Why *do* you wear a dress, Khalor?"

Khalor's eyes hardened. "Would you like to rephrase that question, Kreuter—while you still have your health?"

"They're called kilts, Lady Astarell," Chief Albron explained to the young lady. "Each clan has a different pattern woven into the kilts its members wear. That way we can immediately recognize friends on the battlefield."

"It's not really unattractive, Chief Albron," she said, eying his bare legs. "Did you know that you have dimples on your knees?" she asked.

Chief Albron blushed, and Astarell broke out in peals of silvery laughter.

"Why don't we get in out of the sun?" Althalus stepped in. "We've got some business to discuss, so let's find someplace where we can sit down and be comfortable."

"I'd like to help, Khalor," Kreuter said after he and Althalus had settled accounts in a tent near the cave mouth. He hefted the bag of gold coins he'd just received. "The pay's good, but I've got this little family problem I'll have to clear up first. I'm not sure how long it'll take me to track down my nephew, and I'll need to deal with him before I can leave Astarell unprotected."

"I can take care of myself, Uncle," Astarell asserted. "I know how to use a knife, and if that stinking old lecher who bought me from my brother comes anywhere near me, I'll carve out his tripe."

"She's a little tiger, isn't she?" Dreigon said to Gebhel.

"Spirited," Gebhel agreed.

"There *might* be a solution to the problem," Chief Albron observed. "I know of a safe place where Lady Astarell can sit out the war in Treborea. There are other ladies there, so there won't be any improprieties, and *nobody* can get past the defenses of *that* house."

"We can't take her *there*, my Chief!" Khalor protested.

"Why not? She's a member of Chief Kreuter's family, and we're Kreuter's allies. Her safety should be as much our concern as it is his."

Khalor looked quickly at Althalus. "What do you think?"

"Maybe," Althalus replied, "if we sort of neglect to mention it in advance." Then he glanced quickly at Albron, whose attention seemed totally fixed on Astarell. "You know Albron better than I do," he murmured softly to Khalor. "Am I reading him right? He seems quite taken with Kreuter's niece."

"I noticed that myself," Khalor agreed. "We might want to encourage that. If I can get him married off, maybe he'll settle down and quit pestering me while I'm working."

"If I put it to Dweia in those terms, I might be able to float it past her. She's got an abiding interest in arranging these things."

"I think you're going to get yourself yelled at, Althalus," Khalor predicted.

Althalus shrugged. "It won't be the first time."

"Bheid kept blushing," Gher reported when Althalus and Eliar returned to the House, "and sometimes his eyes almost popped out.

Of course, he was just one, and there were three girl people—probably coming at him from three different directions all at the same time. I don't think he sees the world the same as he used to."

"I'm sure he doesn't," Eliar said. "I know *I* don't." The young Arum frowned slightly. "Of course, I think I started changing quite a while back—along about the time when Andine started feeding me."

"Brother Bheid had some opinions about women that needed to be changed," Althalus noted. "Regardless of what his teachers may have told him, women *do* have minds. They don't always work the way ours do, but they *are* there. I want the two of you to stay on your toes during supper. I'm going to try to float something past Emmy."

"That Astarell business?" Eliar surmised.

"Exactly."

"Who's Astarell?" Gher asked.

"Kreuter's niece," Althalus replied. "She and Chief Albron are sort of interested in each other, and Sergeant Khalor *really* wants to get Albron married off. Albron wants us to bring Astarell here to the House—for reasons of safety, he says, but I'm sure it goes quite a bit further."

"The boy-people and girl-people thing?" Gher asked, making a slight face.

"There's quite a bit of that involved, yes, but there are some military reasons as well. We're going to need Kreuter later on, I think, and he's very worried about his niece. If she's safe, he'll be available; if she's not, he won't."

"I don't see any particular problem with it, pet," Dweia agreed after Althalus had presented his case to her at the supper table.

"No arguments?" he asked in a surprised tone. "No hissing or fluffing out your tail? You're taking a lot of the fun out of this, Em."

"It *does* make sense, Althalus, and I can make sure that Kreuter's niece doesn't find out *too* many things about our House. I gather that Chief Albron will be coming here with her?"

"From what I saw, I don't think you could get him more than ten feet away from her with a team of oxen, Emmy," Eliar said. "He seems to have a real bad case of the boy-girl business."

"That's nice," she purred.

"Do you suppose I might ask a favor, Dweia?" Bheid asked at that point.

"Have you been good today?"

"I've certainly tried—of course, it's a bit hard *not* to be good with three ladies camped on my shoulder." Then Bheid squinted thoughtfully at the ceiling. "As long as we're opening certain doors here, I was wondering if we could bring that shepherd Salkan here. I'd like to have a long talk with that young fellow. I'm getting a sense of an enormous potential there, and I'd hate to see it go to waste. Taking care of sheep is all very nice, I suppose, but it hardly challenges Salkan very much."

"Are we recruiting new priests, Brother Bheid?" Leitha asked with a slightly raised eyebrow.

"We get that hammered into us during our novitiate, Leitha," he replied. "Searching out talent is one of our primary responsibilities."

"And just *which* religion did you have in mind for that young man, Bheid?" Dweia asked archly.

"I'm not entirely sure," he admitted, "but I don't think we should let him get away."

"All in all, it came together fairly well," the silver-haired Dreigon summed up the following morning when the Generals gathered with Eliar and Althalus in a large tent near the cave mouth.

"Except that I had to abandon my trenches," Gebhel said sourly.

"Quit complaining, Gebhel," Khalor told him. "This mountain was even better than your trenches were."

"My men wasted a lot of effort digging those trenches."

"They got paid, didn't they?"

"How long is it likely to take your Chief and my niece to reach that house, Khalor?" Kreuter asked.

"A week or so," Khalor replied evasively. "I sent troops with them to make sure they get there safely, and I guarantee that your nephew won't even be able to find the place."

"Good. Now then, you've been hinting around the edges of another campaign. What's afoot—and where?"

Khalor shrugged. "Things are heating up in Treborea again. That's the war we were originally hired to work. The one we polished off here yesterday was sort of a sideshow. Let's be honest, gentlemen. None of us took this one very seriously. There was a certain strategic connection, but that's about all."

"It's all the same war, then?" Kreuter asked.

"The same enemy," Khalor conceded, "at the top, anyway. The main troublemaker's in Nekweros. I'd imagine that eventually we'll have to go there and ask him to stop stirring things up."

"And put ourselves out of work?" Gebhel snorted. "Don't be silly, Khalor. Is the thing in Treborea a continuation of the argument between Kanthon and Osthos?"

"Pretty much, yes."

"You worked for the Kanthons last time, didn't you, Khalor? Are we going back in on their side?"

"No, Gebhel. We've changed sides. The Arya of Osthos offered better pay," Khalor replied.

"That's good enough for me," Kreuter said. "I work for the money, not for the entertainment. Is there likely to be anything unusual?"

"Probably not," Khalor said. "Everything I've picked up so far has 'conventional' written all over it. One thing's certain, I'm going to need more cavalry."

"I can take care of that," Kreuter assured him. "I'll go back to Plakand and hire more men and horses." He looked at Althalus. "I'll need a few kegs of your gold, though," he added.

Althalus shrugged. "I had a feeling that might crop up."

" 'Money makes the mare go,' " Kreuter quoted.

"Wouldn't she settle for oats?"

"She might, but I won't."

Khalor leaned back in his chair, squinting at the tent roof. "I haven't looked at the situation in Treborea recently," he told them, "but unless there are surprises, this one should be fairly standard. I've got access to some clans that aren't quite so far away, so I'll use those during the initial stages of the war. If you gentlemen start moving in the general direction of Osthos, you can join in farther on down the line. The treasury of Osthos is bulging, so there'll be money enough for all of us. I'd imagine that things should be more or less stabilized by the time you arrive, and then you'll be able to step in and tip the balance."

"I think I could use those shepherds," Dreigon said.

"Wait a minute," Gebhel protested. "Those slingers are mine."

"I thought you didn't want to play this time," Khalor said.

Gebhel shrugged. "I'll be going that way anyway, and I'm fairly sure Gweti's going to want to get involved." Then he grinned. "Besides, if I get there late enough, I won't have to sit out any long, boring sieges. I'll come to your rescue, Khalor, so you can be grateful—and generous—after I pull your backside out of the fire."

"How closely are you related to Chief Gweti, Gebhel?" Khalor asked suspiciously.

"We're third cousins," Gebhel admitted.

"I thought it might be something like that. Certain characteristics run in families."

"Everybody likes money, Khalor. My family just likes it a little bit more, that's all."

"Obtaining Yeudon's permission to take Salkan and his young boys out of Wekti might be just a bit difficult," Bheid warned them.

"Permission my foot," Gebhel snorted. "I'll just offer them gold, and they'll drop sheep herding like hot rock."

"Then I guess I'll have to offer them more." Dreigon sighed.

"You wouldn't!" Gebhel exclaimed.

"Watch me," Dreigon said, grinning broadly.

It was late that afternoon when Eliar led Althalus and Bheid through the main door of the temple in Keiwon.

"What news from the war?" the white-robed priest in Exarch Yeudon's waiting room asked eagerly.

"I guess you could say that we won," Eliar told him.

"Praise Deiwos!" the white-robed priest exclaimed.

"I don't think Deiwos had very much to do with it," Eliar said. "We had a better army, that's all."

"Is Exarch Yeudon busy?" Bheid asked politely.

"Not when you come to call, Scopas Bheid," the white-robed priest replied. "He's left instructions that you're to be admitted immediately. He's been very concerned about the invasion."

"I think he can stop worrying now," Althalus murmured. "Would you mind letting him know that we're here?"

"I'll announce you at once." The priest went to the door behind his table, opened it, and leaned into the Exarch's study. "Scopas Bheid is here, your Eminence."

"Show him in at once, Brother Akhas." Yeudon's voice cracked.

"Yes, your Eminence." The priest opened the door wider and bowed to Bheid. "This way, Scopas Bheid." His tone was respectful, almost fawning, and he no longer looked down his nose.

Bheid led his friends into Yeudon's ornate study and bowed rather perfunctorily. "Good news, your Eminence," he announced. "The invaders have been beaten back. The danger is past."

"We are saved!" Yeudon exclaimed, his lined face breaking into a smile of gratitude.

"For the moment, anyway," Althalus amended.

"You believe that the invaders may return?"

"With what? There aren't that many of them left. Sergeant Khalor's a very thorough sort of man. He didn't just beat the Ansus. He ground them into dog meat. Still, it might not hurt to put some men along that frontier to keep an eye on things—just to be on the safe side."

"Do you think Salkan and the other shepherds might be able to hold that frontier?" Yeudon asked.

"There's a little problem with that, your Eminence," Althalus said. "Our Generals were very impressed with your shepherds, so they've sort of appropriated them for a war that's breaking out over in Treborea."

"I forbid it!" Yeudon exclaimed, coming to his feet. "I will *not* have my children exposed to the heresies of the west. No Wekti can leave our motherland without my express permission."

"Is your faith *that* insecure, your Eminence?" Bheid asked. "Are you so afraid of different ideas and beliefs that you feel you must chain your people to the walls?"

"Gentlemen," Althalus stepped in, "let's not get bogged down in theological debate here. We're talking about business, pure and simple. We came here and saved your bacon, Exarch, and we're taking Salkan and the shepherds as payment. Nothing's free, Yeudon. When you get something, you have to pay for it. What's happening in Treborea's part of the same war we fought here, if that's any comfort to you. Our ultimate enemy's still Daeva, so Salkan's shepherds are your contribution to the struggle between good and evil. Doesn't that make you proud?"

Yeudon glowered at him. Then his eyes narrowed, and he looked at Bheid. "There's something I don't quite understand, Scopas Bheid," he said. "Perhaps you could explain it to me."

"I'll certainly try, your Eminence."

"I sent a message expressing my gratitude to Exarch Emdahl, and he didn't seem to have the faintest idea of what I was talking about. In fact, it seems that he's never heard of you. Isn't that peculiar?"

"I wouldn't blame Bheid for that, Yeudon," Althalus said blandly. "He didn't really want to deceive you, but I compelled him to do it that way—largely because it was simpler and quicker. We *could* have told you what's *really* going on, but that might have shaken your foundations just a bit."

"Then this has all been a deception," Yeudon accused.

"Not entirely, no. Bheid told you that we were following the orders of a higher authority, and that part *was* the truth. He fibbed just a little when he told you that Exarch Emdahl was the authority we were talking about. When you get right down to it, our orders come from an authority that's several cuts above Emdahl—or you, for that matter."

"Deiwos, I suppose?" Yeudon said sardonically.

"No, actually it's his sister. This war that's tearing the world apart is an extension of a family squabble. Deiwos has a brother and a sister who don't really get along. The Book explains it all in great detail."

"Book?"

"The white Book. I wouldn't put too much faith in what the black Book says, if I were you. Of course, I couldn't read when Ghend showed me the black Book, so I'm not familiar with what it says. Dweia tells me that it's a distortion, though. I guess Daeva wrote it to try to take credit for creating the universe."

"You've actually *seen* the Books?" Yeudon's face had gone pasty white, and his hands were shaking.

"None of this would make much sense if I hadn't."

"I thought the Books were just an old myth."

"No, they're very real, Yeudon. I've read the white one from cover to cover—because I had the Goddess Dweia standing over me with a club to make sure that I didn't miss a single line."

"I don't understand."

"Good—Dweia tells me that's the first step toward wisdom. The Gods don't see the world as we do, Yeudon, and no matter how much we try to twist them around to make them arrange things for our own personal benefit, they get their own way, and *we're* the ones who get twisted around. Like it or not, we're going to do things *their* way."

"I take it that you're the high priest of the Goddess Dweia?" Yeudon suggested.

Bheid suddenly burst out laughing.

"Did I say something funny?" Yeudon asked, his eyes narrowing suspiciously.

"Althalus here's the least priestly man in the whole world, your Eminence," Bheid told him, still laughing. "He's a liar, a thief, and a murderer, and every time Dweia tells him to do something, he argues with her about it."

Althalus shrugged. "Nobody's perfect," he said. "I wouldn't go quite so far as to call myself a priest, though. I'm Dweia's agent—in the same way that Ghend's Daeva's agent. When this all started, I was working for Ghend, but that changed when I met Dweia. I work for her now, though she doesn't always approve of my methods. I'm a plain, simple man, and I still think that my answer to this whole business is better than hers."

"That's blasphemy!" Yeudon exclaimed.

"So what? I think she'll forgive me when it's all over. All I really have to do to put an end to all this nonsense is to chase Ghend down and kill him. Dweia's probably going to scold me about that for a few hundred years, but she's done that before, and she always settles down—eventually."

"You would dare to disobey your God?"

"It isn't really disobedience, Yeudon. She wants something done, and I'm going to do it. How I go about getting it done is *my* business, not hers. When you get right down to it, the Gods are really very simple. Divinity seems to make them a bit childish. Maybe that's because they always get what they want—and *maybe* that's why I'm around. If I disappoint Dweia every now and then, it might help her grow up."

Yeudon stared at him in horror.

"He'll probably lie to her," Bheid added. "She might not believe him right at first, but Althalus can talk very fast when he needs to, so she'll probably end up believing him."

"I'd love to stay and discuss this further, Exarch Yeudon," Althalus said, "but Dweia's waiting for us back home, and she absolutely *hates* to be kept waiting."

"That was quick," Dweia said when the three of them returned to the tower through Eliar's special door.

Bheid glanced quickly around the tower room. "Where are Chief Albron and Lady Astarell?" he asked cautiously.

"They're down in the dining room with Leitha, Andine, and Gher," Dweia replied. "I don't think it serves any purpose for them to spend too much time here in the tower. How did things go in Keiwon?"

"I was trying to be diplomatic," Bheid reported, "but Althalus pushed me off to one side and exposed poor Yeudon to a little bit more truth than he was ready for. Althalus can be very blunt when he's in a hurry."

"Yeudon makes me tired," Althalus said. "He's just a little too impressed with his own holiness. Have we more or less decided to bring Salkan here to our private part of the House?"

"Brother Bheid thinks it might be a good idea," Dweia said, "and it shouldn't be *too* much trouble—as long as we keep him out of the tower, along with Astarell and Albron."

"Let's hold off until he's in one of the corridors here in the House with Gebhel and Dreigon, Em," Althalus suggested. "Then Eliar and I can snatch him and bring him here with no one the wiser. We could probably grab him right now, but I'd have to spread assorted lies around to keep everybody happy, and that gets a bit tedious after a while."

"Whatever works best for you, pet," she agreed. "Oh, by the way, Andine wants to pay a call on Lord Dhakan in Osthos. She's positive that the Kanthons will invade soon. Take Sergeant Khalor along to explain our present strategy."

"Anything you say, Em," he agreed.

It was early evening when Eliar led Althalus, Andine, and Khalor into the corridor outside Lord Dhakan's study in the palace at Osthos. Then he rapped on the Chamberlain's door.

"I'm busy," Dhakan's voice responded. "Go away."

"It's me, Dhakan," Andine called to him. "I have some good news for you."

Dhakan opened the door. "Sorry, my Arya," he apologized with a deep bow. "I've had people hammering on my door with *bad* news all day. Come in. Come in."

"Isn't he a dear?" Andine said fondly.

"This is Sergeant Khalor, Dhakan," Althalus said. "We were on our way back to that other war we mentioned during our last visit, and we met him near the Equero border. He'd polished off that other war, and his forces are on the march right now. He wants to know how things stand here currently."

"Sergeant." Dhakan greeted the stern-faced Khalor with a slight nod. "Things here haven't been going very well, I'm afraid."

"The Kanthons have invaded?"

Dhakan nodded. "Several days ago. They have a huge army, and our forces haven't been able to delay them very much."

Khalor gestured toward the large map on the wall behind Dhakan's desk. "Show me," he suggested.

Dhakan nodded. "The border country's not the richest land in the whole of Treborea, so we've never made an issue of who really owns it. The Kanthons invaded our lands here to the north of that lake, and they had a sizable army of mercenary soldiers."

"Horsemen or foot soldiers?"

"Both, Sergeant."

"Have you got any ideas about where those mercenaries came from?"

"It's a little hard to say, Sergeant. Most Treboreans can't tell the difference between Arums and Kagwhers."

"I might recognize them when I see them." Then Khalor pointed at three names written on the map. "Are these places towns? Or are they just farming villages?"

"They're cities, actually."

"Are they walled?"

Dhakan nodded. "The walls of Kadon and Mawor are quite substantial, but those around Poma have sort of fallen into disrepair. Technically, those three cities are a part of the Osthos Alliance. They were independent city-states some centuries back, and when the Kanthons began having imperial urges for the first time, we all joined together to repel them. The Dukes of those three cities still maintain the fiction of independence, but when you get right down to the bottom of things, they take orders from Osthos."

Khalor shook his head. "The politics of the low countries are even more complicated than their religions."

"Complication is part of the joy of being civilized, Sergeant Khalor," Dhakan said drily. Then his face grew somber. "We've fought wars with the Kanthons quite a few times during the past several centuries, and those wars have always concentrated on the cities, because that's where all the wealth is. This time's quite a bit different. The invaders are killing everybody they encounter."

"Not the peasants, certainly?" Andine exclaimed.

"I'm afraid so, my Arya," Dhakan told her.

"That's idiocy! The peasants don't have anything to do with the wars between the cities! Nobody's ever killed the peasants before. They're an asset. If you don't have peasants, who's going to grow your food?"

"That doesn't seem to concern the invaders, my Arya," Dhakan told her. "The peasants are fleeing in panic, of course, and they're clogging every road that leads south."

"Maybe that's what the invaders want," Khalor mused. "If those three cities are jammed full of refugees when the sieges begin, the food won't last very long, and the cities won't either."

"That's a brutal way to make war, Sergeant," Dhakan protested.

"We're dealing with a brutal enemy, Lord Dhakan." Khalor squinted at the map. "Let me guess, my Lord. Could it possibly be that one of the generals of the invading army just happens to be a woman?"

"How do you know *that*?"

"We've met her before. Her name's Gelta, and she calls herself 'the Queen of the Night.' She's a raving maniac with shoulders like a bull, and she loves the taste of blood."

"A *woman*?" Dhakan exclaimed.

"She's no ordinary woman, my Lord," Althalus said, "and this isn't any ordinary war. The Aryo of Kanthon's hardly more than a puppet, and somebody else is pulling his strings."

"My armies are on the way, Lord Dhakan," Khalor said. "I'll want to go have a look at those cities, but the most important thing at the moment is to get forces up there to delay the invaders and give me time to see to the defenses. Let's get somebody between Gelta and those cities. I *don't* want to sit down to dinner with her."

"Smeugor and Tauri, I think," Althalus suggested.

"Not those two, certainly!" Andine exclaimed. "They're turncoats, Althalus! They'll betray us every chance they get!"

"They'll *try* to betray us, little girl," Althalus replied, "but I'll be several steps ahead of them all along the way. Whether they like it or not, Smeugor and Tauri *are* going to make a major contribution to our victory."

The leaves were red—red as blood—when the Queen of the Night ascended to the throne of mighty Osthos. And, behold, the captive Arya of Osthos was brought in chains to kneel before the dreaded Queen who had o'erthrown all who stood in her path.

"Submit unto me, frail child," the dark Queen commanded, "and should thy submission please me, mayhap I shall spare thy life." And the haunted wail filled the room.

And Arya Andine knelt to signify her submission.

"On thy face!" stern Gelta commanded. "Grovel before me that I may know that thy submission is absolute!"

And, weeping, did Arya Andine lower her face to the very stones of the floor.

And the heart of Gelta was full, and the taste of victory on her tongue was sweet, sweet.

And placed she then her rough-booted foot upon the soft neck of groveling Andine in exultant triumph, declaring, "All that was yours is now mine, Andine, yea, verily, even thy life and all thy blood."

And the triumphant cry of the Queen of the Night echoed down the marble-clad palace of the fallen Arya of Osthos, and the despairing wail echoed also.

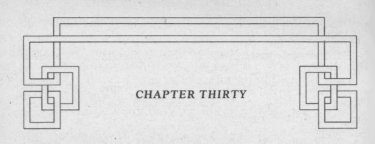

CHAPTER THIRTY

"What a terrible nightmare I had!" Astarell exclaimed the next morning at breakfast.

"I didn't sleep very well myself," Chief Albron admitted.

Dweia looked at the two of them, and then she made a slight gesture with one hand. *"Drem,"* she said softly.

Albron and Astarell immediately froze in position, their eyes open and vacant.

Sergeant Khalor looked slightly puzzled, and he waved one hand in front of his Chief's face. Albron's face remained frozen and his eyes blank. "What's going on here?" Khalor demanded.

"We need to talk, Sergeant," Althalus told him, "and Albron and Astarell don't really need to listen in."

"Witchcraft?" Khalor asked in a startled tone.

"That's hardly the term I'd use, but it's something along those lines. You should have guessed by now that many of the things that happen here in the House are a little out of the ordinary. Astarell and your Chief can take a little nap while we're busy. We might use that now and then to keep certain other things from going *too* far."

"Kreuter probably *would* be unhappy if things went too far between Chief Albron and his niece," Khalor conceded.

"Exactly. And after certain formalities, they'll both be well rested. You might want to raise that issue the next time you talk with Kreuter."

"It *would* solve quite a few problems, wouldn't it?" Khalor agreed. "What was all that talk about nightmares?"

"Did you dream last night, Sergeant?" Dweia asked him.

"A little," Khalor admitted. "It didn't make any sense, but dreams never do."

"Oh, it made sense, Sergeant," Dweia disagreed. "It made a *lot* of sense."

"What's Ghend up to?" Bheid asked in some perplexity. "I thought he was trying to change the past, but that dream last night was in the future, wasn't it?"

"He might be getting a little desperate," Dweia mused. "He hasn't had much luck with his visions of the past, and I'm catching a strong odor of dissatisfaction from my brother. I think Ghend might be staring down the throat of an ultimatum of some sort. Tampering with the future's a very risky sort of business." She turned slightly. "Could you touch Gelta's mind during that dream, Leitha?" she asked.

Leitha nodded. "A lot of it was playacting," she replied. "Gelta was adding things that weren't entirely true. The war wasn't going nearly as well for her as that dream vision suggested."

"This isn't the first time you've all had the same dream, I gather," Khalor said.

"The bad people are trying to play with our thoughts, Mister Khalor," Gher told him. "The Ghend fellow sticks silly things that didn't really happen into our dreams to make us believe that they really *did* happen. That dream we all had last night wasn't way back then like the rest of them have been, though. I think this one's supposed to happen a month or so from now."

"How did you come to *that* conclusion, Gher?" Bheid asked.

"The leaves on the trees outside the room where Andine was sprawled out on the floor were all sort of red. Doesn't that mean that it was in autumn?"

Khalor's eyes narrowed. "They *were*, weren't they?" he said. "That means that this is all supposed to happen about six weeks from now." He looked at Dweia. "Is that thing set in stone?" he asked her. "Or could this Ghend fellow sneak back, put snow on the ground, and then make us dream it all over again?"

"I don't think he'd dare, Sergeant," she replied. "Part of the danger of jumping around in time in a dream vision is the possibility of paradox. If two entirely different things happen in the same place at the same time, reality starts to come apart, and we really don't want that to happen. Changing the past is fairly safe—if you don't go too far. Changing the future is an entirely different matter."

"The past has already happened, Dweia," Bheid objected. "It *can't* be changed."

"It doesn't *have* to be, Brother Bheid," she told him. "The dream vision changes our *memory* of the past. In the world of reality, Gelta never attained total domination of Ansu. She butchered her way to the thrones of about six clans in southern Ansu, and then the rest of the clans joined forces and overwhelmed her. She was on her way to the headsman's block when Pekhal rescued her. That's not the way she remembers it, though. She *believes* that she came to own all of Ansu, and Ghend can use dream visions to make everybody in Ansu believe the same thing. *That's* why the Ansus attacked Wekti when she commanded them to."

"Did that make any sense to anybody else?" Eliar asked plaintively.

"It's not really all that complicated, Eliar," Gher told him. "The dream things are flimflams, that's all."

"That might actually be the best way to look at them," Dweia conceded. "It's a little more complex than that, but 'flimflam' isn't too far off the mark when the dream visions are set in the past. This time, though, Ghend's trying to sneak a future one by us."

"How can we prevent it?" Andine demanded.

"I don't think we'll want to, dear," Dweia replied fondly. "I think we might want to just play along with that dream."

"No!" Andine's voice soared. "I *will* not bow down to that pockmarked cow!"

"You're missing the point, Andine," Dweia told her. "I believe the Knife said 'obey' when you saw it, didn't it?"

"It surely didn't mean that I'm supposed to obey *Gelta*!"

"The meanings of the words on the Knife are a little obscure, dear. It told Eliar to 'lead,' but it didn't mean that he's supposed to command the army. What it really meant was that he's the one who opens the doors. It told Leitha to 'listen,' but she doesn't listen with her ears. When it told you to 'obey,' it was giving you the means to defeat Gelta."

"I *won't* do it! I'd sooner die!"

"That option's not open to you, dear. You don't have to *like* it, Andine, you just have to *do* it."

"I'm sure you folks can deal with these little matters without any help from me," Sergeant Khalor suggested. "Right now I'd probably better go look at those three cities."

"Hold tight for a few minutes, Sergeant," Althalus said. "I want to go talk with Smeugor and Tauri. I think it's time to put some forces out there to slow the invasion." He squinted at Leitha. "You'd better come along," he told her. "I want to know exactly what those two are thinking before I turn them loose."

"It shall be as you command, O glorious leader," Leitha replied with an exaggerated curtsy.

"Would you talk to her about that, Bheid?" Althalus asked the black-robed priest. "I've got enough on my mind already without all these little tweaks and gouges to brighten up my day."

"Why, Althalus," Leitha said in mock astonishment, "what a terrible thing to say."

Althalus and Leitha walked through the silent corridors of the House toward the southeast wing, and Althalus explained a few peculiarities as they went. "They don't see the walls or the floor, Leitha. They think they're in Kagwher—up in the mountains."

"How are you managing that, Althalus?" the blond girl asked.

"I'm not the one who's doing it, so don't ask *me* about it. Emmy takes care of that."

"You love her very much, don't you?"

"It goes quite a ways past that. Anyway, the two clans are sort of lounging around in what they *think* is a mountain pass. I'll station you in a doorway that won't be very far from their encampment, and then I'll go on in and give them their marching orders. I'll need to know what their reactions are and just exactly how they'll try to avoid doing what I tell them to do. We don't want any surprises."

"I'll see what I can find out," she promised.

They turned into an intersecting corridor, and Althalus saw an army of Arums just ahead. "This should be far enough, Leitha," he told her. "Wait here."

There was, as always, a peculiar sense of dislocation when Althalus approached the camp. He could see the corridor clearly enough, but at the same time, he could see the mountains of Kagwher out of the corners of his eyes, and the corridor and the mountains seemed to blur together. Distances weren't exactly the same, so the kilted sentries did a lot of walking in place as they escorted Althalus to the headquarters pavilion.

"Good morning, gentlemen," Althalus greeted the pair as he entered the pavilion. "What cheer?"

"Not much cheer," the pimple-faced Smeugor replied sourly. "This is intolerable, Althalus. We're Clan Chiefs, and you've got us roughing things with the common soldiers. It's insulting."

"You took the money, Chief Smeugor," Althalus told him. "Now you get to earn it."

"What's afoot?" the yellow-haired Tauri asked.

"The Kanthons have invaded Osthos territory," Althalus replied, "so it looks like we're off to the races. You'd better summon your army commanders. I'll need to discuss the details with them."

"We're the Clan Chiefs, Althalus," Smeugor declared with a haughty expression. "*We'll* pass the orders on to our troop commanders."

"Forgive me if I speak bluntly, Chief Smeugor," Althalus said, "but you two don't know beans about military operations. I want to be positive that your commanders know exactly what's going on and what I need them to do. We don't want any misunderstandings."

"You go too far, Althalus," Tauri declared. "*We'll* decide what orders to give our men."

"The pay stops right now, then. Turn around and go back to Arum."

"We have an agreement!" Smeugor exclaimed. "You can't just back out of it like this!"

"I just did. Either send for those commanders or start packing for the trip home. I speak for Arya Andine. You *will* do as I tell you to do, or I'll dismiss you right here and now."

Tauri turned to the sentry posted at the front of the pavilion. "You—what's your name?—go fetch Wendan and Gelun, and be quick about it."

"Yes, my Chief," the sentry replied. Althalus noticed a slight sneer cross the sentry's face as Tauri turned away. The two renegade Chiefs were obviously not highly regarded by their clansmen.

"Exactly what have you got in mind for us, Althalus?" Smeugor asked, his hard eyes narrowing.

"The invaders are moving faster than we want them to move. We're preparing a welcome for them, and we don't want them to arrive early. I want you two to slow them down."

"It's a long way off, Althalus," Tauri protested. "How are we supposed to get there in time to make any difference?"

"The procedure's known as 'running,' Chief Tauri. It's a bit like walking, but you do it faster."

"I don't care for your tone, Althalus."

"That's too bad, isn't it? You've been on the march for almost a month now, and you haven't really covered very much ground. Now you're going to make up for that. This is a war, gentlemen, not an afternoon stroll. You'd better pass the word to your men to start breaking camp. You'll be leaving here within the hour."

"You sent for us, my Chief?" a lean, professional-looking soldier inquired as he and a very tall man entered.

"Yes, Gelun," Tauri replied. "This is Althalus, one of our employer's underlings. He has some instructions for you—outside, if you don't mind. Chief Smeugor and I are about to have breakfast, and we'd rather not be disturbed."

"As you command, my Chief," Captain Gelun replied, saluting. "If you'll come with us, Althalus, we can discuss this in greater detail."

"Of course," Althalus replied. Then he bowed curtly to Smeugor and Tauri. "Enjoy your breakfast, gentlemen, but don't be at it too long." Then he followed the two soldiers out of the pavilion.

"Is it just my imagination, or did I catch a faint smell of hostility in the air just now?" the tall soldier with Captain Gelun asked mildly.

"You're Captain Wendan, aren't you?" Althalus asked.

"At your service, Althalus," the tall man replied extravagantly.

"I certainly hope so. I wasn't having much luck getting through to that pair."

"What an amazing thing," Gelun said sardonically. "Wendan and I don't have any trouble at all persuading them that we should move along—unless we get careless and suggest that we should cover more than a mile a day."

"What possessed your Arya to saddle us with that worthless pair, Althalus?" Wendan demanded.

"Careful, Wendan," Gelun warned. "You shouldn't let the men hear you talking that way about our revered Chieftains. It's bad for their morale."

"Arya Andine doesn't entirely understand Arum social structure, gentlemen," Althalus said glibly. "She thought that all the clans functioned the way Twengor's clan does. Twengor leads his men personally. I tried to explain to her that Smeugor and Tauri don't do that, but I couldn't get through to her. She still seems to think that *they're* the Generals. She's very young."

"Everybody gets over that eventually," Gelun said. "Here's our tent, Althalus. Come on inside, and we'll get down to business."

"I brought a map," Althalus said as they entered a tent that stood no more than ten feet from the pavilion. He reached inside his tunic and drew out one of Khalor's carefully drawn maps. Then he unrolled it and spread it out on the rough table in the tent. "The army of the Kanthons invaded last week, and they're advancing on these three cities. We need to have you slow them down."

"Who's the Overgeneral of our forces?" Wendan asked.

"You know Sergeant Khalor?"

"Oh, yes," Wendan replied. "He and I've been on opposite

sides in a couple of wars. When you get right down to it, if you've got Khalor, you don't *need* any of the rest of us."

"Is he that good?" Gelun asked.

"You don't want to go up against him if you can possibly avoid it."

Gelun grunted. "You *do* know what's involved in a delaying action, don't you, Althalus?" he asked.

"Mostly ambushes and knocking down bridges, isn't it?"

"Stick to politics and diplomacy, Althalus," Wendan said. "Wars are just a little different. Soldiers get hungry several times a day, so they have to be fed. The best way to slow them down is to make sure that you don't leave any food lying around for them. It's almost harvest time now—which is probably why the Kanthons waited to start their invasion. I hope your Arya isn't *too* attached to this year's wheat crop, because it won't be there anymore after Gelun and I reach that border country. We'll burn everything in sight for fifty miles on either side of the line."

"And poison every well we come across," Gelun added.

"Poison?" That startled Althalus.

"It amounts to that," Gelun explained. "If you take a horse or a cow that's been dead for a week and drop it down a well, the water won't be fit to drink."

"And if you can't find suitable cattle, there are always dead people lying around during a war. Dead people stink even worse than dead cows do," Wendan added.

Althalus shuddered. "Do you think you'll be able to keep Chief Smeugor and Chief Tauri from interfering?"

"Anything more than a mile from where their pavilion's set up might as well be on the other side of the world," Gelun sneered. "Our glorious leaders aren't very fond of exercise. Wendan and I just salute smartly when they tell us to do something, but as soon as we get out of sight—and earshot—we do what really needs to be done instead. Tell Sergeant Khalor that we're going to send him invaders who'll be terribly hungry and thirsty. He'll know what to do with them."

"Leave the map, though," the lanky Wendan added. "Now if

you'll excuse us, we'd better go give the men their marching orders."

"Have a nice trip," Althalus said. And then he left the tent.

"You still have a lot of rough bark left on you, Althalus," Leitha observed when he rejoined her. "Weren't you just a bit abrupt with Smeugor and Tauri?"

"It could have been worse. What did they say after I left?"

"They're terribly upset and extremely worried. They haven't been able to get in touch with Ghend since the conclave, so they don't really know what they're supposed to do. Normally, Argan carries messages back and forth, but they haven't seen him for weeks. They're totally baffled and very much afraid. If they do something wrong, they know that Ghend's very likely to punish them—fatally."

"What a shame," Althalus replied, smirking. "We'd better get back to the tower before Khalor starts climbing the walls."

"There's something else going on, Althalus," Leitha said with a slightly worried frown, "and I can't quite get hold of it."

"Oh?"

"Argan's the one who recruits Ghend's spies—usually by offering them bribes. At least that's what he did in Wekti. He's doing something different in Treborea. He's still bribing various officials, but I kept catching the word 'conversion' from Smeugor and Tauri, and it terrifies them. They're happy to take money from Argan, but he seems to be attaching a few strings to his bribes."

"That's *all* we need," Althalus replied. "I *hate* it when religion gets involved in politics."

"I just thought you should know, Althalus."

"Thanks a lot." Then he stopped. "How's Bheid coming along? Gher said he looked a bit upset when you opened certain doors for him—you know what I mean."

She giggled. "He wasn't quite ready for some of the things that were involved. He didn't mind passing *ideas* back and forth, but *feelings* bothered him quite a bit."

"Would you mind a suggestion, Leitha?" Althalus said carefully as they approached the tower stairs.

"That depends on the suggestion."

"Would you go a little easier on Bheid for a while?"

"How do you mean 'easier'?"

"Quit trying to make him blush every time he turns around. Back away from the 'vile thoughts' business—at least until he gets more accustomed to having strangers inside his head."

"But he's so adorable when he blushes," she protested.

"Find some other entertainment for the time being. I've got a strong suspicion that we'll need him to have his wits about him before long, so give the swishing and innuendos a rest. He isn't going to get away from you, Leitha, so behave yourself."

"Yes, Papa," she replied obediently.

"What's that supposed to mean?"

"You were being paternal, Althalus. You do that all the time, you know—probably because you think of the rest of us as children. You aren't really much of a father, but you're the only one we've got—Daddy dear."

"That will *do*, Leitha!"

"Are you going to spank me—with your own personal bare hand?" she asked enthusiastically, fluttering her eyelashes at him.

"Quit that!"

"Yes, Daddy," she replied obediently.

The guards at the gates of Kadon questioned Althalus, Eliar, and Sergeant Khalor at some length before allowing them to enter the city, and Althalus was fuming as the three of them walked through the narrow streets toward the palace of Duke Olkar.

"It *is* wartime, Althalus," Sergeant Khalor explained. "Those men wouldn't have been attending to business if they'd just waved us through."

"I had this pass with Andine's signature on it," Althalus objected, waving the sheet of paper.

"That's very impressive, I'm sure, but you won't find too many common soldiers who know how to read. The guards were doing what they're supposed to do. Quit worrying about it."

"The walls looked fairly good to me," Eliar observed.

"Solid enough," Khalor agreed. "A little pedestrian, maybe, but a few innovations should take care of that."

"What kind of innovations?"

"Think, Eliar. What do you add to a wall to make life difficult for somebody who wants to get into your city?"

"An overhang, maybe?"

"It wouldn't hurt. Flat walls make for easy climbing. Anything else?"

"Redoubts, maybe? Those turret things that stick out from the corners so that archers can shoot arrows at anybody climbing a scaling ladder?"

"Those might be useful, too."

"Why do you do that, Khalor?" Althalus asked.

"Do what?"

"Give tests all the time."

Khalor shrugged. "I'm supposed to be a teacher, Althalus. Teachers give tests. The enemy gives the final examination, though. If my pupil's still alive when the battle's over, he's passed the test. You'd better keep that pass Andine gave you handy. There's the palace of the Duke right over there, and we're a little too busy to spend much time cooling our heels in some waiting room."

Andine's note gained them immediate entry into the opulent office of Duke Olkar. The Duke of Kadon was a somewhat stodgy man of middle years who wore conservative clothes and a somewhat pompous expression. "This is all very bad for business, Lord Althalus," he complained after they'd been seated. "My entire city's clogged with rural bumpkins who expect me to feed them."

"The invaders are killing them out in the countryside, your Grace," Althalus pointed out. "If all the peasants are dead next spring, who's going to plant the crops?"

"There *is* that, I suppose," Olkar conceded grudgingly. "This war won't last *too* long, will it? I've got merchandise I *must* move, and the roads aren't safe right now."

"It's likely to grow worse, your Grace," Khalor told him bluntly. "You'll probably be under siege within a week or ten days. Your walls are going to need strengthening, and you'd better lay in a goodly supply of food. I've got forces who'll come in and lift the siege in a while, but you'd better have enough supplies on hand to carry you through until autumn."

"Autumn?" Olkar exclaimed. "That'd destroy any hope of profit for this entire year!"

"At least you'll be alive when next year rolls around," Althalus pointed out. "Everybody has a bad year now and then."

"I'll need to talk with your engineers, your Grace," Khalor said then. "They'd better get to work on your city walls, and I want to make some suggestions. Oh, there's another thing, too. There's an army of Arum mercenaries on the way here to defend your city. They'll need quarters."

"Can't they just set up camp outside the walls?" Olkar asked plaintively.

Khalor didn't reply, but gave Olkar a long, hard look instead.

"No," Olkar conceded, "I suppose they couldn't at that, now that I think about it." He sighed. "Arums are so *noisy!*" he complained. "And so rowdy. Do you think you might be able to persuade them to mind their manners while they're here in Kadon? The citizens of Kadon are quite proper, and they take offense at rowdies."

Khalor shrugged. "If you think the Arums are going to be *too* offensive, you can always defend your *own* city."

"No, that's quite all right, Sergeant," Olkar replied quickly.

"I rather thought you might see it that way, your Grace," Khalor said. "Now if you'll send for your engineers, I'll get down to business. I still have a lot of things to do today."

"Which clan do you want to have defend Kadon?" Althalus asked Khalor as the three of them left the city.

"Laiwon, I think," Khalor replied. "He's almost as good as Twengor, and he's got better sense. Laiwon's clan's been involved in a few sieges, so he knows what to do. I *don't* want him to drive off the besiegers. This city and that stuffy Duke are going to lock a third of the invading army in place for as long as I want them to." He glanced back over his shoulder at the city. "I don't think they can see us now. Let's go to Poma, Eliar."

"Yes, Sergeant," Eliar replied.

They passed briefly through the House and emerged inside the city of Poma. "It's a way to avoid the gate guards," Eliar explained.

Sergeant Khalor was staring down the street at the city wall with a look of stunned incredulity. "What are they *thinking* of?" he exclaimed.

Althalus squinted at the wall. "Not very good, is it?" he suggested.

"A good sneeze would knock that silly thing down!" Khalor burst out. "Who's running this place, anyway?"

"I think Dhakan called him Bherdor," Althalus replied.

"I'm likely to call him a few other names," Khalor said. "Let's go talk with this imbecile."

The palace of Duke Bherdor of Poma had a decidedly shabby look about it. Several broken windows had been boarded up rather than reglazed, and the courtyard evidently hadn't been swept—or shoveled—for a month or more.

Andine's message once again gained them immediate entry into a distinctly unimpressive office, and into the equally unimpressive presence of the youthful Duke.

Bherdor was hardly more than a boy, and he had a weak chin—and a disposition to match. "I know that things aren't quite up to standard, Lord Althalus," he apologized tremulously when Althalus took him to task for the condition of his city walls, "but my poor, poor city's teetering on the brink of total bankruptcy. I'd raise taxes to repair them, but the merchants have all warned me that a tax increase would send the local economy into total collapse."

"What *is* your current rate, your Grace?" Althalus asked.

"Three and a half percent, Lord Althalus," Bherdor replied tremulously. "Do you think that's too high?" he added with some apprehension.

"*Eighty* percent is high, your Grace. Three and a half percent is a joke. No wonder you're living in a pigsty."

"It's too late to do much about it now," Khalor said. "Those walls won't last for more than a couple of days. I think I'd better put Twengor here. There's going to be fighting in the streets, I'm afraid, and Twengor's the right man for that—if he's sober." He looked at the frightened Duke Bherdor. "Your stingy merchants are likely to get a quick lesson about the necessity for reasonable tax rates, your Grace. There won't be very much left of Poma after a few weeks of house-to-house fighting—and all the incidental looting by both armies. Your merchants swindled you, my Lord, but they won't have anything to show for it after the war."

"Good God!" Khalor exclaimed when he saw the walls of Mawor. "Would you *look* at those?"

"They *are* just a bit intimidating, aren't they?" Althalus agreed, staring at the massive and elaborate defenses of Mawor.

"Intimidating? There isn't enough money in the world to persuade *me* to lay siege to that place! I'd really hate to be a taxpayer in that town, though. What's that Duke's name again?"

"Lord Dhakan called him Nitral, I think," Eliar replied. "I think he said that Nitral's an architect. From what I understand, he's been rebuilding the entire city for the last twenty years."

"Well, we certainly won't have to do anything about the walls." Khalor squinted at the city. "I'd say that Mawor comes close to being totally unassailable. I think I'll want to put somebody here who'll know how to take advantage of that."

"What about Iron Jaw?" Eliar suggested.

"My very thought, Eliar," Khalor agreed. "He'd be perfect for this place."

"Who's 'Iron Jaw'?" Althalus asked.

"He's the Chief with a lower jaw that sticks out past his nose," Khalor replied. "He almost never talks, and he's the most stubborn man in all of Arum. Once he grabs something, he never lets go of it. If we put Koleika Iron Jaw here in Mawor, Gelta might lay siege to the place, but she won't get into the city, and she won't be able to leave."

"I don't quite follow that," Althalus admitted.

"As soon as she turns around to leave, Koleika'll come

blasting out through the gates and cut her army all to pieces. He'll lock them in place right here." Khalor squinted. "It sort of matches what Leitha told us about what Gelta was thinking in that dream. There was *something* that was preventing the invaders from marching on Osthos, and I think it might just have been the combination of *this* fortress and Iron Jaw. Put those two together, and this is a natural trap. The invasion stops right here. They won't be able to get in, and they won't be able to leave. It's perfect." Khalor actually began to laugh. "I almost feel sorry for them. Let's go on inside and meet this architectural genius. We'll let him know that Koleika's coming and roughly what to expect. Then we can go back to Osthos, and I'll have a chat with the Commanders of Andine's army."

It was late summer by now, and the heat in Osthos was oppressive. At Andine's request, Lord Dhakan had summoned the Generals. They had gathered in her throne room, where they stood sweating and idly chatting as they awaited the appearance of their Arya.

"Give them a little time to get settled down, my Arya," Lord Dhakan suggested, peering out through the doorway at the back of the throne room.

"Is the army of Osthos so big that you need *that* many Generals?" Khalor asked.

"Rank is hereditary here in Osthos, Sergeant," Dhakan replied. "Over the centuries, our army's gotten a little top-heavy. About the only advantage to having so many Generals is the remote possibility that at least one of them might know what he's doing."

"You're a cynic, my Lord."

"One of the advantages of a long life, Sergeant," Dhakan said with a faint smile. "Would you be offended if I introduced you as a Field Marshal?"

"Why would you want to do that?"

"Sergeants don't rank very high in our army, my friend. Our Colonels and Generals and exalted poo-bahs might not hold a mere Sergeant in very high regard."

"I'll cure them of that in a hurry," Khalor promised with a bleak smile. He looked at Andine, who was sweating in her robes of state. "Would it bother you very much if I broke up some of the furniture, little girl?"

"Enjoy yourself, Sergeant," she replied with an impish little smile. "Should we go in now, Dhakan?"

"We might as well. Please don't kill *too* many of them, Sergeant. State funerals are terribly expensive."

"I'll try to control myself," Khalor promised. Then he stepped over to one of the armored sentries at the door. "May I borrow your ax, soldier?" he asked politely.

The sentry looked quickly at Lord Dhakan for instructions.

Dhakan winced. "Go ahead and give him the ax," he ordered.

"Yes, Lord Dhakan," the soldier said, handing his long-handled battle-ax to the Sergeant.

Khalor hefted it. "Good weight," he noted. Then he tested the edge with his thumb. "You take good care of it, too." He patted the sentry's arm. "You're a good soldier," he said.

"Thank you, sir," the sentry said, straightening proudly.

"I suppose we'd better get on with this before it gets too much hotter," Khalor suggested. "Why don't you all go on down front? Then Lord Dhakan can let the Generals know who I am, and I'll take it from there."

"Try not to get *too* much blood on the floor, Sergeant," Andine said half seriously. "Marble stains *so* badly."

"I'll try my best to be neat," Khalor promised.

Dhakan signaled the waiting trumpeters, and they blew a lengthy, somewhat involved fanfare.

Then imperious Andine, with armored Eliar in close attendance, marched stately and slowly to her throne while the now-silent Generals bowed.

"Keep yours ears open, Leitha," Althalus murmured to the blond girl. "It's almost certain that Argan's recruited some of the Generals."

"I'll locate them," Leitha promised.

Emmy the cat was sitting on Andine's throne, carefully bathing her face. She meowed inquiringly as Andine approached.

"There you are," Andine said, gathering Emmy up in her arms. "Where have you been hiding, you naughty cat?" Then, with Emmy in her arms, she seated herself on the throne, even as the Generals went back to their conversations.

There was a speaker's lectern directly in front of the dais, and Lord Dhakan positioned himself behind it and rapped his knuckles on the slanted top of the lectern. "Your attention, please, gentlemen."

The Generals largely ignored him and continued their conversations.

"Be silent!" Andine commanded in her soaring voice.

The Generals stopped talking immediately.

"Thank you, my Arya," Dhakan murmured.

"What's this all about, Dhakan?" a bulky general in a gilded breastplate demanded.

"We seem to have this little war going on, General Terkor," Dhakan replied. "Had you noticed that?"

The General smiled faintly. "I'm sure you'll get to the point here eventually, Dhakan," he said, "hopefully before it gets too much hotter in this room."

"You take so much of the fun out of my life when you do that, Terkor," Dhakan complained. "Anyway, I'd like to introduce you all to a certain Sergeant Khalor. I'd strongly suggest that you all make every effort to be polite to him, since he's a bit short-tempered, and you *will* be taking orders from him."

"I'm a General, Dhakan," Terkor snapped. "I *don't* take orders from Sergeants."

"We'll miss you terribly, General Terkor," Dhakan murmured. "We'll give you a nice funeral, though."

Then Khalor stepped through the door and strolled almost casually toward the dais, negligently carrying the battle-ax. "If I may?" he said to Lord Dhakan, pointing at the lectern.

"Of course, Sergeant Khalor," Dhakan said politely, stepping aside.

Khalor took his place behind the lectern, and he stood there silently listening to the outraged Generals babble to each other.

The sound the ax made as it splintered the lectern immediately stopped all conversation.

"There goes the furniture," Andine murmured, rolling her eyes upward.

"Good morning, gentlemen," Khalor roared in a voice that could have been heard all the way across a parade ground. "We've got a lot to cover here, so shut up and pay attention."

"Who do you think you are?" General Terkor demanded, drawing himself up.

"I'm the man who's going to split you right down the middle if you open your mouth again," Khalor barked. "Let's get all this silly nonsense about rank and titles out of the way right now. I'm an Arum, and our titles of rank don't mean the same things they mean down here in the low country. In my clan, 'Sergeant' means 'Commander in Chief,' but let's lay that aside for now." He held up the battle-ax. "Do you see this?" he said. "*This* is my rank, and it puts me in charge of this little get-together. If any of you wants to object, I'll be more than happy to fight him—right here and now."

"He makes that same speech all the time," Eliar said quietly to the others on the dais. "Nobody ever takes him up on it, for some reason."

The Generals were all staring at the ax Khalor was holding over his head.

"Excellent, gentlemen," Khalor said. "We're getting along just fine, aren't we? Now, then, you've recently been invaded by the hired army of the idiot in Kanthon, and your charming little Arya has hired me to tell them to go home. Our enemy—at least on the surface—is the Aryo of Kanthon. I know him very well, since I led his armies the last time he declared war on Osthos. His name's Pelghat, and he hasn't got a brain in his head. I hope this won't offend you gentlemen, but this perpetual war here in Treborea's beginning to bore me, so this time I'm going to finish it once and for all. *Your* concern will be the defense of *this* city, and nothing more. Don't interfere with anything I'm doing in the other cities or out in the countryside, because I'll climb all over you if you try. Arya Andine hired *me* to fight this war, and I'll take care of it for her. The young fellow standing beside her throne is Corporal Eliar, and he works for me. When he tells you something, he's speaking for me, so don't argue with him. I've laid out this campaign in great detail, and I'm bringing in armies from places you've probably never even heard of. I know exactly what I'm doing, and I don't need any advice—or interference—from amateurs. First, I'm going to annihilate the invading armies, and then I'm going to go destroy the city of Kanthon. This *will* be the last war in Treborea, gentlemen, so enjoy it while you can, and let's concentrate on doing it right."

Then Khalor rubbed his thumb along the edge of the battle-ax. "Nicked it a little," he noted. He looked at the sentry standing at the door to the throne room. "I'm sorry I dented your ax, soldier," he apologized. "I thank you for the use of it, and use lots of water on the grindstone when you're polishing the nick out of the blade."

"Yes, my Sergeant!" the soldier barked, snapping to attention.

"You gentlemen are lucky to have people like that boy in your army," he told the Generals. Then he shifted his grip on the ax handle. "Here, soldier, catch!" he called to the sentry. Then he swung his arm back and sent the ax spinning over the heads of the cringing Generals, and the sentry expertly snared the whirling weapon out of the air.

"Nice catch," Khalor called.

The sentry grinned at him and resumed his post beside the door.

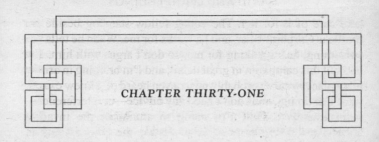

CHAPTER THIRTY-ONE

After the shaken Generals had been dismissed, Andine led the way to her private quarters. "If you'll all excuse me for a moment," she said to them, "I've *got* to get out of this." She plucked at the front of her royal robe. "I'm starting to melt all over the floor. Brocade's attractive, I suppose, but it's *not* meant for summer."

The rest of them sat down in comfortable chairs in the Arya's sitting room. "Your approach to the Generals might have been a trifle abrupt, Sergeant Khalor," Lord Dhakan observed, "but it definitely got your point across to them."

"I'm glad you liked it, my Lord," Khalor replied with a broad grin.

"You wouldn't really have slaughtered them all, would you?"

"Oh, probably not," Khalor admitted, "but *they* didn't know that, did they?"

"Growing up in a warrior culture must be very exciting."

"It has its high points, my Lord. The difficult part is living long enough to grow up. A young fellow whose beard's just starting to sprout tends to boast a lot, and sooner or later he's going to have to back up his boasting. That usually involves fights, and it's not a good idea to let little boys start fighting with all those swords and axes lying around." Khalor squinted at Althalus. "I think I'd better talk with your wife, Althalus."

"I didn't know you were married, Lord Althalus," Lord Dhakan said with some surprise.

"She's a homebody." Althalus shrugged it off.

"You have a house somewhere?"

"It's her House, actually. It's just a nice, cozy little place that we like to call home."

Emmy the cat came padding across the floor and stopped in front of Sergeant Khalor's chair. She looked up at him with her intense green eyes and meowed inquiringly.

"Don't do that, Em," Althalus scolded her.

She gave him a cold look, laying her ears back.

"That is the *strangest* cat," Khalor said.

"We all owe her a great deal, Sergeant," Dhakan said. "She actually saved young Eliar's life a year or so ago."

Andine returned wearing a filmy, sleeveless smock. She sat down and patted her lap. "Come here, Emmy," she said fondly.

Emmy gave Althalus a superior sort of look that spoke volumes and then went immediately to Andine.

"Good kitty," Andine said warmly. Then she looked at Sergeant Khalor. "What next?" she asked him.

"I need to take a look at the invaders, little lady," he replied. "I can recognize most of the armies of the world on sight, and every army has its peculiarities. Getting to know the enemy's very important when you're fighting a war. I know Gelta quite well after that war in Wekti, but I'd like to have a look at her soldiers before I make too many more decisions."

"Won't that be sort of dangerous?" Dhakan asked. "You're much too valuable a man to have running around in plain sight of the enemy."

"I know of a way to observe without being seen, my Lord," Khalor replied. "It's a procedure that's either very new or so old that the rest of mankind's forgotten it. Althalus' wife introduced us to it back in Wekti. That's why I need to talk with her—fairly soon, I think."

Where's Gher? Eliar asked silently when they returned to the tower.

He's playing, Leitha's voice replied, speaking—it seemed—inside Althalus' head.

"Do you have to do that?" Althalus asked them. "Can't you keep these little discussions to yourselves?"

Eliar's new at this, pet, Dweia murmured. *If I remember correctly, it took you quite a while to learn not to shout.*

What's Gher up to now? Eliar asked a bit more quietly.

He's off in the east corridor, Leitha replied, *with Sergeant Gebhel's men. Salkan's teaching him how to use a sling.*

"It was my suggestion, Althalus," Bheid admitted. "Gher and Salkan are off by themselves. I thought that might be the smoothest way to bring Salkan here to this part of the House."

"I'll need to use your windows, ma'am," Khalor told Dweia. "Arya Andine's Generals are just a bit vague about the composition of the invading army, so I'd better have a look at them for myself."

"Of course, Sergeant," Dweia agreed.

Khalor glanced around quickly. "You haven't left my Chief and Kreuter's niece alone, have you?" he asked.

"They're taking another little nap, Sergeant."

Why don't you go fetch Gher and Salkan, Eliar? Althalus suggested silently. *If we're going to break Salkan to harness, we might as well get started.*

Go with him, pet, Dweia murmured.

Me? Why?

Let's keep Gher from revealing too much right at first. We want to ease Salkan into his harness. Gher tends to rush things now and then.

Good point, Em, Althalus agreed.

"That's what it's really all about, Gher," Salkan was saying as Eliar and Althalus approached them in the east corridor of the House. "Any fool can whirl a sling around in the air over his head. Knowing exactly when to let go is the key. Your eye and hand have to work together."

"It's a lot more complicated than it looks, isn't it?" Gher said.

"Ah, there you are, Gher," Althalus said. "We've been looking all over for you."

"Is something wrong?" Gher asked.

"No, not really. Emmy says that since you're so close to her

House, you might as well pay her a visit. You might want to come along, too, Salkan."

"I didn't know there were any houses up here in the mountains," Salkan said.

"We sort of like to keep it that way, Salkan," Eliar told the young redhead. "Emmy likes her privacy."

Salkan looked around. "I don't even see any roads or paths," he said.

"We try not to leave tracks," Althalus told him. "Emmy's House is fairly splendid, and there *are* bandits up here in the mountains." He turned and gestured at the corridor behind him. "The House is over on the far side of that little notch in this ridge. It's almost suppertime anyway, and Emmy can cook much better than Sergeant Gebhel's field cooks can. Let's go have a decent meal, shall we?"

"There's quite a bit more involved in fighting a war than swords and arrows and slings, Salkan," Sergeant Khalor told the young Wekti as they were all finishing up a supper of near-banquet proportions. He tapped his forehead. "The really important part of a war goes on in here. You have to think faster than your enemy does."

"I'm not really a soldier, General Khalor," Salkan replied. "I lose my temper now and then, but mostly I just take care of my sheep."

"I think you underestimate yourself, lad," Chief Albron told him. "You mobilized the closest thing Wekti has to an army in a very short period of time, and your boys made a large contribution to our success."

"Like it or not, Salkan," Althalus told the young redhead, "you *do* command troops, so I think maybe you'd better stay here for a while and get a few pointers from Khalor."

"If you say so, Master Althalus," Salkan agreed. "After we finish with supper, maybe Eliar can take me back to General Gebhel's camp so I can pick up my things and have a talk with my friends."

"We'll take care of it, Salkan," Eliar said.

That was slick, Dweia murmured to Althalus.

Not really, Em. Young Salkan's eager to please people, so he'll usually go along—if you give him a fairly sound reason. Now that he's here in the House, everybody's going to have access to him—*Bheid, Khalor, you, Gher, and maybe even me. We'll convert him to* something *before the summer's out.*

The skies over central Treborea were obscured by smoke from the burning crops the following morning, and the roads were choked with fleeing peasants. Sergeant Khalor's face was bleak as he surveyed the devastation from the window. "I think I'm getting a little too old for this," he muttered, half to himself.

"You didn't invent war, Sergeant," Dweia told him, her face pensive. "Can you see well enough from this height?"

Khalor looked down at the burning fields below. "Let's go a little farther north before we drop down a bit," he suggested. "There are probably things going on down there that I'd rather not see in too much detail."

"Truly," she agreed.

There was no sense of movement in the tower, but the view from the south window was constantly changing.

"Could we go a little lower here, ma'am?" Khalor asked Dweia. "I'd like to get a closer look at those soldiers."

"Of course, Sergeant."

Althalus joined them at the window.

"Their infantry units seem to be mostly Kwerons and Regwos," Khalor observed. "I see a few Kagwhers, but not too many."

"What about those horsemen?" Althalus asked him.

"They're mostly cattlemen from the borderland between Perquaine and Regwos," Khalor replied. "They ride horses well enough, but I'd hardly call them cavalry of the first order. Kreuter's Plakands won't have much trouble with them. There *are* some people mixed up with the rest of them that I can't really identify, though. Who are the ones in that black armor who seem to be giving the orders?"

"Those are Nekweros, Sergeant," Dweia replied. "Ghend likes to have his own officers in charge of the mercenaries."

"I don't believe I've ever seen a Nekweros before."

"You've been lucky, then."

"Do they paint their armor to make it black like that?"

"Not really. It has to do with the way it's forged—and the place *where* it's forged. Those particular people aren't entirely human, Sergeant, and their armor's not so much to protect them as it is to hide their real appearance. You don't really want to see them."

Eliar and Gher came up the stairs from the dining room to join them in the tower. "The ladies are talking about clothes again," Gher reported, "and Bheid and Salkan are talking about sheep. Eliar and I didn't find anything exciting about what any of them were saying, so we came up here to see how the war was going."

"What's my Chief doing?" Khalor asked.

"The same thing he's been doing for the past few days, Sergeant," Eliar replied. "He's sitting there looking at Lady Astarell." Then Eliar blinked and put his hand to the hilt of the Knife. "Is that Treborea down there?" he asked, coming to the window.

"Yes," Althalus replied. "Your Sergeant wanted to have a look at the enemy troops."

"Ghend's down there somewhere!" Eliar said sharply. "The Knife almost jumped out from under my belt just now."

"Can you locate him?" Khalor demanded.

"That burned-out village off to the east, I think."

The ground blurred beneath them slightly, and Althalus felt a slight giddiness as his eyes told him that he was moving and the rest of his body insisted that he wasn't.

"There he is," Eliar whispered, pointing at two figures standing near the still-smoldering remains of a peasant house.

"Who's that with him?" Khalor asked quietly.

"Argan," Dweia replied shortly.

"The defrocked priest?" Eliar asked.

"Yes. Ghend doesn't really like Argan very much. Argan's overly civilized, and when you get to the bottom of things,

Ghend's a barbarian. Argan's also ambitious, and he seems to believe that his blond hair is a sign of some sort of racial superiority. That's what got him expelled from the priesthood."

"I need to hear them, ma'am," Khalor said urgently.

She nodded, and Ghend's voice became audible. "I don't care *how* you find them, Argan," he snarled, "but get to them and tell them to order their soldiers to stop burning the fields. They'll starve my army if they don't quit."

"Didn't the notion of bringing supplies along ever occur to Gelta and the other mercenaries?" Argan asked.

"They're primitives, and primitives graze off the land like cattle."

"Gelta *does* rather resemble a cow, doesn't she?" Argan noted. "And she even smells like one. I'll go order Smeugor and Tauri to stop the burning, but I don't think it'll do much good."

"What are you talking about?"

"You really ought to pay more attention to the hired help, old boy. You wasted a lot of good gold on those two. They have titles, but no real authority. Their army commanders are the ones making the decisions."

"Then order them to get off their backsides and take personal command. I want those fires stopped."

"I'll tell them what you said, old boy—if you think it's going to do any good. I think you're wrong, but that's between you and the master, isn't it?"

"Are you keeping in touch with Yakhag?" Ghend demanded.

"Naturally, old boy. I've got him well trained. Yakhag doesn't scratch his nose without my permission."

"Tell him to keep a tight leash on the Nekweros. I *don't* want Althalus finding out about them until much later."

"I *do* know what I'm doing, Ghend."

"Are you making any progress in Osthos?"

"Some. *Our* brand of religion has a certain appeal among assorted aristocrats. The word 'humility' doesn't sit too well with the highborn, and that works out quite well for us."

"Stay on top of those fools, Argan," Ghend told him, "but go wake up Smeugor and Tauri first."

"At once, great leader," Argan replied with a mocking bow.

"Is there some way that we can kill Argan before he has a chance to meet with Smeugor and Tauri?" Khalor asked Dweia.

"No, Sergeant. Argan has some other things to do farther on down the line, so let's keep him alive."

"We've *got* to prevent that meeting," Khalor insisted. "If those two turncoats take personal command, the fires are going to go out, and it's the lack of food that's holding back the invaders."

"Excuse me," Gher said tentatively.

"Go ahead, boy," Khalor said.

"Why not just keep Smeugor and what's-his-name in some room here in the House? That priest fellow couldn't get near them, could he?"

"It's a thought, Khalor," Althalus said.

"Indeed it is, but I'm not sure exactly how we'd explain it to Wendan and Gelun."

"Why not just tell everybody that the Argan fellow's a hired killer?" Gher suggested. "Sort of tell them that burning all the wheat fields is making Gelta real mad, and she's paid Argan to find Smeugor and what's-his-name and cut their throats. That'd scare those two right out of their shoes, and they'd start looking for someplace to hide. Then we find some real strong fort, you see—way up on top of some hill. Then we tell them they'll be safe there—lots of guards around to keep Argan from getting to them and all that. But even though they *think* they're in that fort, they really aren't. They're here in the House instead. The guards are going to think that Argan's trying to get in so that he can kill them, so they'll be on the lookout for him—and *he's* going to think that they're hiding in the fort to keep Ghend from killing them for burning all that wheat and stuff. Wouldn't that sort of work?"

"Since you won't sell this boy to me, Althalus, what if I adopt him instead?" Khalor said just a bit plaintively.

"No, Sergeant," Dweia said, gathering Gher in her arms possessively. "He's *mine*, and he's going to *stay* mine."

"Did I do good, Emmy?" Gher asked her.

"You did just fine, Gher," she assured him, nestling her cheek against his tousled hair.

"*Let* him," Gelun said flatly. "I'll even lend him my knife if he wants to kill them *that* much."

"Not right in the middle of a war, Gelun," the tall Captain Wendan objected. "Everything'd get all tangled up in arguments about succession. I'll grant you that our clansmen would be a lot happier without Smeugor and Tauri, but we can attend to that *after* the war."

"Am I starting to hear rumblings of mutiny here?" Althalus asked slyly.

"Rumble-rumble-rumble," Gelun said sourly. "Satisfied? But Wendan's right. Much as I'd like to attend a couple of state funerals right now, this isn't the time or the place."

"Khalor's located a safe place for your Chieftains, gentlemen," Althalus told them. "It's an old abandoned fortress that dates back several hundred years. There's always been trouble along this frontier, so there are lots of fortified ruins around. This particular one's fairly intimidating, so a company of guards ought to be able to keep the hired killer out. You might have to repair the roof a bit, but otherwise it's not too bad."

"With stout walls and a lot of guards about, it's almost like a prison, isn't it?" Wendan mused. "It'll *seem* to be a place designed to keep the assassin *out*, but it might really be a place to keep Smeugor and Tauri *in*."

"And maybe we could sort of forget where we put them when the time comes for us to go home," Gelun added.

"My memory for details *has* been slipping a little here lately," Wendan said with a slight smirk.

"That's to be expected, Captain Wendan," Althalus said. "You've got a lot on your mind right now. Keep those welcoming fires burning, gentlemen. After the invaders have eaten all their horses, they'll probably start on their shoes, and barefoot men don't march very fast. Circulate that drawing of the assassin so that all your men know what he looks like. If you should get lucky and kill him, though, I don't know that you'd need to tell Smeugor and Tauri about it."

"They're important men with important things on their minds, Althalus," Wendan said piously. "We wouldn't *dream* of bothering them with picky little details like that."

"You're the very soul of courtesy, Captain Wendan," Althalus said with an extravagant bow. "I'll keep in touch, gentlemen. You have a nice war now, you hear?"

"They're starting to get a little desperate," Sergeant Khalor observed from his post at the south window of the tower. "There's nothing to eat out in the countryside. If they don't take a city— soon—they'll starve to death. I think we'd better get Laiwon and his clan inside the walls of Kadon. See to it, Eliar."

"Yes, my Sergeant," Eliar replied with a smart salute.

"I'll go with him," Althalus said. "Chief Laiwon and Duke Olkar look at the world differently, and there might be a little friction between them."

"A *little*?" Andine murmured. "I don't think Laiwon has the faintest notion of the meaning of the word 'diplomacy,' does he?"

"He *is* a bit blunt," Khalor conceded.

"I'll keep him in line," Althalus assured them. "Let's go get him, Eliar."

"Right," the young man agreed. "His clan's in the southwest wing of the House."

"How are you and Andine getting along?" Althalus asked his young friend as they went down the stairs.

Eliar rolled his eyes upward. "Remember how I used to be hungry all the time?"

Althalus laughed. "Oh, yes. I was almost afraid to take you into a forest, because I was sure that if I happened to doze off, I'd wake up and find that you'd eaten most of the trees."

"I wasn't quite *that* bad," Eliar objected.

"You were close," Althalus disagreed.

"Andine's pretty much cured me of that. Sometimes just the sight of food makes me sick. Every time I turn around, it seems, she's standing there with food in her hand, ready to poke it in my mouth."

"She loves you, Eliar," Althalus said, "and in the minds of some women—and all birds—food is love."

"Maybe, but sometimes I wish she'd find some other way to demonstrate her affection."

"I'm almost sure she will, Eliar, but Dweia's sort of keeping a lid on that for the time being. I think that when that lid comes off, you'd better watch out."

Eliar's face turned red. "Do you suppose we could talk about something else?" he asked.

"Of course, Eliar," Althalus replied with an amused look. "The weather, maybe?"

They went along the dim hallway toward the southwest wing of the House and found Laiwon's clan plodding along the corridor with that now-familiar vacant look on their faces. "They believe they're in the foothills of southern Kagwher," Eliar quietly told Althalus. "Emmy told me when we first started this how to get people's minds ready before I jump them from one place to another. I'm not sure how she does it, but when I tell them that something's already happened, she fixes it so that they remember it as if they'd actually lived through it. She made a big fuss about the names of places. She told me to always say the name. As soon as I do that, they see it, and they remember walking for a month or two to get there."

"I had a feeling it might be something like that. So she really came down hard on the point of saying the names of places, eh?"

"She went on and on about it. I guess that if I don't say the name of the place, the people I'm taking there won't even see it."

"Words are very important to the Gods, I guess. Isn't that Laiwon's clan up ahead?"

Eliar peered down the corridor. "They've got Laiwon's plaid on their kilts, right enough. You've got to be a little careful about that. Laiwon's pattern's very close to Twengor's, and we probably wouldn't want to make a mistake and put Twengor inside the walls of Kadon."

"You've got that right," Althalus agreed. "Sergeant Khalor'd jump all over you, and Dweia would probably talk to *me* about it for months on end."

They were intercepted by kilted clansmen not long after that, and after a brief discussion, they were taken to Chief Laiwon. "What are *you* doing here, Chamberlain Althalus?" Laiwon demanded.

"Looking for you, actually," Althalus replied.

"We've found you now, though," Eliar stepped in rather quickly. "You made better time than we thought you would. The city of Kadon's just over that next hill, and since you're the closest to it, Sergeant Khalor wants you to reinforce the garrison there. The invaders are just a couple of days away, and they're certain to lay siege to the place. Did you encounter any trouble on your way here from Kagwher?"

"Nothing significant," Laiwon replied with a shrug. "The Kanthons seem to be concentrating on their invasion. We sort of tiptoed through their territory. How's the war going? I've been a bit out of touch."

"The invaders are a little gaunt," Althalus told him. "The clans of Smeugor and Tauri have set fire to the fields, so there isn't much for the invaders to eat."

"I wouldn't have thought Smeugor and Tauri have enough brains to come up with that."

"They don't, really. Their troop commanders took care of it."

"I should have known. How good are the walls of this Kadon place?"

"Better than they were before Sergeant Khalor made a few suggestions," Eliar replied.

"That's Khalor for you," Laiwon said drily. "I take it that he wants me to just sit out this siege?"

"Right," Althalus told him. "As long as you hold Kadon, you'll keep a third of the invading army tied up."

"Rather boring," Laiwon observed.

"You're getting paid to be bored, Chief Laiwon."

"Where are you going to put my uncle?"

"There's a town called Poma a ways off to the east," Althalus replied. "The walls of Poma are a joke, so the invaders won't have much trouble getting in. Khalor thought that your uncle Twengor might enjoy a bit of house-to-house fighting."

Laiwon sighed. "He gets all the fun," he said mournfully.

Althalus went on ahead to advise Duke Olkar of Laiwon's approach, and the sober businessman seemed a bit apprehensive. "They won't tear down my town, will they?" he asked.

"I doubt it," Althalus assured him. "They might break a few windows and smash up the furniture in a few taverns, but they probably won't burn down *too* many buildings."

Duke Olkar stared at him in horror.

"Only joking, your Grace." Althalus chuckled. "Chief Laiwon keeps a fairly tight grip on his clansmen. Keep track of the damages and send me a bill when the war's over."

Olkar's expression turned shrewd at that.

"An *accurate* bill, your Grace," Althalus told him quite firmly. "Don't get creative on me. I'll want to see the pieces of every broken dish. You're not going to get away with trying to bamboozle me, Duke Olkar, so don't even try. Now, why don't we go to your front gate and welcome the brave defenders of your beautiful city?"

Duke Olkar and Chief Laiwon didn't hit it off very well, and Althalus was forced to concede that some of that might have been his fault. For one thing, he'd neglected to mention the kilts, and Duke Olkar's reaction to the traditional Arum costume was quite audible. "They're wearing *dresses*!" had echoed off the walls of Kadon when Duke Olkar first laid eyes on the approaching army. That definitely didn't get things off to a good start. Chief Laiwon's face was like a thundercloud as he approached the city gate, and Althalus was forced to talk very fast to prevent bloodshed.

Then there was the smoke. The prevailing winds for the past several weeks had streamed from west to east, carrying the smoke from the burning crops away from the city of Kadon, but the winds had died down during the night, and as Chief Laiwon's clan approached the city, tall columns of dense smoke mounted behind them toward the very heavens.

"What's burning out there?" Duke Olkar demanded suspiciously.

"Wheat fields, I'd imagine," Laiwon replied indifferently.

"Are you *mad*?" Olkar almost screamed.

"It's possible," Laiwon replied. "If I'd been in my right mind, I'd never have accepted this job in the first place. That's part of what wars are all about. I thought everybody knew that. You're being invaded, city man, and there are a couple of clans out there delaying the invaders. Setting fire to croplands is standard practice in situations like this. Most armies prefer not to march through fire, but that's not really why we do it."

"You people are burning *millions*!"

Laiwon shrugged. "What difference does it make? That's enemy territory now, so you wouldn't be able to harvest the wheat anyway. You lost that harvest as soon as they invaded. It's theirs now, and they'd probably planned to feed their army with it. They won't be able to do that now, so they'll be on very short rations. Every enemy soldier who starves to death is one less that we have to kill when they attack your city. Did you actually believe they'd let you harvest this year's crop?"

"But it's *mine*," Olkar protested. "I paid for it already."

"You could try to take them to court, I suppose," Laiwon replied with an amused look. "You'd need a few hundred thousand bailiffs to drag them before a judge, though. We have other fish to fry right now. Where do you want me to billet my men?"

"There are some empty warehouses over on the far side of town—down by the lakeshore," Olkar replied. "They should be good enough for your people. I don't want you disrupting things in the main part of the city, though, so go around to the back gate."

"*That* does it!" Laiwon said abruptly. "I'll take my pay right here and now, Althalus, and we'll call it quits. I don't go in through *anybody's* back gate!" He turned to face his kilted clansmen. "We're finished here, brothers," he bellowed. "Let's turn around and go back home to Arum!"

"You can't do that!" Olkar protested.

"I don't like your attitude, little man. Defend your own stinking city."

It took Althalus a good hour to clear up *that* little misunderstanding, and he had to lean on Duke Olkar quite heavily in the process. Olkar stalked off in a huff, and Chief Laiwon spat on the place where the stuffy Treborean had stood. "Lock him up in his palace if you have to, Althalus," the Chief insisted, "but keep that self-important jackass away from me, or I'll kill him. Now let's go have a look at the walls. I'll probably have to add a few modifications."

"It shall be as you command, Chief Laiwon," Althalus replied, bowing.

"Oh, stop that!" Laiwon told him irritably.

"Your Captains have spies out, gentlemen," Althalus told Smeugor and Tauri, "and their spies have picked up some strong hints that the invaders are plotting to have the two of you murdered. This fort will protect you."

"Murdered?" the pimple-faced Smeugor exclaimed.

"It's not uncommon during a war, Chief Smeugor," Althalus replied blandly. "You might even look upon it as a compliment. If your enemy hates you so much that he wants to murder you, it's a sure sign that you're doing *something* right."

"We haven't really done all that much," Tauri protested.

"Nothing all that much out of the ordinary," Althalus conceded. "I suppose it's because your people are doing their job very well."

"Exactly what *are* Wendan and Gelun doing?" Smeugor demanded.

Althalus shrugged. "The invasion started in the late summer, and that's not really a coincidence, you understand. The wheat fields are ripe now, and the Aryo of Kanthon's mercenaries were planning to live off the land while they marched south. Wendan and Gelun have arranged things so that there's nothing out there to eat—except for maybe the dirt itself. They set fire to the wheat fields and the pastures. There's nothing to eat for men or horses for fifty miles in any direction. The invaders and their horses are quietly starving to death."

"We didn't order that!" Tauri exclaimed, his face going suddenly pale.

"You didn't have to order it, Chief Tauri. It's common practice. The word 'delay' usually means 'burn.' I thought you knew that."

"I've never heard of such a thing! Go tell Wendan and Gelun to stop that immediately!"

"Oh? Why would I want to do that? It's working, Tauri. It's slowing the invaders and giving our armies time to get ready. Your men are doing exactly what I'm paying you two to take care of."

"But . . . but . . ." Tauri tried to protest.

Then Smeugor jabbed him sharply in the ribs with his elbow. "We're pleased that our men are doing so well," he said—just a bit unconvincingly.

"I'd stay away from that window, gentlemen," Althalus cautioned. "Some archer out there might get in a lucky shot." He reached inside his tunic and took out a piece of paper. "One of our spies out there's fairly talented," he said. "This is a drawing of the fellow who's been hired to murder you. Your guards here in this fort have copies of the drawing, so they know who to look for. You're safe here, but I wouldn't go outside very much. Now, if you'll excuse me, I've got a million things to do today."

"Did it work, Master Althalus?" Gher asked eagerly when Althalus returned to the tower from the room where Smeugor and Tauri were imprisoned.

"Slicker than a fresh-caught eel, Gher." Althalus chuckled. "They both recognized that drawing of Argan, and they know that he's probably bringing them a message from Ghend. Our little fiction that Argan's an assassin fully justifies locking them up for their own protection, so they can't object without arousing suspicion. To make it even worse for them, they know that if they don't explain to Ghend that burning the wheat fields wasn't *their* idea, he probably *will* send somebody to kill them. I'd guess that right now they don't know which way to turn."

"I'll bet that's making them crazy." Gher smirked.

"It's sending them right up the wall. We could probably just go ahead and tell them that we've found out that they're working for Ghend and that we've locked them up for it."

"That'd spoil it, Master Althalus. Isn't it a lot funner to just keep them in the dark?"

"It is indeed, Gher—much, much funner." Althalus looked across the tower room. "What are the ladies up to over there?"

"Emmy's teaching Andine how to playact," Gher explained. "It's got something to do with that dream we all had when the bad lady was standing on Andine's neck. Andine got *real* mad when Leitha told her that a couple of her Generals were working for Ghend. She was going to have them taken out and skun alive."

"Skun?"

"Have all their skin peeled off, I guess. But Emmy told her no. Emmy wants her to pretend to be kind of wishy-washy—sort of young and timid, scared of her own shadow and like that."

"Andine? Timid?"

"She's not very good at it yet," Gher admitted. "She's having a lot of trouble with her voice. Emmy wants her to sound sort of weepy and scared, but Andine can't quite seem to get the hang of it. She keeps trying to knock the glass out of the windows with her voice. She's awful cute when she gets mad, isn't she?"

"That sort of depends on where you're standing, Gher," Althalus said. "If you happen to be standing right in front of her when she unleashes that voice, 'cute' isn't the first word that's going to pop into your mind."

"I think you're probably right about that. She's yelled at me a few times, and I didn't really like it a whole lot."

"Where's Chief Albron?"

"He's downstairs with the horse lady. She's teaching him some of the tricks the horse soldiers use when they fight wars. I don't think he's learning very much, though. He likes to look at her for some reason I haven't quite figured out yet, and he's so busy looking that I don't think he's listening too good."

"Probably not, no."

"It's some more of that boy-people and girl-people stuff, isn't it?" Gher asked. "I really wish they wouldn't do that when I'm around. It always makes me real jumpy. Most of the time I don't know *what* they're going to do next."

Althalus scratched his cheek thoughtfully. "I think we're getting quite a bit closer to having an important little talk, Gher."

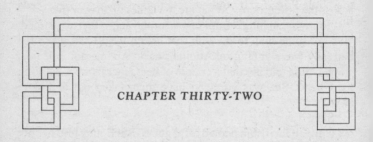

CHAPTER THIRTY-TWO

I just can't do this! Andine's silent voice echoed through their minds. *I won't bow down to that pockmarked hag, no matter what she does to me.*

It's not working, Em, Althalus murmured in a deeper, more private part of their shared awareness. *Why don't you let me deal with it?*

Why can't she just do as she's told? Dweia flared.

I'll take care of it, little kitten. Go wash your face or something. You're very good at sneaking, but this is a little more complicated. Then he stopped. *Stay out of here, Leitha,* he added.

Leitha, who was sitting at the marble table leafing through the Book, gave him a look of wide-eyed innocence.

I mean it, Leitha, Althalus chided. *Don't come in here unless you've been invited.* Then he looked at Andine, who was still fuming near the north window of the tower. "Let's talk a bit," he said to her, speaking aloud.

"It's not going to do you any good, Althalus," she flared, speaking aloud. "I *won't* do this!"

"Why not?"

"I'm the Arya of Osthos, and Gelta's nothing more than an animal."

"Wouldn't that suggest that you're more clever than she is?"

"Of course I am."

"It doesn't show very much right now, Andine."

"What's that supposed to mean?"

"When you're setting a trap for an animal, you have to bait the trap, little Princess. If you're trying to trap a bird, you use seeds for bait. If you're after a wolf or a bear, meat works fairly well. Gelta's a different sort of animal, so you'll have to use a different bait. We *do* want to have baked Gelta for supper, don't we?"

"That's disgusting, Althalus!"

"I was speaking figuratively, Andine. You'd need a lot of spice to make Gelta edible. The bait we're going to use to trap her has to be so alluring that she won't be able to resist it. That's your job. Be irresistible, Andine. Be soft and tender and delicious—right up until she touches you. *That's* when we spring the trap and send her off to the bake oven."

Andine's eyes narrowed as she considered that. "On one condition, Althalus," she countered.

"Oh?"

"I get her heart."

"Andine!" Leitha gasped. "You're even worse than Gelta!"

"Figuratively speaking, of course," Andine amended.

She'll be just fine, Althalus, Dweia murmured. *Don't change a thing.*

"Why?" Salkan demanded of Bheid, continuing a discussion that had obviously been going on for most of the morning as Althalus came by the dining room looking for Eliar.

"That's the way it's always been," Bheid told the young shepherd.

"That doesn't mean that it's right, Brother Bheid," Salkan declared. "If somebody wants to talk with God, he should be able to do it anytime or anyplace he wants to. He shouldn't have to go to a temple and pay some greedy priest to carry his messages for him. I'm not trying to insult you, Brother Bheid, but from what

I've seen, the priests are more interested in money than they are in God—or in the well-being of the people."

"I think he's got you there, Bheid," Eliar said. "Priests always seem to have their hands out for money."

"Not the *real* priests," Bheid objected.

"Maybe not," Salkan conceded, "but how can you tell the *real* priests from the false ones? They all wear the same clothes, don't they? I'll stick to taking care of my sheep. I don't think I'd make a very good priest. I've never learned how to cheat."

I wouldn't push it, Bheid, Althalus suggested silently. *Salkan's not ready yet—and neither are you.*

What's that supposed to mean? Bheid demanded.

Your theological position changed quite a bit last summer, as I recall. I think you'd better have a long talk with Emmy before you dash out to start converting the heathens. Then Althalus looked across the table at Eliar. "Your Sergeant needs us, Eliar," he said, speaking aloud.

"All right," Eliar agreed, standing up and coming around the table.

"What's Bheid up to in there?" Althalus asked once they were out in the hall.

"I'm not really sure," Eliar admitted. "His thinking's sort of scrambled right now. Emmy left a big hole in his mind when she told him that astrology's pure nonsense, and things got a lot worse for him when Leitha dragged him into the family."

"That 'family' notion might have been a mistake," Althalus conceded.

"It's fairly accurate, though. I didn't really think it was such a good idea at first, but after Leitha, Andine, and I got back to the House, I started getting more comfortable with it."

"You've changed a bit since you got swallowed up, Eliar."

"Didn't *you* change after Emmy swallowed you?"

"I suppose I did at that. It takes some getting used to, doesn't it?"

"Oh, yes," Eliar said fervently. "You had it easy, Althalus. The only one *you* had to deal with right at first was Emmy. I had *three* of them crawling around inside my head." He changed the subject. "Just exactly what is it that Sergeant Khalor needs me for?"

"He wants to talk with Kreuter and Dreigon, and he isn't sure just exactly which part of the House they're wandering through. You don't need to make an issue of this, Eliar, but I think the House still makes your Sergeant a little uncomfortable. Your doors are fine—as long as *you're* the one who opens them. I don't think Khalor wants to take any chances. He got a quick glimpse of Nahgharash when Gelta ran up behind you with her ax, and he'd *really* rather not make a mistake and open *that* particular door."

"They believe that they're camped on the west shore of Lake Daso in Equero," Althalus told Sergeant Khalor as Eliar led them along the east corridor toward a fairly extensive encampment. "We probably shouldn't say anything that disagrees with that. Let's not confuse them."

"*I'm* fairly confused," Khalor said. "Why should *they* be any different?" Then he smiled. "Sorry, Althalus. I couldn't resist that one."

They met with Kreuter and the kilted Dreigon in a canvas tent in the center of the corridor, and Khalor handed over the map he'd carefully prepared for them.

"You draw good maps, Khalor," the silver-haired Dreigon noted. "Are these distances close?"

Khalor nodded. "As close as I could get them. The map I was working from wasn't *too* accurate, so I had to make a few corrections."

"Can those three cities hold out?" Kreuter asked.

"Kadon's good for probably three months," Khalor replied. "Laiwon's holding that one, and he knows how to make things expensive for besiegers."

"That he does," Dreigon agreed.

"I'm going to put Koleika Iron Jaw in Mawor," Khalor continued. "The Duke of Mawor evidently decided to make his city stand out as the best-fortified place in the world. The houses inside are a little shoddy, but you wouldn't want to take a run at those walls. I think the combination of walls like that and

Koleika, the most stubborn man in the world, should stop the invaders dead in their tracks."

"What about that other city—Poma?" Kreuter asked.

"That's where we've got a problem," Khalor admitted. "A light spring breeze would probably tumble the walls of Poma. I'm going to put Twengor there. I'm positive that there's going to be house-to-house fighting in Poma, and Twengor's very good at that sort of thing."

"If he's sober," Dreigon added.

"Does this Twengor have problems with drink?" Kreuter asked.

"No, not really," Dreigon replied. "He can usually polish off a barrel of good ale before lunchtime. Of course, he can't stand up in the afternoon, but he doesn't see *that* as a problem. He has a tendency to wreck every town he enters, though. He's as big as a house himself, and he bumps into things when he walks. Usually, whatever he bumps into falls down."

"I *hate* working with a drunkard," Kreuter said.

"I'll sober him up," Althalus promised.

"I don't know," Kreuter said dubiously. "I've never known a confirmed drunk who was able to put it aside."

"Trust me on this one, General Kreuter," Althalus said.

"How's Astarell?" Kreuter asked Sergeant Khalor.

"Oh, she's doing just fine, Kreuter. My Chief's absolutely smitten with her."

"Really? *That's* something we might want to think about. I suppose I *could* just go ahead and kill her rascally brother and the old fool who tried to buy her, but that'd probably start wars all over Plakand. Maybe I should talk with her and see how *she* feels about the idea. Your Chief *is* a handsome sort of devil, and maybe she has feelings for him as well. Let's keep it in mind, Khalor. It might just solve a lot of our problems."

"My thought exactly, Kreuter. If I can get my Chief married off, maybe he'll stay home and get out of my hair."

Chief Twengor was roaring drunk when Althalus and Khalor came down the north corridor of the House the following morning. The burly Arum Clan Chief was sprawled out in a massive chair at the head of a long plank-and-trestle table in the center of his encampment with an open ale keg in front of him, and he was singing—sort of.

"It'll take us all day to sober him up," Khalor muttered to Althalus as they were escorted into the drunken man's presence.

"Maybe not," Althalus disagreed, rummaging back through his education.

"Ho, Khalor!" Twengor bellowed, waving his drinking horn. "Sit you down and get started! You've got some catching up to do!"

"You've got quite a big head start, Chief Twengor," Khalor agreed.

"I should have." Twengor chortled. "I've been working on this one for three days now."

That was useful. If it had taken Twengor three days to drink himself into his present condition, it might be quicker to take him on out through the far end than it'd be to turn him around and take him back. Althalus looked at Twengor's beet-red face and muttered *"egwrio"* under his breath.

Chief Twengor's eyes rolled back in his head, and he slid limply out of his chair. His snores began to rumble under the table.

"I think our Chief just outran you altogether, Khalor!" one of Twengor's sub-Chiefs declared, roaring with drunken laughter.

Althalus expanded the idea—and the ancient word—that had just struck down the vast-bearded Twengor, and a sudden silence, punctuated only by snores, fell over the encampment in the north corridor.

"What did you just do?" Khalor demanded.

Althalus shrugged. "I think it's called 'speeding things up,' " he replied. "They were all wandering off in this direction anyway, but it might have taken them the rest of the day to get where they are now."

"It'll still take them a day or so to sleep it off," Khalor pointed out.

"No, not really," Althalus disagreed. He turned to look back along the corridor. "You can come on in now, Eliar," he called.

The blond young fellow joined them. He waved one hand in front of his face. "They don't smell too good, do they?" he said.

"Take shallow breaths," Althalus suggested. "Which door would put us on the road right outside Poma?"

Eliar pointed to a nearby door. "That one right there."

"Go ahead and open it. I'll start these men moving."

"They're all asleep, Althalus."

"You and I know that, Eliar, but *they* don't."

"That doesn't make any sense at all, Althalus," Khalor protested.

"It will in a minute, I think." Althalus squinted at Eliar. "I'm going to need the door to last week as well as the door to the Poma road," he said.

"Last week?" Eliar asked in a puzzled tone.

"Time's the only thing that'll sober a drunk man up, so I'll need a week at least. I'm going to start our sodden friends here to walking in their sleep. Then I want you to lead them into last week and back. *Then* we'll take them through the Poma road door."

"Wouldn't it be simpler to just make it the same door?"

"Can you *do* that?" Althalus was startled.

"I think so," Eliar said. He put his hand on the hilt of the Knife and concentrated. "Yes," he said confidently. "*Now* I remember how to do it. It's the door frame. I always have to remind myself about that. Place is in the door, but time's in the door frame."

"Do you have any idea at all what he's talking about?" Khalor asked Althalus.

"Sort of," Althalus replied. "Twengor and his men will go to last week and back while they're passing through the doorway. They'll be drunk as lords *here*, and sober as judges *there*, because they'll have had two weeks to get sober during that single step through the doorway. *And,* since they'll be walking in their sleep, they won't really know what's happened."

"Just *do* it, gentlemen; don't explain it," Khalor said. "Sometimes you two are as bad as Gher is."

* * *

"They're not *serious*!" Chief Twengor exploded when he first caught sight of the walls of Poma.

"Duke Bherdor doesn't have much in the way of a backbone, Chief Twengor," Sergeant Khalor admitted. "The local merchants don't really want to pay taxes, and Bherdor's too spineless to insist."

"I want a free hand here, Althalus," the now-sober Twengor said flatly. "Don't interfere with me."

"Just exactly what did you have in mind, Chief Twengor?"

"I'm going to make those merchants pay their taxes in sweat. *They're* the ones who are going to reinforce those walls."

"I don't think they'll agree to that."

"I've got a whip someplace," Twengor said darkly. "They'll agree, Althalus. Believe me when I say they'll agree. Let's go talk to this jellyfish Duke."

They entered the city, and Chief Twengor grew more and more irritated as they passed through the commercial district, where the shops more closely resembled palaces than places of business. Twengor's face was steel hard when they entered Duke Bherdor's run-down palace.

"This is Chief Twengor, your Grace," Khalor introduced the hulking Arum to the weak-chinned Duke of Poma. "He'll be defending your city."

"Praise the Gods!" the young Bherdor exclaimed in his tremulous voice.

"I'm going to need a few things, your Grace," Twengor said brusquely. "We *are* going to cooperate with each other, aren't we?"

"Oh, of course, Chief Twengor. Of course."

"Good. I want every citizen of Poma in that square in front of your palace in half an hour. I need to talk with them."

"I don't know if they'll come, Chief Twengor. The merchants don't like it when I do anything that interrupts normal business."

"Oh, they'll come, Duke Bherdor," Twengor said confidently. "Tell them that my clansmen will hang anybody who refuses— right from the signs that stick out over the front doors of all those fancy shops."

"You *wouldn't*!"

"Watch me."

"He's a different man when he's sober, isn't he?" Eliar said quietly to Sergeant Khalor.

"Oh, yes," Khalor agreed. "This is the way he *used* to be—before he started swimming down to the bottom of every ale barrel he came across. His mind hasn't been this clear for the past ten years."

Twengor sent some of his men to accompany the palace guards out into the city to summon the citizens to the square, and by noon, more or less everybody in Poma had gathered there. The richly dressed merchants seemed quite indignant, for some reason, and they were talking among themselves angrily.

"Ah—excuse me," Duke Bherdor said weakly from the balcony at the front of his palace. "Excuse me."

The crowd ignored him.

"Let me do this, your Grace," Twengor said. Then, ax in hand, he stepped to the front of the balcony. "Be silent!" he roared in a huge voice.

All sound in the square stopped immediately.

"The lands of the Arya of Osthos have been invaded by the Kanthons," Twengor announced briskly. "Some of you may have heard about that, but no matter. I'm Twengor of Arum, and I've been hired to defend your city. This means that *I* give the orders, and I'll hang any man who doesn't obey."

"You can't do that!" one of the merchants exclaimed.

"Try me. Look around you, city man. The men with swords and axes are *my* clansmen, and they do as I tell them to do. This puts *me* in charge of Poma, and our first order of business is to do something about your walls."

"That's Duke Bherdor's responsibility, not ours," another merchant declared.

"What town do you live in?" Twengor asked bluntly. "If the Kanthons break down the walls, they'll burn Poma to the ground and kill everybody who lives here. Doesn't that make those walls *your* responsibility?" Twengor paused to let that sink in. "You all cleverly advised your Duke that you couldn't afford a ten-percent tax. The Kanthons are likely to impose a one hundred–percent tax. After they've looted the city, you won't have anything left. But dead men don't need anything, do they? Now, let's go to work on the walls."

"Where can we find building stone?" someone in the crowd asked.

Twengor looked out over the city. "I can see all sorts of building stone from right here: houses, shops, warehouses, that sort of thing. You may all be living in tents when this is over, but you'll still be alive. That's the best offer I can make. Now, let's get cracking."

"Good speech," Khalor noted.

"I've always had this way with words," Twengor replied modestly.

"You've *got* to see this, Master Althalus!" Gher was chortling from the window when Althalus, Khalor, and Eliar returned to the tower. "That Argan fellow's trying to sneak into the fort to get to Smeugor and what's-his-name. His face is probably going to fall off when he finds out that they aren't really there."

"How did things go at Poma?" Andine asked.

"Twengor was moderately offensive, little lady," Khalor replied. "But he managed to get the point across. The citizens are all practicing a new trade now. They aren't very *good* stone-masons, but they're enthusiastic about it."

"Will the walls hold?"

"Not a chance." Khalor snorted. "I snitched some of Salkan's shepherds from Dreigon and Gebhel, so Twengor's got slingers as well as his own archers. What he's really doing in Poma is opening up avenues to give those boys clear shots at the enemy after they get inside the city. He's giving himself fighting room, and there won't be much left of Poma when he's done."

Althalus and Gher were looking out at the hilltop fort where Smeugor and Tauri were supposedly hiding. "Where's Argan?" Althalus asked. "I don't seem to be able to see him."

"He's hiding in that clump of bushes on the west side," Gher

replied. "He sneaks real good. He's waiting for it to get dark before he goes inside to tell Smeugor and what's-his-name to stop
setting fire to those wheat fields. He won't find them in there, of
course, but he *will* find the note Eliar and I put there."

"Note?"

"Didn't Eliar tell you about it? I thought he was going to take
care of that."

"It must have slipped his mind. Why don't *you* tell me about
it, Gher?"

"Well, we were talking about Smeugor and what's-his-name
the other day. I was asking Eliar why those two Generals didn't
just go ahead and kill their Chiefs, since they really don't like
them. Eliar explained that if they did that, it'd start an awful
fight. Arums seem to have a lot of funny ideas about that sort of
thing, don't they?"

"Arums have a lot of funny ideas, Gher. Why don't you tell me
about the note?"

"Oh. Right. Anyway, I got to thinking about how we told
Smeugor and what's-his-name that Ghend was real mad at them
for setting all those fires, and a whole bunch of stuff sort of
clicked together. If we fixed it so that Ghend *believed* some wild
story about Smeugor and what's-his-name, then he really *would*
want to kill them, and if *Ghend* kills them instead of the Generals doing it, there wouldn't be any fights among the Arums.
They'd be mad at Ghend instead. Does that make any sense at
all?"

"The note, Gher," Althalus said firmly. "Tell me about the
note. Stick to the point."

"I was only trying to explain why we did it, Master Althalus,"
Gher said defensively. "Anyway, that Argan fellow sneaks so
good that he *is* going to get inside the fort, no matter how many
guards there are, so Eliar and I put together a note that's *supposed* to have been wrote down by Sergeant Khalor. Eliar put it
down on paper, since I don't write too good yet. We had to do it
about four or five times to make sure we got it just right. The note
tells Smeugor and what's-his-name to keep on pretending that
they're still working for Ghend and to blame their Generals for

all the fires that're burning up Ghend's food. Then it tells them to weasel Ghend's war plan out of some of Ghend's other sneaky people and to pass it on so that we'll know what they're going to do before they do it. Then Eliar and I put in some stuff about how much gold we're going to pay those two. Then we fluffed it up by saying that our side's *really* worried about the war and stuff like that, and we finished it up by saying some *real* nasty things about Emmy's brother. Do you think it might work, Master Althalus?"

"If it confuses Ghend as much as it just confused *me*, it probably will."

"Oh, I left something out; I got a little rattled when you kept wanting to know about the note."

"I'll bite out my tongue," Althalus told the boy. "What was this thing you left out?"

"Well, after we win this war, there won't be much point in keeping Smeugor and what's-his-name here in the House, will there?"

"Probably not, no."

"Eliar and I thought it might be kind of neat to just shove them through a door into someplace where Ghend can find them real quick. Ghend's going to be mad because he just lost another war, so he'll probably do some real mean things to those two while he's killing them. That'll pay them back for trying to swindle *us*, and since Ghend's going to do the killing, the two Generals won't get their hands dirty and there won't be no fights in Arum. Doesn't that all sort of fit together?"

"I don't see any great big holes in it," Althalus admitted.

"That was why I called you over here to the window to watch," Gher said. "I wanted you to *see* that Argan fellow's face fall off when he reads that note. And later on—if we're not too busy— maybe we can watch *Ghend's* face fall off when Argan shows *him* the note. Did I do good?"

"You did *real* good, Gher," Althalus said, and then he burst out laughing.

Right after breakfast the next morning, Eliar, Althalus, and Sergeant Khalor went through the corridors of the House to the encampment of Chief Koleika Iron Jaw and took the big-chinned Clan Chief to the road leading to the city of Mawor.

"Great Gods!" the usually taciturn Koleika exclaimed. "Would you *look* at those walls!"

"Impressive," Khalor agreed.

"It must have cost a *fortune* to build something like that!"

"As I understand it, Duke Nitral's been studying architecture for most of his life," Althalus told him. "He's made special trips to Deika and Awes and various other cities just to make drawings of the public buildings and the outer walls. Mawor sits on the River Osthos, and it's a very prosperous city. When Duke Nitral ascended the throne there, he decided to indulge his hobby. He's determined to make Mawor the most splendid city in all of Treborea."

"I'd say he's getting close," Iron Jaw said. "I'm glad we're on his side. I'd hate to have to attack *that* place."

"You won't have to," Khalor told him. "How long do you think you can hold Mawor?"

"With that river right beside the walls, there'll always be plenty of water, and if there's enough food in the storehouses, I can hold for ten years, at least."

"Let's hope it doesn't last *that* long," Althalus said. "What's more important than holding the city, though, is keeping the enemy from just giving up and moving on to Osthos."

"Once they've engaged here, I can *keep* them here," Koleika asserted, his lower jaw jutting out even more. "This place is a perfect trap. I'll let them approach and start the siege. If they try to back away, though, I'll *ruin* them. They'll have to keep their entire army right here, because the minute they try to withdraw, I'll come out of that fortress like the wrath of God and tromp them into mud puddles all over this plain. They *won't* get past me, Althalus. I can guarantee that."

"I think that might just be the longest speech I've ever heard you make, Chief Koleika," Khalor noted.

"Sorry," Koleika apologized shortly. "I guess I got a little carried away. Those walls *really* impressed me."

"Let's go on into the city," Althalus suggested. "We'll introduce you to Duke Nitral, and then you two can get down to business."

Duke Nitral was not in his palace when they arrived there, however. "His Grace is down by the river," one of the palace guards advised them. "He's supervising some construction. I think it's got something to do with the docks."

"Now, that's unusual," Khalor noted. "Most noblemen don't get involved in that sort of thing."

The guard laughed. "You don't know our Duke," he said. "When he really gets excited about one of his projects, he'll peel off his coat and start laying bricks right alongside the common stonemasons. I'm told that he's at least as good at it as most of the men who do it for a living. He ruins a lot of very expensive clothes that way, but he doesn't seem to care."

"Now, *this* is a man I want to meet," Koleika said. "If he's willing to get his own hands dirty, that means that he's an artist. *That's* why those walls are so beautiful."

They went down to the riverside gate, passed out through it, and found a wide, paved sort of highway under the looming wall. Piers jutted out into the river, and hordes of workmen were busily erecting vaults over the piers.

"Nitral?" a foreman replied when Khalor told him that they were looking for the Duke. "He's at the upper pier. The crew up there's having trouble seating the pilings."

When Althalus and his friends reached the northern pier, they found the crew anxiously looking down into the muddy water.

Then a man Althalus recognized as Nitral came bursting to the surface with a great splash, gasping for air. "We've hit bedrock down there," he told the men on the pier. "We'll have to drill, I'm afraid. We *have* to seat those footings."

"There are some strangers here who want to talk with you, my Lord," one of the workmen called down to the man in the water.

"Tell them I'm busy."

"Ah . . . they're right here, my Lord."

Koleika, however, was already pulling off his clothes. "Watch yourself," he called to the Duke. "I'm coming in." Then he made a long, smooth dive off the pier and disappeared under the surface of the river.

It seemed to Althalus that Koleika was down forever, and he realized that he was holding his own breath.

Then Iron Jaw burst to the surface about twenty feet out from the pier. "You can set in your footings out here, your Grace," he said when he'd caught his breath. "There's a three-foot crevice in the bedrock right below me."

Duke Nitral was treading water near the pier. "Mark that place!" he shouted up to his workmen.

"Yes, my Lord," the foreman of the crew shouted back.

Iron Jaw swam back to the pier. "I gather these vaults are designed to protect supply ships while they're unloading?" he asked the mostly submerged Duke of Mawor.

"Exactly," Nitral replied. "I've got a friend over on the other side of the river, and he's going to buy wheat from the Perquaines and ship it across to me once Mawor's under siege. I don't want any enemy ships disrupting my bread supply. You seem to know quite a bit about constructing fortifications, my friend."

"I can build them if I have to," Koleika replied. "My job's a lot easier, though, if they're already in place. My name's Koleika, and I've been hired to give your enemies a good trouncing."

"I'm delighted to meet you, Chief Koleika," Duke Nitral said, extending his hand.

"Could we hold off on shaking hands, your Grace?" Koleika said. "I'm not really a very good swimmer, and my hands are kind of busy right now. Have we more or less finished?"

"I think we've just about covered everything," Nitral replied.

"Why don't we get out of the water, then? This river's very cold, and I'm *freezing* down here."

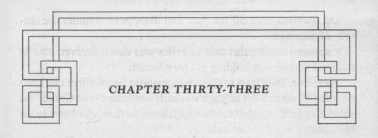

CHAPTER THIRTY-THREE

It had to do with the shape of her arm, Althalus decided as he studied Dweia, who sat pensively at the table with one hand idly resting on the Book. There was an almost infinite perfection in the subtly rounded contours of Dweia's arms that made his knees go weak.

"You're staring again, Althie," she said, not even looking up.

"I know. I've got a permit, though. You've got very pretty arms, did you know that?"

"Yes."

"The rest of you is pretty, too, but your arms always seem to catch my eye when I look at you."

"I'm glad you enjoy them. Please think about something else, Althie. You're distracting me. Call the children, pet. I need to talk with them. Oh, you might as well put Albron, Astarell, and Salkan to sleep for a while—just to be on the safe side."

"Whatever you say, Em." Althalus sent his thought out to touch the still-strange new group awareness. *Emmy wants to see us in the tower,* he silently announced.

"You're shouting again, Althalus," Dweia noted.

"I'm still not used to this, Em," he explained. "Reaching out to the others isn't exactly the same as it was when it was just you and me."

"Ours goes just a bit deeper, love."

"I've noticed that—and we can still talk privately, can't we?"

"Naturally."

"Why 'naturally'? I thought that once somebody was in, he was in all the way."

"Oh, good grief, no, Althalus. That particular link is very private. At this point, *nobody* can go that deep except you and me. I'd imagine there'll be a couple of other private links before very long."

"An Eliar-Andine link, and a Leitha-Bheid link?"

"Exactly. Don't tell them, love. Let them discover it for themselves. I'm just a bit curious to find out how long it's going to take them."

"If that's the way you want it, Em." Then a sudden thought came to him. "What are we going to do about Salkan? Bheid's spending a lot of time and effort trying to convert that boy, and I'm not sure it serves any purpose. I don't think Salkan would make a good priest. He's a little too independent, for one thing, and his opinion of the priesthood isn't very high."

"Let it go for right now, pet. Bheid's going through a personal crisis."

"Oh?"

"You and Eliar ripped him out of the traditional Black Robe priesthood, and he's feeling guilty. I think his attempts to convert Salkan might be a form of expiation."

"That went by just a little fast, Em."

"Bheid feels that he's abandoned his order and violated his vows. I think he might be trying to offer his order a replacement."

"He's trying to buy his way out of the priesthood with Salkan?"

"That's a crude way to put it, but it comes fairly close. Just leave them alone, Althalus. Bheid's not hurting Salkan, and right now he's dealing with a private problem. The time's not too far off when Bheid's going to have to have his head on straight, and if preaching to Salkan's all it'll take, let him preach. Now, encourage Albron, Astarell, and Salkan to take a little nap. You and I and the children have work to do."

"I've been meaning to talk with you about something, Dweia," Andine said when they'd all gathered in the tower. "Couldn't we stay in my palace in Osthos instead of here in the House? I really should be there—just in case Dhakan needs me if an emergency turns up."

"If anything happens, I'll know about it, Andine," Dweia assured her. "There are reasons for us to be *here* instead of in your palace. There aren't any spies here, for one thing."

"If you'd just let Leitha tell me who those spies are, I could clean them out, you know."

"*That's* one of the things we're going to talk about right now," Dweia told her. The Goddess looked around at them. "You've all been coming up with assorted schemes in the past few days," she said. "Some of the schemes are quite clever, and some are just a little silly, but that's beside the point. I want you all to understand right here and now that you will *not* set any of those schemes in motion until *after* Gelta enters the palace in Osthos." She looked quite sternly at Bheid. "Are you listening, Brother Bheid?"

"Of course, Divinity," he said quickly.

"Then call off your assassins."

Althalus looked at the young priest with a certain astonishment. "Just what have you been up to, Bheid?" he asked curiously.

Bheid flushed slightly. "I'm really not supposed to talk about it, Althalus," he said.

"You have my permission to reveal it, Brother Bheid," Dweia told him in a flat, unfriendly voice.

Bheid winced. "Well," he said in an uncomfortable tone, "Church politics sometimes get a little murky, and occasionally— not too often, you understand—somebody gets out of line and makes himself sort of inconvenient. There are legal procedures to deal with those people, but sometimes public trials and the like might embarrass members of the hierarchy. The Church has an alternative of last resort to fall back on in those situations."

"Hired killers, I gather," Althalus said.

"That's an awkward sort of description, Althalus," Bheid objected.

"Who are you planning to have murdered?"

"I wish you wouldn't use that particular word, Althalus," Bheid said uncomfortably.

"It's a technical term that we professionals use. Give, Brother Bheid. Who's your target?"

"Aryo Pelghat of Kanthon. As long as he remains on the throne of Kanthon, there'll be turmoil in Treborea, and Ghend thrives on turmoil."

"What a wonderful idea!" Andine exclaimed.

"Let's establish some rules right here and now," Dweia said sternly. "No murders, no armies out of nowhere, no rounding up of spies, and no mutinies among the Arum clans until *after* Gelta enters Andine's throne room in Osthos. You will do *nothing* to interfere with that dream vision. If any one of you slaps me across the face with a paradox, I'll be very cross with you."

"If those dream things are *that* important, why don't we make up some of our own?" Gher asked.

She gave him a slightly amused look. "Why do you think we're all here, Gher?" she asked him.

"Well, isn't it because Master Althalus hunted us all down and *made* us come here?"

"And why did he do that?"

"I don't know. Maybe *you* made him do it."

"Why would he take orders from me?"

"*Everybody* takes orders from *you*, Emmy."

"Why?"

"We *have* to. I don't know exactly why, but we just have to."

"Exactly. Daeva's dream visions are very blatant. Mine are far more subtle. It doesn't really take very much to alter reality, Gher. Sometimes something as simple as a word can change things enormously. It already has, as a matter of fact." She looked at Andine. "What word did you read on the Knife, dear?" she asked.

" 'Obey,' " Andine replied.

"And what's going to happen to Gelta after you obey her when she tells you to kneel down before her?"

"She'll end up in my dungeon."

"Any more questions, Gher?" Dweia asked the boy.

He grinned at her. "Not a one, Emmy," he replied. "I think I've got it all straight now."

"That's nice," she said fondly.

* * *

The invasion from Kanthon had quite literally stopped cold until long strings of supply wagons began streaming south with food for the starving army. Gelun and Wendan stopped burning fields at that point and began ambushing the supply columns instead. Enough of the wagons evaded the ambushes to feed the invaders minimally, however, so the advance on the city of Kadon resumed, and Kadon was soon encircled.

Both Eliar and Sergeant Khalor grew increasingly grouchy as the invaders closed on Kadon.

"You two *could* take turns, you know," Leitha suggested. "You *both* don't have to stay awake day and night."

"She's right, Eliar," Khalor said. "Why don't you go get some sleep?" Khalor was looking down at Kadon from the window.

"Why don't *you*, my Sergeant?" Eliar replied. "All they're doing right now is setting up their encampments and bringing in their siege engines."

"You'll wake me immediately if anything unusual happens?"

"I've stood watch fairly often, Sergeant," Eliar told him, "so I have a pretty good idea what I'm supposed to do."

"I *am* a little tired," Khalor admitted.

"Then go to bed."

"Yes, *sir*," Khalor replied with a faint smile.

"Taking care of my superior's health is part of my job, Sergeant."

"Don't push it." Khalor yawned.

"Sweet dreams, Sergeant," Leitha told him.

"I think I'd rather not dream at all, under these circumstances," he said, going to the head of the stairs. "The notion of having Gelta climb into bed with me makes my blood run cold, for some reason." He yawned again and went down the stairs.

"I *really* want to see if it worked, Eliar," Gher was saying. "It shouldn't really take all *that* long."

"I'm sorry, Gher," Eliar told him, "but my Sergeant would skin me alive if I deserted my post."

"What are you two bickering about now?" Dweia asked them.

"Gher wants me to leave my post so that we can follow Argan," Eliar replied.

"It's sort of important, Emmy," Gher told her. "We left that letter from Sergeant Khalor in the fort where Smeugor and what's-his-name are supposed to be hiding. Shouldn't we find out if the letter really works the way we want it to?"

"He's got a point there, Em," Althalus said. "If the letter persuades Ghend that Smeugor and Tauri have changed sides again, then *he'll* take care of them, and Gelun and Wendan won't have to. Mutiny during a war isn't really a good idea. There are blood relationships involved in the Arum clans, and if a few second cousins start coming down with family loyalties and the like, those two clans might stop fighting the invaders and start fighting amongst themselves. We wouldn't want that, would we?"

"The window *has* to stay right where it is," Eliar insisted stubbornly.

Dweia sighed. "Men," she said to Leitha.

"Discouraging, isn't it?" the pale blond girl replied. Then she smiled offensively at Althalus. "I see three other windows here in the tower, Daddy," she said in a patronizing tone. "Hadn't you noticed them?"

"Make her stop that, Dweia," Althalus pleaded.

"You *did* catch her point, though, didn't you?"

"Can you really *do* that?"

"Of course. Didn't you know that?"

"Sometimes Daddy doesn't pay very close attention," Leitha observed.

"I'm starting to get just a little tired of that 'Daddy' business, Leitha," Althalus scolded her.

"Oh," Leitha said mockingly, "what a shame."

"Moving right along here—" Dweia cut off Althalus' retort. "—why don't we leave Eliar at his post and go watch Ghend's face fall off?" Then she led the rest of them to the north window.

"I don't think I recognize that place," Bheid noted, staring through the window at a night-shrouded encampment. "Just exactly where is it, Dweia?"

"I'm not entirely sure," she replied. "I was concentrating on Ghend, not any specific location, so the window went directly to Ghend without getting tangled up in geography."

"What a neat window!" Gher exclaimed.

"I'm rather fond of it," Dweia agreed.

"Isn't that Argan?" Leitha said, pointing at a lone horseman approaching the encampment.

"Probably," Dweia replied.

"Is it only a coincidence that we started watching just as Argan reached that place down there?" Andine asked.

"No, not really," Dweia said. "What we're seeing actually happened two days ago." She smiled faintly. "I've had a lot of practice with that procedure. It's a much more interesting way to study history than plodding through some dusty old book."

Argan galloped his exhausted horse into the center of the encampment, reined in, and swung down. "Take me to Ghend immediately!" he snapped at one of the black-armored soldiers Dweia had identified as Nekweros.

"Yes, your Worship!" the soldier replied in a hollow-sounding voice.

Ghend, however, had just emerged from the garishly colored central pavilion. "Where have you been?" he demanded harshly of Argan.

"I was looking for Smeugor and Tauri," Argan replied. "Isn't that what you told me to do?"

"Did you pass my orders on to them?"

"Would have, old boy, but I couldn't seem to find them. As it turned out, they're not in that fort."

"What are you talking about?"

"I searched the place from top to bottom, mighty leader, and there wasn't a sign of them—except for this." Argan held out a sheet of paper.

"What's that?" Ghend asked.

"Read it," Argan suggested. "It sort of speaks for itself, I'd say."

Ghend took the paper over to a sputtering torch and read "Sergeant Khalor's" letter. "Impossible!" he burst out.

"Point your finger at Koman, old boy," Argan said a bit smugly. "He's the one who missed it, not me."

"Those two imbeciles aren't clever enough to have deceived Koman!" Ghend insisted.

"They might have had help, Ghend," Argan said very seriously. "Koman isn't the *only* mind leech in the world, you know. The witch-woman from Kweron has blocked him out before, if I remember correctly."

"I'll make them pay for this!" Ghend fumed.

"You'll have to find them first, I think. They *definitely* aren't inside that fort. You might want to start looking down rat holes, but that might take quite a while. I'd imagine that staying out of your reach is their main goal in life right now. They took your money and then turned around and took money from this Khalor person to turn on you. They've swindled you out of quite a bit of gold, Ghend. They smiled and nodded, and then they quite nearly starved your entire army to death. They know how you'll feel about that, I'd imagine, so they won't be easy to find."

"I'll find them, Argan," Ghend replied, his eyes burning. "Believe me, I'll find them."

"Yakhag could probably locate them for you," Argan suggested.

"No. Keep Yakhag out of sight. I'll take care of Smeugor and Tauri myself."

"Whatever you say, old boy," Argan replied.

The south window in the tower looked out over the city of Kanthon, and Bheid gave Eliar directions to a rather nondescript tavern in the commercial district.

"I won't leave the door open while you two are inside that tavern," Eliar told Bheid and Althalus, "so whistle when you want to come home."

"You don't really have to come with me, Althalus," Bheid said with a slightly anxious took.

"What's bothering you, Brother Bheid?" Althalus asked.

"Well . . ." Bheid said uncomfortably, "I'm really not supposed to tell anybody about these people. It's one of the most closely guarded secrets of the Church."

"I wish you'd get your loyalties straightened out, Bheid," Althalus told him bluntly. "Dweia's a little peeved about this scheme of yours, and I'm going along to unruffle her feathers. Personally, I'm not as upset with your notion as she is, but I *would* sort of like to have a look at your assassins to find out for myself whether they're professionals or just religious enthusiasts."

"All right," Bheid said, throwing up his hands. "Anything you say, Althalus."

"Let's go then."

They went through the door and emerged in the alleyway behind the tavern. They were both wearing ordinary clothes to avoid notice, and they moved out into the street to mingle with the few passersby.

The outside of the tavern appeared sedate, even slightly stuffy, and a pair of what seemed to be ordinary tradesmen were standing in the doorway talking about the weather. Bheid stepped slightly in front of Althalus, making a peculiar gesture with his fingers, and the two men politely stepped aside for him. "It's just a precaution," Bheid said quietly to Althalus as they entered. "The proprietor's not very enthusiastic about random patrons walking in off the street." Then he smiled faintly. "I should probably warn you in advance about something. I wouldn't drink too deeply of the ale that's served here."

"Oh?"

"It's strictly for show, and it doesn't taste very good. People who have no business here may stop by once, but they almost never come back."

"Is it that bad?"

"Worse, actually. This establishment is supposed to *look* like a tavern, but that's not really why it's here." Bheid led the way to a table near the back. "I'll fetch us a couple of tankards and speak with the proprietor. He'll send for Sarwin and Mengh."

"Your hired killers?"

Bheid nodded. "I'll be right back."

Althalus sat down and looked curiously around at the counterfeit tavern. The few patrons were all soberly dressed, and their ale tankards for the most part sat untouched on the tables while they idly talked with each other in quiet tones. Almost in spite of himself, Althalus was very impressed. The entire tavern, including most of the patrons, was an elaborate sham, and he was fairly certain that if someone who wasn't supposed to be here entered, an argument—quickly followed by a brawl—would break out.

Bheid returned to the table with two ale tankards, and one sniff was all it took to persuade Althalus not to taste whatever was in the tankard.

"Awful, isn't it?" Bheid said.

"It might be all right for washing your socks," Althalus agreed. "How long has this place been here?"

"Several centuries, at least. The Treborean clergy's essentially Black Robe—which is to say that they worship the correct God—but they refuse to accept the authority of our Holy Exarch. We've tried for thousands of years to persuade them that their position verges on heresy, but they seem to be blessed with invincible ignorance, and—" Bheid stopped, looking at the faint smile that had come across Althalus' face. "What?" he demanded.

"Think, Bheid," Althalus told him. "Hasn't your theological position changed just a bit here recently?"

"I was only trying—" Then Bheid laughed ruefully. "It's a habit, I guess," he admitted. "Maybe I'm overtrained. My responses are almost automatic. When you get right down to the core of it, there's not much difference between Treborean theology and that of Medyo. We disagree on matters of Church politics, and that's about all, really. Anyway, this tavern is a sort of hidden outpost of the true religion—if there really *is* such a thing—and it gives us a place where we can further Black Robe policies."

"Which occasionally involve murders, I suppose?" Althalus added.

"Now and then, yes. We don't do that sort of thing very often, of course, but the option *is* there."

"You don't have to be so apologetic with *me*, Bheid," Althalus told him. "I'm very tolerant about things like that. I gather that your murderers are on a salary of some kind?"

"A yearly retainer with a bonus for each murder, yes."

"Then they aren't just assorted fanatics who kill for their God?"

"Good heavens no! Fanatics *want* to be captured and executed. That makes them martyrs, and martyrs are rewarded in heaven. Our assassins are thoroughgoing professionals who *never* get caught."

"Good policy. Never hire amateurs when you can get professionals."

"There they are now," Bheid said, looking toward the back of the tavern.

The two men who had just entered the tavern through the back door were so nondescript as to be virtually invisible. The word "medium" covered almost every aspect of their appearance. They were neither tall nor short, light nor dark, and their clothing was neither ragged nor elegant. "I just can't understand what's come over Engena here lately, Mengh," one of them was saying to the other as they approached the table. "Nothing seems to suit her anymore. She doesn't like our house, she doesn't like the neighbors, and she doesn't even like our dog."

"Women get strange on you sometimes, Sarwin," Mengh replied sagely. "They don't think the same way we do. Buy her some presents and make a bit of a fuss over her. That's what *I* do when Pelquella starts getting grouchy on me. It's not really the gift that matters so much. It's the attention. When you stop paying attention to your wife, you're in for trouble." Mengh looked quickly at Bheid. "Well, hello there, Mister Bheid," he said. "We haven't seen you here for quite some time."

"I've been just a bit busy," Bheid explained. "Why don't you gentlemen join us?"

"We'd be happy to, Mister Bheid," Sarwin said.

The assassins seated themselves at the table and signaled to the proprietor for tankards of ale.

"I'm glad you gentlemen happened by," Bheid told them. "There's something we need to talk about."

"Oh?" Mengh said. "What was that?"

"That business matter we were discussing the last time I was here."

The two murderers both looked pointedly at Althalus.

"This is my partner, Althalus," Bheid said, "my *silent* partner, usually. Something's come up here recently, and he wanted to speak with you personally. Our plans have changed just a bit."

"Changed?" Sarwin said sharply. "Are you saying that you don't need our services anymore?" His eyes grew hard.

"That's not what he said, friend," Althalus said. "The timing's changed, that's all. The pay's still the same, and so's the job. We just want you to hold off a bit—market conditions, you understand. Several things have to happen before we'll be able to go ahead, and if you gentlemen just happened to be a little premature, it might alert our competitors. We're out to make a big coup in the market, so to speak, and we don't want the competition to know what we're up to. I'm handling the details in several other cities, and Mister Bheid is taking care of things here. Timing's absolutely crucial in our particular business."

"That's the advantage *we* have in our profession," Mengh said with a perfectly straight face. "Time's not really very important when *we* set out to make a coup. We can hold off, if that's what you want. Just have Mister Bheid give us the word when you want the job done. Would you gentlemen like to drink to that?" He lifted his tankard inquiringly.

Althalus made a face. "I really think I'd rather not," he replied.

"I was rather hoping you'd say that," Sarwin said, pushing his tankard as far away as he possibly could.

"Are you busy, Althalus?" Sergeant Khalor asked the following morning.

"No, not really. Why?"

"Do you suppose you could look in on Twengor over in Poma? I'm not really worried—Twengor knows what he's doing—but I like to keep abreast of things. If the invaders are doing things right, they've committed about a third of their army to Poma, but house-to-house fighting's very tricky, and if they beat Twengor—or manage to slip away—Gelta's going to have an extra hundred thousand or more troops to throw at Mawor. I'd go myself, but I'm rather busy right now. If Twengor thinks those people might be able to get away from him, I want to know about it." He hesitated a moment. "This is just between you and me, Althalus, but what I *really* want to know is whether or not Twengor's still sober. If he's backsliding, I should probably know about it. I wouldn't talk about it, if I were you, but you know what to look for."

"I'll go wake Eliar," Althalus said, turning toward the stairs.

"I just now got to sleep," Eliar complained when Althalus woke him.

"This won't take too long, boy," Althalus told him.

"I'm going to talk with Dweia about this," Eliar grumbled. "Everybody's making sure that Sergeant Khalor gets enough sleep, but nobody ever thinks about me."

"You're the doorman, Eliar. Quit complaining. We'll use the regular door to Poma."

"Why not use the special door in the tower?"

"There's fighting in the streets in Poma, Eliar. I don't think I want to come out in the wrong house. Besides, Sergeant Khalor's using that window beside the door."

"I see what you mean. The regular door's in the east corridor."

"You'd better bring your sword."

"Right."

They went through the quiet house to the east corridor and peered through several doors until they located chief Twengor's command post. The city was largely in ruins by now, and many of the houses and shops were burning.

"What's afoot, Althalus?" Twengor asked when one of his kilted clansmen escorted Althalus and Eliar into the room where the burly Chief crouched beside a window.

"Nothing all that unusual, Twengor," Althalus replied. "We just stopped by to see how things were going."

"There's nothing really unusual happening here. Oh, I'd keep my head down, if I were you. There's an archer in that house across the street who's quite a bit better than average. He's come very close to parting my hair a couple of times. I've got some of those Wekti shepherds up on the third floor trying to get a clear shot at him."

"How are they working out?"

"Not bad at all. I've got several archers who are almost as good, but archers need a supply of arrows, and all a slinger needs is a rock that he can pick up anyplace."

"How much of the city have the invaders overrun so far?"

"They're more or less in control of the northern quarter."

"More or less?"

"Things are sort of fluid. They mass up troops and make an assault on some house or shop. My archers and those shepherds make it very expensive for them when they attack. We hold the house for a while and then pull back." Then the bearded Chief chuckled. "Our enemies have learned not to hold any victory celebrations at that point, though."

"Oh?"

"The capture of a house that might just collapse on top of you is a hollow sort of victory, wouldn't you say? My men had enough time before the invaders broke down the walls to weaken the walls and ceilings in nearly every building in Poma. We brace them up with timbers while *we* occupy those buildings, but we take those timbers with us when we leave. I think if it got down to a count, the houses have killed more of the enemy than my men have. First the invaders have to fight their way into the house, and then the house falls down on top of them. I've told my men that it's perfectly all right to laugh loud enough for the enemy to hear when that happens."

"You've got an evil mind, Twengor."

"I know, and I enjoy every minute of it."

"If none of the houses or shops are safe, the citizens won't really dare to come back when the war's over, though, will they?" Eliar asked.

"That's too bad," Twengor replied indifferently. "If those skin-flint merchants had paid their taxes, the walls might have held and we wouldn't have to do it this way. By the time this is over, there won't be much of Poma left, but that's really none of my concern."

"Is there much of a possibility that the invaders will just give up on Poma and move on?" Althalus asked. "Khalor's a bit concerned about that. He doesn't want these people to march on Mawor—or just bypass Mawor and move on to Osthos."

"I've pretty much got them locked in place here, Althalus," Twengor replied. "I gave them several neighborhoods near the breach in the north wall just to lure them into the city far enough that pulling back out is going to be almost impossible—particularly when my archers and those Wektis with their slings are on top of every roof in that part of town. They're trapped here." Twengor glanced out the window, and then he started to chuckle an evil sort of laugh. "Come here and watch this," he invited them.

Althalus and Eliar joined him at the window.

"My men just signaled. That house across the street's been irritating me for the last three days. One of the boys just took care of that."

An arrow buzzed spitefully through the window.

"*That's* what's been irritating me," Twengor said. "Nobody's been able to get a clear shot at that fellow. Watch."

Clouds of oily smoke began to billow out through the windows of the half-ruined house across the street.

"That's a stone building," Althalus noted. "How did your men manage to set it on fire?"

"It's not the building that's burning, my friend," Twengor chortled. "One of the biggest tax evaders in Poma just happened to be a wool merchant. We emptied out his warehouse and filled the cellars of a goodly number of these houses with wool. Then we soaked that wool down with lamp oil, melted lard, and naphtha. One of my archers just put a fire arrow through the cellar window of that house. Breathing in smoke isn't very good for a man, I'm told, but what *really* tops it all off is the fact that the house that just got turned into a chimney used to be the palace of the wool merchant."

"I'd say that his taxes just went *way* up." Althalus chuckled.

"That they did, Althalus. That they did. Tell Khalor that I've got everything under control here in Poma. I'm dispensing justice and tying down the enemy."

"I'll pass that on. Could you drive the invaders out of town if necessary?"

"That wouldn't be much of a problem. But why? I thought Khalor wanted me to hold them here."

"Just temporarily, Chief Twengor. We've got some cavalry in reserve to mop things up when the leaves have all turned red. I'll let you know when the time's right. Then you can invite your visitors to leave, and they'll be out in the open to provide entertainment for the cavalry."

"We should all be home by winter, then."

"That was roughly what we had in mind. Winter wars are so boring."

"I've noticed that myself. Just say the word, Althalus, and I'll kick our unwanted guests out of Poma and start packing up all the odds and ends we've picked up here for the trip home."

"No victory celebration, Twengor?"

"I don't think so this time," Twengor replied. "Waking up in the morning without a blinding headache's sort of a novelty. I think I might like to enjoy it for a little longer. Go tell Khalor that I'm still sober and that I can drive the enemy out of town at a moment's notice. Isn't that more or less what he wanted to know?"

"You were way ahead of me, weren't you?"

"Of course I was. Now that I'm not seeing double anymore, I can see very clearly. Get out of here, Althalus. I'm busy."

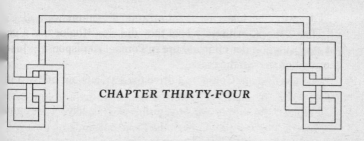

CHAPTER THIRTY-FOUR

"How did you three get past that army out there?" the jut-jawed Koleika demanded when Althalus, Eliar, and Khalor were admitted to Duke Nitral's palace in Mawor.

"We came across from the other side of the river in one of your supply ships," Althalus lied glibly. "It took a bit of fast talking, but we finally persuaded the ship Captain that we were friends."

"How are Kadon and Poma holding out?" Duke Nitral asked.

"Things are going much more smoothly in Kadon now that Laiwon's confined Duke Olkar to his palace, your Grace," Khalor replied.

"He did *what*?" Nitral exclaimed.

"Olkar kept trying to interfere, Duke Nitral," Althalus explained. "He'd come unraveled every time a shop window got broken or Laiwon commandeered part of the workforce. I don't think Duke Olkar quite grasps the meaning of the word 'war,' for some reason."

"Laiwon got tired of all his interference and sent him to his room," Khalor said with a faint smirk. "The walls of Kadon are holding, so the city's not in any real danger."

"What about Poma?"

"That's a different story. They're fighting from house to house there. There won't be much left of Poma by the time Twengor gets through."

"Poor Bherdor." Nitral sighed.

"It's his own fault, your Grace. If he'd been a bit more firm, he might have been able to do something about the walls. From a strategic point of view, though, those insignificant walls are a godsend. The besiegers got *into* Poma, but Twengor's busy making sure that they'll never get out—until I'm ready for them to come out."

The door opened, and a heavily armed Treborean soldier entered. "They're mounting another attack near the main gate your Grace," the soldier reported with a smart salute.

"Time to go to work, I guess," the Duke said, picking up an ornate helmet from his desk.

They all trooped out of the Duke's study.

"Have they been attacking very often, Chief Koleika?" Eliar asked as they left the palace courtyard and came out into the street.

"Three or four times a day," Koleika replied almost indifferently. "They don't really know what they're doing, so they're wasting a lot of their men."

"A stupid enemy is a gift from God," Khalor said in a sententious voice.

"This particular enemy has more than pure stupidity working against it," Koleika added. "One of their Generals is a woman."

"A big, ugly woman with a loud voice?" Khalor asked.

"That's the one."

"Don't underestimate Gelta, Koleika," Althalus cautioned. "She's no ordinary woman."

"You've come up against her before?"

"In Wekti, yes. The lives of her soldiers don't mean anything at all to Gelta. She'll throw away her entire army to get what she wants."

"That's insane!" Koleika said.

"That's a fairly accurate description of her," Althalus agreed. "Pekhal could control her, but I believe he's not with her anymore."

The Queen of the Night was in full voice when Althalus and the others reached the battlements on the eastern side of the city, and her catapults were hurling boulders at the walls of Mawor with a monotonous thudding sound. "I'm starting to get a bellyful of that," Duke Nitral growled. "I spent a fortune on that marble sheathing on the outer wall, and she's breaking it all to pieces with those accursed engines. Excuse me, gentlemen. I'm going to do something about that right now." He went on down the parapet to a cluster of peculiar-looking engines.

"What are those things?" Eliar asked curiously.

"Nitral calls them arbalests," Koleika replied. "They're sort of an oversized bow. They'll throw a spear for half a mile. Nitral and I've come up with a way to make life very interesting for those catapult crews out there."

Duke Nitral barked a sharp command to the men around the arbalests, and a sheet of spears trailing fire shot out in long arcs from the high walls of Mawor.

"Colorful," Khalor noted, "but I don't quite see—"

"Watch," Koleika said gleefully, rubbing his hands together.

The fiery spears began their almost graceful descent, and then they fell amongst the invaders' siege engines. Sheets of fire immediately burst out in all directions from the spears, engulfing the catapults.

"What happened?" Eliar exclaimed in astonishment.

"I saw right off that one spear would only kill one man," Koleika replied modestly, "and only *if* it happened to hit him. I suggested to Nitral that replacing the steel points with earthenware jugs filled with boiling pitch might be an improvement." Then he made a wry face. "You've got to be careful about making suggestions to Nitral. He takes a good, sound idea and immediately starts to expand it. He went me one—or maybe three—better. He liked the pitch idea so much that he added naphtha, sulphur, and something his brewers boil out of good strong beer. One spark is all it takes to set fire to that mixture, and you probably noticed that each spear had a burning rag tied around the shaft."

Burning men were running from the sudden bonfires that had engulfed the siege engines, and the men were shrieking in agony.

"That's mostly because of the pitch in the mix," Koleika explained. "Boiling pitch sticks to anything it touches, and when the jug breaks, the mix splashes all over everything—and everybody—in the vicinity. Then that burning rag sets fire to the whole mess." He squinted out at the horror on the field below.

"They look almost like comets in the night sky. Rather pretty, isn't it?"

"They didn't seem to expect it," Khalor observed.

"I don't imagine they did. This is the first time we've tried it."

"How did you manage that kind of accuracy, then?"

"That was Nitral," Koleika replied shortly. "He's an architect, and computations get involved in that, I guess. He spent two days telling me all about angles of declination, arcs, triangulation, and numbers that he stacked up like cordwood. I couldn't make much sense of it, but he assured me that it'd work."

"It looks to me like he guessed it pretty close, Chief Koleika," Khalor said, gesturing at the bonfires around the siege engines. "As a favor to me, would you see if you can coax the recipe out of him? I've got a sneaking hunch that splashing fire all over people might be a quick way to settle a lot of arguments. Have you worked out the details of how you're going to keep the besiegers from disengaging here and marching on Osthos?"

"They'll lose more than half their army if they try," Koleika told him. "I've got that river at the back door, and Osthos is downriver from here. I can send men down by boat to ambush any columns marching south, and as soon as they weaken the force around Mawor, I'll open the front gate and charge out to engage them. Nitral's fire just added some finishing touches, I think. I'll keep them so busy that they won't have time to disengage, and winter's snapping at their heels."

"That's all it'll take, Chief Koleika," Althalus said. "If they don't reach Osthos before the snow flies, we've won us a war."

Dweia was alone in the tower when Althalus, Eliar, and Khalor returned. Her face was pensive, almost melancholy, and her voice was subdued when she spoke. "I think it's time to call in Kreuter and Dreigon, Sergeant Khalor," she said. "You might want to go start them moving. Let's make absolutely sure that Gelta can't scrape together a *real* army when she goes to Osthos. If Leitha was reading her correctly during that dream, she couldn't have more than two regiments at her back, and we'll want to keep it that way."

"I still don't quite understand how she expects to get into the city with only two regiments," Khalor said.

"Althalus and I are going to investigate that while you and Eliar are visiting with Kreuter and Dreigon, Sergeant. The leaves are starting to turn, so Gelta *has* to move very soon. I think we'll want to be absolutely certain she doesn't have any surprises for us."

"Good thinking," Khalor agreed. "Let's go talk with Kreuter and Dreigon, Eliar."

"Yes, my Sergeant," Eliar replied.

"You seem sad, Em," Althalus said after Eliar and his Sergeant had left.

She sighed. "Autumn's always a sad time for me, love," she replied. "The world grows old in the autumn, and winter lurks just over the edge of next week." She stretched and yawned. "Then, too, before humans came along, I always used to sleep through the winter."

"The way bears do?" That startled him.

"Bears are more clever than they look, Althalus. There isn't really anything to do in the winter, so it's a good time to catch up on your sleep. After this is all over, we might want to try that now and then." Then her expression became more businesslike. "Come to the window, Althalus. Let's do some snooping, shall we?"

"Anything you say, Em."

There was turmoil in the enemy encampment outside the walls of Mawor, and most of the turmoil was centered around the Queen of the Night. Gelta seemed on the verge of homicidal fury, bellowing curses and brandishing her ax. A well-armed Kanthon General was trying to placate her, but she didn't seem to be listening.

Then Argan, accompanied by a figure in the black armor of the Nekweros, came out of one of the tents. "What's wrong with her now, General Ghoru?" Argan demanded of the Kanthon.

"Things haven't been going exactly the way she wants them to go, Argan, and that always seems to set her brains on fire."

"You've noticed," Argan said drily. "Is there any way we can possibly disengage here?"

"Not a chance, Argan. I can't take the city, and if I try to pull my troops clear, the men inside the walls will rush out and destroy my entire army. Tell Ghend that he didn't give me enough men to take this place."

Gelta continued to bellow curses.

"Make her be quiet, Yakhag!" Argan snapped irritably.

Argan's companion raised the visor of his black helmet and approached the raging Queen of the Night, ignoring her stone ax.

"I thought the Nekweros were all demons," Althalus said to Dweia. "That one seems to be human."

"Look again, Althalus," she replied in a chill voice. "That's Yakhag, and he's worse than any demon in Nahgharash."

Althalus looked more closely at the man in black armor. Yakhag's face was pallid white, and he had sunken cheeks. There was a chilling deadness in his eyes, and no expression on his face. He spoke very quietly to the Queen of the Night, and she shrank away from him, trembling.

"She's afraid of him!" Althalus exclaimed. "I didn't think Gelta knew *how* to be afraid."

"Everybody in Nahgharash is afraid of Yakhag, Althalus," Dweia replied. "I think he even makes Ghend a bit nervous."

"Why isn't he one of that inner circle, then?"

"Probably because Ghend can't control him. Yakhag only answers to Daeva. He's a monster."

"He seems to be taking orders from Argan, though."

"You don't really want to start looking into the politics of Nahgharash, Althalus. It's the ultimate madhouse."

"Gelta absolutely *must* be in Osthos in three days, Ghoru," Argan was saying, "and she'll need *something* in the nature of an army to go with her. How many troops can you spare?"

"Maybe two regiments, but no more, and that's hardly enough to take Osthos."

"We'll see," Argan said shortly. "Two regiments should serve my purposes. I have access to certain illusions that should persuade the defenders of Osthos to come to the negotiating table."

"Illusions?" Ghoru scoffed. "You can't win a war with imaginary soldiers, Argan."

"Don't be too sure about that, Ghoru. Start those two regiments marching toward Osthos. I need to talk with Ghend; then Gelta, Yakhag, and I'll catch up with our forces."

Ghoru spread his hands. "Anything you say, Argan."

"Lord Dhakan!" a richly garbed courtier shouted, bursting into the Chamberlain's office. "The enemy approaches!"

"Calm yourself, man," Dhakan said. "Give me some details. Don't just stand there screaming. How many and how far away?"

"Millions, my Lord!"

"Weiko, you couldn't count up to a million if your life depended on it."

"The advancing army stretches from horizon to horizon, my Lord!" the flustered courtier declared. "We are lost!"

"You may go, Weiko," Dhakan told him coldly.

"But—"

"*Now,* Weiko, and don't slam the door behind you."

The courtier looked almost as if he wanted to argue, but then he changed his mind and left the room.

"He's another one," Leitha told Andine.

"Really?" Andine seemed surprised. "Ghend's scraping the bottom of the barrel, then. Nobody in the entire court takes Weiko very seriously."

"He's just a bit more clever than he lets on," Leitha told her friend. "He's a member of one of those cults Argan's been establishing here in the low country. He's been promised a high position in the new government of Osthos, and Argan's ordered him to encourage panic. The whole plan is to persuade you to surrender without a fight."

"That word 'cult' keeps cropping up," Bheid noted. "Just exactly what's involved in those little secret religions, Leitha?"

"Are you sure you want to know?" she asked him.

"I think I should, don't you? Sooner or later, I'm the one who'll have to counter them."

"Just take everything you've ever been taught and turn it upside down, Brother Bheid," she replied. "You'll be fairly close.

Argan's very good at promising rewards to his followers. Everyone has certain unwholesome desires—money, power, sex—all the usual nastiness. Argan preaches the fulfillment of those desires. Just about everything *you* look upon as sin is a virtue in Argan's new religion. I can go into greater detail, if you'd like," she offered archly.

"Ah . . . no, Leitha," he declined, blushing slightly. "I think that's sufficient."

"You're no fun," she accused.

Let it lie, Leitha, Althalus chided silently.

Andine rose and went to the window. "The leaves are just about the right color," she observed, "and the nights *are* getting chillier. How long should we drag out the negotiations, Althalus?"

"I'd try to hold out for the rest of today," he advised her. "Tomorrow's the day when it's all supposed to happen, and I think we want our timetable and Gelta's to match. If you surrender today—or the day after tomorrow—Emmy's very likely to tie her tail in a knot."

"You'd better send an emissary out to meet the scar-faced hag, Dhakan," Andine suggested.

"We've never surrendered before, my Arya," Dhakan said. "Do you happen to know where I might be able to put my hands on a white flag?"

"You could lend him one of your petticoats, dear," Leitha suggested slyly. "That might add a personal touch to the whole affair."

"Very funny, Leitha," Andine said sarcastically. Then she turned to look at her Chamberlain. "I forbid *you* to go out there, Dhakan," she told the elderly man quite firmly.

"That's not what we've got in mind, Andine," Althalus told her.

"Who's going to be our emissary then? It's *got* to be somebody who knows what's going on."

"I know," Althalus replied. "That's why *I'm* going to take care of it."

* * *

The Queen of the Night was riding at the head of the column, and she reined in when Althalus and Eliar, accompanied by a platoon of Andine's soldiers, came out through the main gate under a white flag. Gelta barked a few orders, and her soldiers hastily erected a garishly colored pavilion for the incipient parlay. Althalus gave the illusory army at her back a rather cursory glance. From the walls of Osthos that vast army had looked quite substantial, but now that he was closer, Althalus noticed that it didn't move so much as an inch. It was as static as a picture. *Ghend needs more practice,* he muttered silently to Eliar.

I didn't quite follow that, Althalus, the boy confessed.

When you get a little closer to his illusion, it starts to fall apart. Some of those horses out there have all four feet off the ground, and the flags stick out from the lances they're attached to as if they were made of wood. It's a picture of an army, Eliar, and that's all. These two regiments around that striped tent are the entire extent of Gelta's army. Keep your hand close to the hilt of your Knife when we go into that tent, boy. Gelta's not entirely sane, so you might have to show her the Knife to bring her back to her senses.

I'll watch her, Eliar replied.

They dismounted in front of the pavilion, and Althalus drew the white toga he'd borrowed from Lord Dhakan up over one shoulder and assumed a supercilious expression. "You, there— fellow," he said to one of Gelta's Generals in an arrogant voice, "take me to your leader, and be quick about it."

The General's eyes bulged indignantly, but he held his tongue. He stepped to the front of the striped tent and held the flap open. Althalus tossed a copper penny on the ground at the General's feet with a negligent gesture as he and Eliar entered the pavilion. "For your trouble, my man," he said in his best "down the nose" tone of voice.

"Aren't you pushing it just a little?" Eliar whispered in a choked voice.

"Just getting into character," Althalus murmured.

The Queen of the Night was seated on a rough camp chair inside the tent, and she was obviously trying to look regal.

Althalus gave her a perfunctory sort of bow. "I am Trag," he announced, "and I represent her Majesty Andine, Arya of Osthos. What are your demands?"

"Open your gates," Gelta rasped.

"Not until we've discussed the terms, madam." Althalus gave her another "down the nose" look.

"I might let you keep your head if you do exactly as I tell you," Gelta replied. Now that he was closer to her, Althalus could see how truly ugly she really was. Her face was a mass of deeply indented pockmarks, and her big nose had obviously been broken several times. She had piglike little eyes and more than a hint of a mustache. She also had shoulders like an ox and a rancid fragrance about her.

"Madam," Althalus said coldly, "this is neither the time nor the place for threats. Circumstances have given you a slight advantage, and my Arya has instructed me to inquire as to your terms."

"There *are* no terms, you silly fop!" Gelta flared. "Open your gates to me, or I will destroy your city!"

"Try to maintain your perspective, madam," Althalus replied. "Take a moment, if you wish, to go outside and have a look at the walls of Osthos. Our city will stand, no matter what you throw at those walls. A prolonged siege, however, would inconvenience the citizens slightly. To put it to you bluntly, how much will you take to go away?"

"You are very clever—and very brave—Lord Trag," Gelta almost purred. "You will not provoke me, however. Your city cannot withstand my forces. I *will* be in the palace of your Arya by noon tomorrow."

Althalus maintained his expression of bored superiority, despite a sudden urge to dance on the table. Gelta had just inadvertently pinpointed the exact time of Ghend's dream vision. "That has not been determined as yet," he replied in a lofty tone. "Winter approaches, and the walls of Osthos can surely hold until spring. The spring of which *year* might still be in question. To avoid unnecessary bloodshed, however, my Arya has agreed to capitulate and give you our city to pillage as you see fit for *one* week—no more. In return for her most generous offer, you will stand aside until midmorning tomorrow to permit the citizens to depart."

Gelta's face darkened, but the somber-eyed Yakhag, who stood behind her impromptu throne, grasped her shoulder in one mailed fist and leaned forward to whisper to her.

Gelta shrank momentarily from Yakhag's grasp, but then she recovered, and her expression became transparently cunning. "Your ordinary people would just be in my way anyhow," she said in her harsh voice. "Your Arya and her officials, however, will remain in the palace and will surrender to me before noon tomorrow."

"That seems to be a reasonable request," Althalus replied.

"It wasn't a request," Gelta snapped harshly.

"A linguistic variation, perhaps," Althalus murmured urbanely. "Your accent seems to suggest an Ansu background, madam, and the language as spoken here in Treborea has progressed quite noticeably in the past several eons. I shall advise my Arya of your demands, and I shall return before sunset with her response. One more thing, however. No burning. If you will not agree to that stipulation, these talks break off right here and now."

"Why would I want to burn that which is mine?"

"Good question. I'm sure you'll find your stay in my Arya's palace most pleasing. It has many amenities to which you may not be accustomed. I strongly suggest that you take fullest advantage of the baths while you are there."

The faintest hint of a smile touched dead-eyed Yakhag's lips, and Althalus shuddered.

Then he shook off that momentary chill and bowed to the Queen of the Night again. "Until tomorrow, then, Madam Gelta," he said politely, and then he and Eliar left the pavilion before the meaning of the remark that had amused the somber Yakhag had fully dawned on his hostess.

"She let it slip, Em," Althalus reported when he and Eliar rejoined the others in the tower. "I don't think she even realizes that she did it. I'm sure Yakhag caught it, though. *That* one tends to freeze my blood, and I don't think *anything* slips past him. Anyway, Gelta's little charade is scheduled for noon tomorrow."

"Can we have everything in place by then, Sergeant?" Dweia asked Khalor.

"Eliar probably won't get much sleep tonight," Khalor replied, "but I think we'll be ready."

"I'll need to borrow him for about half an hour, Sergeant," Bheid noted. "I should pass this on to my assassins in Kanthon."

Dweia nodded. "And we might want to return Smeugor and Tauri to that fort as well," she added. "Since Ghend's going to take care of them for us, we might as well make it easy for him. Were you able to get any sense of what Yakhag's planning, Leitha?"

"He was blocking me, Dweia," Leitha replied, "and I'm not sure exactly how. It's almost as if he were dead."

"In a certain sense, he *is* dead, Leitha," Dweia replied. "I don't think you should try to break through his barrier, dear. He's even older and more corrupt than Ghend."

"Gelta's afraid of him," Eliar said. "I could see that every time he spoke to her."

"They're *all* afraid of Yakhag," Dweia said solemnly. "Even Ghend's afraid of that one. Daeva holds Yakhag in reserve in Nahgharash for emergencies."

"Doesn't it make you proud to be an emergency, dear?" Leitha asked Andine archly.

"Not really," Andine replied. Then she turned to Dweia. "When should I have Dhakan round up all the spies and cultists in my palace?" she asked.

"Let's get that out of the way tonight," Dweia decided. "As soon as they're all safely in your dungeon, Sergeant Khalor can start bringing in reinforcements to scoop up Gelta's soldiers the minute she enters your palace."

"Everything's coming together real neat, isn't it?" Gher said enthusiastically. "The bad people are all going to think they've got the world by the tail until about noon tomorrow, and then it's all going to turn into a bucketful of worms, isn't it?"

"That's the ultimate reward of a good deception, Gher," Althalus told him. "It's not the money or property you get, so much as it's the satisfaction of outsmarting your victim—and the way he feels when he finally realizes what you've done to him. By this time tomorrow, Ghend's going to be eating his own liver."

"You're a terrible person, Althalus," Dweia chided.

"Be honest, Em," he replied. "Doesn't the notion of Daeva eating *his* liver sort of warm the cockles of *your* heart just a little?"

"That's entirely different," she sniffed with a toss of her head.

"I wouldn't pursue that, Althalus," Leitha advised.

During the night they put on some show of evacuating Osthos. Long, torchlit columns of civilians streamed out through the south gate of the city for Gelta's entertainment; and once the streets were largely deserted, Lord Dhakan's officials quietly gathered up the assorted people in the palace that Leitha had identified as agents of the enemy. Then, about two hours before dawn, Eliar and Sergeant Khalor brought the bald-headed Sergeant Gebhel and six regiments of Gweti's infantry into Osthos.

"I'd guess that most of them are going to throw down their weapons as soon as they see you, Gebhel," Khalor told the bald soldier. "There might be a few enthusiasts, though. Make an example of them, and the rest should get the point."

"You're being obvious, Khalor," Gebhel growled. "What do you want me to do with them after I've rounded them up?"

"I couldn't care less," Khalor replied. "You'll have about ten thousand prisoners on your hands. Maybe you'll get lucky and come across a slave trader."

Gebhel's eyes brightened. "It's a thought," he said.

"I get twenty percent," Khalor advised him.

"Don't be ridiculous. Five at the most."

"Fifteen."

"You *knew* it was going to be ten percent, Khalor," Gebhel said in an exasperated tone. "Why did you start out with that absurd number in the first place?"

Khalor shrugged. "It was worth a try," he said.

"Go away, Khalor. I've got to get my men into position."

"Just be sure they stay out of sight until I give you the signal."

"And did you want me to order them to put their shoes on, too, O mighty military genius?"

"You can be *very* offensive sometimes, Gebhel."

"Then quit trying to tell me how to do my job. Get out of my face, Khalor."

Khalor was laughing when he and Althalus returned to the palace. "I *like* him," he said.

"I never would have guessed," Althalus murmured.

The day dawned clear and bright, and autumn had filled the world with color.

"Don't bite your fingernails, Andine," Leitha told her small friend.

"I'm just a little nervous, Leitha," Andine replied.

"Dweia won't let anything happen to you, dear."

"I'm not worried about *that*, Leitha. Do you think we should run through the performance one more time?"

"Andine, dear, we've practiced it dozens of times already. If you haven't got it right by now, you never will."

"I always get so *nervous* before I make a public appearance," Andine admitted. "Once I get started, I'm all right, but the waiting is awful." She held out her visibly shaking right hand. "Look at that," she said. "It happens every single time."

"You'll do just fine, dear," Leitha said, taking the smaller girl in her arms.

Eliar came into Dhakan's study. "They're stirring up their cooking fires right now, Althalus," he reported. "As soon as Gelta's regiments eat breakfast, they'll be ready to move."

"*They* might be, but I think Gelta may want to hold off just a bit," Althalus replied with a slight frown. "She's supposed to put her foot on Andine's neck at noon, and if she does it too early, it'll probably make things fall apart in the same way they would if she did it late."

"I wish Emmy was here."

"She is, Eliar," Althalus assured him. "We might not be able to see her, but she's here, all the same."

The morning dragged on, lasting, it seemed, forever. Then, perhaps two hours before noon, the Queen of the Night emerged from her pavilion bellowing orders. Her soldiers scurried to their horses, mounted, and formed up. Then Gelta pulled herself up into her saddle and sat, quite obviously waiting for something.

Then Argan and the somber-faced Yakhag came out of the garish pavilion. Argan spoke briefly with the Queen of the Night, and a short argument broke out between them.

Yakhag, however, clashed his mailed fist against his black-armored chest, and Gelta and Argan both fell silent with slightly apprehensive expressions.

Yakhag spoke to the both of them at some length, his face expressionless and his eyes dead.

Gelta started to object once, but Yakhag once again smashed his fist against his armor.

"That's a novel way to tell people to shut up," Sergeant Khalor observed. "There must be some sort of threat involved."

"Probably so," Althalus agreed. "Emmy doesn't want to talk about Yakhag, but I've seen him bully Gelta once or twice. She's *really* afraid of that one."

"Why do you and Eliar and Gher always call your wife 'Emmy'?"

"It's one of those pet names married people come up with now and then," Althalus replied. "It sort of rubbed off on Eliar and Gher. Keep an eye on Yakhag, Khalor. Ghend and Argan are up to something, and Yakhag's the key to whatever it is. There's something going on here that I don't understand, and that always makes me jumpy."

The gates of Osthos stood open and unguarded to suggest to the enemy that the city was deserted. Gelta and Yakhag rode triumphantly into the city and along the broad avenue that led to the palace with the two Kanthonese regiments drawn up in close order behind them.

"She didn't leave any men to secure the gates," Khalor said incredulously.

"Gelta's a country girl, Sergeant," Althalus replied lightly. "She hasn't had much experience with cities. She *did* put her shoes on, though."

"Very funny, Althalus," Khalor said sardonically.

When the Queen of the Night reached the palace, she barked out several commands, and her regiments surrounded the huge structure.

"We could call Gebhel in right now, you know," Khalor suggested. "That'd put an end to all this nonsense before it went any further."

"We'd spoil Andine's whole day if we did that, and she'd go on about it for weeks."

"Good point. She's got a pretty voice, I suppose, but I hate it when she points it in my direction."

When they reached the throne room, Andine was practicing her cringing for all she was worth.

"Isn't she overdoing that just a bit?" Khalor quietly asked.

"Her audience isn't going to be very sophisticated," Althalus replied. "Now, Sergeant, listen rather carefully. Andine's going to kneel down in front of Gelta, and that's your signal to start the ball rolling. As soon as Andine's knees touch the floor, I want Gebhel's troops to move on the men surrounding the palace, and I'll want the men you've got hidden here to overpower Gelta's bodyguards. You're going to be hearing some peculiar sounds, but don't pay any attention to them."

"Your wife's already explained all this to me, Althalus," Khalor said.

"She *did*? She didn't tell *me* she was going to do that."

"Maybe she was trying to surprise you. I know where I'm supposed to be and what I'm supposed to do. Now why don't you go on inside and let *me* take care of things out here?"

Althalus went on to the throne room, grumbling to himself.

It may have been pure coincidence, but it probably wasn't, that the long-familiar wailing sound began to echo through the halls of Andine's palace the moment Althalus entered the throne room, and no more than a moment later the Queen of the Night appeared in the doorway with Argan and the dead-eyed Yakhag close behind her. "What wench is this who doth defile my seat?" Gelta demanded harshly.

"I . . . I am Andine, Arya of Osthos," Andine replied in a quavering voice.

"Thou wert! But no more! Let the wench be bound in chains, and let this task fall to her own servants, so that they who loyally follow me be not defiled by touching this abomination!"

"Would you do the honors, Lord Trag?" Argan suggested to Althalus in a faintly amused voice.

"As you wish, Reverend Sir," Althalus replied, bowing slightly.

Something wasn't right here. Neither Argan nor Yakhag had been present during the original dream vision. He moved quickly to the throne, however. Andine was well rehearsed, but still . . . *Keep your mouth shut and your eyes on the floor,* he silently advised. *Gelta's trying to goad you into some kind of flare-up.*

I'll kill her! Andine shouted silently in reply.

Althalus had prudently concealed a set of chains identical to those Andine had worn in the original dream, and he quickly clapped them around the Arya's wrists and ankles. *Don't wiggle!* he sent his thought through the curtain of her rage. *The chains aren't locked.* Then he took her roughly by the arm and dragged her from her throne.

"Thy service shall not go unrewarded, Lord Trag," Gelta told him, striding toward the throne. "Advise all others herein that submission unto me is the path to life."

"It shall be as thou dost command, O Queen of the Night," Althalus replied, bowing deeply.

The wailing rose to shake the very walls.

Then Gelta, Queen of the Night, mounted the dais and sat upon the golden throne of Osthos with imperious demeanor and bleak satisfaction.

"And now shalt thou kneel and submit unto me, frail child," ox-shouldered Gelta said, "and should thy submission please me, mayhap I shall spare thy life."

Althalus once again seized Andine's arm and dragged her up onto the dais. *You know what to do,* he sent to her. *Do it.*

Andine dropped to her knees. "Do with me as thou wilt, mighty Queen," she said in her best throbbing voice, "but I pray thee, spare my beloved city."

Keep talking! Althalus hissed. *Every word you speak is disrupting Ghend's original version of this.*

"Be merciful, dread Queen!" Andine's voice soared, covering another sound that had begun to intrude upon the wailing that always accompanied Ghend's dream visions.

Althalus looked sharply at Eliar, who was standing with Bheid and Salkan among the cowering courtiers. The young man's face was grim, and he had the Knife half drawn. Dweia had evidently been issuing instructions to the others, and it seemed that she'd neglected to include Althalus.

"On thy face!" stern Gelta commanded the kneeling Arya. "Grovel before me that I may know that thy submission is absolute!"

Then Althalus heard some muffled shouts coming from outside the palace, shouts concealed beneath the competing wail and the song of the Knife. Sergeant Gebhel, it appeared, was right on schedule.

Then Leitha's voice sounded sharply inside his head. *Althalus!* she shouted. *They're real! It's not an illusion!*

What isn't?

That army outside the walls! It's real! There are thousands of them, and they're marching on the gates!

Althalus began silently cursing his own inattention. Ghend had his own doors and his own doorkeeper. Yakhag was obviously involved in some way, but events were already moving too fast to worry about that now. Ghend's dream vision was already in full swing.

And, weeping, Arya Andine lowered her face to the very stones of the floor as the wailing rose to a shriek.

And the heart of Gelta was full, and the taste of victory on her tongue was sweet, sweet.

And she placed her rough-booted foot upon the soft neck of

groveling Andine in exultant triumph, declaring, "All that was yours is now mine, Andine, yea, verily, even thy life and all thy blood!"

And the triumphant cry of the Queen of the Night echoed down the marble-clad palace of the fallen Arya of Osthos.

Khalor's soldiers were supposed to be removing Gelta's sentries at this point, but the black-armored Nekweros were still in place in every doorway of the throne room, and sounds coming from the corridors suggested that Khalor's men were encountering some unexpected opposition.

What's going on, Althalus? Bheid's silent voice was shrill. *Why are those enemy soldiers still guarding the doorways?*

It's Yakhag! Althalus sent his thought back sharply. *He's slipped an army into Osthos while we weren't watching!*

The song of the Knife faltered as the wail rose to a triumphant shriek.

"Tripped you up, didn't I, old boy?" Argan said smugly to Althalus. "You should really pay closer attention, you know. You might be a match for Ghend, but you're out of your class when you come up against me." Then he turned to look at Bheid. "Well, Brother, we meet at last. Awfully good of you to put in an appearance. You've saved me all the time and trouble of hunting you down. It's really a shame that we won't have time for a nice chat, but I'm dreadfully busy right now." Then he turned to his black-armored companion. "Yakhag," he said in an offhand manner, "*do* be a good fellow and kill that priest for me, would you?"

Yakhag nodded expressionlessly and advanced on Bheid, his heavy sword at the ready.

Salkan, however, snatched Eliar's sword from its sheath and jumped in front of his teacher. "You'll have to get through me first!" the fiery young redhead shouted, awkwardly brandishing Eliar's sword.

Yakhag shrugged expressionlessly, flicked his sword slightly to tap the sword the shepherd was waving off to one side, and then drove his sword completely through Salkan's body.

Salkan doubled over sharply, and Eliar's sword went skittering across the floor of Andine's throne room.

"Get out of my way, Bheid!" Eliar shouted as both of them rushed after the sliding sword.

Bheid, however, had already snatched up the sword. Shoving Eliar aside, he rushed at Yakhag, who was struggling to free his sword from Salkan's limp body.

Althalus saw immediately that Bheid had probably never held a sword before, since he was swinging it much as he would an ax, grasping the hilt in both hands and chopping at Yakhag's helmet.

Bheid's third stroke sent the visor of Yakhag's helmet flying, and Yakhag raised his arms to cover his head.

"Stab, Bheid!" Eliar shouted. "Stab! Stab!"

Bheid awkwardly reversed his grip on the hilt of Eliar's sword and drove the point against the black breastplate of Yakhag's armor. The sword point penetrated only slightly, but Bheid wrenched the sword from side to side, grinding more than cutting as he worked the blade to enlarge the hole in the steel. Then, still holding the sword in place, he lunged, throwing his full weight against the hilt. Then he lunged again, and bright blood burst forth from Yakhag's mouth.

Yakhag cried out and desperately grabbed the blade Bheid was methodically driving through his body.

Bheid's face contorted with hate, and he lunged against the sword hilt yet again.

Yakhag screamed, and his hands fell away from the sword blade.

Bheid lunged one last time, and Althalus clearly heard the scrape of the sword point against the steel backplate of Yakhag's armor.

For a very brief instant Althalus saw a faint hint of something that looked almost like gratitude touch Yakhag's eyes, and then the black-armored savage shuddered and collapsed beside Salkan's inert body.

Bheid stared in horror at the man he had just killed and at the one who had died for him, and then he wept, sobbing like a broken-hearted child.

Once again, there was that peculiar flicker, and Khnom burst out of nowhere, grasped the stunned Argan by the arm, and dragged him through a doorway that had flames behind it.

And then the doorway vanished—and so did the black-armored Nekweros who had been guarding every door in the throne room.

"Get your foot off me, you stinking hag!" Andine's soaring voice broke through the stunned silence that had fallen over the throne room, even as the wild wailing faltered and the song of the Knife soared.

Gelta's eyes widened in astonishment, and her hand flashed toward her sword hilt.

"I wouldn't," Sergeant Khalor advised her. "There are ten arrows aimed directly at your heart, ma'am. If your sword comes out so much as an inch, you're dead meat."

Gelta froze.

"Get off my throne!" Andine commanded, rising to her feet and discarding her chains.

Gelta stared at her in open disbelief. "This can't happen!" she exclaimed.

"It just did!" Andine told her. "Now move, or I'll take an ax to you myself."

"I have an army!" Gelta blustered. "They'll destroy this entire city!"

"Weren't you watching just now?" Althalus said. "Your army vanished when Yakhag died. You're all alone, Gelta."

"Chain this foul-smelling cow!" Andine commanded. "And drag her down to my dungeon!"

The palace guards swarmed over the struggling Queen of the Night, and Althalus neatly locked Andine's discarded chains about Gelta's wrists and ankles.

The guards dragged Gelta toward a side door, but the song of the Knife continued to soar.

"Just a moment, please," Eliar said, wrenching his sword from Yakhag's inert body. "There's something I need to show to the prisoner."

Gelta turned, her back to the door.

Eliar sheathed his sword and drew the Knife. "I thought you should see this before you leave," Eliar said bleakly. Then he held the Knife out with the flat of the blade directly in front of her eyes.

Gelta shrieked in agony, trying to raise her chained arms so that she could cover her eyes. She flinched back against the door, and it swung smoothly open.

The Queen of the Night fell backward through the door—and vanished.

"What did you *do*?" Andine demanded of Eliar, her voice rattling the windows.

"Emmy told me to do it, Andine." Eliar tried to shift the blame. "It wasn't *my* idea."

"I wanted to put that stinking cow in my dungeon."

"I think Emmy just stole your doormat, dear," Leitha murmured. "Now you'll have to wipe your feet on something else."

"Where *is* she, Eliar?" Andine insisted. "Where did that door take her?"

"She's in the House now, Andine," Eliar replied. "Emmy fixed up a special room for her. It's a fairly *nice* room—except that it doesn't have a door. From what Emmy told me, I guess that Gelta's managed to break out of jails before. She won't break out of *that* one, though."

"How long does Emmy plan to keep her there?"

"She didn't say," Eliar said, shrugging, "but the look on her face when she told me what to do had 'forever' written all over it."

"Forever!" Andine's eyes widened in horror.

"At least forever," Eliar said. "Or maybe just a little while longer."

There was a sudden silence in Andine's throne room, broken only by Brother Bheid's hopeless sobbing.

Part Six

LEITHA

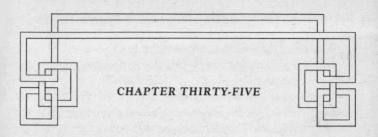

CHAPTER THIRTY-FIVE

"Not a chance, Althalus," Sergeant Khalor said bleakly. "He's gone."

The Sergeant's right, Althalus, Dweia's voice murmured. *We've lost Salkan.*

Isn't there anything you can do, Em?

No, I'm afraid not.

Althalus swore.

"My sentiments exactly," Khalor said. "I really liked that boy. I think we all did."

"Bheid seems to be taking it strangely. I can't figure him out."

"He did the right thing, though," Khalor nudged the sprawled body of the black-armored Yakhag with his foot. "Who was this fellow, anyway?"

"I'm not completely sure, Sergeant," Althalus admitted. "He seems to have been some kind of outsider who only answered to Argan. I don't think Ghend had any control over him. There was quite a bit going on that I didn't understand."

"We won, though. That's all that really matters." Then Khalor frowned. "I thought priests weren't supposed to kill people," he added. "Isn't that one of the things that aren't permitted?"

"I'm not all that familiar with Church law myself," Althalus replied, "but Brother Bheid seems to have gone a little crazy after Yakhag killed Salkan."

"It happens," Khalor said, shrugging. "You might want to keep a close eye on him for a while. He's not an Arum, so he hasn't had much training. An Arum doesn't get upset when he

has to kill an enemy. A priest from the low country, though . . .
Well, I'm sure you get my point."

"You don't have to beat me over the head with it," Althalus
replied. He squinted at Bheid. "He doesn't seem to be too awfully upset, though."

"That's what I'm talking about, Althalus. He *should* be. He
just lost a very close friend, and then he did something that's absolutely forbidden. That blank expression on his face is making
me a bit edgy. I wouldn't let him get close to anything with a
sharp point for a while."

"He wouldn't do anything like that," Althalus scoffed.

"Not if he's in his right mind, probably. But I don't think he *is*
in his right mind at the moment."

"I'll watch him," Althalus agreed. "Let's get those two bodies
out of his sight for right now. Then I think maybe Eliar and I
should take Bheid back to the House and turn him over to
Emmy."

"That might be best," Khalor agreed.

"It may take a while, my Arya," Lord Dhakan said in a weary
voice two days later when they all gathered in Andine's throne
room. "We didn't explain very much to the members of the court
before that barbaric woman rode into Osthos."

"We couldn't really, Dhakan," Andine said from her throne.
"The palace was absolutely *infested* with spies."

"Not anymore," Leitha murmured.

"Unfortunately, that's *also* contributed to this outbreak of
skittishness," Dhakan pointed out. "I'm sure they were all on the
enemy payroll, but throwing footmen and stable boys into the
dungeon along with high-ranking members of the court lays a
strong odor of arbitrary capriciousness over the whole procedure, and there's no really rational explanation for some of those
arrests." Dhakan passed a weary hand across his face. "I'm sure
that Leitha was right in her identifications of those enemy
agents, but it's not the sort of thing you'd want to take into any
law court." He sighed.

"You're exhausted, aren't you, Dhakan?" Andine asked sympathetically.

"I *am* just a bit worn down, my Arya," he admitted. "It's been fairly hectic here lately."

"Why don't you go eat and then get some sleep?"

"There are so many things left to do," he protested.

"They'll wait. Get to bed, Dhakan."

"But—"

She drew herself up on her throne. "Go to your room! Now!" she commanded, pointing to the door.

"Yes, Mother," he replied with a faint smile. Then he turned and wearily shuffled from the room.

"I *love* that old man," Andine murmured fondly.

"I never would have guessed," Leitha said.

Then Eliar and Gher entered Andine's throne room. "It's all finished up at Poma," Eliar advised them. "Twengor ran the enemy forces out of town and Kreuter and Dreigon rolled right over the top of them."

"Where's Khalor?" Althalus asked.

"He's stuck to that window," Gher replied. "I don't think you could drag him away from it with a team of horses."

"He wants me to come right back," Eliar added, "in case he needs to use the door. I'm supposed to tell you that Twengor's coming here for his money. The Sergeant thinks we should probably have a conference after Kreuter and Dreigon finish up at Kadon and Mawor."

"That might not be a bad idea," Althalus agreed. "How's Bheid?"

"He's been sleeping quite a lot," Gher replied. "Emmy says that's the best way to calm him down."

"He *is* going to be all right, isn't he?" Leitha asked in a worried voice.

"He acts a little strange whenever Emmy lets him wake up," Gher told her. "He talks about stuff that I don't quite understand. Emmy lets him go on and on about it while he's eating, and then she puts him back to sleep again. Don't worry, Leitha. Emmy's not going to let him stay strange. She'll fix him, even if she has to take him apart and put him back together again."

Leitha shuddered. "What a gruesome thought."

"You know our Emmy," Gher told her.

The citizens who had fled at Gelta's approach began to filter back into the city, and life in Osthos had almost returned to normal by the time Chief Twengor, accompanied by Duke Bherdor, reached the main gate. Althalus was a bit surprised to discover that Twengor was still avoiding strong ale. "Where's Khalor?" the vastly bearded Chief asked after he and Althalus had settled accounts.

"He's away—on business," Althalus replied evasively.

"He certainly moves around a lot."

"He's got a fairly big war on his hands."

"That's what I wanted to talk with him about. He was making loud noises about doing something sort of permanent to Kanthon after we'd mauled their armies. Since I'll be going in that direction on my way home anyway, I thought that maybe he and I should have a little talk."

"It probably wouldn't hurt. I see you've brought Duke Bherdor with you."

Twengor nodded. "He's a good boy, but he's such an innocent that the merchants in his town were able to bamboozle him about taxes. Now that Poma's in ruins, he'll get to start all over from the ground up. I told him that it might go a little smoother if he issued certain commands from Osthos for a while. If he's going to rebuild Poma, he's going to need money, and that means taxes. Bherdor wants the people of Poma to like him, and if I'd left him there, the merchants would have been all over him like a flock of vultures. He needs to study 'firm' for a while, and this might be the best place for him to get that kind of training."

"You've changed quite a bit, Chief Twengor."

"Now that I'm sober, you mean?"

"That might have something to do with it, yes."

"I was very sorry to hear about that redheaded shepherd,"

Twengor said. "It really upset those Wekti boys I had working for me. Did anybody get around to doing anything about it?"

"Brother Bheid took care of it."

"I wasn't talking about a funeral, Althalus."

"Neither was I. Bheid pounded a sword through the man who killed Salkan."

"A priest?" Twengor demanded incredulously. "I thought they weren't supposed to do that."

"I guess Bheid thought it was a special situation."

"I will *never* understand the lowlanders," Twengor said.

The chill of autumn had stripped the trees of their leaves by the time the invading armies had been driven out of Andine's realm, and the Dukes and Arum Clan Chiefs gathered in Osthos to consider further action.

"What it finally boils down to is the food supply," Duke Nitral observed in the conference room late one gloomy afternoon. "Burning off the wheat fields in central Treborea made good sense when we were being invaded, but now that winter's almost here, I think we're all having second thoughts about it."

"I might have an answer to that," Duke Olkar of Kadon said. "I have quite a few contacts among the grain merchants of Maghu. I'm sure they'll nudge their prices up just a bit, but there's plenty of wheat in Perquaine."

"We have to feed the peasants first," Andine declared. "I *won't* let my children starve."

"Your *children*?" Eliar sounded startled.

"Emmy's been talking to her, Eliar," Gher advised his friend, "and you know how Emmy is about things like that."

"You'll strip the treasury, my Arya," Lord Dhakan cautioned.

"That's just too bad. This is an emergency."

"The mother of Treborea hath spoken," Leitha intoned. "Pay heed unto her, lest she send you all to bed without any supper."

"That's not funny, Leitha," Andine snapped.

"I sort of liked it," Gher said, grinning impudently at Andine.

"Things might be a little chaotic in Perquaine at the moment," Duke Nitral cautioned Olkar. "Most of the invaders to the west of the River Osthos fled over into Perquaine after Kreuter and Dreigon raised the siege at Mawor, plus there's some peculiar religious turmoil over there."

"They're arguing about *religion*?" Twengor demanded incredulously. "Isn't that sort of like arguing about the weather?"

"The Perquaines get peculiar every so often," Nitral said, shrugging. "Sitting around listening to wheat grow gives them too much time for idle thought."

"The grain merchants in Maghu worship money," Olkar said. "I speak the same language, so we'll get along all right."

"I think this situation all boils down to short rations," Sergeant Khalor observed. "I know it's not customary, and it goes against most of what we've been taught, but I think we'd all better saddle up and move on Kanthon right now."

"A war in wintertime?" Koleika Iron Jaw said dubiously. "That's the wrong time of year, isn't it?"

"It's not going to be much of a war, Koleika," Twengor told him. "All the mercenaries who were working for the Kanthons ran away after Kreuter and Dreigon mauled them, and the Aryo of Kanthon himself turned up mysteriously dead one morning last week. All we really have to do is swing by Kanthon on our way back home to Arum and invite them to surrender. I don't think they're going to argue with us, do you?"

"Twengor's got a good point, gentlemen," Chief Albron said. "Let's get out of Treborea as soon as we can." He smiled faintly. "I'm sure the mother of Treborea will miss us terribly, but if we start rummaging around in her pantry, she might get a little grumpy with us."

Lady Astarell, who sat at Albron's side, nudged him with her elbow.

"Yes?" he said, smiling fondly at her.

"Ask my uncle," she said shortly. "Do it now."

"This isn't really the proper time, dear."

"Do it, Albron, before you forget."

"Shouldn't we do that in private?"

"Did you plan to keep it a secret?"

"Well, no, but—"

"Just do it, Albron."

"Yes, dear." Albron cleared his throat. "Chief Kreuter," he said rather formally.

"Yes, Chief Albron," Kreuter replied. "What can I do for you?" The blond-bearded Plakander had a faint smile hovering about his lips.

"This is serious, Uncle," Astarell scolded him.

"Sorry, dear. I take it that you have a request of some kind, Chief Albron?"

"I beseech you, mighty Chief, to grant me the hand of your niece, Astarell, in marriage," Albron declared.

"What an amazing notion!" Kreuter said. "That idea never would have occurred to me in a thousand years."

"*Will* you stop that, Uncle?" Astarell flared.

"Just teasing, child." Kreuter grinned broadly at her. "What's *your* opinion in this matter? You *could* do worse, you know. Chief Albron doesn't know very much about horses, but otherwise, he's not bad."

"Oh," Astarell said with a mischievous little smile, "I *guess* he'll do."

"Astarell!" Albron objected.

"All right, Astarell," Kreuter said, "if this is what you really want, I'll be happy to oblige. Chief Albron, you have my permission to marry my niece. Does that make everybody happy?"

"A thousand horses, I think," Astarell said thoughtfully.

"I didn't quite follow that, dear," Kreuter confessed.

"My dowry, Uncle. A thousand horses seems about right to me—along with my wedding dress, of course."

"A *thousand*?" Kreuter almost screamed. "Are you out of your mind?"

"You *do* love me, don't you, Uncle? You're not just getting rid of me, are you?"

"Of course I love you, Astarell, but a *thousand* horses?"

"It lets everybody in Plakand know how much you value me, dear Uncle Kreuter," she said sweetly.

"Did you put her up to this, Albron?" Kreuter demanded.

"Actually, it's the first I've heard about it." Albron looked at

Astarell in total bafflement. "What in the world am I supposed to do with a thousand horses?" he demanded.

"I don't really care, Albron. The number establishes my value. I'm *not* some beggar girl at the side of the road."

Albron and Kreuter exchanged a helpless took. "Yes, Astarell," they both said almost in perfect unison.

Winter had settled over central Treborea as the royal party rode north out of Osthos, and dirty clouds scudded chill and somber across the war-ravaged region.

They stopped briefly in Mawor, then rounded the lake to the city of Kadon. "I'll leave you now, my Arya," Duke Olkar said. "I'll negotiate as best I can with the grain merchants in Maghu, but I'm certain they'll try to skin me."

"I'm afraid that can't be helped, Olkar," she said. "I *must* have bread for my people."

"I think you both might be overlooking something," Althalus said. "There *are* granaries in Kanthon, and there hasn't been a war there—yet. When we take the city, the granaries become our property. You might want to mention that when you're negotiating with the bloodsuckers in Maghu, Duke Olkar. I wouldn't throw words like 'emergency' or 'starvation' around, if I were you. Try 'contingency' or 'possible spoilage' instead."

"You've done this sort of thing yourself, haven't you, Lord Althalus?" Olkar suggested.

"I've pulled off a few fairly elaborate flimflams on occasion, your Grace, yes," Althalus admitted, "and there's not really much difference between what *you* do and what I *used* to do, now is there?"

Olkar suddenly grinned at him. "That's supposed to be a secret, Lord Althalus," he chided.

He'll do just fine, Andine, Althalus assured the Arya of Osthos. Then he looked back at Olkar. "You might want to keep the negotiations sort of tenuous, your Grace," he suggested. "After we take Kanthon, I'll have a quick look at their granaries, and then I'll join you in Maghu. Let's find out where we *really* stand before we start throwing money away."

"My thought exactly, Lord Althalus," Olkar agreed.

When they reached the palace of Duke Olkar, they found Captains Gelun and Wendan waiting for them. "It grieves us to report that the Chieftains of our mighty clans fell heroically in the recent war," the tall Captain Wendan announced with no hint whatsoever of a smile.

"All of Arum grieves with you, noble Captain," Albron intoned.

"Does that more or less cover the formalities?" Captain Gelun asked.

"I'd say so," Twengor advised. "We wouldn't want our grief to overwhelm us, would we?"

"I'm bearing up fairly well," Gelun replied.

"Who's going to replace them?" Koleika Iron Jaw demanded abruptly.

"That's just a bit murky right now, I'm afraid," Wendan reported. "There's no clear and direct line of succession—some second cousins and a few nephews is about all."

"Is anybody any good at making speeches?" Koleika asked, looking around at the other Clan Chiefs.

"Albron's about the best," Laiwon suggested. "At least he knows how to read, so maybe he could quote some poetry."

"Am I missing something here?" Andine asked with a puzzled expression. "Here in Treborea, succession's determined by bloodline—consanguinity, I think it's called."

"We're a bit more relaxed in Arum, little mother," Twengor said with a faint smile. "In situations like this one, the other Clan Chiefs can serve in an advisory capacity. *We* have to be able to get along with the new Chiefs, so our 'suggestions' carry quite bit of weight." He looked at his fellow Chiefs. "Would I be overstepping any rules to suggest Gelun and Wendan as the best candidates?" he asked.

"I think *I* could live with them," Laiwon agreed.

"I thought we'd already made that decision," Koleika said. "Are we all agreed, then?"

The other Chiefs nodded.

"I'll start working on my speech," Albron said. He looked at

Captain Wendan. "Just exactly how did Smeugor and Tauri die?" he asked. "Maybe I should work that into my oration."

"I wouldn't, if I were you," Wendan replied. "It wasn't particularly pleasant. There was fire involved, and some long iron skewers." The Captain glanced at Andine, Leitha, and Astarell. "I don't think the ladies would want to hear the details," he added.

"Ah . . . no," Albron agreed, "probably not. I'll gloss over what happened and let it go as 'heroic.' "

"That might be best," Captain Gelun agreed.

"Where are your clansmen currently?" Twengor asked.

"Up near the frontier," Wendan replied. "I *doubt* the Kanthons are going to try anything, but it doesn't hurt to be on the safe side."

"Good thinking," Twengor said approvingly. "Why don't we go up there and take care of the formalities? Then we can march on Kanthon so that we can get the coronation out of the way before we all go home."

"Which coronation was that, Chief Twengor?" Andine asked with a puzzled frown.

"Yours, little mother," he said with a fond smile. "I thought it might be sort of nice to crown you Empress of Treborea—right after we've sacked and burned the city of Kanthon."

"Empress?" Andine's eyes went very wide.

"It has a nice ring to it, wouldn't you say?" Twengor suggested with a sly look.

"All hail her Imperial Majesty, Andine of Treborea," Leitha intoned.

"Well, now," Andine said. "Isn't *that* an interesting idea?"

"Don't bite your nails, dear," Leitha told her. "It makes them look terrible."

Chief Albron's funeral oration was suitably sad and flowery, and it glossed over the character defects of the departed Smeugor and Tauri. Then each Clan Chief and Sergeant of the armies of Arum rose to recommend Gelun and Wendan as interim Chiefs—until after things settled down a bit.

"Interim?" Leitha murmured to Althalus.

"A few centuries or so," Althalus explained. "It's a fairly common sort of thing in Arum. Distant relatives usually don't take offense when a new Chief has 'interim' tacked onto his title. It tends to be dropped after a few generations."

"Do men *ever* grow up?" she asked.

"Not if we can avoid it, no."

There were some conferences among the now-leaderless clansmen of south Arum, and some heated arguments about terminology. "Interim" ultimately won out over "temporary," and the entire matter was settled with hardly any bloodshed.

Then Chief Albron once again rose to address the assembled clans. "Gentlemen," he announced, "our gracious employer has a few thoughts she'd like to share with us."

"What's this?" Althalus demanded of Leitha.

"Andine's going to make a speech, Daddy," Leitha replied. "Doesn't that just thrill you all to pieces?"

"Do you *have* to do that, Leitha?"

"Every now and then, yes. It's one of those things I just can't seem to keep bottled up."

Tiny Andine climbed up into an abandoned farm cart so that the towering men of Arum could see her. "My dear friends," she said in her soaring voice, "the warriors of the fair mountains of Arum are without peers in the known world, and I am quite overwhelmed by the magnificent victory you have presented to me. My enemies have been crushed, and now we march on Kanthon. I had thought to lay waste that city, but your demonstration of sweet reason here today has caused me to reconsider that course. My enemy, the Aryo of Kanthon, now lies dead. The stones of Kanthon did nothing to offend me, and spanking stones wouldn't really accomplish very much, now would it?"

They laughed at that.

"With all of Arum at my back, I could ride roughshod over Kanthon and impose my will upon her citizens, but what would that accomplish—except to arouse eternal enmity? I watched with astonishment this day when the most warlike people on earth bowed to reason and averted a return to the clan wars of antiquity. I am but a foolish girl, but the lesson you have presented this day has impressed itself upon me indelibly. Therefore, I go to Kanthon not as a conqueror, but as a liberator. We will *not* burn Kanthon, nor will we slaughter the citizens, nor loot the city. Sweet reason shall be our guide—even as it was *your* guide in your discussions this day. I *will* follow your example, my brave warriors—braver still in that you chose *not* to fight this day."

The laughter had faded by now, and there was a stony silence as Andine left her impromptu platform.

Then Chief Twengor rose. "She's the one who's paying us," he announced bluntly, "so we'll all do things her way, won't we? If anybody has any problems with that, come and see me. I'll explain it—in detail, if that's the way you want it."

"Nice speech," Leitha murmured.

"Which one?" Althalus asked her.

"Take your pick, Daddy dear," she suggested. "If I know Andine—and I *do*—she wrote both of them. Twengor's epilogue fit onto the end of *her* speech just a little too neatly to be a pure accident, don't you think?"

Late that evening Althalus reached out to Dweia. *We need to talk, Em,* he sent.

Problems? her voice responded.

I'm starting to lose my grip on Leitha. She's getting more erratic every day. She's trying to hide it, but she's desperately concerned about Bheid. How's he doing?

About the same. I've been letting him sleep—well, forcing him, actually. Every time I bring him back, he starts off again.

How long has it been there?

A month at least.

And he still *hasn't come around?*

Not noticeably. He's overwhelmed with guilt, Althalus. He's blaming himself for Salkan's death, and he's horrified by what he did to Yakhag. I'm having trouble getting around his early training.

He has *to be able to function, Em. Perquaine's right on the verge of boiling over, and we'll be going there before very long, won't we?*

Probably, yes.

The Perquaines are getting involved in a religious controversy, and something like that has "Argan" written all over it. Bheid's the one who's supposed to deal with Argan, isn't he?

Probably so, yes.

Then he has to get over this—soon. If we lose Bheid, we'll lose Leitha as well. She's the most fragile one in the group, and without Bheid, she'll come apart.

You're more perceptive than I'd thought, love.

It's no big thing, Em. I used to make my living by reading people, remember? Give it a few more days, and a loud noise will shatter Leitha like a pane of glass.

I'm working on it, pet. Bheid may be quite a bit older the next time you see him, but that won't matter as long as he's here. If he needs years to get over this, I'll see to it that he has those years.

The gates of Kanthon stood open and unguarded, and the streets were deserted as Andine rode at the head of her escort to the palace. Sergeant Gebhel ran his hand over his bald head with a regretful sigh. "We could have picked up a fortune here," he lamented.

"And continued a war we're sick of fighting in the process," Khalor reminded him.

"Chief Gweti isn't going to be *too* happy when peace breaks out here in Treborea."

"Into each life some rain must fall, Sergeant," Leitha told him solemnly.

"I've noticed that," Gebhel replied, "and Gweti's likely to cloud up and rain all over me when I tell him that the Treborean wars have ended."

Sergeant Khalor dispatched several platoons of soldiers to search the palace thoroughly for any hidden pockets of armed men and to summon any remaining officials to the throne room, "to confer with the Liberatress."

"Ah, Lord Aidhru." Dhakan greeted an elderly official who

was standing rather apprehensively off to one side as Imperial Andine entered the throne room with her entourage. "I see you managed to survive the recent unpleasantness."

"Barely," the old man replied. "What are *you* doing here, Dhakan? I'd have thought you'd be in your dotage by now."

"You're at least as old as I am, Aidhru," Dhakan reminded him. "Why on earth did you let Pelghat push this stupid war as far as he did?"

The old Kanthonese statesman spread his hands helplessly. "I lost control of him, Dhakan. He wriggled out from under my thumb." Aidhru blinked suddenly. "Is that you, Sergeant Khalor?" he asked with some astonishment. "I thought you'd gotten yourself killed in the last war down here."

"I'm fairly hard to kill, Lord Aidhru."

"You've changed sides, I see."

"Better pay, my Lord," Khalor explained.

"You've not met our divine Arya, have you, Aidhru?" Dhakan said.

Aidhru looked at Andine. "She's only a child," he observed. "I'd heard that she was thirty feet tall."

"That's her voice, my friend," Dhakan said. "Andine herself is quite tiny, but she *does* manage to make herself heard on occasion."

"Be nice," Andine chided gently.

"Yes, Mother," Dhakan replied with a slight bow.

"I *do* wish you'd all stop that," Andine complained

"Sorry, your Majesty," Dhakan apologized. "It's Leitha's doing, you know." Then his tone turned formal. "Lord Aidhru, I have the honor to present my Arya, her Majesty, Andine of Osthos."

Aidhru bowed deeply.

"And this, my Arya, is Chamberlain Aidhru of Kanthon, who was chief advisor to Aryo Pelghat until that ruler's recent demise."

"You might want to add 'ignored' in there someplace, Dhakan," Aidhru suggested. "Toward the end there, Pelghat refused even to see me. There were some foreigners who'd set up camp here in the throne room, and Pelghat only listened to them."

"We were more or less aware of that," Althalus stepped in. "When you get down to the meat of things, this recent war didn't really involve the Kanthons at all. It was one of the end results of a very old disagreement between me and a man named Ghend."

"Ah," Aidhru said. "*That* one. It chilled my blood just being in the same room with him." Then the Kanthonese statesman indicated the throne. "Would you care to try your new seat, Arya Andine?" he asked politely.

"No, Lord Aidhru," she replied, "I don't really think so. It *is* just a bit massive for my tastes, and I haven't really come here to Kanthon as a conqueror. As Lord Althalus just explained, the *real* war was the one between him and the man named Ghend." She smiled winsomely. "In reality, Lord Aidhru, Kanthon and Osthos were little more than innocent bystanders. Right now, we have more important things to do than sitting around chewing old soup. The major battleground of the recent unpleasantness was central Treborea, and we've pretty much lost this year's wheat crop. We're staring in the face of a long, hungry winter, my Lord, and even if it bankrupts both Kanthon and Osthos, I will *not* let the people starve."

"We're in total agreement on that issue, Arya Andine."

"Is there some conference room nearby?" Dhakan asked. "My feet are starting to hurt, and I rather believe we'll be at this for quite some time, so we might as well get comfortable."

"May I ask a few specialists to sit in, Arya Andine?" Aidhru asked.

"Certainly, my Lord," she replied quickly. "You and Dhakan and I could sit around and speculate all day and not really get anywhere. That's why we have experts in the first place, isn't it?"

"You lucky devil," Aidhru said to Dhakan. "Not only is your Arya pleasant to look at, but she's also got her head on straight. You wouldn't *believe* how unpleasant things were here in Kanthon after Pelghat ascended the throne. If I could find out exactly who arranged that maniac's death, I'd fall down and lick our benefactor's feet."

Andine lifted one of her tiny feet and looked at it critically. "They aren't really that clean right now, Lord Aidhru," she told him with a coy little smile. "Maybe after I bathe, we could talk about that."

Aidhru blinked, and then he suddenly laughed. "I should have guessed," he said. "Why don't we find a nice, soft chair in a warm room for our cranky old friend here? Then we can talk about assassinations, forms of government, and just how the devil we're going to feed the people of Treborea until next spring."

The conference room to which Chamberlain Aidhru led them was large and well appointed. "I could send for some ale," Aidhru suggested, glancing at the hulking Arums.

"None for me, thanks all the same," Chief Twengor said shortly. "Maybe something to eat, though."

"Aren't you well, Uncle?" Chief Laiwon asked in a startled voice.

"Actually, I am, Laiwon," Twengor replied, "and I plan to stay that way. I'm not sure exactly how Althalus here boiled all the residue of ten years of heavy drinking out of my blood, but I haven't felt this good since I was a boy—and I'm not going to take any chances with it."

"Would you be offended if *I* had some?" Laiwon asked.

"It's your belly—and your head. If you want to tear them apart, that's up to you."

They all took seats around a long conference table. Althalus opened the discussion. "I think we're going to need some precise numbers. We'll want a fairly accurate count of how many mouths we'll have to feed *and* just how much wheat's stored in the granaries of Kanthon, Osthos, and all the other cities in Treborea. Once we start putting those numbers together, we'll know just how short we are." He looked at Aidhru. "Our little mother has already taken some steps to get things rolling," he advised.

"*Will* you all stop that!" Andine's voice soared. "I am *not* anybody's 'little mother'!"

"She might spank you," Leitha noted, "but probably not too hard."

"Getting back to the point," Althalus said, "Arya Andine has already dispatched a certain Duke Olkar to Maghu over in Perquaine. Olkar's a merchant himself, and he's acquainted with most of the grain merchants in Maghu. Once I know just how much of a shortfall we're facing, I'll run on over to Maghu and tell Olkar how many tons of wheat we're going to need. I don't think we'll want to buy this year's *entire* crop."

"Lord, no!" Aidhru said. "That'd wipe out every treasury in Treborea." He looked nervously at Andine. "Before I make too many more of these imperial announcements, Arya Andine, just exactly what's my status here? Am I a prisoner of war, a captive being held for ransom, a potential slave, or what?"

"We'll invent a title for you, Lord Aidhru," she replied.

" 'Imperial Advisor' sounds sort of nice," Leitha suggested. "Our Andine's quite fond of the term 'Empress of Treborea,' aren't you, dear?"

"Not anymore, Leitha," Andine said. "That particular delusion wore off rather quickly. For the time being, let's just say that Kanthon's a 'protectorate.' It's a suitably vague term that won't hurt too many feelings—and it's only a temporary sort of thing. Let's get through the coming winter and root out all of Ghend's underlings before we move on into a more permanent arrangement. The 'protectorate' isn't going to last, of course. It's just something interim—until things settle down."

"Which probably won't take more than a couple of centuries," Chief Twengor murmured to his nephew, Laiwon.

"Or maybe three," Laiwon amended. "Five at the very most."

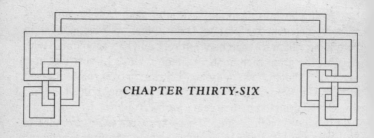

CHAPTER THIRTY-SIX

"It's not quite as bad as Andine seems to think it is, Em," Althalus told the Goddess when he and Eliar stopped briefly in the tower on their way to Maghu to speak with Duke Olkar. "Dhakan evidently keeps a running inventory in his head every year. When we added the wheat in the granaries of Kanthon, we're not as short as everyone seems to have believed we were. Would it be all right if I stopped by our private gold mine to help buy what we'll need?"

"Why would you want to do that, pet?" she asked.

"A fair number of Andine's people will starve if I don't, Em, and she'll weep and wail about that for years if *somebody* doesn't lend her a hand."

"And?"

"What do you mean, 'and'?"

"It's not entirely Andine's concerns that moved you to suggest this, was it, love?"

"The money's right there in that hole, Em, and it isn't doing anything useful. It's not exactly as if it *meant* anything to me."

"You absolutely *refuse* to come right out and admit it, don't you, Althalus?"

"Admit what?"

"You're as concerned about the well-being of the ordinary people of Treborea as Andine is. Compassion's not a sin, Althalus. You don't have to be ashamed of it."

"Aren't we getting just a little syrupy here, Em?"

She threw her hands in the air. "I give up!" she said. "I was trying to compliment you, you dunce!"

"I'd take it as a favor if you didn't noise it around *too* much, Em," he told her. "I *do* have a reputation to maintain, after all, and soft-heartedness could ruin people's opinion of me."

"Is Bheid starting to get his senses back at all?" Eliar asked.

"It varies," Dweia replied. "Sometimes he seems almost normal, then he flies apart again for no particular reason."

"Where *is* Bheid, by the way?" Althalus asked.

"He's gone into seclusion—in an empty room. I suppose I could tamper with him, but I'd really rather not do that. If he can work his way through this on his own, it'll be better in the long run. Sooner or later, he's going to have to face what happened in Osthos and come to grips with it. If I start smoothing things over for him, his problems might sink below the surface and then pop up again right in the middle of some emergency."

"How long is it likely to take for him to get well?" Eliar asked. "Leitha *really* misses him, and she can't even feel his thoughts anymore."

"He's doing that on purpose, Eliar," Dweia explained. "He's going through something that's fairly awful right now, and he doesn't want it to involve her. I've more or less suspended time for him. If all he needs to recover is time, I can give him all he needs." Then she straightened and looked at Althalus. "Keep your eyes and ears open when you get to Maghu, love," she instructed. "There's something going on in Perquaine that's not quite natural. See if you can get some specifics."

"Duke Nitral said something about religious arguments, Emmy," Eliar recalled. "Could that have anything to do with what's got everybody there all stirred up?"

"It's possible. Where are the rest of the children, Althalus?"

"They're going up into Arum with the Clan Chiefs for the wedding of Albron and Astarell," he replied.

"That's nice," she said approvingly.

"Weddings mean a lot to you, don't they, Em?"

"You haven't forgotten who I *am*, have you, Althie?"

"Not *too* likely," he said. "Let's go to Maghu, Eliar. I need about ten thousand tons of wheat, so we'd better get to buying before the price goes up."

* * *

"It's a manageable number, Althalus," Duke Olkar conceded. "If I spread my purchases and delivery times out a bit, I should be able to acquire that much without causing a sudden rise in price—*and* if I buy in thousand-ton lots, I should probably even be able to get a discount."

"You're an even bigger thief than I am, Olkar," Althalus accused the Duke of Kadon.

"Thank you," Olkar replied with a shrewd smirk.

"Is there something going on here in Perquaine?" Althalus asked. "Duke Nitral was saying that there's some kind of religious controversy boiling to the surface."

"I hadn't heard that religion was involved in it," Olkar replied. "There's a certain amount of unrest among the peasantry, I'm told, but that crops up every ten years or so. It's the fault of the property owners, when you get right down to it. Perquaines tend to be egomaniacs who spend millions building palaces. The peasants live in hovels, and the differences between 'your palace' and 'my hovel' are very obvious. The notion of 'comfortable but not showy' hasn't occurred to the Perquaines yet. The property owners show off, and the peasants resent it. There's nothing new about that."

"I'll nose around a bit," Althalus advised him. "If there's likely to be an all-out peasant rebellion before long, we'd better buy our wheat and get it across the border before the fires break out."

Olkar scoffed. "It never goes quite *that* far, Althalus."

"Let's not take any chances, Duke Olkar. If we happen to blunder on this one, Arya Andine's going to talk to us about it—and I'm sure we'll hear her even if she doesn't bother to leave her throne in Osthos."

"You could be right about that," Olkar agreed. "Maybe I'd better go hire a few hundred wagons."

"I would, if I were you. Eliar here can lend you a hand. I think I'll do some snooping around. I want to find out what's *really* going on here in Perquaine."

* * *

"My great-great grandfather was probably one of the best burglars in the world in those days," Althalus boasted to the other patrons in the seedy tavern near the riverfront, "but he was a country boy from up in the mountains, and he'd never seen paper money before. Where *he* came from, money was round, yellow, and it went *clink*. He didn't have any idea at all that he had *millions* right there in his hands, so he just turned around and walked away from it."

"Tragic," one of the professional men in the tavern observed, shaking his head.

"Indeed it was," Althalus agreed. "According to my father, nobody in our family's done an honest day's work in ten generations—except for one black-sheep great uncle, who was a carpenter—and the incident here in Maghu was the one time in hundreds of years that any of my relatives *ever* came that close to real money. It's a stain on the family honor, so I've come to Perquaine to pull off something that'll sponge that stain away."

"What line do you follow?" a nimble-fingered pickpocket asked.

"Oh, a bit of this, a bit of that. I'm fairly ecumenical. I know that most businessmen believe they should stick to one trade, but if the authorities are looking for a daring highwayman and they've got hanging on their minds, it's time for the highwayman to sell his horse and plumed hat, and move into some city where he can pick pockets for a while."

"That *does* sort of make sense," a wiry burglar with a long nose agreed. "You might have picked a bad time to come to Perquaine, though. Things are sort of stirred up just now."

"That's what somebody was telling me when I first got here. He wasn't altogether sober, though, so I couldn't make much sense out of what he was saying. He kept going on about religion. Does anybody take religion *that* seriously?"

"Not anybody who's got his head on straight," the burglar agreed, "but on down to the south there seems to be some kind of new order in the priesthood. We've all seen White Robes, Brown Robes, and Black Robes, but from what I've heard, this new order of priests wears red robes, and they're preaching sermons about 'social justice,' 'oppressive landowners,' and 'starving peasants.' It's all absolute nonsense, of course, but the peasants are lapping it up. But then, peasants don't have much in the way of brains, or they wouldn't keep on being peasants, would they?"

"*I* certainly wouldn't," Althalus agreed. "It's probably the same here in Perquaine as it is everywhere else. The landowners gouge the peasants, the merchants gouge the landowners, and *we* gouge the merchants. That's why *we* stand at the very top of the social order."

"I *like* his way of thinking," the long-nosed burglar said to the other thieves. "If we look at it that way, wouldn't you say that pretty much makes us the true noblemen?"

"Not in front of strangers, I wouldn't," the pickpocket replied.

"Is anything significant likely to come out of this peasant unrest?" Althalus asked.

"Some fancy houses are probably going to burn down, and a few fat landowners will get their throats cut," the burglar said with a shrug. "Then there'll be quite a bit of looting—but the Red Robes will eventually preach all the loot away from the peasants. Every priest alive believes that about half of all the wealth in the world rightfully belongs to him, so you won't find very many priests in poor countries. This so-called 'peasant revolt' is nothing more than a hoax. The Red Robes will preach the peasants into a frenzy; the peasants will run around yelling, and waving shovels and rakes, and stealing everything that isn't nailed down; and then the Red Robes will cheat the peasants out of everything they've stolen."

Althalus shook his head sadly. "Where will it end?" He sighed.

The long-nosed burglar laughed cynically. "The nobility will see which way the wind's blowing, and they'll buy off these new priests," he predicted. "Then the sermons will change. 'Social justice' goes out the window at that point, and 'peace and tranquility' becomes all the rage. 'Getting your fair share' gets replaced by 'getting your reward in heaven.' It's the same old swindle it's always been, my friend. Then the priests will quietly point out each and every leader of the revolt to the authorities as a 'civic duty,' and before long, every tree in all of Perquaine's going to be decorated with dangling peasants. Revolutions always end that way."

"You've got a very cynical way of looking at the world, haven't you, my friend?" Althalus noted.

"I've looked deeply into the hearts of my fellow men," the burglar replied eloquently, "and to be honest with you, I'd rather look into a cesspool."

"You just raised an interesting possibility, though," Althalus mused. "If we were all to put on green robes, or maybe blue ones, and then go out and tell all the peasants that we speak for some *new* God—or better yet, a very *old* one that people have forgotten about—we could pull off exactly the same hoax these Red Robes have. It appears that there's money to be made in religion."

"I think I've got just the God you want," the pickpocket said with a broad grin.

"Oh?"

"What about Dweia?"

Althalus nearly choked at that.

"She *was* the Goddess of Perquaine a few thousand years back, you know," the pickpocket explained, "and her temple still stands in the center of Maghu—except that the Brown Robes have sort of usurped it. If I'm not mistaken, there's still a statue of her back in some dusty corner of the temple. She'd be perfect for your scheme."

The long-nosed burglar laughed delightedly. Then he struck a pose with one hand lifted aloft as if in benediction. "Gather, O my children," he intoned in a rich, oratorical voice, "and lift your voices in prayer and song to Divine Dweia—the once and future Goddess of fertile Perquaine. Beseech her, O my brethren, to return and cast out the unbelievers and return our dear Perquaine unto the glory of the past."

"Amen!" the pickpocket said fervently, and then he howled with laughter.

Althalus was trembling violently when he left the tavern.

* * *

"So *that's* it," Dweia said when Althalus told her of what he had learned in the thieves' den.

"That's what, dear?"

"Ghend's crowding the edges just a bit. The priests of Daeva in Nekweros wear scarlet robes."

"Then this peasant revolt goes a little deeper than a hoax by a group of opportunists, doesn't it? It's an effort to convert the peasants to the worship of your brother."

"It's not impossible, Althalus. Ghend hasn't had too much luck with conventional wars. Now he's trying to mix social revolution with religious controversy."

"He's cooking up a very strange stew, then."

"Indeed he is, love. I'm not sure how he plans to pass Daeva off as the friend of the masses, though. Daeva's even worse than Deiwos when you start talking about sheer arrogance. I think we'd better get Albron's wedding out of the way in a hurry so that we can get back to Maghu before all of Perquaine catches on fire." Dweia looked at Eliar. "We'll use the doors to get all the wedding guests to Albron's Hall."

"I don't think the weather's going to cooperate, Emmy," Eliar said dubiously. "If we made the trip on the ground instead of through the House, it'd be the dead of winter before we reached my Chief's Hall. It might help if you could stir up a blizzard or two."

"I'd really rather not. Those glaciers are starting to melt, and I don't want to tamper with that. Tell the others to mention 'unusual weather' and 'a very mild winter' every so often. That should cover our tail feathers."

"How's Bheid doing?" Eliar asked.

"About the same," she replied. "He's still wallowing in his guilt."

"How long does he think he's been here?"

"He's not really sure. He's starting to mix real time with House time."

"That's a novel term, Em," Althalus noted. "I sort of like it, though. 'House time'—yes. It gets right to the point, doesn't it?"

"I'm glad you approve, pet."

"Let's get started, then," Althalus said to Eliar. "The sooner we get your Chief married, the sooner we can go back to Perquaine and spoke Ghend's wheel." He grinned. "That's starting to turn into my favorite hobby," he said.

Eliar and Althalus joined the others in the foothills of Arum, and then their "resident hero" smoothly led them through a door into a corridor in the north wing of the House.

"You're getting better and better at that, Eliar," Sergeant Khalor observed. "I knew exactly what you were doing, and even then *I* couldn't tell precisely when we stepped through that door."

"Practice, my Sergeant," Eliar replied modestly. "If you do something often enough, you're bound to get better at it."

"Where are we going to come out, Althalus?"

"Just a few miles south of Chief Albron's Hall. Emmy wants to get this wedding out of the way so that we can concentrate on that revolution in Perquaine. Oh, I almost forgot, we're supposed to act surprised at how mild this winter is. We're coming home about six weeks before we possibly could if we actually had to cover the real distance, so it won't be as cold as it should be, and there won't be as much snow piled up as everybody's going to expect."

"I'll practice my look of astonishment," Khalor said drily.

"I'd really like to introduce you to her, Andine," Eliar said earnestly to the tiny Arya the next morning at the breakfast table in Albron's Hall. "One of these days before too much longer, she *is* going to be one of your relations, after all."

"I think you'll like Eliar's mother, Andine," Chief Albron said. "She's a beautiful lady."

"Why doesn't your mother live in the village, Eliar?" Gher asked curiously.

Eliar shrugged. "My father built the cottage just outside of town, and I don't think the idea of moving's ever occurred to my mother. She says it's where she belongs."

Chief Albron sighed. "It's one of the great tragedies of our clan," he said sadly. "Eliar's father, Agus, was one of the greatest warriors in our history. He and Khalor were almost like brothers."

"Yes," Khalor agreed. "We were very close." There was a kind of flatness in the way he said it that seemed strange to Althalus.

"If I had any kind of literary talent, I could pen an epic romance about the first meeting between Agus and Alaia—that's her name, of course," Chief Albron said.

"It's a beautiful name," Leitha noted in a very sad tone.

"Indeed it is," Albron agreed, "and it's quite clear that Agus was Eliar's father. It was Khalor, I think, who introduced them. I happened to be there at the time, and I've never *seen* anything like it. No sooner had they laid eyes on each other when it became obvious that they were both hopelessly in love. Wasn't it, Khalor?"

Sergeant Khalor nodded, not even bothering to speak.

"We haven't intruded on Alaia," Albron continued. "I think she's still in mourning."

"Well, not entirely, my Chief," Eliar said. "She's always glad to see me, and she doesn't send people away when they come by the house."

"I think I'd like to meet this lady myself," Astarell said. "Why don't we all pay her a short visit and invite her to our wedding?"

"What a splendid idea," Albron said enthusiastically. "Eliar, why don't you and Sergeant Khalor go tell your mother that we'll be paying her a call? It wouldn't be very polite if we all just showed up unannounced on her doorstep, now would it?"

"We'll go tell her right now, my Chief," Eliar replied enthusiastically. Sergeant Khalor, however, looked just a bit gloomy.

Alaia's cottage was a small, neat structure built of carefully squared-off logs, and it had a steeply pitched shake roof. It stood a short distance outside the village that was tightly clustered around the walls of Albron's stone fortress, and there was a small garden outside the kitchen door.

Eliar's mother was a fairly tall woman in her late thirties. She had chestnut-colored hair, and her eyes were a deep, deep blue. "She's gorgeous!" Andine murmured nervously to Leitha.

"I noticed that, yes," Leitha replied.

"Do I look all right?" Andine asked with some slight apprehension.

"You'll do just fine, dear," Leitha assured her. "Don't be nervous."

"She *is* Eliar's mother, Leitha, and I *do* want her to like me."

"Everybody likes you, Andine. You've got *tons* of adorability leaking out of every pore."

"*Will* you stop teasing me, Leitha!" Andine exclaimed.

"Probably not, no. It's my favorite hobby."

Alaia greeted the leader of the clan with a formal and very graceful curtsy. "Chief Albron, my house is honored by your presence." Her voice was rich and full.

"It is we who are honored, Alaia," Albron replied, bowing.

"And this is my Andine, Mother," Eliar introduced the Arya of Osthos.

Alaia's smile was rather like the sun coming up. Probably without even thinking, she held out her arms to the tiny girl.

Andine ran to her, and they embraced warmly.

"My, aren't you the tiny one?" Alaia said fondly. "Eliar told me that you weren't very big, but I hadn't expected you to be quite *this* small."

"Would it help at all if I stood on my tiptoes?" Andine suggested.

"You're just fine the way you are, Andine," Alaia told her. "Don't change a thing. Eliar says you've undertaken the chore of feeding him."

"It's my life's work now," Andine replied.

"It's a very large chore for one so small."

"I try to stay ahead of him, Alaia. I've found that if I always have food in my hand ready to pop into his mouth, I can keep him from eating the furniture."

They both laughed and looked fondly at the young man.

"I think we need to talk, Althalus," Leitha suggested. "There's something you should know about."

"All right. Is it urgent?"

"Probably not, but let's go talk about it right now, shall we? It won't really take very long, and I don't think we'll be missed for a bit."

"You're being cryptic again," he said as they quietly left the cottage.

"Don't be such an old grouch, Daddy," she chided him.

They crossed Alaia's small garden and entered a grove of towering trees near the river gorge.

"All right, Leitha," Althalus said, "what's bothering you?'

"Sergeant Khalor's very uncomfortable, Althalus."

"Are you saying that he doesn't like Eliar's mother?"

"No, just the opposite. He and Alaia had been 'walking out together,' as the saying goes, before he introduced her to Eliar's father, Agus."

"Oh?"

"You heard Chief Albron's description, didn't you? When Agus and Alaia met, it was one of those 'love at first sight' things. Khalor's very perceptive, and he immediately saw what was happening. He loved Alaia—and still does—but he and Agus were as close as brothers, so he hid his feelings and stepped aside."

"This is one of those gloomy stories, isn't it?"

"It gets worse. After Agus was killed in some meaningless war down in the low country, Khalor thought there might be room for some hope, but Alaia was absolutely crushed by her husband's death, and she's been in almost total seclusion for all these years. When Eliar began to train for his life as a soldier, Khalor sort of took him under his wing. If you pay close attention to them, you'll probably notice that they're more like father and son than Sergeant and Corporal."

"Khalor *does* sort of look out for Eliar, now that you mention it. Does Alaia have any feelings at all for Khalor?"

"She thinks of him as her oldest friend, but I caught a few hints from her that it might go just a bit further—*if* Khalor would just relax a bit."

"That's *all* we need right now!" Althalus growled. "I think I'd have been happier if you hadn't told me about this, Leitha."

"I'm trying to keep your tail feathers out of the soup, Daddy," she told him.

"What's that supposed to mean?"

"It's a situation that Dweia might find *very* interesting, don't you think? And if you neglect to bring it to her attention, she might be a little put out with you, wouldn't you say?"

"I wouldn't have *known* about it if you hadn't dragged me out here and told me this sad little story."

"Why, Daddy," she said in mock astonishment, "you didn't think I'd keep any secrets from *you*, did you? Then, of course, if I hadn't told *you*, it might have been *my* tail feathers that'd get dunked in the soup. I love you dearly, Daddy, but not *that* much. Now that I've handed it to you, *you* get to take care of it. Aren't you proud of how sneaky I can be?"

"I'd really be a lot happier if you'd drop this 'daddy' business, Leitha," he said plaintively.

She gave him a sudden, stricken look, and then she began to cry, burying her face in her hands.

"Now what?" he demanded.

"Leave me alone." She sobbed. "Go away, Althalus."

"No, Leitha, I won't do that. What's wrong?"

"I thought you were different. Go away." She continued to sob.

Without even really thinking about it, he put his arms around her. She struggled just a bit, but then she wailed and clung to him, sobbing uncontrollably.

She was obviously too distraught to talk coherently, so Althalus reluctantly decided to do it "the other way."

Leitha's thoughts were chaotic as Althalus very gently intruded into her awareness.

Stay away! Stay away! she pleaded silently.

"No, I won't do that," he said aloud, still searching.

A myriad of her memories from the village of Peteleya in Kweron flooded over him, and her overwhelming loneliness cut into him like a knife. Despite her "gift," Leitha had grown up in almost total isolation. Her father had died before she'd been born, and her mother had been insane—not raving mad, perhaps, but "strange." The other children in Peteleya had been about half afraid of Leitha and her uncanny-seeming ability to know what they were thinking, so she'd had no real friends as a child, and she'd grown up in nearly total isolation.

And in fear. The shadow of the harsh-faced priest, Brother Ambho, still hung dark and menacing over all her memories, his lustful hatred of her growing stronger with each passing year. Her attempts to avoid him had been fruitless, since he'd followed her wherever she'd gone, and the dreadful image that crawled through his imagination had filled her with terror, a terror that had virtually erased her ability to think or to act.

Though she had known his intentions, she'd been quite helpless. In time, his accusation and the mockery he'd called a trial had taken place, and her inevitable condemnation to the flames had come about.

And then Bheid had come to Peteleya with earthquakes and avalanches in his wake to save her from the fire.

"It wasn't entirely his idea, Leitha," Althalus told her, speaking aloud. "Emmy sent us, and the Knife was involved as well."

"I know that now, Daddy," she replied, "but I was wound just a little tight that day for some reason. Then, after Eliar showed me the Knife, I wasn't alone anymore. I was suddenly up to my ears in family, and Bheid had made that possible—at least that's the way I saw it."

"And now you love him."

"I thought that was fairly obvious, Daddy."

"There's that word again."

"You don't listen very well, do you, Althalus? That's part of what the word 'family' means, isn't it? When we were back in Wekti and Eliar couldn't see, you kept beating me over the head with 'family,' 'brothers and sisters,' and all those other clever reasons you invented to persuade me to lower my defenses and let Eliar into my mind. Didn't you realize that you were offering yourself as my father when you did that? I really need a father, and you volunteered. It's too late for you to back out now."

He surrendered. "I guess there's a sort of perverse logic to what you're saying, Leitha. All right, if it's 'daddy' you want, 'daddy' it is."

"Oh, good!" she said with feigned enthusiasm. "Now, what are we going to do about poor Brother Bheid?"

"Emmy's taking care of it."

"No, Daddy, she isn't. She's waiting for you to realize that it's *your* responsibility."

"Where did you come up with *that* peculiar idea?"

"I have my sources, Daddy. Trust me." Then her pale face grew pensive. "A day's coming when Bheid and I are going to have to do some dreadful things to certain people, and we'll both need somebody to hold on to. I think you just got the job."

"Could you be a bit more specific, Leitha? 'Dreadful things' is a little vague."

"It's the best I can do for right now, Daddy. Dweia knows, and she's trying to conceal it from me, but I'm catching some hints. You've *got* to bring Bheid back to his senses, Althalus. He *must* be able to function. I can't do this alone!"

And then she began to cry again, and without even thinking, Althalus took her in his arms and held her until it had passed.

"I need to go back to the House," Althalus told Eliar as the party was returning to Chief Albron's Hall from Alaia's cottage.

"Is it urgent?"

"Probably. I need to talk with Emmy. She's been playing games again, and she's starting to irritate me."

"You're going to get yourself in trouble, Althalus."

"It won't be the first time. When we get there, I think you'd better wait in the dining room."

"It's going to be one of *those*?"

"Probably so, and you don't want to be around once Emmy and I get started."

Althalus and Eliar dropped back as Chief Albron and the others moved up through the village, and then they stepped into an alleyway, where Eliar opened a door that only he could see. "Good luck," Eliar told Althalus at the foot of the stairs leading up to Dweia's tower.

Althalus grunted and stomped up the stairs.

"What a delightful surprise," Dweia said pleasantly when Althalus banged the tower door open.

"Stop that, Em," he said shortly. "You knew I was coming, and you know exactly why."

"My, aren't we peevish today."

"Quit. Why didn't you tell me what you wanted me to do?"

"Bheid wasn't ready yet, love."

"That's too bad. I'll *make* him ready. Between the two of you, you've just about destroyed Leitha, and I *won't* permit that!"

"You're taking this 'daddy' business seriously, aren't you, Althie?"

"Yes, as a matter of fact, I am. Now where's Bheid?"

"You're not going to hurt him, are you?"

"That depends on how stubborn he gets. I might have to slam him up against a wall a few times, but I *will* get through to him. Then you and I are going to have a nice, long talk."

Her green eyes narrowed. "I don't care for your tone, Althalus."

"You'll probably get over it. Where's Bheid?"

"Two doors down the corridor from the dining room—on the left. I don't think he'll let you in, though."

"How's he going to stop me?" Then Althalus turned and went down the tower stairs two at a time.

"No hitting!" Dweia called after him.

Althalus reached Bheid's door and stopped briefly to get his anger under control. "Bheid," he said then, "it's me—Althalus. Open the door."

There was no answer.

"Bheid! Open it! Now!"

There was still a profound silence.

Althalus decided at the last instant *not* to use any one of a half-dozen words from the Book to open Bheid's locked door. He kicked it to pieces instead.

Bheid, blank eyed and unshaven, huddled in one corner of the cell-like room, rhythmically banging his head against the stone wall.

"Stop that," Althalus told him, "and get on your feet."

"I am lost," Bheid moaned. "I have killed."

"Yes, I noticed that," Althalus replied, shrugging. "It wasn't very neat, but it got the job done. If you're going to make a habit of it, you should practice a bit."

Bheid blinked incredulously. "Don't you understand?" he demanded. "I'm a priest. Killing is forbidden."

"You didn't have any problems with hiring those assassins to kill the Aryo of Kanthon."

"That wasn't the same at all."

"Really? What's the difference?"

"I didn't personally kill the Aryo."

"That's pure sophistry, Bheid, and you know it. Sin—if that's what you want to call it—lies in the intent, not in the technicality of just who ran the knife into the victim. Yakhag killed Salkan, and what you did was exactly right. You're *supposed* to kill the people who kill your friends."

"But I'm a priest."

"I noticed that. Which religion, though? You can talk it over with Emmy, but I think she sees the world a bit differently from the way her brother does. This is all beside the point, though. If you don't open the door to your mind to Leitha, I'll do exactly the same thing to *that* door as I did to the one to this room. Your silly wallowing in guilt and self-pity's destroying Leitha, you blithering idiot. I don't care *how* many people you kill, Bheid, but if you hurt Leitha anymore, I'll reach down your throat and jerk out your heart!"

"It's my fault that Salkan was killed."

"Yes, it was. So what?"

Bheid stared at him in horror.

"You didn't think I was going to excuse you, did you? If something's been done, it's done. There aren't any punishments or rewards, Bheid—only consequences. You made a mistake; now you have to live with it—on your own. I won't let you slop your guilt all over the rest of the family. If you're going to eat your liver, do it on your own time and someplace private."

"I'm a murderer," Bheid declared.

"Not a very good one, though. Now quit this sniveling and come back to work." Althalus looked around the cluttered cell. "Clean up this mess and then clean yourself up as well. You and I are going back to Chief Albron's hall. You have a wedding ceremony to perform."

"I can't!"

"Oh, yes you can, Brother Bheid, and you *will*—even if I have to stand behind you with a club. Now, *move!*"

The wedding day of Albron and Astarell dawned clear and cold. Because of the season, the decorations in the hall were largely limited to evergreen boughs and bright-colored cloth bows.

The traditional bachelor party for Chief Albron the previous evening had left the assorted Clan Chiefs, Sergeants, and visiting nobles feeling a bit delicate that morning, and for some reason Chief Twengor found that vastly amusing.

Alaia had more or less taken charge of the young ladies in the bridal party, whose activities during the week leading up to the wedding had consisted, so far as Althalus could tell, largely of dressmaking and giggling.

Chief Gweti and the ancient Chief Delur had journeyed to Albron's hall for the ceremony, since the wedding of a Clan Chief traditionally required the presence of all the Chiefs of Arum. Gweti largely kept to himself during the festivities. Andine's decision *not* to loot the city of Kanthon had put the pinch-faced Chief's nose out of joint, and he obviously found scant reason to celebrate.

The ceremony was scheduled for noon. Althalus gathered that this was an ancient Arum custom—designed primarily to give the celebrants time to recover from the previous evening's entertainments, *and* not to interfere too much with the postceremony celebration. Arums appeared to take their parties very seriously.

There had been a certain amount of religious controversy about the wedding, since the God of the Arums was the mountain God Bherghos, while the Plakands worshiped Kherdhos, the herd God.

"Brother Bheid's going to perform the ceremony," Althalus announced in a tone that ended the discussion rather abruptly.

And so it was that as noon approached, Bheid, garbed in his black priestly robe, stood at the front of Albron's central hall with Chief Albron, Sergeant Khalor, and Chief Kreuter awaiting the entrance of the bride and her attendants, Andine and Leitha.

Althalus stood with the other guests in the hall to witness the ceremony, and just as the great door at the back of the hall opened for Astarell and her ladies in waiting, he caught a very familiar fragrance. Startled, he turned to look full in the face of Dweia. "What are you *doing*?" he demanded in a choked voice.

"It's all right, love," she replied. "I've been invited."

"That's not what I'm talking about. I didn't think you could leave the House in your real form."

"Whatever gave you *that* ridiculous notion?"

"You never have before. You've always changed into Emmy the cat. I thought your *real* form wasn't allowed out of the House."

"*Nobody* tells me what I can or can't do, you ninny. I thought you knew that." Then she pursed her perfect lips. "I'll admit that I don't do it very often," she conceded. "I seem to attract a lot of attention in my real form."

"I wonder why," he murmured.

"Be nice, Althalus." Then she paused. "Have you recovered from the peeves yet?"

"Peeves?"

"You seemed a bit grouchy the last time you came by the House."

"I took my peeves out on Bheid."

"You didn't really slam him against the wall, did you?"

"Not *too* hard, no. Here comes Astarell."

Astarell was radiant as she marched to the front of the central hall, and Chief Albron's expression was one of vapid adoration.

"Give me your handkerchief, Althalus," Dweia said, sniffling slightly.

He looked at her sharply. "Are you crying, Em?" he asked in a startled voice.

"I always cry at weddings, Althalus. Don't you?"

"I haven't really attended all that many weddings, Em," he confessed.

"You'd probably better get used to them, pet. In *my* view of the world, weddings are *very* important. Now just be quiet and give me your handkerchief."

"Yes, dear," he replied.

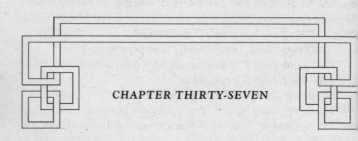

CHAPTER THIRTY-SEVEN

"Do you really have to leave, Althalus?" Chief Albron said two days later.

"I'm afraid so, Albron," Althalus replied, leaning back in his chair in one of the upper rooms in Albron's hall. "There's trouble brewing in Perquaine, and I don't want it getting out of hand. If it's all right—and probably even if it's not—I'm going to keep Sergeant Khalor. I might need him on down the line, and I may not have time to come back and fetch him."

"It's all right with me, Althalus. It might go a little ways toward paying what I owe you."

"Do you owe me for something?"

"Don't be coy, Althalus. You had a very large hand in arranging my marriage to Astarell."

"It solved a number of problems," Althalus replied, shrugging.

"What's *really* going on in Perquaine?"

"A peasant rebellion—at least on the surface."

Albron shook his head mournfully. "The lowlanders just don't understand ordinary people, do they?"

"They haven't got a clue. The aristocrats spend so much time admiring themselves in their mirrors that they don't pay much attention to the commoners. From what I've heard, these rebellions break out every ten years or so. You'd think that after five or six times, the aristocrats might start to realize that they're doing something wrong."

"I certainly *hope* not. If the lowlanders start behaving like rational human beings, the clans of Arum are going to be out of work."

"I've got another favor I'd like to ask of you, Albron."

"All you have to do is ask."

"Could you keep Andine and Leitha here for a while?"

"Of course, but why? They'd be safe in the House, wouldn't they?"

"I'd like to keep Leitha away from Brother Bheid for right now. He's going through a crisis of sorts, and I think it might be best if he suffered his way through it on his own. Leitha doesn't really need to get involved. Bheid and I—along with Eliar and Sergeant Khalor—are going to be passing through the House fairly often, so it might be best if the young ladies are somewhere else for a while."

"Gher, too?" Albron asked.

"No, I think I'll keep Gher with me. Every so often he comes up with some very interesting ideas."

"Doesn't he?" Albron smiled. "Oh, one other thing. If trouble breaks out in Perquaine, send Eliar here. I'll have an army in the hallways of Dweia's House before you can blink twice."

"I'll keep that in mind, Chief Albron," Althalus said, rising to his feet. "You'd better get your men to working on the corrals, though. As soon as Kreuter gets back to Plakand, he's going to start herding Astarell's dowry here. You'll be overrun with horses before too long."

"Thanks for reminding me," Albron said in a flat tone.

"Don't mention it, mighty Chief." Althalus was chuckling as he left the room.

* * *

"The Perquaines are basically an outgrowth of the Treboreans,"
Dweia told Althalus and the others that evening in the tower.
"The Osthos sent ships to the west to establish new colonies and
open new land for farming early in the eighth millennium, and
the Kanthons went overland to set up *their* colonies. The more-
or-less perpetual war between Kanthon and Osthos didn't really
mean all that much to the Perquaines, so they stayed clear of it
and concentrated on tending their crops and getting rich. The
turmoil in Treborea relaxed certain social restrictions, so the
Treborean peasantry has quite a bit more freedom than the peasants of Perquaine do. The Perquaine peasantry aren't *quite* serfs,
but they come very close."

"What's a serf, Emmy?" Gher asked in a puzzled tone.

"They're chattel, Gher—a part of the land itself. When
someone buys a tract of land in a country where serfdom's a part
of the social structure, he comes into possession of the people
who live there as well."

"They're slaves, then?" Eliar asked.

"Not quite," Dweia replied. "They're part of the land, that's
all. A serf's slightly better off than a slave, but not very much."

"I certainly wouldn't put up with something like *that*," Gher
said. "I'd be across the mountains before anybody knew that I'd
left."

"That *does* happen every so often," Dweia agreed.

"Is it all one country?" Sergeant Khalor asked. "Or are there
all those baronies and duchies and the like? What I'm getting at
is whether or not there's a central government."

"In theory, Maghu's the capital city," she replied, "but nobody
pays very much attention to that. Most of the power in Perquaine
lies in the hands of the clergy."

"Yes," Bheid agreed, "and the clergy of Perquaine's the worst
of the lot. The Brown Robes are dominant there, and the Brown
Robe order is far more interested in wealth and privilege than it
is in the well-being of the lower classes. The Black Robes—my
order—have a presence there, and so do the White Robes, but
we're fairly minimal in the overall social structure. Over the cen-

uries the three orders have developed a sort of tacit agreement
hat we won't poach on each other's territory."

"I visited a thieves' tavern in Maghu a while back," Althalus
old them, "and the thieves there were discussing the situation in
:outhern Perquaine. Evidently, Ghend's taking advantage of the
·light of the Perquaine peasantry. There's a group of self-
rdained priests in the seacoast cities preaching revolution and
:tirring up the peasants."

"Self-ordained?" Bheid asked sharply.

"The thieves were fairly certain that these troublemakers
weren't really priests. They wear scarlet robes, and they deliver
:ermons about social justice, greedy aristocrats, and corrupt
:lergy. Unfortunately, most of what they're saying is true—
·articularly in Perquaine. The peasants *aren't* treated very well,
ind the Brown Robe priests *do* support the aristocracy in
:rinding the poor."

Bheid scoffed, "There's no such thing as a Red Robe order."

"Oh, yes there is, Brother Bheid," Dweia disagreed. "The
·riests of Nekweros wear scarlet robes. My brother's always
·een fond of bright colors."

"Are you saying that the peasants of Perquaine are being con-
·verted to the worship of the Demon Daeva?"

"Probably not," she replied with a shrug. "Not yet, at least.
That might be the ultimate goal, but for right now the Red Robes
in southern Perquaine seem to be concentrating on social change.
There are many injustices in a system based on an aristocracy—
·robably because aristocrats view the peasants as subhuman.
Revolutions have broken out many times in the past, and they've
never really worked, largely because the leaders of those revolutions were only interested in gaining the positions and privileges
of the nobles they denounce. The only thing a revolution ever
really changes is the terminology."

Althalus considered it. "Who's the headman of the Brown
Robes, Bheid?" he asked.

"Exarch Aleikon," Bheid told him. "The Brown Robes' main
temple used to be in Deika over in Equero, but after the fall of

the Deikan Empire, they set up shop in Maghu. Their temple
quite splendid."

"Thank you," Dweia said with a faint smile.

"I'm not sure I follow you," Bheid confessed with a
puzzled look.

"It's *my* temple, Bheid. The Brown Robes usurped it a few
thousand years ago."

"I hadn't heard about that," Bheid admitted.

"The Brown Robes don't like to admit it. The notion of a Goddess seems to upset them, for some reason."

"Are things really *that* bad for the peasants?" Sergeant Khalor
asked. "There are always malcontents who spend their time
grumbling, but that's usually brought on by greed and envy."

"The window's right there, Sergeant," Dweia told him. "Go
look for yourself."

"I think maybe I will," Khalor replied. "I'd like to know what
we're *really* up against."

The vista beyond the south window blurred and gradually grew
lighter to reveal a wintry field overlooking a grey, angry sea.
"Southern Perquaine," Dweia identified the location, "not far
from the seaport at Egni."

"Why is it still daytime there when it's nighttime here?" Gher
asked curiously.

"We're farther north," Dweia replied.

"What's that got to do with anything?" the boy asked.

"Althalus can explain it," she told him with a faint smile.

"You're wrong, Em," Althalus disagreed. "I can tell him that it
happens every year, but I still don't know exactly why."

"I explained it all to you a long time ago, pet."

"I know. I still don't understand, though."

"You *told* me that you did."

He shrugged. "I lied. It was easier than listening to you explain it for the third time."

"I'm ashamed of you," she chided.

"It seems to be late afternoon," Sergeant Khalor observed,

quinting at the western horizon. "What are those peasants
loing out in the fields in the winter?"

"Nothing very meaningful," Dweia replied. "The nobleman
vho owns that field likes to keep his peasants busy, that's all."

The peasants were garbed in burlap rags tied together with
its of string, and they were gaunt and dirty. They were hacking
vearily at the frozen earth with crude mattocks under the
vatchful eye of a mounted overseer with a grim face and a whip.

Then a richly dressed nobleman rode up to the overseer. "Is
hat as far as they've gotten today?" he demanded.

"The ground's frozen, my Lord," the overseer explained.
'This is just a waste of time, you know."

"Their time is *mine*," the nobleman declared. "If I order them
o dig, they'll dig. They don't need to know why."

"I understand that, my Lord," the overseer replied, "but it
night help if *I* knew why."

"There are agitators out there, Alkos," the noble said. "We're
;oing to keep our peasants so busy that they don't have time to
isten to speeches."

"Ah," the overseer said. "I guess that makes sense. You're
;oing to have to feed them a little more, though. I've had a dozen
of them collapse today."

"Nonsense." The nobleman snorted. "They're playacting.
That's what your whip's for, Alkos. Keep them moving until
lark. Then let them go eat. Tell them to come back at first light
omorrow."

"My Lord," the overseer objected, "they don't *have* anything
o eat. Most of them are eating grass."

"That's what cattle do, Alkos. Stay on top of them. I have to
;et back to my manor house. It's almost suppertime, and I'm ab-
iolutely famished."

You just made that up, didn't you, Em? Althalus silently
iccused.

No, pet, she replied sadly. *I didn't have to. It's really
iappening—and it gets worse.*

*   *   *

The region beyond the window blurred again, and Althalus an the others found themselves looking into an opulent room wher a pouchy-eyed nobleman was lounging on a padded bench, ab sently toying with a gilt-handled dagger.

There was a knock at the door, and a burly soldier entered "He said 'no,' my Lord," the soldier reported.

"What do you mean, 'no'?" the nobleman exclaimed.

"He's very stubborn, my Lord, and he seems to be very at tached to his daughter."

"Kill him, then! I want that girl here in my chamber befor nightfall!"

"The High Sheriff says we can't kill the peasants anymore, my Lord," the soldier said. "Those troublemaker priests grab up every incidental killing and use it to keep the rest of the peasant stirred up."

"That's the most ridiculous thing I've ever heard!"

"I know, but the High Sheriff will be pounding on your doo before morning if I kill that stubborn old fool." Then the sol dier's eyes narrowed. "There's another way, my Lord," he said "The girl's father's a cripple. A plow horse kicked him and brok his leg last year. He can't work, and he's got eight other childre besides that pretty daughter."

"So?"

"Why don't I just tell him that you'll evict him from that stick and-wattle hut of his unless he hands his daughter over to you It's winter now, and his whole family will starve—or freeze t death—without shelter or food. I think he'll come around."

"Brilliant!" The nobleman smirked. "Go ahead, Sergeant. Tel him to start packing. If his daughter isn't here by nightfall, h leaves at first light tomorrow."

"Can you find the door to that place, Eliar?" Sergeant Khalo asked bleakly.

"Almost immediately, my Sergeant," Eliar replied in a steel voice. "Should I bring my sword?"

"Probably so, yes."

"Not now, gentlemen," Dweia told them. "We haven't quit finished yet."

* * *

The window moved once again, and Althalus and the others found themselves looking into yet another house. A lean, hard-faced nobleman was seated at a table covered with documents, and he was conferring with a brown-robed priest. "I've been through these a dozen times, Brother Sawel," the nobleman declared, "and I can't find any way around the problem. The tradition seems to be locked in stone. I *want* that well, but it has belonged to the people of that village for a thousand years. I have hundreds of acres I could plant if I had access to that water."

"Calm yourself, my Lord Baron," the priest replied. "If you can't find a document that suits your purposes, we'll just have to put one together."

"Would it stand up in court?"

"Of course it will, my Lord. My Scopas will be presiding, and he owes me several favors. When I present him my 'startling new discovery,' he'll make his ruling. The village—and its well—will pass into your hands, and the authorities will send the villagers packing. Then you can tear down their houses—or use them for cattle barns if you want."

"Can we actually get away with that, Brother Sawel?" the Baron asked dubiously.

The priest shrugged. "Who's going to stop us, my Lord?" he asked. "The aristocracy controls the land, and the Church controls the courts. Between us, we can do just about anything we want to do."

"Well, Sergeant?" Dweia asked the hard-faced Arum soldier. "Does that answer your question?"

"Pretty much, ma'am, yes," Khalor replied, "but it raises another one. Why are we getting involved in this? From what I've just seen, I'd say that a rebellion's long overdue. Why don't we just seal the borders of Perquaine and let the peasantry run all over the top of the nobility and the priesthood?"

"Because the wrong people are leading the rebellion."

"So we're going to just walk in and steal it out from under them?" Gher suggested.

"Approximately, yes."

"If we're going to steal their revolution, wouldn't it be sort of useful to look in on the people who are stirring it up?" Khalor suggested. "Now that Pekhal and Gelta have been eliminated, somebody else is in charge, and getting to know the enemy's fairly important."

"Good point, Sergeant," Dweia agreed. "Let's nose around just a bit, shall we?"

Althalus stepped back just a bit and sent a probing thought at Bheid. The young priest's mind was a mass of conflicting emotions. His grief and guilt were still there, of course, but a seething rage had begun to grow just below the surface. The obvious injustices of Perquaine society were beginning to intrude upon Bheid's self-loathing.

It's a start, pet, Dweia's voice murmured. *Don't push him just yet. I think he's starting to come around on his own.*

You've been exaggerating a few things, haven't you, Em? Althalus suggested.

A little, yes, she admitted. *The thoughts of most of the people we've been watching aren't quite as blatant as what we saw and heard, so they probably wouldn't come right out and say them aloud.*

You're cheating again, Em.

I know, she admitted, *but if that's all it takes to bring Bheid around, it's acceptable.*

Your sense of morality's very flexible, I've noticed.

What a shocking thing to suggest. Watch Bheid very closely, pet. He's about to see and hear a few things that might just put his feet back on the ground.

The blur beyond the south window shifted and came into focus again, and Althalus and the others found themselves looking into the ruins of a long-abandoned house on a hilltop overlooking the sea far to the south. There was a tent inside the tumbled ruins and a small, well-concealed fire. Argan, the yellow-haired former priest, stood near the fire irritably kicking at a pile of tumbled building blocks.

A harsh voice came out of the darkness. "You'll wear out your shoes doing that."

"Where have you been?" Argan demanded as the grizzled Koman came into the firelight.

"Looking around," Koman replied. "Isn't that what you wanted me to do?"

"Did you find anything?"

"Nobody's invaded yet, if that's what's got you so worried. I don't think they fully understand what you're doing, Argan. I couldn't find Althalus, but that's not unusual. He's probably hiding out in that castle at the End of the World, and that place is out of my reach. Have you heard from Ghend?"

"No. He's in Nahgharash, trying to placate the Master."

A faint smile touched Koman's harshly lined face. "You're slick, Argan, I'll give you that. *You're* the one who pulled Yakhag out of Nahgharash and got him killed, but Ghend's getting the blame for it."

"That's because he took the credit for my idea, old boy," Argan replied with a lofty smirk. "Ghend's greedy for the Master's approval."

"You've noticed," Koman said drily.

"The plan *would* have worked, though," Argan declared. "Yakhag was the perfect answer to the elaborate scheme Althalus devised to trap Gelta, but then that idiot Bheid lost his head and butchered Yakhag before any of us could stop him."

"I tried to warn you about him, Argan, but you wouldn't listen to me."

"I didn't think he'd *go* that far," Argan said almost plaintively. "It was a complete violation of one of the cardinal rules. I got myself defrocked for something much less significant."

"I don't think I'm going to miss Yakhag all that much, though," Koman added. "Just the sight of him chilled my blood. Even Ghend was afraid of that one. The Master was the only one who was comfortable around Yakhag."

"I know," Argan replied moodily, "but with him to back me, I could have pushed Ghend aside and taken his place. Everything was going so well—but then that maniac in the black robe took up a sword and slaughtered my key to power."

Koman shrugged. "If you feel that way about it, go kill him. Khnom could probably get you into Dweia's House."

"Quit trying to be funny, Koman. I wouldn't go into that place any more than you would."

"It was only a suggestion, Reverend Argan," Koman said sardonically. "Since you're so bent on killing that Black Robe, I didn't think you'd mind getting yourself obliterated in the process."

"Revenge is sweet, old boy," Argan told him, "but you have to be alive to taste it. I'll deal with Bheid in good time. Right now, I'm going to need more Scarlet Robes to keep this uprising cooking. Go to Nahgharash and get as many as the Master will release. I want to be in the temple in Maghu before spring. If we loiter too much along the way, Althalus is likely to have an army waiting before we get there."

"It shall be as thou hast commanded, Revered Leader," Koman replied with a mocking bow.

"Just exactly who *was* that Yakhag fellow, ma'am?" Sergeant Khalor asked. "I know that Gelta was afraid of him, but I didn't think Ghend was as well."

"He was a creature with absolutely no emotions," Dweia replied with a slight shudder. "He had no love, no hate, no fear, no ambition—nothing. He was totally empty."

"A man of ice?" Gher suggested.

"That's very close, Gher," she agreed. "If he'd lived, it's entirely possible that Argan's scheme to push Ghend aside might have succeeded."

"The bad people don't get along with each other the way we always have, do they?" the boy observed. "We try to help each other, but they seem to spend all their time trying to stab each other in the back."

"Daeva prefers it that way, Gher," Dweia replied. "In my brother's eyes, Yakhag was the perfect man."

"Yakhag didn't see it that way," Althalus observed. "The only thing he really wanted was to die."

"That's what Nahgharash is all about, love," Dweia said.

"Sooner or later we're going to have to do something about that place," Sergeant Khalor said bleakly.

"What did you have in mind, Sergeant?" Dweia asked him.

"I don't know. We could march in and put out the fire, I suppose. I think you ought to know that I'm not really too enthusiastic about this particular war, ma'am. Unless something changes, we're going to come in on the wrong side. This revolt is long overdue—no matter *who* stirs it up."

"I'm working on that right now, Sergeant," Althalus told him. "I think our first step should involve getting access to the Exarch of the Brown Robes—didn't you say his name's Aleikon, Bheid?"

Bheid nodded. "My Exarch has some other names for him, but we probably shouldn't mention those in the presence of the ladies."

"If Aleikon approves of the things we saw a little while ago, your Exarch's probably understating things, Brother Bheid," Khalor added. "Where are you going with this, Althalus?"

Althalus shrugged. "The Brown Robes are greedy, and I'm very good at swindling greedy people. The first thing I'll need to do is get Exarch Aleikon's undivided attention. Let's suppose that some fabulously wealthy nobleman from someplace over in Equero—or maybe Medyo—came to Maghu on a religious pilgrimage of some kind. Would he have very much trouble getting an audience with the Brown Robe Exarch, Brother Bheid?"

"I doubt it—particularly if his pilgrimage were one of atonement for past sins. The word 'atonement' has a golden sort of ring to it in the ears of high-ranking Brown Robe churchmen."

"I had a feeling it might get their attention," Althalus said. "I'll put on some expensive clothing, look down my nose at everybody, and buy—or rent—a fancy house. Then my personal chaplain can drop by the temple and get me an appointment with Exarch Aleikan."

"I take it that *I* get to be your chaplain?" Bheid guessed.

"What a splendid notion, Bheid!" Althalus said. "How *do* you keep coming up with all these clever ideas?"

"It's a gift," Bheid said drily.

"Where are you going to say you came from, Master Althalus?" Gher asked.

Althalus shrugged. "It doesn't really matter—as long as it's far, far away."

"Try Kenthaigne, love," Dweia suggested.

He frowned. "It seems that I've heard of a place called Kenthaigne. Just exactly where is it?"

"It's a very ancient name for the region between Lake Apsa and Lake Meida in Equero. It hasn't been used for several eons now."

He shrugged. "It's got a nice sound to it," he said. "All right, then, I'll be the Duke of Kenthaigne, and I murdered my way to the throne. My conscience is bothering me now, so I'm in need of divine forgiveness. Does anybody see any holes in that?" He looked around at the rest of them.

"He does this all the time, doesn't he?" Sergeant Khalor noted. "Why not just tell people the truth, Althalus?"

"Khalor, if I walked into Maghu and announced that I'm the emissary of the Goddess Dweia, they'd lock me up as a madman, wouldn't they? The truth doesn't work very often."

I think it's time to bring Leitha and Andine back home, love, Dweia suggested silently.

Is Bheid ready, Em? If he's still coming apart at the seams, I don't want Leitha anywhere near him.

He's coming along just fine, pet. He's beginning to understand just exactly what Yakhag was, so he's past the worst of it. Let's get Leitha back before he wanders off again.

Whatever you say, Em, Althalus agreed.

"I *will* need the money almost immediately, your Grace," the seedy-looking Count Baskoi said anxiously. "I'm in debt to some people who aren't really very patient."

"The dice haven't been very friendly lately, I gather," Althalus surmised.

"You wouldn't *believe* how unfriendly they've been," Baskoi lamented.

"Your house suits me quite well, Baskoi," Althalus told him, looking around at the opulent parlor. "I may have to stay here in Maghu for quite some time, and I'd really rather not stay in some shabby inn with cockroaches for neighbors and bedbugs under my pillow. Let's say half a year for right now. If the priests at the temple tell me that my penance is going to take longer, we might want to make more permanent arrangements."

"Anything you say, Duke Althalus. Would it be all right if I stored my personal belongings in the attic?"

"Of course, Count Baskoi. And as soon as you've finished up with that, talk with my chaplain, Brother Bheid, and he'll pay you our rent."

"Are you absolutely certain that I can't stay in the attic—or maybe down in the cellar?" Baskoi asked plaintively.

"That wouldn't really be a good idea, Count Baskoi," Althalus told him. "I've got some enemies who make your creditors look like kittens by comparison. You *don't* want to be in the house if they should happen to pay me a call someday."

"I suppose I can find a room at some inn," Baskoi said mournfully.

"I'd avoid any of them where dice games are popular, Count," Althalus advised. "When the dice don't like you, it's best to stay away from them."

"Truly," Count Baskoi agreed sadly.

"You're the Duke of *what*?" Duke Olkar of Kadon asked incredulously.

"Kenthaigne," Althalus replied.

"You just made that up, didn't you, Althalus?"

"Pretty much so, yes. How are we doing in the wheat market?"

"Quite well, actually," Olkar said a bit smugly. "Last summer was one of the best in the last dozen years. They had a bumper crop here in Perquaine, and that pushes the price down. I've already freighted four thousand tons toward Kanthon, and paid for another three thousand. I'm having some trouble finding enough wagons, though. If this peasant rebellion just holds off for another month, I'll have all the wheat we'll need over in Treborea."

"Andine's going to be very happy to hear that, Olkar."

"What's this 'Duke of Kenthaigne' business, Althalus?"

"It's the bait I'm using in a fishing trip, your Grace. I need information that's probably going to come from the priesthood. If you happen to think of it, you might mention the fact that the Duke of Kenthaigne, who's so rich that he carries a solid gold handkerchief to sneeze into, is suffering from a very guilty conscience about some really serious sins, and he's come to Maghu to buy forgiveness."

"You'll have every priest in Perquaine camped on your doorstep by morning if *that* gets around, Althalus," Olkar warned.

"That was roughly what I had in mind, your Grace," Althalus replied with a sly grin. "That way, I won't have to go looking for *them*. They'll come to *me*."

"It'll cost you, Althalus."

"Money doesn't really mean anything, Olkar."

"Bite your tongue!" Olkar exclaimed.

"Word of your spiritual crisis has reached the ears of our holy Exarch Aleikon, Duke Althalus," the brown-robed priest who'd come knocking at daybreak the following morning announced.

"I was praying that it might," Althalus said, piously rolling his eyes heavenward.

"Holy Aleikon is much moved by your plight, your Grace," the priest declared, "and our Exarch is quite probably the most charitable man alive. Thus has he granted you immediate audience in his private chapel in the central temple."

"I'm quite overwhelmed by this honor, your Reverence. I pray you, return directly to the temple and advise your Holy Exarch that I and my retainers shall answer his call straightway."

"I shall do so immediately, your Grace. Pray tell me, when should I advise Exarch Aleikon that he may expect you?"

"I'd hustle right back to the temple, your Reverence," Althalus suggested. "If you dawdle even just a little, I'll get there before you do. My burden of sin is heavy, and I must put it down, lest it break my back."

"I shall run, your Grace," the priest promised.

Sergeant Khalor was trying, without much success, to muffle his laughter as the Brown Robe left.

"Are you having some sort of problem, Sergeant?" Leitha asked him.

"His Grace here was spooning it on just a little thick," Khalor laughed.

"It's one of Daddy's failings," she conceded. "He never wastes time with a spoon when there's a shovel handy."

The ancient temple of Dweia was clearly the most magnificent building in Maghu. The Brown Robes had made some effort to conceal the more blatant suggestions that the temple had been erected for the worship of a fertility Goddess, and the excessively bosomed statue had been removed from the altar.

The priest who'd visited them that morning came hustling out through a door behind the altar to greet them. He looked just a bit confused when he saw the party accompanying Althalus.

"My sins have made enemies for me, your Reverence," Althalus explained. "It wouldn't have been prudent to leave my daughters unprotected. There are some other reasons that I won't let them out of my sight, but it probably wouldn't be very proper for me to mention them to a man who's taken a vow of chastity."

The Brown Robe blinked, and then he flushed slightly. "Oh," he said, and then he let the subject drop. He turned instead, led them through the door into a dimly lighted corridor and on down to a dark, heavy, cherry-wood door. "The private chapel of our Holy Exarch," he said. Then he rapped on the door.

"Enter," a voice responded from behind that door.

The brown-robed priest opened the door and led Althalus and his companions into the chapel. "Holy Aleikon," he said, kneeling briefly, "I am honored to present his Grace, Duke Althalus of Kenthaigne." Then he rose and backed from the small chapel, bowing at every other step.

Exarch Aleikon was a plump man with close-cropped blond hair and a serious demeanor. "I am honored, your Grace," he said rather perfunctorily to Althalus, "but I had thought you wished a private audience that we might more fully explore the seriousness of your sins."

"Privacy's a luxury I cannot afford, your Eminence," Althalus replied glibly. "Holy men speak of sins, but more worldly men speak of crimes. Ambition drove me during my rise to the ducal throne, and my methods made me many enemies. The two lovely young ladies are my daughters, Leitha and Andine. The child is their personal page boy. The Black Robe is Brother Bheid, my personal chaplain. My entire party lives in constant danger and must be protected at all times by my personal bodyguards Khalor and Eliar, the two greatest warriors in all of Kenthaigne."

"The duchy of Kenthaigne is thousands of years old, your Eminence," Althalus was telling Exarch Aleikon a while later in the Exarch's study, "and over all the endless centuries, we've raised corruption to an art form. I've got every judge in my pocket, and the clergy dances to my tune. All it takes is money, and I control the treasury. My subjects have learned not to cross me. If I want something, I take it; and if anyone objects, he quietly disappears. Everything would be just fine—if it weren't for the dreadful nightmares I've been having here lately."

"Nightmares?" the Brown Robe Exarch asked.

"Have you ever heard of a place called Nahgharash, your Eminence?"

Aleikon's face blanched.

"Ah," Althalus said, "I see that you *have* heard of it. Well, I've seen it, and you wouldn't want to visit *that* place. The buildings are made of fire, and the people dance in the streets as flickering little flames, screaming and writhing in perpetual agony. It's the screaming that sets my teeth on edge, and I hear it all the time now—even when I'm awake. I have everything any man could possibly want—except for a good night's sleep. That's why I've come to Maghu, your Eminence. If you can banish those nightmares, I'll pay anything you ask."

"Are you truly repentant, my son?" Aleikon asked.

"Repentant? Don't be absurd. I did what I had to do to get what I wanted. Just tell your God that I'll pay him anything he wants if he'll just make those dreams go away."

He's wavering, Daddy, Leitha's soft voice murmured. *He really wants your money, but he knows he can't drive those "nightmares" away.*

Good. Things seem to be going according to plan, then.

Just exactly what is your plan, Althalus? Bheid asked in silent curiosity.

Watch, Brother Bheid. Watch and learn.

"I will pray for guidance, Duke Althalus," Exarch Aleikon declared in a troubled voice. "And if you return tomorrow, we will discuss a suitable penance."

Althalus stood up. "I am at your command, Exarch Aleikon," he declared with a pious bow. "And I will return at first light tomorrow with as much gold as I can conveniently carry—*if* I sleep well tonight."

That's dreadful, Daddy, Leitha murmured.

I rather liked it myself, Althalus replied smugly.

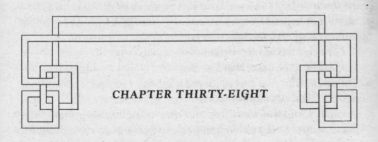

CHAPTER THIRTY-EIGHT

"His Eminence is . . . ah . . . indisposed, your Grace," the priest who'd originally come to Count Baskoi's house told Althalus the next morning at the temple.

"Oh?"

"Something he ate, no doubt," the priest added hastily.

"There's been a lot of that going around here lately," Althalus noted. "How long do you think it might take for him to pull himself together? Later on today, perhaps?"

"I don't really think so, your Grace. Tomorrow, perhaps."

He's very upset, Daddy, Leitha silently reported. *Exarch Aleikon woke up screaming just before dawn, and he's still screaming. The Brown Robes are afraid that he's gone mad.*

Althalus reached out to Dweia. *What have you been up to, Em?*

I snitched your idea, love, she purred her reply. *It was just too good to pass up. How in the* world *did you come up with the idea of nightmares?*

I needed something to get Aleikon's attention, Em. Our imaginary Duke of Kenthaigne was too much of a scoundrel to start getting all weepy about assorted indiscretions in his past. I needed something fairly awful to explain why I'd come to Maghu to beg for help. After I'd given it some thought, I decided to hang the whole thing on nightmares about Nahgharash.

Ah, I see. You just scraped it off the wall.

There might have been some of that involved, yes. From what I understand, a sizable part of the education of novice priests of all three orders involves lurid descriptions of Nahgharash, so I threw it in to get Aleikon's attention. Actually, it was sort of in the nature of an afterthought—or maybe divine inspiration.

Let's call it a stroke of pure genius, pet.

I wouldn't go quite that far, Em.

I would. You just sort of tossed it off, but I picked it up and ran with it. You've caught occasional glimpses of Nahgharash through Khnom's doorways, but they've just been a view from the outside. Aleikon's nightmares put him inside the city itself, and Nahgharash is a place of absolute despair. That's why Yakhag was grateful when Bheid killed him. Death is a release from Nahgharash.

Aleikon's going to recover from his little siege of horrors, isn't he? I think I'm going to need him on down the line.

Why don't we let him simmer for a while, pet—cook him until he's tender. After a week or so of these nightmares, he'll agree to

*almost anything. Why don't you bring the children home, Al-
thalus? We need to talk.*

The streets of Maghu were literally teeming with heavily armed
soldiers as Althalus and his friends returned to Count Baskoi's
house. The soldiers all seemed a bit edgy, and they stayed together in tight little groups. Althalus stopped a street vendor
who was pushing a cartload of turnips along a cobblestoned
street. "What's afoot here, neighbor?" he asked the vendor.

The cart man shrugged. "Prince Marwain's flexing his
muscles, I think," he replied. "You've heard about the peasant
unrest, I suppose."

"I just arrived in Maghu last night," Althalus said.

"Oh? Where are you from?"

"Equero. I'm in town on business. What's got the peasants all
stirred up?"

"The usual sort of thing. Every so often they get excited about
how badly the world's treating them. Prince Marwain puts his
troops out in the streets of Maghu every time that happens. He
wants everybody in town to know who's in charge."

"City folks don't get involved in these country bumpkin matters, do they?"

The turnip vendor snorted. "Of course we don't. There are always a few malcontents in the grubbier parts of town, though.
Our noble Prince wants to be sure they understand the *real* situation here. As long as you mind your own business, the soldiers
won't bother you. Could I interest you in some turnips?"

"Sorry, neighbor, but turnips don't agree with me, for some
reason. You wouldn't *believe* the bellyache one bite of a turnip
gives me."

"Ah," the peddler said. "Onions do the same thing to me."

"It's good to know that I'm not the only one with a delicate
tummy. You have a nice day, hear?"

"I've heard of this Prince Marwain, Althalus," Andine said as
they crossed the street to the front of Count Baskoi's house.
"He's a ruthless tyrant with an exaggerated notion of his own
importance."

"We might have to cure him of that particular delusion," Sergeant Khalor said.

"We've got a certain amount of time," Dweia told them when they gathered in the tower. "Argan's moving carefully and consolidating his control over each city before he moves on to the next. A revolution's not like an invasion from the outside. What's the customary procedure when an Exarch's unable to function, Bheid?"

Bheid leaned back, squinting at the ceiling. "In normal circumstances, the hierarchy would maintain the fiction that the Exarch's 'indisposed,' Dweia," he replied. "The bureaucracy of the Church makes most of the day-to-day decisions anyway, so the Exarch's actually little more than a figurehead. The current situation's not normal, though. The peasant revolt in southern Perquaine is an emergency of the first order, so as soon as it becomes obvious that Exarch Aleikon isn't going to come to his senses, some high-ranking Scopas will send an appeal to Exarchs Emdahl and Yeudon for a meeting of the high council of the faith."

"Something on the order of a conclave of the Clan Chiefs of Arum?" Sergeant Khalor suggested.

"Exactly," Bheid agreed. "If it's determined that there's a crisis of the faith, the high council can override normal procedures. Emdahl and Yeudon could replace Aleikon, or possibly even go so far as to absorb the Brown Robes into their own orders. I don't *think* they'd go quite that far, though. It'd probably start a religious war that'd turn the civilized world inside out."

"And Argan could ride *that* particular horse directly into an imperial seat," Althalus added.

"He might *think* so," Dweia disagreed. "It has some possibilities, I think. We eliminated Pekhal with Sergeant Khalor's mountain—and the river that ran in two directions—and we lured Gelta into Osthos with Andine's seeming submission. Trickery *does* seem to work on occasion."

"I *knew* you'd come around to my way of thinking eventually, Em," Althalus said smugly.

"I didn't quite follow that," Andine said.

"It's an old debate, little Princess," Althalus explained. "Emmy set out to teach me truth, justice, and morality; I offered to teach her how to lie, cheat, and steal. I seem to be just a bit ahead of her."

Dweia shrugged. "Whatever works," she said. "For right now, I think we'll want Exarch Aleikon to keep dreaming about Nahgharash. Go back to the temple, Brother Bheid. I need to know who's making the decisions for the Brown Robes now that Aleikon's not able to function. I need to know everything about him you can find out so that I'll be able to nudge him into sending an appeal to Emdahl and Yeudon. I want those two in Maghu just as soon as we can get them here."

"His name's Eyosra, Althalus," Bheid reported that evening when he returned to Count Baskoi's house. "He's a Scopas in the Brown Robe order, and he specializes in details—and numbers. The rest of the hierarchy hates him, probably because he keeps finding discrepancies in their account books. He's tall, very thin, and as pale as a ghost."

"That doesn't sound very encouraging," Althalus said. "A bean counter doesn't usually have that much power."

"Scopas Eyosra controls the Brown Robe treasury, Althalus," Bheid said with a faint smile. "In a religious order controlled by greed, the man who holds the purse strings rules."

"Good point. What do you think it'll take to nudge him into screaming for help?"

"Extravagance of some sort, probably. If Dweia can push Aleikon in the direction of spending a lot of money, Eyosra's likely to go up in flames."

"I'll take it up with Em," Althalus promised. "I'm sure she'll be able to come up with something."

"He seems to be coming around, Em," Althalus reported when he and Eliar had returned to the House. "Keeping him busy's probably the best way to deal with his problem."

"It's better than slamming him up against a wall," she agreed.

"Did you really do that, Althalus?" Eliar asked.

"Not all *that* hard," Althalus replied. "I just wanted to get his attention. Anyway, Brother Bheid tells me that we'll want to stir up a certain Scopas Eyosra. He controls the treasury of the Brown Robes, and he's one of those penny-pinchers. Bheid seems to think that a sudden outburst of extravagance by Exarch Aleikon would send Scopas Eyosra running to the other Exarchs almost immediately."

"Some renovations of my temple, perhaps?" she suggested.

Althalus wobbled his hand dubiously. "Maybe," he said. "I think it might depend on what you've got in mind, Em."

"The restoration of the altar sort of leaps to mind. Back in the good old days, my altar was sheathed in gold. The Brown Robes peeled the sheathing off when they usurped my temple. If I planted the notion of putting it back into Aleikon's mind . . ." She left it hanging.

"As I remember, that altar's fairly large," Althalus said. "It *would* take quite a bit of gold to resheathe it, wouldn't it?"

"Yes, definitely—several tons, at least."

"I'll see what Bheid has to say, but I think that might just turn the trick, Em. Pulling that much gold out of the Brown Robe treasury should send Scopas Eyosra straight up into the air, and he'll probably come down running."

"Argan's more or less consolidated his hold on those coastal cities—Egni, Athal, Pella, and Bhago," Sergeant Khalor reported about a week later when they all gathered again in the tower room. "He's sent various agitators upriver from Athal to Leida and overland from Bhago to Dail to stir up the peasants in those regions."

"How much longer do you think it might be until he starts the march on Maghu?" Bheid asked.

"A couple of months at least," Khalor replied. "He's not rushing things. Argan's an entirely different breed of cat from Pekhal and Gelta. He's very cautious. I *do* think we might want to speed up the journey of those two other Exarchs, though. Religious people do a lot of talking before they make decisions, I've noticed—no offense intended, Brother Bheid."

"That's all right, Sergeant," Bheid told him. "We *do* tend to babble on fairly often. Perhaps it's an attempt to *avoid* making decisions." Then Bheid looked at Dweia. "The Sergeant's probably right, though. I think we *should* get Exarchs Emdahl and Yeudon here before too much more time passes. They have some important decisions to make, and Argan's already on the move."

Dweia pursed her lips. "I'll tamper with a few people's memories, and then Eliar can bring the Exarchs through the House and put them down in Maghu. All *we're* doing right now is marking time. We can't really make any decisions until Emdahl and Yeudon reach Maghu."

"Argan's rabble's starting upriver from Egni toward Leida," Sergeant Khalor reported the next morning. "They aren't moving very fast, but they're going in that general direction."

"What's delaying them?" Eliar asked.

"Looting, for the most part." Khalor made a sour face. "Unleashing an undisciplined army in a land where there are towns and villages is just about the best way I know of to arrive at your destination without any troops."

"Didn't you once say that a stupid enemy's a gift from the Gods?" Eliar said slyly.

"Maybe I did, Eliar, but it still rubs me the wrong way. It's unprofessional."

"Have they left Bhago to march toward Dail yet?" Althalus asked.

Khalor shook his head. "They're still looting in Bhago," he replied. "Somebody's going to have to set fire to the town before the peasants will even *think* about leaving."

Bheid gave the Sergeant a startled look. "Is *that* why looted towns are always burned?" he asked.

"Of course, Brother Bheid. I thought everybody knew that. A dedicated looter wouldn't even consider leaving a town until the flames are licking at his tail feathers. Fire's just about the only way to start an army moving after they've taken a town."

"Don't worry about it, Althalus," Dweia said.

"The numbers don't match, Em," he protested. "Eyosra's messenger's going to take several weeks to reach the Black Robe temple in Deika and even longer to get to Keiwon. If Emdahl and Yeudon arrive in Maghu tomorrow morning, Eyosra's likely to start getting *very* suspicious."

She sighed, rolling her eyes upward.

"I wish you wouldn't do that, Em," he complained.

"Then quit being so obvious, pet. I know all about the problem of elapsed time, and I've already taken care of it. We've been tampering with time and distance for quite a while now, so you should know by now that miles and minutes mean what I *want* them to mean. Nobody's going to notice anything, Althalus, so stop worrying."

He gave up. "All right, Em, anything you say. Is Aleikon still having nightmares?"

"Occasionally, yes. We want him to be nice and pliable when Emdahl and Yeudon start making some decisions."

"What kind of decisions?"

"Watch, Althalus. Watch and learn."

Exarch Emdahl was a burly clergyman with a deeply lined face and a harsh voice. He and Exarch Yeudon arrived in Maghu late one chill afternoon, and they went immediately into an extended conference with Scopas Eyosra and the other high-ranking Brown Robe clergymen.

"He's like a bull, Daddy," Leitha reported. "He's overriding everybody in the temple, and he seems to know a great deal more than he really should."

"Our order specializes in gathering information," Bheid explained. "There's very little that happens in the world that isn't brought to the attention of my Exarch. I'm told that he tends to be just a bit abrupt in emergencies. I think we'll want to step around him rather carefully."

"Maybe," Althalus said, "but then again, maybe not. If he just happens to want truth, I'm in a position to give him more truth than he can handle. Exarch Emdahl might be a bull, but I've got bigger horns than he has."

The summoner arrived at Count Baskoi's house the following morning with a document "requesting" the presence of the Duke of Kenthaigne at the temple.

"Do be a good fellow and run on back to the temple and advise the Exarchs that we'll be along just as soon as it's convenient," Althalus told the somewhat self-important official in his haughtiest tone of voice.

Bheid winced. *You're getting off to a bad start, Althalus,* he silently warned.

Not really, Althalus replied. *I want to jerk Emdahl's chain just a little. Let's give it about half an hour. Then we'll drop by the temple. I think maybe you should stay in the background just a bit, Brother Bheid. I'm going to pull Emdahl up short, and I'd rather he didn't take his dissatisfaction out on you.*

They waited for a while in Baskoi's comfortable parlor. "That's long enough," Althalus decided finally. "Let's go to the temple and educate a few clergymen, shall we?"

"Aren't you pushing things just a bit?" Andine suggested.

"Naturally," Althalus replied gaily. "I want Emdahl's undivided attention."

They left the house and went across town to the temple, and there were a fair number of unfriendly looks cast in their direction as they entered. Althalus ignored the obvious hostility and marched through the temple to Aleikon's private chapel. "Are they in there?" he demanded of the priest who'd originally come to Baskoi's house.

"Ah . . . no, your Grace," the priest replied nervously. "Exarch Aleikon's still indisposed, and Exarchs Emdahl and Yeudon are conferring in the library."

"I think you'd better take me to them at once," Althalus said.

The priest scurried on ahead, and Althalus and the rest marched on behind, Althalus drawing an icy calm about himself.

"It shouldn't be more than a few minutes, your Grace," the nervous priest reported when they reached an arched door.

"You've been quite helpful in the past several weeks, young man," Althalus said, "so I don't want to get you in trouble. Isn't there some important duty you just absolutely *must* see to in another part of the temple?"

"I'll think of something, your Grace," the priest replied gratefully, and then he scurried away.

What are you up to? Dweia's voice demanded.

I'm going to get their attention, Em. I'm going to ignore some customary courtesies and bull my way into the presence of Yeudon and Emdahl. I'm not going to dance to their tune as they most likely expect me to. Then he slammed open the library door and marched into the presence of Emdahl and Yeudon. "Don't get up, gentlemen. I'm told you want to see me," he announced to the two startled clergymen. "Well, here I am. What's your problem?"

"What kept you?" the harsh-faced Emdahl demanded.

"Courtesy, your Eminence," Althalus replied with a florid bow. "Since it's customary to keep visitors cooling their heels in an anteroom for a certain amount of time, I took care of that in more comfortable surroundings. We have a great deal to discuss, gentlemen, so let's get down to business, shall we? What is it that you want to know?"

"Let's start with everything," Emdahl replied in his gravelly voice, "and we'll go on from there. Just who *are* you? There's been a great deal of turmoil in the world here lately, and you and your people seem to have been at the center of most of it. You've been running roughshod over people who outrank you everywhere you go, and that disrupts the natural order of things. The Church wants to know what your intentions are."

Althalus seated himself at the opposite end of the table, motioned the others to sit, and leaned back in his chair. "How much truth are you prepared to deal with, Exarch Emdahl?"

"As much—or more—than you're ready to give me. Let's start with who you are."

Althalus shrugged. "Is that all? This shouldn't take very long, then. My name's Althalus, but you already know that. I'm a thief and a swindler, and if the money's right, a sometime murderer. I was born a very, very long time ago, and I was having a long spell of bad luck when this all started. I was approached by a man named Ghend—a disciple of the demon Daeva—who hired me to go to Kagwher to steal something he called a book. I went to the House at the End of the World where the Book was, and there was a cat there—except that she wasn't really a cat. She's the Goddess Dweia, the sister of Deiwos and Daeva." He paused slightly. "You *did* know that Deiwos and Daeva are brothers, didn't you, Emdahl? Anyway, the cat, who I call Emmy, taught me how to read the Book of Deiwos, and then about two years ago, she and I left the House to pick up certain people: a young Arum named Eliar; Andine, the Arya of Osthos; a Black Robe priest named Bheid; a boy-thief named Gher; and the mind leech Leitha. Then we all went to the House and saw the *real* form of the Goddess Dweia. She explained some things to us, and then we came out of the House to deal with Ghend and his underlings in the inevitable war between good and evil. That's what we're doing right now. We've already eliminated two of Ghend's underlings—Pekhal and Gelta—and we've come to Perquaine to deal with Argan, who is a defrocked priest, and Koman, who is Ghend's mind leech. You gentlemen can either lend a hand or back off and leave me alone. That's entirely up to you, but I should probably advise you that if you try to interfere with me in any way, I'll destroy you and anything you gather up to try to resist me. I can do things you can't even begin to imagine, so get out of my way and let me get on with my work." Althalus paused. "Was that bald enough for you, Emdahl?" he asked.

Exarch Emdahl's eyes were bulging.

"Oh, one other thing," Althalus added. "Dweia tampered with Exarch Aleikon just a bit to get your attention. The poor fellow hasn't *really* gone crazy. Dweia's been filling his dreams with visions of Nahgharash, that's all. It only takes a little bit of Nahgharash to get somebody's total attention."

"Nahgharash is only a metaphor, Althalus," Yeudon objected. "It's a way to explain a spiritual condition."

"I think you've got it upside down, Yeudon," Althalus disagreed. "Nahgharash is much more real than your sometimes-obscure definition of sin. It's *not* just a state of mind. I've caught a few glimpses of it—usually when Ghend was trying to surprise me."

"Just exactly where is it?"

"It's supposed to be a vast cave filled with fire under the mountains of Nekweros. Actually, it's wherever Ghend wants it to be. It's very similar to the House at the End of the World, which can be Everywhere and Everywhen all at the same time." Althalus smiled faintly. "There's an alternative to Everywhere and Everywhen, but we aren't even supposed to *think* about it. Gher started playing with the notion of 'Nowhere and Nowhen' once, and it sent Dweia right straight up the wall. I guess there's a chaos out beyond good and evil that's so hungry that it can swallow the universe. Let's get back to the question of reality, though. When you get right down to the core of things, the House and Nahgharash are the ultimate realities, and what *we* call the real world is just a reflection of them. That almost suggests that *we're* the metaphors—concepts, if you wish—designed to act out the realities of the struggle between Dweia and Daeva." He laughed. "We could discuss that for several centuries, couldn't we? Right now, though, we've got this little war on our hands, so maybe we should concentrate on that. In those other realities, time and distance aren't constant in the same way they are in the ordinary world. Scopas Eyosra sent a message to you two gentlemen urging you to come to Maghu because Exarch Aleikon was starting to come unhinged. In *this* world, that message would have taken about six weeks to reach you, and it would have taken you another six weeks to come here to Maghu. If you wanted to investigate a little, though, I think you'd find that Eyosra's message left here early last week. Emmy *could* have done it even faster, but she prefers not to make big splashes and all kinds of noise." He looked at Emdahl and Yeudon. "I don't seem to be getting through to you gentlemen," he noted.

"I think you're even crazier than Aleikon," Emdahl rasped.

"Aleikon isn't crazy, Exarch Emdahl," Leitha told him. "He's

having nightmares about Nahgharash, that's all, and those nightmares aren't coming from his own mind. Dweia's giving them to
him. The whole idea was to make him *appear* to be insane so that
the two of you would come here. It seems to have worked, so I'd
imagine that Aleikon will recover almost immediately."

"You're the witch-woman, aren't you?" Emdahl demanded.

"That's beginning to make me *very* tired," Leitha told him in a
flat, unfriendly voice.

"I'd be awful careful right here, Mister High Priest," Gher
cautioned. "Leitha's not afraid of anything—or anybody—and if
you make her mad at you, she'll melt your brains down into a
mud puddle."

"This is all nonsense!" Emdahl exploded. "I think you people
all belong in a madhouse somewhere. *We* are the leaders of the
faith, and *we* tell you what you can or cannot believe."

"I think you'd better show him how wrong he is, Leitha," Althalus suggested, speaking aloud.

"Yes, Daddy," she agreed. "Maybe I should at that." She
looked at the harsh-faced Exarch of the Black Robes. Then she
sighed. "How very sad," she said. "Deiwos *is* real, your Eminence," she told him. "He's not just some fiction the priesthood
invented to foist off on the gullible among the population. Your
uncertainty and your anguish are unnecessary. Don't keep pun-
ishing yourself about your doubts."

Emdahl's expression was suddenly stricken, and he began to
tremble violently. "How . . ." he started, but left it hanging.

"Leitha is gifted, my Exarch," Bheid explained gently. "She
can hear your innermost thoughts."

"I *do* wish you people would stop calling it a gift," Leitha
complained. "It's more like a curse. I don't *want* to hear most of
what comes to me unbidden."

Dweia's voice crackled in Althalus' mind. *This is tiresome as
well as annoying, Althalus. Stand clear. I'll take care of it.*

Then one wall of Aleikon's high-vaulted library was no longer
there. Where the wall had been was the perfect face of Dweia:
calm, beautiful, and so enormous that Althalus flinched back in
near panic. Her perfect arms were crossed on what had been the

floor, and her chin was resting pensively on those arms. "I sometimes forget how small you people are," she murmured. "So tiny,
so imperfect." She reached out with one vast hand and gently
picked up the rigid body of Exarch Emdahl and placed him on
the palm of her other hand. Then she took up Yeudon and stood
him beside Emdahl. "Does this put things in perspective for you
gentlemen?" she asked.

The two clergymen clung to each other, squeaking almost like
mice.

"Oh, stop that," she scolded in a voice that seemed oddly
gentle. "I'm not going to hurt you. Althalus isn't the most reli-
able person in the world, but this time he's telling you the truth. I
am who he told you that I am, and this is *not* an illusion or some
kind of trick. I want you both to behave yourselves and to do exactly as Althalus tells you to do. We aren't going to argue about
this, are we, gentlemen?"

Emdahl and Yeudon, still clinging to each other in panic, both
shook their heads violently.

"I knew all along that you were good boys," she murmured.
Then she reached out one enormous finger and touched each of
them with a kind of gently stroking motion. "So tiny," she murmured again. "So very, very tiny." Then she took each of them in
turn and set them back down in their chairs. "Bring them here,
Althalus," she said, "and fetch Aleikon as well. They have some
decisions to make, and it might take them quite a while to make
them. Once they're in the House, I can give them as much time
as they'll need."

Exarch Aleikon was trembling violently when Althalus and Eliar
led him through the door into the tower. *You might have gone
just a little too far with him, Em,* Althalus silently suggested. *The
nightmares pushed him very close to the edge, and dropping the
House on him like this might just be more than he can handle.*

Bring him to me, pet, she replied. *I'll bring him back to his
senses.*

Althalus rather gently took Exarch Aleikon by the arm and led
him to the marble table where Dweia sat with Emdahl and

Yeudon. He noted that the Book was covered with a piece of heavy cloth.

"You aren't looking too well, Aleikon," Emdahl rasped.

"Where are we?" Aleikon asked, looking around in confusion.

"We're not entirely sure, Aleikon," the silver-haired Yeudon told him. "Reality seems to be very far away right now."

"That might depend on your definition of reality," Emdahl said. "Can you put Aleikon's head back together, Divinity?" he asked Dweia. "The three of us have to make some decisions, and Aleikon's not functioning very well right now."

"Perhaps we *did* push him a little far," Dweia conceded, looking at Aleikon's anguished face. "Your nightmares are over now, Aleikon," she told the Brown Robe Exarch. "They've served their purpose, so let's get rid of them." She reached out and uncovered the Book. "Give me your hand, Aleikon," she told him.

The Brown Robe Exarch held out his trembling hand, and Dweia gently took it and placed it palm down on the white, leather-bound Book. "Just relax," she told him. "My brother's Book will banish all memory of your nightmares."

"Is that . . . ?" Yeudon started in an awed voice.

"It's the Book of Deiwos, yes," Althalus told him. "It's really quite interesting—once you get into it. It's a bit tedious right at first. Dweia's brother has a little trouble sticking to the point."

"Be nice," Dweia scolded.

"Sorry," Althalus apologized.

A look of wonder had come over Exarch Aleikon's face.

"That should be enough for right now," Dweia noted clinically. "We don't want to go *too* fast here. You gentlemen need to discuss practicalities, and religious ecstasy isn't the best route to that."

"Could I . . . ?" Yeudon pleaded, reaching his hand out toward the Book with a look of longing.

"Let them touch it, Em," Althalus suggested. "It's all they'll think about if you don't, and we've got work to do."

Dweia gave the Exarchs a stern look. "If you really think you *must* touch the Book, I suppose it's all right," she told them, "but no peeking."

Althalus burst out laughing at that.

"What's so funny?" Dweia demanded.

"Nothing, Em," he replied with mock innocence. "Something just struck me as sort of funny, that's all."

Exarch Emdahl's harshly lined face was pensive as he sat at the marble table in the tower of the House. "There's no question that the Church has strayed from her original purpose, gentlemen," he said sadly to Aleikon and Yeudon. "We sought to impress the wealthy and powerful by imitating them, and in the end, we became more arrogant and filled with pride than they were. We've totally lost contact with the commoners, and that opened the door for the enemy."

"Face reality, Emdahl," the plump-faced Aleikon told him abruptly. "The Church has to live in the real world, imperfect though it may be. Without the aid of the aristocracy we'd never have been able to perform our task."

"Have we really succeeded all *that* well, Aleikon?" Emdahl asked him. "From where I sit, it rather looks as if it's all falling down around our ears."

"I think we're straying just a bit," Althalus suggested. "When your house is on fire, you don't really have time to argue about which kind of bucket you should use to throw water on the flames. Why don't we have a look at the faces of the people who're setting the fires? It might be useful to get to know them."

"I don't think we have the time, Althalus," Yeudon disagreed.

"Time doesn't mean anything here in Emmy's House," Gher told him, "and neither does distance, but that's only natural, I guess, since time and distance are the same thing. Everything in the world's always moving, since the world's part of the sky, and the sky moves all the time. When we talk about miles, what we're really talking about is hours—how long it takes to get from here to there. I think that might be why nobody can see Emmy's House, since, even though it's always here, Emmy can make it be here somewhen else."

"Is this boy all right in the head, Althalus?" Emdahl asked.

"He just thinks faster than anybody else can, Exarch Emdahl," Althalus replied, "and he takes ideas further than the rest of us do. If you talk with him for a while, I think you'll come away with your eyes popping."

"Or with your brain turned inside out," Sergeant Khalor added. "I don't think Gher even lives in the same world with the rest of us. His mind moves so fast that nobody but Dweia can keep up with him."

The three Exarchs looked speculatively at the little boy.

"Never mind," Dweia told them firmly. "Don't get any ideas, gentlemen. The boy's mine, and he's going to *stay* mine. Tell them about the windows, Gher."

"All right, Emmy." Gher looked earnestly at the three. "Since the House is Everywhere, the windows look out at any place Emmy wants them to, so we can find out what the bad people are doing and what they're going to try to do next. The great thing about the windows is that we can see and hear the bad people, and they don't even know we're right behind them—except that we really aren't." Gher frowned. "This is awful hard to explain," he told them. "*I* know what's happening, but I just don't know the right words to make it clear to anybody else. If the House is Everywhere, then wouldn't that sort of mean that it's Nowhere? I mean, not really Nowhere, but only sort of Nowhere. At least it's Nowhere enough so that the bad people can't see us while we're watching them."

"I think the word you're looking for is 'omnipresence,' boy," Emdahl suggested. "It's part of the standard definition of God. If God's Everywhere, man can't hide from him."

"That makes me feel a lot better, Mister Priest," Gher said gratefully. "I thought I was the only one who'd ever had these ideas, and that's a really lonesome sort of feeling."

"I think that maybe you'd better get used to that, boy," Emdahl told him. "You seem to be able to grasp instinctively concepts that others can only touch the edges of after a lifetime of study." Emdahl sighed regretfully. "What a theologian we could have made of this boy if we'd gotten to him first."

"He's doing just fine on his own, Emdahl," Dweia said. "Don't tamper with him."

"Unguided thought can be very dangerous," Emdahl declared.

"Both of my brothers feel the same way," she said. "It's lucky for Gher that I'm the one who found him."

"Are they *really* your brothers, Dweia?" he asked in a strangely subdued voice.

"It's a bit more complex than that, Emdahl, but the word 'brother' comes fairly close. Now then, why don't we all go over to the window and find out what 'the bad people' are up to?"

The light outside the window blurred and grew darker.

"What's going on?" Yeudon demanded in an alarmed voice.

"The window's moving, your Eminence," Bheid explained. "It's going from here to there—and I'd judge that it's also going from when to when, considering the change in the light." He glanced at Dweia. "Just exactly what are we looking at, Divinity?" he asked her.

"It's the town of Leida in south central Perquaine," she replied, "and we're looking at yesterday evening."

"That's Koman sneaking down that alley, isn't it, Em?" Althalus asked, peering through the fading light.

"It seems to be, yes," she replied "I was looking for Argan, but the House has a mind of its own. Sometimes Deiwos is a little lazy, so the House goes out of its way to make things easier."

"There's a concept for you, Brother Bheid," Leitha said slyly. "Consider the notion of a lazy God for a while."

"Please don't do that, Leitha," Bheid pleaded. "I'm having enough trouble already—and stay out of my head right now. You don't want to see what's in there."

Exarch Emdahl looked speculatively at Bheid and Leitha, but he didn't say anything.

Then in the littered and half-dark alleyway below, Koman opened a battered door and entered a building.

The light blurred again as the window followed Ghend's mind

leech into a shabby room where Argan sat waiting. "Did you find anything useful?" Argan asked.

The white-bearded Koman sat down. "The local ruler calls himself a Duke," he replied. "His name's Arekad, and he's as stupid as the others have been."

"Didn't really expect anything else, old boy," the blond priest in the scarlet robe replied. "What about the local Scopas?"

"He's a fairly typical Brown Robe churchman. He fawns all over the Duke and squeezes every penny he can get out of the commoners. This pot's already simmering, Argan. One good sermon should bring it to a boil."

Argan smiled faintly. "You don't necessarily need to pass this on to Ghend, old chap, but I never had much confidence in those open military campaigns. It's always been easier to work from within. Pekhal and Gelta should have stayed in the dark ages where they belonged. If Ghend had listened to me in the first place, we'd already have Wekti and Treborea in our pockets, and the rest of the lands would be opening their doors to welcome us."

"Possibly, but it doesn't matter all that much to you and me, Argan. Ghend's the one who has to explain it to the Master. I rather think the Master's growing impatient. We don't really have forever to finish up. Those military campaigns in Wekti and Treborea were a waste of time, and that was Ghend's fault, not ours."

"Couldn't agree more, old boy," Argan said. "We want men's hearts and minds, not their bodies, and the key to that is the temple of Dweia in Maghu. If you and I can present that place to the Master as a gift, he might just send our 'glorious leader' packing."

"My, aren't *we* ambitious?" Koman observed.

"I'm better suited for the job than Ghend ever could be, old chap. You know that as well as I do. When we're done with this, I'll sit at the right hand of Daeva in Nahgharash, and you'll sit at his left, and the world will bow down to us."

"It's a pretty picture, Argan, but you still have to get past Ghend, and that might take a bit of doing."

"Althalus got around him without too much trouble."

"You're good, Argan, but you're not *that* good."

"We'll discover that in time, old boy. Are you with me in this?"

"Up to a point. If Ghend finds out what you're doing, though, you're on your own."

"Wouldn't have it any other way, old boy. Let's go report our progress to Ghend. I wouldn't make things sound *too* easy, though, if you get my drift."

Althalus rolled over in his bed and punched his pillow a few times. Then, grumbling to himself, he settled down and slowly drifted off to sleep.

The vast temple in Maghu seemed deserted, and then two cleaning ladies with brooms and mops and dust rags entered. They wore aprons, and their hair was protected by kerchiefs. And as they entered, the song of the Knife serenaded them.

One scrubwoman was pale blond Leitha, and the other was perfect Dweia. And pale Leitha, weeping, did seat herself upon the stones of the temple floor, and she took up a garment of finest weave. Still sobbing, she tore one sleeve from the garment and cast it up into the silent air, and the Knife cried out also as the sleeve vanished in the air.

And the face of Dweia was sad.

And, weeping still, did pale Leitha tear the other sleeve from the garment of finest weave, and once again cast she that torn sleeve into the air, and once again the Knife cried and the sleeve vanished.

And then did Leitha, with tears upon her face, rip the garment of finest weave into fragments small, casting each in turn after the vanished sleeves. And when she was done, the garment of finest weave was no more, and pale Leitha cast herself facedown on the floor before the altar and wept, even as a brokenhearted child.

But perfect Dweia comforted her not, but proceeded unto the altar. Then stopped she there and brushed the top of the altar with meticulous care, catching her brushing in one perfect hand.

And then did she cast the fruit of her brushing into the air, and it was even as dust.

Then caused she that window that men call Bheid to be opened. And behold, a great wind did issue forth from the window Bheid. And the Knife sang, and the dust was there no more.

And then the Goddess looked about with calm satisfaction. "And now," she spake, "my temple is once more immaculate and undefiled."

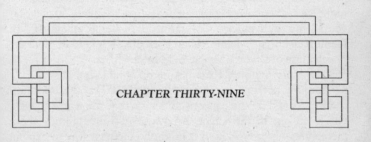

CHAPTER THIRTY-NINE

"Did you sleep well, gentlemen?" Althalus slyly asked the Exarchs the next morning as they gathered in the dining hall.

"Quite well, actually," the silver-haired Yeudon replied, "all except for a rather peculiar dream I had. I can't seem to get it out of my mind, for some reason."

"Let me guess. Two cleaning ladies were tidying up the temple. One of them was ripping up a shirt, and the other one was dusting off the altar. Was that roughly the way it went?"

"How did you know that?" Yeudon asked in a startled tone.

"You aren't the only one who was dreaming last night. This has happened before, but this time the dream was probably a gift from Dweia. We've all had these peculiar dreams before, but the other ones came from Daeva. You don't really want to start having *those* dreams."

"You should know all about dreams, Yeudon," Exarch Emdahl rasped. "You White Robes make more money interpreting dreams than you do casting horoscopes. What was that peculiar noise in the dream, Althalus?"

"The song of the Knife, Emdahl. The dreams of Daeva have an entirely different sound. Most dreams don't really mean too much, but when they start singing to you, it's time to pay attention. The dream visions are usually an alternative to reality. The ones we've encountered before were Ghend's attempts to modify certain events in the past in order to change what happened next. Sometimes they're fairly blatant, but that one last night was about as complicated as they're likely to get. Of course, Emmy's much more subtle than her brothers. If I'm reading last night's dream vision correctly, it had to do with the purification of Dweia's temple in Maghu."

"That's *our* temple!" Exarch Aleikon objected.

"For now, perhaps, but it was the temple of Dweia a few thousand years ago. If she happens to decide that she wants it back, you'll be out in the street. Anyway, we were talking about metaphors yesterday, and that might be the best way to explain last night's dream. Dweia and Leitha *are* going to clean out the temple, right enough, but it's not going to involve dusting and mopping. Over the years your order has grown corrupt. You're just a little too interested in money and power, and your treatment of the commoners has opened the door for Ghend's underling, Argan. He's a defrocked priest, so he knows how to preach. His sermons are mostly denunciations of the injustices of your order, and he's reaching a very willing audience. Ghend tried invasions by armies in Wekti and Treborea. Now he's trying social revolution, and that's far more dangerous. Evidently, Dweia's going to step in personally this time, and when *she* cleans house, she goes all the way down to bedrock. She'll sweep away everything that offends her, and you Brown Robes might very well wind up on the dustheap with Argan and Koman."

"Deiwos wouldn't permit that!" Aleikon exclaimed.

"I wouldn't be too sure about that, your Eminence. Dweia and her brother argue quite often, but they *do* love each other. Deiwos is a distant God, but Dweia gets personally involved. If you offend her, she *will* take steps, and Deiwos won't interfere."

The three Exarchs looked uneasily at Dweia, but she smiled faintly and said nothing.

"Emmy was reaching on up ahead with her dream thing, wasn't she?" Gher suggested to Althalus. "I mean, it hasn't happened yet, has it? Wasn't it sort of like that one we all had when the bad lady was standing on Andine's neck?"

"You're probably right, Gher," Althalus agreed. "Emmy jumps around in time fairly often, so sometimes it's a little hard to know exactly when she is. This time it *did* have a sort of 'not yet' feel to it, and I get a strong feeling that Brother Bheid's going to be involved somehow."

Not yet, love, Dweia's voice murmured. *A few things have to happen before we get to that. Right after breakfast, let's go up to the tower and see what Argan's doing.*

If that's what you want, Em, Althalus agreed.

"Where is that, Sergeant Khalor?" Bheid asked when they joined the hard-bitten Arum at the west window of the tower.

"Dail," Khalor replied. "After somebody finally woke up and set fire to Bhago, the peasants packed up all their loot and marched in a more-or-less northeasterly direction. The defenses of Dail are a joke, so I don't imagine the city'll hold out for very long. Argan and Koman are there, and I think Argan's getting ready to make a speech to fire up the peasants."

"It's called a sermon, Sergeant," Bheid said with a slightly pained expression.

Khalor shrugged. "Whatever," he replied indifferently. "I'm an Arum, so I'm not too well versed in religious terminology. When some idiot jumps up and starts shouting, 'My God's better than your God,' I don't pay very much attention—except to hide my purse."

"Wise precaution," Althalus murmured. "I'm just a bit curious to see how good Argan really is, though. He *has* managed to stir things up here in Perquaine, so he's probably fairly eloquent."

"Here they come," Eliar reported from the window.

"I think you gentlemen might want to listen to the competition," Althalus suggested to the Exarchs. "I'm sure he'll do his best to touch as many sore spots as he can manage."

A vast mob of ragged peasants flowed across the frozen fields of northern Perquaine toward the grim walls of the city of Dail. Here and there the crowd was dotted with more splendidly dressed individuals, fairly clear evidence that the clothing of assorted nobles had been a part of the loot taken from the coastal cities.

Exarch Aleikon's face had turned pale. "I didn't know there were *that* many," he said with a certain dismay. "They go on *forever*!"

"It's wintertime, Aleikon," Emdahl rasped. "They don't really have anything else to do."

Sergeant Khalor was looking at the ocean of peasants advancing on Dail. "I think we're in trouble," he said bleakly. "They don't know how to fight, and the only thing they're really interested in is looting, but it looks as if just about every peasant in Perquaine's joining the rebellion. Fighting that mob's out of the question. There aren't enough professional soldiers in all of Arum to stand up to that crowd, and no Clan Chief's stupid enough to even try. The aristocracy always seems to forget just how many peasants there really are. Once the peasantry's been aroused and given some sort of goal, there's no way to stop them."

"It looks to me as if you might have picked the wrong side, Aleikon," Yeudon observed rather smugly. "The nobility of Perquaine has all the money, but the peasants have the numbers. I'd make a run for it, if I were you."

"Koman," Leitha said rather cryptically, "and Argan."

"Where?" Bheid asked her.

"Up at the front of the crowd," she replied, peering out the window. "There," she said, pointing. "They're riding in that farm wagon."

"Can we get a bit closer, ma'am?" Khalor asked Dweia. "I think we might want to listen to them."

"Of course, Sergeant," she agreed, making a sort of gesture at the window.

The scene below blurred briefly, and then it cleared again, and they seemed to be just above a rickety farm wagon that was jolting over the frozen ground as the pair of weary-looking oxen drawing it plodded toward Dail.

"Do your people know what they're supposed to do?" Argan was asking Koman. Argan was dressed in an artfully patched red robe, and he'd obviously not shaved for several weeks.

"You worry too much," Koman replied. "Everything's set up exactly the way you want it." Koman was dressed in burlap rags tied here and there with bits of twine. "Just ask the questions, Argan; you'll get the answers you want. I think you'd better fire these dirt balls up a bit. The enthusiasm's starting to fade, and that uncontrolled looting in the coastal cities is starting to cut into your numbers. Peasants with nothing to lose will follow just about anybody, but a peasant who's just filled his purse with gold usually wants to live long enough to spend it."

"I can set fire to them again, old boy," Argan replied confidently. "I can preach the birds down out of trees, if I really want to. Is Ghend around anywhere nearby?"

Koman shook his grizzled head. "Not close enough for me to find him. I think he's still in Nahgharash trying to smooth over the death of Yakhag. That's not sitting very well with the Master."

"What a shame," Argan replied sardonically. "Things are going rather well for us, aren't they? Once we present the Master with Dweia's temple in Maghu, I think he might just decide that he doesn't really need Ghend anymore."

Let's wait until we take Maghu before we start celebrating, Argan," Koman replied. "Althalus is still out there, you know, and he's outsmarted Ghend at every turn. You'll have to get past him to take the temple in Maghu, and I'm not sure that you're up to it."

"You seem to have quite a reputation in the enemy camp, Althalus," Emdahl rasped.

"I'm good," Althalus replied deprecatingly. "Everybody knows that."

"Turn aside, Koman," Argan instructed when their wagon was about half a mile from the gates of Dail. "Let's get up on top of that little knoll so they can all see me."

"Right," Koman agreed.

"Make sure they can all hear me," Argan added.

"No problem," Koman said, reining their tired oxen around.

"I didn't quite follow that," Exarch Emdahl rasped. "That mob's spread out for miles, and nobody can talk loud enough to make himself heard *that* far."

"Koman's going to take care of that, your Eminence," Leitha told him.

"How?"

She shrugged. "I'm not entirely certain," she admitted.

"It's one of those little tricks, Emdahl," Althalus said.

"Could you do it?"

"Probably, if I really wanted to. I'd have to get the proper word from Emmy, though. The Books are involved, and that always gets a little complicated."

"Some sort of miracle, then?"

"Well, in a way. We can talk about it some other time, though. Let's see what Argan has to say right now."

When their rickety wagon reached the top of the knoll, the blond Argan pulled his ragged hood up to conceal his face and rose to stand pensively in the wagon while Koman's people quieted the unruly crowd. After a certain degree of order had been established, Argan pushed back his hood and raised his head with an expression of noble suffering on his face. "My brothers and sisters," he said in a voice throbbing with emotion.

The crowd fell silent.

"My brothers and sisters," Argan repeated. "Much have we suffered in our quest for justice. Now is the very dead of winter, and the cold north wind bites our flesh while the frozen ground bruises our feet. Unshod and poorly clad, we have struggled our way across Perquaine while cruel winter swirls about us. We hunger and thirst, but not for bread and water. Our hunger and our thirst go far deeper. And what is the unattainable goal we seek?"

"Justice!" a stout peasant bellowed in a voice like a crack of thunder.

"A well-chosen word, my brother," Argan agreed. "Justice, indeed. But who stands athwart our path to simple justice?"

"The nobility!" another peasant shouted.

"Ah, yes," Argan agreed, "the ones who call themselves noble. In truth, however, I see very little nobility in what they have done to us down the endless centuries. The fair land of Perquaine is fertile, and she brings forth food in abundance. But how much of that food is allotted to us?"

"None!" a slatternly woman with wild, matted hair shrieked.

"Well said, my sister," Argan agreed. "None is our allotment. None is our breakfast, and none is our supper. We gorge ourselves on none. We expend our lives in wresting food from the rich land of Perquaine, and whole bushels of none is our only reward. Those who call themselves noble have taken from us all that we have, and they still demand more. And when there is no more to surrender up to them, then are we beaten with whip and club—not to satisfy their greed, but rather to fulfill their lust for cruelty. And is *this* noble?"

"No!" a hundred voices burst forth.

"And should we respect these foul villains?"

"No!"

"We starve in the midst of plenty, my brothers and sisters, and they who call themselves noble oppress us beyond reason, for they believe it is their God-given right to do so. Better by far to be a horse or a dog than a commoner in Perquaine. But let us consider this but yet a bit further, my brothers and sisters. We have lived out our lives under the heels of our oppressors, and we know them well. Has anyone here ever seen a noble who could with any certainty tell his right hand from his left?"

The crowd roared with laughter.

"Or tie his own shoes?"

They laughed again.

"Or scratch his own backside when it itches?"

"He's pushing that a little," Emdahl growled.

"He's playing to his audience, your Eminence," Althalus explained. "Peasants tend to be a little earthy."

"Since our unspeakably noble nobility is too stupid to tell night from day," Argan continued, "it's fairly obvious that *someone* or something is leading them down the path of oppression and injustice. Who or what do you suppose that might be, brothers and sisters?"

"The Church!" a deep voice came from the center of the throng.

"That was smooth," Exarch Yeudon noted.

"Surely you don't agree with that apostate!" Aleikon said in a shocked voice.

"I was talking about his skill, not his message, Aleikon," Yeudon explained. "He's good. There's no question about that."

"Then cruelty and oppression are a part of the nature of the true God?" Argan asked the crowd.

"No!" a dozen voices responded.

"Then it would seem that the Church of Perquaine has strayed from the true course set forth by God himself. That's not particularly surprising, though. The Brown Robes are notorious for twisting the words and intent of God in their quest for wealth and power. They preach submission to us and oppression to the nobility. We are dressed in rags and live in crude hovels that cannot protect us from the weather, but the nobility wears velvet and rich furs, and their houses are palaces. And just who has told the pampered—and stupid—nobility that this is right and proper?"

"The Brown Robes!" a voice thundered from the midst of the crowd.

"Our womenfolk are forced to submit to highborn lechers, and who tells the aristocracy that the rape of peasants is no sin?"

"The Brown Robes!" the crowd shouted.

"And what must we do to follow the true teachings of the God of all mankind?"

"Kill!" a solitary voice barked.

"And who is it that we must kill?"

"The nobles!"

"And who shares the guilt of the nobles?"

"The Brown Robes!"

"Then must we also kill the Brown Robes?"

"Yes!"

"But man *must* have priests, lest he stray from the true path. Tell me, citizens of Perquaine, into the hands of which order would you place your souls?"

"The Red Robes!" Koman's well-placed underlings responded.

Then a stout fellow with a deep, thunderous voice stepped out of the crowd. "Lead us, Brother Argan!" he pleaded. "Tell us what we must do, lest we die in the clutches of our oppressors."

Argan's face took on an expression of exaggerated humility. "I am unworthy, my brother," he replied meekly.

"Not as unworthy as Exarch Aleikon, Brother Argan," the stout man disagreed. "Free us from our oppressors. Give us justice!"

"And is this the will of all here assembled?"

"Yes!" The great shout echoed across the frozen plain.

"Then follow me, my brothers and sisters, through the gates of Dail, and when Dail has been purified, whither shall we go?"

"Maghu!"

And the vast mob surged forward, and the gates of Dail could not withstand them.

"He twisted everything," Exarch Aleikon protested weakly. "Things aren't really all *that* bad in Perquaine."

"Oh, *really*?" Exarch Yeudon said with heavy sarcasm. "You Brown Robes are notorious for your greed. I hate to admit it, but that fellow in the red robe was telling the absolute truth, and if we were the least bit honest, we'd be forced to admit that this peasant rebellion's fully justified."

"Not here, Yeudon," Emdahl rasped. "I think it's time for the three of us to discuss this situation—extensively, and in private."

He looked at Althalus. "We need a room where we can talk, Althalus—quite some distance from here, I think."

"The tower at the far end of the west corridor, I think," Dweia suggested. "Why don't you show them the way, Eliar?"

Eliar nodded. "Come with me, gentlemen."

Emdahl looked intently at Leitha, and then he gave her a sly wink.

"What was that all about?" Bheid asked the pale girl after the churchmen had followed Eliar from the room.

"Your Exarch just invited me to sit in during their conference," Leitha replied. "He knew I was going to do it anyway, but he actually *wants* me to eavesdrop. He's planning what Althalus calls a 'flimflam,' and he wants us to go along with it."

"Could you be a little more specific, Leitha?" Andine asked her friend.

"Emdahl views this current unrest in Perquaine as a golden opportunity, dear," Leitha explained. "The Brown Robe order's totally corrupt, and Emdahl has a sort of grand plan to jerk the Brown Robe power base right out from under Aleikon. Without the support of the nobility of Perquaine, the Brown Robes are likely to be reduced to a mendicant order, begging at the roadside."

"What a splendid idea," Andine giggled. "How does Emdahl plan to pull that off?"

"He's still working on the details, but in a general sort of way he wants to use Argan's sermon to frighten Aleikon into pulling all his priests out of Perquaine. He'll throw the words 'temporary' and 'interim' around to keep Aleikon from realizing that he *won't* be coming back to Perquaine when this is all over."

"My Exarch's very shrewd," Bheid said proudly. "When things quiet down here in Perquaine, Aleikon's going to discover that the Black Robes have replaced him."

"Not exactly," Leitha said with a sly little smile. "Emdahl's still working on some details, but a direct, open confrontation between the Black Robes and the Brown Robes would probably start a war that'd make the peasant revolt look like a stroll in the park by comparison, wouldn't it?"

"You're hiding something from me, Leitha," Bheid accused.

"Would I do that?" she said with feigned, wide-eyed innocence. "Little old me?"

Bheid threw his hands in the air. "Women!" he said.

The conference in the tower at the end of the west corridor lasted for several days, and Eliar, who'd been carrying meals to the three ecclesiasts, reported that it was a fairly lively affair.

Then, about midafternoon on a snowy day, the churchmen returned to Dweia's tower. Exarch Aleikon looked a bit sullen, but Emdahl and Yeudon wore expressions of bleak satisfaction. "We are agreed," Emdahl announced. "The crisis in Perquaine is the direct result of our policies. Aleikon's *most* responsible, of course, but there's enough blame to go around. We've all concentrated our efforts on powerful men and neglected the commoners. We'd thought that men of power could *command* the commoners to accept our doctrines, but that, of course, was a mistake. Powerful men can command the *actions* of weaker men, but not their thoughts or beliefs. The Scarlet Robe Argan has saddled our blunder, and he'll ride it straight through the doors of the temple in Maghu unless we take certain steps immediately."

"Immediately might not be quite soon enough, Exalted One," Andine said rather pointedly. "The aristocracy of Perquaine's notorious for its treatment of the poor, and the Brown Robe order's been painted with the same brush. I may be just a silly girl, but even *I* know that the well-being of any society depends far more on the peasantry and the city laborers than it does on the nobility. The three orders have betrayed the commoners so often that they'll never trust you."

"My point exactly," Emdahl replied. Then he smirked at Yeudon and Aleikon. "Notice, dear friends, that even this tiny child has seen directly to the core of our blunder."

"All right, Emdahl," Aleikon said acidly, "you don't have to beat us over the head with it. Get to the point and let's get on with this."

"What a splendid idea, Aleikon," Emdahl agreed. "We need

someone to counter the exaggerations of this Argan, and no commoner in his right mind would ever believe anything that came from the mouth of any member of the established clergy."

"That pretty well sums it up, yes," Althalus agreed. "What are you gentlemen going to do about it?"

"We need a new voice, that's all," Emdahl said, shrugging, "a voice untainted by our past mistakes."

"What exactly *is* this surprise you have for us, Emdahl?" Dweia asked.

"We've founded a new order of clergy. The new order will wear different robes from ours, so they'll be uncontaminated by the things we've done in the past. They'll minister to the poor and the despised, they won't live in palaces, and they won't associate with the aristocracy."

"It's a start, perhaps," Bheid noted a bit dubiously, "but if you'll excuse me, my Exarch, will there be time enough for this new order to counter the preachings of Argan? He's already gathered a multitude of followers, and he'll be leading them toward Maghu before the week's out."

"I expect it'll take a certain amount of inspired preaching, Brother Bheid," Emdahl agreed, "but I'm positive that you're up to it."

Bheid's face went suddenly dead white. *"Me?"* he gasped.

"It was one of the few things we agreed upon, Exarch Bheid," Yeudon told him. "You're the only possible choice. Your order will wear robes of grey, and they'll take vows of poverty. The issue of chastity came up during our discussions, but we decided that we might offend Divine Dweia if we were to insist."

"Wise decision," Leitha observed.

"Absolutely out of the question," Bheid announced quite firmly. "I'm not even a priest anymore."

"The vow is permanent," Emdahl rasped. "You can't give it and then take it back."

"I murdered a man, my Exarch," Bheid said in a flat, emotionless voice.

"You did *what*?"

"I drove a sword through a man in Arya Andine's throne room. I am damned."

"Well, now," Aleikon said, his plump face suddenly creased with a broad smile. "That changes everything, doesn't it, Emdahl? I guess I won't be leaving Maghu after all."

"This *is* a problem, Emdahl," Yeudon said gravely. "A murder automatically disqualifies any priest."

"Be serious, Yeudon," Emdahl rasped. "We've all arranged occasional assassinations."

"But we don't personally do the killing. It's a technicality, probably, but it *is* one of the hard and fast rules. Until Brother Bheid's sin is expiated—some sort of penance, I'd imagine—he most certainly can't be elevated."

"Who was this fellow you killed, Bheid?" Emdahl demanded.

"His name was Yakhag, your Eminence," Andine stepped in, "and I think Brother Bheid was exaggerating. Yakhag was *not* a man in the usual sense of the word. He was more demon than man. Even Ghend was afraid of that one. Then, too, Yakhag had just butchered a young fellow Brother Bheid was grooming for the priesthood. Exarch Yeudon can tell you about the young man. He was a shepherd from Wekti named Salkan."

"Salkan is dead?" Yeudon exclaimed in a stricken voice.

"I'm afraid so, your Eminence," Andine replied. "Argan ordered Yakhag to kill Brother Bheid, but Salkan grabbed Eliar's sword and jumped in front of Bheid to protect him. Yakhag killed him, and then Bheid killed Yakhag. Since it happened in Treborea, *our* laws would take precedence, and in Treborean law, what happened was *not* murder. It was fully justified."

"Brother Bheid's subject to *Church* law," Aleikon said stubbornly. "Until he has served out his penance, he cannot hold any office in any order." He smirked at Emdahl. "Your clever scheme just flew out the window, didn't it?" he said smugly.

Emdahl scowled at him.

"Perhaps not," Yeudon said. "Define the word 'penance,' Aleikon."

"Prayer, fasting, isolation, hard labor—whatever punishment

his Exarch decides is appropriate. Stop trying to get around this, Yeudon."

"Let's take a look at 'hard labor,' shall we?" Yeudon said smoothly. "The present situation in Perquaine sort of suggests to me that the Exarch of the Grey Robes will have to work harder than just about any other man in the world. Brother Bheid can expiate his crime by taking on the most difficult job in the world."

"Expiation through service," Emdahl agreed. "Brilliant, Yeudon."

"That's pure sophistry!" Aleikon protested.

"Of course it is," Emdahl agreed, "but it's *good* sophistry. Brother Bheid is still technically a Black Robe, so that gives *me* final authority over him, doesn't it?"

"Well . . . technically, I suppose," Aleikon reluctantly agreed.

"Very well, then. Let's take care of certain formalities before we go any further. May I use your table, Divinity?" he asked Dweia.

"Of course, Exarch Emdahl," she replied.

The harsh-faced Emdahl seated himself at the marble table and pulled up his hood. "Would you be so good as to present the charges to the court, Yeudon?"

"That's not the way it's done," Aleikon protested.

"That depends entirely on who's running things, Aleikon," Emdahl said. "Brother Bheid's a Black Robe, and that puts him under *my* jurisdiction. The trial—and the final judgment—is in *my* hands. The court will hear the charges, Exarch Yeudon."

Yeudon rose to his feet, also pulling up his hood. "The prisoner is charged with murder, Holy Emdahl," he intoned, "and freely has he confessed to this crime."

"How says the prisoner?" Emdahl demanded sternly. "Quickly, quickly, Bheid. It's almost suppertime."

"I am guilty, my Exarch," Bheid answered in a broken voice, "for I deliberately killed the man called Yakhag."

"And will you submit to the judgment of this court?"

"In all things, my Exarch," Bheid agreed.

"The prisoner will kneel to hear the judgment of the court," Emdahl announced sternly.

Trembling, Bheid sank to his knees.

Emdahl absently placed his hand on the Book. "The prisoner stands convicted of the crime of murder," he announced in a formal tone. "Has the prisoner anything to say before the court passes judgment?"

"I . . ." Bheid faltered.

Emdahl cut him off. "I didn't think so. It is the judgment of this court that you shall serve out the remainder of your life at hard labor, and, moreover, the labor which you shall undertake shall be to serve as the Exarch of the Grey Robe order—and may the Gods have mercy on your miserable soul."

"But—"

"Shut up, Bheid," Emdahl snapped. "Now get on your feet and go to work."

"That was slick, Emdahl," Althalus complimented the Black Robe Exarch as they followed the others downstairs to supper.

"I'm glad you liked it." Emdahl smirked. "I can't take all the credit, though. Expiation through hard labor was Yeudon's idea in the first place. I'm surprised you didn't think of it yourself."

"I don't look at the world in quite the same way you priests do," Althalus replied. "I'm a professional criminal, so I don't get very worked up about my assorted sins. Yakhag needed killing, but I couldn't quite get that across to Bheid. I had a certain amount of success by slamming him against a wall, though."

"Interesting variation," Emdahl noted. "Bheid was suffering from his sense of guilt. We needed him in a certain position, so all I did was define that position as a punishment. He *wanted* to be punished, so now we're both getting exactly what we want."

"And I'm getting what *I* want as well."

"That went by a little fast."

"Bheid's sense of his guilt was separating him from Leitha, and that was starting to make her come unraveled."

"The witch? I didn't think *anything* could bother *that* one. She's made of steel, isn't she?"

"Not really, Emdahl. She's very fragile, and she needs love. She's chosen me to be her father. *Me,* of all people."

"She could do worse," Emdahl noted. "You've got more than your share of faults, Althalus, but you *do* love everybody in your little group of followers. With a little training, you'd make a good priest—of course that's what you really are, isn't it? You're the Exarch of the Church of Dweia, aren't you?"

"We aren't quite that formal, Emdahl. Emmy's a lot more relaxed than her brothers are. As long as we love her, she's perfectly happy. She even purrs."

"Purrs?"

"It'd take much too long to explain," Althalus told him.

"It's probably the best we can do on such short notice, Bheid," Emdahl said when they'd all returned to the temple at Maghu a few days later. "Aleikon wasn't very happy about it, but we all finally agreed that our orders were going to have to give the Grey Robes a free hand. Your order won't be very large. That vow of poverty makes most priests start to choke, so you won't have very many voluntary followers at first."

"There'll be some, though, who'll be involuntary," Yeudon added drily.

"No," Bheid declared adamantly. "You gentlemen *aren't* going to use the Grey Robes as a garbage heap for your undesirables."

"Now, wait a minute, Exarch Bheid," Aleikon said. "Your order's less than a week old. You're definitely subordinate to the three of us."

"Then we can just forget the whole idea," Bheid said, his face hardening. "If all you three are trying to do is throw a sop to the commoners to quiet the current unrest, I'll have no part in it. Something along those lines would just be a perpetuation of the blunder that opened the door to Argan in the first place. Can't you see that?"

"He's got a point there," Emdahl conceded grudgingly. Then he shook his head and made a wry face. "I think I may have let one of the good ones get away. If I'd been paying attention the way I'm supposed to, I could have groomed Brother Bheid to be my successor."

"Not if I'd seen him first, Emdahl," Yeudon disagreed.

"Emmy wants to talk with you, Althalus," Eliar said quietly as they were all leaving Exarch Aleikon's ornate office.

"Oh? Am I in trouble again?"

"She didn't say. I don't think so, though. Why don't we use the door to your room? I'll stand guard outside."

"All right."

They went along the corridor of the temple where the quarters Exarch Aleikon had provided them were located, and Eliar opened the door to the room assigned to Althalus. Just beyond that door were the familiar stairs.

Dweia was waiting in the tower room when Althalus came up the steps. She held her arms out to him, and they wordlessly embraced. "Is something amiss, Em?" he asked her.

"No, actually things are going rather well. Bheid's turning out even better than I'd expected. That's something I wanted to explain to you. I think it's important for you to know what's really happening."

"I thought it was fairly obvious, Em."

"Not entirely, pet. The words on the Knife are just a bit more complex than they appear on the surface. What did it tell *you* to do?"

"Seek. Didn't that mean that I was supposed to wander around and find the others?"

"It goes perhaps a bit further than that, love. You were *also* supposed to find me."

"I'd already done that, hadn't I?"

"Not really. You'd found Emmy the cat, but you hadn't found me yet when you first saw the Knife."

"I suppose I hadn't at that. Where are we going here?"

"We'll get to it, Althalus. When Eliar saw the word 'lead,' he thought it meant that he was supposed to command an army, but that's not what it meant at all. Andine read 'obey' and that's how she defeated Gelta."

"All right, I can follow you so far. Leitha's supposed to 'listen,' except that she doesn't do it with her ears. We've already used that particular capability of hers any number of times."

"It's going to be just a bit more complicated than that when she meets Koman."

"I sort of gathered that. She knows what she's going to have to do, and she doesn't like it one little bit. She cried all over the front of my tunic after she'd tacked that 'daddy' on to me. Just exactly what is it that she's supposed to do to Koman?"

"She'll listen, Althalus, and when *she* listens, *Koman* won't be able to hear anymore. It's a very subtle sort of procedure."

"But awful?"

"Very, very awful. That's why Leitha needs you so desperately. Don't scold her when she calls you 'daddy.' She's crying out for help. Comfort her as much as you can."

"In that dream you wished off on all of us, what the deuce was that shirt she was tearing apart?"

"That was Koman, love."

"She's going to rip him all to pieces? Isn't that just a little gruesome?"

"Quite a bit worse than gruesome, love," Dweia said sadly, "but it has to be done. Next we come to Bheid. 'Illuminate' might just be the most complicated word of the lot. Ultimately, Bheid's going to expose Argan and his Scarlet Robes for what they really are—the priesthood of Daeva."

"I didn't see anything like that in the dream vision."

"Then you weren't watching, Althalus. What was I doing?"

"You brushed all the dust off the altar into your hand. Then you tossed it up into the air, and a breeze from the window blew it away." He frowned. "But that window was Bheid in some peculiar way. That was the part that *really* confused me."

"Bheid's task is to 'illuminate,' Althalus, and that's what windows are for. They let in light—but they *also* let a breeze come in. The dream turned Argan into dust, I tossed him up into the air, and the breeze that came through the window we call Bheid blew the dust that was Argan away. Look upon the dream vision I gave you as a metaphor." She paused. "That is the most *useful* word. All *sorts* of things can be explained as metaphors."

"In a nonmetaphorical sense, what's *really* going to happen to Argan?"

"His body will lose its cohesion, and the tiny bits that were originally Argan will float in the air. Then the window we know as Bheid will let in a breeze. A good, stiff breeze clears the air and lets in the truth. That's another kind of 'illumination,' isn't it?"

"Will Argan ever come back together again?"

"I don't think so, no."

"So Bheid kills again, right? He was just practicing when he killed Yakhag. His *real* task is to kill Argan. Why all this beating around the bush, Em? Why didn't you just come right out and tell me that you want Bheid to murder Argan?"

Her green eyes narrowed, and she hissed at him.

He laughed delightedly. "Oh, I *do* love you, Em!" he declared, taking her in his arms and affectionately nuzzling at the side of her neck.

She suddenly giggled almost girlishly and tried to pull away and to hunch up her shoulder to cover her neck. "Please don't do that, Althalus," she said.

"Why not?" he asked with wide-eyed innocence.

"Because it tickles, that's why."

"Are you ticklish, Em?"

"We'll discuss that some other time."

He grinned at her slyly. "I can hardly wait," he said, laughing.

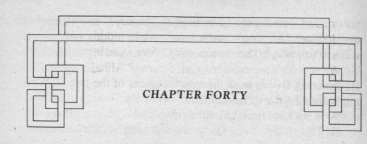

CHAPTER FORTY

Brother Bheid looked distinctly uncomfortable in the ornate chair in Exarch Aleikon's former office. "Do I really have to use this room, Althalus?" he asked a bit plaintively after they'd been in Maghu for about a week.

Althalus shrugged. "Not if it bothers you, Bheid. What's wrong with it?"

"It's too luxurious. I'm trying to recruit priests for an order that's supposed to take a vow of poverty. This isn't really the place for that."

"Select another room, then. How's the recruiting coming along?"

"Not too well, really," Bheid admitted. "Most of the applicants still believe that joining the clergy is an easy road to wealth and power. As soon as I tell them what's going to be expected of them, they lose interest. The ones who keep smiling and nodding are usually Brown Robes in disguise. Aleikon's doing his best to infiltrate my order, but Leitha's been weeding his people out for me. When we get to the bottom of it, though, it's a good day when I manage to get three acceptable candidates."

"I think you might have to start raiding seminaries, Bheid," Althalus suggested. "Catch them when they're still young and idealistic."

The door opened, and Leitha stood a bit hesitantly in the doorway. "Are you busy?" she asked.

"Not noticeably," Bheid said. "The word seems to be getting around that when I say 'poverty,' I mean just that. Come in."

Leitha entered and crossed the large room. "Is there some way for you to block out the eavesdroppers, Daddy?" she whispered to Althalus. "Aleikon's got several people hidden behind the walls of this place. They're reporting every word back to him."

"We should have expected that, I guess," Althalus observed. He frowned, roving back through the pages of the Book. "This might turn the trick," he muttered.

"Why not ask Dweia?" Leitha suggested.

"I'd like to see if I can find one on my own," Althalus replied. Then he said, "*Kadh-leu*," waving one hand in the air.

"*Kadh-leu*"? Dweia's voice echoed incredulously in his mind.

I have trouble with negatives, Em, he admitted. *I can usually come up with the right word when I want to tell somebody to do something. Telling him* not *to do it gets a little confusing. Did it work?*

Well, in a way. Aleikon's spies will still hear you, but they won't pay any attention to what you're saying—or to what anybody else says, for that matter. They're going to be a little strange from now on.

All priests are strange. No offense intended, Bheid.

"There's something else," Leitha told him. "Aleikon isn't too happy about what Emdahl and Yeudon rammed down his throat back in the House, so he's hiding many of his Brown Robes among the general population of Maghu—in disguise, of course. He hasn't advised Prince Marwain that Brother Bheid's taking over in Perquaine yet. I don't think it's very far off, though. Marwain's not the brightest fellow in the world, I guess, and Aleikon's made a career out of manipulating him. He seems to be fairly sure he can persuade Marwain to *pretend* to accept the Grey Robes, but as soon as Bheid's eliminated Argan and put down the peasant revolt, Aleikon plans to have Marwain march back into Maghu, resume his former position, stamp out the Grey Robe order—vigorously—and hand Perquaine back to the Brown Robes."

"They want me to pull their irons out of the fire, and then they come back and get rid of me, I suppose?" Bheid asked bleakly.

"Why don't we get rid of *them* first?" Althalus suggested.

"I'm not too interested in general murder, Althalus."

"That isn't what I had in mind, Brother Bheid," Althalus said with a wicked grin. "Maybe it's time for Exarch Aleikon and Prince Marwain to take a little trip."

"Oh?" Bheid said. "Where do you plan to send them?"

"Somewhere a lot farther away than just across the border into western Treborea. I think we might prefer it for them to be far enough away that they'll be very old before they reach Maghu again. Let's gather up the rest of the children and go home. Emmy can use the windows to help us find a new residence for Aleikon and Marwain—the far side of the moon, maybe."

"Why not just kill them?" Gher asked when they reached the House. "That's the easiest way to get bad people out from under-foot, isn't it?"

"Have you been talking with this boy again, Althalus?" Dweia asked accusingly.

"Not recently, Em," Althalus replied. "Gher can come up with ideas without too much help from me. All *I* really want to do is put those two so far away that they won't come back for fifty or sixty years."

"I think Dhweria might be the place you're looking for, pet."

"Where's Dhweria?"

"It's on beyond the east coast of Plakand."

"Plakand has a coast?" Eliar asked. "I thought it was just grassland that just went on forever."

"Nothing goes on forever, Eliar," Dweia told him. "The world's a globe—a round ball. Anyway, the east coast of Plakand is about a thousand miles from Kherdon. Dhweria's a very large island a couple thousand miles from that coast."

"What's it like?" Bheid asked.

"Very much like Hule—primeval forest with enormous trees and lots of wild animals."

"No people?" Gher asked.

"Oh, there are people there," she replied, "but Aleikon and Marwain won't be able to talk with them, since the people there wouldn't understand what they're saying."

"Are they stupid or something?" Gher asked.

"No. They speak a different language, that's all."

"People talk is people talk, Emmy," the boy objected. "Dogs talk with bow-wows; birds talk with tweet-tweets; and people talk with words. Everybody knows that."

"No, Gher," she said gently. "Actually, there are dozens of different human languages. Maybe hundreds."

"That's silly!"

" 'Silly' is part of the definition of humans, Gher. Anyway, the island's a bit larger than Treborea, and it's all one vast forest. The people there are very primitive—stone tools, animal-skin clothes, and very little in the way of farming."

"No boats?" Althalus asked.

"Rafts are about all."

"It might be quite difficult for two men to row a raft across two thousand miles of open water," Andine suggested.

"Almost impossible, dear," Dweia agreed. "That's the main reason I suggested Dhweria. Aleikon's a churchman, and Marwain's a noble. Neither of them know anything about tools, so they'd never be able to build a real boat. If we put them there, that's where they'll stay—permanently."

"We'll miss them something awful, though, won't we?" Gher smirked.

"We'll just have to be brave about it, I suppose." Leitha sighed in false resignation.

"I'm pretty brave, Leitha," Gher told her. "If I grit my teeth real hard, I can probably stand it."

"I love this boy," Leitha said fondly.

"What are you talking about, Bheid?" Aleikon demanded when the Exarchs responded to Bheid's summons the next morning.

"I'm trying to save your lives, Aleikon," Bheid explained. "You heard Argan's sermon at Dail. The peasants are butchering every priest they find. I *must* get you gentlemen to safety."

Aleikon scoffed. "There are safe places where we can hide."

"Oh, really?" Althalus asked. "The peasants and city laborers are everywhere, Exarch Aleikon, and all it'd take to expose you and your Brown Robes would be one set of curious eyes. Bheid's right. If you want to live, leave—and take Prince Marwain with you."

"I think you'd better listen to him, Aleikon," Exarch Emdahl rasped. "And maybe you and I'd better listen, too, Yeudon. We selected Bheid to deal with the situation here in Perquaine, so why don't we just pack up and leave so that he can do his job?"

"It might be best," Yeudon agreed.

A weary-looking priest entered the office and spoke with Aleikon. "Prince Marwain is here, my Exarch," he announced. "He demands an immediate audience."

"We aren't quite through here yet, Brother," Bheid told the priest. "Tell Marwain that he'll have to wait."

Aleikon's pudgy face went pale, and his eyes bulged. "You can't *do* that!" he gasped. "Marwain's the ruler of Maghu. *Nobody* keeps him waiting!"

"Nothing ever stays the same, Aleikon," Althalus said philosophically. "It'll be good for Marwain to discover that."

"Nobody's going to take Bheid's Grey Robes seriously with the rest of us lurking around every corner," Emdahl rasped. "We hired him to do a job, so now let's get out of his way and let him do it."

"But—" Aleikon started to protest.

"Your house is on fire, Aleikon," Yeudon pointed out. "You'd better leave while you still can—and take all your Brown Robes with you. We aren't dealing with ordinary people here. I had to come to grips with that during the Ansu invasion of Wekti. What's happening here in Perquaine's a continuation of that war, and our enemies aren't all human. The gates of Nahgharash have been opened, Aleikon, and you know what that means."

Aleikon's face blanched at Yeudon's mention of Nahgharash. Evidently his nightmares still haunted him.

"One other thing, Exarch Aleikon," Leitha said pleasantly. "You might as well call in the Brown Robes you've been trying to conceal in the general population. They can't really hide, you know. Koman can sniff them out, and Argan will use them for firewood. Brother Bheid's the only one who can deal with Argan, so you and your Brown Robes had better run while you can."

"I think we've just about exhausted the possibilities of this particular conversation," Emdahl observed. "We should call in Marwain before he boils over. Let's give him his marching orders and get him out from underfoot, shall we?"

Prince Marwain appeared to be on the verge of apoplexy as he stormed into the office. "How *dare* you?" he almost screamed. "Don't you know who I am? I've never been so insulted in my entire life."

Aleikon tried to smooth things over. "We had a problem to deal with, your Highness. We do have a crisis of sorts on our hands."

"This peasant uprising?" Marwain sneered. "You frighten too easily, Aleikon. I'll crush their rebellion the moment they approach Maghu. One word from me, and they all die."

"Not too likely, Prince Marwain," Emdahl said bluntly. "The peasants outnumber your forces by about a thousand to one."

"Who is this man, Aleikon?" Marwain demanded.

"This is Exarch Emdahl of the Black Robes, your Highness," Aleikon replied.

"Let's clear the air here right now," Emdahl rasped. "We've just concluded a meeting of the high council of the Church, and the Church isn't answerable to secular authorities in purely religious matters. The Church is being realigned in response to the current crisis. The Brown Robe order will depart, and the Grey Robes will replace them."

"Why wasn't I consulted?" Marwain exclaimed. "You can't *do* this without my permission."

"We just did."

"I forbid it!"

Yeudon stepped in. "Forbid all you want, Prince Marwain. The Brown Robes no longer have any authority in Perquaine. If you have any religious questions, you'll have to take them up with Exarch Bheid of the Grey Robe order."

"I'll call out the guard!" Marwain blustered. "I'll have you all clapped into my dungeon! Nobody makes decisions like this without my permission!"

"Well, Bheid," Emdahl said slyly, "how do you plan to deal with this little problem?"

"Firmly," Bheid answered in a voice quite nearly as harsh as Emdahl's. His face turned bleak as he looked at the spluttering nobleman. "The high council of the Church has made its decision, Prince Marwain, and that decision is final. The other orders are leaving Perquaine even now, and the Grey Robes are replacing them. *We* are the Church now, and I'm the voice of the Church, so you'd better shut your mouth and listen to me."

Exarch Aleikon winced.

"I don't have the time to be diplomatic, Prince Marwain," Bheid continued, "so I'm going to put this to you rather bluntly. You and the rest of the aristocracy—with the connivance of the Brown Robe order—have been running roughshod over the commoners for a long time, and now it's coming home to roost. Your arrogance and outright brutality have opened the door for certain people you *really* don't want to meet. Those people have stirred up the commoners of Perquaine to the point that nothing's going to satisfy them but blood, and it's *your* blood they want."

Prince Marwain's face turned pale.

"You seem to have grasped my point," Bheid said. "That isn't an army that's marching on Maghu, Prince Marwain. It's an undisciplined sea of people, and they'll walk right over any force you could possibly raise. They'll swarm into Maghu like a horde of ants, killing anybody who gets in their way. I wouldn't be at all surprised if their first order of business is going to be putting your head on a pole over the city gate, and then they'll probably loot Maghu right down to the cobblestones. After that, they'll most likely burn the city to the ground."

"God wouldn't permit that!" Marwain asserted.

"I wouldn't make any large wagers on that, your Highness," Bheid told him. "I'm fairly well acquainted with God, and he doesn't usually involve himself in the affairs of people."

"This is starting to get tiresome," Althalus muttered. "Have you got the location of the door to the island Em told us about locked in your mind, Eliar?"

"Pretty much, yes," the kilted young Arum replied. "We aren't going to use it *now*, though, are we?"

"I can't see any reason why not. I'll blow some smoke in Marwain's ear about a secret tunnel down in the cellar. Then we'll take him and Aleikon downstairs. Pick any door down there that suits you and lead us on through into the House. Then you can lead them to their new home. Pay fairly close attention to what I tell Marwain and make things sort of match up. All right?"

"Anything you say, Althalus," Eliar agreed.

Then Althalus rose and crossed the room to the richly dressed Prince Marwain. "Excuse me, your Highness," he said politely. "My name's Althalus, and I'm sometimes known as the Duke of Kenthaigne."

"I've heard of you, your Grace," Marwain said with a slight bow.

"Your Highness." Althalus also bowed. "I had to set aside my personal business to assist Exarch Bheid with certain courtesies and practicalities. Churches sometimes seem to have trouble with those—or had you noticed?"

Marwain laughed. "Many, many times, your Grace," he replied.

"I thought you might have." Althalus threw a quick glance at Exarch Aleikon. The high churchman's wooden expression strongly suggested that Dweia had already closed down his mind. Althalus spoke again to Marwain. "Anyway, when I heard the news about this human sea marching on Maghu, I started looking for an escape route. Exarch Bheid might believe that he can pray his way out of this mess, but I think I'd prefer to look after myself. I snooped around here in the temple, and I found an ideal way to leave Maghu, completely unnoticed. Since we're both noblemen, courtesy obliges me to share that information with you." He sighed theatrically. "Sometimes I'm so courteous that I can barely stand myself."

Marwain grinned broadly. "You and I are going to get along just fine, Duke Althalus," he said.

"I'm sure of it. There's no real hurry at the moment, since the rebels haven't found their way here yet, but when things start getting noisy here in Maghu, we might get separated, so maybe I'd better show you—and Exarch Aleikon—this quick way out of town right now, so that you'll be able to find it yourselves in the event of an emergency."

"Excellent idea, Duke Althalus. Where's your escape route located?"

"In the cellar, of course. Underground passages almost always start in a cellar. This one hasn't been used for centuries, if the cobwebs I had to wade through are any indication. It goes under the streets of Maghu and comes out in some woods out beyond the city walls. Nobody'll see us leave, and nobody'll see us when we come out of the tunnel."

"We may never need it," Marwain said, "but it might not be a bad idea to have a look at it, eh, Aleikon?"

"As your Highness commands," Aleikon said in a numb voice.

"Lead the way then, Eliar," Althalus said.

"Right," Eliar replied, starting toward the door.

What are they seeing? Althalus sent his quick thought to Eliar.

Cobwebs, torchlight, a few mice, the young man replied. *If you've seen one tunnel, you've pretty much seen them all.*

You're probably right. How much farther?

Just a little way. The door opens into a small clearing in the woods. When we get to it, give me a moment to adjust the door frame. It's morning in Maghu, but it's already nighttime in Dhweria. I'll have to arrange for us to come out at pretty much the same time of day so Marwain doesn't get suspicious.

Good idea, Althalus agreed.

Eliar moved quickly on ahead, paused for a few moments, and then looked back. "Here it is," he called back.

"Well, *finally*," Marwain said. "I was starting to think your tunnel went on forever, Duke Althalus."

"Maghu *is* a fairly big city, your Highness," Althalus reminded him. "Now, as soon as we come out in the woods, we'd better take a quick look around to make certain that nobody's watching us. Why don't you and the Exarch push on through to the far edge of the grove of trees while Eliar and I go back to the side facing the city walls? We don't want some peasant with a big mouth telling everybody in town that he just saw us, do we?"

"Not even the least little bit," Marwain agreed. "A thorough search is definitely in order. After we've taken a look around, we'll meet back at the mouth of the tunnel, right?"

"Exactly," Althalus agreed. "When you get to the edge of the trees, you might want to see if there's a ravine or a brushy lane leading off to the east. If we need to be sneaky when we leave town, we should plan ahead."

"You're very good at this, Duke Althalus."

"I had a fairly exciting boyhood, your Highness. The Duchy of Kenthaigne was a lively place to grow up. We'll see you in a half hour or so."

"Right," Marwain agreed. "Come along, Aleikon." Then the two of them crossed the clearing and entered the woods.

Em, Althalus called silently.

Her voice came back immediately. *Yes, love?*

You might want to keep Aleikon's head turned off for a little while. Let those two wander around in the woods for a bit before Marwain finds out the bad news.

Whatever makes you happy, dear.

Althalus reached out and thoughtfully patted the open door. "Keep the location of this one in mind, Eliar," he suggested. "It might be very useful on down the line. Emmy's tail fluffs out when I kill people, and this gives me an alternative. Let's go back to Maghu and pick up the others. I think we'll need to have a little private conference."

"Right," Eliar agreed. Then he led Althalus back into the east corridor of the House and quietly closed the door behind them.

Sergeant Khalor had been at the window in Dweia's tower all day, and his face was bleak when Althalus and the others came up the stairs. "My best guess is two weeks," he reported. "They're consolidating their positions as they move north, and that's not really an army down there. It's an undisciplined mob, and most of them are much more interested in looting than they are in religion or social change."

"Revolutions tend to turn out that way," Dweia said rather sadly. "The theorists make high-minded speeches. Their followers cheer and applaud—briefly—and then they get back to the business of appropriating everything of value."

"You're in a cynical humor this evening, Em," Althalus noted.

"I've seen this all before, Althalus," she replied wearily, "many, many times. An idea that's born in glory starts to tarnish almost immediately." She sighed and then seemed to shake off her gloom. "There are a few things you'll all need to know. The dream I gave you established what and where."

"I know that you and Leitha were in the temple in Maghu," Andine said, "but exactly what were you doing?"

"Cleaning house," Dweia replied simply. "Leitha disposed of Koman, Bheid and I dealt with Argan."

"That's the where and the what, Emmy," Gher said, "but what about the when? Ghend always seems to play around with the when part when he comes up with one of those dream things. Did your dream thing happen now? Or is it maybe in some other when?"

"It wasn't in the world of now, Gher. In order for a dream vision to really work, it has to be either in the past or in the future. Their purpose is to change things. It's remotely possible to make changes by altering now, but it's easier if you go back—or forward."

"That seems to have gone right past me," Andine admitted.

"That's probably because Emmy hasn't really made up her mind yet," Gher said. "I'd guess that a few more things are going to have to happen before she can be sure about the when part. She knows about what and where, but she can't exactly nail down the when part until the bad people get to the town with the funny name."

"Maghu," Leitha supplied.

"I guess so," Gher said. "Anyway, I think Emmy's waiting until Argan and the other one walk into the church before she picks out the when. I kind of think it was like that time in Wekti when we all dreamed about somewhen when the bad lady's ax was made out of a sharp rock."

"I *love* this boy," Leitha said fondly. "I could ponder the meaning of 'somewhen' for weeks on end. You should learn how to write, Gher. You have the soul of a poet."

Gher flushed. "Not really," he admitted. "It's just that I don't know the right words for what I'm thinking, so I have to make words up. Anyway, Argan and his friend—except that they aren't really friends—are going to dash into the church, but when they go through the door, it won't be now inside. The ordinary people who are coming along behind them are going to get a real big surprise, I think, because it'll look like their leaders just got themselves turned into nothing. That'll scare the teeth out of that crowd, I'll bet, and they'll probably decide that this revolution stuff isn't very much fun anymore. Then they'll all pack up and go back home, and we won't have to kill hardly any of them at all. That's really just about the best way there is to fight a war, don't you think?"

"You should stop and take a breath once in a while, Gher," Andine said fondly. "You get so enthusiastic sometimes."

"Have you chosen which time you're going to use, Emmy?" Eliar asked.

"A time when the temple is mine," she replied.

"Back in the past?"

"Perhaps," she said with a mysterious little smile, "or it might be in the future instead."

"Are you planning to return to your temple, Dweia?" Bheid asked, sounding a bit worried.

"I never left, Bheid. The temple's still mine, and it always will be. I'm just letting you use it for the time being." She gave him a sly look. "Maybe someday when you're not too busy we should take up the matter of the back rent your Church owes me for the use of my building. It's been mounting up for quite some time, you know."

"How did they change their faces, Emmy?" Gher asked curiously as they watched from the window while several scarlet-robed priests moved through the vast mob of peasants and day laborers camped outside the gates of Maghu about sixteen days later. "They had those steel things hanging off their helmets over in Equero, but their faces are right out in the open over here in Perquaine."

"It's just an illusion, Gher. Daeva's very good at illusions, and he's taught his priests how to do it."

"How are we going to make them look the way they really are when the time comes?"

"*We* won't have to," she replied. "Eliar's Knife will strip away the illusions when he shows it to them."

"I sure wish *I* had a knife like that."

"You don't really need one, Gher. You can see and understand reality better than anyone else in the world."

"Well, maybe not yet, but I'm working on it."

"Have you managed to empty out the city yet, Brother Bheid?" Sergeant Khalor asked.

"More or less, Sergeant. There are quite a few hiding in cellars and attics in the shabbier parts of town." Bheid smiled faintly. "Those are the ones who'll join Argan's people as soon as they come through the city gates. They're just getting an early start on the looting, I guess."

"Why must they always set fires?" Bheid asked Althalus as the two of them stood on the portico of the temple waiting and watching the columns of smoke rising from various quarters of the city.

"I'm not really sure, Bheid," Althalus confessed. "It might just be accidental. Looters are usually fairly excited, and sometimes they get careless. My best guess, though, is that the fires are being set deliberately to punish the noblemen for their bad habits."

"That's pure stupidity, Althalus," Bheid objected.

"Of course it is. It's the nature of mobs to be stupid. A mob's only as clever as its stupidest member."

Bheid reached out tentatively as if to touch something directly in front of him.

"Quit worrying about it, Bheid," Althalus told him. "The

hield's still in place, and nothing can penetrate it—except for
our voice, of course."

"You're sure?"

"Trust me, Bheid. Nobody's going to shoot you full of arrows
or split your skull with a pickax. Leitha'd set my brain on fire if I
et anything happen to you. Are your people in place?"

Bheid nodded. "They'll filter into that crowd along with the
ocal rebels." He sighed regretfully. "I wish we didn't have to do
t this way, Althalus. It seems so dishonest."

"So? Isn't it better to control a crowd my way rather than
Prince Marwain's?"

"I can't argue with that," Bheid admitted.

"They're coming," Althalus warned, pointing toward the other
side of the square, where several men armed with farm tools had
ust appeared. "I'd better get out of sight now. I'll be at the
window. It's right behind you and about four feet above your
head. If something starts to go wrong, I'll pull you out. Let's go
over this one more time: it's an elaborate little dance, so let's be
sure we've got the steps right."

"We've been through it a dozen times already, Althalus,"
Bheid said.

"Humor me, Brother Bheid. You start out on the portico to
greet Argan and Koman when they reach the steps. Eliar's going
to be at the temple door. Argan and Koman will come across the
square, and they'll bluster at you."

"And Koman will be listening to my every thought," Bheid
added.

"No, actually he won't. Leitha's going to blot him out. She'll
fill his other set of ears with noise. Now, here's where it starts to
get tricky. Argan demands to be admitted to the temple, and you
invite him to go inside. That's when you move back to your right,
clearing the way for them."

"Yes, I know, and that's when Eliar opens the temple door and
goes over to the left side of the portico."

"You actually remembered," Althalus said drily. "Amazing.
The whole point of our little dance is to put Eliar between Argan
and Koman and that mob that's following them. When he raises

the Knife, Argan and Koman are going to run one way, and th
mob's going to run the other. Emmy doesn't want a crowd in th
temple while she's working. Then you get to preach your littl
sermon to the crowd, say 'Amen,' and join the ladies in th
temple. Don't dawdle, Bheid. Emmy can't start evaporatin
Argan until you're in place. Have you got it all straight?"

"As many times as we've been through it, I could probably d
it in my sleep."

"I'd really rather you didn't, Brother Bheid. Keep your eye
and ears open. If something unexpected crops up, we might hav
to modify things a bit, and if I tell you to jump, just jump. I'm no
inviting you to an extended debate."

Aren't you being just a bit obvious, love? Dweia's voic
murmured.

Sometimes it's necessary to keep Bheid on a tight leash, Em
he replied. *Every so often he breaks out in a rash of creativity
How's Leitha holding out?*

*She knows that what she has to do is absolutely necessary
Help her as much as you possibly can, Althalus.*

He nodded and took his place at the window.

Argan's red-clad henchmen were in the forefront of the ad
vancing crowd as the square before the steps of the temple fille
with eager commoners. Then Argan and Koman pushed thei
way forward. "On to the temple!" Argan shouted.

"Hold steady, Bheid," Althalus told his friend. "They can't ge
to you, no matter what they do."

"Right," Bheid answered.

Then Althalus turned slightly. "You'd better go on down now,'
he told Eliar. "Try to be sort of inconspicuous."

"I know what to do, Althalus," Eliar replied, drawing up th
cowl of the priestly grey robe he wore. Then he opened the doo
beside the window and stepped through to a position in th
entryway of the temple.

Argan and Koman reached the foot of the temple steps. "Stan
aside if you value your life!" Argan shouted to Bheid.

"What is it that you want?" Bheid asked in an oddly formal ton

"That should be obvious by now, old boy," Argan replied sar

lonically. "We're taking the temple. Now move aside while you still can. The Red Robes are now the Church of Perquaine!"

The belligerent crowd roared and began to surge forward.

"Are you certain that's what you want, Argan?" Bheid asked.

"It's what I will *have*! Maghu is mine now, and I will rule Perquaine from the temple."

Bheid bowed slightly. "I am here but to serve," he said. "The temple awaits you." He stepped off to his right to leave the path to the temple door open for them.

Argan and Koman started up the steps with the commoners and the Red Robes close behind them.

Bheid turned slightly and nodded to Eliar.

The young Arum put his hands to the massive temple doors and opened them wide. Then he stepped to the left, his head bowed in apparent subservience.

Argan and Koman flinched back. Beyond the open door there was fire, and hollow, despairing screams came echoing out into the square before the temple. The commoners recoiled, their faces filled with horror.

"And will you enter now?" Bheid asked the now-terrified crowd.

"It's a deception!" Argan declared, his voice shrill. "That's nothing but an illusion!"

"You've been in Nahgharash before, Brother Argan," Bheid said. "You know that what you're seeing is reality, not an illusion."

Eliar was moving unobtrusively among the columns on the left side of the portico. When he reached the spot Althalus had marked with paint on the marble surface, he glanced toward the window and nodded.

"Preach, Bheid," Althalus commanded.

Bheid nodded and stepped back to his former position, placing himself between the crowd and Ghend's two henchmen. He raised his voice to speak to the terrified crowd in the square. "Pay heed to this revelation, my children!" he warned. "Hell itself awaits you, and the demons are already among you!" He motioned to Eliar, and the young man joined him at the front of the portico. "Look around you, my children," Bheid intoned, "and behold the *real* faces of the Red Robes."

Eliar took out his Knife and held it out before him, turning slowly so that all in the square could see it.

Argan and Koman shrieked, covering their eyes with shaking hands.

There were other shrieks in the crowd as well, and Argan's scarlet-robed underlings recoiled in agony, their commonplace features dissolving like melting wax.

Althalus winced. *Is that what they* really *look like?* he demanded of Dweia.

They're worse actually, love, she replied calmly. *That's only the surface of what they really are.*

The creatures in scarlet robes were hideous. Their skin was scaly and covered with slime, and dripping fangs protruded from their mouths as their bodies swelled and expanded into enormity.

"Behold the promise of Argan, my children!" Bheid thundered. "Follow him if you will, or come to the Grey Robes. *We* will guide and protect you from the demons of Nahgharash and from the injustice of those who call themselves your masters. Choose, my children! Choose!"

"It's Exarch Bheid!" a disguised Grey Robe priest declared. "He's the holiest man alive."

"Listen to him!" another cried. "The Grey Robes are the only friends we have!"

The word spread quickly through the terrified crowd even as, one by one, the demons began to vanish.

Eliar turned, still holding the Knife before him, and advanced on the shrinking pair in front of the temple door.

With a despairing wail, Koman turned, and with his eyes still covered, he ran directly into the temple, with Argan close behind him.

But as they ran through the temple doorway, they vanished.

And the Knife sang in joyous fulfillment as it returned once again unto its home, and behold, the temple of Dweia was once more sanctified by the song of the Knife. And flowers bedecked the walls of the Temple, and offerings of bread and fruits and golden wheat did rest upon the altar before the titanic marble statue of the Goddess of fruit and grain and of rebirth also.

Althalus, still at the window in the House at the End of the World, tried to push away the lyricism of his perceptions of the temple. *It's just a building,* he muttered. *It's made of stone, not poetry.*

Will you stop *that, Althalus!* Dweia's voice in his mind sounded peevish, and, oddly, it seemed to be coming from the marble statue behind the altar.

One of us has to keep a grip on reality, Em, he replied.

This is *reality, love. Stop trying to contaminate it.*

And pale Leitha, her gentle eyes brimming with tears, did cast a beseeching look to the window. "Help me, Father!" she cried out unto the watching Althalus. "Help me, or I shall surely die!"

"Not while I have breath, my daughter," he assured her. "Open thy mind unto me that I may join thee in the performance of this stern task."

Much better, Dweia murmured with the voice of a soft spring breeze.

You're going to insist, I take it? Althalus forced the words out in a flat tone.

Be guided by me in this, beloved. Better by far to be gently guided than forcibly driven.

Methinks I did note a faintly threatening odor in thy voice, Emerald, spake Althalus. If Dweia wanted to play, it wouldn't really cost him anything to go along with her.

We will speak of this anon, Althalus. Now lend thy thought and all thy care unto our pale daughter. Her need for thee is great in her dreadful task.

And so it was that the mind of Althalus was softly joined with the mind of his gentle and reluctant daughter, and their thoughts became as one.

And the song of the Knife soared joyfully.

And with the joining of their thought did Althalus share his daughter's pain, and harkened his thought back some brief span

of time when pale Leitha had first encountered that emptiness
which doth surround all others, but which she had not known
before.

And then at last understanding came to him, and he perceived
the true horror of his daughter's dreadful task. "Come to me, my
beloved child," he spake unto her, "and I will care for thee."

And her thought that flooded over him was filled with gratitude, and with love.

Then bent they their intertwined thought upon the hapless
Koman. And the mind of Koman was awash with sound that
was not sound, for behold, the mind of Koman had never known
silence.

Murmuring, murmuring, the thoughts of they who were beyond the temple did wash over Koman even as the thoughts of
others had sung in the vaults of his mind since first he drew
breath.

And then pale Leitha did approach the servant of Ghend, and
warily did he bend his thought upon her, forsaking the random
thought from beyond the temple walls.

And, sorrowing, Leitha did gently close that door behind wary
Koman.

And startled Koman did reach forth, seeking with his mind
the sound that had been with him always.

But behold, it was no longer within his grasp, and the mind of
Koman shrank back from the horror of silence. Then clung he
with his thought to the mind of Argan, even though he held the
defrocked priest in great despite.

But pale Leitha, with tears coursing down her cheeks, did put
forth her gentle thought, and behold, the open door between
Koman's thought and Argan's did also softly close.

And Koman screamed as even greater emptiness did settle
around him.

And he fell to the floor of the holy temple of the Goddess
Dweia, and clung he in terror-stricken desperation to the thought
of she who even now closed each door that had always stood
open for him.

And the soul of Althalus was wrenched with pity.

I beseech thee, my beloved father, pale Leitha's thought cried out in anguish, *bend not thy despite upon me for this cruelty. The cruelty is not mine, but is that of necessity.*

And Althalus hardened his heart toward hapless Koman and stood sternly by as pale Leitha did perform the final act compelled of her by stern necessity.

"Fare thee well, my unfortunate brother." Leitha wept as, with gentle finality, she withdrew her thought from the servant of Ghend.

And behold, endless emptiness and eternal silence did descend upon the mind of hapless Koman as he lay upon the polished temple floor. And his shriek was a shriek of absolute despair, for he was alone and had never been so before. Then curled he his limbs and body tightly, even as though he were yet unborn, and his voice fell silent, and his mind also.

And Leitha cried out, wailing in horror, and Althalus, unthinking, did enfold her in his comforting thought to hold her back from the awful finality of what she had done.

Now flaxen-haired Argan's incomprehension was writ large upon his face even as the mind of his companion departed forever.

But from the altar came the voice of the Goddess Dweia. Sternly spake she, saying, "Thy very presence doth defile mine holy temple, Argan, servant of Ghend."

And behold, that which had been cold marble was now warm flesh, and gigantic did Dweia descend upon him who was no longer a priest.

And verily was Argan confounded and unable to move so much as one finger.

Then spake the Goddess further, saying, "Thou wert cast out from the priesthood, Argan, and all temples have been forbidden unto thee, because thou art unclean. Now must I cleanse this holy and sanctified house of worship of thy corruption."

Then considered Divine Dweia the wretch who stood trembling before her. "Methinks this will be no great task," mused she, pursing her lips. "Thou art only as dust, apostate priest, and dust is easily removed." Then stretched she forth her rounded arm and raised her hand as if she lifted that which was of no moment.

And behold, flaxen-haired, apostate Argan was borne aloft to stand on air alone before the Goddess who had judged him and found him wanting. And the servant of Ghend grew as insubstantial as glittering motes of dust that still clung to the form of that which had once been the reality called Argan.

"Come to the window, Bheid," Althalus suggested. "It's all yours—or maybe the window *is* you. Emmy's dream was just a little complicated."

Bheid, pale and trembling, joined Althalus at the window. "What am I supposed to do, Divinity?" he asked humbly.

"Just open the window, Bheid," she instructed. "The temple needs to be aired out."

Bheid obediently opened the window, and then from directly behind him a great wind sprang up and howled about his shoulders to pass through the window into the temple of Dweia.

And the glittering motes of that which had been Argan were swept away in that great wind, leaving behind only the faint echoes of his despairing scream to mingle with the song of the Knife.

And the face of Divine Dweia was filled with satisfaction, and spake she. "And now is my temple once more immaculate."

And the song of the Knife soared in indescribable beauty as it sang its blessing upon the holy place.

Part Seven

GHER

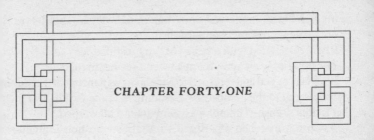

CHAPTER FORTY-ONE

Althalus sat alone in Dweia's tower watching the shimmering rise and fall of God's fire out beyond the Edge of the World with a kind of absent bemusement. So far as he knew, God's fire served no useful purpose, but it was pretty to look at. Watching it play across the northern sky was peculiarly relaxing, and Althalus needed some relaxation at this point.

The peasant rebellion in Perquaine had faltered without the presence of Argan's Red Robes, but Bheid had moved with surprising and uncharacteristic speed to install his Grey Robes in positions of authority. Bheid's tendency to agonize over every decision seemed to vanish, and he started to bull his way through any opposition almost like a junior version of Exarch Emdahl. At first, the nobility of Perquaine had viewed Bheid as their own champion, but he'd rather quickly disabused them of *that* misconception. The Perquaine aristocracy was shocked to discover that Grey Robe churchmen were neither interested in bribes nor intimidated by threats.

As winter receded and spring approached, the nobles of Perquaine began to realize that Exarch Bheid had the upper hand. Planting time was rapidly approaching, and the peasantry let it be generally known that no seeds would touch the ground without Bheid's permission—and Bheid didn't seem to be in a permitting frame of mind. At first, the nobles blustered indignantly.

Bheid ignored them.

Spring began to arrive in southern Perquaine, and the nobility in that region began to grow more and more desperate as their fields remained unplowed and unplanted. Their appeals to Exarch Bheid grew increasingly shrill.

Bheid responded with a series of "suggestions."

The nobility went up in flames when they heard them.

Bheid shrugged and returned to Maghu to wait them out. Leitha slyly referred to the process as "Bheiding his time." Althalus felt that Leitha's sense of humor was sometimes a bit warped.

As spring marched on, Bheid's initial "suggestions" graduated to "demands," and one by one the nobles of southern Perquaine began to capitulate. Aided by the onset of spring, Bheid had wrung concession after concession out of the panicky aristocrats of southern Perquaine. Then he moved inexorably north, riding springtime like a warhorse and vanquishing all in his path. Several of the more arrogant nobles refused Bheid's demands as "outrageous." Bheid smiled briefly and then made examples of them. It soon became very clear that when Exarch Bheid said "final offer," he meant exactly that. A number of very large estates in central Perquaine remained fallow that year.

After a few weeks, Bheid had stopped trying to explain his seeming ability to be in three or four places at the same time, and wild stories about the new Exarch spread across the land. By early summer, almost everybody in Perquaine stood in awe of "Holy Bheid." The nobility wasn't too happy about the way Bheid was disrupting "the way things ought to be," but they were careful not to make an issue of their disagreement.

"Whatever works, I guess," Althalus muttered to himself.

"Have we taken to talking to ourself, Daddy?" Leitha asked from the doorway at the top of the stairs.

"Just thinking out loud," he replied.

"Ah. If everybody did that, I'd be out of a job, wouldn't I? Dweia says that it's time for supper." Her tone was subdued.

Althalus stood up and looked at the pale-haired girl. "Are you still having trouble with what happened in Maghu?" he asked her sympathetically.

She shrugged. "It had to be done," she replied. "I just wish I hadn't been the one who had to do it."

"It'll pass in time, Leitha," he assured her.

"That doesn't make me feel much better right now," she replied. "We'd better go down to supper. You know how Dweia feels when we're late."

"Oh, yes," he agreed as they went to the head of the stairs. "Did Bheid get any sleep? He looked as if he was starting to come unraveled when he came back from Maghu this morning."

"He rested," she replied. "I don't know how much he slept. He has a lot on his mind right now."

"I'm sure he does. Sooner or later, though, he'll have to learn how to delegate authority. He can't do *everything* himself."

"He hasn't quite grasped that yet," Leitha observed.

"It's too bad Sergeant Khalor's not here," Althalus said. "He could probably explain the process better than any of the rest of us."

"I don't think I'd suggest that to Dweia, Daddy. When she sent Khalor home, she gave him some very specific instructions regarding Eliar's mother, and asking her to bring him back wouldn't make you very popular."

"I was wondering why he'd left so soon."

"Now you know. I'd keep my nose out of it, if I were you."

"I shall be guided by you in this," he said extravagantly.

"Oh, stop that," she scolded.

Dweia had prepared a baked ham for that evening's supper, and it was superb, as always. So far as Althalus had been able to determine, there was no kitchen in the House. For obvious reasons, Dweia didn't really need one.

Exarch Bheid still looked totally exhausted by events in Perquaine, but Althalus decided not to start giving out advice. It was obviously something Bheid was going to have to work out for himself.

Gher had wolfed down his supper as he usually did, and now he sat fidgeting, kept in his seat by Dweia's ironclad rule that nobody was to leave the table until after they'd all finished eating.

Althalus didn't really have anything else to do, so he pushed back his plate and idly reached back into his memories, looking for something that might keep Gher out of mischief. "Did I ever tell you the story about my wolf-eared tunic, Gher?" he asked the bored little boy.

"I don't think so," Gher replied. "Is it a good story?"

"All my stories are good stories, Gher," Althalus assured him. "You should know that by now."

"Is it a true story?" Gher asked. "Or is it one you just make up as you go along? I like the true ones better, but the made-up ones are pretty good, too."

"How can you tell the difference, Gher?" Leitha asked. "Once Althalus gets started, his stories seem to run away with him."

"How does it go, Althalus?" Gher asked eagerly.

Althalus leaned back in his chair. "Well, this all happened a long, long time ago—before I'd even heard about Emmy's House or the Edge of the World or Books or any of the things that we've come across here lately. I'd gone on down into the low country to have a look at civilization—and more importantly, at the rich men who lived down there. Back in those days, I found rich people absolutely fascinating."

"Was that the time those dogs chased you and when you first found out about paper money?"

"That was the trip, all right. Well, as you can probably imagine, I wasn't in a very good humor when I gave up on civilization and started back toward Hule where I belonged. Nothing I'd tried down there in the low country had worked out the way it'd been supposed to, so I was feeling grumpy, to say the very least." Althalus glanced casually around the table and saw that Gher wasn't the only one who was listening to the story. It was nice to know that he hadn't lost his touch.

"Anyway," he continued, "I had to go through Arum to get back to Hule, but that didn't bother me too much, since I've always gotten along fairly well with the Arums. Well, I was sort of plodding my way up into the foothills of southern Arum late that summer, and when I happened to pass a wayside tavern, I decided to stop in for a cup or two of good, rich mead. The lowlanders evidently didn't know how to brew mead, because all I'd been able to get down there had been wine, and wine leaves a sour taste in my mouth—almost as sour as the taste of all the things that'd gone wrong for me down there."

"You *are* going to get to the point here eventually, aren't you, Althalus?" Dweia interjected.

"It's my story, Em," he replied complacently, "so I'll tell it the way it's supposed to be told. You don't have to listen, if you don't want to."

"Get *on* with it, Althalus," she said impatiently.

"Anything you say, Em," he replied blandly. "Well, Gher, as it so happened, there was a half-drunk loafer in the tavern who was babbling on and on about some Clan Chief who was supposed to be the richest man in Arum. I didn't really pay all that much attention to his story, because at any given time there are probably forty or fifty 'richest men in Arum' floating around."

"The subject *does* come up fairly often," Eliar conceded.

"I'll be the first to admit that I find the subject of money fairly interesting," Althalus admitted, "but on this particular occasion, I was a bit more interested in the wolf-skin tunic that tavern loafer was wearing. Now, back in those days, it wasn't really unusual to see people wearing clothes made out of the skins of wild animals, but this particular tunic was just a bit odd. Whoever had made it in the first place had left the ears on the wolf skin, and they stuck up from the hood of the tunic in a perky sort of way that looked kind of dashing—even elegant. Well, the fellow who was wearing it was a fairly typical Arum tavern loafer—drunk, stupid, and none too clean. The front of that fine tunic was all spotted with gravy he'd spilled on it, and it obviously hadn't had a good brushing since the day he'd first put it on. It was clearly much too fine a garment for a man like that to be wearing, so I decided that maybe I should do something about that."

"And I'll bet I know exactly what you had in mind." Gher chuckled.

"Don't get ahead of the story, Gher," Althalus chided. "Well, as I said before, the fellow in the tunic was already half-drunk to start with, so I bought him enough good, rich mead to push him on along the rest of the way, and by the time it got dark outside, he was far gone. I decided that we might as well get on with this, so I suggested that we might step outside for a breath of fresh air to clear our heads. He thought that was a wonderful idea, and so we went outside. He stumbled along until we got out a ways from the tavern. I took a quick look around to make sure nobody was watching, and then I whanged him on the head a couple of times with the hilt of my sword. He went down as if somebody had just cut the ground out from under him."

Gher laughed delightedly. "This is a *real* good story, Althalus," he said enthusiastically. "What happened then?"

"Those of us in the profession call it 'the transfer of ownership.' First I peeled my fine new tunic off him, and then I took his purse. The purse wasn't really very heavy, but mine was quite a bit lighter. Then I took a good look at his shoes. They weren't new, by any stretch of the imagination, but mine were so badly worn that if I'd held them up, daylight would've shown through. After I'd gathered up all my new possessions, the sour taste of civilization began to fade from my mouth."

"Whatever happened to that tunic?" Gher asked.

Althalus sighed. "I had to throw it away," he said sadly. "As I went on farther up into Arum, I came across other people who told me stories about that same rich Clan Chief."

"The story isn't over yet, is it?" Gher asked eagerly. "I really like stories that keep on going like this one does."

"Most younger people prefer those stories," Althalus agreed, "and some who aren't so young. Some stories have a beginning, a middle, and an end. Other stories never end, maybe because they're alive."

"Those are the kind *I* like," Gher declared. "What happened next?"

"Well, what happened *might* have been a coincidence, but when Emmy's around, the word 'coincidence' almost never describes what's really happening. As it turned out, that rich Clan Chief the former owner of my tunic had been talking about just *happened* to be the Chief of Albron's clan back then. His name was Gosti Big Belly, and he had a toll bridge that was almost like a gold mine—or so the fellows in a little village tavern told me."

"Have you ever heard about this Gosti fellow, Eliar?" Gher asked curiously. "Since he was the Chief of your clan back then, you've probably heard stories about him."

"Oh, yes," Eliar said. "The one everybody tells the most often is probably the one Althalus is telling you right now. All of *our* stories call Althalus a scoundrel. His version might be a little different, though."

"Well, now," Althalus said, picking up his story again, "every place I turned in Arum, somebody was telling me about how fabulously rich this Gosti was, and it was in that little village tavern that I finally decided that it might be worth my while to pay a call on this rich fat man to see if there was any truth to those stories."

"And then to rob him?" Gher demanded enthusiastically.

"If the opportunity arose, probably so. Anyway, I went to Gosti's fort and talked my way inside. This was a very long time ago, and things were a little crude back then. Albron's hall is pretty much a castle, with stone walls and marble floors. Gosti Big Belly lived in a log fort with dirt floors, and he kept pigs in his dining room."

Andine made a gagging sound.

"There was a certain practicality there, Andine," Althalus explained. "If you've got pigs in the dining room, you don't have to keep carrying scraps out to the garbage heap."

"Will you *stop* that?" Andine scolded him.

"Sorry," Althalus said. "Anyway, I spent all that winter telling Gosti stories and jokes and eating at his table—*and* locating his strong room and examining the lock, of course."

"Naturally," Gher said with a knowing little smirk.

"Well, when spring arrived and melted all the snow off the passes, I decided that it was time to say good-bye to Gosti and his pet pigs, so late one night I visited his strong room and got the shock of my life. As it turned out, all the talk about unlimited wealth was just that: talk. There wasn't any gold in the strong room—only copper pennies and a few tarnished brass coins. I'd just wasted a whole winter, and I was going to come away with very little to show for it. Anyway, I took as much of Gosti's brass and copper as I could conveniently carry and left the place before dawn."

"What did this have to do with throwing away your tunic?"

"I was just getting to that, Gher. Gosti was really nothing but the fat Chief of a very minor clan, and he desperately yearned for fame and recognition. I gave him exactly what he wanted. He sent out word that a master thief had just robbed his strong room and carried off a dozen bags of gold. He offered a reward for my capture, and the description he circulated all over Arum described my fine tunic right down to the last whisker. I didn't have any choice at that point. I *had* to get rid of that tunic."

"Tragic," Leitha murmured.

"That story didn't turn out too happy," Gher objected.

"Not every story has a happy ending, my boy," Althalus said philosophically, "and this is one of them."

"Why don't we just fix it so that it turns out the way it should?"

"I suppose I *could* change a few things the next time I tell it to make it come out a little better," Althalus conceded.

"That wasn't what I meant, Althalus. I wasn't talking about just changing the story. I was talking about changing the things that happened back then so that the story—and the things the story tells about—come out the way we want them to." Then Gher frowned slightly. "You hadn't met Ghend yet when all this happened, had you?"

"No. I didn't meet Ghend until I finally got away from Arum and went to Nabjor's camp in Hule. I didn't even *know* about Ghend back then, but I guess he knew about me. When he came into Nabjor's camp, he told me that he'd been following me for months. What's Ghend got to do with this, though?"

"You said he was following you?"

"That's what he told me."

"Then my idea might work after all. As long as he's right there following after you, maybe we could use him to make the story better."

"Gher," Bheid said with a pained expression, "I wish you'd make up your mind. Are you talking about 'story' or 'reality' here?"

"Aren't they the same thing, Mister Bheid? A really good storyteller always changes his story to make it better, and since we've got those doors right here in the House, we can do the same thing to reality, can't we?"

"You can't go back and change the past, Gher," Andine objected.

"Why not? Ghend's been doing it right from the start, hasn't

he? Why should *he* have all the fun?" Gher scratched thoughtfully at his tousled hair. "Let me work on this a little bit, Althalus," he said. "I've got a sort of hunch that we'll be able to fix
things so that you'll get to keep that tunic you liked so much, and
maybe if I think real hard, we might be able to have something
pretty awful happen to Ghend at the same time."

"I don't know about the rest of you," Eliar said with a great
yawn, "but I'm just about ready for bed."

"Why don't we all go to bed now," Dweia agreed, "*before* Althalus launches into another story."

Althalus slept very well that night, but Gher's eyes were puffy
as he sat down to breakfast, and he was yawning.

"Are you all right?" Dweia asked him.

"I didn't sleep too good, Emmy," he replied. "It's real hard to
get to sleep when you've got a lot on your mind."

"You need your sleep, Gher," she scolded.

"I'll be able to catch up once I've straightened out a few kinks
in the thing I'm working on."

"What's bothering you so much, Gher?" Andine asked the boy.

"Well, it all started with that wolf-skin tunic Althalus was
telling us about last night. He had to throw it away after he
robbed the fat man, because the fat man was describing it to
everybody he met. If we want to fix it so that Althalus doesn't
have to throw away, then we have to come up with some way to
make sure that the fat man didn't talk about it."

"That might have taken a bit of doing, Gher," Althalus said
dubiously. "Gosti didn't care anything about the money, because
it was almost worthless. All he was really doing was bragging
because I'd taken the trouble to rob him."

"Oh, I saw that right off, Althalus," the boy replied, "and I'd
already come up with a way to get around that. All you'd really
need is somebody to help with the robbery."

"I didn't really know anybody that well in Arum back in those
days, Gher, and you don't just pick up a perfect stranger to be
your accomplice."

"But there was somebody you met later who'd have fit right in.
You keep forgetting about the doors, Althalus."

"All right, who was it that I met later who'd have made a good accomplice?"

"I was sort of thinking of Ghend. He knew you, even if you didn't know him. He wanted to get on your good side so that he could persuade you to go steal the Book for him, so he'd almost have to go along with you if you suggested that he should join you when you went to rob the fat man, wouldn't he?"

"Maybe so, but I didn't even so much as see him back then."

"Couldn't we fix that with one of those dream things? That was my first idea. I thought that he was probably sneaking around behind you everywhere you went, and we could use Emmy's window to find just the right time to do it. Let's say you went into one of those taverns when people were talking about the fat man, and maybe Ghend's outside listening. Then Emmy does the dream thing, and Ghend's not outside anymore; he's inside the tavern instead. Every thief in the world knows another thief almost as soon as he lays eyes on him, doesn't he?"

"I've never had much trouble picking out other businessmen."

"There you have it, then. After you two hear about that rich fat man, you take Ghend aside and suggest that maybe you two ought to go visit that Big Belly fellow. Ghend's stuck right there. He wouldn't dare to say no, because then you might say no when he talked about the Book later on."

"I *love* the way this boy's mind works," Leitha said. "It'd be perfect. Ghend wouldn't have any choice but to go along with your scheme."

"I didn't really need any help, Gher," Althalus objected.

"Not with the robbery, maybe, but it wasn't the robbery that caused the problem. It was getting away that fixed it so that you had to throw your tunic away, wasn't it?"

"How would having Ghend as my partner change that?"

"If you did it right, you wouldn't have to even *try* to get away. Let's say that you and Ghend steal a bunch of gold out of that storeroom."

"But there *wasn't* any gold, Gher. I told you that."

"We could fix that in a minute. We've still got some of those kegs that we used to hire the Arums with up in Emmy's tower, haven't we? We sneak one of the kegs into that storeroom, see, and then you and Ghend break in and steal it. The fat man doesn't even know it's there, but that won't make any difference, because he's not the one you're swindling. It's Ghend you're after. After you two steal that keg of gold, you divide it up, see, and then you tell Ghend that it might confuse people if each of you ran off in a different direction. Then you jump on your horse and ride off one way, and Ghend rides off in another. As soon as you're out of sight, you give your share of the gold to Eliar to bring back here, and then you double back to Gosti's place and act like you never went anywhere at all. Then you go wake up Gosti and tell him that you saw Ghend break into that storeroom to steal stuff. Now, Gosti doesn't know about the gold we snuck into his storeroom, so he thinks that all there is in there is pennies. He wants people to think he's rich, though, so he makes a big fuss about how mad he is that Ghend robbed him, and he describes Ghend to everybody he meets instead of describing you. So it's *Ghend* who's out there running for his life, and you're still loafing around in Gosti's place like you hadn't done anything at all. You sit in front of the fireplace eating chicken and telling stories like you did all winter long while everybody in Arum's chasing Ghend as hard as they can because they think he's got a lot of gold they'd like to steal from him. Then after a week or so, you tell Gosti you've got some business you have to take care of, so you tell him good-bye and ride on up to Hule to meet up with Ghend like you two planned in the beginning. *This* time, though, you've still got that tunic you liked so much. When you get to Hule, you tell Ghend that you got away easy, and when he tells you about what a bad time he had, you put on a long face and go 'tsk, tsk, tsk.' He doesn't know that you fooled him, so he still thinks you're his friend. Then when he hires you to go steal the Book for him, you make him pay you with *his* share of all that gold you two stole from Gosti's place— only you didn't really steal it, because we're the ones who put it in that storeroom to begin with. Wouldn't that sort of work?"

"Could you follow any of that?" Andine asked Althalus with a baffled expression on her face.

"Most of it, yes," he replied. "There are a couple of twists and turns that I haven't quite figured out yet, but I caught the broad outline." He looked at Dweia. "Could we actually *do* that, Em?" he asked her. "The notion of bamboozling Ghend that way lights a warm little fire in my heart."

"It's not impossible," she replied. "It doesn't make very much sense, but we *could* do it."

"Dweia!" Bheid exclaimed. "That's tampering with reality. If you change the past, who knows what's going to happen to the present?"

"We've already seen what *this* now looks like, Bheid," Gher said, "and there's a lot of stuff about it that we don't like very much. Wouldn't it be funner to make up a different now? If we keep tinkering with way back then, sooner or later we're bound to come up with a *new* now that suits us right down to the ground and puts Ghend's nose out of joint at the same time. That's what Ghend's been doing with *his* dream things, isn't it? He tries to make now come out the way *he* wants it to. All we'd be doing would be changing back then enough to make now come out the way *we* want it to instead of Ghend's way. And if we do it like this, Althalus gets to keep that tunic he liked so much."

"But if we keep tinkering with the past, nothing's ever permanent."

"Where's your sense of adventure, Bheid?" Leitha asked him. "Permanence is so boring sometimes, isn't it? Wouldn't it be funner to live in a world Gher can change any time he wants to?"

"Funner?" he asked.

"Isn't it logical to believe that language would change as well as circumstances? Welcome to the world of Gher, Exarch Bheid."

"I think that's about enough of that, Leitha," Dweia said absently. Althalus noticed that she was looking at Gher in a peculiar sort of way, however.

The following day after supper, Dweia pushed her plate back and looked around the table. "There's something I've been considering for most of the day," she told them, "and I think maybe we should all take a look at it."

"Is Ghend up to something else?" Eliar asked.

"Not as far as I know. Of course, with Ghend you can never be sure. This has to do with variations. A rather peculiar idea came to me while we were all listening to Althalus and Gher trying to tamper with reality."

"We were only fooling around, Em," Althalus told her. "We weren't really serious about it."

"We weren't?" Gher objected. "I thought it was a real good idea."

"It *was*, Gher," Dweia told him. "You just didn't take it quite far enough, that's all."

"What did I miss?"

"You were concentrating too much attention on that ridiculous tunic."

"Now, wait a minute," Althalus protested.

"If you *really* want another tunic with ears, dear heart, I'll make you one. How would donkey ears suit you?"

"You *wouldn't*!"

"Not if you stop interrupting me, I won't," she said sweetly. "Now, then," she continued, "as soon as someone tells Gher a story, he immediately starts thinking of ways to improve it. *This* time he raised a very interesting possibility. If we were to create a dream vision at some place and time back there when Althalus was just a common thief, it's entirely possible that he'd be able to cozen poor Ghend into being his accomplice during the famous robbery of Gosti Big Belly. The main goal of Gher's original scheme was to arrange things so that Althalus could keep that silly tunic, but that's not really much of a goal, is it? It's almost like building an entire castle just so that you'll have a hook to hang your hat on in one of the rooms. Gher's scheme's just too good to waste on something that small, don't you think?"

"*I* thought it was kind of fun," Gher said defensively.

"I think I know of a way to make it funner," she said with a fond little smile. "I liked the part where Althalus tricks Ghend into being his accomplice, and I *loved* the part where Althalus betrays Ghend to Gosti so that Ghend has to run for his life. But after that, it doesn't go anyplace. A great scheme like yours should have a greater goal than some silly shirt, shouldn't it?"

"Althalus *would* get all the gold in my plan," Gher said.

"But it's *his* gold in the first place isn't it?"

"Well . . . yes, I suppose so, but the idea was to let Ghend hold it for a while and then trick him out of it."

"Why not use the scheme to steal something from Ghend that's *much* more important than gold?"

"What *is* there that's more important than gold, Emmy?" Gher demanded in a baffled tone of voice.

"We'll get to that in just a moment, Gher. I've noticed that you always start these schemes of yours by saying, 'What would happen if . . .' I came up with a different 'if' than you did, though. What if Althalus used your scheme *not* to keep his tunic or to swindle Ghend out of his share of the gold that belonged to Althalus in the first place, but to steal Ghend's Book instead?"

"Dear God!" Bheid exclaimed.

"I'm a little busy right now, Exarch Bheid," Dweia told him. "Was it something important?"

"Things *would* sort of fly apart for Ghend if Althalus stole his Book and threw it into a fire, wouldn't they?" Eliar mused.

"That's not what I had in mind, Eliar," Dweia replied. "Ghend's Book wouldn't burn, for one thing. The entire procedure's a little more complex. Ghend's scheme probably involved taking the Book of Deiwos to Nahgharash. It wouldn't have worked, of course. He'd have had the *two* Books, but he wouldn't have had the third one."

"There are only two Books, Dweia," Bheid protested.

"You're wrong, Brother Bheid," she told him. "There are three—the Book of Deiwos, the Book of Daeva, and *my* Book."

"*Your* Book? I'd never even *heard* that you have a Book." Bheid's eyes had gone very wide. "Where is it?"

"It's right here," she said calmly. "Eliar has it tucked under his belt at the moment."

"That's a Knife, not a Book," Bheid objected.

She sighed. "What exactly is a Book, Bheid?" she asked.

"It's a document—pages with writing on them."

"The Knife has writing on its blade, doesn't it?"

"But it's only one word!"

"Only one that *you* can read. Althalus read a different word, Eliar read another, and Andine and Leitha each read something else. The Books of my brothers speak in broad generalities. My Book's very specific. It told each of you one word, and you'll each spend your entire lifetime reaching out to understand that word. The Book of Deiwos stays here, where it's absolutely safe. *My* Book had to go out into the world, so I disguised it in order to protect it. Why do you think Pekhal and the others couldn't bear to look at it? They've all seen knives before, and this one isn't all that much different from thousands of others. It's not the Knife they see when Eliar holds it in front of them, it's my Book. *That's* what terrifies them so much. They can't look at my Book, because it judges them."

Eliar had taken the Knife from his belt and was carefully examining it. "It still only looks like a Knife to me, Emmy," he said.

"It's supposed to."

"What color is it?" Gher asked. "When it goes back to being a Book, I mean. The one Ghend carries around is black, and that one on the table's white. What color is yours?"

"Gold, naturally. It *is* the most valuable one of the three, after all."

"Could we see it? In its real shape, I mean?" Bheid's voice had a kind of hunger in it.

"Not yet, Bheid. It's not time yet. Several things have to happen before I let it revert to its real form. That's what we're here to talk about. If we follow Gher's plan and use a dream vision to compel Ghend to join Althalus in the robbery of Gosti, Ghend would *have* to go to Gosti's fort. And where Ghend goes, the Book of Daeva goes."

"Oh, *now* I see where you're going with this, Emmy," Gher said. "While Althalus and Ghend are both at Gosti's fort, Althalus slips into the place where Ghend sleeps and steals his Book."

Dweia shook her head. "No, Althalus doesn't steal the black Book until he meets Ghend in Nabjor's camp in Hule."

"Then why do we go through all that folderol in Gosti's fort?" Bheid demanded. "Why not just leave the past alone for the most part and just concentrate on stealing the black Book when Ghend goes to Hule?"

"Because if Ghend wakes up and finds that his Book is gone,

he'll be on the trail of Althalus before he takes another breath. We have to come up with a way to delay him, and I think an imitation Book might turn the trick. I can *make* that imitation, but I have to see—and touch—the real one first."

"If you've already got the Book *here*, why bother to put it back in Ghend's saddlebag at all?" Althalus asked her. "Just give me the imitation. I'll put it in his bag, and he'll never know the difference."

"No, love," she disagreed. "Sooner or later, Ghend's going to open that Book and read it. The moment he does *that*, he'll know immediately that it isn't the real one. I don't want him to do that until *after* he hires you to steal the white Book. A few picky little changes in the past won't really alter the present very much, but if Ghend calls Daeva out of Nahgharash to recover the black Book, the present won't even be recognizable anymore. That's why Althalus *must* have a duplicate to take the place of the Book he steals, and I'm the only one who can produce a believable duplicate. Besides, I'm sure it'll be more fun if we do it this way."

"Fun?" Bheid objected. "What's fun got to do with this?"

"Althalus always does things better when he's enjoying himself, Bheid," Dweia said with a sly little smile. "And when you get right down to it, most other people do as well." Then she looked archly at Althalus. "If I remember correctly, you and I made a little compact when we first started out. I was supposed to teach you how to use the Book, and you were supposed to teach me how to lie, cheat, and steal. It seems that there might even have been some talk of a wager."

"Now that you mention it, I do sort of remember a conversation along those lines, yes," he replied.

"Well, pet, what do you think? Is my little scheme devious enough to suit you?"

"It's so devious that it confuses even *me*," he admitted.

"Then I done good?" she demanded in an obvious imitation of Gher's favorite question.

He laughed. "You done real good, Em. When you get right down to it, I think you done perfect."

"Naturally," she said with a little toss of her head. "I'm always perfect. Didn't you know that?"

"I don't quite get the point of this," Andine said with a baffled sort of look. "What do we do with Ghend's Book after Althalus steals it? If it won't burn, how are we going to destroy it?"

Dweia's expression grew very serious. "We bring it here," she replied. "That's what all of this has been about. When the three Books are brought together in the same place and time, something very important's going to happen."

"Oh?" Bheid asked. "What's that?"

"I'm not entirely certain; it's never happened before. My brothers and I've had our little squabbles in the past, but the Books have never been involved. The Books are elemental forces, and there's no way to know what's going to happen when they come together. If there were only two, this would be fairly predictable, but since there are three . . ." She shrugged and spread her hands. "Who knows?"

"Wouldn't it be better not to risk it, then?" Bheid asked, sounding worried.

"That option's not open anymore, Bheid," she said. "I'm not sure exactly why Daeva decided to involve the Books this time, but he did, and our choices went out the window the moment he told Ghend to hire Althalus to steal the Book of Deiwos. Now we have to play it out and see what happens."

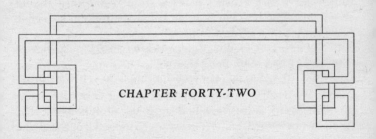

CHAPTER FORTY-TWO

Now it came to pass that upon a certain day in early autumn did Althalus the thief and his youthful companion ride boldly up into the tree-clad mountains of Arum with the gentle song of the Knife singing about them all the way. And the heart of Althalus was content, for once more garbed was he in a garment of splendor wrought of luxurious fur.

And came they of a golden morning unto a wayside inn deep in the mountains, and there did they pause to refresh themselves from the rigors of their journey, and entered they a low-beamed room alight with the golden sun of morning and besat themselves at a finely wrought table awash with light and called out unto the innkeeper for bright, foamy mead even as the song of the Knife caressed their ears.

And ever-watchful Althalus did cast his eyes about, and lo, there at a table across the room did he espy a familiar face. Puzzled was Althalus the thief, for try though he might he could not recall that face nor summon up any memory of his meeting with the man. Lank and black and greasy was the familiar stranger's hair, and deep-sunk and burning were his eyes. And the stranger's companion was a smaller man with a sly face and manner ingratiating.

And behold, others there were in that place, and spake they in good-humored wise concerning a certain Clan Chief of Arum known throughout the land most improbably as "Gosti Big Belly."

"Truly have I heard of him ere this day," spake Althalus, "but baffled am I that a Chief of even small significance should choose to allow his clan to address him so, for surely such a name carries with it scant respect."

" 'Tis but one of Gosti's peculiarities, wayfarer," spake one of they who tarried there upon that golden morning. "Correct art thou that such nomenclature would offend each and every Clan Chief in all of Arum, save this one. But Gosti doth view his paunch with great pride, and laughingly doth he boast that he hath not espied his feet in years." Amused appeared the speaker, and twinkled his eyes with delighted good humor.

"Men say that he is wealthy beyond belief," ventured Althalus the thief, ever alert for the main chance.

"Wealthy doth not e'en begin to describe the richness of Gosti," spake yet another of they who lingered there.

"Hath it been some fortunate discovery of a heretofore unknown pocket of gold which hath enriched him?" besought Althalus in hopeful query.

Then laughed yet another of they who lingered there, e'en as the song of the Knife transmuted itself into a minor key. "Nay, traveler," spake he. " 'Twas not the clan of Gosti upon which good fortune smiled, though methinks some slight corner of her smile did flicker across them. Some few years back did a wayfarer in the mountains above the lands of the clan of Gosti stumble across an outcropping of finest gold. Slender were the wits of the wayfarer, and spake he long and loud of his good fortune to sundry others in places where good rich mead is sold, and word of his discovery did soon spread far and wide o'er all the lands of Arum. And many were they who went to seek their fortunes above the lands of Gosti."

And puzzled was the face of Althalus the thief.

" 'Tis but a simple thing, wayfarer," bespake yet another in the wayside tavern. "Some few years back was ponderous Gosti's father slain in a clan war, and thus was Gosti elevated. Some there were in that clan who gravely doubted Gosti's ability, but Gosti's paternal cousin Galbak—a man of towering stature and the temperament of an angry bear—did stand behind him, and others in the clan wisely chose to remain silent concerning Gosti's slender qualifications. Common is the opinion that men of great girth have small brains, but such is not true of Chief Gosti. His ancestral home doth stand on the bank of a raging river so swift that some believe it can snatch away a man's shadow, and no man is so brave—or so foolish—that he would venture to attempt a crossing, e'en though it be five days hard travel in either direction to safer fords. Therefore did shrewd Gosti and titanic Galbak devise a scheme whereby they did erect a bridge across that savage river, and then did they cruelly extort money from they who sought to cross. Their benefit at first was meager, for they extorted merely copper, but following the discovery of gold in the nearby mountains, commenced Gosti's unprincipled clan to demand gold rather than copper. Now, the mountains of Arum are beautiful to behold, but a man who hath just passed a tedious year tunneling inch by inch into obdurate stone hath scant interest in scenery. His thirst for good, rich mead is strong, and he hungers greatly for the companionship of lithesome ladies who care not a farthing if a man be dirty and unkempt so long as his purse be filled with gold. As thou canst well imagine, such men will pay gladly whatever is asked of them to cross shrewd Gosti's bridge to the pleasures that lie beyond, and thus it is that Gosti's strong room doth bulge with good yellow gold that others most cheerfully wrest from the mountains for his benefit."

"Stretch forth thine eyes and look upon the face of Ghend," bespake youthful Gher in sibilant whisper. "Methinks his thought doth follow closely upon thine, O my teacher."

And puzzled was Althalus the thief, for his companion Gher bespake himself in a manner most unusual, for truly, youthful Gher was unlettered and unpolished. But clever Althalus pondered not this peculiarity but bent his eyes instead upon the face of Ghend, and recognized he there such signs of open avarice as were common among those who followed the profession so dear to the heart of Althalus himself.

"Mayhap it would be wise of us to seek out the familiar stranger Ghend," shrewdly whispered youthful Gher. "For should it come to pass that his thought is e'en as thine—as methinks it surely is—shall ye both not stumble o'er each other in pursuit of this common goal?"

And it seemèd Althalus that youthful Gher spake wisely, and resolvèd he then and there to pursue the child's cunning advice.

"It didn't happen that way," Althalus muttered, coming half awake in his bed.

"Hush," Dweia's voice commanded. "Go back to sleep, or we'll never get this finished."

"Yes, dear," he replied with a long sigh, and then he plunged back into his dream.

Now it came to pass that e'en as golden morning turned to golden noon that lank-haired Ghend and his small, sly companion Khnom did quaff the dregs of their mead and arise to go their way.

Then arose also cunning Althalus and youthful Gher, and went they also from that place.

And as it chanced to happen, their horses were tethered near unto each other, and clever Althalus spake most casually unto fire-eyed Ghend, saying, "Methinks thy thought is e'en as mine, forasmuch as the rumor of gold, it seemeth me, doth strike sparks from thy mind e'en as it doth from mine."

"Truly," replied harsh-voiced Ghend, "for gold doth shine prettily in mine eyes and ring winsomely in mine ears."

"It is e'en so with me," confessed wily Althalus, "but prudence doth suggest that wisely might we confer regarding this matter, for should we separately follow a self-same course, it were probable that we should encounter each other at every turn, and thus may our design be confounded."

"Thy thought hath merit," spake Ghend. "Let us go apart from this place and speak further concerning this matter. It seemeth me that thou dost propose an alliance in this venture, and I do confess me, thy proposal doth titillate mine imagination."

"Well?" Dweia said the next morning at the breakfast table. "Does that give you enough to work with?"

"What were you doing to my mouth, Emmy?" Gher demanded in a baffled tone. "I don't even know what some of those words *mean*."

"It was absolutely beautiful, Gher," Andine declared. "You spoke almost like a poet."

"It wasn't *me* who was talking like that, Andine," Gher said. "I think Emmy stuck one of her paws in my mouth and sprained my tongue."

"It was what's called 'High Style,' Gher," Bheid explained. "I doubt if *anybody's* ever actually spoken that way."

"It's been quite some time since it was common," Dweia said. "Let's set the language aside for the moment, though, and stick to the event itself. Will you be able to build on what I gave you, Althalus, or are you going to need more?"

"I think there was enough for me to work with, Em. Ghend was there, and he was interested. That's all I'll really need."

"As long as we're going to go through with this, it doesn't really matter that I was spitting 'thees' on the table and 'thous' on the floor, does it?" Gher said.

"It seemeth me that thou hast hittethèd the nail right upon its head, winsome Gher," Leitha said brightly.

"Make her stop that, Emmy," Gher complained.

"But none of that could have happened," Eliar objected. "There *wasn't* any new gold discovery back then."

"There is—or *was*—now," Dweia disagreed. "It wasn't really all that big a change, Eliar. The gold deposit was all mined out in a dozen or so years, and nothing really significant came of it. The only thing of any real meaning that grows out of it is going to be Ghend's involvement in the robbery. The sun will continue his journey, and the earth and the moon theirs. A slight dislocation in human history won't alter the universe. There *is* one thing you should keep in mind, Althalus. *Our* dream vision happened now. You and Gher will remember it, because you were here in the House last night. When the two of you go back to the past, Ghend *won't* remember it, because for him it hasn't happened yet."

Althalus chuckled evilly. "That's all I need, Em," he boasted. "I'll have him for lunch. When do we start?"

"Did you have anything particularly important you wanted to do today?"

"Not a thing, Em. Not a thing."

"Then we can start right after breakfast."

Their preparations weren't very extensive. Althalus had to discard his steel sword, of course, but he didn't mind that: the bronze sword he'd worn when he'd first come to the House was a dear old friend anyway. Dweia modified the clothing Althalus and Gher wore to eliminate the buttons, and Eliar made a quick trip to Chief Albron's hall to fetch a couple of horses. He was grinning broadly when he returned. "Sergeant Khalor sends his regards, Emmy," he said, "and I'm supposed to tell you that everything's going pretty much the way you wanted it to."

"That's nice," she said with a faint smile. "Do you have enough money, Althalus?" she asked then.

"I think so," Althalus replied. "If I need more, I'll just pick somebody's pocket."

"I'd rather you didn't," she said disapprovingly.

"It's part of your education, Em," he said piously. "Now that you've decided to lie, cheat, and steal, I'm just going to give you some demonstrations. Watch and learn, Em."

"Go Althalus," she commanded, pointing at the door. "Go now."

"Yes, ma'am."

Eliar took Althalus and Gher through his "special door" to a trail that wandered up into the mountains of southern Arum. "I've got your horses picketed right over there," he told them, pointing toward a nearby thicket.

Althalus nodded. "You'd better get out of sight, Eliar," he said. "Ghend's probably nearby, and I don't think we want him to see you."

Eliar nodded. "I'll be at the window," he said. "If you need anything, give me a shout."

"Right," Althalus said.

Eliar turned and then stepped out of sight.

"That's spooky," Gher, dressed once more in rags, said. "Even though I know what he's doing, watching him just poof out of sight like that gives me the collywobbles."

Althalus looked around to get his bearings. "This is the way we're going to do this, Gher," he said quite seriously. "There should be a crossroad about a half mile on up ahead. I'll keep plodding along this trail while you get the horses and take them through the woods to that crossroad. We'll meet there and make some show of acting as if we'd planned it that way a long time ago."

Gher looked puzzled. "Why do it that way?" he asked.

"Because Ghend told me in Nabjor's camp that he'd been following me. He might be somewhere nearby, or he might not, but I'm not going to take any chances. I was alone and on foot when I left Maghu, and if Ghend was following me, I don't want anything to happen that doesn't have a logical explanation. If he's just stumping along behind me, he's probably about half asleep, and I want him to stay that way. If he wakes up, he might start noticing things I'd rather he didn't."

"You're awful good at this kind of stuff," Gher said.

Althalus shrugged. "I'm the best," he said modestly. "Oh, one other thing. I know that Andine and Leitha have been trying to teach you correct language. Forget about it. I want you to go back to 'country boy.' Start saying 'he done,' and 'we was' and 'didn't mean nothing.' If you talk *that* way, maybe Ghend won't realize how clever you are."

Gher went back into the thicket, and Althalus walked on along the trail trying to remember every single detail of certain events that had happened some twenty-five centuries ago so that he could alter them slightly. He kept repeating the word "slightly" to himself as he plodded along.

Gher was sitting on a log at the crossroad, and the horses were tied to nearby bushes.

"I see you got my message," Althalus called out.

"Well," Gher said, "sort of. You didn't pick such a good messenger, Althalus. He was pretty drunk when he told me what you wanted, so I wasn't *too* sure I was getting it right."

"He was the only one I could find on short notice. It looks to me as if you got enough of the message to meet me here."

"I had to do a lot of guessing. Where are we going from here?"

"I want to go back to Hule, where I belong. I've had about as much of civilization as I can stand. Did you happen to see any taverns on your way here? I've been walking for a long time now, and I've worked up a powerful thirst."

"There's a village a few miles on up ahead," Gher said, rising to his feet. "Anyplace where there's a village, there's bound to be a tavern."

"Right," Althalus agreed. "Let's mount up and go see if we can find it."

They went to the horses and prepared to mount. "Did I do all right, Althalus?" Gher whispered.

"You did fine, Gher. If Ghend *was* listening, our little talk covered everything we want him to know."

"What if he *wasn't* listening?"

"I'll take care of that when we get to the tavern," Althalus assured him.

You won't have to do that, Eliar's voice silently spoke to Althalus. *Ghend's about twenty feet away from where you are, and he's got Khnom with him.*

Everything's going the way it's supposed to, then, Althalus sent his thought back. *Thanks, Eliar.*

Don't mention it, Dweia's voice murmured. *Oh, by the way, I encouraged Khnom to think about "thirsty," so he and Ghend are probably going to be in that tavern when you two arrive.*

Encouraged?

Someday I'll show you how to do it, love. It's not really very hard.

Good. "Let's go, Gher," Althalus said, nudging his horse.

The tavern was much as Althalus remembered it—except for a shaggy grey horse and a tired-looking bay tied to a rail near the front door. "The grey's Ghend's horse," Althalus told his young friend quietly as they dismounted. "Let's tie ours to that same rail."

"Right," Gher agreed. "Do I get to drink mead, too?"

No. Dweia's voice was very firm.

Althalus overrode her. *Sorry, Em. If he doesn't drink something, it might arouse suspicions in Ghend's mind. I'll see to it that our boy doesn't drink too much.*

You and I are going to talk about this, Althalus, she told him ominously.

It's always a pleasure talking with you, Em, he said blandly.

Althalus and Gher tethered their horses to the rail and went into the tavern. "They're right over there," Gher said quietly, thrusting his chin at a table off to one side.

"Right," Althalus agreed. "Let's not sit too close."

They sat down at a crude table near the door, and Althalus called for mead.

"That's a fine-looking tunic you've got there, friend," the tavern keeper said, placing two large earthenware cups of mead on the table.

Althalus shrugged. "It keeps the wind off my back," he replied.

"He charges *how* much?" one of the patrons of the tavern demanded incredulously of a man who'd evidently just said something astonishing.

"One full ounce of gold," the other man replied, "and Gosti Big Belly's got a dozen men with battle-axes standing right there to make sure you pay before you cross that bridge."

"That's outrageous!"

"It beats trying to swim, and there's no place where you can ford the river for five days' ride in either direction. That bridge is Gosti's license to steal. All the gold diggings are over on the other side of that river, but nobody's going to get to them—or get back out—unless he pays what Gosti Big Belly demands."

"Excuse me," Althalus said to them. "I wasn't eavesdropping or anything, but my young friend and I are on our way to Hule, and I think that we might have to pick another route if that bridge you were just talking about happens to stand in our way on this particular trail."

"If you're going to Hule, you won't have no problems, traveler. The Hule road runs along *this* side of that river, and you won't have to pay nobody to use it. It's the *other* side of the river that'll bite big chunks out of your purse. There's gold on that side, and Gosti Big Belly's going to make certain sure that anybody who wants to go a-looking for that gold is going to pay to get there."

"Where in the world did a Clan Chief get a name like that?" Althalus asked. "It doesn't sound very respectful to me."

"You'd almost have to know Gosti to understand," another tavern patron explained. "You're right about how a name like that would offend *most* of the Clan Chiefs of Arum, but Gosti's very proud of that belly of his. He even laughs out loud when he brags that he hasn't seen his feet in years."

"If he's charging people an ounce of gold to cross over that bridge of his, he must be getting fairly close to rich by now."

"Oh, he's rich, all right," the man who'd announced the amount of the toll confirmed. "He's way, way *past* rich."

"Did he have his men build that bridge as soon as he heard about that pocket of gold up there in the mountains?"

"No, he had his bridge in place even before word of the gold leaked out. It all started some years back. There was this clan war you see, and Gosti's father—who was Chief back then—got hisself killed in that war. That made Gosti the Chief, whether anybody liked it or not—and most of them didn't. Gosti weren't none too popular, since a Clan Chief's supposed to be some kind of hero, and a real fat man don't look none too heroic. Gosti's got a cousin, though—Galbak his name is—and Galbak's about seven feet tall and he's meaner than a snake. Nobody in his right mind crosses Galbak. Now, Gosti's not the most energetic fellow in the world, since he's real, real fat, and like most fat men, he's dog-bone lazy. Now, every so often, a Clan Chief has to visit other Clan Chiefs, and a five-day ride to the nearest river ford didn't hardly set Gosti's heart all aglow, so he ordered his men to build him a bridge across that river. Then, after it was finished, he came up with the idea of making anybody who wasn't a member of his clan pay to use his bridge. Right at first, the price was only a penny, but after the discovery of gold up in the mountains, the price went up considerable."

"A full ounce of gold goes beyond considerable, my friend," Althalus said drily. "Why would anybody in his right mind pay that kind of price?"

"They're *glad* to pay it. A man who's just spent six months digging a hole into a mountainside starts to get powerful thirsty, and he starts to get real lonesome for the company of pretty women who don't care how bad a fellow smells as long as he's got a pocket full of gold. Gosti's camped right across the only way out of the mountains, so he gets his share of every speck of gold that's dug up, and he don't even have to get his hands dirty. I don't think anybody's even come up with a word yet to describe just how rich Gosti Big Belly really is."

Gher nudged Althalus with his elbow. "Look at Ghend!" he hissed. "He's actually drooling!"

Althalus let his eyes casually drift across the faces of the other tavern patrons, giving Ghend only a quick glance in passing. The lank-haired man with burning eyes was pale, and the expression on his face was a grotesque exaggeration of undisguised yearning.

"I think he just swallowed our hook, Althalus," Gher said smugly. "All we have to do now is pull him in."

"Just exactly where is this toll bridge?" Ghend asked carefully in his harsh voice. "My friend and I are going north ourselves—probably in the same general direction as those two other travelers—and if this Gosti fellow's as greedy as you say, he might just start collecting toll on the Hule road as well as on that bridge of his."

"I don't think he'd go quite *that* far, traveler," the fellow who'd just recounted Gosti's history declared. "The other Clan Chiefs wouldn't stand for it, and that'd start a war."

"Maybe," Ghend said, "but I think my friend and I might want to get past the greedy man's territory before he happens to think of expanding his little empire." He drained his mead cup and stood up. "It's been a pleasure, gentlemen," he said sardonically, "and we'll have to do this again one of these days." And then he and Khnom left the tavern.

"Let's go," Althalus said quietly to Gher.

"I haven't finished my mead yet," the boy protested.

"Yes, you have. We're leaving right now."

They went out through the tavern door to join Ghend and Khnom at the rail where their horses were tethered. "Have you got a moment, friend?" Althalus asked.

"We're in sort of a hurry," Khnom told him.

"This won't take but a minute," Althalus assured him. Then he looked directly at Ghend. "If I read your face correctly—and I usually do—you found the story about Gosti Big Belly and all that gold that's piling up around him *very* interesting."

"It got my attention," Ghend admitted shortly.

"I thought it might have. You've got the look of a businessman about you."

"Which business are we talking about? I don't sell pots and pans or sheep, if that's what you mean."

"Neither do I, friend. I was referring to the business that involves the transfer of ownership of this, that, and the other thing."

"Oh, *that* business. My associate and I dabble in that now and then."

"I sort of thought you might. I saw the way your eyes lit up when those country bumpkins started talking about the fat man and his toll bridge. I'll tell you right out in front that those stories lit a little fire in *my* belly, too."

"So?"

"If it just happened that we both went to visit the fat man with the idea of transferring ownership of part of his gold, we'd probably be tripping over each other at every turn, right?"

"It's possible," Ghend conceded.

"Now, I *am* going to pay Gosti a call, and if you are, too, mightn't it be better if we joined forces instead of going into competition with each other? If I'm trying to outsmart you and you're trying to outsmart me, the fat man's likely to outsmart the both of us, and we could both end up getting ourselves hung."

"That *does* make sense," Ghend admitted. "Are you any good?"

"He's the best there is," Gher said proudly. "You wouldn't *believe* how much he's charging my family for my education. Althalus here could probably even steal things from God."

"Now *that's* something I'd like to see," Khnom chortled.

"Just point Althalus in the direction of God's house and get out of his way," Gher boasted.

"I think maybe we'd better talk about this just a little bit more," Ghend said. "Let's move away from here, though. The doorstep of a tavern's not the best place for this kind of discussion."

"I was just about to suggest that myself," Althalus said. "You've got good instincts."

They all mounted their horses and rode through the village, into the woods beyond.

"Find us a good place, Gher," Althalus told the boy.

"Right." Gher dug his heels into his horse's flanks and galloped off.

"He seems to be a very clever boy," Khnom observed.

"He's so clever he makes my teeth hurt," Althalus said sourly. "Every time I come up with a simple plan for a simple robbery, he starts adding complications."

"Oh, by the way," Ghend said, removing his peculiar bronze helmet, "my name's Ghend, and this is Khnom."

"That might be useful to know. My name's Althalus, and the boy's Gher."

"Pleased to meet you," Ghend said with a faint smile.

"I think I seen a good place," Gher called from just on ahead. "There's a meadow with a clump of trees in the middle. We can talk there without nobody seeing us together, and nobody can't sneak up on us to listen to what we're saying."

"Lead the way," Althalus told him.

"It's over there," Gher said, pointing off to the left.

The meadow was steeply sloped, and the small grove of trees in its center was several hundred yards from the edge of the surrounding forest.

"Are we going to do this like we usually do?" Gher asked as they dismounted in the grove. "You know—tenlike we don't know each other when we get there?"

" 'Tenlike'?" Khnom asked with a look of bafflement.

"Gher makes up words sometimes," Althalus explained. "What he actually means is 'pretend like'—and he's probably right. We don't want Gosti to start thinking of us as a group. I think we should behave as if we're strangers and sort of avoid each other while we're inside Gosti's main building. We'll have to gain his confidence, and that's going to take a while. We'll need to make up a few fairly convincing lies, but that's no problem for professionals."

"Not really," Ghend acknowledged. "Then we should probably split up right here."

"Right," Althalus agreed. "Why don't you and Khnom ride out from this grove and go north? Then Gher and I'll wait for about an hour and ride off toward the east. If anybody's watching, he won't realize that we're together."

"You *are* good, Althalus," Ghend said admiringly. "You've got an excellent eye for details. When this is all over, we might want to talk again. I might just have a business proposition for you— but let's rob Gosti first, shall we?"

"One thing at a time, certainly. All right, have you got gold enough to buy your way across that bridge?"

"I've got plenty," Ghend replied. "Do you need some?" The question was slyly put.

"And if I happened to say 'yes,' our partnership would end right here, wouldn't it?"

"Probably, yes."

"That went by real quick, didn't it?" Gher said to Khnom.

"If we'd blinked, we'd have missed it," Khnom agreed. "We're dealing with a pair of masters here, my boy. We can tenlike we don't know it, but we'd better keep our eyes open."

"You're right about that."

"Gher and I'll cross Gosti's bridge a day or so after you and Khnom do," Althalus continued. "And we'll keep away from you when we get to Gosti's place. Have you noticed my tunic?"

"How could I miss it?" Ghend replied.

"Most of the time, I'll just leave the hood pushed back. If I pull it up and you can see the wolf ears sticking out, it means that I need to talk to you, all right?"

Ghend nodded. "And I'll use my bronze helmet the same way. Most of the time, it'll be hanging on my belt. If I've got it on my head, it'll mean that *I* want to talk to *you*."

"This is all coming together very well," Althalus said. "This is probably as far as we need to go for right now. We'll need to get the lay of the land a bit before we come up with any more details. Once we know where the fat man's strong room is and how well it's guarded, we'll be able to polish the details."

"Agreed," Ghend said shortly.

"Do we need to talk about anything else?"

"I think that covers it," Ghend said.

"All right, then," Althalus said. "You two had better get moving. We'll see you again in Gosti's fort."

"Only we'll tenlike we never laid eyes on each other before," Khnom said, grinning broadly at Gher.

"He learns quick, don't he?" Gher said to Althalus. "Maybe if we steal enough gold, I'll be able to buy him and teach him the business."

That startled even Althalus.

"Don't get worried none, Althalus," Gher said with an impudent grin. "You're *still* the best. I probably won't get to be better than you are for at least another month or two—maybe even as long as three."

Ghend was laughing as he and Khnom mounted their horses and rode out of the grove toward the north.

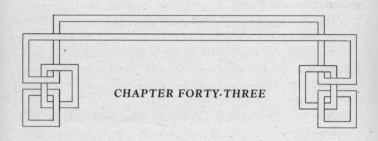

CHAPTER FORTY-THREE

"It definitely goes against my grain, Ghend," Khnom was saying to his confederate as Althalus and the others stood at the window watching the pair riding north toward the lands of Gosti's clan. "Do we *have* to let that grubby thief get away with half of the gold?"

"We need him, Khnom," Ghend replied. "Unless *you* want to go to the House of Deiwos and steal his Book."

"Not very likely," Khnom said, shuddering. "I've heard a few stories about what Dweia does to people who annoy her, and they make swimming in boiling pitch sound pleasant by comparison." Then Khnom squinted slyly sideways at Ghend. "What about *after* he's stolen the Book for us? We won't need him anymore then, so we could cut his throat and take his share of the gold we steal from Gosti, couldn't we? Once he's delivered the Book, we're done with him."

Ghend laughed sardonically. "You have no loyalties whatsoever, do you, Khnom?"

"Not when they get in my way," Khnom admitted. "I like gold, Ghend, and I won't stop until it's all mine."

"Except for *my* share," Ghend told him. "You weren't planning to steal *mine*, were you?"

"Of course not," Khnom replied just a bit too quickly. "Althalus and that clever little boy are another matter. You and I are like brothers, but those two aren't much more than a convenience. Their only reason for existence is to help us rob the fat man and then to go steal the Book for us. Once they've done that, we can dispose of them."

"Remind me never to turn my back on you, Khnom," Ghend said.

"You haven't got a thing to worry about, dear brother," Khnom declared with mock sincerity.

"Not yet, anyway," Ghend added.

"They aren't really very friendly to each other, are they?" Gher said.

"Not particularly, no," Dweia replied. "Ghend saved Khnom's life after he was expelled from Ledan, but gratitude's an alien concept for Khnom. Watch him very carefully, Gher. He's devious, sly, and completely unscrupulous; and he's *your* responsibility."

"Mine?"

"Of course. Eliar dealt with Pekhal in Wekti, Andine outwitted Gelta in Treborea, and Leitha and Bheid eliminated Argan and Koman in Perquaine. Now it's your turn, and Khnom's the one you're after."

"I don't think he'll give me too much trouble, Emmy," the boy said. "The Knife told me to 'deceive,' didn't it? Doesn't that mean that I'm supposed to trick him? I already did that when I came up with the idea of the dream thing that made him and Ghend help me and Althalus rob Gosti, didn't I? I'm already so far ahead of Khnom that he doesn't even know which way I'm going."

"Don't get overconfident, Gher," she chided. "Khnom's more clever than he appears to be. Keep things simple. If you get *too* exotic, he'll start to catch a faint odor of something that's not quite right, and that'll put him on his guard. He already knows

how clever you are. You have to make sure that he keeps believing that you're concentrating on tricking Gosti instead of
Ghend."

"I'll remember that, Emmy," Gher promised.

It was late morning two days later when Ghend and Khnom
reached Gosti's toll bridge, and they were obliged to wait while
the burly toll taker was engaged in a heated argument with a
would-be prospector in ragged clothes.

"What if I promise to come back and pay after I find gold?"
the prospector suggested plaintively.

"Don't be silly," the tattooed toll taker said in a voice filled
with contempt. "You pay now, or you don't cross the bridge."

"It's just not fair," the ragged man complained. "There's all
that gold up there, and you won't let me cross the river to get my
share."

"You don't have any money at all, do you?"

"Well, not yet, but I'll be rich as soon as I find gold."

"You're just wasting my time. Stand aside and let the paying
customers through."

"I've got as much right to be here as they do."

"Guards!" the toll taker shouted over his shoulder to two fur-
clad men armed with bronze axes lounging nearby. "This fool's
blocking the bridge. He wants to cross the river. Why don't you
throw him in, and we'll find out how good a swimmer he is."

The two burly guards grinned broadly and started toward the
prospector.

"I'll tell my Clan Chief about this!" the fellow threatened,
backing away. Then he turned and ran, shouting curses back over
his shoulder.

"Does that happen often?" Ghend asked the tattooed man.

"All the time. You wouldn't believe some of the promises I've
heard. Only about one in ten has the money to cross the bridge."

"How much?" Ghend asked shortly.

"One gold ounce apiece," the tattooed man replied.

Ghend opened his purse almost negligently and took out two

coins. "How do I go about getting in to see your Chief?" he asked. "I need to talk business with him."

"He's in that fort over on the other side of the river," the toll taker replied. "Most probably in the dining hall."

"I wouldn't want to disturb him while he's eating."

"You'll wait a long time, then. Gosti eats steadily from morning to night. I wouldn't worry about it. He can eat and listen at the same time."

One of the guards laughed. "It's eating and talking at the same time that gives Gosti problems," he said. "He sprays a lot when he tries to talk, so it gets kind of messy out in front of him."

"I'll keep that in mind and stand back a bit," Ghend said, and then he and Khnom made their way across the bridge.

"They don't look the least bit like Arums," Eliar protested. "Why aren't they wearing kilts like real Arums do?"

"The trade routes between Arum and Wekti hadn't been established yet," Dweia explained.

"What's that got to do with their clothes?"

"Kilts are made of wool, Eliar," she replied, "and Arums aren't very interested in raising sheep. This *is* happening twenty-five hundred years ago, you realize. Back then, most of the people living in the mountains wore animal-skin clothing, and their weapons were all made of bronze."

"What a strange way to live," Eliar said disapprovingly.

"That's a better bridge than the old one," Althalus observed. "A good sneeze would've collapsed the old bridge."

"Was that fellow with the drawings on his skin the same one you met last time?" Gher asked.

"It's the same man," Althalus replied, "but he's acting more official, now that the price has gone up." Then he squinted at the fort across the river. "It's bigger than it was when I came here last time. Could we get a bit closer, Em? I'd like to see just exactly what's been modified."

"Of course, love."

There was a brief blur beyond the window, and Althalus found that he was looking down at Gosti's fort from above. "They *have* made some changes," he observed. "Last time, that barn at the north end was outside the walls, and the pigs were just wandering around in the courtyard. I see that they're penned up now."

All in all, Gosti's fort was much more orderly than it'd been before. The main structure was now a fairly substantial log fort that overlooked the river and the toll bridge, rather than the rickety building Althalus remembered. The walled-in courtyard was lined with various workshops and animal pens. The stables were attached to the old hay barn on the north side of the court, and the smithy, tannery, and carpenter's shed ran along the east wall from the fort to the barn. "Once we get there, we'll have to do some exploring," Althalus told Gher. "There are a lot of changes we'll need to know about."

"I'll snoop around," Gher said. "Nobody pays much attention to curious boys."

"Good idea."

"They're taking Ghend inside the fort to meet Gosti," Leitha told Althalus. "You might want to eavesdrop."

"Maybe so. I don't want Ghend getting exotic at this point."

The ground below blurred, and Althalus found himself looking down at Gosti and his table.

"He's grotesque!" Andine exclaimed in a voice filled with revulsion.

"They don't call him 'Gosti Big Belly' for nothing, that's for certain," Eliar agreed.

"How can anybody that fat even *move*?" Andine demanded.

"He doesn't," Althalus told her. "He sleeps in that chair—and he usually keeps eating right through his naps."

A fur-clad clansman with a bronze-tipped spear escorted Ghend and Khnom into the fat man's presence. "These strangers want to talk with you, Gosti," he announced. "They say it's about business."

"Show them in," Gosti commanded, wiping his greasy hands on the front of his vast robe. "I'm always ready to talk business."

"This one says his name's Ghend," the clansman said. "He's the one who wants to speak with you."

"I'm pleased to meet you, Ghend." Gosti belched. "What kind of business do you have in mind?"

"It's nothing very important, Chief Gosti," Ghend said. "I have some things to attend to in Equero. Normally, I'd travel there through Perquaine and Treborea, but there are some people down there who aren't really very fond of me, so my servant and I decided to go to Equero by the northern route. We got a late start, though, so we won't be able to get across the mountains before the snow flies. I was wondering if I might be able to persuade you to put us up for the winter."

"Persuade?" Gosti asked, gnawing at a bone.

"He means 'pay,' Chief Gosti," Khnom translated.

"That's the word dearest to my heart," Gosti chortled, spraying pork fat all across the table. "Talk to my cousin Galbak, and he'll see to your accommodations." Gosti turned slightly and gestured toward a giant of a man with a close-cropped beard and agate-hard eyes. "Look after their needs, Galbak," he ordered.

"Yes, cousin," Galbak replied in a deep, rumbling voice.

"He's a big one, isn't he?" Eliar noted.

"Bigger'n a house," Gher agreed. "I don't think we'd want to get on the wrong side of him—except that I don't really see no *good* side on that one."

"You're lapsing, Gher," Andine scolded. "You've been taught to speak more correctly."

"It's part of the swindle, Andine," he explained. "Althalus wants me to talk 'country' so Ghend and Khnom don't get no ideas about how slick I really am. I'm supposed to be smart but act dumb. I don't know exactly how come, but if that's the way he wants it, I'll do 'er that way."

"It's colorful, if nothing else," Leitha noted.

"When are *we* going in, Althalus?" Gher asked.

"Let's wait a few days. We want to give Ghend and Khnom time to get settled in—and for everybody in Gosti's hall to get used to having them around. If we go in too soon, somebody might see some kind of connection between us. I want everybody there to believe that I've never seen Ghend before."

Althalus and Gher spent the next two days carefully watching Ghend and Khnom grow acquainted with Gosti. "That should do it," Althalus told the boy on the afternoon of the second day. "We'll go in about midmorning tomorrow."

"Anything you say, Althalus."

They gathered in the dining room at the foot of the stairs for breakfast the next morning, and Dweia gave Althalus and Gher a great deal of advice—most of which Althalus planned to ignore.

"She does that a lot, doesn't she?" Gher asked Althalus as they followed Eliar to the south wing of the House, where their horses were stabled.

Althalus shrugged. "It doesn't cost us anything to sit and listen to her, and if it makes her happy—"

"But you don't never do exactly what she tells you to."

"Not very often, no," Althalus admitted. "We'll want to come out on the trail about ten miles south of that toll bridge, Eliar—just in case Gosti's got lookouts posted near his fort."

"Right," Eliar agreed.

The willow trees along the tumbling river had turned, and their leaves were red as Althalus and Gher rode north through Arum toward Gosti's fort. "Let me do the talking when we get to the bridge, Gher," Althalus cautioned. "There's something I need to set up."

"All right," Gher agreed.

It was almost noon when they reached the bridge, and the toll taker stopped them to demand two ounces of gold. "That's a fine-looking tunic you've got there friend," the tattooed fellow noted after Althalus had paid him.

"It keeps the weather off," Althalus replied with a casual shrug.

"Where did you come by it?"

"Up in Hule," Althalus replied, even as he had the last time. "I happened across this wolf, you see, and he was about to jump on me and tear out my throat so that he could have me for supper. Now, I've always sort of liked wolves—they sing so prettily—but I don't like them well enough to provide supper for them, particularly when I'm going to be the main course. Well, I just happened to have this pair of bone dice with me, and I persuaded the wolf that it might be more interesting if we played dice to decide the matter instead of rolling around on the ground trying to rip each other apart."

Even as he had the previous time, the toll taker became totally engrossed in the wild story about the dice game with the wolf, and Gher appeared to be caught up in it as well. Althalus was pleased that he hadn't lost his touch, and he expanded the story, adding more outrageous details as he went along.

"Oh, that's a rare story, friend!" the chortling toll taker said at the conclusion, clapping Althalus on the back with one meaty hand. "Gosti's *got* to hear this one!" He turned to one of the broadly grinning guards. "Take over here," he ordered. "I want to introduce our friend here to Gosti."

"Right," the guard agreed.

"That was a terrible good story, Althalus," Gher said admiringly as they followed the toll taker across the bridge.

"I'm glad you liked it."

"Was that the same one you told him last time?"

"More or less. I embellished it a little, though."

They followed the fur-clad man up through the village, through the gates of the fort, and then on into the dining hall, where Gosti sat ripping chunks from the haunch of roasted pork.

"Ho, Gosti!" their guide said loudly to get the fat man's attention. "This is Althalus. Have him tell you the story of how he came by this fine wolf-eared tunic of his."

"All right," Gosti replied, taking a gulp of mead from his drinking horn. "You don't mind if I keep eating while you tell me the story, do you?

"Not at all, Gosti," Althalus replied. "I certainly wouldn't want you to start wasting away right in front of my eyes."

Gosti blinked, and then he roared with laughter, spewing greasy pork all over the table.

Althalus glanced quickly around the smoky dining hall, and he saw Ghend and Khnom seated near the fire pit. Ghend nodded slightly and put on his peculiar bronze helmet.

Althalus launched into a much-expanded version of his story

about the dice game with the wolf, and by late afternoon he and Gher were firmly ensconced in chairs beside the enormous fat man.

After sunset, Gosti drifted off to sleep, and the tall, bearded Galbak leaned across the table. "If you and your boy have finished, Althalus, I'll take you to a place where you can get some sleep. When Gosti starts to snore, nobody sleeps."

"I *am* a little tired, Galbak," Althalus admitted. "Telling stories can be exhausting."

Galbak let out a bit of a laugh. "Don't play games with me, Althalus. You loved every minute of it."

Althalus grinned at him as he and Gher rose from their seats. "You seem to be Gosti's right hand, Galbak," he told the towering Arum as they crossed the dining hall.

"Well, more like his left one," Galbak rumbled. "He *eats* with his right hand." Galbak sighed then. "That's what's going to kill him in the end, I'm afraid. It's probably all right to be *sort of* fat, but Gosti's taken it too far. He can't sleep lying down anymore, and there are times when he can barely get his breath."

"You're likely to be the one who succeeds him, aren't you?"

"Probably so, but I'm not looking forward to it very much. Gosti and I are like brothers, and I'm more or less forced to stand and watch while he eats himself to death."

Ghend rose from the bench upon which he and Khnom had been sitting. "That was quite some story, stranger," he complimented Althalus.

"This is Ghend," Galbak introduced them, "and that's his servant, Khnom. They're from Regwos, and they're wintering here."

"Pleased to meet you, Ghend," Althalus murmured perfunctorily. "Maybe we'll have time to get better acquainted during the winter."

"Maybe," Ghend agreed, sitting back down.

Galbak led Althalus and Gher on toward the dining room door. "I wouldn't get my hopes up too much about that one, Althalus," he suggested. "Ghend keeps pretty much to himself, and you could tell him the funniest joke in the world and he wouldn't so much as crack a smile. I've never heard him laugh once since he came here."

Althalus shrugged. "Some people are like that." He glanced back over his shoulder and saw Khnom exaggeratedly mouth the word "stables." Althalus nodded briefly and then followed Galbak on out of the dining hall.

The room to which Gosti's cousin led them had no door, nor any significant furniture. There was a pile of straw in one corner that was evidently intended to serve as a bed. "It isn't much," Galbak apologized, "but Gosti hates to spend money on furniture instead of food."

"It'll be just fine," Althalus assured him. "The boy and I can go to the stable and pick up our blankets, and then we'll settle in."

"I'll see you in the morning, then," Galbak said, and then he retraced his steps back toward the dining hall.

"It's working out pretty good, isn't it, Althalus?" Gher noted as the two of them walked through the fort toward the stables. "You got some plans about that real tall fellow, don't you?"

"I get a feeling that he's going to be useful later on," Althalus replied. "It seems that Gosti concentrates on eating and leaves details up to his cousin. That could be important before this is over."

They left the main building and passed through the various workmen's open-fronted sheds to the hay barn on the northeast corner of the enclosure. Then they entered the stables that were butted up against the north wall. Ghend and Khnom were waiting there in the dim light.

"You took your time getting here," Ghend growled.

"There's no real rush," Althalus replied. "There's already snow in the passes, so we aren't going anywhere until spring."

"I know that, Althalus," Ghend said, "but I was starting to wonder if you'd changed your mind."

"And leave all of Gosti's gold for you? Don't be silly. Have you located the strong room yet?"

Ghend nodded. "It's on the main floor—past the dining hall and up a very short flight of stairs. I haven't had a chance to look inside yet, but I'd guess that it's got a wooden floor—probably split logs. Nobody in his right mind stores gold in a room with a dirt floor."

"Truly," Althalus agreed. "Particularly in a region where everybody's carrying mining tools. Is it guarded?"

"All the time, but that shouldn't be much of a problem. The guards who watch the door at night usually take a couple of flagons of mead to work with them. If we go in after midnight, they'll probably be dozing. We'll be able to kill them quietly."

Althalus nodded. "Could you see the lock?" he asked.

"It won't be a problem," Khnom assured him. "I could undo that one in my sleep. We *could* do this tonight, you know."

"Too dangerous," Gher said quickly. "You fellows only got here a few days ago, and me and Althalus came today. They're probably watching us sort of careful because we're still strangers, and that big, mean Galbak's almost certain sure told the guards that they'd get skun alive if they drank theirselves to sleep. I think we ought to wait until they get used to us—and by then the snow'll be belly deep on a tall horse."

"He's right," Althalus said. "I want lots of open running room out there after we steal that gold. Galbak's got long legs, and he can probably run like a deer for at least a day and a half before he gets winded. No robbery's complete until you've gotten away."

"You're very good at this, Althalus," Ghend observed.

"I learned a long time ago that good planning makes for good robberies. We've got a long winter ahead of us, but we've got plenty of work to keep us busy. We need to go over every inch of this fort so that we can find our way in the dark. Our main problem is that we're inside a walled-in group of buildings. Getting inside was easy. Getting out with the gold might be a lot more difficult."

"I've had some luck with fire," Khnom suggested. "The fort *is* made of wood, you know, and people whose houses are on fire are too busy to pay attention to anything but the fire."

"It's a possibility," Althalus conceded, "but let's see if we can find some other way. A fire would only give us a two-hour head start—at most—and that's cutting things a little fine. I can lie my way past the front gate if that's our only way out, but we *don't* want to kill the guards. Blood attracts almost as much attention as fire, and we don't want to destroy the strong-room lock, either. If we do this right, they won't know they've been robbed for at least a day. If we've got a full day's head start, we're home free; if it's only five minutes, we're in trouble."

"And we should always tenlike we don't know each other," Gher added. "Don't get seen talking to each other and like that."

"We've got a whole winter to work out the details," Althalus said confidently. "I won't be able to help very much, because I'll have to spend the winter entertaining Gosti and the others in that hall with jokes and funny stories. That leaves most of the work up to you three. Now we'd all better get back to the main building. We *are* being watched, and if we stay out of sight for *too* long, somebody's liable to come looking for us."

Ghend's eyes were burning as he peered at Althalus in the dim light. "When this is all over, let's stay in touch," he said in his harsh voice. "I think we might want to talk about that business proposition I mentioned before."

"I'm always ready to listen, my friend," Althalus replied. "For now, though, let's get back to the main fort before somebody starts getting curious about where we are."

Althalus and Gher picked up their blankets and crossed the open courtyard to the main fort. "This must seem real strange to you, Althalus," Gher said as they were spreading their blankets on the pile of hay in the corner of their room. "I mean, you went through all this before, didn't you?"

"There are enough differences to make it interesting," Althalus replied. "When you get right down to it, we're pulling off a *double* swindle here. We're swindling Gosti in one direction and Ghend in another. That should be enough to keep me on my toes."

The weather closed in about a week after Althalus and Gher had reached Gosti's fort, and a series of savage snowstorms with howling winds and driving snow clawed at the buildings. It was warm and dry inside, however, and Althalus entertained Gosti and his men in the dining hall with jokes and stories. He also went out of his way to become better acquainted with the towering Galbak. The big man with agate-hard eyes seemed to be habitually melancholy, and it wasn't hard to see why. Arums are intensely loyal to begin with, and Galbak's close kinship to Gosti greatly increased his attachment to his Chief. It was obvious to anyone with eyes that Gosti's health was deteriorating. The fat man wheezed a great deal whenever he spoke, and he needed help to rise from his chair.

"I give him maybe two more years, Althalus," Galbak said one snowy afternoon when the two of them had gone to the stable to check the horses. "Three at the very most. Gosti was never what you'd call skinny, but ten years of steady eating have turned him into a mountain. It'd be easier to jump over him than it'd be to walk around him."

"He's no midget, that's certain," Althalus agreed.

"He wasn't always like this," Galbak said sadly. "When we were just boys, he'd run and play like any other boy, but after his older brother died, Gosti realized that he'd be the next Clan Chief, and he started to indulge himself. The more he ate, the more he wanted, and now he can't stop. He *has* to eat constantly."

"It's very sad, Galbak, but what can you do?"

"Not very much. He doesn't really pay much attention to any-thing that's happening around him, so I've been sort of obliged to take over for him. I keep a running count of the gold that's piling up in his strong room. He doesn't even look at his gold anymore. I give him a number every week or so, and that always sends him off into another celebration." Galbak shrugged. "He's fat, but he's happy."

Althalus altered his plan slightly at that point. Quite obvi-ously, Gosti was not much more than a figurehead. Galbak was the real Clan Chief here, and it'd be Galbak who'd give the or-ders after the robbery. In some ways, that made things easier. Waking Gosti from a sound sleep might have proved to be well-nigh impossible, and trying to explain that there'd been a rob-bery would most likely take an hour or two. Galbak's reaction should be almost instantaneous.

The winter dragged on, and Althalus concentrated most of his attention on keeping Gosti entertained, leaving the other business to Gher, Khnom, and Ghend. Then one night when the fire in the pit just in front of Gosti's table had burned low, Althalus chanced to overhear an argument between a pair of white-haired old Arums.

"Yer an idjut, Egnis," one of the creaky old warriors was saying scornfully. "There hain't no other door in the hay barn."

"There certainly *is*," Egnis retorted hotly. "Course you wouldn't know about it, Merg, 'cause you never done no honest work in yer whole life. You bin planted on yer backside right here fer forty years. I hauled hay through that back door every summer when I was a young feller."

Merg scoffed. "You can't remember that far back. You can't even remember this morning."

"There's a back door in the barn."

"No, there ain't."

"Is too."

"Is not."

Gosti was snoring loudly while Egnis and Merg continued to spit "is toos" and "is nots" at each other.

There was a way to settle the argument, of course, but Althalus decided not to suggest it. The two old codgers were having fun, so why spoil it for them? He rose quietly to his feet instead, and went to have a look for himself.

There was hay piled against the back wall of the barn, and Althalus scrambled up onto the stack and felt around under the hay. After a few moments, he found what he was looking for. Evidently, Egnis had been right. Althalus could feel a round pole that passed through a fair-sized hole in a jutting plank. He fumbled around some more, and he finally found the other one. Then he took hold of the pole and pushed it first toward one side and then toward the other. It slid back and forth quite easily. "Well, well, well," Althalus murmured softly to himself. "Isn't *that* interesting?" Then he climbed down from the haystack, brushed himself off, and went looking for Gher.

He found the boy in the kitchen, pilfering.

"Let that go for now, Gher," he instructed. "Go find Ghend and tell him that I'd like to speak with him."

"In the stables again?"

"No, let's meet in the hay barn instead. There's something there that's going to make things a lot easier for us."

"I'll see if I can find him," Gher said promptly.

"Do that," Althalus said, rather absently taking up a piece of bread and dipping it into a pot of still-warm gravy.

It was no more than a quarter of an hour later when Gher led Ghend and Khnom into the hay barn.

"What's afoot, Althalus?" Ghend asked. "Has something gone awry?"

"No, actually we've just had a stroke of luck. I happened to overhear an argument between a couple of old men."

"What a peculiar way for you to pass the time," Khnom said. "What were they arguing about?"

"This barn, actually," Althalus replied.

"How can you argue about a barn?" Ghend asked in a faintly derisive tone.

"They probably didn't have anything better to do. Anyway, they were busy remembering 'the good old days' the way old coots usually do, and somehow the question of barn doors came up. One of them said there was only one; the other insisted that there were two. I came out and had a look for myself, and it seems that the second coot was right. You see that haystack against the back wall?"

Ghend peered at the wall in the dim light. "Barely," he said. "You should have brought a torch here."

"In a hay barn? That's a quick way to attract a lot of attention, Ghend, old boy. Anyway, I climbed up that stack and stuck my hand down through the hay. There's a bar that runs across that back wall, and nobody I've ever heard of bars a blank wall. If there's a bar, there's a door, and if we can get that door open, we *won't* have to carry our newfound fortune out through the front gate after we *find* our newfound fortune."

"That *is* a bit of luck," Khnom agreed. "That's one of the things I've been a little worried about."

"Judging from the condition of the logs in the walls here, this barn's probably several generations older than the log palisade around the fort. This is only a guess, but I think Gosti's people built the palisade *after* gold was discovered back in the mountains and the price Gosti charged to cross his bridge went up just a bit. There was no need for a palisade before that, because there wasn't anything here to steal. Now there is. The hay in that stack is old. The newer hay—last summer's crop—is up in the loft. I'm just guessing, but I suspect that haystack's been there for several years—probably since before they built the palisade. Since the barn wall was already there, they probably just included it in the palisade. There wouldn't have been much point to building a new wall where one was already in place, but Gher can go outside tomorrow to play in the snow or something, and have a look. If there *is* a door—and if we can get it open—we can lead our horses out *that* way and be long gone before anybody knows that we aren't here anymore."

"That's another reason to wait until after the snow melts before we visit Gosti's strong room," Khnom said. "Tracks in the snow are a dead giveaway. I think our chances of success just doubled."

"Play in the snow?" Gher objected.

"Make a snowman or something," Khnom suggested. "Little boys do that all the time, don't they?"

"Only if they don't have nothing better to do," Gher retorted. "I'd rather spend my time learning how to steal stuff. I don't think I even know *how* to make a snowman."

"Take Khnom with you, Gher," Althalus suggested. "He'll show you how it's done."

"Thanks, Althalus," Khnom said in a flat, unfriendly tone.

"Don't mention it," Althalus replied grinning. "I want you two to check that outside wall *very* carefully. We don't want to wait until *after* we've done what we came here to do before we find out whether or not we can open that door, now do we?"

Khnom sighed. "I guess not," he said.

Althalus pushed on. "Now, then, after we've finished up and slipped out through that back door, I think we'd better split up. Gher and I'll go south, and we'll make sure that we leave a lot of tracks. The ground's soft in the springtime, so we shouldn't have much trouble churning up the trail that runs south on this side of the river. Ghend, you and Khnom go north, but stay *off* the trail. Ride north back in the brush a ways so that there won't be any tracks on the trail. Gher and I'll gallop through any villages we come across and make all kinds of noise."

"You two'll get yourselves caught and hung," Khnom warned.

Althalus scoffed. "Not a chance. I know of a rocky stretch on that trail, and there *won't* be any tracks there. That's where we'll turn and go on up into the mountains. Gosti's people won't even know we've left the main trail. They'll keep going south, and by the time they wake up, Gher and I'll be a long way away."

"Why are *you* taking all the chances, Althalus?" Ghend asked suspiciously.

"Because I'm better at this than you are. I know that *I* can get away with it; *you* might not be able to pull it off. Just keep on going north up into Hule. Then ask anybody you meet how to find the camp of a man named Nabjor. Gher and I'll meet you two there. You mentioned a business proposition of some kind a while back, and I think I'd like to hear more about it—*after* we've finished up our business here."

"One steal at a time, right?" Khnom suggested.

"Exactly. Let's get this one out of the way first. *Then* we can talk about the next one."

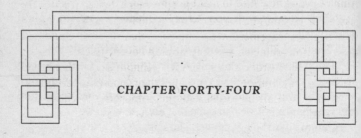

CHAPTER FORTY-FOUR

The winter plodded on until it was finally spring, and by then the thieves knew every corner of Big Belly's hall intimately. All that was left to do now was wait for the snow to melt.

Althalus began to make excuses for frequent trips out to the courtyard, since he'd arbitrarily selected a snowdrift in a nearby mountain pass as a signal. "When that one disappears, so do we," he'd told his fellow thieves.

It might have been sheer coincidence—although Althalus had become reluctant to use that word—but Galbak advised him that the clan customarily celebrated a certain event every spring. "Gosti was born in the early spring," Galbak said. "We Arums don't really keep very close track of days and months the way lowlanders do, so we celebrate Gosti's natal day when the last of the snow melts off those hills across the river. It might not be very precise, but it's close enough, I suppose."

"It's the thought that counts," Althalus replied piously, pulling up the hood of his wolf-eared tunic.

"Are you cold?" Galbak asked.

"I'm getting a little draft on the back of my neck, that's all."

It was about a quarter of an hour later that the four thieves met in the stables. "Is something wrong?" Ghend asked.

"No, just the opposite," Althalus replied. "I was talking with Galbak a while ago, and he tells me that it's customary here to celebrate Gosti's birthday, and as it so happens, the big party takes place when the snow melts off the surrounding hills. When an Arum says 'celebrate,' he's talking about some fairly serious drinking, and the timing couldn't be much better for us. By sunset, there won't be a sober Arum in the fort, and by midnight, they'll all be snoring and so stupefied that the fort could fall down around their ears and they wouldn't even notice."

"It's made to order for us, isn't it?" Khnom said with a broad grin. "*Our* celebration starts just after theirs comes to an end."

"And they'll all be too sick the next morning to chase us," Gher exulted.

"It's a peculiar sort of birthday present," Ghend said with an evil grin, "but it *will* make this birthday one that Gosti won't ever forget."

"He's been good to us," Althalus observed, "so we *do* sort of owe him *something*, don't we? The preparations should take them about a week, and that'll give us plenty of time for *our* preparations. The back door of the hay barn might not be quite as important now, but let's go ahead and use it anyway. There's not much point in riding through that village outside the walls if we don't have to. We'll want to leave tracks on the ground, not in some wide-awake villager's memory. Oh, there's something else, too. After a winter of lounging around in this stable, our horses are probably going to be a little frisky, so we'll want to ride that out of them before the big day rolls around. We'll be in a bit of a hurry, I expect, so we won't have the time to explain things to our horses."

"You think of everything, don't you, Althalus?" Ghend said.

"I certainly try. It's the best way I know of to stay unhung."

"How about decorations?" Gher suggested.

"That one went right past me, boy," Khnom admitted.

"If we was to tenlike we was going out to get tree branches and other stuff to decorate that big room where they do all their eating and drinking, it'd give us a good excuse to ride off into the woods to work the kinks out of our horses, wouldn't it? We'd be helping with the big party, and so we'd kind of fit right in, and nobody'd have no reason to guess we were thinking about anything but having a real good time."

"Shrewd, Gher," Ghend said. "Very shrewd. It'd also give us a chance to look over our escape routes in broad daylight."

"I'll suggest it to Galbak," Althalus said. "We'd better get back before somebody misses us. Let's all keep our eyes and ears open. We're getting closer, so it's time to start paying attention to what's happening around us. We don't want any surprises on Gosti's birthday."

Althalus and Gher waited in the stable while Ghend and Khnom crossed the courtyard, and then they sauntered into the hay barn. "Have you ever jumped out of a hayloft, Gher?" Althalus asked the boy.

"Why would anybody want to jump out of a hayloft?"

"For fun. You want a pile of soft hay to land on, though, so you'd probably better move this pile that's in front of the back door and pile it up under the edge of the loft."

"That's a *lot* of hay to move, Althalus," Gher protested.

"You can take your time, if you want. You don't really have to get it out from in front of that door until the day of the party. If somebody comes in and catches you at it, just tell him that you're moving the hay to give yourself something soft to break your fall."

"This sounds like an awful lot of work, Althalus."

"The pay's pretty good. I'll explain what you're doing to Galbak—'little boys get all fidgety by the end of winter,' or something along those lines. If Galbak knows why you're doing it, he won't get excited about it."

"Why am *I* always the one who gets stuck with these chores?"

"It's part of your education, Gher. Besides, the exercise might be good for you."

"You're a mean person, Althalus."

"It's part of my job, Gher. Somebody has to get that haystack out from in front of that door. If Ghend and I do it, the Arums are going to get curious. If *you* do it and tell them *why* you're doing it, they won't even pay any attention to you. They'll think you're just playing."

It was about noon the following day when Galbak went out into the courtyard, squinted at the hills rising steeply from the river gorge, and said, "Close enough. Gosti's birthday's five days from today."

The clansmen all cheered.

"Is everything going to be ready?" Khnom asked that evening when the thieves met in the stable.

"Pretty much so, yes," Althalus replied. "We still need to work the kinks out of our horses, but that's about all. We won't want to ride out in a group, though. Now that we're getting closer to the time, we don't want to be seen together, even for a few minutes. How's your haystack coming, Gher?"

"I've still got quite a ways to go, Althalus," the boy replied. "There's an *awful* lot of hay piled up in front of that door."

"I'll see if I can get you some help."

"How are you going to manage that?"

"Watch me, Gher." Althalus smirked at him. "Watch and learn."

When they returned to the great hall, Althalus was chuckling and shaking his head.

"What's so funny, Althalus?" Galbak asked curiously.

"My young friend. Have you ever noticed that when you ask a little boy to do almost any kind of work, he starts sulking and complaining?"

"I'd never really paid that much attention. Now that you mention it, though, I suppose the idea of work *does* sort of rub little boys the wrong way."

"When it comes to something that involves play, though, they'll try to move a mountain. I was telling Gher about something my brothers and I used to do when we were boys, and it seems to have set his imagination on fire. We had a rickety old hay barn on our farm, and my brothers and I used to spend whole winters jumping out of the loft into the soft hay down below. Falling *is* sort of fun, *if* there's something soft to come down on. Anyway, Gher decided that he'd *really* like to try it, and he's been spending just about every waking moment moving that big haystack out in the barn over in front of the loft."

"The devil you say!" Galbak laughed.

"You wouldn't *believe* how he makes the hay fly."

"What did you do after you'd jumped out of the loft, Althalus?" one of the other clansmen asked curiously.

"We'd climb back up the ladder and jump again," Althalus replied. "We could use up whole weeks that way. It's just about the closest thing to flying that anybody who doesn't happen to have wings is ever going to get."

"Well, now," the clansman said speculatively.

The next morning, Gher went out to the hay barn and discovered that he had all kinds of help moving the haystack out from in front of that long-forgotten door. Then the jumping started, and the hay barn quickly became the most popular place in the compound. Gher was just a bit sullen about that. "I can't even get up into the hayloft," he muttered. "The Arums are lined up on the ladder all day long, so I never get a chance to jump."

"Stop complaining," Althalus told him. "They did your work for you, didn't they? Let's go run some of the kinks out of our horses. I need to talk with Emmy anyway."

They rode out of the fort "to look for decorations," and as

ɔon as they were back into the trees, Althalus looked up. "I need ɔ see you, Em," he said into the vacant air above him.

"Bring them home, Eliar," he heard her say just over his head, nd a moment later, Eliar was standing on the trail ahead.

Althalus and Gher tethered their horses and followed the oung Arum back into the tower room in the House.

"*Was* there something?" Dweia asked impishly.

"How long are you going to need Ghend's Book, Em?" Althalus asked her. "If it's going to be more than a few moments, we ight have to come up with a way for Gher to distract Khnom."

"You worry too much about that, love," she told him. "You now that time's not the same here as it is out there, but you always seem to forget."

"So beat me. I just want to be sure that we won't have any ɔose ends dangling about, Em. Let me run this through for you, nd you can tell me if I've left anything out."

"All right, pet."

"We're going to rob Gosti about midnight on his birthday. By hen, everybody in his fort should be dead to the world; I'll see to at personally."

"I've been meaning to ask you about that, Althalus," Bheid inːrrupted. "I've come across a few men who can swill down strong ɪe for a straight week and still be able to stand up. What's going to appen if one of Gosti's men suffers from that same peculiarity?"

"I'm already working on that, Brother Bheid," Althalus mirked. "You remember Nitral, don't you?"

"Of course. He's the Duke of Mawor—the fellow who used quid fire on the besiegers of his city."

"That's the one. That 'liquid fire' was a mixture of boiling itch, sulphur, naphtha, and some fluid brewers can boil out of orːinary beer. *That's* the fluid that gives beer or wine or mead its unch and makes men wobbly in the knees and fuzzy in the head. 'm going to see to it that the mead the partygoers are drinking at ɟosti's birthday party is strong enough to stand up by itself ⅾithout any help from a cup. If that's what they drink that eveːing, I'll flat guarantee that nobody'll be awake by midnight."

"Typically devious," Leitha observed.

"I won't *force* anybody to drink it, Leitha," he said with feigned look of wide-eyed innocence. "If they want to drink it that's up to them, isn't it? Pushing on, then. I'm going to suggest to Ghend that he and I should take care of the actual robbery while Gher and Khnom saddle up the horses and get the back door of the hay barn open. I'll make sure that the robbery takes long enough for Gher to 'deceive' Khnom, pass Ghend's Book to Eliar, and then stick it back in Ghend's saddlebag after Emmy finished with it. Then Ghend and I can carry the gold to the stable, tie it to our saddles, and we'll all ride out through the back door. Once we're clear of the fort, we'll split up. Ghend and Khnom will ride north toward Hule, and Gher and I'll 'tenlike we're riding south toward Treborea. As soon as Ghend and Khnom are out of sight, though, Gher and I'll pass our share of the gold to Eliar so that he can bring it back here, and then we'll slip back into the fort and go to bed." He paused. "Can anybody see any holes so far?" He looked around, but no one replied.

"All right, then," he continued, "when morning rolls around, I'll make some show of feeling delicate, and just 'happen' to notice that Ghend and Khnom don't seem to be around anymore. Then I'll just happen to 'remember' that I saw Ghend sneaking across the court yard about midnight carrying something that seemed very heavy."

"Will that be enough?" Andine asked. "If you're going to poison everybody, they'll be even more 'delicate' than you'll be."

"It's not exactly poison, Andine," he objected.

"Oh, *really*?" the tiny girl said. "My point was that if you're *too* subtle, they won't realize what you're telling them."

"Then I'll have to be more obvious. I'll get my point across, Andine, believe me. By the time the sun's well up, Gosti's men'll be hot on Ghend's trail."

"*There's* a hole, Daddy," Leitha said triumphantly. "Didn' you tell Ghend to stay off that north trail?"

"Of course I did. I don't want him to see the tracks *I'm* goin to lay down on that trail for Gosti's men to find—*or* the track I'm going to leave running from the back door of the hay barn to the north trail. I'll fix it so that even a blind man could follow Ghend. I think that takes care of *my* part. The rest is up to Gher.

"And what are *your* plans, Gher?" Leitha asked the boy.

"I'm not too sure yet," Gher admitted. "I'll come up with omething, though." Then the tousle-haired boy gave Leitha a ly, sidelong glance. "Trust me," he added in a fair imitation of Althalus' favorite pronouncement.

"Oh, dear," Leitha sighed. "Not you, too."

Gher smirked. "It's part of my education."

The day before Gosti's birthday was clear and bright, but Galbak's face seemed mournful.

"What's the trouble, my friend?" Althalus asked him.

"I was planning a surprise for Gosti," the tall Arum said, "but 'm afraid it won't work out."

"What sort of surprise?"

"I thought it might be sort of fun if we woke him up on the norning of his birthday, carried him out to the hay barn, and hrew him out of the loft."

"It might have been fun for *you*, Galbak, but I don't think Gosti'd have enjoyed it all that much. What made you change our mind?"

"The floor of the hayloft isn't strong enough to support his veight. Jumping into that haystack is great fun, but crashing hrough the floor of the loft and coming down in the manure pile vouldn't entertain Gosti very much."

"You're probably right," Althalus agreed. "It *would* have been un to see the expression on his face, though."

As Althalus and Gher were returning to the bare room where hey slept, Eliar spoke silently to Althalus. *I just finished adding our concoction to the mead,* the young Arum advised.

Not all *the mead, I hope,* Althalus replied.

No, Eliar said. *The only crocks I doctored were the ten at the very back of that storeroom. The crocks at the front are only holding ordinary mead. They'll drink those all down by evening. They won't get into your "special mead" until after supper to-norrow evening.*

Perfect, Althalus gloated, rubbing his hands together. *I don't vant them to get completely frazzled until evening. A man who*

drinks himself to sleep by noon could wake up before midnigh
Did you taste any of the "special" mead?

Emmy wouldn't let me, Eliar replied a bit disconsolately.

*I guess I'd better stop by the kitchen and find out if it's as
strong as it's supposed to be.* He hesitated slightly. *You don
necessarily have to tell Emmy about that, though,* he added.

She's standing right beside me, Althalus.

Oh? Althalus said. *Hello, there, Em. How's your day gone so far.*

Mine *hasn't been too bad,* her voice replied. Yours *might star
going to pot if you get carried away with your sampling, though*

Is that a threat, Em?

No, Althalus. It's a promise.

Althalus turned and went back to the kitchen with Gher close
behind him. When they got there, Althalus dipped one drinking
horn into one of the crocks near the front of the storage room and
another into one from the back. The first horn of mead tasted
fine; the second left him gasping and filled his eyes with tears.

"Did Eliar get it right?" Gher whispered.

"Oh, yes," Althalus wheezed, trying to catch his breath.

"Won't Gosti's men notice the difference?"

"I doubt it. They'll already be half drunk by the time they ge
to those last ten crocks. They'll be too fuzzy-headed to know
what they're drinking." Althalus squinted toward the kitchen
door. "When we start getting on toward the end of the day, you
might want to take a few horns of mead to the guards standing in
front of the door to the strong room," he suggested. "Start ou
with the ordinary stuff and switch to the strong stuff later on
Ghend's a little too quick with his knife sometimes, so I don'
want those guards awake when the time for the robbery roll
around. I doubt that anybody in Gosti's hall's going to be sobe
enough to check on those guards, but let's stay on the safe side. I
the guards have had their throats cut, even the drunkest Arum'
likely to raise the alarm."

"Are there always so many details in a robbery?" Gher asked
"Here lately, it seems like you've even been counting the leave
on that tree just outside the gate."

"Well, I haven't gone quite *that* far," Althalus said, "but whe ou're planning a robbery, you should always try to cover every possibility. The thief who thinks ahead, stays ahead."

"I'll remember that."

"Good. Let's go mingle with the clansmen. Gosti should be waking up soon. He hasn't had anything to eat for six hours, and that's usually about as long as he can go."

"That's why he sleeps in his chair at the table, isn't it?"

"It's one of the reasons, yes. The more important one is probably that he can't walk anymore. He doesn't get much exercise, and he weighs as much as a horse. I don't think his legs would hold him anymore."

The birthday celebration was fairly formal at the outset. Galbak made a rather stuffy speech to start things moving, and he concluded by proposing a toast to their huge Chief.

The word "toast" was received with much enthusiasm.

Gosti beamed briefly, and then he fell ravenously upon his breakfast.

Althalus bided his time until the fat man had taken the edge off his hunger with about half a ham, and then he leaned back in his chair and began. "Ho, Gosti, did I ever tell you the story about the crazy man I met once up in northern Kagwher?"

"I don't think you ever did, Althalus," Gosti replied, munching thoughtfully. "How were you able to tell that he was crazy, though? I've never met a Kagwher who wasn't a little strange."

"This particular Kagwher was stranger than most, Gosti," Althalus told him. "He wandered around up there near the Edge of the World, and he spent most of his time talking to God. I've heard that a lot of people do that, but this fellow believed that God talked back to him."

"That's crazy, all right," Galbak agreed.

"Tell us the story, Althalus," another clansman urged.

"Well," Althalus began, "it was quite some time ago, and I'd gone up out of Hule into Kagwher on a business trip, you see, and one morning up there near the Edge of the World, I woke up when I heard somebody talking." He went on to describe the bent old crazy man at some length and then jumped off into a pure fantasy that was related to the truth only by implication.

The party grew increasingly rowdy through the morning and early afternoon, and then the fights began. Good humor returned at suppertime, when the first of the doctored crocks of mead were broached.

The singing began about an hour later, and the snoring not long after that.

"Go take some more of the strong mead to the guards in front of the strong room, Gher," Althalus instructed quietly. "Then go to the stables and saddle the horses."

"Right," Gher agreed.

"Do you know what you're going to do? You've got to distract Khnom for long enough to slip Ghend's Book to Emmy."

"I'll take care of it, Althalus," Gher assured him.

Khnom slipped out of Gosti's great hall shortly after Gher had left, and after a few moments, Althalus gestured curtly at Ghend.

The fire-eyed man rose, put on his bronze helmet, and quietly left the room.

Althalus slowly counted to one hundred, and then he also rose, looked around at the sodden Arums, and went to the door.

"Why the delay?" Ghend whispered.

"Just making sure that nobody was still awake," Althalus replied. "Let's get to work."

They went down the corridor to the three steps leading up to the strong-room door. The guards were sprawled on the floor just in front of the steps, and they were both snoring.

"Should we kill them?" Ghend asked.

"Absolutely not," Althalus said firmly. "Dead men attract attention, and that's the last thing we want. After we steal the gold, I'll lock the strong-room door again and leave it just the way we found it. With any luck at all, it'll be two or three days before anybody even looks inside, and that'll give us a long head start."

"Clever," Ghend said admiringly.

"I'm glad you liked it." Althalus went up the three steps to the strong-room door and examined the crude lock.

"Is it going to give you any trouble?" Ghend asked nervously.

Althalus snorted. "*Gher* could open *this* lock," he said derisively. He reached down and drew a long bronze needle out of his boot, probed at the lock for a moment, and was rewarded with a loud click. "We're in," he said tersely, opening the heavy door slightly. "Get inside. I'll pull the door mostly shut behind us."

Ghend nodded and slipped through the partially open doorway.

Althalus reached up, took the burning torch from the bronze ring beside the door, and followed Ghend into the room, carefully pulling the door closed behind him. Then he held the torch aloft, and the two of them looked around the strong room for the first time.

There were animal-skin bags piled along the wall, and there seemed to be quite a few of them. "This might take us a while," Ghend noted.

"I doubt it," Althalus disagreed. "Not even a man as messy as Gosti is would pile gold and copper together in the same stack." He set the butt of the torch into a bronze ring jutting from the wall behind the crudely built table, went to the pile of bags, picked one up, and shook it. "Copper," he said.

"How can you tell?"

"The sound. Copper pennies make a different sound. Gold's more musical." Althalus rummaged through the bags. "Here we go," he said triumphantly. "This one feels as if it's full of sand, and it's much heavier than those others."

"Sand?"

"Those miners up in the mountains don't have the equipment to melt their gold down to make bars, so they have to pay their toll in gold flakes when they cross Gosti's bridge. The ones who are going the other way are the ones who pay in coins." Althalus untied the top of the bag, poked his hand inside, and took out a handful of bright yellow flakes. Then he let the flakes spill back into the bag in a glittering golden shower. "Pretty, isn't it?"

Ghend seemed almost paralyzed, and his eyes were blazing.

"Help me sort these out," Althalus told him. "We don't want to carry off a bag of copper pennies by mistake."

"Right," Ghend agreed.

It took them about a quarter of an hour to sort through the bags, and they piled the ones containing gold on the crude table in the center of the room.

"I think that's all of it," Althalus said finally. Then he thought-fully hefted one of the bags of golden sand. "About fifty pounds," he mused.

"So what?" Ghend demanded.

"We've got four horses, partner, and if Gosti's men happen to wake up early and start chasing us, we'll want our horses to be able to run like frightened deer. I don't think we'll want to put more than two bags on each horse—maybe four on Gher's horse, but that might start some arguments later. Let's just take eight bags and let it go at that."

"But there are almost twenty bags here!" Ghend protested.

"Take as many as you want, Ghend, but if the extra weight slows your horse down and Gosti's men catch up to you, you'll never get a chance to spend any of your gold."

"There are lots of other horses in the stables."

"And missing horses attract almost as much attention as dead guards do. We've got a very good chance at having a three-day lead. If we start killing Gosti's people and stealing his horses, we can kiss that lead good-bye. I'd rather travel light and stay alive, but what you do is up to you."

Ghend sighed. "I guess you're right," he agreed mournfully.

"The gold coins are in separate bags," Althalus told his lank-haired accomplice. "Let's take those bags rather than the ones filled with sand. Coins are ready to spend, but we'd have to melt down the sand, and I've never been very good at that." Althalus went to the door and looked out into the corridor. "It's still clear," he announced. "Let's get started. We'll haul the ones we're stealing down to the end of the hall and stack them in the kitchen. As soon as we've got our gold out of here, I'll close the door and lock it again. Then we'll take our loot down through the sheds to the hay barn. I don't *think* anybody in the fort's awake, but let's stay in the shadows, just to be on the safe side."

"Right," Ghend agreed. "Let's get cracking."

They each took up two of the heavy bags, quickly lugged them down the corridor to the kitchen, and returned for two more. When they came out of the room, Althalus set his bags down on the top step. "Go on ahead," he instructed. "I'll catch up in a minute."

"What are you going to do?"

"I want to make that room look exactly the way it looked before we went in. If Galbak happens to glance in, I don't want anything to be out of place. If we're lucky, he might not even notice that Gosti's been robbed for a week or so."

"Very shrewd, Althalus," Ghend said admiringly. "Don't be too long, though." He turned and carried his bags of gold toward the kitchen as Althalus went back into the strong room, closing the door behind him. Then he quickly untied several bags of pennies and dumped them on the floor. He seasoned that pile with the contents of one of the bags of flakes and then tipped over the table. "That should do it," he muttered. Then he went back out, put the torch back into the bronze ring, and carefully relocked the door.

"That didn't take long," Ghend observed when Althalus joined him in the kitchen.

"I can move very fast when I have to," Althalus replied. "If Galbak opens that door tomorrow, he'll see exactly what I want him to see. Let's haul our loot to the hay barn. We want to be a long way from here by sunrise."

"You won't get any arguments from me on that score," Ghend agreed.

They each took up two of the heavy bags again and went out through the kitchen door. Then they moved carefully through the dense shadows in the open-fronted workshops along the east wall of the fort.

"What took you so long?" Gher demanded, his hoarse whisper sounding shrill. "I been going crazy in here!"

"Calm down, Gher," Althalus said. "What's got you all tied up in knots?"

"We've got trouble, Althalus!"

"Keep your voice down," Ghend hissed. "What's wrong?"

"*That's* what's wrong," Gher said in a strained voice. He pointed at a motionless figure lying near the stable door. "That's Khnom, in case you don't recognize him. We had the horses all saddled and ready, and we was waiting for you when this drunk Arum came stumbling in mumbling something about jumping out of the hayloft. Khnom was trying to come up with some story to explain why we was here, but the Arum was too drunk to listen. He seemed to think we wanted to jump before he did, so he banged Khnom on the head with that wooden bucket over there, and Khnom went down like somebody'd just cut the ground out from under him. Then the drunk Arum climbed up the ladder and jumped out of the hayloft. He didn't come down where he was supposed to, though, and he landed all wrong. I think he broke his neck, because he's not breathing anymore. I couldn't think of nothing else to do, so I just covered him up with hay. Khnom's still breathing, but I can't wake him up. What are we going to do?"

"Get that back door open," Althalus told him. "Ghend and I'll go get the rest of our gold. We'll decide what to do about Khnom when we get back."

Ghend was muttering curses as he and Althalus retraced their steps to the kitchen door. "What a stupid thing to have happen!" he flared hoarsely.

"Maybe we can wake Khnom if we throw water on him," Althalus said. "If that doesn't bring him around, we might have to tie him to his saddle and you'll have to lead his horse. We don't dare leave him behind. Galbak could probably squeeze the truth out of him in about half a minute. Let's get the rest of our gold first. Then we'll decide what to do about Khnom."

They picked up the other four bags of gold and returned to the hay barn. "Is he moving at all yet?" Ghend demanded of Gher.

"Not even a twitch," Gher replied. "I dumped cold water in his face, but he didn't come around. That Arum banged him real good with that bucket."

Ghend knelt beside his friend and began pinching his nose and slapping him across the cheeks.

"What *really* happened here, Gher?" Althalus whispered.

"It was *me* who hit Khnom with that bucket, Althalus," Gher admitted. "Khnom's real sneaky, and I got to thinking that he'd probably expect *me* to be sneaky, too—like maybe tiptoe up behind him and stab him in the back, or something like that. I sort of figured that the best way to be sneaky was to *not* be sneaky, so I just walked up to him carrying that bucket like I didn't even remember that it was still in my hand. He was looking right straight at me when I came up to him, and he was even smiling at me. I didn't even blink or nothing. I just swung that bucket at his head as hard as I could. He looked awful surprised when he fell down. Then I hit him on the head some more until Emmy told me to stop. She must have thought it was funny, because she was laughing. Then she told me that she'd fix it so that Khnom won't remember that I hit him." Gher looked just a bit ashamed. "It wasn't a very fancy cheat, Althalus," he apologized. "I didn't sneak or tiptoe or nothing like that the way I guess I was supposed to. I just walked right straight up to Khnom and whacked him on the head with that bucket, is all."

Althalus was trying very hard to keep from laughing out loud. "You done good, Gher," he said, fighting back his laughter. "You done *real* good."

"Eliar took Ghend's Book to Emmy, and then he came right back with it in the blink of an eye," Gher reported. "I guess she done what she needed to do, and the Book's right back where it was before I hit Khnom with the bucket."

"We did what we were supposed to do, then, and that's all that really matters. Let's get our gold tied to our saddles and get ready to leave."

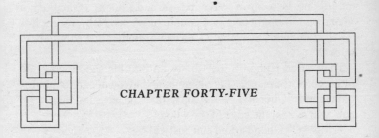

CHAPTER FORTY-FIVE

Ghend was fuming as they tied the bags of gold to their saddles, muttering swearwords in a dialect Althalus couldn't quite recognize. "It could have been worse, Ghend," Althalus told him. "It might be a little awkward leading Khnom's horse, but if he's tied to his saddle, he won't fall off. Gher and I'll see to it that nobody's following you, so you won't have to gallop."

"Maybe," Ghend growled. "Everything was going so well, though, and then *this* turned up."

Althalus shrugged. "These things happen sometimes. You can't anticipate everything. It could have been worse. The Arum could have killed Khnom and then raised the alarm."

"I suppose you're right." Ghend went to the open back door of the hay barn and squinted up at the star-studded night sky. "How long do you make it until morning?"

"Four hours anyway. We've still got lots of time."

"Are you sure you'll be coming to Hule later?" Ghend asked. "There's still that other matter I'd like to discuss with you."

"We'll get there," Althalus promised. "You and Khnom go on ahead, and we'll all get together again in Nabjor's camp. We work very well together, Ghend, and the notion of a partnership's starting to look better and better."

"How long do you think it'll be until you and Gher reach that camp?"

"A lot of that depends on how soon Gosti's people recover from the birthday party. If I've got a two-day head start, Gher and I'll only be a day or so behind you and Khnom. If they're hot on our trail, it might take us a couple of weeks. Nabjor's got lots of entertainments available in his camp, so the time should pass quickly."

They lifted Khnom's inert body up into his saddle and tied him securely in place. "Take Khnom and go on ahead," Althalus told Ghend. "Gher and I'll tidy up here in the barn and then we'll meet you over at the edge of the woods."

"Tidy up?" Ghend asked curiously

"We'll make everything here look exactly as it did before the party. If anything's out of place, somebody might start getting curious."

"What are you going to do with that dead Arum?"

"We'll just pile some more hay on top of him. The weather's still cool enough to keep him from spoiling for the next few days. After

Galbak discovers our little visit to the strong room, it won't really make much difference anyway. Have you got any cord, Ghend?"

"Cord?"

"I'll have to come up with a way to slip that bar back into place from the outside. We don't want to ride off and leave that door open and swinging in the wind."

"You're probably right." Ghend rummaged around in his saddlebags, taking out his Book in the process.

Althalus held his breath.

"Would this work?" Ghend asked, holding out a long leather thong.

"It should. Thanks."

"Don't mention it." Ghend put the Book back in the bag and then tied the bag shut. "Don't be too long here, Althalus," he said, swinging up into his saddle. "I'd like to be a long way from here by morning." Then he rode out through the door, leading Khnom's horse behind him.

"Why were you so jumpy just now?" Gher asked.

"I wasn't completely sure that he couldn't feel some slight difference in his Book," Althalus admitted. "Emmy's touch might have changed it."

"You're not really going to lock that door, are you?"

"Of course not. I just wanted to come up with the idea before Ghend did." He made some show of fumbling around with the bar on the door. Starlight isn't too bright, but Ghend had very strange eyes, and Althalus wasn't exactly sure just how well his enemy could see in the dark. Then he and Gher mounted their horses, crossed the brushy area between the wall of Gosti's fort and the nearby forest, and joined Ghend and the still-comatose Khnom. "That's about everything," he said. "I think you'd better hold your horse down to a walk, Ghend. If Khnom's horse starts to gallop, our sleeping friend might slide around until he trips the poor beast, and you'd have to stop and straighten him up again. You'll make better time after Khnom wakes up. Stay off that main trail, and move quietly when you're near any villages. Gher and I'll leave plenty of tracks and make enough noise to convince Galbak that we all rode south. You shouldn't have any trouble, but be careful anyway."

"Right," Ghend agreed. "We'll see you in Nabjor's camp, then."

"Have a nice trip," Althalus told him. Then he turned his horse. "Let's go south, Gher."

"Yes, sir," Gher replied.

After Ghend and his unconscious companion were out of sight, though, Althalus reined in his horse. "Are you there, Eliar?" he called back over his shoulder.

"Where did you think I'd be?" Eliar's voice came from just behind them.

"I thought that maybe Andine or Bheid had commandeered you. I'll pass our gold up to you. Put it in a safe place."

"I'll take good care of it," Eliar promised.

"Althalus," Dweia's voice murmured.

"Yes, Em?"

"You *could* return the gold to the strong room, you know."

"Don't be silly," he chided her.

"You don't really need it, love. You *do* have your own gold mine, you know."

"I worked hard for this gold, and I'm not about to give it back."

"Somehow I knew you were going to say that."

Althalus hefted the bags up over his head one by one, and Eliar's arms came out of nowhere to take them. Then Althalus and Gher returned to the unlocked back door of the hay barn, opened it, and went inside. "Let's get our horses back into the stable and unsaddled," Althalus said quietly as he barred the door. "Then we'll go to Gosti's hall and wake Galbak. I don't want Ghend to get too far ahead of him."

"Are there horse tracks on that trail so that Galbak and his men won't have much trouble?" Gher asked.

"There are two sets of tracks going north from the back door of the barn to the edge of Gosti's territory. They're so obvious that a child could follow them."

"Are you certain sure you'll be able to wake up Galbak?" Gher asked as he unsaddled his horse. "He was awful drunk when we left that big room where the party was."

"Eliar's already taken care of that," Althalus assured him, lifting off his own saddle. "It was something along the lines of what he did to Chief Twengor. Galbak took a quick trip to the day after tomorrow, and when Eliar brought him back, the worst of the effects of the party'd worn off. He still won't be feeling very well, but he'll understand what I'm trying to tell him." Althalus patted his horse's rump, and the animal obediently went back into its stall. Althalus looked around to make sure that nothing was out of place. "I guess that's got it," he said. "Let's go turn the tables on Ghend, shall we?"

"I thought we'd never get to that," Gher said eagerly.

"Once we're in the hall, I want you to slip inside and lie down somewhere close to Galbak."

"Tenlike I'm asleep, you mean?"

"Exactly. I'm going to spin a little story for Galbak that won't involve you. Just lie still and keep your eyes closed until Galbak starts screaming—which he *will* do after I tell him the story."

Gosti was snoring in his massive chair at the head of his table, and his clansmen were mostly sprawled on the floor. Althalus noticed that the general snoring was now punctuated with a few groans. "They seem to be coming around," Althalus told the boy. "Get to your place and try to look like you're asleep."

"Right," Gher said, moving quickly to a place not far from where Galbak lay stirring restlessly.

Althalus shambled toward the table, holding his head and contorting his face into an expression of suffering. He knelt beside Gosti's cousin, reached out and shook him slightly. "Galbak," he said in a wheezy sort of voice, "I think you'd better wake up."

Galbak snored.

Althalus shook him harder. "Galbak," he said a little louder. "Wake up. I think something's wrong."

Galbak groaned. "Oh, Gods!" he swore, putting one trembling hand to his forehead.

"Galbak!" Althalus said, urgently shaking him again. "Wake up!"

"Althalus?" Galbak said, his bleary eyes coming open. "What's wrong?"

"I think we got into a bad batch of mead," Althalus told him.

"I've been as sick as a dog for the last half hour. I just saw something out in the courtyard I think you ought to know about."

"My head's coming apart," Galbak groaned. "Let me go back to sleep. You can tell me about it in the morning."

"That might be too late," Althalus said in a worried voice. "Something's afoot here that isn't right, and I think you'd better look into it right now. I could be wrong, but I believe you've just been robbed."

"What!" Galbak came to a half-sitting position and grabbed the sides of his head with both hands. "God's blood!" he groaned. "What are you talking about, Althalus?"

"I woke up with my belly on fire a little while ago," Althalus told him. "I crawled out to the courtyard and turned my stomach inside out. I've been sick a few times before, but never like this. Anyway, right after I'd heaved up my toenails, I saw somebody sneaking across the yard. There were two of them, and they seemed to be carrying some bags that looked very heavy. They went past one of the torches out there, and I saw that it was Ghend and his servant Khnom. From the way they kept looking around, it was fairly obvious that they didn't want anybody to see them. Then Khnom dropped one of the bags he was carrying, and it made a jingling sort of sound. I can't swear to this, Galbak, but it sounded to me like a bagful of money."

Galbak jerked his hands away from his face and stared incredulously at Althalus.

"Anyway," Althalus hurried on, "they went into the stable, and after a couple of minutes, I heard a creaking sort of sound—like a door being opened. The sound seemed to be coming from the back of the hay barn. Then I heard a couple of horses galloping away. I think maybe you'd better go take a quick look at Gosti's strong room. My head wasn't any too clear, so I might have been imagining all that, but you should probably go have a look at the strong room, just to make sure."

Galbak scrambled to his feet. Then he doubled over, retching violently. "Come with me!" he barked at Althalus when he'd recovered.

They rushed to the corridor and on to the steps in front of the strong-room door. The guards were still snoring peacefully, and Galbak stepped over them and tried the door. Then he laughed weakly. "You scared me out of a year's growth there, Althalus," he said. "The door's still locked, though, so everything's still all right. You must have been having a nightmare of some kind."

"I think you'd better take a look inside, Galbak," Althalus suggested. "I've had a lot of nightmares before, but if that *was* a nightmare, it's the first one I've ever had that involved throwing up. I'd feel a lot better if you took a look to make sure everything's still all right."

"Maybe you're right," Galbak conceded, "and it won't cost anything to look." He took a large bronze key from the pouch at his waist, unlocked the strong-room door, and took the torch from the ring beside the door. Then he pulled the door open, raised the torch, and stepped inside.

Althalus concealed a sly smile. The pile of pennies on the floor and the overturned table should get Galbak's immediate attention.

Galbak was cursing when he came running out of the strong room. "You were right, Althalus!" he half shouted. "Come with me!"

Althalus nodded and followed the tall Arum back to the great hall. "On your feet!" Galbak roared, savagely kicking the clansmen awake. "We've been robbed!"

"What are you saying, Galbak?" Gosti demanded in a voice blurred with sleep.

"Your strong room's been opened, Gosti!" Galbak shouted to his cousin. "Somebody undid the lock and got inside! There are coins all over the floor, and several bags of gold are missing!"

Gosti scoffed. "You're drunk, Galbak. The main gate's locked. Nobody could get into the fort to rob me."

"He was already inside the fort, you dunce!" Galbak snapped. "It was Ghend and that man of his who robbed you! Althalus here saw them sneaking out with bags of your gold." He went back to kicking clansmen to their feet. "Get to the stables and saddle the horses! The robbers can't be far ahead of us! Move!"

"Will somebody tell me what's going on?" Gosti demanded.

"Tell him what you told me, Althalus," Galbak said.

"I woke up sick, Gosti," Althalus reported. "I stumbled out to the courtyard, and I was busy throwing away a lot of very good mead when I saw that fellow Ghend—the one who says he comes from Regwos. He and his friend were tiptoeing across your courtyard like a pair of chicken thieves sneaking out of a coop. People don't sneak that way unless they've got something to hide, so I watched them. Just before they got to the stable, Khnom dropped something he'd been carrying, and it made a sort of jingling sound when it hit the ground. They went on into the stable, and a minute or so later, I heard some horses galloping off to the north."

"Did you see them go out through the main gate?" Gosti demanded.

"No, actually I didn't, but I *did* hear horses galloping away."

"It must have been somebody else, then," Gosti said. "The main gate's the only way out of the fort."

"You're wrong, Gosti," the grey-haired old clansman Althalus recognized disagreed. "There's a back door in the hay barn. Nobody's used it for years, but it's still there. It might have been boarded up, but that Ghend fellow has been here long enough to have pried the boards loose."

"Galbak!" Gosti shouted. "Go look into the strong room!"

"I told you, Gosti," Galbak shouted back, "I already did! You've been robbed, cousin!"

"Chase the scoundrels down!" Gosti roared. "Get my gold back!"

"That's what I'm trying to do, you fat dolt!"

"Neat," Gher murmured to Althalus.

"I'm glad you liked it."

"What do we do now?"

"You stay here. If anybody asks, tell them that I've gone back outside to be sick again. We *don't* want to join the chase. I don't want Ghend to see us among his pursuers."

Galbak roused the rest of the clansmen with kicks and curses, and about a quarter of an hour later they were mounted and milling around in the courtyard. Galbak's scouts had found the tracks Althalus had carefully put down from the back of the hay barn to the trail that followed the river gorge. The main gate swung open, and Galbak led his men out in pursuit of the thieves.

Although everything had gone exactly according to his plan, Althalus felt a peculiar sort of discontent as he reentered Gosti's great hall. He genuinely liked Galbak, and he wasn't particularly proud of the way he'd deceived Gosti's tall cousin. It'd been a necessary part of the scheme, of course, and the ultimate goal of the scheme was commendable, but still . . .

"Galbak's got a good chance of catching the thieves, Gosti," he reported. "Ghend and Khnom haven't got much more than an hour's head start, and they're not as familiar with the surrounding territory as Galbak is." He gave the grossly fat Clan Chief a wry sort of smile. "It's a peculiar sort of thing to say, but Ghend's greed is actually working for *us*."

"I didn't follow that, Althalus," Gosti admitted.

"Gold's very heavy, Gosti," Althalus explained, "and from what Galbak was saying, there are about eight bags of it missing from your strong room."

Gosti groaned. "Eight bags!" he grieved.

"It'd be better if Ghend's greed had gone even further, but eight should be enough. Ghend and Khnom only have two horses, and the dead weight of those bags is going to slow those horses down. Galbak and his men are traveling light, so they'll be able to move faster. I'd guess that they'll catch up with those thieves by midafternoon."

"That makes very good sense, Althalus," Gosti said, his sweaty face breaking into a broad grin of relief.

"Evidently, your gold's very fond of you, Gosti. Notice how it cooperates with you and Galbak in the capture of those thieves."

"It *does*, doesn't it? I hadn't thought of that."

"You were meant to have that gold, Gosti, and now it's going out of its way to come back to you."

"I like your way of thinking, Althalus."

"It never hurts to look on the bright side."

Althalus and Gher remained in Gosti's hall for several days

after the robbery. Their fat host grew more and more unhappy as the messengers from Galbak failed to bring good news.

"I think it's just about time for us to move on," Althalus told Gher on the morning of the third day. "We'll cross Gosti's bridge and meet Eliar over on the other side of the river. Then we can go back to the House."

"I thought we'd be going to Hule to wait for Ghend."

"I want to talk with Emmy about that. We've tampered with reality quite a bit here lately, and I think we might want things to go back to the way they were last time before we wander off too much more. As far as I can tell, we've only opened up *one* new possibility. If we keep fooling around with it, a dozen or so more might crop up. I can handle two, but twelve or fourteen might stretch me a little thin."

"It'd be a lot funner, though," Gher said, his eyes brightening.

"Never mind," Althalus told him firmly.

They gathered up their belongings and went to Gosti's great hall. "We'd really like to stay, Gosti," Althalus apologized, "but I'm supposed to meet a fellow in Maghu this spring, and he'll be very put out with me if I leave him cooling his heels down there until summer. We've got some business to attend to, and he's a grouchy sort of man who hates delays."

"I understand, Althalus," Gosti replied.

"We'd like to cross your bridge, but I'm a little short of money right now. Do you suppose . . ." Althalus left it hanging.

"I'll send word to the men at the bridge," Gosti replied. "I think I owe you that much. Your stories brightened a long, dreary winter, and you *did* report the robbery. If you hadn't seen Ghend sneaking out of the fort, it might have been a week before we'd have known that he'd robbed us."

"I was hoping you'd see it that way. We'll stop by the next time we come through Arum. Then *you* can tell *me* the story of how Galbak caught Ghend and nailed him to a tree so that the wolves could eat him."

"I don't think Galbak would do that, Althalus."

"You might suggest it to him the next time you send a messenger in his direction."

Gosti's answering grin was evil. "It *would* make a pretty good story, wouldn't it?" he said.

"It would indeed, and if it got around, it'd probably be a long, long time before the notion of robbing you even occurred to anybody else."

Then Althalus and Gher went to the stable, saddled their horses, and rode out of Gosti's fort. The toll taker at the bridge waved them through, and they crossed the river in the bright spring sunshine.

"It went off pretty good, didn't it, Althalus?" Gher said proudly.

"Close to perfect, Gher," Althalus agreed. "I just wish we hadn't been forced to bamboozle Galbak in the process."

"Why should that bother you?"

Althalus shrugged. "I like him, and cheating him the way we did left a sour taste in my mouth."

"Eliar's just up ahead," Gher said, pointing. "If we sort of hurry right along maybe Emmy can fix us something to eat. I sure missed her cooking last winter."

"So did I, Gher."

Eliar beckoned them, and they followed him back into the woods. "Emmy's very impressed, Althalus," the young man said. "I didn't think she really approved of what you were doing, but she was laughing all the time while you two were leading Ghend around by the nose."

"She has an artistic temperament, Eliar," Althalus explained, "and the swindle Gher and I just put over on Ghend was a work of art. Give me just a little more time, and I'll make her one of the best thieves in the world."

They led their horses through the door that opened in the south wing of the House, and they were soon climbing the stairs to Dweia's tower.

"All hail the conquering hero," Leitha said.

"Why do you have to do that?" he asked her.

"It's a form of affection, Daddy." She gave him a radiant smile.

"Could I have a look at the imitation Book you made, Em?" he asked.

"It's over there on that marble bench, pet," she replied, pointing.

Althalus went to the bench and picked up the black Book. "The cover matches the real Book perfectly," he observed.

"Naturally."

He opened the lid of the box and took out the first sheet of parchment. He looked at the sheet closely. "It seems different, for some reason," he noted.

"That's probably because you can read it now," Dweia suggested.

"Maybe *that's* it. Back when Ghend showed me the real Book, none of it made any sense to me. I see that some of the words are still written in red." He frowned. "I thought I could read just about anything anybody'd written down, but I can't seem to get the meaning of those red words on this sheet."

"You don't really want to. Put it back in the box."

"Could we see how Ghend's doing, Emmy?" Gher asked hopefully. "I'll bet he's awful miserable by now."

"Moderately miserable, yes," Andine said with a wicked little giggle.

"Weren't you just a bit direct with Khnom, Gher?" Bheid asked. "The Knife told you to 'deceive,' not to 'bang him on the head.' "

"I had to work on that," Gher admitted as they crossed the room to the south window. "I didn't want to disappoint the Knife, but I had to get Khnom out of the way for long enough for me to grab Ghend's Book. Then it sort of came to me that 'deceive' *might* mean 'do something Khnom wouldn't expect me to do,' and getting thumped on the head was just about the last thing he expected."

"There's a weird sort of logic to that, I suppose," Bheid conceded.

"Things are definitely going to pot for poor Ghend," Leitha reported from the window. "Galbak's running him ragged down there."

"What a shame," Althalus said absently.

"What's troubling you, Althalus?" Dweia asked him. "I thought you'd be pleased at the way this turned out."

"I am—up to a point," he replied. "I just wish I'd been able to do it a little differently, that's all."

"It bothers Althalus that he had to trick Galbak while we were tricking Ghend," Gher explained. "Althalus and Galbak got along real good, and Althalus doesn't like to trick friends."

"Morality, Althalus?" Dweia asked in mock amazement.

"Ethics, Em," he corrected her. "There's a difference between ethics and morality. You *did* realize that, didn't you?"

"My perspective's a bit different, love," she replied. "Maybe when this is all over, we can discuss that issue for a few centuries."

"Doesn't Khnom do the same stuff Eliar does?" Gher asked suddenly. "I mean, isn't he Ghend's door opener?"

"Sort of," Dweia replied.

"What's giving them so much trouble down there, then? If we were the ones trying to run away, all we'd have to do is yell for Eliar and he'd pop open a door for us, we'd zip on through, and then we'd pop out someplace a hundred or maybe even a thousand miles away."

"It's not entirely their fault, Gher. Daeva keeps *his* agents on a very tight leash. He doesn't care for creativity, and he's extremely sensitive about the doors in Nahgharash. He doesn't want his people using them without his permission, and there are some rather extreme punishments for anybody who uses a door in Nahgharash *without* that permission."

"That's just silly, Emmy," Gher objected.

"That more or less describes my brother, yes," she agreed. "Both of them, actually."

"Dweia!" Bheid protested.

"They're silly in different ways, Bheid," she said, "but silly is silly, no matter how much we try to pretty it up. Both Deiwos and Daeva tinker with things—and people—most of the time. I'm just a bit more relaxed than they are. I've found that as long as my people love me, things are probably going to turn out the way I want them to." Then she looked at Althalus. "Were you planning to go to Hule sometime in the near future, love?" she asked pleasantly.

"I think we should talk about that, Em," he replied seriously. "Haven't we tampered just about enough?"

"I don't quite follow you."

"It was early autumn when Ghend came to Nabjor's camp last time. How much can change if he arrives in early summer? If he hires me to steal the Book then, won't I come to the House about three months early? And if I do, how many other things will change?"

She frowned slightly. "You may have a point, Althalus. There are a number of things that should stay more or less just the way they are."

"It shouldn't really be too hard to do it, Emmy," Gher said. "All we have to do is fix it so that Ghend and Khnom don't get away from Galbak quite so easy. We can watch him from your window, and every time he brushes out his horse tracks so that Galbak can't find his trail, Eliar can come along behind him and put down new tracks for Galbak to find. That way, Ghend ought to have a real nervous summer, and he won't get to Nabjor's camp until pretty close to the right time."

"It's worth a try, Em," Althalus agreed. "And if we do it that way, there's no particular urgency about getting to Nabjor's camp. That'll give me enough time to take a bath and put on some clean clothes at least."

"I think I'll faint."

"Quit trying to be funny, Em. After a few centuries, bathing gets to be a habit."

"You *are* planning to get rid of that ridiculous tunic, aren't you?"

"Not on your life. I just spent an entire winter arranging things so that I could *keep* my tunic instead of throwing it away."

"I thought the whole point of this past winter was to trick Ghend so that you could steal his Book."

"Well, there's that, too, but keeping this tunic was the main thing."

She sighed. "We've got further to go than I thought," she said.

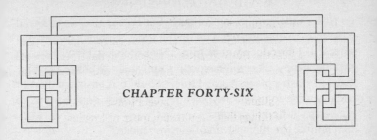

CHAPTER FORTY-SIX

"It's good to be home again," Gher said as he and Althalus rode north through deep-forested Hule in early autumn. "I sort of missed the trees." Then he frowned. "But they aren't really the same trees, are they?"

"Some of the smaller ones might be," Althalus replied.

"Do trees really live for that long?"

"Some of them do."

"And they just keep getting bigger and bigger, don't they?"

"Oh, I'd imagine there's some kind of limit."

"Just exactly where's this place where we're going?"

"You'll probably recognize it, Gher. It's the place where you joined us—right after Eliar and I caught you trying to steal our horses. It's one of those 'significant places' we come across from time to time."

"That's spooky," Gher said.

"You'll have to talk with Emmy about that." Althalus looked up at the massive trees around them. "We've changed a lot of things as we've gone along, but the trees are still the same, and I'm sure Nabjor's camp hasn't changed all that much either." Then he grinned. "I *do* feel better this time, though. I was in a foul humor last time. I'd just gone through a year of incredibly bad luck." Then he cocked his head to listen to a sound they'd been hearing since they'd first ridden through the door that had led them to Hule. "That's *also* a definite difference. Last time it was the wailing noise we used to hear every time we turned around. This time it's Eliar's Knife."

"That means that we're going to win, doesn't it?"

745

"It's a little hard to say for sure, but I'd say that we're ahead this time." Althalus peered on up the trail. "Nabjor's camp's just ahead. I'll introduce you to him. You'd probably better keep on talking sloppy. Ghend'll be along soon, and you talked that way back at Gosti's place. A good thief should be consistent. Part of what you're doing when you're trying to trick somebody is to make up a different person."

"Tenlike I'm him instead of me, you mean?"

"Exactly. There are a lot of tenlike people in every thief's saddlebags. You get to know them after a while, and you can pull out whichever one's going to work best." Then Althalus scratched his cheek thoughtfully. "I think I'd better use the happy tenlike Althalus this time. Last time I didn't have anything to talk about but my bad luck, but this time I'm up to my ears in good luck."

"That sort of means that you're in charge, doesn't it?"

"I think that was the whole idea, Gher. Last time, Ghend was running things; this time it's me. Go along with the story I'm going to spin for Nabjor. There won't be much truth to it, but that's not too important."

"I sort of think you're wrong, Althalus," Gher said. "We're changing things, so any story you tell anybody is true this time, isn't it? You're not really tenliking, are you?"

Althalus blinked.

"If I was you, the first thing I'd do is get rid of them dogs in that rich man's house in Deika. If he don't have dogs, things'll turn out a lot different, won't they? The neat part of this is that you can change anything that happened back then that you didn't like. This is *your* dream thing, so you can make it come out any way you want it to. No matter what kind of story you tell, it'll turn out to be the truth."

"You're starting to give me a headache again, Gher."

"It's not really *that* hard, Althalus. It'll be easy if you just remember that anything you say is the truth. You *can't* lie—even if you want to."

"You're making it worse." Althalus reined in his horse. "I'd better let Nabjor know that we're coming. He doesn't like to have people just ride into his camp without any kind of warning." He raised his voice then. "Ho, Nabjor," he called. "It's me—Althalus. Don't get excited. I'm coming in."

"Ho! Althalus!" Nabjor bellowed. "Welcome! I was starting to think that maybe the Equeros or the Treboreans had caught you and hung you up on a tree down there."

"Not a chance, Nabjor," Althalus called back. "You should know by now that nobody ever catches me. Is your mead ripe yet? That batch you had last time I passed through was just a trifle green."

"Come on in and try some," Nabjor invited. "This new batch came out rather well."

Althalus and Gher rode forward into the clearing, and Althalus looked at his old friend with a peculiar sense of sadness as "then" and "now" clashed in his mind. He knew that Nabjor was long dead in the world from which he and Gher had come to revisit the past, but there was Nabjor the same as always—big, burly, squinty eyed, and dressed in a shaggy bearskin tunic.

Althalus dismounted, and he and Nabjor clasped hands warmly. "Who's the boy?" Nabjor asked curiously.

"His name's Gher," Althalus replied, "and I've sort of taken him under my wing as an apprentice. He shows quite a bit of promise."

"Welcome, Gher," Nabjor said. "Sit you down, gentlemen. I'll fetch us some mead and you can tell me all about the splendors of civilization."

"Ah, no mead for the boy," Althalus said quickly. "Gher's got an older sister who doesn't really approve of drinking. She doesn't get upset about lying, cheating, or stealing, but she can go on for weeks about some of the simpler pleasures of life. If word happened to get back to her that I was leading Gher astray, she might haul him back home."

"I've met a few like that," Nabjor said. "Sometimes women get a little strange. I've got some cider that hasn't turned yet. Would that be all right for your apprentice?"

"I don't think she'd find any fault with cider."

"Good. Mead for us and cider for Gher, then. That's a haunch of forest bison on that spit over the fire. Help yourselves to some of it. I'll bring a loaf of bread, too."

Althalus and Gher seated themselves on a log by the fire and carved some chunks of meat from the spitted haunch while Nabjor filled two cups with foaming mead and a third with golden cider. "How did things do down there in civilization?" he asked.

Althalus realized that *this* was the important moment. This would change things. "It went beyond my wildest expectations, Nabjor," he replied expansively. "My luck was smiling at me every step of the way. She still absolutely adores me." He took a long drink of his mead. "You got a good run on this batch, my friend," he complimented Nabjor.

"I thought you might like it."

"It's good to come home where I can get mead to drink. Down there in civilization, they don't seem to know how to brew it. The only thing you can buy in their taverns is sour wine. How's business been?"

"Not bad at all," Nabjor replied expansively. "Word's getting around about my place. Just about everybody in Hule knows by now that if he wants a good cup of mead at a reasonable price, Nabjor's camp is the place to go. If he wants the companionship of a pretty lady, this is the place. If he's stumbled across something valuable that he wants to sell with no embarrassing questions about how he came by it, he knows that if he comes here, I'll be glad to discuss it with him."

"You're going to fool around and die rich, Nabjor."

"If it's all the same to you, I'd rather live rich. All right, since that's out of the way, tell me what happened down there in the low country. I haven't seen you for more than a year, so we've got a lot of catching up to do."

"You're not going to believe just how well things went, Nabjor," Althalus replied with a broad grin. "Everything I touched down there turned to gold." He laid an affectionate hand on Gher's shoulder. "This boy here has luck that's at least as good as mine, and when you pour both of them into the same pot, we just can't possibly lose—as we discovered when we got to Deika. After we'd looked at all their fancy stone buildings, we just 'happened' to overhear talk about a rich salt merchant named Kweso. I'm positive that it wasn't really a coincidence. My luck was herding us from one direction, and Gher's was coming from the other. Anyway, if you've bought any salt lately, I'm sure you can understand how a salt merchant can end up richer than any gold miner in the world."

"Oh, yes," Nabjor agreed. "They're the worst gougers there are."

"Well," Althalus went on, "we located this Kweso fellow's house, and I sent Gher up to the door to ask for directions to the place where one of the neighbors lived—*and* to have a close look at the latch on Kweso's door."

"It wasn't much of a latch, Mister Nabjor," Gher added. "It *looked* big and strong, but I could have sprung it open with my thumbnail."

"Is this boy *that* good?" Nabjor asked Althalus.

"Why do you think I took him on as my apprentice?" Althalus replied. "Well, to cut it short, we went to Kweso's house along about midnight a couple of days later, undid that latch, and went on inside. Kweso's servants were all asleep, and Kweso himself was filling all the corners of his bedroom with snores. He stopped snoring when I set the point of my knife against his throat, though, and he was very cooperative. There's nothing quite like a knife point to get somebody's attention. A few minutes later, Gher and I came into a great deal of money. We thanked Kweso for his hospitality, tied him up, and stuffed a rag into his mouth to keep him from disturbing the sleep of his servants. Then we left the splendid city of Deika. We even bought some horses. Now that we were rich, we didn't have to walk anymore."

"Where did you go next, Althalus?" Nabjor asked eagerly.

"We made our next stop in Kanthon," Althalus replied. "That's a city up in northern Treborea. There's a new ruler in the city, and he's got some peculiar ideas about taxes."

"What are taxes?"

"I'm not entirely sure. The way it seems to work is that people have to pay to live in their own houses and breathe all the precious air that the ruler of the place so generously provides.

Breathing's *very* expensive in Kanthon—about half of everything a man owns usually covers most of it. The local rich men seem to think that it's not a very good idea to *look* rich. Shabby, broken-down furniture's very expensive in Kanthon, and rich men take lessons from stonemasons to learn how to lay flagstones very neatly, so that the tax collectors can't identify the flat rock that covers the hole in the floor where the rich man hides his gold. My luck—and Gher's—herded us into a tavern where the stonemasons of Kanthon did their drinking, and they just *happened* to be talking about a fellow who'd just inherited a fortune from his uncle. Those masons were laughing themselves sick over the sloppy job he'd done laying that particularly important rock. From what they were saying, the fellow was one of those ne'er-do-wells who spend all their nights carousing around in the seedier establishments down by the river, and I guess his hands were a bit shaky the day he set the stone in place. To make things even better for us, the fellow's servants had appetites of their own that were the same as his. They'd piously promise to look after things while he was out enjoying himself, but a quarter of an hour after he went out the front door, his house was deserted."

Nabjor chuckled. "What a shame."

"Well, Gher and I just happened to come into *more* money that very same evening. By now, we had so much money that carrying it was turning into quite a chore, so after we left Kanthon, we found a secluded place and buried it—and that wasn't the last time, either. We've got money buried in a half dozen places down there, because we had more than we could carry, and every time we turned around, more of it kept piling up on us."

Nabjor laughed. "You know, I just can't seem to remember the last time I had *that* problem."

Althalus glossed over his encounter with paper money, since the concept was a little exotic for Nabjor. "I could go on for days telling you about all the swindles and robberies we pulled off down there, but our biggest success was in Arum, of all places."

"I've heard that they've struck gold down there," Nabjor said.

"Don't tell me that you finally broke down and started digging your own gold."

"Not *this* old dog," Althalus replied. "I let somebody else take care of that for me. Gher and I'd come up out of Perquaine and we were hotfooting our way back here to Hule. Well, we stopped in a wayside tavern, and there was this fellow who had a splendid tunic—wolf skin, it was, and the ears decorated the hood of that tunic."

"I see that some ownership got transferred," Nabjor said, eying the tunic Althalus was wearing. "Did you swindle that fellow out of it, or did you just break down and buy it from him?"

"Bite your tongue! I *steal* gold, Nabjor; I don't spend it. Anyway, the loafers in the tavern were talking about a rich man called Gosti Big Belly who owns and operates a toll bridge that just *happens* to be the only way to cross a certain river that stands between the rest of Arum and the region where gold's just been discovered. The price Gosti charges to cross is outrageous, but people are glad to pay it, and this Gosti is getting richer by the hour. Well, I'm not one to pass up an opportunity like that, so I decided to look into the matter."

"*After* you'd transferred some ownership?" Nabjor asked slyly, looking at the wolf-skin tunic.

Gher smirked. "That didn't hardly take no time at all, Mister Nabjor. The fellow in the tunic went outside the tavern after a while, and Althalus followed him, popped him on the head with the handle of his sword, and took his tunic and his shoes."

Nabjor raised one eyebrow.

"I'll admit it went a little far," Althalus conceded apologetically, "but my shoes were just about ready to fall apart. That fellow didn't really need shoes all that much: he wasn't too likely to walk very far away from that tavern. Anyway, Gher and I mounted up and rode on. After a day or so we stopped at another tavern, and the people there were talking about Gosti Big Belly, the same as the ones in the other tavern had been. Gher and I picked up some more details, and I began to realize that robbing Gosti might go a little further than a simple "smash and grab" sort of thing, so we were probably going to need some help. That's where our luck stepped in again. My luck's always been sort of sneaky, and Gher's is even worse. There were two other fellows in that tavern, and I'd noticed them the minute we walked in, because I could tell by their looks that they weren't Arums. Their eyes lit up like torches every time somebody said the word 'gold,' so I was fairly sure they were in the same business as we are. We talked with them after we all left the tavern, and we decided to go into partnership instead of competing with each other."

"We went into Gosti's place separate, though," Gher added. "Our idea was to tenlike we didn't know each other. The other stealers was named Ghend and Khnom, and we didn't even go near them—not out where any of Gosti's people could see us, anyway—but we'd meet late at night in the stables or the hay barn to make our plans. We spent a whole winter there and got to know every log in the place by its first name. Then Althalus happened to hear a couple of old coots arguing about a back door to the barn with one coot saying there was one and the other saying there wasn't, even though all they'd have had to do was go to the barn and look, but they was having so much fun arguing that they didn't want to spoil it. Me and Althalus weren't having no argument, though, so we *did* go look, and it turned out that the coot who said 'was' was right, and the coot who said 'wasn't' wasn't—except that there was a haystack piled up in front of that old door. I was the one who got to move that haystack, because Althalus told me I was supposed to tenlike I wanted to jump out of the loft into it. I wasn't too happy that I was the one who was going to have to do all the work—except that it didn't turn out that way at all, because all the Arums heard what I was doing, and they thought that jumping in the hay might be funner than just sitting around watching Gosti eat and get fatter. So they pitched in and helped me move the haystack, but even though I did a lot of the work, I didn't get to jump in the hay more'n two or three times, 'cause the Arums was lined up clear out into the courtyard waiting for their turn to jump. I don't think that was very fair at all, do you?"

Nabjor was staring at Gher with an awestruck expression. "Doesn't he ever stop to breathe?" he asked Althalus.

"I haven't looked too closely, but I think he might have gills or something under his collar. I've heard him talk steadily for two straight hours without stopping once to catch his breath. Once he starts, you'd better lean back and get comfortable, because he's likely to go on for quite a long time." Althalus paused. "Well, to continue, spring finally rolled around, and Gosti's cousin told me that they always celebrated Gosti's birthday when the last of the snow melted off, and that fit into our plans perfectly. The trails would be clear, and everybody in Gosti's hall would be so drunk that an earthquake or a volcano wouldn't attract much attention."

"Beautiful!" Nabjor chuckled.

"We sort of liked it. Anyway, Gher and Khnom went to the stables to saddle the horses while Ghend and I stepped over the two sleeping men who were supposed to be guarding the strong room. We undid that latch that *looked* very impressive but that a child of four could have opened. Then we went into Gosti's strong room to have a look at our new gold."

"Was there very much?" Nabjor asked eagerly.

"More than we could carry, that's for sure."

"I could carry a lot of gold, Althalus."

"Not *that* much, you couldn't. It took me a while to explain to Ghend that a robbery isn't a success until you've gotten away. He had wild ideas about stealing horses to carry the excess and other absurdities, but I finally managed to persuade him that staying unhung was going to be a major goal in our lives after we'd taken a few bags out of the strong room, and that attracting attention wouldn't be the best way to achieve that goal."

"Whatever happened to that Ghend fellow?" Nabjor asked.

"I'm not entirely sure. We split up after we left Gosti's fort— to confuse anybody who might decide to follow us—but if they managed to get away, he and Khnom are supposed to meet us here. Back at Gosti's fort, Ghend was telling me that he might have a business proposition for me, and I'm always interested in business."

"It sounds to me as if you've made enough money this past year to retire on."

Althalus laughed. "I wouldn't know what to do with myself, Nabjor. Sitting around growing moss isn't my style."

"More mead?" Nabjor suggested.

"I thought you'd *never* get around to asking that," Althalus said, holding out his empty cup.

Nabjor took their cups back to the narrow crevice between two standing boulders where he kept his mead crocks.

Nicely done, pet, Emmy's voice murmured approvingly. *You managed to mix this time and the last time together so smoothly that it's almost impossible to separate them.*

It's a gift, Em. Always mix a certain amount of truth into your lies. Of course, according to Gher, the story I told this time is the truth and last time was the lie.

Quit showing off, Althalus, she chided.

Nabjor brought their cups back, and the three of them sat by the fire talking until well after nightfall. Althalus noticed that his friend had a new wench in camp. She had wicked eyes and a provocative way of walking, and he thought that under different circumstances, it might be sort of nice if they got to know each other a little better. Emmy probably wouldn't approve, though.

After a while, Gher dozed off, but Althalus and Nabjor talked until almost midnight. Then Althalus fetched the blankets he and Gher had carried rolled up behind their saddles. He covered the boy without waking him, and then he rolled up in his own blankets near the dying fire and fell asleep almost immediately.

Gher rose early the next morning, but Althalus slept late. There wasn't really anything very pressing to take care of, so he felt that it was a good time to catch up on his sleep. He was fairly sure he'd want his wits about him when Ghend and Khnom arrived, and a man who's been missing sleep for a while tends to be a bit fuzzy-minded at times when it's important for him to be on his toes.

It was about midmorning when he finally arose, and when he was going to the brook to splash some water on his face, he saw Gher seated on a log beside the naughty-eyed wench. The boy's hair was wet as if it'd just been washed, and the wench appeared to be darning one of his socks. Althalus shook his head in bafflement. There seemed to be something about Gher that made every woman he came across automatically want to mother him. Andine had done it, and to a lesser degree, so had Leitha. Emmy didn't really count, of course, because Emmy mothered everybody.

Althalus and Gher loafed around Nabjor's camp for at least a week, and then one blustery day when the racing clouds overhead were blotting out the sun, Ghend and Khnom rode into camp.

"Well, *finally*," Althalus said by way of greeting. "What took you so long to get here?"

"I thought you were supposed to keep Galbak off our tails, Althalus," Ghend replied, wearily swinging down from his exhausted horse. "He was hot on our trail before the sun was fully up."

"The devil you say!" Althalus replied. "Are you sure you stayed away from the Hule road?"

"We did everything just the way you suggested," Khnom told him, "and none of it worked the way it was supposed to. I think that accursed Galbak's part bloodhound. Every time we passed over soft ground, we were careful to brush out our tracks, but he followed us anyway. This has been the worst summer in my life. We even tried wading twenty miles up a river, and Galbak *still* followed us. How did you two get away?"

Althalus shrugged. "It was easy. We rode south a ways—leaving plenty of tracks—and then we picked a rocky place to leave the road, crossed the mountains into Kagwher, and came to Hule from that direction. We were positive that you two had gotten away clean, too. Why would Galbak follow a road with no signs, instead of the one that was littered with tracks?"

"I think he outsmarted us, Althalus," Ghend said mournfully. "Maybe we were just a little too obvious. Evidently Galbak's shrewd enough to be suspicious about a trail that jumps up and hits him right in the face."

"I can't for the life of me see how Galbak was able to get on your trail so fast," Althalus said. "He was dead to the world when I left the dining hall. I was positive he wouldn't wake up before noon, and when he *did* wake up, he should have been too sick to even care about Gosti's gold."

"I think we both overlooked just how big Galbak is," Ghend said. "A big man can soak up a lot more strong drink than a smaller man can."

"Well, at least you two were finally able to get clear, and that's what matters. You're safe here, so you can sit down and relax." He turned slightly. "Mead, Nabjor," he called, "and keep it coming. These are the two friends I told you about, and they've had a very bad summer."

Ghend wearily seated himself on one of the logs by the fire pit and rubbed at his face. "I could sleep for a week," he said.

"This is a good place for it," Althalus told him. "How did you two finally manage to shake off Galbak?"

"Pure luck, more than anything else," Khnom replied. "Arums do a lot of hunting in those mountains of theirs—deer, bear, and those big stags with huge horns—so they're expert trackers. No matter what we did, we couldn't seem to shake them off. We holed up for a week in a cave that was back behind a waterfall, and then one of those summer storms came along— the kind of storm that even rains straight up. I'm sure we left tracks when we rode out of the cave, but our tracks were gone almost before we put them down. We made it up to the ridgeline, and after that, it was easy."

Nabjor brought mead, and Ghend and Khnom started to relax. "Help yourselves to a bit of that haunch on the spit," Nabjor told them.

"How much is it going to cost us?" Khnom asked.

"Don't worry about it. Althalus has already taken care of it."

"Why, thank you, Althalus," Khnom said. "That was considerate."

"Well, I *did* sort of invite you two to come here," Althalus reminded him. "Besides, since we're all so stinking rich now, the money doesn't really mean anything, does it?"

"Bite your tongue," Khnom said. "Did you two actually bring your share of that gold into a place like this?"

"Do I really look *that* stupid, Khnom?" Althalus replied. "We just took out enough for current expenses and put the rest in a safe place."

"Oh? Where might that be?"

"It wouldn't really be a safe place if we went around talking about it, now would it?"

A sudden flash of bitter disappointment crossed Khnom's face before he could conceal it, and Althalus smiled inwardly. The knowledge that four bags of gold were hidden somewhere nearby and that there was no way he could find out exactly where was probably causing Khnom more pain than Gher's bucket had.

They had a few more cups of mead and several slabs of roast bison, and after Ghend and Khnom relaxed a bit, Althalus decided that it was time to get down to business. "You were saying something about a business proposition last winter, Ghend," he said. "Has that fallen by the wayside, or would you still like to discuss it?"

"No," Ghend replied, "it's still roaming around in the back of my mind. As it happens, there's someone in Nekweros who's holding some obligations over my head, and he's not the sort of fellow anybody in his right mind wants to disappoint—if you take my meaning."

"One of *those*, I take it?"

"He's the one who invented 'those,' my friend. People who cross *that* one usually live just long enough to regret it. Anyway, there's something he *really* wants, and he strongly suggested that he'd like to have me go get it for him. Unfortunately, the thing he wants is in a house over in Kagwher, and that puts me in a very tight spot. I'm not terribly popular in Kagwher just now. Khnom and I had a very successful season there a couple of years ago, and Kagwhers tend to hold grudges. There are a couple of fellows over there who make Galbak look gentle by comparison, and those fellows would *really* like to see me again."

"I can see your problem, Ghend. There are quite a few places that *I* should probably avoid, too."

"Exactly. You're a very good thief, Althalus, so I know I can depend on you. I think you're just the man I've been looking for."

"I'm the best," Althalus said with a deprecating shrug.

"He's right about that, Ghend," Nabjor said, bringing them cups of fresh mead. "Althalus here can steal anything with two ends."

"That might be a slight exaggeration," Althalus said. "I've

never stolen a river. What exactly is it that this terror over in Nekweros wants you to steal for him? Is it some jewel, or what?"

"No, it's not a jewel," Ghend replied with a hungry look. "What he wants—and will pay for—is a book."

"I like the word 'pay' well enough," Althalus said, "but now we come to the hard part. What in blazes is a book?"

Ghend looked sharply at him. "You don't know how to read, do you?"

"Reading's for priests, Ghend, and I don't have any dealings with priests if I can avoid it."

Ghend frowned. "This might complicate things just a bit," he said.

"Ghend, old friend, I don't know a thing about stone cutting, but I've stolen a lot of jewels in my time; and I haven't got the faintest idea of how to cook gold out of rocks, but I still manage to pick up quite a bit of it from time to time. Just tell me what this book thing looks like, and I'll go steal it for you—if the price is right, and if you tell me where I'll find it."

"You probably could at that," Ghend agreed. "I just happen to have a book with me. If I show it to you, you'll know what you're looking for."

"Exactly," Althalus said. "Why don't you trot your book out, and Gher and I'll have a look. We don't have to know what it says to be able to steal it, do we?"

"No," Ghend agreed, "I guess you don't at that." He rose to his feet, went over to his horse, reached inside the leather bag tied to his saddle, and took out his black Book. Then he brought it back to the fire.

"It's just a leather box, isn't it?" Gher observed.

"It's what's inside that's important," Ghend said, opening the lid. He took out a sheet of parchment and handed it to Althalus. "That's what writing looks like," he said. "When you find a box like this one, you'd better open it before you steal it to make sure it has sheets like that one inside instead of buttons or knitting needles."

Althalus held up the sheet and looked at it, feigning a look of blank incomprehension. "Is this what writing's supposed to look like?" he demanded. "It looks to me like meaningless scrawling."

"You've got it upside down," Khnom told him.

"Oh." Althalus turned the page and looked at it blankly for a while. "It still doesn't make any sense," he said.

It was all he could do, however, to keep from throwing the dreadful sheet into the fire. The Book of Daeva was not something for the faint at heart, and some of the words on the page seemed almost to leap into flame right before his eyes. "I still can't make any sense out of this," he lied, handing the sheet of parchment back to Ghend, "but that's not important. All I really need to know is that I'm looking for a black box with leather sheets inside."

"The box we want is white," Ghend corrected as he reverently replaced the sheet in the box. "Well," he said then, "are you interested in the proposition?"

"I'll need a few more details," Althalus replied. "Just exactly where is this book, and how well is it guarded?"

"It's in the House at the End of the World over in Kagwher."

"I know where Kagwher is," Althalus said, "but exactly where in Kagwher is this place?"

"Up north. It's up in that part of Kagwher that doesn't see the sun in the winter and where there isn't any night in summer."

"That's a peculiar place for somebody to live."

"Truly. The owner of the book doesn't live there anymore, though, so there won't be anybody there to interfere with you when you go inside the House to steal the book."

"That's convenient. Can you give me any kind of landmarks? I can move faster if I know where I'm going."

"Just follow the Edge of the World. When you see a House, you'll know it's the right place. It's the only House up there."

Althalus drank off his mead. "That sounds simple enough," he said. "Now, then, after I've stolen the book, how do I find you to get my pay?"

"I'll find you, Althalus." Ghend's deep-sunk eyes burned even hotter. "Believe me, I'll find you."

"I'll think about it."

"You'll do it, then?"

"I said I'd think about it. Now, why don't we have some more of Nabjor's mead? I seem to have come into some money here lately, so we can afford to have a good time."

They talked and drank mead until well after sundown, and after a while, Nabjor began to yawn rather ostentatiously.

"Why don't you go to bed, Nabjor?" Althalus suggested.

"I have to mind the store, Althalus."

"Just mark the side of the crock, Mister Nabjor," Gher suggested. "Put a line where the mead is now and another line where it is in the morning. That way you'll know how much we drank. I can carry their cups to them."

Nabjor threw a quick glance at Althalus.

Althalus nodded, and then he winked.

"I *am* just a little tired," Nabjor admitted. "You gentlemen wouldn't mind if I left you to take care of yourselves, would you?"

"Not a bit," Khnom told him. "We're all old friends here, so we won't start brawling and breaking up your furniture."

Nabjor laughed. "I'd hardly call a few peeled logs furniture," he said. "Good night then, gentlemen." He crossed the clearing to the roughly built hut where he slept.

Gher took over the chore of bringing mead to the men at the fire, and Althalus soon noticed that *his* mead had been watered down noticeably; he suspected that the mead Ghend and Khnom were drinking had also been altered, but *not* with water.

It didn't really take very long for the doctored mead Ghend and Khnom were drinking to begin to show some results. They'd been exhausted when they'd come into camp anyway, and the mead Gher was serving them soon pushed them over the edge. The fire in Ghend's eyes grew dim, and Khnom began to sway from side to side on the log where he sat. After two more cups of the doctored mead they both slid off the log and began to snore.

"Where did you get the special mead?" Althalus asked Gher.

"The lady who's been darning my socks told me about it. Nabjor uses it on some of his customers now and then—*if* they've got a lot of money, but don't want to spend it."

"Just exactly what are you up to, Althalus?" Nabjor demanded in a hoarse whisper as he came out of his hut. "Aren't those two your friends?"

"I wouldn't go quite *that* far, Nabjor," Althalus replied. "Business associates, yes, but not exactly friends. Ghend's trying to bamboozle me into stealing something for him that's a lot more valuable than he cares to admit, and it's in a place that's so dangerous that he's afraid to go steal it himself. That's hardly the act of a friend, now is it?"

"Not hardly," Nabjor agreed. "If you're going to kill them, don't do it here."

"Oh, we're not going to kill them, Nabjor," Althalus said with a wicked grin. "I'm just going to prove to Ghend that I'm a lot slicker than he is. Go fetch our imitation Book, Gher."

"Right," Gher said, grinning broadly.

"I thought you didn't know what a book was," Nabjor said. "You certainly made quite a show of that."

"It's called 'playing dumb,' Mister Nabjor," Gher said. "It's always easy to swindle somebody who thinks he's smarter than you are." Gher went to where their saddles were and took out the book Dweia had given them. "Do you want me to switch them now, Althalus?" he asked.

"That's your job, Gher. Just make sure that Ghend's saddlebag looks the same when you're finished."

"And did you want to show me how to walk, too?" Gher asked.

"That boy's got a very clever mouth, doesn't he?" Nabjor said.

"I know," Althalus agreed. "He's good though, so I put up with him." He fished a gold coin out of his purse and held it up for Nabjor to see. "Do me a favor, old friend. Ghend and Khnom drank quite a bit of your special mead before they drifted off, and they won't be feeling very good when they wake up. They'll need some medicine to make them feel better. Give them as much of that doctored mead as they can drink, and if they're feeling delicate again the day after tomorrow, get them well again with the same medicine."

"How did you find out about my special mead?"

"I've used doctored mead occasionally myself, Nabjor, so I recognize the effects."

"Are you going to steal their gold, too?"

"No, I don't want them to get excited and start looking at Ghend's book *too* closely. It's a fairly good copy, but it's not entirely the same. Keep the two of them drunk and happy, and if they ask, tell them that I've gone to Kagwher to steal that other book for them."

"After this is all over, come on back and tell me how it all turned out," Nabjor said with a broad grin.

"I'll do that," Althalus promised, even though he knew that this was the last time he'd ever see Nabjor. "Be the friendly tavern keeper, my friend," he said. "Cure Ghend and Khnom of any unwholesome urges to follow Gher and me. I don't like to be followed when I'm working, so make them good and drunk right here, so that I don't have to make them both good and dead somewhere up in the mountains."

"You can depend on me, Althalus," Nabjor said, eagerly snatching the gold coin from his friend's fingers.

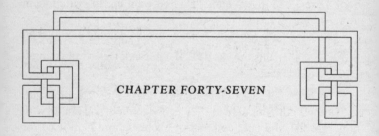

CHAPTER FORTY-SEVEN

Althalus had a peculiar sense of dislocation as he and Gher rode east from Nabjor's camp through the tag end of night. Their elaborate modification of the past had gone well—almost too well, perhaps. Their alterations hadn't really been all that extensive, but they'd set some things in motion that Althalus didn't fully understand.

"You're awful quiet," Gher said as they rode through the forest.

"I'm just a little edgy, that's all," Althalus told him. "I think we might have opened some doors that we didn't really want to."

"Emmy can take care of it."

"I'm not sure she's supposed to. I get the feeling that *I'm* the one who'll have to deal with it."

"How much longer are we going to keep poking along like this?" Gher asked. "We could just give Eliar a shout and go home in a blink, you know."

"I don't think we should, Gher. It's only a hunch, but I think there are some things that happened last time that we'd better not step over."

"Like what?"

"I don't *know*. That's what's making me edgy. I think we'd better just stay on the ground."

"Did you float this past Emmy?"

"Not yet. I'll get around to it—one of these days."

"You're going to get yourself yelled at, Althalus."

Althalus shrugged. "It won't be the first time. I think we've changed just about enough of the past. We swindled Ghend, I got to keep my tunic, and we stole the Book of Daeva. I don't think we want to change anything else. Something happened last time that *has* to happen this time as well. If it doesn't, this whole thing might fall apart on us."

"Are you certain sure you didn't get hold of Ghend's cup by mistake back there in Nabjor's camp? You're not making much sense right now."

"We'll see."

The dawn came up murky and sullen over deep-forested Hule, and Althalus and Gher rode east among the gigantic trees. "We need to watch out for wolves," Althalus cautioned.

"Wolves?" Gher sounded a bit surprised. "I hadn't heard that there are any wolves in Hule."

"There were—are—now. We're in a different Hule right now. This isn't the place you're familiar with. It's a lot wilder than it's going to be later on. The wolves shouldn't be much of a problem, since we've got horses this time and we'll be able to outrun them, but keep your eyes and ears open."

"It was real exciting back then, wasn't it?"

"It had its moments. Let's move right along, Gher. If Nabjor does what he's supposed to do, it should be quite some time before Ghend wakes up to what we've done, but I want to get a long way ahead of him—just to be on the safe side."

"What could he do?"

"Put an army out in front of us, possibly. He still has access to Pekhal and Gelta at this particular time, you know."

"I hadn't thought of that," Gher admitted.

"I didn't think you had."

"Maybe we should gallop for a while."

"Excellent idea, Gher."

Because they were mounted, they covered the distance between Nabjor's camp and the edge of the vast forest in less than half the time it'd taken Althalus before. The trees thinned as they moved up into the highlands of Kagwher and turned north, retracing the route Althalus had taken some twenty-five centuries ago rather closely.

The air turned chill as they moved north, and then one frosty night as they sat near their campfire, Althalus saw a familiar sight in the northern sky. "I think we're getting closer," he told Gher.

"Oh?"

Althalus pointed to the north. "God's fire," he said. "I couldn't swear to it, but I think we're getting closer to one of those things that has to happen this time in more or less the way it did last time."

"I wish you could give me some hints about what we're supposed to be looking for."

"So do I. I just hope we'll recognize it when it comes along."

"Well, I hope so, too. We're getting awful close to winter, you know, and we're still a long way from home."

"We'll make it in time, Gher," Althalus assured him. "That's one thing I can be sure of. I've been through this before, you know."

Just before sunrise the next morning, they were awakened by a human voice—a voice Althalus recognized. "Don't be alarmed," he told Gher quietly. "This is that crazy man I told Gosti about. He's not dangerous."

He was a bent and crooked old man, and he was shambling along with the aid of a staff. His hair and beard were silvery white, and he was garbed in animal skins. His face was deeply lined, and his eyes were shrewd and alert. He was talking in a resonant voice, speaking in a language Althalus could not quite recognize.

"Ho, there," Althalus called to the crazy man. "We mean you no harm, so don't get excited."

"Who's that?" the old man demanded, seizing his staff in both hands and brandishing it.

"We're just travelers, and we seem to have lost our way."

The old man lowered his staff. "Don't see many travelers around here," he said. "They don't seem to like our sky."

"We noticed that fire in the sky ourselves, just last night. Why does it do that?"

"People say it's supposed to be a warning. Some think that the world ends a few miles to the north of here, and that God set the night sky on fire to warn everybody to stay back."

Althalus frowned slightly. The crazy old man didn't seem to be quite as crazy as he'd been last time, and he didn't look quite the same either. "It sounds to me as if you don't quite agree with those who say that the world ends someplace around here," he noted.

The old man shrugged. "People can believe anything they want to," he said. "They're wrong, of course, but that's none of *my* business, is it?"

"Who were you talking to just now?" Althalus asked, trying to wrench the conversation back to the track he remembered.

"I was talking to myself, of course. Do you see anybody else out there for me to talk to?" Then the old man straightened and indifferently tossed his staff away. "It's not going to work, Althalus," he said. "You've changed too many things. Our conversation won't be the same as it was last time." He made a wry face.

"Of course, it was fairly silly last time, if I remember it correctly, and we have more important things to discuss. When you get back to the House and see my sister, tell her that I love her." He smiled faintly. "Dweia and I don't agree about too many things, but I love her just the same. Tell her that I said to be *very* careful this time. This scheme you all cooked up was clever, certainly, but it's extremely dangerous. Our brother's shrewd enough to have guessed what you've been up to by now, so he won't let Dweia get away with what she's planning without a fight."

"Are you who I think you are?" Althalus choked.

"Can't you accept the obvious without asking all these idiotic questions, Althalus? I'd have thought that Dweia'd slapped that out of you by now."

"Were *you* the one I met here last time as well?"

"Obviously. Dweia was waiting for you in the House, and she hates to be kept waiting—or had you noticed that? You needed directions, so I came here and gave them to you. That's part of my job. You already know the way this time, so I'm here to give you some advice instead."

"Advice? Don't you mean commands?"

"That isn't the way it works, Althalus. You have to make your own decisions—and accept the consequences, of course."

"Dweia gives us orders all the time."

"I know. She even tries to give *me* orders. I usually ignore her, though."

"Doesn't that make things awful noisy?" Gher asked.

"*Very* noisy, but that's part of the fun. She's absolutely adorable when she flares up like that, so I nudge her in that direction every so often. It's a game we've been playing for a long, long time, but that's a family matter that doesn't really involve you." Then the old man's face grew deadly serious. "You haven't seen the last of Ghend, Althalus. You'll meet him one more time, so you'd better be ready for him."

"What am I supposed to do?"

"You'll have to decide that for yourself. When you chose to go back and change things, you changed other things as well. Your scheme was very clever, I'll grant that, but it's also very dangerous. When Ghend comes at you, he'll be so desperate that he'll be opening doors that aren't supposed to be opened, and you'll have to respond in kind. If you stop and think about it, you'll know what has to be done. Please be careful when you do it, though. I spent a lot of time and effort on this place, and I'd rather you didn't nullify it."

"Nullify?"

"The word isn't too accurate, but there *isn't* a word that describes what'll happen if you aren't careful. Now, then, if I were you, I'd stay away from those doors right now. You've been using them to alter reality, and you're starting to dislocate some things that'd be better left alone. It wouldn't be a good idea to shift the seasons right now."

"I was sort of wondering about that myself, even before we left Hule."

"You managed to get *something* right, at least. You reached the House at the onset of winter last time. I'd keep it that way *this* time. Everything has a proper time and season, and the more important something is, the more crucial the time is. You don't want to reach the House late, of course, but getting there early could be just as dangerous."

"I had a feeling it might be. I'll make sure we reach the House at exactly the same time."

"Good." Then the old man looked rather quizzically at Althalus. "I can't really see why Dweia objects to your tunic so much," he said. "I think it looks rather splendid myself."

"I've always liked it."

"I don't suppose you'd care to sell it?"

Althalus floundered a bit.

"Never mind, Althalus. I won't make an issue of it. There's something I *will* make an issue of, however."

"Oh?"

"Treat my sister well. If you disappoint her, or hurt her, you'll answer to *me* for it. Do I make myself clear?"

Althalus swallowed hard and nodded.

"I'm glad we understand each other. It's been very nice

talking with you, Althalus. You have a nice day now, hear?" And then the old man sauntered off, whistling as he went.

"Now *that's* something that doesn't happen every day," Gher said in a shaky sort of voice. "You said that something important was going to happen on our way back to the House. This was it, wasn't it?"

"I don't think anything's likely to come along to top it."

"Do you think we ought to holler at Eliar and have him tell Emmy that we're going to be a little late?"

"Not *this* old dog," Althalus replied. "The old man kept using the word 'advice,' but I got his point. He told us to stay away from the doors—and he probably meant the windows as well. I'm not going to take any chances at this point."

"Emmy was probably watching from the window anyway, don't you think?"

"Almost certainly. She likes to keep an eye on me. Let's gather up our things and get ready to move out. We still have a ways to go, and we don't want to be late."

They took a quick breakfast and rode north toward the precipice Althalus still thought of as the Edge of the World.

"I thought that tree was dead, Althalus," Gher said, frowning. "It doesn't look very dead to me."

Althalus looked sharply at the Edge of the World. The tree was still gnarled and twisted, and it was still bone white. It had leaves now, however—autumn leaves of red and gold that crowned the tree in glory.

"It wasn't like that before, was it?" Gher asked.

"No," Althalus replied in a puzzled voice.

"What do you suppose made it come alive?"

"I haven't the foggiest idea, Gher."

"Do you think it means something?"

"I don't know. Now I've got something else to worry about."

"Should we stop and see if something happens?"

"We don't have time. Let's keep going." Althalus turned his horse in an easterly direction to follow the edge of the precipice.

"It looks different out there," Gher said after a while, pointing north. "It didn't look that way from Emmy's House."

"No ice," Althalus told him.

"There isn't, is there? What happened to all the ice we used to see off to the north?"

"It hasn't got here yet. We're still back 'then.' 'Now' won't get here for a couple thousand years." He broke off. "Now you've got *me* doing it," he scolded the boy. "This fooling around with time does funny things to a man's head."

Gher grinned at him. "That's what makes it so much fun."

"I think I've had enough fun for a while." Althalus looked around. "Keep your eyes open for rabbits or marmots. We didn't bring very much food with us, so we'll have to live off the land for the rest of the trip."

Evening was settling in over the far north, and Althalus and Gher were rounding a jutting spur of rock when they saw a campfire in a small grove of stunted pines just ahead. "We'd better be just a little careful," Althalus cautioned. "That fire's something new. It wasn't there last time."

They scouted around, but there didn't seem to be anyone in the vicinity.

"Who built that fire, Althalus?" Gher demanded. "Fires don't just start themselves, do they?"

A familiar odor coming from the campfire, however, hinted at a distinct possibility. "Supper's ready, Gher," Althalus told the boy. "We'd better go eat it before it gets cold. You know how Emmy is when we're late for supper."

Gher gave him a puzzled look, and then his eyes widened. "You know, sometimes Emmy's so clever she makes me sick. She wanted to let us know that she saw us talking with her brother without coming here and telling us right to our faces, so she fixed us supper instead."

Althalus sniffed at the fragrance coming from the fire. "She's managed to get *my* attention," he said, swinging down from his horse. "Let's eat."

"I'm ready," Gher agreed. "When you get right down to it, I'm way past ready."

There was no question about who'd prepared the feast at the

lonely campfire, since every bite had the familiar taste of Dweia's cooking. There were also several large bags of additional food near the fire. Althalus and Gher both ate too much, but it'd been quite some time since either of them had tasted decent food, so their enthusiasm was quite natural.

They continued along the Edge of the World for a week or more while autumn marched inexorably toward winter. Then one evening after they'd eaten, Gher looked off toward the north. "That fire out there seems awful bright tonight, doesn't it?" he said.

"Why don't we go have a look?" Althalus suggested, standing up.

"Why not?" Gher said.

They left their camp just as the moon was rising and walked over to the Edge of the World.

The moon gently caressed the misty cloud tops far below, setting them all aglow. Althalus had seen this before, of course, but it was different here. The moon in her nightly passage drinks all color from the land and sea and sky, but she could not drink the color from God's fire, and the seething waves of rainbow light in the northern sky also burnished the tops of the clouds below. It seemed that they almost played there among the cloud tops with the moon's pale light encouraging the amorous advances of the rainbow fire. All bemused by the flicker and play of colored light that seemed almost to surround and enclose them, Althalus and Gher lay in the soft brown grass to watch the courtship of the moon and the fire of God.

And then, far back in the mountains of Kagwher, they heard the sweet sound of the song of Eliar's Knife. Althalus smiled. All manner of things were different this time.

He fell asleep easily that night. The fire of God in the northern sky and the song of the Knife rising from the forest seemed perfectly matched, and everything fit together just as it should. It must have been along toward dawn when thoughts of shimmering fire and aching song were banished by yet another dream.

Her hair was the color of autumn, and her limbs were rounded with a perfection that made his heart ache. She was garbed in a short, archaic tunic, and her autumn hair was plaited elaborately.

Her features were somehow alien in their perfect serenity. On his recent trip to the civilized lands of the south, he had viewed ancient statues, and his dream visitor's face more closely resembled the faces of yore than the faces of the people of the mundane world. Her brow was broad and straight, and her nose continued the line of her forehead unbroken. Her lips were sensual, intricately curved, and as ripe as cherries. Her eyes were large and very green, and it seemed that she looked into his very soul with those eyes.

A faint smile touched those lips, and she held her hand out to him. "Come," she said in a soft voice. "Come with me. I will care for you."

"I wish I could," he found himself saying, and he cursed his tongue. "I would go gladly, but it's very hard to get away."

"If you come with me, you shall never return," she told him in her throbbing voice. "For we shall walk among the stars, and fortune will never betray you more. And your days will be filled with sun and your nights with love. Come. Come with me, my beloved. I will care for you." And she beckoned and turned to lead him.

And, all bemused, he followed her, and they walked out among the clouds, and the moon and the fire of God welcomed them and blessed their love.

And when he awoke the next morning, his heart was filled with contentment.

The days grew shorter and the nights more chill as Althalus and Gher followed the Edge of the World toward the northeast, and after about a week, they entered a region that was very familiar. "We're getting close to the House, aren't we?" Gher said one evening after supper.

Althalus nodded. "We'll probably get there about noon tomorrow. We'll have to wait a bit before we can go inside, though."

"What for?"

"I didn't go across the bridge to the House until late in the day last time, and I think we'd better keep it that way. Ghend's been using these dream visions since the beginning, and every one has fallen apart on him. It sort of looks to me as if *something* doesn't like it when we start playing with things that're all over and done with. That's why I'm going to make this time turn out as close to last time as I can—put my feet in the same places, scratch my nose at the same time, and all that. I'd like to get back on the good side of whatever it is out there that doesn't like tampering with the past. Once we're both back inside the House, we'll be all right, but as long as we're outside, I think we'd better be very careful."

They arrived at home late the following morning, and Althalus realized that he hadn't looked at the House from the outside for quite some time. He knew that it was much larger than it appeared to be from out here, but it was still an imposing place. Its location on that promontory, separated from the narrow plateau by the chasm the drawbridge crossed, silently suggested that it was separated from the rest of the world as well. Althalus was fairly certain that the House would remain exactly where it was, even if the rest of the world happened to vanish.

They dismounted and sat down on the rock behind which Althalus had hidden twenty-five centuries before.

At noon, Andine and Leitha came across the bridge with a large wicker basket. "Lunchtime," Leitha called.

"Is Emmy mad at us or anything?" Gher asked apprehensively.

"No," Andine replied. "Actually, she seems to be rather pleased about the way things turned out."

"Dweia wants you to wait a bit before you cross the bridge," Leitha told them. "It's not quite time yet."

Althalus nodded. "I know," he said.

"Keep an eye on the tower window," Leitha instructed. "Bheid's going to flash a lantern to let you know when you're supposed to come home." She smiled briefly. "That's part of his job, isn't it?"

"I think I missed that one," Gher admitted.

"The Knife told him to illuminate, didn't it?"

"Are you trying to be funny?"

"Would I do that?" Then she smiled again. "Poor Bheid's been staring at the floor ever since he saw you two talking with Dweia's brother," she told Althalus. "He definitely wasn't expecting that."

"Neither was I," Althalus replied, "and I'm going to have a very long talk with Emmy about it. I'm sure she recognized him last time, but she didn't bother to tell me just exactly who the crazy man was. Why don't you girls go on back home? It's a bit chilly out here."

Althalus and Gher ate lunch, and then they sat waiting and casting frequent glances up at the tower window.

The sun was low over the southern horizon when they saw the flicker of light in the window. "That's it, Gher," Althalus said, rising to his feet. "Let's go home."

"I'm ready," Gher agreed.

They led their horses across the bridge and into the courtyard, where Eliar was waiting. "I'll take care of your horses," he told them. "Emmy wants to see you in the tower. Take Ghend's Book with you."

"Right," Althalus said. "Bring the Book, Gher."

They went into the House and made their way to the stairs leading up to the tower.

Dweia was standing at the top of the stairs, and Althalus felt a peculiar twisting inside. He hadn't fully realized just how much he'd missed her. "Have you got the Book?" she demanded.

"I'm awfully sorry, Em," Althalus told her. "We used it to start fires along the way."

"Very funny, Althalus."

"I've got it right here, Emmy," Gher told her, patting the leather bag he was carrying.

"Good. Bring it upstairs, but leave it inside the bag for now."

Althalus and Gher climbed up the stairs, and Dweia fiercely embraced Althalus at the top. "Don't go away anymore," she told him quite firmly.

"Not if I can help it, Em," he agreed.

"May we see the Book?" Bheid asked eagerly as they entered the tower room.

"No," Dweia said. "That's not necessary."

"Dweia!" he protested.

"I don't want you to touch it, and I most definitely don't want you to read any part of it. We brought it here to destroy it, not to read it."

"What do you want me to do with it, Emmy?" Gher asked.

"Toss it under the bed for now," she replied indifferently.

"Why not get rid of the dreadful thing right now?" Andine demanded.

"Not until morning, dear," Dweia told her. "We *definitely* want plenty of daylight around when we bring the Books together. I want all traces of night gone before we start."

"You're cruel, Dweia," Bheid accused.

"She's protecting you, Bheid," Leitha told him. "She knows all about your hunger for books—even for *this* one. There are things in Ghend's Book that you *don't* want to know about."

"Are you telling me that *you* know what's in it?"

"Only in general terms, Bheid. I'm staying as far away from it as I possibly can."

"This discussion isn't really going anywhere," Dweia told them. "Why don't we all go down to supper?"

"Do you want me to stay here and guard the Book, Emmy?" Eliar asked.

"Why?"

"Well, shouldn't somebody stay here and keep an eye on it—just in case Ghend tries to sneak in and steal it back?"

"Ghend can't enter the House, Eliar," she replied, "not unless somebody invites him in."

Several things clicked together for Althalus at that point. He knew what he had to do now. "There's something I'll need to discuss with you, Eliar," he told the young Arum as they all started toward the stairs. "Later on, probably."

"Anything you say, Althalus."

"Are you sure you know what you're doing, love?" Dweia asked Althalus later, when they were alone.

"More or less," he replied. "Your brother hinted around the edges of it, and I know Ghend well enough to have a fair idea of what he'll probably try to do. Please don't interfere, Em. Ghend's *my* responsibility, and I'll deal with him in my own way."

"No killing in my House, Althalus," she said flatly.

"I wasn't planning to kill him, Em. Actually, I'm going to do something worse."

"It's dangerous, isn't it?"

"It won't be a casual stroll in the park," he admitted. "The timing's going to be crucial, so don't interrupt me or distract me—and keep the others out from underfoot. I know what has to be done, and I don't need any interference."

"Are you certain you'll be able to handle it?"

"Your brother seemed to think so. Oh, by the way, he sent his love."

"Are you trying to be funny?"

"Didn't you hear him?"

"Not very clearly, no."

"You missed the good part of the conversation, then. When you get right down to it, you've got your brother wrapped around your little finger. He absolutely adores you."

She started to purr. "Tell me more," she urged.

"We might as well get on with this," Dweia told them the next morning after breakfast. "It's broad daylight now, so let's go upstairs and get started."

They rose from the table and started toward the door. But Althalus motioned to Eliar, and the two of them lingered in the dining room. "Pay very close attention, Eliar," Althalus told the young man. "This is crucial."

"What do you want me to do, Althalus?"

"When we get to the tower room, I want you to go over to the window where your special door's located. Be sort of casual about it, and as soon as you're sure that nobody's watching, I want you to unlatch that door and leave it just slightly ajar."

"Is that a good idea? I mean, if Ghend's looking for a way to get inside the House, and if that door's unlatched—"

"I *want* him to see that the door's not locked. When he comes at me, I want him to come through *that* door. I *don't* want him coming at me from behind my back."

"Oh, now I see what you're getting at. When did you want me to do that other thing?"

"Wait for my signal. Just be ready when I give you the word. We'll only have a few seconds, so stay on your toes. If Emmy starts screaming at you, just ignore her and do what *I* tell you to do."

"You're going to get me in trouble, Althalus."

"I'll explain it to her after it's all over. It's essential that you only listen to *me* once this gets started. If we don't do it exactly right, none of us'll be here to see the sun go down—and that's assuming that there'll still *be* a sun, or anything for it to go down behind."

"You're starting to make me nervous, Althalus."

"Good. At least I'm not alone."

"*Will* you two stop dawdling?" Dweia called down the stairs.

"We're coming, Em," Althalus called back. "Don't get excited."

"Now, then," Dweia told them all after Althalus and Eliar had joined them in the tower room, "when this starts, I want you all to stay back. This might be dangerous. All right, Gher, fetch Ghend's Book."

"Anything you say, Emmy," the boy replied, going to the bed. He knelt and groped around under the marble platform until he found the leather bag. Then he stood up and brought the bag to her. "Here it is," he said, holding it out to her.

"Take it out of the bag, Gher," she told him, putting her hands behind her back.

"It won't hurt you, Emmy," he assured her. "It feels a little funny, but it's not scalding hot or anything like that."

"That probably depends on who you are, Gher," she told him. "Take the Book out of the bag and lay it on the table beside our Book. Don't let them touch each other, though."

"If that's the way you want it," he said, untying the thong that held the bag shut. Then he reached in and pulled out the large, black leather box. "It seems a little heavier," he noted. Then he laid the box on the gleaming marble table. "Is that just about where you want it?" he asked.

"Move it just a bit closer to the white one," Dweia replied.

He slid the black box across the table top toward the white one. "Is that about right?"

She squinted at the two boxes. "Close enough, I think."

"Nothing's happening, Dweia," Bheid said.

"Not yet," she said. "That's because it's not complete yet. Give me your Knife, Eliar."

"All right, Emmy," he replied, drawing out his dagger.

Althalus glanced quickly toward the south window and saw that the door was slightly ajar, even as Eliar reversed his Knife and offered the hilt to Dweia.

"Not that way," she told him, extending both of her hands, palms up. "Just lay it across my hands."

"Whatever you say." Eliar placed the Knife on her outstretched hands.

She turned to face the table then and stood holding the Knife over the two books. "Now we wait," she said.

"Wait for what, Emmy?" Gher asked curiously.

"The right moment."

"Is a bell going to ring, or something like that?"

"Not exactly. I'm sure we'll all notice it, though. They'll probably notice it on the other side of the world."

"Oh, one of *those* things."

" '*Those* things' as you put it, are a sort of family tradition. We do that a lot in my family."

Then the House itself seemed to shudder, almost as if shaken by a distant peal of thunder, and the sky outside darkened.

The Knife lying across Dweia's palms seemed to shift and blur, and its aching song rose in triumph. Then it expanded into a formless sort of mist.

"What's happening?" Bheid's voice was alarmed.

Dweia, however, did not answer as the blurred mist above her hands coalesced. Then a slender golden box lay glowing where Eliar's Knife had been.

The darkness that had descended on the House was quite suddenly pushed back by the golden glow that seemed to emanate from Dweia's Book. The inky black clouds that had temporarily obscured the light roiled titanic along the horizon as the golden light of the Book and the rainbow light of God's fire engulfed them.

"I've missed you," Dweia said fondly to her Book. "The time's finally come for you to do what I made you to do at the very beginning." And she gently placed the golden Book atop the other Books on the table, meticulously shifting it so that it bridged the gap between the Book of Deiwos and the Book of Daeva.

The shuddering of the House intensified, and from deep in the earth there came a sound so low that it was felt rather than heard. And from the sky and the nearby mountains came that familiar wail of despair commingled with the song of the Knife.

"Oh, hush," Dweia said absently. "Both of you. I'm trying to concentrate."

The golden light of the Book intensified, enveloping the entire table in a blinding intensity. "Get back!" Dweia cautioned them. "It's starting!"

A tendril of smoke began to rise out of the shimmering light that enveloped the table.

"Are the Books on fire?" Bheid exclaimed in a shrill voice.

"Ghend's Book is," Dweia replied. "That was the purpose of this from the beginning."

"I thought you said it wouldn't burn," Andine said in a frightened voice.

"Not in an ordinary fire, dear," Dweia replied. "That fire on the table *isn't* really fire."

"It's truth, Andine," Leitha told her.

"But—"

"Hush, dear," the pale girl told her, "and get back." Then she looked quickly at Althalus. "He's coming!" she warned.

"I know," Althalus said grimly. "I've been expecting him."

Eliar's door crashed open, and Ghend, all in flame, was there, with burning Khnom just behind him. Garbed in armor of fire were they, and armed with swords of flame.

"I have come to reclaim that which is mine!" Ghend declared in a voice of thunder, and his burning eyes were incandescent and filled with madness.

The flaming pair bulked large in Eliar's doorway, but beyond them it seemed that another door opened on absolute horror. It appeared to Althalus that the door beyond Eliar's door looked out over a city of fire. The buildings were columns of flame, and the streets were rivers of liquid fire. Multitudes howled and burned in the streets of fire, and lightning seethed around them.

Ghend raised his sword of flame. "Behold the instrument of thy doom, thief!" he roared with lightning seething about his face and with his burning hair wreathing up around his head. And then, with pace inexorable, Ghend marched toward Althalus and toward the table bathed in golden light, and footprints of fire marked his passage across the marble floor.

But Althalus raised his hand, saying, *"Leoht!"* And a wall of purest light barred Ghend from his goal. Ghend howled, and all the flaming hosts of Nahgharash howled with him.

Caught up in desperate frenzy, Ghend slashed at the wall of light that barred his way, as lightning seethed about him and his sword of flame rang hollowly against the barrier Althalus had placed before him with but a single word.

"You'll break your sword, Ghend," Althalus told him, forcing all traces of archaism from his speech. "You won't get through unless I let you through. Are you ready to listen?"

Ghend, still bathed in fire, seized the hilt of his burning sword of flame with both hands and struck mighty blows at the wall of light.

"You're wasting time, Ghend," Althalus told him, "and you don't have much time left."

"What are you *doing*?" Dweia demanded.

"Stay out of this, Em!" Althalus snapped. "This is between Ghend and me!"

Ghend lowered his sword of flame, but his eyes burned even hotter, and the shrieks of the hordes of Nahgharash howled about him.

"You have a choice to make, Ghend," Althalus told his frenzied enemy, "and you have to make it now. You can persist in this idiocy and suffer the consequences, or you can turn around and close that door."

"Are you mad?" Ghend shrieked, as flames seethed hotter about him.

"Close the door, Ghend," Althalus told him. "The fire will go out if you close the door. Pull your mind together and close that door. Shut out Nahgharash and Daeva. This is your only chance to escape."

"Escape?" Ghend shrieked. "The world is within my grasp you fool! I can have it all—forever!"

"Not without your Book, you can't, and you'll never reach that Book in time to use it. You've lost, Ghend. I've beaten you If you'll admit that, you might live. If you refuse, you haven't go a chance. Choose, Ghend. Make your choice now, so that we car get on with this. Time's running out."

"I *will* have my Book!"

"Are you sure?"

Ghend renewed his attack on the wall of light, and Althalus felt a sudden sense of relief as certain restrictions were lifted from his shoulders. "Somebody's going to hear about this," he muttered, even as he lowered his hand. *"Ghes!"* he said.

Ghend, still burning, stumbled forward as the barrier of golden light flickered and vanished and the wails of the multitudes of Nahgharash rose to shrieks of triumph.

Althalus stepped aside as his desperate enemy rushed to the table. Ghend, wreathed in flame, hesitated a moment, and then he cast his fiery sword aside and reached out with both arms as if to seize up all three Books. But as his hands plunged into the golden light, the song of the Knife soared, and with a startled oath Ghend jerked his hands back.

"You didn't really, *really* think I'd let you do that, did you?" Althalus said. "You can take *your* Book, if you think you must, but ours stay right where they are. Quickly, Ghend. Time's almost run out."

Ghend's answering snarl was almost bestial as he snatched up the smoldering black Book. "You haven't heard the last of this, Althalus!" he shouted as he turned back toward the door.

"Oh, yes we have, brother." The voice was not the voice of Althalus, even though it came from his lips. Then the voice cracked like thunder. "Now, Eliar!"

There was a sudden hollow sound as the door beside Dweia's window vanished. The archway that had enclosed it became a

ormless hole filled with the empty darkness of Nowhere and
Nowhen.

Beyond that formless hole, Althalus could see the buildings of
Name and the wailing creatures of fire that were the sum and
essence of Nahgharash sinking and liquefying into the rivers of
fire that were the streets of the city of the damned; and the rivers
ran fast to spill over some unimaginable brink to cascade into the
abyss of absolute nothingness. And now, all commingled and
aware, the streets and the buildings and they who dwelt in flame
shrieked out in despair, and their shrieks faded down and down
and down into that utter silence.

Khnom, all aflame and gibbering in panic, tried to catch at the
sides of the formless hole as he was inexorably drawn into the
nothing that lay beyond the doorway, but that, of course, was
hopeless. Khnom passed through the doorway of this world and
vanished.

Ghend, armored in fire and still clutching his burning Book,
flailed about with his free arm, desperately seeking something
he could cling to as the emptiness beyond the doorway drew him
across the smooth marble floor of the tower room. Shrieking and
cursing, he clawed at the marble, but still he slid inexorably
toward his fate. And at the last moment, he looked with pleading
eyes at the face of his enemy and reached out a supplicating
hand. "Althalus!" he cried. "Help me!"

And then he vanished through that awful doorway with his
Book still clutched to his breast, and his scream faded behind him
as he fell forever into the nothing that had finally claimed him.

"Close the door, Eliar," Althalus said with profound sadness.
"We're finished with it now."

"It was one of those things you have to see to believe, Twengor," the bald Gebhel told the vastly bearded Clan Chief as Althalus and his friends all sat reminiscing in Albron's hall on the evening before the wedding of Khalor and Alaia early the following summer. "The silly thing stuck up out of the plain of North Wekti like a huge tree stump—except that you don't very often come across a tree stump that's a thousand feet high."

"I still don't understand what possessed you to abandon your trenches, Gebhel," the recently elevated Chief Wendan said. "You'd just finished tearing up the Ansu cavalry and wiping out that surprise attack from the rear. Why didn't you just sit tight? Your trenches seem to have worked out very well."

"Khalor's scouts told us that the Ansus had reinforcements coming, and it was fairly obvious that they'd reach our trenches long before Kreuter and Dreigon could possibly make it," Gebhel explained. "Trenches are all right, but only if you're not too badly outnumbered. When the numbers start moving into the neighborhood of five to one against you, it's time to cut and run, I always say."

"It all turned out for the best," Sergeant Khalor said. "I had a few doubts about that tower myself, to be perfectly honest with you, but that artesian spring and all the food supplies in that cave sort of tipped the balance."

"Oh, yes," Gebhel agreed with a broad grin. "If you gentlemen don't mind a bit of advice, I wouldn't play dice with Khalor if you can avoid it. He's had a run of unbelievably good luck here lately. Even nature seems to be on his side."

"Oh?" Koleika Iron Jaw said.

"A wind storm pops out of a dead-calm morning just when he needs it to fan a grass fire. Then there's that earthquake that opened a ditch across the top of that tower right in front of the crazy man who was charging our position. And to cap it all, there was the river that ran in both directions and washed an entire enemy army away." Gebhel absently rubbed his hand over his bald head. "There were a lot of things going on that I couldn't understand," he admitted.

"Would you consider the possibility of divine intervention, Sergeant?" Bheid asked slyly.

"I'm an Arum, Brother Bheid," Gebhel said. "We prefer not to think about that sort of thing." Then he shrugged. "I don't know exactly how all those lucky things happened. I'm just glad that Khalor was on my side during *that* particular war."

"I'd say that his lucky streak hasn't run itself out yet," Twengor said, grinning. "I've seen the lady he's going to marry tomorrow, and *that's* about as lucky as any man's likely to get."

Althalus leaned back in his chair, smiling faintly. Any time there was a gathering of more than three Arums, they always seemed to start telling each other war stories, and the stories inevitably got better with every telling. After a few seasons, the stories would slip over the line to become legends, and legends tended to gloss over the more blatant impossibilities. Given a few years, the Arums would shrug off rivers that ran in two directions, a Knife that knew how to sing, and a blond girl who could hear the thoughts of the people around her. The events of the past couple of years would enter the realm of folklore, and Emmy would slip away on soft paws. Nobody would know just exactly how much she'd tampered with possibility or reality.

You'll still know, though, won't you, pet? her soft voice purred in his mind.

I don't really count, Em, he replied. *Somewhere along the line I seem to have misplaced the definition of the word "impossible." I don't really get excited about much of anything anymore.*

I think I'll be able to come up with something *that'll change your mind, love,* she purred.

* * *

Brother Bheid officiated at the wedding of Khalor and Alaia Dweia, only marginally disguised, attended; and after the cere mony, she joined the well-wishers clustered about the bride an groom in Albron's hall.

I think I've just come up with a way to solve a certain problem pet, her silent voice murmured to Althalus.

Oh? Which problem was that, Em?

We'll get to it, love. We've got a couple more weddings to ge out of the way first.

"I'm not their father, Em," Althalus protested a few days late when they were alone in the tower.

"Don't argue with me, Althalus. Just sit there, look paternal and give your permission. It's an ancient ritual, and rituals are very important to ladies. Don't try to turn it into a joke, Althalus I'm warning you."

"All right, Em. Don't tie your tail in a knot about it."

"Those 'knotty tail' remarks are starting to wear a little thin. Althie," she said tartly. "They weren't very funny to begin with, and they get less amusing each time you come up with some feeble excuse to make them."

"You're in a grouchy sort of humor today, Em. What's bothering you?"

"Our children are leaving us, Althalus," she replied pensively. "Eliar and Andine will go back to Osthos, and Bheid and Leitha will be in Maghu."

"We'll still have Gher, Em. It'll be a while before *he* grows up."

"That's something we'd better talk about, pet. Gher's never had anything even remotely resembling a normal childhood, and I think we should do something about that—*after* the wedding."

"We've got *two* weddings, Em."

"Let's do just one, love. Separation's painful enough to begin with, so let's not drag it out."

"Who do you think should officiate? Emdahl, maybe?"

"Not in *my* temple, he won't."

Althalus blinked. "You're going to do it yourself?" he demanded incredulously.

"Of course I am, you ninny. They *are* my children, after all, and I want to be sure it's done right."

He surrendered. "Whatever you say, Em."

Althalus sat in the tower on a golden summer morning making some pretext at reading the Book while Dweia, garbed in splendor, sat enthroned beside the south window.

The stairway door opened, and Gher, once more in his pageboy costume, entered. "I'm supposed to say that they want to see you, Althalus," he said. "Andine made up a speech for me. You didn't really want to hear it, did you?"

"Let's go through the motions, Gher," Dweia told him. "Speak the speech in formal wise."

"Do I really have to, Emmy?" he said with some distaste.

"The ladies would prefer it that way, Gher."

Gher sighed. "All right, Emmy, anything you say." He cleared his throat. "All-powerful father," he addressed Althalus, "thy children entreat thee to give them a hearing in a matter of utmost importance."

"Do it right, Althalus," Dweia said firmly.

"If that's the way you want it, Em." Althalus straightened. "Advise my noble offspring that I will hear their petition, my son," he told Gher, "and—barring unforeseen demands in their presentation—gladly will I grant their each and every request, as our dearly beloved Goddess giveth me strength."

"Unforeseen demands?" Dweia asked.

"Just a precaution, Em. Let's keep the dowries at a reasonable level."

Arm in arm, Andine and Eliar, both in formal garb, entered the tower room, closely followed by Leitha and Bheid.

The bows and curtsies were a trifle florid.

"We have come this day to lay our petition before thee, our noble and beloved father," Andine announced, "forasmuch as we are—and must be—guided by you in all things. Noble Eliar and Holy Bheid will speak of this anon, but know full well that my

beloved sister and I do add our plea to theirs in this matter. Lon
and hard have we considered this, and it doth appear clearly ev
dent that much benefit shall accrue to all peoples shouldst tho
graciously accede to our humble request."

"And is it thine intent, glorious Arya, to dwell upon this in pe
petuity?" Althalus asked, deliberately exaggerating the forma
speech Andine had addressed to him, "for should thine oratio
continue at greater length, might not it be more humane to perm
brave Eliar and righteous Bheid to beseat themselves?"

"You're not supposed to say that!" Andine flared. "Make hin
stop that, Dweia!"

"Be nice, Althalus," Dweia chided. "Go on, Andine."

The tiny orator pushed bravely on, and Althalus stifled severa
yawns.

"I would not presume to attempt to outdo our dear, dea
Arya," Leitha announced. "Thus must I speak in simple terms
The Exarch of the Grey Robes hath caught mine eye, deares
Daddy. I want him. Give him to me."

"Leitha!" Andine gasped. "That's not the way it's supposed tc
be done!"

"Well, gentlemen?" Althalus said to Eliar and Bheid. "How
do you feel about this?"

"Andine and I want to get married," Eliar said simply. "Is that
all right?"

"It is with me," Althalus replied. "How do *you* feel about
it, Em?"

"I can live with it," she said with a faint smile.

"That settles that, then. Was there something you'd like to add,
Bheid?"

"I don't think there's much left for me to say, Althalus," Bheid
noted. "I want Leitha as much as she wants me—or maybe just a
little more. A formal wedding might be a good idea, because certain things *will* start to happen—with or *without* the ceremony."

"He's *definitely* making progress, isn't he?" Leitha said with a
sly little smirk.

"How says mighty Althalus to our humble request?" Andine

manded, trying to salvage some small remnant of formality
ut of the wreckage.

"Would 'yes' upset anybody?" Althalus asked.

"That's all?" Andine flared. "Just 'yes'? Nothing more?"

"It *does* have a certain abrupt charm," Leitha observed. "Now,
nobody objects *too* much, I think Brother Bheid and I ought to
vestigate the notion of 'with or without the ceremony' just a bit
urther, wouldn't you say?"

Bheid blushed furiously.

Now it came to pass that upon a certain day when golden autumn
ad spread her glory across the land did sundry people from
cross the length and breadth of all lands come together in the
igh temple of the Goddess Dweia in stately Maghu. And fra-
rant were the flowers that did bedeck the altar, and exceeding
lad were all they who gathered there to witness the joining that
vas to come on that happy day.

And the Goddess Dweia, mother and perpetrator of all life,
miled, and with her smile were all cares banished, and all they
vho were there were caught up in rapture.

And behold, she who mothers all was filled with love, and her
gentle face did expand into enormity, for no shape of humankind
could contain a love so vast. And spake she then in language ancient, for even as Dweia was the mother of love, so that tongue
which she spake was mother of all speech wheresoever or when-
soever people dwelt. Strange and alien sounded the language in
which she spake, and yet did all they who were there clearly per-
ceive her meaning, for Dweia spake unto their hearts and minds,
and not unto their ears.

And the mother of love spake of love unto they who had come
before her that she might bless their union. And behold, she did
open doors between them which had ne'er been opened before,
and tall Eliar's mind was forever linked with the mind of tiny Andine, and their minds did merge in that ancient language, never
again to be separate, and thus were they wed.

Then turned Divine Dweia her attention to holy Bheid and pale
Leitha. Troubled was the mind and heart of Bheid forasmuch as

in a moment of rage had he struck down with mortal blow
fellow human, and his guilt lay heavy upon his soul. And behol
the Goddess Dweia did freely and with love boundless absol
the fallen priest of his sin, and his soul was cleansed. And then
like manner did the divine Goddess extend her boundless fo
giveness to pale Leitha. Great had been the pain of Leitha t
reason of acts compelled of her by necessity, and the suffering
Koman still gnawed at the heart of gentle Leitha. Softly did d
vine Dweia remove all memory of the fate of Koman from he
pale daughter's mind, that she might be whole again, and th
were the troubled pair freed of their pain, and their minds an
hearts were bound together, and so they too were wed.

And the very stones of Dweia's ancient temple did burst fort
in song, casting away the stern and somber humor of the pries
hood that had usurped that holy place and turned it aside from i
intended purpose, which was and is yet love and joy.

And all of Maghu resounded with the rejoicing of Dweia
temple.

"The whole point here, Gher, is that we can't be entirely positiv
that all the fuss and bother of the past few years was Ghend'
doing, or if it just grew out of the natural wrongheadedness of a lo
of other people out there in what they call 'the real world.' I thin
we're going to have to keep a close watch on them for the next sev
eral years. I've had just about enough of all these silly wars."

"Why don't you let me take care of that, Althalus?" Gher vol
unteered. "If you leave the House to go roaming around th
world looking for troublemakers, Emmy's going to yell at you
She wants you right here, I think."

"She'll yell at me even more if I send you out there on you
own."

Gher frowned for a minute, and then he snapped his fingers. "
think I just came up with the answer, Althalus," he said.

"I certainly hope so. I can't seem to come up with anything
that won't set Emmy off. What's this idea of yours?"

"After what's happened in the last couple of years, if som
bonehead wants to start a war, the very first thing he's going t

is look up Sergeant Khalor, isn't he? I mean, when we were
at there fighting *our* war, Khalor tromped all over anybody who
ot in his way. If somebody wants to start a war and he wants to
in, Khalor'd be the one to see."

"*We* helped a little bit, didn't we?"

"Of course we did, but the boneheads don't know that, because
e sort of stayed out of sight. I'll bet that by now, everybody out
ere believes that Khalor's a hundred feet tall, he can walk on
ater, and he can break a mountain in two with his bare fist."

"Where are we going with this, Gher?"

"Well, I was sort of thinking that if you want me to be some-
lace where I can sniff out trouble before it even gets started, I
hould probably stick closer to Khalor than his own shadow does."

"It wouldn't bother you to leave the House and go live with
Khalor and his new wife, then?"

"Me and Khalor get along real good, Althalus, and I can have
Eliar's mother wrapped around my finger in a flat minute. All I have
o do to get any woman in the world to mother me to pieces is put
on my 'poor little orphan boy' look. She'll take to me like a duck
akes to water. It won't hardly take me no time at all to get settled
down in Eliar's old room, and I won't make no big fuss about how
ast I can think. I'll just sit around kind of blank eyed like nothing
vas going on in my head. I'll keep my nose to the wind and my ears
vide open, though, so if somebody comes to Khalor or Chief Al-
oron to rent Arums for some war someplace, I'll be right there, and
quicker'n you can blink, I'll pass that on to you. Then you and me
an go look up the bonehead and tell him that if he doesn't forget
about his war, we'll chop out his liver and feed it to him."

"Won't you sort of miss being here in the House with Emmy
and me?"

"Emmy's got that boy-people and girl-people sort of look on
her face, Althalus. You don't have to tell her I said this, but I
hink I'd sooner be someplace else for a while. If I'm in Arum
vith Khalor and the other fellows, at least I'll have somebody to
alk to once in a while. I think I might start getting a whole lot of
onesome here in the House if I stay. Besides, I'll be doing some-
hing pretty important, won't I?"

"It has a lot of possibilities, Gher," Althalus conceded, tryir to sound dubious. "Let me think it over a bit, and then we'll se what Emmy has to say."

"Oh, that was slick," Dweia said admiringly.

"Naturally," Althalus replied. "When I want somebody to d something, I always maneuver him around so that he thinks it *his* idea. We wanted Gher to go to Arum to live with Khalor an Alaia because that was best for him. All I did was herd him alon until he came up with the idea himself. If we'd *ordered* him t go, he'd have thought we were just throwing him out because w didn't want him anymore. I wouldn't do that to Gher, and neithe would you. This way, Gher gets the permanent home and famil he's never had, and Khalor and Alaia get a son without goin; through the trouble of having one themselves. Everythin; worked out exactly the way you wanted it to, Em, and that's wh you hired me in the first place, wasn't it?"

"You done good, Althie," she said with a radiant smile.

"Don't get me wrong here, Em," he said, leaning back in hi; chair. "I'm very fond of the children, but it's sort of nice to have the House to ourselves again. What are we going to do to pass the time now that we've saved the world and gotten the childrer married off or permanently settled?"

"I'll think of something," she promised in a tone that left little doubt about what she meant.

All as in a dream she came to him amidst the shimmer and play of the courtship of the moon and the fire of God as the song of the Knife serenaded them.

Her hair was the color of autumn, and her limbs were rounded with a perfection that made his heart ache, and her features were somehow alien in their perfect serenity. And she held out her hand to him, saying, "Come. Come with me. I will care for you."

"Most gladly," he replied, "for the world about me tires me, and I am weary of it. And whither shall we go, my beloved? And when shall we return?"

"If you come with me, you will never return," she replied in a

oice of song. "For we shall walk among the stars, and fortune shall
ever betray you more. And your days will be filled with sun and
our nights with love. Come. Come with me, my beloved. I will
are for you." And she took him by the hand and led him up the fa-
niliar stairs to the tower of light where they had dwelt before.

And when they had entered, the door behind them merged
vith the curved wall of the tower, and the door—and all other
loors—were no more.

And content was the heart of Althalus, for now was he once
again home, and no more would he wander.

t was some several seasons—or centuries—later, when spring
had returned to the House at the End of the World, and Althalus
sat idly at the table, leafing through the pages of the Book.

A familiar sound came from the fur-robed bed, and Althalus
glanced over at his wife. "What's that all about, Em?" he asked curiously. "I thought we'd put Emmy the cat more or less behind us."

"What *are* you talking about?" the autumn-haired Dweia
asked.

"You're purring, Em."

She laughed then. "Maybe I am at that," she admitted. "Old
habits are hard to break."

"It's a pleasant sound, Em, and it doesn't really bother me all
that much."

She sat up and stretched luxuriously. "It's probably because
I'm happy. Nothing seems to express happiness quite as much as
purring."

"I'm fairly happy myself, Em, but I manage to get by without
purring."

"Come over here, love," she told him. "I have some news I'd
like to share with you."

He carefully replaced the pages in the white box and went
over to the bed. "Spring came early this year," he noted, glancing
out the south window at the mountains lying off in that direction.

"And it'll probably last quite a bit longer than usual," she
added.

"Oh? Why's that?"

"The world's celebrating, dear," she replied.

"Some special event?" He sat down beside her.

"Very, very special, love," she said, touching his face fondly.

"Were you planning to keep it a secret?"

"It's not the sort of thing that'll stay a secret for very long, pet," she said, smiling mysteriously and gently touching her slightly rounded abdomen.

"I think you might be eating a bit too much, Em," he observed.

"Not really." She gave him a sly, sidelong glance. "You're a bit thick-headed this morning, pet. What is it besides food that causes a woman's waistline to expand?"

"Are you serious?" he exclaimed.

She stroked her tummy again. "If I'm not, *this* is. We're going to have a baby, Althalus."

He stared at her in absolute astonishment. Then he suddenly felt his eyes fill with tears.

"Are you crying, Althalus? I didn't think you knew how."

He took her in his arms then and held her with tears of joy streaming down his face. "Oh, I *do* love you, Em!" was all he could say.

Visit Del Rey Books online and learn more about your favorite authors

There are many ways to visit Del Rey online:

The Del Rey Internet Newsletter (DRIN)
A free monthly publication e-mailed to subscribers.
It features descriptions of new and upcoming books,
essays and interviews with authors and editors,
announcements and news, special promotional offers,
signing/convention calendar for our authors and
editors, and much more.

To subscribe to the DRIN: send a blank e-mail to
join-ibd-dist@list.randomhouse.com
or you can sign up on Del Rey's Web site.

The DRIN is also available for your PDA devices—
go to www.randomhouse.com/partners/avantgo for
more information, or visit http://www.avantgo.com
and search for the Books@Random channel.

Del Rey Digital (www.delreydigital.com)
This is the portal to all the information and
resources available from Del Rey online including:

• Del Rey Books' Web site, including sample chapters
of every new book, a complete online catalog, special
features on selected authors and books, news and
announcements, readers' reviews and more

• Del Rey Digital Writers' Workshop, a members-only,
FREE writers' workshop

Questions? E-mail us...
at delrey@randomhouse.com